GEMINIANI STUDIES

Ad Parnassum Studies 6

★

Advisory Board

★

Published in association with

Centro Studi Opera Omnia Luigi Boccherini-Onlus
Lucca

Geminiani Studies

Edited by

Christopher Hogwood

Ad Parnassum Studies
APS 6
ISBN 978-88-8109-479-0

Printed in Italy 2013 - Global Print S.r.l. - Via degli Abeti 17/1 - Gorgonzola (Mi)

CONTENTS

PREFACE

THE EIGHTEENTH CENTURY had problems with Geminiani, not least with his name: "Geminiany", "Germiniani", "Jeminiani", "Gimeniani", "Geminiary", and even "Mr. Jammaniana" were some of the attempts to pin down a much-admired but elusive genius in their midst. His music proved in the end almost as intractable as his name — initial admiration became more dilute as Geminiani failed to behave as was expected of a star-pupil of Corelli — indeed, he was even reluctant to give public concerts at all. Then there was general suspicion at his open admission that he preferred dealing in paintings to being a musician. And when he turned to writing treatises, public bafflement was complete.

Geminiani himself compounded the problem; Tartini described him as "furibondo" (presumably meaning as a performer), and Sir John Hawkins noted delicately the "versatility of his temper". His unwillingness to appear in public concerts was overcome only, Burney acidly pointed out, when forced by circumstances and he even demurred over playing at Royal command unless Handel were recruited to accompany him (Handel agreed). Throughout his life he valued his independence, turning down a pension from the Prince of Wales and preferring to support himself by art dealing. He was also, it now appears, fiercely litigious — two essays in the present volume provide new evidence of his legal battles with employees who he felt had failed to hold to an agreement.

The conventional verdict on Geminiani's career is that 'he failed to fit accepted norms and therefore fell from public favour'. Today, of course, this might be construed as a measure of his genius, but his most quoted contemporaries decided that it indicated a deficiency of ambition or inspiration (or both). Although Burney once admitted to Thomas Twining that "Handel, Geminiani & Corelli were the sole Divinities of my Youth",[1] in the end his grudging epitaph rose no higher than "[…] he was a great Master of Harmony, & very useful in his Day". Even Hawkins, who knew and supported Geminiani

---

[1] Burney to Thomas Twining, 14 December 1781 in: *The Letters of Dr Charles Burney*, edited by Alvaro Ribeiro, SJ, 4 vols, Oxford, Oxford University Press, 1991, vol. I, p. 328.

rather more enthusiastically than Burney, diagnosed "the want of an active and teeming imagination".

Succeeding generations have accepted the negative verdicts of Burney and Hawkins without noting the discrepancies with other evidence. Burney's view, for example, that Geminiani was a "bad timist" and had (according to hearsay) been demoted on this account in the Naples opera was gleefully repeated, while Mrs Delany's first-hand report of his playing as late as 1760 has been ignored: contrary to Burney, she specifically noted "the sweetness and melody of the tone of his fiddle, his fine and elegant taste, and the perfection of time and tune". Even she, however, subscribed to the public belief that he was 86 when in fact he was a mere 72 — yet another area where Geminiani sowed confusion. It was left to the lesser-known Charles Avison, a pupil of Geminiani, to lead an attempt to preserve and promote his mentor's music. He swept all criticism imperiously aside:

> This extraordinary Man had a Genius in all the Arts of Taste. Music, Painting, and Sculpture, were the principal Objects of his Mind; and he was sensible in them all. He spoke all the European Languages, and his Conversation was lively and entertaining to the latest of his Life time. He had seen many Courts, many Men, many Customs. After all his Long Experience, his general Sentiments were, — "That none should be elated with Praise, when unconscious of deserving it — nor too much depressed, when their Merit is neglected. — And, that the only Power of defeating a Rival, is to excel him." Such were the Sentiments of the ingenious Geminiani. He loved the Arts, and assisted many Artists. I speak for one, and revere his Memory in this very Expression which I have often heard him repeat, — "That Truth and Simplicity are the best Criterion of the fine Arts, as they are of the good Conduct in human Life".[2]

★★★

Geminiani was more international even than Handel, and his speaking "all the European Languages" was, like his art dealing, a necessity rather than a hobby. He can be traced at various periods to Lucca, Rome, Naples, Bologna, London, Edinburgh, Newcastle, Dublin, Paris, Amsterdam and The Hague, and it seems very probable (though not yet investigated) that he would also have visited his brother, who was employed as leader of the royal orchestra in Madrid. Certainly his one recommendation for a textbook on

---

[2] *Newcastle Courant*, 17 September 1768.

harmony and counterpoint — *El Porqué de la musica* by Andres Lorente[3] — optimistically assumed that his English pupils would be as fluent in Spanish as himself. He was equally at home in Italy, France, Holland, England and Ireland, and in the following essays a largely geographical organisation of topics seems natural with so footloose a subject. Disappointingly for national pride, neither London nor Dublin appear to have had much musical effect on Geminiani — certainly less than the strong influence Paris had, both on his music and on its printed appearance.

However, his sheer internationalism and what was seen (in contemporary terms) as the 'hybrid' character of his style had the predictable effect of making him no nation's favourite. John Potter observed in 1762 that "his taste is peculiar to himself",[4] and even Hawkins doubted "whether the talents of Geminiani were of such a kind, as qualified him to give a direction to the national taste" (1776). There were few attempts at critical measurement in any broader sense; William Hayes ventured a brief comparison with the obvious target, concluding that, "In short GEMINIANI may be the *Titian* in Music, but HANDEL is undoubtedly the RUBENS",[5] and only an anonymous 'Scale to Measure the Merits of Musicians' published in *The Gentleman's Magazine and Historical Chronicle* in 1776 attempted any sort of broader rational evaluation: it was noted that, although "an ingenious Frenchman"[6] had some years previously made a table evaluating and comparing the scores for some fifty-six major painters, judging them on their composition, drawing, colour and expression, nothing similar had been attempted for composers. The criteria and score-card (given on pp. xiii-xiv) explain how an otherwise almost equal balance between Handel and Geminiani is upset by the sheer quantity of the former's works — under "quantity published or known" Handel scores 18,

---

[3]   The full title of this treatise is *El Porque de la musica : en que se contiene los quatro artes de ella, canto llano, canto de organo, contrapunto y composicion y en cada uno de ellos nuevas reglas, razon abreviada, en utiles preceptos, aun en las cosas mas dificiles, tocantes a la harmonia musica, numerosos exemplos...* and (for the interested) it can be found in a modern facsimile edition (Alacante, Biblioteca Virtual Miguel de Cervantes, 2006).

[4]   POTTER, John. *Observations on the present state of music and musicians; with general rules for studying music, in a new, easy, and familiar manner; [...] to which is added, A scheme for erecting and supporting a musical academy in this Kingdom*, London, 1762, p. 54. He added in a footnote "I believe he is still alive, but if he is, he must be very old, and past doing any thing now".

[5]   [HAYES, William.] *Remarks on Mr. Avison's Essay on Musical Expression. Wherein The Characters of several great Masters, both Ancient and Modern, are rescued from the Misrepresentations of the above Author; and their real Merit asserted and vindicated. In a Letter from a Gentleman in London to his Friend in the Country...*, London, 1753, p. 128.

[6]   DE PILES, Roger. *Cours de peinture par principes avec un balance de peintres*, Paris, 1708; Caravaggio, interestingly, scores 16 for colour but 0 for expression.

Geminiani only 4. Although a little partiality may be suspected when we find Jackson of Exeter scoring higher than anyone else in most categories, as a measure of contemporary taste this table offers a well-argued system for incorporating both musical and extra-musical criteria.

★★★

Geminiani has benefited surprisingly from modern technology; our first essay lists some of the many recordings that have appeared over the last 45 years and, unexpectedly, we now find a higher proportion of Geminiani's works available in facsimile editions than of any other eighteenth-century composer's output — all his treatises and almost all of his other opus numbers, some several times over; only the miscellaneous concerti (*Select Harmony* and *Unison*) and the arrangements of Corelli Opp. 1 and 3 appear to have missed the net. At the moment he is, in fact, far better represented in facsimile than in modern editions — possibly a compliment to his scrupulous insistence on fine production and accurate engraving, but a certain deterrent to modern performers.

In fact, of all the leading composers of the 18th century, only Geminiani is lacking a complete modern critical edition of his music and writings. The on-going *Geminiani Opera Omnia* is designed to fill this gap, presenting all his works, instrumental, vocal and didactic, in full critical editions, with the composer's first versions, revisions and re-workings presented consecutively by opus number, and including a full critical commentary and facsimiles, together with complete performance material for the orchestral and chamber works. The didactic treatises issued in English are accompanied by Italian, French or German translations of the period, where these exist, together with full commentaries from modern authorities. A thematic catalogue, which will complete the 17 volumes, can already be found in a beta-version online, together with a database calendar of references extracted from newspapers and periodicals published in Britain, France and Holland between 1700 and 1800 (see <http://www.francescogeminiani.com>). The opening and closing essays of the present volume offer two differing views on the 'Geminiani revival' which it is hoped this edition will promote — only with a more widespread circulation of his music can the idiosyncratic composer hope to meet with the necessarily unconventional performer. The final essay in particular focuses on the difficulty of finding suitable proponents and practitioners today.

For academic researchers, Geminiani's life still contains many biographical puzzles and lacunae. There are his so far undocumented travels (just recently it came to light that he was in Bologna in 1749 signing up a young singer for London concerts), few letters and no will. Neither his patrons nor his pupils have been systematically investigated, nor the wider phenomenon of the Italian musician employed in Britain during the eighteenth century. New here are details of his Masonic activities, the complexities of his international publishing operations, his legal tussles with performers, his highly successful dealings in art-works and his fascination with Scotland. His "re-heatings" of earlier works, so derided by Veracini, are re-interpreted here in a more positive light and his constant faith in the power of teaching is underlined in the two essays on violin playing.

Dilemmas and disagreements are also beginning to appear — a sign of health in research and a symptom of "cognitive discord" to be encouraged. Was Geminiani promoting the Corellian model or disputing it? — both theories are espoused in this volume. Was he more French than Italian? Why does so little documentary evidence survive from the four years or more he spent in Paris? Is *The Enchanted Forest* more than simply an enhanced series of concertos? Are the Op. 7 concertos really Geminiani's transformation of Rameau's *Scenes de Ballet*? Do literary programmes perhaps lurk behind his apparently 'abstract' music (as with Tartini)? — we find such a hint in William Hayes' mysterious mention of "his *historical* or *poetical* Plans, which, the Advocates for GEMINIANI are so fond of saying, his Concertos are built upon."[7]

Overarching all these activities is Geminiani's lifelong faith in the power of teaching, and the tractability of intelligent pupils — everything, in his world, could be transmitted by demonstration and example, including good taste, style, technique and musical theory. But even in his own day such faith in the improvability of musical souls was questioned; John Gregory commented in 1774:

> Geminiani, who was both a composer and performer of the highest class, first thought of reducing the art of playing on the Violin with Taste to rules, for which purpose he was obliged to make a great addition to the musical language and characters[.] The scheme was executed with great ingenuity, but has not yet met with the attention it deserved.[8]

This volume therefore offers not a last word on Geminiani but a means of opening the door to further research; as with all essay collections, what we

---

[7]   HAYES, William. *Op. cit.* (see note 5), p. 124.

[8]   GREGORY, John. *A Comparative View of the State and Faculties of Man with Those of the Animal World*, 2 vols, London, 1774, vol. II, pp. 30-31.

have here is a series of snapshots, rather than a rolling film. It is very unlikely that Geminiani will ever meet with unconditional endorsement — as William Blake shrewdly observed, "the tree which moves some to tears of joy is in the Eyes of others only a Green thing that stands in the way"[9] — but while his music may never induce universal tears of joy, we hope these essays may rescue Geminiani from being seen solely as an obstacle to the smooth forward flow of musical history.

Christopher Hogwood
Cambridge (UK), December 2011
hogwood@hogwood.org

Acknowledgements

The editor, publishers and contributors are grateful to the following persons and institutions for permission to reproduce material in their collections: Her Majesty Queen Elizabeth II (The Royal Collection), National Portrait Gallery (London), The Library and Museum of Freemasonry (London), the Victoria and Albert Museum (London), Royal Society of Musicians (London), Royal College of Music (London), The Foundling Museum, Gerald Coke Handel Collection (London), the collection of the Earl of Wemyss, The Frick Collection (New York), Österreichischen Nationalbibliothek (Vienna), Archives of the Court of Justice (The Hague), the Nationalmuseum (Stockholm), Universiteitsbibliotheek (Leiden), and the Sotheby's Picture Library (London).

Also to Heather Jarman and Damian Penfold for editing and production assistance, and to Ryan Mark for fathoming the complexities of house style and footnote formatting.

---

[9] Letter to Rev. John Trusler, 23 August 1799; see *Blake's Poetry and Designs*, edited by Mary Lynn Johnson and John E. Grant, New York, Norton, 1979, p. 448.

Scale to Measure the Merits of Musicians

The Gentleman's Magazine, XLVI (December, 1776), pp. 543-544

Mr. URBAN,

Some years since, an ingenious Frenchman, in his Lives of the Painters, gave us a scale to measure their different abilities, which, of late, has been imitated and applied to poets, orators, and even to beauties. Musicians have as yet been unweighed in the critical balance: but the time is now come for them, and I have undertaken the office; which I shall immediately enter upon, after professing a strict impartiality in the execution of it, (though, no doubt, many will differ from me in opinion,) and explaining a few necessary preliminaries.

All the columns (except one) suppose 20 for the point of ideal perfection, 19 for the utmost pitch of human attainment, and 18 for the greatest height to which it has yet been carried. The second column alone supposes 4 for the maximum. There was a necessity for this difference: for if natural and imitated melody were upon the same proportion, a composer who excels as much in the latter, as another in the former, might seem of equal rank; whereas natural melody is superior to imitated, at least, in the rates of 5 to 1, as I have put it. The seventh column is of more consequence than may at first appear; for many productions shew a fertility of genius, and give a larger scope for criticism. No one can put Gray and Pope upon the same footing, supposing them equal in all other respects, on account of the latter exceeding the former so much in the quantity of his poetical works. Handel seems by this balance to outweigh Geminiani but little, until you throw in the bulk of his works, and then the scale of the latter "kicks the beam."

The sixth column only notices such musicians as have appeared in *public* as performers, otherwise their merit in this respect is supposed to be unknown. The other parts explain themselves.

Yours, &c.
JUSTICE BALANCE.

	Original melody	Imitated melody	Expression	Knowledge	Correctness	Performance	Quantity published or known
	20	4	20	20	20	20	20
	—	—	—	—	—	—	—
Abel	6	3	12	10	8	18	3
Arne	17	2	12	15	14		9
Avison	10	2	10	8	6		4
Bach, John	6	3	13	10	6	13	9
Blow	4	2	4	12	10		4
Boyce	14	1	10	17	17		9
Corelli	18		8	17	18	14	4
Croft	9	1	8	10	12		6
Dibdin	6	3	10	8	6		6
Fischer	6	3	11	8	6	18	1
Garth	10	2	6	9	6		3
Geminiani	17	2	12	17	18	15	4
Giardini	13	3	14	1	1	18	4
Greene	10	2	7	12	13		7
Handel	18	2	12	18	16	18	18
Howard	8	2	4	12	15		4
Jackson	17		18	17	18		5
Marcello	12	2	9	6	4		9
Paradies	11	2	10	12	12	15	1
Piccini	6	3	10	12	14		9
Purcel	16	1	12	15	15		9
Sacchini	9	3	10	12	12		8
Scarlatti, Domenico	14	2	9	12	10	16	1
Schobert	12	3	14	3	4	18	3

Abbreviations

Burney	Burney, Charles. *A General History of Music from the Earliest Ages to the Present Period, to which is prefixed, a Dissertation on the Music of the Ancients*, 4 vols, London, 1776-1789
Careri	Careri, Enrico. *Francesco Geminiani (1687-1762)*, Oxford, Clarendon Press, 1993
DNB	*Oxford Dictionary of National Biography*, edited by Brian Harrison, 60 vols, Oxford, Oxford University Press, 2004 <http://www.oxforddnb.com>
Hawkins	Hawkins, Sir John. *A General History of the Science and Practice of Music*, 5 vols, London, 1776
H.	References to the *Thematic Catalogue of Works by Francesco Geminiani*, complied by Christopher Hogwood (*Geminiani Opera Omnia*, vol. 17). A beta-version of this catalogue can be consulted online at <http://www.francescogeminiani.com/catalogue>
NG	*The New Grove Dictionary of Music and Musicians*, edited by Stanley Sadie, 29 vols, London, Macmillan, ²2001 <http://www.oxfordmusiconline.com>
RISM	*Répertoire International des Sources Musicales*
Smith1	Smith, William C. *A Bibliography of the Musical Works Published by John Walsh during the years 1695–1720*, London, The Bibliographical Society, 1948
Smith2	Smith, William C. – Humphries, Charles. *A Bibliography of the Musical Works Published by the Firm of John Walsh during the years 1721-1766*, London, The Bibliographical Society, 1968

Thoughts on the 250ᵗʰ Anniversary of Geminiani's Death

Enrico Careri
(Naples)

IF WE CONSIDER RECEPTION HISTORY TO BE the degree of interest that the life and works of an artist attract, bearing in mind also the number of writings devoted to him and not only their 'critical' content, then we can certainly say that what I wrote twenty years ago in my Ph.D. dissertation and also in my book on Geminiani still remains substantially valid today, although the present volume and in particular the critical edition of his *Opera Omnia* (Ut Orpheus Edizioni) are important initiatives that will soon bear fruit.[1] Geminiani, I wrote then, has never received from musicology the same level of attention that Handel or Corelli have enjoyed in modern times, although he was considered their peer by his contemporaries.

Before I embarked on my research, the number of publications specifically dedicated to Geminiani was very small. This is what I wrote in the preface of my dissertation:

> When I began my investigation, I soon found how limited the existing knowledge of the composer and his music was: his biography remained largely in the state in which it had been inherited from Hawkins and Burney, his music had been examined only fragmentarily and often very superficially, and nothing resembling a complete catalogue of his works existed. Part of the reason for this unsatisfactory situation was the wide dispersal of the relevant biographical and musical sources, a result of Geminiani's activity in four different countries: Italy, England, France and Ireland. This dispersal encouraged a

---

[1] CARERI, Enrico. *A Controversial Musician: The Violinist, Composer, and Theorist Francesco Geminiani (1687-1762)*, Ph.D. Diss., 2 vols, University of Liverpool, 1990; CARERI, Italian translation, *Francesco Geminiani (1687-1762)*, Lucca, LIM, 1999, repr. 2009.

corresponding fragmentation of research on the part of scholars, who were rarely in a practical position to undertake primary research in situ in more than one or two of those countries. This meant that Geminiani's music was often analysed without due reference to the biographical and historical background, and that his multifarious activities as violinist, composer, theorist, and small-scale entrepreneur were never considered in their full interrelationship.[2]

Once one moved beyond the writings of Hawkins and Burney, there was a truly meagre harvest of musicological studies concerning the composer, and this was certainly one of the reasons why my supervisor, Michael Talbot, suggested this topic to me. The initial basis for research was almost non-existent, and while this made the project more difficult, it also guaranteed its originality. Since the historiographical fortunes of an artist are inevitably linked to the biography of any scholar who decides to devote many years of his life to him, I think it is appropriate to start by outlining the circumstances that at the end of the 1980s led me to trace the path of Geminiani from his native Lucca to Rome, Naples, London, Paris and Dublin.

At the beginning of 1987 I was on the point of finishing a historical-documentary study of the Italian violinist-composer Giuseppe Valentini. My musicological experience at that time was limited to a study of the eighteenth-century cantata in Rome, and a thesis on Italian vocal technique during the sixteenth and seventeenth centuries, an abstract of which had already been published. My article on Valentini was my first mature work; the result of long and arduous studies in many archives and libraries in Rome, Lucca and Florence. For this reason, I sent a copy, before it was published, to one of only two scholars (the other being Albert Dunning) who had worked on Valentini before me: Michael Talbot, at that time and until a few years ago Professor of Music at the University of Liverpool. I was expecting from him merely suggestions, corrections or additions, but he wrote me a letter with an unexpected invitation: to come to Liverpool and write a Ph.D. dissertation under his supervision, with the lure of a scholarship for three years. This was a very good opportunity for me, so in July 1987 I went to Liverpool for a few days to discuss with him what the topic of my dissertation should be. We were in the garden of his house in Liverpool when he suggested that I write a life-and-works study of Francesco Geminiani. I will never forget that I was initially quite puzzled, since I then knew little music by this composer except his Op. 3 concertos and *The Enchanted Forest*, through recordings by

---

[2]   ID. *A Controversial Musician* (see note 1), p. v.

the Academy of Ancient Music and I Solisti Veneti, respectively; this was all that was generally available of Geminiani's music at the time. Only later did I come to understand the reasons behind his suggestion. With my article on Valentini I had demonstrated enough competence in archival research to be able to reconstruct from scratch the life of a composer of whom almost nothing was previously known. To be a native-born Italian was a distinct advantage for my research in Italian archives, primarily those of Lucca and Rome, while my knowledge of English and French would certainly help me to track down and evaluate documentary sources in London, Paris and Dublin. Talbot knew very well something that at that time I did not know; one of the reasons for Geminiani's indifferent critical reception in modern times was the inconvenient dispersal of the relevant sources between Italy, England, Ireland and France, the four countries in which the composer at some point lived. In practical terms, what was needed was a person well versed in archival research, possessing the necessary musicological and linguistic qualifications and young enough to have the time and stamina that such a task demanded.

When, in September 1987, I moved to Liverpool and started to collect sources, my worries increased even further; the bibliography was almost non-existent and mostly unhelpful, particularly on the biographical front. However, I did not lose heart, and after three years of work, thanks to the prompt assistance and valuable suggestions of my supervisor, I was finally able to complete the thesis. It contained three biographical chapters, one dealing with the composer's critical reception, five covering his main compositions (concertos, sonatas, *The Enchanted Forest*, reworkings and transcriptions, vocal music), one on his treatises and, as an appendix, the first ever thematic catalogue of his manuscript and printed works. With minimal changes, this thesis was published as a book, which is still today the standard monograph on Francesco Geminiani.

When I started my research, the biographical studies specifically devoted to Geminiani, leaving aside the references in Hawkins' and Burney's histories and their later incarnations, were limited to a short article by Adolfo Betti (1934), which stopped at the discovery of Geminiani's date of baptism, and a study by William H. Grattan Flood (1910), which conveyed vague information about his activities in England and Ireland.[3] All the biographical information quoted in articles referring to his compositions and treatises repeated uncritically the few things that were already known. I therefore had to start almost *ex novo* by pursuing the few promising leads in a number of European archives,

---

[3]   Betti, Adolfo. *Francesco Geminiani*, Lucca, Giusti, 1934, pp. 7-20; Flood, William Henry Grattan. 'Geminiani in England and Ireland', in: *Sammelbände der Internationalen Musik-gesellschaft*, XII/I (1910), pp. 108-112.

but, of course, this same lack of information about the composer's life had consequences for the quality of the hardly more numerous analytical studies then existing, which examined his music in ignorance of the historical context in which it was written. I am referring here not only to the essay of Newell Jenkins (1967) on *The Enchanted Forest*, in which, for lack of historical reference points, the author mistakenly considered this composition "the largest form Geminiani ever attempted" — thanks to the discovery of various sources, we know today that this work was something quite different[4] — but also to studies of the concertos, sonatas, transcriptions and treatises which, though in part still valid today, are impaired by a lack of in-depth knowledge of the composer's life — in particular his activities as virtuoso, composer, theorist, teacher and dealer in paintings but also his pioneering role as a musician independent of institutions and patrons.

Some studies of Geminiani's compositions also suffered from the defect of repeating the negative prejudices inherited from the eighteenth century without undertaking a new, thorough analysis of the musical sources. The first trace of these prejudices can be found in a letter that Charles Burney wrote to Thomas Twining on 30 August 1773, in which — although conceding that "the advancem' of the Violin, & its Family, towards perfection in this Country, for the 1st 40 or 50 years of this Century, in short, till the arrival of Giardini, was in a great Measure the Work of Geminiani" — he observes:

> As a player, he was always deficient in *Time*; as a composer, *laboured*; & as a Critic, *jamais de bonne Foi,* changing his opinions according to his Interest, as often as Caprice. One Day he w^d set up French Music against all other — the next, English — Scots — Irish, anything but the best Compositions of Handel & Italy. You know, I dare say, how much he preferred the Character of a Picture-dealer, without the least knowledge or Taste in Painting, to that of a Musician, by which he had acquired his reputation & importance. I am afraid there is such a *penchant* in the generality of Italian artists towards Chicane, that they w^d rather trick a Man out of a Guinea than get it fairly, in a John-Trot way. & when Geminiani's Musical decisions ceased to be irrevocable, he tried his Hand at Painting.[5]

The topics contained in Burney's correspondence with Thomas Twining concerning Geminiani later appeared in his *General History of Music* (1776-

---

[4] JENKINS, Newell. 'Geminiani's *The Enchanted Forest*: A Conspectus', in: *Accademia Musicale Chigiana*, XXIV (1967), p. 171.

[5] The letter is quoted in *The Letters of Dr Charles Burney: Volume 1: 1751-1784*, edited by Alvaro Ribeiro, SJ, Oxford, Oxford University Press, 1991, p. 144.

1789), becoming the basis of the composer's critical reception, which can be summarized as follows: rhythmic and melodic irregularity, asymmetry of musical phrases, and above all "a confusion in the effect of the whole, from the too great business and dissimilitude of the several parts".[6] To these we must add Veracini's charges concerning the composer's musical plagiarism and recycling (in *Il trionfo della pratica musicale*, *c*1760),[7] and Hawkins' criticism of his lack of musical imagination: "It is to the want of an active and teeming imagination that we are to attribute the publication of his works in various forms".[8]

These critics had a negative effect on musicological research. At the end of the eighteenth century the only compositions of Geminiani still admired and played were his Op. 3 concertos; soon afterwards the music and the name of the composer underwent a prolonged period of oblivion, never enjoying in modern times a 'rediscovery' comparable to that of Albinoni or Vivaldi.

The prejudices inherited from Burney — asymmetry, irregularity, confusion — were compounded by a clear lack of interest in analysing the scores at first hand, remembering also that most of the latter were not available in libraries. Before 1996, the year of the first modern edition of *The Enchanted Forest*, those who wished to study or perform this work could do so only from Johnson's original printed edition. The difficulty of locating the musical sources certainly bore some of the responsibility for the scant attention given to the composer, but of course this situation creates a vicious circle, for the editors of old music and those who write on it are in most instances the same persons: they are part of the same community. One exception, however, should be made: the dissertation of Marion E. McArtor (1951), who, despite having the same difficulties we have already mentioned — the lack of a biographical framework, a catalogue and access to several scores — was the first scholar to try to understand the style of the composer through analysis of his music. The results of his dissertation are still interesting today, although his methodology is rather mechanical and not linked closely enough to the historical and musical context; nor is there any discussion of Opp. 2, 5 and 7, which amounts to almost one half of Geminiani's musical production.[9]

---

[6]   Burney, IV, p. 645.

[7]   Veracini, Francesco Maria. *Il trionfo della pratica musicale o sia Il maestro dell'arte scientifica dal quale imparasi non solo il contrappunto ma quel che più importa insegna ancora con nuovo e facile metodo l'ordine vero di comporre in musica Studio di Francesco M.ᵃ Veracino Opera III*, manuscript, Florence, Conservatorio di Musica Luigi Cherubini, Biblioteca [I-Fc], f. I. 28/29, II, ff. 381–383.

[8]   Hawkins, V, p. 424.

[9]   McArtor, Marion Emmett. *Francesco Geminiani: Composer and Theorist*, Ph.D. Diss., Ann Arbor (MI), UMI Research Press (51-107), 1951.

Thus, before I started my dissertation, the available research on Geminiani was essentially confined to the biographical studies of Betti and Flood and the analysis of McArtor, to which we should add an article by Robert Hernried on the Op. 3 concertos and one by Mario Fabbri on Geminiani's so-called (by Veracini) *fuga mostruosa* from his Op. 7 concertos.[10]

The treatises had more luck, particularly the most famous among them: *The Art of Playing on the Violin* and *A Treatise of Good Taste in the Art of Musick*, published in facsimile edition by Oxford University Press (1952) and Da Capo Press (1969), and edited by David D. Boyden and Robert Donington respectively, each of whom supplied interesting introductions. Boyden and Donington also contributed to the understanding of Geminiani's theoretical works both in specific articles and in more general publications.[11] To these we should add contributions by Thurston Dart, Bruno Tonazzi, Roger Hickman and Peter Walls.[12]

If we compare this picture with the state of research at the end of the 1980s into the most important confrères of Geminiani, particularly the composers regarded in his time as on the same level — i.e. Handel and Corelli — it is difficult to understand the lack of interest aroused by the Lucchese master. The already mentioned prejudices and the difficulty of finding documentary and musical sources explain only in part the disparity of treatment between these composers; they do not explain why Italian musicology was — and still is — so indifferent towards this composer. Prejudices and difficulties did not respect geographical borders. They discouraged scholars irrespective

---

[10] HERNRIED, Robert. 'Francesco Geminiani's Concerti grossi Op. 3', in: *Acta Musicologica*, IX (1937), pp. 22-30; FABBRI, Mario. 'Le acute censure di Francesco M. Veracini a *L'Arte della Fuga* di Francesco Geminiani', in: *Accademia Musicale Chigiana*, XX (1963), pp. 155-194.

[11] BOYDEN, David Dodge. 'Prelleur, Geminiani, and just Intonation', in: *Journal of the American Musicological Society*, IV/3 (1951), pp. 202-219; ID. 'Geminiani and the First Violin Tutor', in: *Acta Musicologica*, XXXI (1959), pp. 161-170; ID. 'A Postscript to "Geminiani and the First Violin Tutor"', in: *Acta Musicologica*, XXXII (1960), pp. 40-47; ID. *The History of Violin Playing from its Origins to 1761*, Oxford, Oxford University Press, 1965; ID. 'The Corelli "solo" Sonatas and Their Ornamental Additions by Corelli, Geminiani, Dubourg, Tartini, and the "Walsh Anonymous"', in: *Musica Antiqua*, III (1972), pp. 591-606; DONINGTON, Robert. 'Geminiani and the Gremlins', in: *Music and Letters*, LI/2 (1970), pp. 130-155; ID. *Baroque Music: Style and Performance*, London, Faber, 1982.

[12] DART, Thurston. 'Francesco Geminiani and the Rule of Taste', in: *The Consort*, XIX (1962), pp. 122-127; TONAZZI, Bruno. 'L'Arte di Suonare la Chitarra o Cetra di Francesco Geminiani', in: *Il Fronimo*, I (1972), pp. 13-20; HICKMAN, Roger. 'The Censored Publications of *The Art of Playing on the Violin*, or Geminiani Unshaken', in: *Early Music*, XI/1 (1983), pp. 73-76; WALLS, Peter. '"Ill-compliments and Arbitrary Taste"? Geminiani's Directions for Performers', in: *Early Music*, XIV/2 (1986), pp. 221-235.

of their nationalities, places of residence or fields of work. The only Italian contributions prior to my thesis (carried out in England at the behest of an English scholar) were the quoted article by Betti (1934) and Tonazzi's study of Geminiani's treatise on the guitar (1972). True, the difficulty of locating and gaining access to sources affected many coeval composers who, like Geminiani, were active in more than one country, but this did not automatically prove a fatal impediment to research into them. Twenty years after my dissertation, I remain convinced that these difficulties — in particular, the need for several visits abroad for the purpose of research in libraries and archives, entailing the sacrifice of much time, energy and money — certainly played a part in slowing down research. They were accompanied by other, perhaps more fundamental causes; for instance, the lack of pressure from the relevant local communities to encourage and promote the study of the works of their most illustrious citizens: something that Lucca never granted to Geminiani, but which a much smaller community such as Fusignano, with its few thousand residents, gave, and still gives, to Arcangelo Corelli.

Since 1968 the community of Fusignano, a small town close to Ravenna, has organized, approximately every six years, one of the most important Italian musicological congresses. They invite scholars from all parts of the world and cover all their expenses together with the cost of publishing the conference proceedings, which are today an essential reference point for scholars studying the instrumental music of late Baroque era. Corelli conferences have stimulated archival research, analysis, studies of the dissemination and reception of Corelli's works in the world and researches into performance practice. A by-product has been the study of many less well known composers active in Rome during the seventeenth and eighteenth centuries in addition to research into patrons such as the cardinals Ottoboni and Pamphili and the main Roman institutions where music was performed at that time, the Arcadian Academy, and the Accademia del Disegno. The role of Fusignano itself extended not only to sponsoring conferences and publications but also to offering private hospitality to the participants, making them feel welcome in their town. Lucca, in contrast, has done almost nothing to promote the study of Geminiani, as I myself have been able to witness. Obviously, Puccini and Boccherini absorb all the energies of the city.

As I have already mentioned, the earliest monograph on Geminiani, though written by an Italian author, was 'commissioned' in England and was completed and first published there. The main scholarly contributions on Geminiani have all been published in English, as are now all the essays in the present volume and the critical edition of the *Opera Omnia* of Geminiani, both owing to the initiative of Christopher Hogwood. Can this greater degree of interest in the composer be explained by the simple fact that he was active mainly in England, and it was there that his music enjoyed its widest dissemination? I do not think so. Two and a half centuries have passed, and the oblivion has lasted long. I think that Anglo-Saxon musicology has simply been more aware than its Italian counterpart of the role of Geminiani in the history of Western music of the eighteenth century, and of the quality of his music. Michael Talbot had the distinction of being the first person to understand the importance and urgency of studying Geminiani, taking a keen interest in my work at the Music Department of the University of Liverpool as it progressed. Christopher Hogwood, with decades of experience in performing Geminiani's music behind him, has assumed the direction of the edition of the *Opera Omnia*, which is planned to be an essential tool for research and for the future performance of Geminiani's music.

My book on the composer, being a life-and-works study — which is to say a volume aspiring towards completeness of information but unable, for reasons of both space and balance, to examine any single aspect in great depth — represented only a starting point. At the end of the 1980s the priority was to draw the complete outline without filling in all the details. This does not mean that my study was superficial, but only that I had to coax into few words the much more detailed material of my notes and analyses. I hope that a clear enough idea of the man and his music emerged, but I am only too aware that much remains to be done, and that every single line of my book can be refined, added to and possibly also disputed by new analysis and research findings. This was precisely what I was hoping for after my study was published, but obviously I was deceiving myself, for since that time nothing much more has been done. One possible reason was that my monograph, perversely, had the opposite effect on scholars to that I intended, by discouraging new research, as if I had already written everything necessary about the topic. In Italy, the lack of interest in Geminiani, even after the publication in 1999 of an Italian translation, simply carried on as before. As I have remarked, only a few publications concerned specifically with Geminiani have appeared since 1993, and none of them, leaving aside my article on the recently discovered autograph manuscript of the violin treatise, is from the pen of an Italian musicologist.[13] I should also mention in passing the existence of a short article by me, published in 2000 in a non-musicological journal, concerning Geminiani's Masonic activities in Naples, which appear to suggest

---

[13] CARERI, Enrico. 'Un manoscritto ritrovato di Francesco Geminiani, *The Art of Playing on the Violin* (1750)', in: *Studi Musicali*, XXXVII/2 (2008), pp. 387-407.

that the composer was not merely the first Italian to become a Freemason but was also the principal instigator of Freemasonry in Italy.[14]

The most important musicological discovery concerning Geminiani in the last twenty years, the discovery of the autograph manuscript[15] of his violin treatise, was the result of pure serendipity and not the deserved conclusion of long, patient research. Its previous owner, a Londoner, discovered it in a forgotten old wardrobe or trunk, as happens in the dreams of many musicologists, and tried to sell it via Christie's, for which he needed a letter from an expert to confirm its authenticity. In order to find this expert, he merely keyed in 'Geminiani' on Google and found me. But I didn't simply verify its authenticity; I also found a good way of avoiding the strong likelihood that after auction this precious manuscript would immediately disappear into anonymous private hands for another two centuries. I managed to persuade him to sell the manuscript to the Centro Studi Luigi Boccherini of Lucca, which thereby marked its first act of homage towards the Lucchese master.

The modern reception of a composer of the past also needs to be measured in terms of the dissemination of his works through performances and recordings. Here, things are completely different from what I have described in relation to musicological research. When I began my studies, the few available recordings comprised only a small number of works: the Op. 3 concertos, the Op. 5 cello sonatas and *The Enchanted Forest*, together with a few anthologies including selected concertos from Opp. 2 and 7, and the evergreen concerto transcription of Corelli's *Follia*. Today the increasing popularity of Geminiani is evidenced by the increased space allotted to his music on the CD shelves of music shops between Gabrieli and Gershwin, and, above all, by the fact that a complete recording of his concerti grossi (Opp. 2, 3 and 7) is available on the popular Naxos label (Capella Istropolitana conducted by Jaroslav Kreček, 1998). Italy witnessed in 2003 a CD of *The Enchanted Forest* (Cosarara, Giuseppe Camerlingo) sold in news kiosks — something unimaginable only ten years previously. *The Enchanted Forest*, even more than the Op. 3 concertos, has been performed frequently in concert halls, perhaps being today the most celebrated composition by Geminiani. Although it must be said that musicians are generally very lazy and prefer to play music readily available in shops and libraries, I believe that the decisive reason behind this popularity was not the publication in 1996 of the first modern edition of the

---

[14]   ID. 'Francesco Geminiani primo massone italiano', in: *Hiram*, 2 (2000), pp. 63-69.

[15]   But see Peter Walls, in: *Geminiani Opera Omnia*, vols 12 and 13 for doubts on the authenticity of this manuscript.

score, which I myself edited for Libreria Musicale Italiana, Lucca (LIM) — before 1996 they would have had to order the microfilm of Johnson's original edition and then laboriously score it up. I think, rather, that the reason for the success of *The Enchanted Forest* lies above all in its high musical quality and its originality of conception, which makes it so different from works of the same period, although it is clearly beholden to the concerto genre.

So, performers have shown much more interest in Geminiani than musicologists, despite the lack of new editions of his music. Since 1993, musicologists have possessed a standard monograph containing a full thematic catalogue by which to locate the material, however, besides the LIM edition of *The Enchanted Forest*, nothing has been published in recent years except for the first collection of *Pièces de Clavecin* (Ut Orpheus Edizioni, 2003).

Within the space of a few years we have seen many recordings, often of high quality, that by now almost cover the entire production of the Lucchese master. I will cite only a selection.

The Op. 2 concertos have been recorded by Auser Musici (Symphonia) and the already mentioned Capella Istropolitana; Op. 3 by the Academy of Ancient Music conducted by Christopher Hogwood (Decca/L'Oiseau-Lyre), Europa Galante conducted by Fabio Biondi (Opus 111) and the Capella Istropolitana, besides a recently produced version for harpsichord (Tactus); Op. 7 by the Academy of St Martin-in-the-Fields conducted by Iona Brown (ASV) and the Capella Istropolitana; the Op. 5 cello sonatas by Gaetano Nasillo (Symphonia), Bruno Cocset (Alpha), Jaap ter Linden (Brilliant Classics) and Anthony Woodrow (Stradivarius) and it is also available in the version for violin (CPO); *The Enchanted Forest* by Cosarara (Amadeus), the Orchestra Barocca Italiana conducted by Ryo Terakado (Stradivarius) and La Stagione Frankfurt conducted by Michael Schneider (Capriccio); the *Pièces de Clavecin* by Fabio Bonizzoni (Glossa) and Roberto Loreggian (Tactus); the guitar sonatas from Geminiani's *The Art of Playing the Guitar or Cittra* are available in a performance by Giampaolo Bandini (Tactus); the concerto arrangements of Corelli's Op. 5 sonatas have been recorded by the Academy of Ancient Music directed by Andrew Manze (Harmonia Mundi). The two sets of violin sonatas, Opp. 1 and 4, were already less well favoured when they were originally published, respectively in 1716 and 1739, probably because they were difficult to play, especially the first of them (Burney wrote that few violinists besides the author were able to perform them). Only individual violin sonatas are today available in recordings of mixed content, such as that of the Purcell Quartet (Hyperion/ Helios), where we find as partners to the concerto transcription of Corelli's *Follia* sonatas III, IX, XI and XII from Op. 1, and sonata XII from Op. 4; some of these not in the original violin versions but in the subsequently published trio-sonata transcriptions. As often occurs, less well known compositions are recorded alongside very famous ones such as the *Follia*, which usually lends its title to the CD in order to encourage sales, rather as the *Trillo del diavolo* does for Tartini's sonatas, although in the case of the *Follia* the original work was not by Geminiani himself. Further evidence of the vigorous dissemination today of Geminiani's music comes from the large number of anthologies in which his name is joined to those of some better known contemporaries, such as Handel, Vivaldi, Corelli, Veracini and Bononcini.

Is it possible to find an explanation for this fairly lively production of CDs in the absence of any impulse coming from the musicological direction? This is not easy, partly because it demands clear ideas about another hard question; the role of musical studies in the choice of the repertory that is performed and recorded. In countries where theoretical and practical studies are united in a single institution, such as British university music departments (and, increasingly, also British conservatoires), the free exchange of knowledge and experience between musicians and musicologists is much easier than in countries where the studies are segregated in different institutions. As we all know, musicologists would be happy if their writings were read by musicians as well, but this often does not always happen, and sometimes musicians even display a hint of antipathy towards theoretically oriented works. In contrast to the norm, performers of 'ancient' music are, generally speaking, very competent and aware about their musical choices. They are able to read, and even to perform from, old manuscripts and printed editions and they are very conversant with the endless debates about the appropriate way to perform the authors of the past. In other words, they are usually library-goers, and this fact alone gives me the hope that my studies on Geminiani have played a small role in the recent dissemination of his works.

This would be pleasant, but I believe that the choice of the music to sell on CD is ultimately the result of less noble business strategies that are not necessarily connected with musical criteria. The market always seeks to increase its size by offering new products, but it also has to balance what is new with what is famous, as happens similarly in the programming of seasons at concert halls. This means that *Four Seasons* and Fifth Symphonies find themselves yoked together with less well known compositions, albeit preferably not completely obscure ones. Geminiani fits in very well with these strategies, because his music is very accessible, even on the part of those who do not attend performances of early music (and this may explain the decision of the Italian magazine *Amadeus* to sell *The Enchanted Forest* as a supplement), and because he is not completely unknown on account of the relative familiarity of his Op. 3 concertos.

The *Opera Omnia* of Geminiani's music and treatises and the present volume of essays represent an important juncture; a fresh starting point for all the research that is crying out to be done. Some periods of the composer's life are still obscure — particularly his Italian apprenticeship, of which there exist only a few indistinct traces — but even his sojourns in London, Paris and Dublin need much better documentation. Thanks to the contributors to this volume we know much more about Geminiani's activities as an art dealer, publisher of his own compositions and freemason, and I am happy to see that all these new discoveries confirm the originality of his biography with respect to his deep desire of freedom and independence from patronage and institutions, adding more historical evidence to the conclusion to which I myself arrived twenty years ago:

> Geminiani's effort to improve his social and economic status through activities unrelated to music in order to avoid the need for private or institutional patronage is certainly the strangest and most interesting theme to emerge from his biography.[16]

His compositions, too, need more analysis in depth, particularly the Op. 5 cello sonatas, which I personally believe to be Geminiani's most original set of sonatas. But I think that all his works should be better analysed and that music analysis has been and still is the weak point of research.

The critical edition of *The Enchanted Forest* that I edited for the *Opera Omnia* has given me a further opportunity to study Geminiani's dynamic markings, embellishments and slurs, and to think about the meaning that they held for the composer. His treatises still await analysis *in combination with* his music, and I am sure that *The Enchanted Forest* in particular can provide the key to a better understanding of the composer's musical thought, since it is the sole composition by Geminiani for which both an autograph manuscript and an original printed edition exist. Studying it will allow us to make an accurate examination of the function of the expressive markings, which were considered by the composer essential components of musical meaning. I must also mention the last treatise, the *Guida armonica*, over which a big question mark still hangs, since it is not clear whether it is a 'senile folly' or represents a genuine desire to offer a new, original and easy method of composition. We know that Geminiani was a freelance operator who never enjoyed the

---

[16] ID. *A Controversial Musician, op. cit.* (see note 1), p. 45.

economic stability that many of his colleagues possessed, thanks to their patrons or employing institutions, but in the case of his *Guida armonica* I do not believe that the main reason for its publication was to make money, as seems to be much more clearly the case with his so-called 'reheatings' (Veracini's term). I think that this curious treatise, too, deserves closer investigation.

Catalogues, as we know, grow old — this is unavoidable and even desirable, since it implies that new sources have been discovered — and my catalogue of Geminiani's music and treatises is no exception; it needs updating, enlargement and general improvement. Hence the new catalogue prepared in conjunction with the critical edition of Geminiani's *Opera Omnia* that is today available online is very welcome. Scholars are warmly invited to contribute towards its improvement.

A balanced assessment of the twenty years that have elapsed since the publication of my book is no easy task. I can say that it is on the whole positive, but only because the 250th anniversary of his death has given rise to two large-scale enterprises that promise to redeem the lost musicological opportunities of those years: the *Opera Omnia* and the present volume. I am very grateful to Christopher Hogwood and to all the scholars who took part in these initiatives, and I have strong hopes that a new impulse towards more solid research will emerge from it in the immediate future.

Geminiani's Op. 1 and the Early Eighteenth-Century Violin Sonata

Gregory Barnett
(Houston, TX)

When Francesco Geminiani published his Op. 1 *Sonate a violino, violone, e cembalo* in 1716, he was one of several Italian musicians in London contributing to a burgeoning repertory of violin sonatas. Since Nicola Matteis' *Ayrs for the violin* (1676), Londoners had had first-hand access to Italian violin music. Just after the turn of the eighteenth century, Nicola Cosimi, Nicola Francesco Haym, and Gasparo Visconti ("Gasperini") arrived there, and the following decade saw more Italian musicians follow them: Francesco Barsanti, Stefano Carbonelli, Pietro and Prospero Castrucci, and, not least, Geminiani himself.[1] All of these expatriate instrumentalist-composers produced collections of violin music, much of it published by the indefatigable London music printer John Walsh, who augmented that supply by re-issuing works first brought out in Rome, Bologna, Venice, Paris, and Amsterdam.

The early eighteenth-century popularity of Italian violin sonatas was more than just an English (or even Italian) phenomenon. Rather, the genre was esteemed internationally. This was largely due to the fame of Geminiani's teacher, Arcangelo Corelli, and his Op. 5 *Sonate a violino e violone o cimbalo*, which were published in Rome in 1700 and enjoyed immediate and multiple

---

[1] For a detailed account of the Italian musicians who came to London in the first decade of the eighteenth century, see Lindgren, Lowell. 'The Great Influx of Italians and Their Instrumental Music into London, 1701-1710', in: *Arcangelo Corelli: fra mito e realtà storica. Nuove prospettive d'indagine musicologica e interdisciplinare nel 350° anniversario della nascita, Atti del Congresso Internazionale di Studi (Fusignano, 11-14 settembre 2003)*, edited by Gregory Barnett, Antonella D'Ovidio and Stefano La Via, 2 vols, Florence, Olschki, 2007, pp. 419-484. See also Careri, Enrico. 'Francesco Geminiani e il culto inglese per Corelli', in: *Studi corelliani v. Atti del Quinto Congresso Internazionale (Fusignano, 9-11 settembre 1994)*, edited by Stefano La Via, Florence, Olschki, 1996, pp. 347-377.

reprintings in Amsterdam, London, and Paris.[2] At the turn of the century, non-Italian publishers were producing not only re-prints of Italian music but in some cases the first editions. As a result, the sonata was exposed to new influences, particularly French, and English audiences, who consumed sonatas primarily as concert music, were introduced to the Italian distinctions between church and chamber music. This essay focuses on the Italian sonata and its development in response to the new international market in the period between Corelli's remarkably popular Op. 5 and Gemininani's auspicious debut with his Op. 1, itself a complex reaction both to the new conditions and to his teacher's model. An APPENDIX (p. 44) furnishes a brief listing of published solo violin music by Italian composers from 1670 to 1725. In most cases, references to works here are by composer and date; the appendix presents a more complete listing that gives the full title (including that of first London reprints, if applicable), the city of publication, and opus number.

VIOLIN SONATA ENSEMBLES

The titles of Corelli's Op. 5 and Geminiani's Op. 1, although they differ by just one small word (*o* versus *e*; that is, *or* versus *and*), point to an important variation in the bass accompaniment to violin music of the period.[3] Corelli offers the option of using either violone or harpsichord; Geminiani calls for both. The obvious difference of who and how many are the continuo may be connected to the subtler differences of bass function in the violin sonata; that is, whether the bass acted as a contrapuntal partner in a sonata *a 2* or simply

---

[2] CARERI, Enrico. 'Dopo l'opera quinta. Un'indagine sull'evoluzione stilistica della sonata per violino e continuo post-corelliana (1700-1750)', in: *Il Saggiatore Musicale*, VII/2 (2000), pp. 243-278. Reprinted in: ID. *Dopo l'opera quinta. Studi sulla musica italiana del XVIII secolo*, Lucca, Libreria Musicale Italiana, 2008, pp. 3-32. Careri's study furnishes a survey of the formal characteristics of Italian violin sonatas from the first half of the eighteenth century that concentrates particularly on the relative incidence of unitary, binary, and rounded binary forms.

[3] JENSEN, Neils Martin. 'Solo Sonata, Duo Sonata, Trio Sonata: Some Problems of Terminology and Genre in 17th-Century Italian Instrumental Music', in: *Festskrift Jens Peter Larsen*, edited by Nils Schiørring, Henrik Glahn and Carsten E. Hatting, Copenhagen, Hansen, 1972, pp. 83-101; JENSEN, Neils Martin. 'When Is a Solo Sonata Not a Solo Sonata? Corelli's Op. 5 Considered in the Light of the Genre's Tradition', in: *Arcangelo Corelli fra mito e realtà storica. Nuove prospettive d'indagine musicologica e interdisciplinare nel 350° anniversario della nascita. Atti del congresso internazionale (Fusignano, 11-14 settembre 2003), op. cit.* (see note 1), pp. 211-230; WALLS, Peter. 'On Divided Lines: Instrumentation for Bass Parts in Corelli-Era Sonatas', in: *Performance Practice Review*, 13 (2008) <http://ccdl.libraries.claremont.edu/u?/ppr,3021>.

provided harmonic accompaniment to the violin in a more homophonic solo sonata. Contrasting examples between sonatas *a 2* on the one hand, and solo sonatas on the other, can be seen in works from the late seventeenth century. In his Op. 55 sonatas (1670), Maurizio Cazzati included separate part-books for violone and organo, each of which reflected a different role: contrapuntal for the violone and harmonic for the organ (Ex. 1, Cazzati 1670, Sonata 3). Sonatas *a 2*, although not abundant, were hardly rare, and examples that similarly use three part-books (usually violin, bass violin,[4] and keyboard) persisted into the eighteenth century.[5]

In the late 1680s, some composers eliminated the keyboard part to create violin and bass violin duets in which the two players of acoustically matched bowed strings typically share melodic material as contrapuntal equals (Ex. 2, Pegolotti 1698, Sonata 1).[6] The opposite extreme, hinted in titles that specify *a violino solo*, were usually printed in score so that the continuo performer could more easily follow the nuances of the soloist's line as accompanist.[7]

---

[4]   I use the term bass violin to refer to the bass-range instrument of the violin family, whether the larger violone, smaller violoncello, or other variants such as the violoncello da spalla. Two studies of the yet-to-be standardized bass violin of the seventeenth and early eighteenth centuries are BONTA, Stephen. 'From Violone to Violoncello: A Question of Strings?', in: *Journal of the American Musical Instrument Society*, III (1977), pp. 64-99; and BARNETT, Gregory. 'The Violoncello da Spalla: Shouldering the Cello in the Baroque Era', in: *Journal of the American Musical Instrument Society*, XXIV (1998), pp. 81-106.

[5]   A listing of *a 2* sonatas includes Giovanni Bononcini 1687, Antonio Veracini 1696, Tomaso Antonio Vitali 1701, Giuseppe Antonio Aldrovandini 1703 and Giulio Taglietti 1707. All but the last use three part-books, and for the last there are two: a score for violin and violoncello and a separate part for basso continuo.

[6]   The unaccompanied violin and cello duo had a brief vogue in the 1680s and 90s before it was subsumed by the Corellian violin sonata: Giuseppe Torelli 1687-1688, Bartolomeo Laurenti 1691, Giuseppe Jacchini 1695, Attilio Ariosti 1695 and Tomaso Pegolotti 1698. Such pieces probably reflect an established performance practice of using a bass violin for the continuo accompaniment. Evidence of this is found in Giovanni Maria Bononcini 1671, who alerts his readers in the continuo partbook "Si deve avvertire, che farà miglior efetto il violone, che la spinetta, per essere i bassi più proprij dell'uno, che dell'altra [It should be noted that the violone will make a better effect than the spinet because the bass lines are better suited to the one than to the other]". The bass violin — that is, the bass member of the violin family of instruments — comprised several variants of eight-foot, bowed string instrument during the late seventeenth and early eighteenth centuries: the relatively smaller violoncello (tuned C, G, d, a), a term that first appears in a Bolognese print of 1665; the relatively larger violone (sometimes tuned *B flat*, *F*, *c*, *g*) that Corelli names in his Op. 5 violin sonatas; and, among French musicians, the basse de violon (usually tuned to *B flat*, *F*, *c*, *g*).

[7]   Two examples of score-formatted solo sonatas are Angelo Berardi 1670 and Pietro Degli Antonii 1686.

Ex. 1: Cazzati 1670, Sonata III.

Ex. 2: Pegolotti 1698, Sonata 1.

Ex. 3: Corelli 1700, Sonata 1.

Solo and *a 2* genres, however, overlapped frequently, so that bass lines typically switched roles from movement to movement or even within a movement. Likewise, the bass parts in the sonatas of Corelli and Geminiani shift between harmonic accompaniment and contrapuntal dialogue so that they sometimes sonatas *a 2* and sometimes solo sonatas. The *moto perpetuo* movements of Corelli's first sonata and Geminiani's third clearly use a harmonic bass, and one that benefits from the incisive attack and chord-realizing abilities of the harpsichord (Ex. 3, Corelli 1700, Sonata 1; Ex. 4, Geminiani 1716, Sonata 3). But the fugal movements benefit from a melodic bass to sound the third fugal part against the violin's two, and they require less chord-realizing because many of the figures are already realized in the violin.

None of this is to argue that the bass violin cannot realize chords or that the harpsichord cannot play a melodic line; rather, it is to point out how the

Ex. 4: Geminiani 1716, Sonata III.

bass parts of such violin sonatas play alternately to the strengths of one and then the other bass instrument and that this duality has its roots in differing genres of late seventeenth-century sonatas. The difference between Corelli's and Geminiani's designations — or versus and — points to each composer's approach. Corelli leaves it to performers to decide which instrument can best perform the dual function, and most other sonata composers from the period followed his example.[8] A minority, primarily composers working or publishing in Venice required the harpsichord without alternative.[9]

---

8   Nicola Cosimi 1702, Gasparo Visconti 1703, Michele Mascitti 1704 (also 1706 and 1707), Giuseppe Valentini 1706, Francesco Antonio Bonporti 1707, Giorgio Gentili 1707, Tomaso Albinoni c1709 (but not c1712; see n. 10 below), Stefano alli Macarani 1710, Ippolito Marotti 1710, Martino Bitti 1711, Pietro Castrucci 1717, Giovanni Battista Somis 1717 and 1723 and Gaetano Maria Schiassi 1724.

9   Giovanni de Zotti 1707, Antonio Vivaldi 1709 and Lodovico Ferronati 1710.

Geminiani, by contrast, calls for both instruments, but he was nearly alone in doing so.[10] Nor did he make a strong point of it: in the re-published Op. I sonatas of 1739, revised and with ornaments added, the wording reads simply *Le prime sonate a violino, e basso*. This falls into line with the non-specific designations of *basso* or *basso continuo* used in the early eighteenth century that leave the realization of the bass to the performers.[11] Among those that simply call for *basso* is Alberti 1721, which introduces a further complication in the performance practice of continuo realization. Like many Italian sonata collections, this was reprinted in London by John Walsh, who typically described the continuo line as "a thorough bass for the harpsicord or bass violin", irrespective of the wording on the original print.[12] As it happens, the frontispiece of the original includes a violin, cello and harpsichord in its illustration (ILL. 1), and if iconographic evidence is taken into account, it would seem that performers often followed Geminiani's prescription. A portrait from around 1730 of the Somis family of musicians — Giovanni Battista, violin; Lorenzo Francesco, cello; and Cristina, harpsichord — is one example (ILL. 2). Stefano Ghirardini's painting of a musical gathering, *c*1730 (ILL. 3) — featuring a shoulder-held violoncello — illustrates an even larger continuo accompaniment: cello, harpsichord, and lute.[13] In sum, the practice was hardly uniform, but Geminiani's preference may not have been as rare as sonata title-pages suggest. Above all, the variations in bass realization are evidence of the differing functions of the bass. These different roles are most clearly signalled by the distinct genres of late seventeenth-century violin music that were then subsumed as variants within the eighteenth-century violin sonata.

---

[10] Tomaso Albinoni *c*1712 and Francesco Antonio Bonporti 1712 are similar in this respect: Albinoni specifies "à violino, violone e cembalo"; Bonporti, "con l'accompagnamento d'un violoncello e cembalo o liuto".

[11] Carlo Antonio Marini 1705, Giuseppe Fedeli 1715, Francesco Maria Veracini 1721 and Giuseppe Matteo Alberti 1721.

[12] See, for example, Antonio Vivaldi 1709, Martino Bitti 1711, Michele Mascitti 1711 and Francesco Maria Veracini 1721.

[13] I am grateful to Marc Vanscheeuwijck for drawing my attention to this painting, which he reproduces on p. 187 of VANSCHEEUWIJCK, Marc. 'Recent Re-evaluations of the Baroque Cello and What They Might Mean for Performing the Music of J. S. Bach', in: *Early Music*, XXXVIII/2 (2010), pp. 181-192.

ILL. 1: Alberti 1721, frontispiece.

ILL. 2: Giovanni Lorenzo Somis, portrait of the Somis family, c1730, black and white chalk on blue paper. Photo courtesy of Sotheby's Picture Library.

Ill. 3: *Concertino*, attributed to Stefano Ghirardini, *c*1730 (private collection; photo by Stefano Martelli).

Sonata Genres

If there were various ensemble types within the solo violin repertory and different ways of realizing them, there were also differing styles of sonata. Corelli and Geminiani both divided their sonata collections between non-dance and dance genres, and the two types reflect a distinction between sonatas thought to be suited to the church (*da chiesa*) and those suited to household or courtly chambers (*da camera*).[14] The categorisation of genre by venue — church, chamber, theatre — is found in Italian and German writings on music of the seventeenth and eighteenth centuries, and it reflects a generalized connection between musical style and function.[15] The church sonata could be used liturgically,[16] just as the dances could be used at a ball.[17] Sonatas da chiesa, usually titled simply as *sonate* in which the possibility for church use is implied, included a fugal allegro and affective slow movements, and used the bass violin and organ for continuo accompaniment. Sonatas da camera, specifically designated as chamber music, comprised a suite of courtly dances, often introduced with a prelude, and used the bass violin or harpsichord.

That much is textbook defining, the best-known example of which is Sébastian de Brossard's entry on the sonata in his *Dictionnaire de musique*.[18] In practice, Corelli's trio sonatas of the 1680s and '90s were the clearest and most influential exemplars, but the characteristics of the two genres always involved a degree of overlap in which church sonatas featured dance-like binary-form movements and chamber sonatas often included an affective *adagio* or *grave* between the dances. From 1700, that overlap grew more pronounced, starting

---

[14]   ALLSOP, Peter. 'The Italian Sonata and the Concept of the "Churchly"', in: *Barocco padano 1: Atti del IX Convegno Internazionale sulla Musica Sacra nei Secoli XVII-XVIII, Como 16-18 luglio 1999*, Como, Antiquae Musicae Italicae Studiosi, 2002, pp. 239-247. Allsop argues that the designation *sonata da chiesa* was infrequent in Italian music and that church and chamber genres of sonata were more a phenomenon of the eighteenth-century northern European reception of Italian sonatas. BARNETT, Gregory. *Bolognese Instrumental Music, 1660-1710*, Aldershot, Ashgate, 2008, pp. 163-194, points out the widespread use by Italians of the term *sonata da chiesa*, and further argues that Italians typically used *sonata* to mean *sonata da chiesa*.

[15]   PALISCA, Claude. 'The Genesis of Mattheson's Style Classifiction', in: *New Mattheson Studies*, edited by George Buelow and Hans Joachim Marx, Cambridge, Cambridge University Press, 1983, pp. 409-423.

[16]   BONTA, Stephen. 'The Uses of the Sonata da Chiesa', in: *Journal of the American Musicological Society*, XII/1 (1969), pp. 54-84.

[17]   BARNETT, Gregory. *Bolognese Instrumental Music, op. cit.* (see note 14), Chapter 2.

[18]   BROSSARD, Sébastian de. *Dictionnaire de musique*, Amsterdam, Roger, c1708; facsimile edition, Geneva, Minkoff, 1992, pp. 139-140. English translation based on Albion Gruber: "One could say that there is an infinity of styles [of sonata], but the Italians reduce them ordinarily to two types. The first comprises the sonatas *da chiesa* — which is to say proper to the church — that begin usually with a *grave* and *majestic* movement, suited to the dignity and sanctity of the place; after which comes some sort of gay and animated fugue, etc. These are what one properly calls *sonatas*. The second type comprises the sonatas called *da camera* — which is to say, proper to the chamber. These are actually suites of several little pieces suitable for dancing and composed in the same mode or key".

with Corelli's own violin sonatas. The fifth sonata, which stands among the six sonatas that exemplify the sonata da chiesa, ends with a *giga* in name as well as in musical features; the eleventh sonata, which stands among the suites of dances, omits dance titles in all but its last movement. Both details portend further intermingling of the genres in the years after Corelli.

Certainly, suites of courtly dances were strongly represented after 1700,[19] but there was also a weakening of the chamber sonata's distinguishing features. Vivaldi's first collection of violin sonatas (Op. 2 of 1709), comprises suites of dances that usually include dance titles introduced by preludes, but within a print that is generically titled *Sonate a violino* (without *da camera*). In the next year Lodovico Ferronati, a fellow Venetian using the same printer as had Vivaldi, published his Op. 1 *Sonate a violino solo per camera*, which include no dance titles despite the title-page designation of chamber music. Ferronati reveals the more representative trend in the early eighteenth century, and the resulting subgenre of sonata was a tuneful or *arioso* style that comprised mostly homophonic or lightly imitative binary forms and few if any labelled dances.[20] Some collections in this style advertised their suitability for performance on the recorder (flauto) or flute (flauto traverso or German flute) as well as the violin, taking advantage of a restrained virtuosity not strictly idiomatic to one or another instrument.[21] Double-stops, for example, are a rarity in the arioso sonata.

Geminiani's Op. 1, although modelled on Corelli's Op. 5, follows this newer trend. The second half of the publication — the portion that he reserved for chamber sonatas, as had Corelli — comprises homophonic or lightly contrapuntal binary-forms, but all without dance titles. In keeping with the arioso style, moreover, these are easier pieces than those of the first half: there is no double-stopping, and the highest pitch used repeatedly, if sparingly, is *e'''*, the octave harmonic of the violin's highest string. (In a single passage in the last movement of the final sonata, Geminiani works his way up to *f'''* at

---

[19] Nicola Cosimi 1702, Gasparo Visconti 1703, Tomaso Antonio Vitali 1704, Michele Mascitti 1706 and 1707, Francesco Antonio Bonporti 1707, Martino Bitti 1711, Giovanni Antonio Piani 1712, Gaetano Maria Schiassi 1724 and others published suites that comprised the standard dance types, including the allemanda, giga, sarabanda, gavotta, minuetto and corrente.

[20] Sonatas of this type are Stefano alli Macarani 1709, Ippolito Marotti 1710, Tomaso Albinoni *c*1712, Giuseppe Maria Buini 1720, Giuseppe Matteo Alberti 1721 and Giovanni Battista Somis 1717 and 1723.

[21] Those sonatas that may be played on violin or other treble-range instruments are Nicola Francesco Haym and Martino Bitti 1710, Martino Bitti 1711, Giovanni Bononcini 1722, Diogenio Bigaglia *c*1722 and Gaetano Boni *c*1725.

the top of a long scale.) By contrast, the first six of Geminiani's Op. 1 sonatas, the church type, feature intricate double-stopping in the fugues and in some of the slow movements; an unprepared f''' after a rest in the melodic line in the fugal second movement of the second sonata plus a highest note of a''' in the third sonata (see Ex. 4, p. 20, Presto cadenza); and *arpeggio battuto* bowing that does not occur in the chamber sonatas but does conclude a fiercely challenging *moto perpetuo* notated in demisemiquavers (see Ex. 4, end of the third system). Corelli, by contrast, makes no distinction in virtuosity between the church and chamber violin sonatas: both types feature the highest pitch of the Op. 5 collection (e'''), both include double-stopping, and both require the same bowing techniques.

EXPANSIONS AND CONVERGENCES

Dance-like movements without dance titles and actual dance suites differ mostly in the designations added to their movements. Both are the stylistic territory of the sonata da camera, whether they bear the title or not. Indeed, most of the early eighteenth-century repertory for solo violin comprises sonatas with dances or with dance-like binary forms, and this inclination towards the sonata da camera is emphasized by the disappearance of the organ from the continuo accompaniment. From Corelli onwards (including Geminiani), if a keyboard is specified, it is the harpsichord, the continuo instrument associated with the sonata da camera.

The territory of the sonata da camera was also expanded by an impulse toward evocative or colourful movement types. Giuseppe Valentini's fancifully titled *Idee per camera* (1706) and Vivaldi's inclusion of capriccios and fantasias among his 1709 dance suites hint at a more exotic strain of sonata da camera.[22] Likewise, Francesco Antonio Veracini, who divided his *XII Sonate a violino solo*, Op. 1 (1721) between church and chamber types included a giga with *postiglione* (post horn) imitations (Ex. 5, Veracini 1721, Sonata 1), a paesana, a fantasia, and a pastorale among the latter.[23] The evolving conception of chamber sonatas

---

[22] CARERI, Enrico. 'Le idee e gli allettamenti di Giuseppe Valentini tra bizzarria e tradizione', in: *Analecta Musicologica*, XIII (2002), pp. 33-69, reprinted in: *Dopo l'opera quinta. Studi sulla musica italiana del XVIII secolo*, Lucca, Libreria Musicale Italiana, 2008, pp. 33-63, considers Valentini's contributions to the early eighteenth-century violin sonata. For a broader study of Valentini's life and works, see TALBOT, Michael. 'A Rival of Corelli: The Violinist-Composer Giuseppe Valentini', in: *Nuovissimi studi corelliani. Atti del Terzo Congresso Internazionale (Fusignano, 4-7 settembre 1980)*, edited by Sergio Durante and Pierluigi Petrobelli, Florence, Olschki, 1980, pp. 347-365.

[23] HILL, John Walter. *The Life and Works of Francesco Maria Veracini*, Ann Arbor (MI), UMI Research Press, 1979, pp. 153-171, offers a close examination of Veracini's Op. 1 violin sonatas.

can be seen in the distance travelled by Francesco Antonio Bonporti between his Op. 7 *Sonate da camera* (1707), which are dominated by the standard dance types, and his Op. 10 *Inventioni da camera* (1712), whose dances intermingle with movements entitled 'bizaria', scherzo, fantasia, 'ecco', and recitativo. The scherzo from the second *Inventione* centres on rhythmic playfulness with its offbeat repartee between violin and continuo (Ex. 6, Bonporti 1712, Sonata 2), whereas the recitativo offers ornamental melismas and 'parlando' figures in alternation over a mostly static bass (Ex. 7, Bonporti 1712, Sonata 1).

Ex. 5: Veracini 1721, Sonata I.

Ex. 6: Bonporti 1712, Sonata II.

Ex. 7: Bonporti 1712, Sonata 1.

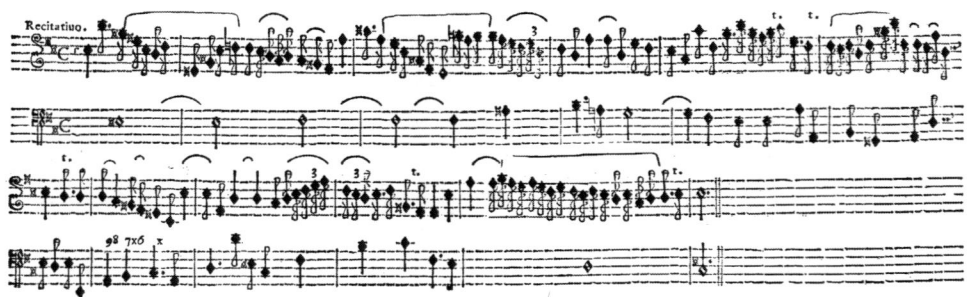

All this illustrates the early eighteenth-century expansion of both the share of the solo violin repertory taken up by sonatas da camera and the conception of the genre itself: no longer simply a suite of dances, the sonata da camera comprehends distinct-but-related styles that stand apart from the sonata da chiesa. For its part, the church sonata persisted only in those printed collections that are divided between church and chamber sonatas: in addition to Corelli and Geminiani, Gasparo Visconti 1703, Michele Mascitti 1704, Giovanni Mossi 1716, Francesco Maria Veracini 1721, Stefano Carbonelli 1729 and Giuseppe Tartini 1734 split their sonatas in this way.[24] Apart from these cases, the church sonata all but disappears from the solo violin repertory, as had the organ from its continuo accompaniment. As mentioned, much of the repertory comprises *sonate da camera*, that is, dance suites or sonatas with dance-like binary-form movements, and the one collection in the repertory that bears the designation of church sonata — Tomaso Albinoni, *Sonate da chiesa a violino solo, e violoncello, o cembalo* (*c*1709) — features mostly binary forms, some with dance titles, calls for the harpsichord, and contains no fugal movements. Albinoni's are church sonatas in name only.

A still further weakening of the traditional distinction between church and chamber is evidenced by the several prints that freely intermingle both kinds of sonata and, in a few examples, mix *da chiesa* and *da camera* movements within individual sonatas. The fifth sonata of Francesco Barsanti's *Sonate a flauto, o violino solo* (1724) is a case in point: the fugue features a simultaneous subject and countersubject whose motifs pervade the second movement (Ex. 8, Barsanti 1724, Sonata 5), while the finale comprises a minuet with six variations (Ex. 9, Barsanti 1724, Sonata 5). Likewise, the fifth sonata in

---

[24] The last two collections in this list fall outside the chronological period covered by the appendix: CARBONELLI, Stefano. *Sonate da camera a violino, e violone, o cembalo*, without opus number, ?London, s.n., 1729; and TARTINI, Giuseppe. *XII sonate et una pastorale a violino, e violoncello, o cembalo*, Op. 1, Amsterdam, Hummel, 1734.

Stefano Carbonelli's *Sonate da camera* (1729) juxtaposes a well-wrought fugue in the *stile antico* (an 'open-note' subject in semibreves and minims in *alla breve* allegro) (Ex. 10, Carbonelli 1729, Sonata 5) and a lively, syncopated giga-finale (Ex. 11, Carbonelli 1729, Sonata 5). These have precedents in Corelli's Op. 5, no. v, which also has a second-movement fugue and a giga finale, but the intermingling, rare in Corelli's oeuvre, becomes commonplace after him.

Ex. 8: Barsanti 1724, Sonata v.

Ex. 9: Barsanti 1724, Sonata v.

Ex. 10: Carbonelli 1729, Sonata v

Ex. 11: Carbonelli 1729, Sonata v.

Carbonelli, one of the composers who divided his sonatas into chiesa and camera types (six of each), offers a peculiar but illustrative case. On the one hand, he had the church/chamber distinction in mind in the overall layout of the collection: all of the church type have a fugue, and all of the chamber type include a dance. On the other hand, the individual sonatas blur that distinction: three of the church type end in dances, and none of the chamber type has more than one dance movement. Michele Mascitti's Op. 1 (1704) offers a similar example: among the six solo violin sonatas of the collection, three are labelled *a violino solo* and three are *da camera a violino solo*, yet here too the movement types within each category reveal an overlap that contradicts the advertised distinction.

Within this context of converging sonata genres, Geminiani's Op. I stands out as an exception in which the distinctions of church and chamber established by Corelli are not only maintained, but thrown into greater relief. As mentioned, Geminiani contrasts the two in the level of virtuosity required to play them. That distinction is underscored by his fugues whose subjects are longer and more rhythmically complex than Corelli's or, to give another comparison, Mascitti's. The result is a more intricately contrapuntal texture of violin double-stops, requiring virtuosity in both composition and performance. This intricacy is further emphasized by the fugues that also employ a countersubject (Ex. 12, Geminiani 1716, Sonata 6). The recherché quality of the Corellian sonata da chiesa — a genre that Brossard described as suited to the dignity and sanctity of the church[25] — is, then, all the more recherché in Geminiani and contrasts his shorter and less technically challenging chamber sonatas all the more sharply.

Ex. 12: Geminiani 1716, Sonata VI.

By contrast, Geminiani's Italian contemporaries in London — Pietro Castrucci (thought to have been a student of Corelli, as was Geminiani),[26] Francesco Barsanti (a fellow native of Lucca), and Stefano Carbonelli — were creating hybrid sonatas. Such an approach harmonized with the English reception of Italian sonata genres — London re-publications of Italian violin

---

[25]   BROSSARD, Sébastian de. *Op. cit.* (see note 18), p. 139.

[26]   Around 1720, the London publisher John Walsh paired works by Geminiani and Castrucci in a collection of flute sonatas: *XII Solos for a German flute, violino or harpsicord.*

repertory tended to erase genre distinctions so that, for example, Mascitti's *Sonate a violino solo col violone ò cimbalo e sonate a due violini*, Op. 1, and his *Sonate da camera a violino solo*, Op. 2, were both reprinted by John Walsh simply as *Solos for a violin*.[27] Church and chamber designations originated in Italian and not English musical culture, after all, and yet Geminiani delineated their distinctions for his English musical consumers.

EMBELLISHING STYLES

From his first publication Geminiani thus appears uniquely *neo*-Corellian in his conception of sonata genres; however, when he revisited these Op. 1 sonatas, re-publishing them in 1739 in revised form, his melodic embellishments were distinctly *post*-Corellian in its adaptation of a wholly different style. Consider the beginning of the third sonata in the 1739 version (Ex. 13, Geminiani 1739, Sonata 3): in these opening bars the melody is ornamented by trills and appoggiaturas, that is, brief and stereotyped additions to the melodic line.

Ex. 13: Geminiani 1739, Sonata III.

Ex. 14: Geminiani 1716, Sonata III.

---

27   See also the titles of the London reprints of Francesco Antonio Bonporti 1707 and Antonio Vivaldi 1709.

32

The original 1716 version, however, illustrates a different melodic embellishment, a unique written-out example in the print. In this earlier version, Geminiani connected first held note to the next with a florid, serpentine, and rhythmically irregular or free *passaggio* (Ex. 14, Geminiani 1716, Sonata 3). This is the Corellian style, and Corelli's own embellishments abound in similar, improvisatory-sounding figures that comprise a varying number of demisemiquavers.[28] Geminiani's brief sampling of it stands alone in the 1716 sonatas.

For much of the eighteenth century, the Op. 5 embellishments said to be Corelli's served as a point of departure both for performers who played his music and added their own embellishments,[29] and for composers writing their own sonatas. Even before their publication in 1710, Giovanni de Zotti 1707 used the same embellishing formula of holding a pitch before allowing it to surge, drop, or wind toward the next held pitch (Ex. 15, de Zotti 1707, Sonata 8). Corelli's Roman colleague (and possibly his student), Giovanni Mossi, produced more flamboyant examples, but in the same basic style (Ex. 16, Mossi 1716, Sonata 1) where Corellian embellishments are grafted onto a French-overture style of opening movement, seeming to grow out of the shorter off-beat figures of the first two bars.[30] Mossi's flourishes sometimes outline a chord, which Corelli's rarely do, but this amounts to an expansion of the idiom rather than a departure from it. A similar expansion of melodic embellishments may be seen in Castrucci (Ex. 17, Castrucci 1717, Sonata 2).

---

[28]   RASCH, Rudolf. 'Migliorare il Perfetto. Le edizioni delle Sonate a tre di Corelli (ed altre edizioni corelliane) stampate ad Amsterdam nel Primo Settecento', in: *Arcangelo Corelli fra mito e realtà storica, op. cit.* (see note 3), pp. 253-268. Rasch (pp. 408-409) makes a strong case for the authenticity of the ornaments that Roger published in 1710, arguing that the surviving contract of 1712 between Roger and Corelli would hardly have come about if Roger had published forgeries. See also RASCH, Rudolf. 'Corelli's Contract: Note of the Publication History of the *Concerti Grossi* [...] *Opera Sesta* [1714]', in: *Tijdschrift van de Koninklijke Vereniging voor Nederlandse Muziekgeschiedenis*, XLVI (1996), pp. 83-136.

[29]   BOYDEN, David Dodge. 'Corelli's Solo Violin Sonatas 'Grac'd' by Dubourg', in: *Festskrift Jens Peter Larsen, op. cit.* (see note 3), pp. 113-126; ID. 'The Corelli "Solo" Sonatas and Their Ornamental Additions by Corelli, Geminiani, Dubourg, Tartini, and the "Walsh Anonymous"', in: *Musica antiqua europae orientalis*, III (1972), pp. 591-606; ZASLAW, Neal. 'Ornaments for Corelli's Violin Sonatas Op. 5', in: *Early Music*, XXIV/1 (1996), pp. 95-115; FIKENTSCHER, Saskia. *Die Verzierungen zu Arcangelo Corellis Violinsonaten Op. 5: Ein analytischer Vergleich unter besonderer Berücksichtigung der Beziehung von Notation und Realisation*, Lucca, Libreria Musicale Italiana, 1997.

[30]   For a study of the life and works of Mossi see SGARIA, Giovanni. 'Giovanni Mossi, musicista romano del primo Settecento', in: *Intorno a Locatelli*, edited by Albert Dunning, 2 vols, Lucca, Libreria Musicale Italiana, 1995, vol. II, pp. 1113-1167.

Ex. 15: de Zotti 1707, Sonata VIII.

Ex. 16: Mossi 1716, Sonata I.

Ex. 17: Castrucci 1717, Sonata II.

By contrast, the brief introductory passage from Geminiani's third sonata in his 1739 version exemplifies a French style of embellishment, which was similarly notated with smaller note shapes and stenographic symbols. In Italian violin music, this reflects not only a new manner of melodic ornamentation that departs from Corelli's style, but also a different kind of slow movement that had emerged in the early eighteenth century. The slow movements of Corelli's Op. 5 are models of melodic simplicity, usually featuring a melodic phrase that is given twice and then followed by a series of repeated motifs (Ex. 18, Corelli 1700, Sonata 3). This melodic reserve allows for the luxuriant embellishments that he added in performance, and in the examples shown here, it is difficult to imagine a performance without embellishment.

Ex. 18: Corelli 1700, Sonata III.

Composers after Corelli, however, began to introduce a busier galant style of slow movement whose intricate rhythms leave less space for Corellian extemporizations. The opening Adagio from the second sonata of Lodovico Ferronati's Op. 1 features demisemiquavers and triplet semiquavers in a melodic line that needs no more embellishment than its indicated trills (Ex. 19, Ferronati, 1710, Sonata 2). The melodic line is itself ornamented, but the style is other than Corellian: where Corelli's embellishings are freely spun and rhythmically irregular,[31] Ferronati's detailed rhythms are conceived in strict metre against the accompanying bass. The prelude from the eighth sonata of Martino Bitti's *Sonate a due* (Ex. 20, Bitti 1711, Sonata 8), and the opening adagio from the first sonata of Giovanni Mossi's *Sonate da camera* (Ex. 21, Mossi Op. 3?, Sonata 1) furnish similar cases of an emerging *stil galant* of rhythmically precise slow movements, a subset of which can be seen in the *notes inégales* imitations of Bitti (Ex. 22, Bitti 1711, Sonata 2), Francesco Barsanti (Ex. 23, Barsanti 1724, Sonata 5), and others.

---

[31]   For example, the opening Grave of Corelli's first solo violin sonata shows seventeen demisemiquavers of embellishment to replace just a quaver's worth of unembellished melody. Later in the same bar a flourish of twelve demisemiquavers replaces the same amount.

Ex. 19: Ferronati 1710, Sonata II.

Ex. 20: Bitti 1711, Sonata VIII.

Ex. 21: Mossi Op. 3(?), Sonata I.

Ex. 22: Bitti 1711, Sonata II.

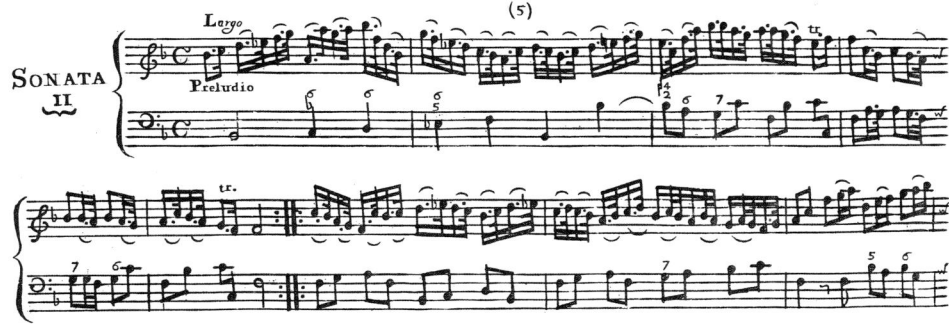

Ex. 23: Barsanti 1724, Sonata V.

Such melodies were more easily embellished through smaller, conventional ornaments: trills, mordents, turns, appoggiaturas, passing tones, slides. As a consequence, a parallel development in the slow movements of Italian violin sonatas was the incorporation of these French-style, stereotypical ornaments along with the French manner of notating them either as smaller notes or with added symbols.[32] The most prolific example is Giovanni Antonio Piani, who began his career in Paris and published his sonatas there. Among the ornaments of the prelude to his seventh sonata are the appoggiatura, mordent (a vertical mark in this print), turn, trill, and passing tone (Ex. 24, Piani 1712, Sonata 7). His approach to performance practice is modelled on the French collections of *pièces* for viol or harpsichord that set forth their ornamentation symbols in a

---

[32] Among the prints of the Italian solo violin repertory that use grace-notes for ornaments are Giovanni Antonio Piani 1712, Giovanni Mossi 1716, Pietro Castrucci 1717, Giuseppe Maria Buini 1720, Giuseppe Matteo Alberti 1721, Francesco Barsanti 1724 and Gaetano Boni c1725.

prefatory table. Pietro Castrucci evidences the same style of slow movement and ornaments with distinct symbols for trill (*t*) and mordent (*m*) and grace-notes for slides, passing notes, and appoggiaturas (Ex. 25, Castrucci 1717, Sonata 12).

Ex. 24: Piani 1712, Sonata VII.

Geminiani's Op. 1 features similar slow movements. The Adagio of the fourth sonata might be Corellian in its melody set over a slowly walking bass, but the ever-moving (and, for Geminiani, typically angular) melody has no parallel in Corelli; Geminiani's embellished version reflects this fundamental difference, with its numerous small-note and stenographic embellishments (Ex. 26, Geminiani 1739, Sonata 4). This is not to argue that French-style embellishments and rhythmically busy slow movements were always connected. The Affettuoso that begins the third sonata of Mossi's *Sonate da camera* (Ex. 27, Mossi, Op. 3?, Sonata 3) and the sixth sonata of Alberti's *Sonate a violino* (Ex. 28, Alberti 1721, Sonata 6) have the long notes that might

Ex. 25: Castrucci 1717, Sonata XII.

well have been embellished in the Corellian style, but Mossi and Alberti's notated ornaments — appoggiaturas, trills, and mordents — stick to the shorter, conventional embellishments. It would be simplistic to divide the Corellian from the French styles of melodic embellishment too cleanly, since some of the apparent differences lie in the different manner of notating similar ornaments. Corelli's Adagio, seen in Ex. 18 above, furnishes a case in point: the brief figure at the end of the first system uses a passing tone; and the third system features a series of one- or two-note ornaments, but all notated with full size notes of definite rhythmic value. Corelli, then, did use a few of the small, stereotyped ornaments, plus the ubiquitous trill, even though his style is otherwise dominated by the free, often metrically irregular, and improvised-sounding *passaggi*.

Ex. 26: Geminiani 1739, Sonata IV.

Ex. 27: Mossi Op. 3(?), Sonata III.

Ex. 28: Alberti 1721, Sonata VI.

Another point that reveals a more nuanced practice than an Italian-versus-French polarity is the hybrid embellishing style of Italian musicians in the early eighteenth century. Although Piani has been quoted here as an exemplar of the French influence, the Largo of his fifth sonata (Ex. 29, Piani 1712, Sonata 5) is more a mixture of conventional small ornaments and florid melodic embellishments, although not quite so florid nor rhythmically free as

Corelli's. Similar hybrids may be seen in the opening movements of Barsanti's second sonata (Ex. 30, Barsanti 1724, Sonata 2), Castrucci's eleventh sonata (Ex. 31, Castrucci 1717, Sonata 11), including bowing indications,[33] and others.[34]

Ex. 29: Piani 1712, Sonata V.

Geminiani's Italian contemporaries were thus eclectic in their practice, often mixing the Italian and French styles. But not Geminiani himself: as seen above, the single Corellian embellishment in the Op. 1 sonatas of 1716 was replaced in the 1739 version, which eschews the Corellian style throughout in favor of French-style ornaments.

---

[33] Castrucci gives indications of bow direction — *giù* for downbow and *sù* for upbow — so that the downward *passaggi* are played with a downbow. The trilled 4-3 suspensions at the cadences that follow, however, are played on either downbow or upbow.

[34] TALBOT, Michael. '"Full of Graces": Anna Maria Receives Ornaments', in: *Arcangelo Corelli: fra mito e realtà storica*, op. cit. (see note 3), pp. 253-268, shows that similar hybrids are found much later in Carlo Zuccari's *The True Method of Playing an Adagio* (London, 1762, facsimile reprint: Launton, Edition HH, 2011 [HH290]) and in a Vivaldi concerto adagio, probably embellished by the composer himself for Anna Maria, who was principal violinist in the Ospedale della Pietà during the 1720s and '30s.

Ex. 30: Barsanti 1724, Sonata II.

Ex. 31: Castrucci 1717, Sonata XI.

***

In his history of music, John Hawkins doubted whether Geminiani could be considered a proper representative of the Italian style because of his peculiarities as a composer: "It is much to be doubted whether the talents of Geminiani were of such a kind, as qualified him to give a direction to the national taste".[35] Indeed, Geminiani was hardly typical among Italian sonata composers: his conception of church and chamber sonatas demonstrated an unusual fidelity to Corelli's precedent at a time when other Italians intermingled the genres, and his marked preference for French embellishing-style over Corellian distinguished him from his colleagues who typically drew on both. Even his preference for both violoncello and harpsichord in the performance of the continuo sets him apart from his colleagues, who tolerated one or the other and were apparently happy to leave the choice to the performers. On each of these points, Geminiani appears intent on distilling genres and styles, and on clarifying how to perform his sonatas, where others tended toward eclecticism or hybridization and a latitude of performing possibilities.

Little wonder, therefore, that Geminiani went on to publish treatises on violin playing, guitar playing, continuo accompaniment, harmony, and "good taste in the art of musick".[36] Geminiani, more than simply being the transmitter of his teacher's style, sought from the first to codify his own.

---

[35] *HAWKINS*, v, p. 239.

[36] These treatises are *A Treatise of Good Taste in the Art of Musick*, London, [the Author], 1749; *The Art of Playing on the Violin*, London, s.n., 1751; *Guida armonica*, London, John Johnson for the Author, 1756; *L'art de bien accompagner du clavecin*, Paris, Aux adresses ordinaires, 1754; and *The Art of Playing the Guitar or Cittra*, Edinburgh, Robert Bremner for the Author, 1760; see *Francesco Geminiani Opera Omnia*, Bologna, Ut Orpheus Edizioni, 2010—, vols 12-16, in preparation.

APPENDIX

PRINTS OF ITALIAN SOLO VIOLIN MUSIC, 1670–1725

YEAR	COMPOSER	TITLE (INCL. LONDON REPRINT)	OPUS	CITY
1670	BERARDI, Angelo	Sinfonie a violino solo	7	Bologna
1670	CAZZATI, Maurizio	Sonate a due istromenti cioè violino, e violone	55	Bologna
1670	DEGLI ANTONII, Pietro	Arie, gighe, balletti, correnti, allemande, e sarabande a violino, e violone, ò spinetta con il secondo violino à beneplacito	1	Bologna
1671	BONONCINI, Giovanni Maria	Arie, correnti, sarabande, gighe, & allemande a violino, e violone, over spinetta, con alcune intavolate per diverse accordature	4	Bologna
1671	DEGLI ANTONII, Pietro	Balletti, correnti, & arie diverse à violino, e violone per camera, & anco per suonare nella spinetta, & altri instromenti	3	Bologna
1673	BONONCINI, Giovanni Maria	Ariette, correnti, gighe, allemande, e sarabande, le quali ponno suonarsi à violino solo; a due, violino e violone, a trè, due violini, e violone, & à quattro, due violini viola, e violone	7	Bologna
1676	DEGLI ANTONII, Pietro	Sonate a violino solo con il basso continuo per l'organo	4	Bologna
1676	MATTEIS, Nicola	Ayrs for the violin preludes allmands sarabands courants gigues divisions and double compositions fitted to all hands and capacities	without opus number	London
1677	BASSANI, Giovanni Battista	Balletti, correnti, gighe, e sarabande à violino, e violone, overo spinetta, con il secondo violino à beneplacito	1	Bologna
1677	DEGLI ANTONII, Giovanni Battista	Balletti, correnti, gighe, e sarabande da camera à violino, e clavicembalo ò violoncello	3	Bologna
1678	VIVIANI, Giovanni Buonaventura	Capricci armonici, da chiesa, e da camera à violino solo cioè sinfonie, toccate, sonate, introduttioni, alemande, corente, gagliarde, sarabande, gighe, balletti, e capricci, et sonate per tromba sola	4	Venice and Rome
1682	ALBERGATI, Pirro	Balletti correnti, sarabande, e gighe, à violino e violone, con il secondo violino à beneplacito	1	Bologna
1684	GABRIELLI, Domenico	Balletti gighe, correnti, alemande, e sarabande, à violino, e violone, con il secondo violino à beneplacito	1	Bologna
1685	MATTEIS, Nicola	Ayrs for the violin to wit preludes, fuges, allmands, sarabands, courants, gigues, fancies divisions. And likewise other passages, introductions and fuges for single and double stops, with divisions somewhat more artificial	without opus number	London
1686	DEGLI ANTONII, Pietro	Suonate a violino solo col basso continuo per l'organo	5	Bologna
1687	BONONCINI, Giovanni	Sinfonie a due strumenti violino, e violoncello, col basso continuo per l'organo	6	Bologna
1687–1688	TORELLI, Giuseppe	Concertino per camera a violino, e violoncello	4	Bologna
1689	DEGLI ANTONII, Giovanni Battista	Ricercate à violino, e violoncello, ò clavicembalo	5	Bologna
1690	DEGLI ANTONII, Giovanni Battista	Balletti a violino, e violoncello, ò clavicembalo	6	Bologna

Year	Composer	Title	No.	Place
1691	LAURENTI, Bartolomeo	Suonate per camera à violino, e violoncello	1	Bologna
<1695	JACCHINI, Giuseppe	Sonate à violino è violoncello, et à violoncello solo per camera	1	Bologna
1695	ARIOSTI, Attilio	Divertimenti da camera à violino, e violoncello	1	Bologna
1696	VERACINI, Antonio	Sonate da camera a due, violino, e violone, à arcileuto, col basso per il cimbalo	3	Modena
1697	JACCHINI, Giuseppe	Concerti per camera à violino, e violoncello solo, e nel fine due sonate à violoncello solo col basso	3	Bologna
1698	PEGOLOTTI, Tomaso	Trattenimenti armonici da camera a violino solo, e violoncello	1	Modena
1700	CORELLI, Arcangelo	Parte prima [-seconda] Sonate a violino e violone o cimbalo; reprinted in London as XII Sonatas by Arcangelo Corelli	5	Rome
1702	COSIMI, Nicola	Sonate da camera a violino e violone ò cembalo	1	London
1703	ALDROVANDINI, Giuseppe Antonio	Concerti à due violino, e violoncello, ò tiorba	4	Bologna
1703	VISCONTI, Gasparo	Sonate à violino e violone o cembalo; reprinted in London as Gasperini's solos for a violin with a thorough bass for the harpsicord or bass violin	1	Amsterdam
1704	MANFREDINI, Francesco	Concertini per camera a violino, e violoncello, o tiorba	1	Bologna
1704	MASCITTI, Michele	Sonate a violino solo col violone à cimbalo e sonate a due violini, violoncello, è basso continuo; reprinted in London as Solos for a violin with a thorough bass for the harpsicord or bass violin	1	Paris
1704	VITALI, Tomaso Antonio	Concerto di sonate a violino, violoncello, e cembalo	4	Modena
1705	MARINI, Carlo Antonio	Sonate a violino solo con il suo basso continuo	8	Venice
1705	TAGLIETTI, Luigi	Sonate da camera a violino, e violoncello col basso continuo	4	Venice
<1705	CANDIDO, Lodovico	Sonate da camera a violino solo con violoncello, arcileuto, o cembalo	lost	Venice
1706	MASCITTI, Michele	Sonate a violino solo col violone o cimbalo; reprinted in London as Solos for a violin with a thorough bass for the harpsicord or bass violin	2	Paris
1706	VALENTINI, Giuseppe	Idee per camera a violino, e violone, o cembalo	4	Rome
1707	BONPORTI, Francesco Antonio	Suonate da camera a violino e violone, o cembalo; reprinted in London as Bomporti's solos for a violin with a thorough bass for yᵉ harpsicord or bass violin, consisting of preludes, allemands, sarabands, &c.	7	Venice
1707	GENTILI, Giorgio	Capricci da camera a violino e violoncello o cimbalo	3	Venice
1707	MASCITTI, Michele	Sonate da camera a violino solo col violone o cembalo; reprinted in London as Solos for a violin with a thorough bass for the harpsicord or bass violin	3	Paris
1707	TAGLIETTI, Giulio	Pensieri musicali a violino, e violoncello col basso continuo a parte. All'uso d'arie cantabili, quali finite si ritorna a capo, e si finisce al mezzo, cioè al segno ⌒	6	Venice
1707	ZOTTI, Giovanni de	Sonate a violino solo col suo basso per il cembalo	1	Venice
c1709	ALBINONI, Tomaso	Sonate da chiesa a violino solo e violoncello o basso continuo; reprinted in London	4	Amsterdam
1709	MACARANI, Stefano alli	Trattenimenti musicali di sonate da camera a violino violone o cembalo	1	Rome

Year	Composer	Title	Opus number	City
1709	VIVALDI, Antonio	Sonate a violino, e basso per il cembalo; reprinted in London as XII Solos for a violin with a thorough bass for the harpsicord or bass violin	2	Venice
1710	BESSEGHI, Angelo Michele	Sonate da camera a violino solo col violone o cembalo	1	Amsterdam
1710	FERRONATI, Lodovico	Sonate a violino solo per camera con il suo basso continuo per il cembalo	1	Venice
1710	HAYM, Nicola Francesco & BITTI, M[artino]	VI Sonate da camera a flauto traversa [sic], hautbois, o violino solo	without opus number	Amsterdam
1710	MAROTTI, Ippolito	Sonate per camera a violino, e violone, ò cembalo	without opus number	Bologna
c1710	CORELLI, Arcangelo	Sonate a violino e violone e cembalo [...] troisieme edition où l'on a joint les agrèmens des adagio de cet ouvrage, composez par Mr. A. Corelli, comme il les joue; reprinted in London as XII Sonata's or solo's for a violin, a bass violin or harpsicord compos'd by Arcangelo Corelli, his fifth opera, this edition has y.e advantage of haveing y.e graces to all y.e adagio's and other places where the author thought proper by Arcangelo Corelli	5	Amsterdam
1711	BITTI, Martino	Sonate a due violino, e basso, per suonarsi con flauto, o'vero violino	without opus number	London
1711	MASCITTI, Michele	Sonate a violino solo e basso. E sonate a due violini, e basso; Nos 1–8 reprinted in London in Solos for a violin with a thorough bass for the harpsicord or bass violin	4	Paris
c1711	TAGLIETTI, Giulio	Arie da suonare col violoncello e spinetta o violone al uso d'arie cantabili le quale finite, si torna da capo, e si finisse al segno	lost	Venice
c1712	ALBINONI, Tomaso	Trattenimenti armonici per camera, divisi in dodici sonate à violino, violone e cembalo; reprinted in London as An entertainment of harmony. Containing twelve solos for a violin with a thorough bass for the harpsicord or bass violin	6	Amsterdam
1712	BONPORTI, Francesco Antonio	Inventioni da camera à violino solo con l'accompagnamento d'un violoncello e cembalo o liuto	10	Bologna
1712	PIANI, Giovanni Antonio	Sonate a violino solo è violoncello col cimbalo	1	Paris
1714	VALENTINI, Giuseppe	Allettamenti per camera a violino, e violoncello, o cembalo; reprinted in London as XII Solos for the violin or violoncello with a thorough bass for the harpsichord	8	Rome
1715	FEDELI, Giuseppe	Sonate a violino è basso	1	Paris
1715	TAGLIETTI, Giulio	Sonate a violino solo per camera col suo basso continuo	13	Bologna
1716	GEMINIANI, Francesco	Sonate a violino, violone, e cembalo; Amsterdam reprint (n.d.): Sonate a violino, violone, e cembalo; London reprint (1739): Le prime sonate a violino, e basso	1	London
1716	MOSSI, Giovanni	Sonate a violino e violone, o cimbalo, parte prima [-seconda]	1	Amsterdam

1716	VIVALDI, Antonio	*VI sonate, quatro à violino solo e basso & due a due violini & basso continuo*	5	Amsterdam
1717	CASTRUCCI, Pietro	*Sonate a violino e violone o cimbalc*; reprinted in London as *XII Solos for a violin with a thorough bass for the harpsicord or bass violin*	1	Amsterdam
1717	SOMIS, Giovanni Battista	*Sonate da camera a violino solo, e violoncello, ò cembalo*	1	Amsterdam
1720	BUINI, Giuseppe Maria	*Suonate per camera da cembalo, ò violino, è violoncello*	1	Bologna
c1720	GEMINIANI, [Francesco] & CASTRUCCI, [Pietro]	*XII Solos for a German flute, violin or harpsicord*	without opus number	London
1721	ALBERTI, Giuseppe Matteo	*Sonate a violino, e basso*; reprinted in London as *XII solos for a violin with a thorough bass for the harpsicord or bass violin*	2	Bologna
1721	VERACINI, Francesco	*Sonate a violino solo, e basso*; reprinted in London as *XII Solos for a violin with a thorough bass for the harpsicord or bass violin*	1	Dresden
1722	BONONCINI, Giovanni	*Divertimenti da camera pel violino, o flauto*; also published in 1722 as *Divertimenti da camera traddotti pel cembalo*	without opus number	London
1722	MASCITTI, Michele	*Sonate a violino solo col violone o cimbalo*	6	Paris
c1722	BIGAGLIA, Diogenio	*XII Sonate a violino solo o sia flauto e violoncello o basso continuo*	1	Amsterdam
1723	SOMIS, Giovanni Battitsa	*Sonate dà camera a violino solo, e violoncello, ò cembalo*	2	Turin
1724	BARSANTI, Francesco	*Sonate a flauto, o violino solo con basso, per violone, o cembalo*	1	London
1724	MANCINI, Francesco	*XII Solos for a violin or flute*; 3rd ed. as *XII Solos for a flute with a thoroughbass for the harpsicord or bass violin*	without opus number	London
1724	SCHIASSI, Gaetano Maria	*Trattenimenti musicali per camera à violino, e violoncello, ò clavicembalo*	1	Bologna
1725	MONTANARO, Francesco [Antonio Montanari?]	*Sei suonate a violino solo e violoncello o basso continuo*	1?	Paris
c1725	BONI, Gaetano	*Divertimenti per camera a violino, violone, cimbalo, flauto, e mandola*	2	Rome
c1725	MOSSI, Giovanni	*Sonate da camera per violino, e violoncello, o cembalo*	3?	Amsterdam

Geminiani in Paris

Neal Zaslaw
(Ithaca, NY)

Geminiani visited Paris on at least four occasions and spent perhaps 40 to 50 months there in total.[1] Given that so many of his works were published in the French capital and that on 15 occasions between 1749 and 1758 his music was heard at the *Concert spirituel*, sometimes played or led by himself,[2] Parisian musicians, music lovers and intellectuals must have known his violin playing, his concertos, his sonatas and his textbooks. And during his final visit to Paris he also became known as the composer of music for a ballet-pantomime, *La Forêt Enchantée* (1754) by Giovanni Niccolò Servandoni.

This multimedia extravaganza is usually said by modern writers to have been considered a failure by the critics in 1754. Certainly the three Parisian reviews reproduced by Enrico Careri[3] suggest a negative reception of *La Forêt Enchantée*. There are, however, two further reviews to consider: one by Élie Fréron in *L'année littéraire, ou Suite des Lettres sur quelques Écrits de ce Temps*[4]

---

[1]   Approximate dates of Geminiani in Paris: late 1732 - 20 September 1733; November 1740 - for about a year; after April 1750 - ? (Leclerc, priv. 7 October 1751; priv. 25 January 1752); before 31 March 1754 - ? (Leclerc, priv. 21 August 1765).

[2]   Pierre, Constant. *Histoire du Concert spirituel 1725-1790*, Paris, Société française de musicologie, 1975, pp. 256-276.

[3]   See Careri, chap. 7 and 'Appendix: The Reviews of *La Forest Enchantée*', pp. 203-211, which contains French texts of: [Le Corvaisier, Pierre-Jean.] *Lettre critique de M. le marquis* ✳✳✳ *à M. de Servandony, chevalier de l'ordre de Christ, peintre & architecte du roy & de son Académie Royal. Au sujet du spectacle qu'il donne au Palais des Thuileries*, n.p., 1754 (Careri, pp. 203-207); Grimm, Friedrich Melchior, Baron von. Private manuscript newsletter of 15 April 1754, published in: *Correspondance littéraire, philosophique et critique par Grimm, Diderot, Raynal, Meister*, edited by Maurice Tourneaux, 16 vols, Paris, Garnier, 1877-1882, vol. II, pp. 343-347 (Careri, pp. 207-210); and [Anon.] Review in: *Annonces, affiches, et avis divers*, 15 (10 April 1754), pp. 59-60 (Careri, pp. 210-211).

[4]   *L'année littéraire, ou Suite des Lettres sur quelques Écrits de ce Temps*, II (1754), pp. 141-144, signed 18 April 1754. My English translation can be found in Appendix B of this article.

and the other, a few pages devoted to *La Forêt Enchantée* in the *Dictionnaire des théâtres de Paris*.[5] Fréron was a conservative literary critic who chastised the writers of the Enlightenment and held up certain seventeenth-century French authors as models; Voltaire wrote a seething satire of him.

That the *Dictionnaire des théâtres* was published in 1767, some 14 years after *La Forêt Enchantée* was on the stage, might seem to reduce its value as an eyewitness account. But reading the essay, we come to understand that it was written in 1764 about an event that was "currently the novelty of Paris", presumably in some kind of diary or theatre chronicle kept by its author, Claude Parfaict. Parfaict offered a description and evaluation of *La Forêt Enchantée*. His political position is revealed by the fact that his patron was Madame de Pompadour, who obtained for him a lifetime pension from the French government.

There is much here that calls for elaboration. Servandoni presented his mute spectacles in the Salle des machines of the Palais des Tuileries during the years 1728-1743 and 1754-1758,[6] so the year of Geminiani's contribution was Servandoni's attempt to revive his displays after an eleven-year hiatus. His ballet-pantomimes provided Paris with wordless entertainment during the three weeks of Lent, when by statute other theatres were closed. The timing avoided competition while the wordless spectacles evaded the monopoly that the royal patent of Académie royale de musique (the Paris Opéra) granted it for sung theatre. In some unexplained way the absence of spoken or sung text also circumvented the Catholic Church's prohibitions against theatre during Lent. With an eye on Handel's contemporaneous Lenten performances in London, we may perhaps consider Servandoni's productions to be wordless oratorios.

Then there was the matter of the auditorium, the Salle des machines (see ILLS. 1-3). Built as an opera house in 1662, it was almost immediately abandoned for that purpose because of its wretched acoustics. The hall was subsequently used on an *ad hoc* basis for other types of entertainment. Hence, unless Servandoni was in a position (highly unlikely!) to hire an orchestra even larger than that of the Paris Opéra, Geminiani's music may have faced a nearly insuperable obstacle to a favourable reception.[7] Still, *something* must have been audible to the public for Servandoni to commission music and pay orchestral musicians, and for any of the critics to have mentioned the music. Neither the *Lettre critique de M. le marquis* ★★★ nor Fréron's review comments

---

[5]   [PARFAICT, Claude.] *Dictionnaire des théâtres de Paris*, 7 vols, Paris, Rozet, 1767, vol. v, pp. 135-139. My English translation can be found in APPENDIX A of this article.

[6]   For details, see Clare Hornsby's essay in this volume, pp. 89-111.

[7]   SPITZER, John - ZASLAW, Neal. *The Birth of the Orchestra: History of an Institution*, Oxford, Oxford University Press, 2004, pp. 184-190.

ILL. 1: Salle des machines in the Palais des Tuileries, Paris. Cross-section showing the proscenium and stage (1662). © Photo: Hans Thorwld/Erik Cornelius/Nationalmuseum, Stockholm.

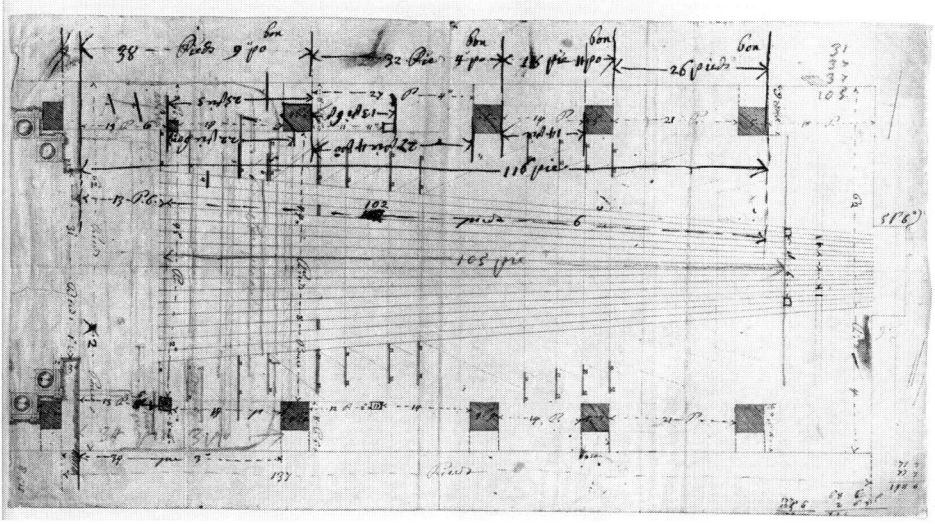

ILL. 2: Salle des machines in the Palais des Tuileries, Paris. Bird's-eye plan of the stage drawn by Servandoni. The scale: 12 pouces = 1 pied de roi = 32.48406 centimeters = 1.06575 feet. © Photo: Hans Thorwld/Erik Cornelius/Nationalmuseum, Stockholm.

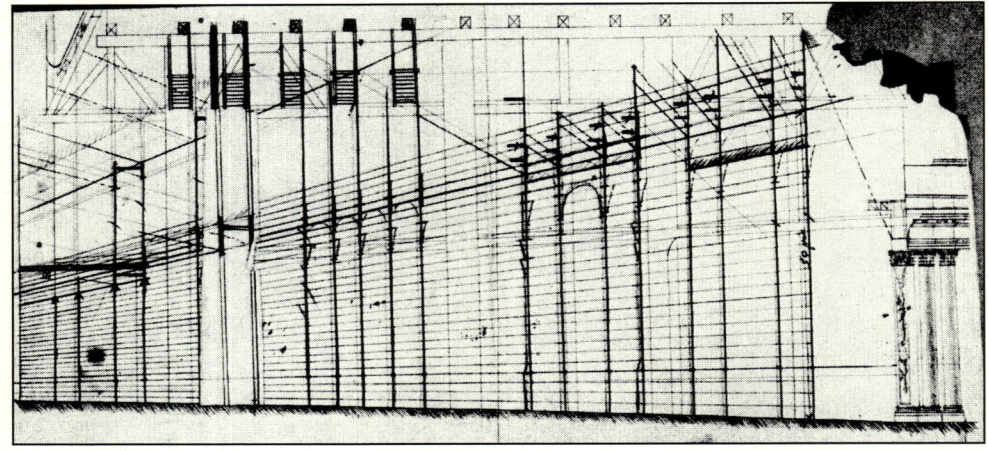

ILL. 3: Salle des machines in the Palais des Tuileries, Paris. Longitudinal section showing the stage, wings, flies and vista stage drawn by Servandoni. As a dashed line indicates, the proscenium represented at the right is drawn to a smaller scale than the tapered wings, flies, stage and vista stage. Note that the nine pairs of wings shown here correspond to the nine shown in ILL. 2. © Photo: Cecilia Heisser/Nationalmuseum, Stockholm.

on the music. Grimm, an experienced theatre critic to whom we shall return, merely dismissed the "miserable music composed by M. Geminiani". But the anonymous critic in the *Annonces, affiches, et avis divers* was more favourable, writing of "expressive music composed by M. Geminiani". And the *Dictionnaire des théâtres* affirmed that the spectacle was "accompanied by music expressing the various actions, composed by Mr. *Geminiani*". John Hawkins, who knew Geminiani, reported the composer's ideas as follows:

> About the same time [1755] he published what he called the Enchanted Forest, an instrumental composition, grounded on a singular notion, which he had long entertained, namely, that between music and the discursive faculty there is a near and natural resemblance; and this he was used to illustrate by a comparison between those musical compositions in which a certain point is assumed in one part, and answered in the other with frequent iterations, and the form and manner of oral conversation. With a view to reduce this notion to practice, Geminiani has endeavoured to represent to the imagination of his hearers the succession of events in that beautiful episode contained in the thirteenth canto of Tasso's Jerusalem, where, by the arts of Ismeno, a pagan magician, a forest is enchanted, and each tree informed with a living spirit, to prevent its being cut down for the purpose of making battering-rams and other engines for carrying on the siege of Jerusalem.[8]

---

[8]   *HAWKINS*, v, pp. 423-424.

John Hawkins was an arch-conservative music historian who in 1776, when his pioneering *History of Music* appeared, thought that music had gone down hill precipitously since Handel's day. He was knighted by the Crown.

All this suggests that perhaps not everyone considered Geminiani's music a failure and, more important for the argument of this essay, that his music was to be understood as programmatic.[9] Why is this important? Because generations of musicologists have written of *La Forêt Enchantée* that, despite its dramatic origins, the score is really nothing more than a series of concerti grossi. This strikes me as wrong-headed. Geminiani might have said so too, as the title page of the work's first edition reveals: *The Inchanted Forrest. An instrumental composition expressive of the same ideas as the poem of Tasso of that title.*[10] Geminiani's best-known and most successful works were unquestionably his concerti grossi, both the original ones and those he arranged from his own and his teacher Corelli's solo and trio sonatas. This is not to deny that there are similarities between Geminiani's concerti grossi and *La Forêt Enchantée* — the late-baroque textures and genres of some of the movements, the division of the strings into concertino and ripieno, and the composer's general stylistic preferences. If that were all there was to say, the circular equation *La Forêt Enchantée* = concerto grosso = *La Forêt Enchantée* would suffice as a critique. But there is much more.

The concertino/ripieno divide in the strings originated in the opera orchestras of Italy in the later seventeenth century, subsequently becoming a useful feature of many types of orchestral music. But even though the concerto grosso exploited that particular feature of early orchestration, it had no monopoly on it. Indeed, the orchestra of the Paris Opéra had its concertino too. The practice was attached to theatre music quite as much as to concerti grossi. It was a feature that, even when not specified by a composer, was adopted by many eighteenth-century orchestras when and where their leaders found it expedient. *La Forêt Enchantée* is not a series of concertos; rather, it is a series of late baroque movements of a programmatic nature. The music mixes styles, including Italianate movements, French-tinged dances, marches and *sinfonies*, and instrumental accompanied recitative. The programmatic intent of the music extends beyond Act v's abrupt changes of key, metre and style — deliberately shocking splices corresponding to twists and turns of Tasso-Servandoni's plot — to encompass all the movements.

Prior to the successful revivals of operas by Lully, Rameau and some of their contemporaries that have occurred since the 1980s, the sounds of French

---

9 In this matter Parfaict was paraphrasing the scenario's title page (see Appendix C).
10 London, J. Johnson, 1755; *RISM* G1485.

dance music played in the French manner (as we understand it nowadays) was not familiar to most of those who have written about *La Forêt Enchant*ée. Twentieth-century performances of French baroque opera and ballet prior to the period of revival were few and far between and (judging by recordings) mostly poor. This is no longer the case. Re-listening to *La Forêt Enchantée* with that in mind, one hears movements tailored by Geminiani to remind his Paris audiences of the great stage dances of French opera and ballet of the first half of the eighteenth century.

TABLE 1

GEMINIANI'S MUSIC HYPOTHETICALLY ALIGNED WITH PLOT ELEMENTS

THE MUSIC	THE STAGE
Geminiani	*Tasso-Mirabeau-Servandoni*
PART I (D minor)	[The Crusaders' siege machine has been destroyed. They want timber to build new machines.]
ACT I	THE FOREST ON THE SHARON PLAIN
1. Andante	Night-time, moonlight
2. Allegro moderato (dance, *inégales*)‡	Gathering of magicians and demons
3. Andante★	*Ismeno* appears and casts a spell on the forest
4. Allegro moderato (march)★‡§	The magicians congratulate him and accompany him back to Jerusalem
ACT II	THE CENTRAL MOSQUE IN JERUSALEM
5. Andante-Adagio	Night-time; *Aladdin* [ruler of Jerusalem!] consults his advisors
6. Allegro moderato (dance, *inégales*)★‡	Each in turn gives him his advice
7. Andante spiritoso (march)★§	*Argante* proposes attacking the Christians; *Ismeno* arrives with news that the forest is now protected by his spell
ACT III	THE SHARON FOREST
8. Adagio Grave (recitativo accomp)	Sunrise, daylight
9. Allegro★‡	Christian workmen flee from monsters
10. Grave (recitativo accompag)	*Alcasto* arrives leading soldiers and workmen
11. Allegro moderato★‡	They flee from demons and a wall of fire

Part II (D major)	[The magicians of Jerusalem led by *Ismeno* have conjured unremitting sun and a parching drought]
ACT IV	THE CHRISTIAN CRUSADERS' ENCAMPMENT
12. Andante affettuoso (chaconne)★	*Godefroy de Bouillon*'s sorrow; his troops are perishing
13. $\frac{6}{8}$ [Moderato]‡	In a vision the *Hermit Peter* counsels the return of the disgraced warrior *Rinaldo*
14. Allegro moderato (march)★§	*Rinaldo* is pardoned and with the aid of a magic sword will lead a Christian counterattack
ACT V	THE SHARON FOREST
15a. Andante spiritoso★‡	Dawn; *Rinaldo* enters the Enchanted Forest, newly verdant and flowering
15b. Allegro assai★	He crosses a stream that becomes a torrent
15c. Andante	He proceeds
15d. Adagio	He spies demons disguised as *Armide* and the Nymphs of Diana
15e. Andante/Affettuoso★‡	The false *Armide* and Nymphs sing, dance, play enchantingly
15f. Allegro	He rejects, unmasks, fights them with the magic sword; thunder, earthquake; the vanquished monsters disappear
15g. Allegro moderato (march)§	Triumph
16. Andante‡	The forest is tranquil
17. Allegro (march)★‡	The Christian troops arrive and celebrate *Rinaldo*'s victory; horse ballet
18. Affettuoso	[?Sober prayer thanking God] [?*Hermit Peter* conjures a drenching rain]
19. 17 da capo (march)★‡§	Ordered to do so, the workmen chop down the forest

★ with flutes
‡ with concertino
§ with 2 horns in Part I, 2 horns + 1 trumpet in Part II

As far as is known, neither Servandoni nor Geminiani left behind a cue sheet to assist in coördinating the former's five acts with the latter's four suites of movements. But whether or not this pairing of music and plot given in TABLE I is precisely right, the basic point remains: Geminiani's contribution comprised programme music, not concertos, even if a number of the movements could perfectly well also have served in a concerto grosso. And if we consider London theatrical practice, with which Geminiani was well familiar, movements of his several concerti grossi in D major and D minor could have served to provide overtures to Parts I and II as well as act tunes.

The condensed story-line given in TABLE I — extracted from the scenario, the documents reproduced by Careri and those in the appendices of this essay — remind us that Servandoni's was a theatre of metamorphoses, of illusions, effects for which the baroque stage was designed. Parfaict's closing sentence speaks of a show "in which nothing has been forgotten that painting, perspective and machines could provide to most fully satisfy the audience". From this it transpires that while we have the scenario and music for *La Forêt Enchantée*, we are missing the visual element — the element which was primarily what audiences paid to experience, and which the story and music served in supporting roles. What, then, can be recaptured of the visual elements of *La Forêt Enchantée*?

War machines (two battering rams and a catapult) can be seen in Servandoni's two stage pictures illustrating before and after the breaching of a walled city; he drew them for an earlier pantomime-ballet. These are reproduced in Clare Hornsby's essay in this volume, which also contains other descriptions that help us to imagine visual aspects of such spectacles. A stylized drawing of the stage and scenery for another of Servandoni's pantomime-ballets, *La descente d'Enée aus enfers* (1740; ILL. 4), reveals the characteristic Torelli, or baroque, stage of the Tuilleries Theatre, with its mechanized wings and exaggeratedly distant single-vanishing-point perspective.[11] If, in light of known staging practices of the period, we apply to *La Forêt Enchantée* what we see in the sketch for *La descente* and in the drawings representing before and after a siege, the following is suggested: Acts I and III of *La Forêt Enchantée* may have used a middle-deep stage to portray the forest on the wings and also with built scenery, opening up to the deepest possible stage with a distant backdrop for Act V, while Acts II and IV used a shallow stage with built scenery in front of a close backdrop. This is somewhat helpful, but still leaves us far from knowing much about the costumes, scenery, miming, dancing and special effects.

---

[11]   In a private collection and reproduced (with permission) from LA GORCE, Jérôme de. 'Une initiative originale d'un artiste italien au XVIIIe siècle: les spectacles de Servandoni dans la salle des machines des Tuileries', in: *Les artistes étrangers à Paris de la fin du Moyen Âge aux années 1920. Actes des journées d'études organisées par le Centre André Chastel les 15 et 16 décembre 2005*, edited by Marie-Claude Chaudonneret, Bern–New York, Peter Lang, 2007, pp. 121-135.

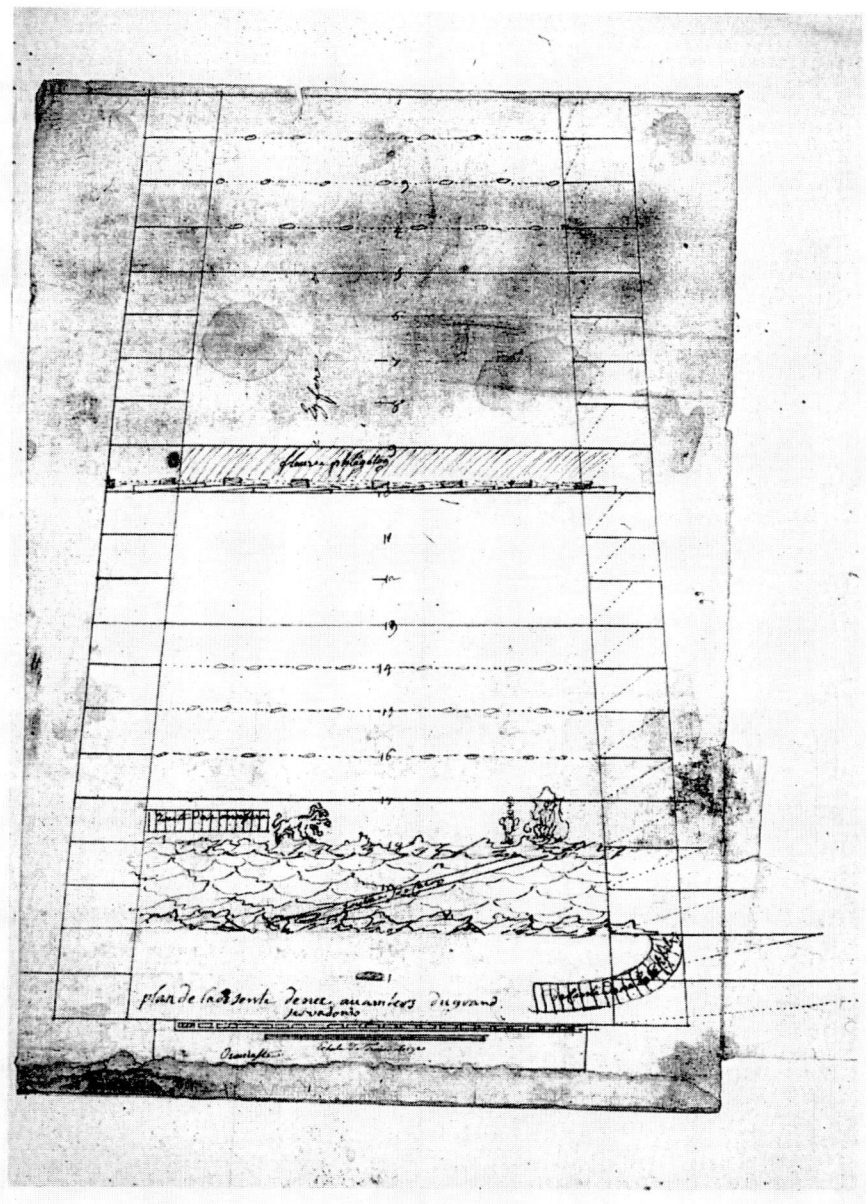

ILL. 4: Servandoni's sketch of stage designs for *La descente d'Enée aus enfers* (1740). Private collection; used by permission.

Fortunately, another previously ignored pamphlet offers additional information. This is the *Lettre de M.* ✱✱✱ *à Madame de* ✱✱✱, my English translation of which is found in APPENDIX B. This *Lettre* begins with a quotation of a passage from Horace:

> Let poetry be like painting. There might be a painting that, if you stand close to it, will hold your attention more, and another painting that holds your attention more if you stand back at a distance; one painting loves a dark corner, while another wants to be seen in the light...

The significance of these sentiments from the *Ars poetica* is twofold: they further confirm that Servandoni's primary goal was visual, not literary or musical. They also demonstrate his basic conservatism since, for instance, Diderot in his writings on the Parisian salons argued the opposite, that "Ut pictura poesis *non* erit".[12]

But what gives us the right to attribute the anonymous author's citation of Horace to Servandoni's aesthetic? The answer to this question is found on the last page of the pamphlet, which reveals that it passed the censorship on 29 March 1754, two days before the premiere of *La Forêt Enchantée* (which was also the day that the final version of the scenario was approved by the same censor); the *Lettre de M.* ✱✱✱ *à Madame de* ✱✱✱ was therefore a puff penned by someone in Servandoni's circle who had been attending rehearsals. Because it emphasizes the visual aspects and relies less than other accounts on paraphrasing the scenario, it reads more like an eye-witness account than the others. Geminiani's music is not mentioned as such, only the general soundscape, accompanying images and actions: rain, waves, thunder, subterranean rumblings, evil birds, burbling streams and early-morning birds, playing, singing and dancing nymphs, and above all, marches — marches to close every act but the third, which ends in disarray. Although no part for them survives, timpani were presumably included in the orchestra along with the brass instruments. One might also hypothesize "Turkish" instruments in the march-finale of Act I, and the action accompanying a section near the end of Act V finale is now revealed to be a horse ballet, said to be the first appearance of horses on a Parisian stage.[13] But whatever the *Lettre de M.* ✱✱✱ *à Madame de* ✱✱✱ may lack in music

---

[12]   COHEN, Huguette. 'Ut Pictura Poesis Non Erit: Diderot's Quest for the Limits of Expression in the Salons', in: *Studies in Eighteenth-Century Culture*, XXVI (1997), pp. 195-207.

[13]   BABEAU, Albert. 'Le Théâtre des Tuileries sous Louis XIV, Louis XV et Louis XVI', in: *Mémoires de la Société de l'histoire de Paris et de l'Île-de-France*, XXII (1895), pp. 130-188: 147-148.

criticism it makes up for with vivid descriptions of the sets, exotic costumes, lighting effects (as emphasized in the citation from Horace), evocations of earth, air, fire and water, metamorphoses and stage actions.

By 1754 sinfonias and overtures in the galant style had been pouring out of Italy for at least two decades. They were performed all over Europe, including Paris of course, and they were imitated by many trans-Alpine composers. The comic intermezzi of Pergolesi and others in that style were on the stage of the Paris Opéra. Vivaldi and Bach had died, Handel and Rameau were nearing their ends, and everywhere but in Britain, concerti grossi were falling from fashion. As a pamphlet war raged in Paris, the Queen (the Polish princess Marie Leczinska) sat in *her* box on one side of the opera house with the supporters of Italian music, the King (Louis XV, grandson of Louis XIV) in *his* box on the other side with the supporters of French music. To Geminiani's critics his *Forêt Enchantée* reeked of the *ancien régime*. He contrived to sound "French" in some movements, but "French" in styles that were on their way out, just as were his concerti grossi. His music was as conservative as Servandoni's productions, which attempted a revival of theatrical conventions popular in an earlier period. Even though the future lay with the Italianists, at that moment the Italian Geminiani was on the losing side of music history.

There is an extensive literature on the so-called *Guerre* or *Querrelle des buffons*, the serio-comical pamphlet battle that roiled Paris in the period 1752-1754 and then simmered for a couple of decades until it was fired up again in the Piccinni versus Gluck debates. Even though 1754 was also the year of *La Forêt Enchantée*, neither that work nor Geminiani nor Servandoni is mentioned in the documents of these literary disputes.[14] What were the disputes really about? Ostensibly about music, art, theatre, culture. In reality, however, also about other things — things by no means limited to 1752-1754.

In music the ongoing disputes were first manifested in France as the "modern" (Lully) versus the "ancient" (a largely imaginary category based on descriptions of music's effects in Greek classical authors). This metamorphosed into the "modern" (French composers from Campra to Rameau) versus the "ancient" (now Lully), then the "modern" (Italian music) versus the "ancient" (Rameau et al), to Lully-Rameau versus Gluck, and finally to Rameau-Gluck

---

[14]   The source documents of both quarrels have been reprinted and are readily available. *La querelle des bouffons. Texte des pamphlets avec introduction, commentaires et index par Denise Launay*, 3 vols, Geneva, Minkoff Reprints, 1973; *Querelle des Gluckistes et des Piccinnistes. Texte des pamphlets avec introduction, commentaires et index par François Lesure*, 2 vols, Geneva, Minkoff, 1984; GOUDAR, Ange. *Le brigandage de la musique italienne*, Paris, 1777; repr. Geneva, Minkoff, 1972.

versus Piccinni. By then Italianized versions of French music in general, and French opera in particular, had largely triumphed, although the literary grumbling continued. The politics of those supporting the second (pro-French French) of each of these binaries tended to the politically conservative or reactionary; they supported the monarchy, the divine right of kings, and a kind of nationalistic isolationism. The politics of the supporters of the first of the binaries, which included a goodly number of the French nobility, favoured a cosmopolitan outlook and the desire to modernize France. Enter the hapless Geminiani, who (whatever his politics may have been) was presumably greatly pleased to be offered a major commission by the internationally famous architect, painter and designer. Servandoni's methods and materials were firmly rooted in the past. In a season when the theatres were otherwise closed, he offered Parisians an artistic synthesis based upon Renaissance vanishing-point perspective, seventeenth-century stage machinery in the high-baroque manner, seventeenth-century optics, and of course well-known stories from ancient and Renaissance histories and epics, which provided the *raisons d'être* that motivated his supernatural stage effects. The only element in Servandoni's productions that might be considered almost up to date was the ballet-pantomime, a genre that originated as an independent genre early in the eighteenth century and enjoyed popularity as the century progressed, although largely in the conservative confines of the Paris Opéra, in the French court at Versailles, and in the provinces.

ENGLISH TRANSLATION OF CLAUDE PARFAICT'S DESCRIPTION OF *LA FORÊT ENCHANTÉE*

LA FORÊT ENCHANTÉE, a show in five acts embellished with machines, brought to life by pantomime actors, and accompanied by music, composed by Mr. *Geminiani*, expressing the various actions. The subject is taken from Tasso's *Jerusalem Delivered*, cantos XIII and XVIII. We hope that no-one will take it amiss at finding here a brief summary drawn equally from the two printed programmes for this show, which is currently the novelty of Paris.

The Mohammedans are besieged in Jerusalem by the Army of the Cross, led by Godefroi de Bouillon, and in a sortie they have burnt the Christians' siege machinery. The magician Ismen enchants the only forest in which the Christian army can hide while making good their losses. Upon Ismen's arrival some magicians, male and female, who had preceded him, draw back out of respect. As the result of the power of his conjuring the moon changes colour, becoming bloody. He places each tree in the forest under the protection of an infernal spirit charged with defending it, and after he has finished casting his spells, the magicians who had stood aside, return to congratulate him and accompany him in triumphal procession back to Jerusalem. This ends the first act during all of which the stage represents the forest that the magician had just put under the protection of the demons. The dense foliage of the forest, which is located in a solitary valley, barely allows the moon's pale light through.

This changes for the second act, which represents the interior of a mosque with its lamps lit, as the scene takes place at night. There we see Aladdin, ruler of Jerusalem, who is consulting his muftis, ministers and generals. They offer different opinions about how to defend the city. Argant requests permission to challenge the besieging general to a duel. At that moment Ismen arrives and reports what has just happened. Aladdin gives thanks to Mohammed, and the second act concludes.

[In the third act] the enchanted forest appears in a new light — broad daylight. A detachment of workers from Godefroi de Bouillon's army arrives, but intimidated by the specters and phantoms, they withdraw. A moment later they return supported by an elite troop led by a warrior named Alcaste. The obstacles increase, with the spectres replaced by ferocious beasts. A defensive wall of fire flanked by fiery towers blocks their passage. Alcaste orders them to attack these remarkable ramparts. The demons hold their ground and spread torrents of fire against the assailants who, despite their commander's efforts to rally them, are finally forced to flee, dragging him with them.

In the fourth act the stage represents the Christians' encampment. We see the interior of Godefroi de Bouillon's tent, in which the general sadly ponders means of warding off the excessive heat of the region, the length of the siege, and the scarcity of water, to all of which his troops cannot fail to be exposed. They are beginning to be troubled by thirst. Alcaste arrives and, in a confused manner, reports to Godefroi the miserable outcome of his commission. The holy hermit Peter then appears and presents Renaud, who had absented himself from the encampment after having in a private dispute killed one of the army's leaders. The Hermit, who knows that Heaven has destined Renaud to disenchant the forest, has been sent to reconcile the two warriors, and he proclaims God's wishes concerning Renaud. The General buckles on the young warrior a sword that an angel had handed him for this very undertaking. But meanwhile the Hermit raises his hands to heaven and procures a pouring rain for the soldiers' relief.[*]

The scenery of the fifth act represents the full extent of the enchanted forest, gradually lit by the sun's rays. Renaud appears at dawn at the spot where the spectres had frightened the most courageous men of the Christian army. He notices nothing of that sort; the forest offers him only a delightful greenness. He hears a sweet concert composed of murmuring waters, nightingales' songs, melodious voices, and the harmony of various instruments. A river blocks his passage, and he hardly begins to look around for a means of overcoming this obstacle when he spots a bridge. He crosses the bridge, and just as he sets foot on the other bank, the river is transformed into a raging torrent, which would permit no-one to attempt the same crossing, if anyone dared to try. As he advances, the trees of the forest, whose foliage the weather had destroyed, leaf out in new greenery. He arrives at a wide-open clearing in the forest in the centre of which stands a myrtle that, from its height and beauty, appears to be the ruler of the forest. It flowers, as do all the trees around it. Charming nymphs appear, who resemble the nymphs of Diana as represented by the painters, except that instead of bows and arrows, they hold musical instruments in their hands. They form a circle around the myrtle and around the nymph who appears to lead, and they enclose Renaud in this circle. To Renaud's eyes the head nymph looks just like Armide, but he is on his guard and does not dance with her. Drawing his sword, he uses it to strike the myrtle. Thunder is heard, the ground dances and responds to the thunder with roars. The false Armide turns into an enormous giant, the nymphs become cyclops. All these monsters attack Renaud who, despite their efforts, finally manages to cut the [myrtle] tree in half. In succumbing to his blows, this tree seems to moan; and its fall puts an end to the enchantment. The thunder ceases to rumble, the myrtle and monsters disappear, etc.

Some soldiers hidden at the edge of the forest gather around Renaud. They are followed by several squadrons of the Army of the Cross. After having disenchanted the forest, the young hero is placed at their head and conducted in triumph back to Godefroi's encampment — just as Ismen, after having enchanted the forest, was conducted in triumph back to Jerusalem by the magicians. At the same time the workers demolish this redoubtable forest, which fills the stage with its debris. And thus ends the show, in which nothing has been forgotten that painting, perspective and machines could provide to most fully satisfy the audience.

* "We have thought it a duty of suppress Tancredi's attempt [an unsuccessful effort to overcome the enchantment related in Tasso], in order to avoid the repetition of things that are nearly alike". Note in one of the programmes.

S E   135

fermés à Paris. En voici les titres & les sujets :

La Représentation de l'Église de S. Pierre de Rome, 1738.

Pandore, 1739.

La Descente d'Énée aux Enfers, 1740.

Les Travaux d'Ulisse, 1741.

Léandre et Héro, 1742.

Et actuellement, depuis le Dimanche 31 Mars 1754.

La Forêt enchantée, Spectacle en cinq actes, orné de machines, animé par des Acteurs Pantomimes, & accompagné d'une Musique de la composition du Sieur *Geminiani*, qui en exprime les différentes actions ; le sujet en est tiré de la *Jérusalem délivrée*, du *Tasse*, chant treizième & dix-huitième. Nous espérons qu'on ne sera pas fâché de trouver ici un court extrait tiré également des deux programmes imprimés de ce Spectacle qui fait actuellement la nouvelle de Paris.

Les Mahométans assiégés dans Jérusalem par l'armée des Croisés, commandée par Godefroi de Bouillon, ayant dans une sortie brulé les machines des assiégeans, le Magicien *Ismen* enchante la seule Forêt d'où l'armée Chrétienne peut tirer du bois pour réparer cette perte ; des Magiciens & Magiciennes le précédent, & se retirent par respect à son arrivée ; la Lune change de couleur, & devient sanglante par la force de ses conjurations ; il met tous les arbres de la forêt chacun sous la garde d'un esprit infernal chargé de le défendre, & son charme fini, les Magiciens & Magiciennes qui s'étoient écartés reviennent pour le féliciter, & l'accom-

136   S E

pagnent comme en triomphe à son retour
à Jérufalem , ce qui finit le premier acte. Le
Théatre repréfente pendant tout cet acte , la
forêt dont le Magicien vient confier la défenfe
aux Démons , qui eft fituée dans un vallon foli-
taire , dont l'épais feuillage ne laiffe qu'une foible entrée à la pale lumiere de la lune. Il change
au fecond , & il repréfente l'intérieur d'une
Mofquée éclairée par des lampes , parce que la
fcéne fe paffe pendant la nuit. On y voit Aladin ,
le Souverain de Jérufalem , qui tient confeil
avec le Muphti & fes Miniftres & Généraux ;
on paroît propofer différens avis pour la défenfe
de la place ; *Argant* demande la permiffion
d'envoyer défier au combat le Général des affié-
geans ; là-deffus *Ifmen* arrive , & rend compte
de ce qu'il vient de faire ; Aladin en remercie
Mahomet , & termine le fecond acte. Le Théatre change pour le troifiéme. La Forêt enchantée paroît dans une nouvelle fituation , & éclairée par le jour. On voit arriver un détachement
de travailleurs de l'armée de Godefroi de Bouillon , qui fe retirent , intimidés par des fpectres
& des fantômes ; ils reviennent un moment
après , foutenus d'une troupe d'élite commandée par un guerrier nommé Alcafte. Les obftacles fe multiplient , des bêtes féroces fuccédent
aux fpectres , une muraille de feu flanquée de
tours auffi enflammées leur ferme le paffage ;
Alcafte les anime à donner l'affaut à ce rempart
fingulier , les Démons défendent le terrein , &
répandent des torrens de feu fur les affaillans ,
qui font forcés de prendre enfin la fuite , & qui
entraînent avec eux leur Chef , malgré qu'il en

S E 137

ait, & quelque effort qu'il faffe pour les ral-
lier. Le Théatre repréfente au quatriéme le
camp des Chrétiens. On y voit l'intérieur du
Pavillon de Godefroi de Bouillon, où ce Général rêve triftement aux moyens de prévenir les
dangers auxquels la chaleur exceffive du climat,
la longueur du fiége, & la difette d'eau ne peuvent manquer d'expofer fes troupes, que la
foif commence à tourmenter. Alcafte arrive, &
lui rend compte avec confufion du mauvais
fuccès de fa commiffion. Le faint Hermite
Pierre paroît enfuite & lui préfente Renaud,
qui s'étoit abfenté du camp après avoir tué un
des Chefs de l'armée dans une querelle particuliere. L'Hermite qui fçait que le défenchan-
tement de la Forêt lui eft deftiné par le Ciel,
l'a envoyé rappeller par deux guerriers, &
annonce à Godefroi quelle eft la volonté de
Dieu fur Renaud. Le Général ceint à ce jeune
guerrier l'épée qu'un Ange lui a remife, & qui
eft deftinée à cette entreprife. Cependant l'Hermite leve les mains au ciel, & obtient en attendant, pour le foulagement des foldats, une
pluie qu'on voit tomber avec abondance (*)

La décoration du cinquiéme acte repréfente
la Forêt enchantée dans toute fon étendue,
éclairée par degrés des rayons du foleil. Renaud paroît avec le point du jour, à l'endroit
où les fpectres ont effrayé les plus courageux
de l'armée Chrétienne ; il ne remarque rien de
femblable. La forêt ne lui offre qu'une verdure

(*) On a cru devoir fupprimer la tentative de Tanetéde
pour éviter la répétition d'objets à peu près femblables.
Note d'un des Programmes.

138   **S¦ E**

charmante ; ſes oreilles ſont frappées d'un doux concert formé par le murmure des eaux , le chant des roſſignols , des voix mélodieuſes , & l'harmonie de différens inſtrumens. Une riviere lui ferme le paſſage , & à peine a t-il cherché des yeux le moyen de franchir cet obſtacle , qu'un pont ſe préſente à ſa vue ; il le traverſe , & dès qu'il a touché l'autre bord de la riviere , elle ſe change en un torrent impétueux, qui ne permettroit à perſonne de tenter le même paſſage,ſi quelqu'un oſoit s'y haſarder ; à meſure qu'il avance , les arbres de la forêt que le temps avoit privés de leurs ornemens , reprennent une nouvelle verdure ; il arrive dans une place ſpatieuſe , au milieu de laquelle ſe préſente un myrthe qui par ſa hauteur & ſa beauté paroît le ſouverain de la forêt. Il s'ouvre , auſſi bien que tous les arbres des environs ; il en ſort des Nymphes charmantes , en tout ſemblables à celles de Diane , telles que les Peintres les repréſentent , excepté qu'au lieu d'arcs & de fléches , elles ont en leurs mains des inſtrumens de Muſique. Elles font un cercle autour du myrthe & de la Nymphe qui ſemble y préſider , & enferment Renaud dans ce cercle. Cette Nymphe ſe montre à ſes yeux avec tous les traits d'Armide , mais il eſt ſur ſes gardes , & n'en eſt point ébranlé. Il tire ſon épée , & ſe met en devoir de frapper le myrthe ; le tonnerre ſe fait entendre , la terre eſt ébranlée , & répond au tonnerre par des mugiſſemens ; la fauſſe Armide devient un géant énorme ; les Nymphes deviennent des Ciclopes ; tous ces monſtres attaquent Renaud, qui parvient enfin malgré leurs efforts à couper

S E 139

l'arbre en deux ; cet arbre femble gémir , en tombant fous fes coups , & fa chute met fin à l'enchantement ; le tonnerre ceffe de gronder ; le mirthe & les monftres difparoiffent , &c. Quelques foldats cachés à l'entrée de la forêt fe raffemblent autour de Renaud ; ils font fuivis de plufieurs efcadrons de l'armée des Croifés ; le jeune héros fe met à leur tête , & eft recon-duit en triomphe au camp de Godefroi , après avoir défenchanté la forêt , comme *Ifmen* a été reconduit par les Magiciens à Jérufalem , après l'avoir enchantée. Pendant ce temps-là les tra-vailleurs détruifent cette forêt redoutable , qui remplit le théatre de fes débris , & c'eft par là qu'eft terminé ce fpectacle , où rien n'eft oublié de tout ce que la peinture , la perfpective & les méchaniques peuvent produire de plus pro-pre à la fatisfaction des Spectateurs.

Nous nous fommes laiffé emporter par les circonftances préfentes , à rendre compte de la reffource prefque unique en ce temps , que M. Servandoni offre aux amateurs des Spectacles ; les bornes que nous nous fommes impofées de ne faire mention que de ceux qui font actuelle-ment exiftants , ne nous ont pas permis de faire des articles féparés de chacun des autres Spec-tacles du même genre que le même Auteur a préfentés au Public dans la même faifon , & qui étoient interrompus depuis longtemps , quand ce Dictionnaire a été entrepris. Nous efpérons réparer ailleurs cette omiffion invo-lontaire.

SERVANDONI, (Jean - Nicolas) né à Gre-noble en Dauphiné ; il eft neveu du précédent ,

English Translation of the *Lettre de M. *** à Madame de ***

*Lettre de M. *** A Madame de *** Sur le nouveau Spectacle donné sur le grand Théâtre du Palais des Thuilleries, le Dimanche 31 Mars 1754. Par le Sieur SERVANDONI, Chevalier de l'Ordre Militaire de Christe, Peintre & Architecte ordinaire du Roi, & de son Académie Royale*, Paris, Ballard, 1754.

> *Ut pictura poesis: erit quæ, si proprius stes,*
> *Te capiat magis, et quædam si longius abstes;*
> *Hæc amat obscurum; volet hæc sub luce videri…*
> HORACE, Ars Poetica, 361-363

["Let poetry be like painting. There might be a painting that, if you stand close to it, will hold your attention more, and another painting that holds your attention more if you stand back at a distance; one painting loves a dark corner, while another wants to be seen in the light…"]

Madame,

In this passage the author of the *Ars poetica* seems to favour painting over poetry, proposing that the latter follow the rules of the former. In truth, these masses, the force of objects, this defacement, these shadows, these flashes of light [in *La foret enchantée*] do appear to belong even more to painting than to poetry. But in this case the painter [Servandoni] is not embarrassed to say that today he borrows from poetry — not only his subject but also the striking images that he offers to put before the public.

The Chevalier Servandoni has drawn his subject from Tasso's poem *Jerusalem Delivered*. He conceives of the new spectacle in five acts, the main action of which will be Renaud's triumph over Ismen's enchantments.

After the miserable success at Lussant[?], when the Christian army was foiled at the walls of Jerusalem and their war machines burnt, [the Muslim magician] Ismeno hopes to bring down the last of [the Christian crusader] Godefroy's remaining troops solely by the force of his art. He hopes by enchanting the forest to make it impossible for them to rebuild their machines, forcing them to lift their siege or to perish wretchedly outside the walls of Jerusalem, where in that season the climate's extreme heat, and even more so the lack of water, would reduce them to a feeble, debilitated state, which could not fail to prove fatal.

In order to realize this aim, Chevalier Servandoni occupied himself primarily with Cantos XIII and XVIII from Tasso's famous poem, as most suitable to provide him with the subject matter of several varied spectacles in which he deployed everything most noble and most surprising that the arts of painting, perspective and machines can provide for carrying out his project.

FIRST ACT

The first act shows the spectators a forest located in a solitary valley. The darkness of night in a mature forest, whose foliage barely allows the moon's light to feebly penetrate, doubles the horror naturally evoked by such a scene. The silence that prevails is broken only by the funereal songs of birds of ill omen. Witches appear from all directions, at first spread out and then assembling to celebrate one of their number with an infernal ceremony; but they draw back out of respect when they spot Ismeno approaching the forest and moving to the front of the stage, in order to carry out his plan by means of enchantments to render the forest forever inaccessible to the Christians.

Hardly has he begun his mysterious magic when the moon, which had been pale, responds to his curses by turning the colour of blood. Proud of his initial success, he redoubles his conjurings. Demons rush toward the sound of his voice; the magician urges them to support his enterprise, and finally the witches, who had distanced themselves out of respect, join Ismeno to congratulate him on the success of his activities. They form a procession, which is a species of homage to this powerful enchanter and a kind of triumph for him.

SECOND ACT

The Second Act takes place in the mosque that constitutes the second stage set. Aladin is seen seated on a throne surrounded by the members of his council. The prince's discouragement is expressed by his physical demeanour and his deeply depressed expression. Various members of his council seek to pull him out of it by their advice. Their varying advice can be distinguished only by the slowness or rapidity each character's varied actions. The Mufti, or religious leader, one of the prince's chief advisors, demonstrates his zeal and devotion, but Argand (who is more impetuous) takes up his weapons and seems to ask Aladin's permission to challenge the most courageous and proudest of the enemies to combat. At that instant the magician Ismeno and his followers appear. He stops Argand and makes him put down his weapons. Waving his wand and pointing to the enthusiasm of his followers, he appears to recount everything he has just done to render powerless any new efforts that the enemies might wish to attempt against the City of Jerusalem.

This council meeting takes place at night in the mosque, lit by lamps. The presence of the religious leader and his followers contributes to the range of personalities, and even more to the action, by engaging in a religious ritual to thank Mohammed for the success that Ismeno has just reported.

THIRD ACT

In the Third Act we see the Enchanted Forest but in a different guise. In place of the thick darkness that made it an object of horror, it is lit by sunlight. We see a gang of workers from the Christian army with the tools needed to fell the trees wanted to build new machines for the siege of Jerusalem. They appear joyful at being able by their labours to contribute to the conquest of that city. Their first concern, however, is to take advantage of the trees' shade to rest. But they are abruptly astonished by steam issuing from the ground, gradually increasing and becoming thicker and blacker. The workers take fright and flee. Monsters emerge from all parts of the forest; they appear to regard the workers' terror and congratulate them on having fled. A few of the workers pause, however, thinking they have noticed something new in the forest. They call out to their co-workers, they gather in a mob, brought together as if frozen in their tracks by their curiosity. Then we see Alcaste appearing at the head of an infantry regiment intended to support the workers. Although manifesting signs of fear, they follow Alcaste's soldiers. At that instant an appalling noise fills them with renewed terror and causes them to halt their forward progress. Alcaste urges them on. They advance. The noise redoubles and comes to resemble the roaring of wind and waves. A multitude of terrifying animals join the din, adding to the situation's horror. The troops stop again and seem inclined to flee. Alcaste quickly leaps in front of them and stops them; they rally. Horrible earthquakes and thunder succeed in discouraging and frightening them.

Alcaste, mad with courage, advances intrepidly, but a wall of flame blocks his passage. Towering flames serve as a bulwark. As soon as the flaming wall collapses, a crowd of demons issues forth to fight Alcaste's solders. The soldiers and the workers finally lose courage and take to their heels. Only Alcaste remains. The monsters throw some fire at him, forcing him to leave in despair, confused, and abandoned by all his followers.

FOURTH ACT

This horrific scene gives way to a new stage set, which presents the audience with Godefroy de Bouillon's encampment. The general is in his tent. He appears consumed by profound sadness brought on not only by the prodigious events in the Enchanted Forest but also by the extreme heat and lack of water, which reduce his army to harsh extremes and have killed a large number of his soldiers. His officers surround him. Alcaste arrives, but he responds to the eagerness and curiosity of the knights who surround him only by hiding his face and avoiding their handshakes, in order to hide his shame and despair at the failure of his mission.
At that moment we see the Hermit Peter arrive leading Renaud, accompanied by Abalde and the Danish Knight. Renaud bows with respect before his General, who receives him with good will. The army officers congratulate one another on the return of this young warrior and embrace him eagerly.
Then Godefroy produces the sword that a Chevalier (on orders from Heaven) had brought to the encampment after the death of the brave Suïne. He bestows it upon Renaud and calls the workers together, presenting Renaud to them as the one who is to lead them to the forest, the one whom Heaven has chosen to enable them to overcome all the enchantments and obstacles that the demons have thus far placed in their paths.

FIFTH AND LAST ACT

We are again in the Enchanted Forest, but its appearance has changed and we can see its full extent. Dawn comes, at first feebly and by degrees. The light increases and produces a beautiful day. Renaud appears advancing toward the Forest. The Forest is no longer sad and savage, inspiring horror and fright: at that moment it appears freshly verdant and smiling; the shadows make it charming, one's ears are struck by the most agreeable sounds. Renaud stops for a moment, then advances a bit slowly to the entrance to the Forest, which he finds surrounded by a river whose waters flow tranquilly. A branch of the river divides the Forest through its middle, and mingles its freshness with the shadows of the trees through which it flows. Seeking to cross the river, Renaud spots a bridge over which he passes, but hardly has he reached the far shore when the water suddenly wells up, causing a violent torrent that disturbs the tranquility of the scene and threatens imminently to destroy the bridge. Without being frightened by this prodigious happening, Renaud continues deeper into the Forest. A path leads him straight to a spacious opening, in the middle of which grows a myrtle tree, which by its height and beauty seems to be the King of all the surrounding trees. As Renaud goes directly to this spot, one of the neighbouring trees splits open and from it emerges a beautiful but false dryad, dressed in a remarkable fashion. The other nearby trees proffer the same spectacle. From each tree emerges a nymph; their dresses are turned up, their hair falls in great ringlets about their shoulders, they are shod in half-boots. In place of bows and arrows, like those carried by the Nymphs of Diana, they are armed only with lyres, systrums and other musical instruments. They form a circle around Renaud. At the same time the myrtle opens up in its turn, presenting to the warrior's gaze a demon disguised as Armide. Far from allowing himself to be seduced by such dangerous enchantments, he draws his sword and advances toward the myrtle. The false Nymphs try in vain to hold him back, tying him with garlands of flowers with which they hope to restrain his courage. Renaud breaks these feeble chains and raises his arms to strike the Myrtle. At that point horrible thunderclaps are heard, the ground appears to shake violently, terrifying bellowing issues forth, and the false Armide is replaced by a Giant. The Nymphs change into Cyclops. Despite all the efforts of these monsters, the intrepid warrior strikes the Myrtle repeatedly with his redoubtable sward. The tree trembles, Renaud redoubles his efforts and finally cuts down the fatal tree. In an instant all of the enchantment ceases; the demons leave the Forest, some of them fleeing, others bumping into them in their terror. Soon the Forest returns to tranquility and its natural state. This allows Renaud to spy some soldiers coming to see what the success of his undertaking has been. We hear a war-like noise, the troops advance, the workers arrive armed with hatchets and wedges. The Forest resounds to their blows. The warriors approach Renaud. A page presents him with a horse richly accoutered. He mounts the horse and causes it to make some movements. To the noise of warlike instruments, three companies of cavalry with several generals, in the richest and most brilliant equipage, come forward to escort Renaud in triumph to Godefroy de Bouillon's encampment. At the moment that he disappears in the distance, all the trees of the forest are felled, falling with a crash and filling the stage with their debris.

Such, Madame, is more or less the notion that I am able to convey to you of the spectacle that the Chevalier Servandoni is offering the public.

I have the honour to be, &c.

LETTRE

DE M. ***,

A MADAME DE ***,

*Sur le nouveau Spectacle donné sur le grand
Théâtre du Palais des Thuilleries, le
Dimanche 31 Mars 1754.*

Par le Sieur SERVANDONI, Chevalier de
l'Ordre Militaire de Christe, Peintre & Architecte
ordinaire du Roi, & de son Académie Royale.

Prix 12 s.

A PARIS,

De l'Imprimerie de BALLARD, Seul Imprimeur du Roy
pour la Musique, & Noteur de la Chapelle de Sa
Majesté, Rue S. Jean de Beauvais, à Ste. Cécile.

M. DCC. LIV.

Avec Approbation & Permission.

Ut Pictura Poësis erit quæ si propius stes;

Te capiat magis . & quædam si longius obstes;

Hæc amat obscurum volet hæc sub luce videri.
                    Q. Horat. Fl. de Arte Poët.

LETTRE

DE M. ***,

A MADAME DE ***,

 ADAME,

L'AUTEUR de l'Art Poëtique semble ici donner quelque avantage à la Peinture sur la Poësie, en proposant à celle-ci l'Art & les regles de la Peinture pour modèle. En effet, ces masses, cette force des objets, cette dégradation, ces ombres, ces coups de lumière paroissent encore plus apparte-

A ij

[4]

nir à la Peinture qu'à la Poësie. Mais ici le Peintre ne rougira point d'avouer qu'il emprunte aujourd'hui de la Poësie, non-seulement le sujet, mais encore les images frappantes, qu'il se propose d'exposer aux yeux du Public.

C'est dans le Poëme de la Jérusalem délivrée, du Tasse, que le Chevalier Servandoni a puisé son sujet; il a divisé ce nouveau Spectacle en cinq Actes, dont la principale action doit être le triomphe de Renaud sur les enchantemens d'Ismen.

Après le mauvais succès de Lussant, donné aux murs de Jérusalem par l'armée des Chrétiens, & la déroute que leur causa le renversement & l'incendie de leurs machines de guerre, Ismen se flatta de réduire à la derniere extrêmité les troupes de Godefroi, par la seule force de son art: il espera de les mettre par l'enchantement de la forêt, dans l'impossibilité de construire de nouvelles machines, & dans la nécessité de lever le Siége, ou de périr misérablement sous les murs de Jérusalem, où les excessives chaleurs du climat & de la saison, & plus encore la disette des eaux, les tenoient dans un état de foi-

[5]

blessé & de langueur, qui ne pouvoit manquer de leur devenir funeste.

C'est pour remplir cette idée que le Chevalier Servandoni s'est principalement atta-
ché aux Chants XIII & XVIII du fameux
Poëme du Tasse, comme plus propres à lui
fournir la matiere de plusieurs spectacles
variés, dans lesquels il a déployé tout ce
que l'Art de la Peinture, de la Perspective,
& des Méchaniques peut fournir de plus
noble & de plus surprenant pour l'exécu-
tion de son projet.

PREMIER ACTE.

Le premier Acte offre aux yeux des spectateurs une Forêt située dans un valon
solitaire : la nuit qui y regne redouble encore l'horreur qu'inspire naturellement un
bois antique, dont l'épais feuillage ne laisse
qu'une foible entrée à la seule lumiere de
la Lune. Le silence qui y regne n'est inter-
rompu que par les chants funebres des Oi-
seaux de mauvais augure. On y voit arriver
de toutes parts des Magiciennes, d'abord
dispersées, qui semblent s'y rassembler pour
célébrer quelques-unes de leurs cérémo-

[6]

nies infernales ; mais elles s'éloignent par respect lorsqu'elles apperçoivent Ismen qui s'achemine vers la Forêt , par le devant de la Scene, pour exécuter le projet qu'il a formé de rendre à jamais cette Forêt inaccessible aux Chrétiens par la force de ses enchantemens.

A peine a-t-il commencé ses mysteres magiques , que la Lune qui étoit pâle , se teint de couleur de sang à ses imprécations. Fier de ce premier succès il redouble ses conjurations ; les Démons accourent à sa voix ; l'enchanteur les engage à favoriser son entreprise ; & enfin les Magiciennes qui s'étoient éloignées par respect , reviennent en foule féliciter Ismen sur le succès de ses opérations, & forment une marche qui est un espece d'hommage qu'elles rendent à ce puissant enchanteur , & qui est pour lui une sorte de triomphe.

SECOND ACTE.

Le second Acte se passe dans la Mosquée , qui forme la seconde Décoration ; Aladin y paroît assis sur un thrône entouré par ceux qui composent son Conseil. L'ab-

[7]

battement de ce Prince est exprimé par son attitude & sa profonde rêverie. Les différens Membres de son Conseil semblent chercher à l'en tirer par leurs conseils, dont la différence ne peut être marquée que par la lenteur ou par la vivacité de leurs actions. Le Muphti ou Chef de la Loi est un des principaux Conseillers de ce Prince, & marque comme les autres son zèle & son ardeur; mais Argand plus impétueux, prend ses armes, semble venir demander à Aladin la permission d'aller défier au combat les plus courageux & les plus fiers des ennemis. Dans ce moment l'enchanteur Ismen paroît avec sa suite; il arrête Argand, & l'oblige à lui remettre ses armes. C'est en montrant sa baguette & en faisant remarquer le zèle des Magiciens qui le suivent, qu'il paroît rendre compte de tout ce qu'il vient de faire pour rendre à jamais impuissans les nouveaux efforts que les ennemis voudroient tenter contre la Ville de Jérusalem.

Ce conseil se tient de nuit dans la Mosquée, éclairée par des lampes. Non-seulement le Chef de la Loi & sa suite contribueront à la variété des personnages, mais

[8]

encore à celle de l'action, en faisant quelques cérémonies de leur Loi, pour rendre graces à Mahomet des succès dont Ismen vient de rendre compte.

TROISIEME ACTE.

On apperçoit dans le troisiéme Acte la Forêt enchantée, mais dans une autre situation. Au lieu des épaisses ténébres qui en faisoient un objet d'horreur, elle paroit ici éclairée des rayons du jour : on y voit une troupe de travailleurs de l'armée Chrétienne, avec les instrumens necessaires pour y couper les arbres dont on doit construire de nouvelles machines pour le Siége de Jérusalem. Ils paroissent animés de la joie qu'ils ont de pouvoir contribuer par leurs travaux à la prise de cette Ville : leur premier soin est pourtant de profiter de l'ombre des arbres pour se reposer ; mais tout-à-coup des vapeurs qui sortent de la terre les étonnent : ces vapeurs augmentent & deviennent de plus en plus épaisses & noires. Les travailleurs s'effrayent & prennent la fuite ; des Monstres sortent de toutes parts de la Forêt ; ils paroissent suivre de l'œil les travail-

[9]

leurs épouvantés, & se féliciter de les avoir
mis en fuite : cependant quelques-uns des
Ouvriers s'arrêtent, croyant appercevoir
quelque chose de nouveau dans la Forêt,
ils appellent leurs camarades ; ils s'attrou-
pent, & se groupent comme arrêtés par
leur curiosité : alors on voit arriver Alcaste à la tête d'une troupe d'Infanterie de-
stinée à soutenir les travailleurs. Ceux-ci
suivent les Soldats d'Alcaste ; mais c'est
avec les démonstrations de leur frayeur ;
dans cet instant un bruit épouvantable les
frappe d'une nouvelle terreur, & les oblige
à suspendre leur marche. Alcaste les rani-
me, ils avancent ; alors le bruit redouble,
& devient semblable à celui des vents &
des flots en fureur. Une multitude d'ani-
maux terribles se mêlent à ces bruits, &
en augmentent l'horreur ; la troupe s'arrête
encore, & paroît disposée à prendre la
fuite. Alcaste court au-devant d'eux, & les
arrête ; il les rallie : d'affreux tremblemens
de terre & d'horribles coups de tonnerre
achevent de les décourager & de les ef-
frayer.

Alcaste emporté par son courage avance
avec intrépidité ; mais une muraille enflam-

[10]

mée s'oppose à son passage; des tours de
feu servent de rempart: aussi-tôt la muraille
s'écroule, & il sort une foule de Démons
qui livrent le combat aux soldats d'Alcaste: ceux-ci avec les travailleurs perdent
enfin courage, & prennent la fuite; Alcaste
reste seul, & les Monstres jettant du feu,
l'obligent à se retirer, désespéré, confus &
abandonné de tous les siens.

QUATRIEME ACTE.

Cette Scene d'horreur fait place à une
nouvelle décoration, qui présente aux spectateurs le Camp de Godefroy de Bouillon:
ce Général est dans sa tente; il y paroit en-
seveli dans la profonde douleur que lui
causent non-seulement les prodiges de la
Forêt enchantée; mais encore l'excessive
chaleur & le défaut des eaux, qui réduit
son armée dans une cruelle extrêmité, &
fait périr un grand nombre de ses soldats.
Tous les Chefs de l'armée sont autour de
lui; Alcaste y arrive; mais il ne répond à
l'empressement & à la curiosité des Che-
valiers qui l'entourent qu'en se cachant le
visage, & en s'échappant de leurs mains

[11]

pour aller cacher fa honte & fon défefpoir ;
qui ne décellent que trop le peu de fuccès
de fon entreprife.

Alors on voit arriver l'Hermite Pierre
qui conduit Renaud, accompagné d'Abalde
& du Chevalier Danois ; Renaud s'incline
avec refpect devant fon Général : celui-ci
le reçoit avec bonté. Tous les Chefs de
l'armée fe félicitent du retour de ce jeune
Guerrier, & s'empreffent à l'embraffer.

Alors Godefroy fait apporter l'épée qu'un
Chevalier, par un ordre du Ciel, avoit
apportée au camp après la mort du brave
Suine ; il la remet à Renaud ; & faifant
affembler les travailleurs, il leur montre
Renaud comme celui qui doit les conduire
à la Forêt, & que le Ciel a choifi pour
leur faire furmonter tous les enchantemens
& tous les obftacles que les Démons leur
avoient jufques à ce moment oppofés.

CINQUIEME & *dernier* ACTE.

C'eft encore ici la Forêt enchantée, mais
fous un nouvel afpect, & dans toute fon
étendue. L'Aurore éclaire d'abord foible-
ment & par degrés ; la lumiere augmente

[12]

& forme un beau jour. Renaud paroît s'a-
vancer vers la Forêt. Ce n'eſt plus cette
Forêt triſte & ſauvage, inſpirant l'horreur
& l'effroi ; elle paroît en ce moment d'une
verdure fraîche & riante ; les ombrages en
font charmans ; les oreilles y ſont frappées
par les ſons les plus agréables. Renaud ſuſ-
pend un moment ſa marche ; bientôt il s'a-
vance quoique lentement, juſqu'à l'entrée
de la Forêt ; il la trouve environnée d'une
riviere dont les eaux coulent avec tranqui-
lité. Un bras de cette riviere en ſe parta-
geant, prend ſon cours par le milieu de la
Forêt, & joint ſa fraîcheur à l'ombre des
arbres qu'elle arroſe. Renaud en cherchant
le moyen de traverſer cette riviere, apperçoit un Pont, ſur lequel il paſſe ; mais à
peine a-t-il touché l'autre bord, que tout-à-
coup les eaux enflées & les efforts d'un torrent impétueux viennent troubler la tran-
quilité de cette belle riviere, & menacer le
Pont d'une ruine prochaine.

Renaud ſans être épouvanté de ce premier prodige, s'avance dans la Forêt ; un
ſentier étroit le conduit à une place aſſez
ſpacieuſe, au milieu de laquelle s'éleve un
Myrthe, qui par ſa hauteur & ſa beauté

[13]

femble être le Roi de tous les arbres qui
l'environnent. Renaud va droit à cette place:
alors un des arbres voisins s'entr'ouvre; il
en fort une belle, mais fauſſe Driade, vê-
tue d'une façon finguliere. Les autres arbres voiſins lui offrent le même ſpectacle.
De chacun de ces arbres il fort autant de
Nymphes ; leurs robbes ſont retrouſſées ;
leurs cheveux tombent en groſſes boucles
ſur leurs épaules ; leurs chauſſures ſont des
brodequins ; au lieu d'arcs & de flèches,
comme en portent les Nymphes de Diane.
Elles ne ſont armées que de Lyres, de Sy-
ſtres, & d'autres inſtrumens de Muſique.
Elles forment un cercle autour de Renaud.
En même-temps le Myrthe s'ouvre à ſon
tour, & préſente aux yeux du Guerrier un
Démon ſous la figure d'Armide. Le Héros
loin de ſe laiſſer ſéduire par un enchantement ſi dangereux, s'arme de ſon épée, &
s'avance vers le Myrthe. Les fauſſes Nymphes tentent en vain de le retenir, en l'en-
tourant de guirlandes de fleurs dont elles
voudroient enchaîner ſon courage. Renaud
briſe ces foibles chaînes, leve le bras pour
frapper le Myrthe : alors d'horribles éclats
de tonnerre ſe font entendre, la terre pa-

[14]

toit violemment ébranlée ; Il en fort d'affreux mugiſſemens ; un énorme Géant prend la place de la fauſſe Armide ; les Nymphes font changées en autant de Cyclopes. L'intrépide Guerrier malgré tous les efforts de ces Monſtres , laiſſe tomber ſur le Myrthe les coups de ſa redoutable épée. L'arbre gémit, Renaud redouble ſes efforts, & coupe enfin l'arbre fatal. En un inſtant tout enchantement ceſſe , les Démons quittent la Forêt ; les uns s'envolent , & les autres la traverſent avec épouvante. Auſſi-tôt la Forêt redevient tranquile , & dans ſon état naturel ; elle laiſſe appercevoir à Renaud quelques ſoldats qui s'étoient avancés pour voir quel ſeroit le ſuccès de ſon entrepriſe. Bien-tôt on entend un bruit de guerre , les troupes s'avancent , les ouvriers arrivent armés de haches & de coignées. La Forêt retentit de leurs coups ; les Guerriers s'approchent de Renaud. Un Page lui préſente un cheval richement enharnaché ; il le monte , & lui fait faire quelques mouvemens. Au bruit des inſtrumens de guerre , trois Compagnies de Cavalerie avec pluſieurs Généraux , dans le plus riche & le plus brillant équipage , viennent prendre

[15]

Renaud pour le conduire en triomphe au Camp de Godefroy de Bouillon ; & dans le moment qu'il s'eft éloigné , tous les arbres de la Forêt font abbattus, tombent avec fracas , & rempliffent le Théâtre de leurs débris.

Telle eft à peu-près , Madame, l'idée que je puis vous donner du Spectacle que le Chevalier Servandoni donne au Public.

J'ai l'honneur d'être , &c.

<hr>

APPROBATION.

J'AI lû , par ordre de Monfeigneur le Lieutenant-Général de Police , un écrit intitulé : *Lettre de M.***, à Madame de ***.* Et je crois que l'on peut en permettre l'impreffion. A Paris ce 29 Mars 1754.

CRE'BILLON.

Vû l'Approbation ; permis d'imprimer. Ce 29 Mars 1754.

BERRYER.

Appendix C

The Three States of the Printed Scenario

I. Early state

La Forest enchantée, représentation tirée du poëme italien de la Jérusalem délivrée, spectacle orné de machines [...] accompagné d'une musique de la composition de M. Geminiani [...] exécuté sur le grand théâtre du Palais des Thuilleries, pour la première fois le dimanche 31 mars 1754 [...]
(Paris, Ballard, 1754).
octavo; 16 p.
Copies: Lyon BM 361116 CGA; Le Mans BL 8★ 2721 Fonds anciens.

II. Early state

Description du nouveau spectacle, donné sur le grand théâtre du Palais des Thuilleries, le [...] 31 mar 1754 par le sieur Servandoni [...]
(Paris, Ballard, 1754).
octavo; 15 p.
Copies: Paris BnF 8-Yth-4704; Grenoble F.6521.

III. Final state

La Forêt enchantée, représentation tirée du poème italien de la Jérusalem délivrée, spectacle orné de machines, animé d'acteurs pantomimes & accompagné d'une musique (de la composition de M. Geminiani,) qui en exprime les différentes actions; exécuté sur le grand théâtre du Palais des Thuilleries, pour la première fois le Dimanche 31 mars 1754 [...]
(Paris, Ballard, 1754).
octavo; 24 p.
Copies: Paris BnF 8-YTH-7448 Tolbiac - Rez de jardin - Magasin (this copy is available on line at <http://gallica.bnf.fr/ark:/12148/bpt6k5771989s.r=Servandoni.langEN>); Rouen BM Mt p 13148 Fonds Cas; Paris BnF Microfiche 8-YTH-7448 Tolbiac - Rez de jardin - Magasin; Paris BnF P93/4200 Tolbiac - Haut de jardin - communication en banque de salle; Paris BnF 8-RT-11876 (3) Richelieu - Arts du spectacle - Magasin; Paris BnF 8-BL-13787 (4) Arsenal - Magasin; Paris BnF GD-23286 Arsenal - Magasin; Paris BnF NUMM-5771989.

Geminiani's Artistic Collaborator in Paris, Giovanni Niccolò Servandoni

Clare Hornsby
(London)

GIOVANNI SERVANDONI (FLORENCE 1695 – PARIS 1766) was the Franco-Italian architect, stage set designer and painter who engaged Geminiani to write music for *La Forêt Enchantée*.[1] He was the designer for all the productions staged in the large performance space within the Tuileries palace, the Salle des Machines — there were ten in total; and he was also the entrepreneur who risked (and incurred) financial failure. As impresario, he was responsible for the whole, bringing together artists from different fields — painters, designers, librettists, poets and musicians — many of whom he had worked with in other contexts, and in other cities.

Looking back at earlier periods of his career and beyond the boundaries of France, it will be seen that in his work with Geminiani in 1754, Servandoni was using an artistic vocabulary that was wholly within the framework of his previous achievements — a point that might also be made for Geminiani's musical component of *La Forêt Enchantée*[2] — and thus we are able to see this *spectacle* not as an isolated curiosity but as forming part of the tradition of

---

[1]   Much of the material for this paper was first gathered while researching my doctoral thesis *The Life and Work of Giovanni Niccolò Servandoni 1695-1766*, University of Bristol, 1989. This has not been published as a whole, but several articles on various aspects of the wide-ranging and long career of Servandoni have appeared in journals over the years. I am very grateful to Christopher Hogwood for inviting me to contribute to this volume and giving me the opportunity to refresh my ideas on Servandoni's work in a musicological context. His name is given variously in the French and Italian forms. Since he was born and baptised in Italy, the Italian form is more correct.

[2]   CARERI, p. 116: "the music for the first four acts is supplied by nothing other than four separate concerti grossi of conventional type". For a dissenting view see Neal Zaslaw's essay in this volume, pp. 49-87.

decorative stage performances in western Europe that existed until 1789, for his part in which Servandoni received such high praise from contemporaries.

He was trained as a painter of architecture and perspective in Rome under Gianpaolo Panini and others; under Panini, Servandoni would have learned the skills of decorative and illusionistic painting, and may have participated on the early stages of the commission his teacher received for decorating the Villa Patrizi. Alternatively he may have worked with his co-student Antonio Joli in the studio of Benedetto Luti.[3] The early part of his professional life is very unclear, but it would appear that from the beginning he was associated with musicians. He is reported as having left Rome for Lisbon with the members of the Italian opera,[4] but it is certain that he was in London in their company by 1721[5] when he began his set painting and designing career.[6] Geminiani was eight years older than Servandoni, and during the years leading up to 1714 he was in Rome where he was at some time a pupil of Corelli.[7] Without having archival evidence in support, it is conceivable that Servandoni met Geminiani during these years at the illustrious court of the opera and music *aficionado* and patron of art, Cardinal Pietro Ottoboni,[8] where he might also have encountered Rolli, Bononcini and Handel — all of whom spent some time there and later collaborated in London in the opera founded in 1720. Their example, along with Geminiani's, may have influenced Servandoni to seek his fortune in London.[9] The architect and

---

[3] MIDDLETON, Robin D. *J. N. Servandoni and the Architecture of the 'Anciens'*, unpublished seminar paper, n.d.; OZZOLA, Leandro. *Gian Paolo Pannini: Pittore*, Turin, E. Celanza, 1921; CROFT-MURRAY, Edward. *Decorative Painting in England 1537-1837*, 2 vols, London, Country Life, 1962-1970, vol. II, p. 274.

[4] Bataille in DIMIER, Louis. *Les Peintres français du XVIIIe siècle*, 2 vols, Paris-Brussels, G. van Oest, 1928-1930, vol. II, p. 380; NAGLER, Georg K. *Neues allgemeines künstler Lexicon*, Munich, E. A. Fleischmann, 1835-1852, p. 300; DI MATTEO, Colette. *Servandoni décorateur d'Opéra*, *Maîtrise specialisée de l'histoire de l'art*, Paris, s.n., 1970, appendix, p. 1.

[5] ROSENFELD, Sybil - CROFT-MURRAY, Edward. 'A Checklist of Scene Painters Working in Great Britain and Northern Ireland in the 18th Century', in: *Theatre Notebook*, XIX/1 (Autumn 1964), p. 19.

[6] The account of this comes from his first appearance in the French press, *Mercure de France*, October 1726, p. 234.

[7] *CARERI*, pp. 5-7.

[8] OLSZEWSKI, Edward J. 'The Enlightened Patronage of Cardinal Pietro Ottoboni (1667-1740)', in: *Artibus et Historiae*, XXIII/45 (2002), pp. 148-150.

[9] Antonio Joli, his fellow student in Rome, who later decorated the Richmond house of Heidegger, the director of the King's Theatre, and made sets for the opera from 1744 to 1748, may have made an early trip with him. The literature on these Italian opera collaborators in London includes: LINDGREN, Lowell. 'Handel's London - Italian Musicians and Librettists', in: *The Cambridge Companion to Handel*, edited by Donald Burrows, Cambridge, Cambridge

scene designer Filippo Juvarra, who made sets for the productions at the Ottoboni private theatre, was in Lisbon in 1719 and then in London before he settled in Turin to pursue an architectural career; these are the same journeys as Servandoni is often supposed by biographers to have undertaken in the same years; they may indeed have travelled together.[10]

Once in London his connections with the Royal Academy Italian opera extended beyond theatre work to a commission for a decorative painting in collaboration with Dietrich Ernst André, the German grisaille artist, which is dated to sometime before 1722. The work was destined for a house on the estate of Lord Burlington, the founder-subscriber of the Italian opera and patron of Handel, at 34 Old Burlington Street in central London, leased to Burlington's close friend Richard Arundell.[11] Geminiani also was naturally associated with the Italian circle in London; a letter from the singer Berenstadt to the merchant and diplomat Zamboni in London sends compliments to Geminiani and Rolli.[12] Zamboni and Berenstadt both dealt in art, objects and books and made money with their dealing, as did Geminiani and Servandoni. Whether or not the two future collaborators on *La Forêt Enchantée* knew each other well prior to the launch of Servandoni's public career in Paris in 1725, it can be clearly seen that both artists lived and worked in the same milieu, a diaspora of Italian artists and musicians in London.

Servandoni's first successes with set design in Paris were reported in 1726 and from 1728, he was appointed to the prestigious position of *Premier*

University Press, 1997, pp. 78-91, especially pp. 85-86; STREATFIELD, Richard Alexander. 'Handel, Rolli, and Italian Opera in London in the Eighteenth Century', in: *The Musical Quarterly*, III/3 (July 1917), pp. 428-445; LINDGREN, Lowell. 'The Three Great Noises "Fatal to the Interests of Bononcini'", in: *The Musical Quarterly*, LXI/4 (October 1975), pp. 560-583; HUME, Robert D. 'Handel and Opera Management in London in the 1730s', in: *Music & Letters*, LXVII/4 (October 1986), pp. 347-362; LINDGREN, Lowell. 'Musicians and Librettists in the Correspondence of Gio. Giacomo Zamboni (Oxford, Bodleian Library, MSS Rawlinson Letters 116-38)', in: *Royal Musical Association Research Chronicle*, XXIV (1991), pp. 1-194.

[10] VIALE FERRERO, Mercedes. *Filippo Juvarra: Scenografo e architetto teatrale*, Turin, Edizioni d'arte Fratelli Pozzo, 1970.

[11] See 'Cork Street and Savile Row Area: Old Burlington Street', in: *Survey of London: volumes 31 and 32: St James Westminster, Part 2*, edited by F. H. W. Sheppard, London, 1963, pp. 495-517 <http://www.britishhistory.ac.uk/report.aspx?compid=41491>; VERTUE, George. *Notebooks*, 6 vols, London, The Walpole Society, 1929-1950, vol. III (The Walpole Society, 22), p. 68; CROFT-MURRAY, Edward. *Op. cit.* (see note 3), p. 275; HARRIS, John. 'Dietrich André', in: *The Connoisseur*, April 1965, p. 253. Middleton suggests that when Servandoni left London for Paris in 1724, it was in the company of André. Servandoni was certainly married in London to an Englishwoman, Anne Roots, before that date.

[12] LINDGREN, Lowell. 'Musicians and Librettists [...]', *op. cit.* (see note 9), p. 20; CARERI, pp. 11-12.

peintre décorateur for the Académie Royale de Musique, the state bureaucratic body that controlled public opera performance and which ran the Théâtre du Palais Royale — otherwise known as the Opéra.[13] Like his later venture at the Tuileries, he received much praise from some quarters and criticism from others. However at the Opéra, the criticism concerned only his lavish spending (an enduring theme wherever he worked) and not the style and the manner of his designs. It is instructive to take just one example to see how taste changed from the 1730s — his most successful decade at the Opéra — to the mid fifties, the era of his collaboration with Geminiani.

One of the years of greatest expenditure on set decorations was 1735, when Servandoni worked on the new opera-ballet written by Jean-Philippe Rameau, *Les Indes Galantes*. The set designed for the third *entrée*, *Les Fleurs*, was Servandoni's masterpiece,[14] designed by Servandoni himself and described at length in two issues of the *Mercure de France* (in September and October of that year); it was one of the two revived for special performance in Bordeaux for the marriage of the Dauphin in 1745. The costs of the decorations came to 10,118 *livres*, doubling the total of the previous year.[15] There was adverse criticism of the lack of adherence to the classical unities of time and place in the drama but it was noted that these did not concern the correctness of the art of Servandoni, "Qui a fait en bonne partie la petite fortune de cet opera".[16]

---

[13] See BOUCHÉ, Jeanne. 'Servandoni', in: *Gazette des Beaux Arts*, no. 638 (August 1910), p. 121 and HEYBROCK, Christel. *Jean-Nicolas Servandoni - Eine Untersuchung seiner Pariser Bühnenwerke*, Inaugural Dissertation, Universität Köln, 1970. Most recently and with full bibliography, LA GORCE, Jérôme de. 'Décors et machines à l'Opéra de Paris au temps de Rameau, inventaire de 1748', in: *Recherches sur la musique française classique*, XXI (1983), pp. 145-157; and ID. 'Un grand décorateur à l'Opéra au temps de Rameau, Giovanni Niccolò Servandoni', in: *Jean-Philippe Rameau. Colloque international organisé par la Société Rameau, (Dijon, 21-24 septembre 1983)*, edited by Jérôme de La Gorce, Paris-Geneva, Champion-Slatkine, 1987, p. 579.

[14] Description of the flower garden set for *Entrée des Fleurs* of Rameau's *Les Indes Galantes* 1735: "A large and magnificent garden — an avenue of trees mixed with yews terminates in a large arbour formed by very high trees — there is a distant view through this to an arbour. In the shape of a half hexagon on the right and the left are five arcades supporting five more on an upper level all decorated with vases and swags of flowers. The lower porticoes have a flight of three steps along them for musicians — about 100 with the men on the higher steps and the women below. From the centre of each arcade of the portico hangs a crystal lamp decorated with flowers — and the same on the upper level. The cypresses have candelabra aligned with these lamps"; *Mercure de France*, October 1735, p. 2287 (author's translation).

[15] Bibliothèque de la Musée de l'Opéra, Archives 18/20, p. 76, *Liste annotée et détaillée du personnel 1730/40 Noms de ceux qui composent l'Ecole Le Chev. Servandoni pour les peintures de decoration | 1734-1735 Peintures de décoration 4660. 19. 6. | 1735-1736 [...] 10118. 9. / | 1736-1737 [...] 13300. /. /. | 1737-1738 [...] 9026. /. /.*

[16] *Mercure de France*, December 1735, p. 2372.

However, a critique of this type of operatic production, as employing the ingenuities or trickery of the scenic arts, is expressed by the time we reach the Enlightened intellectual context of 1755:

> Ces murmures, ces bruits, ces champêtres concerts
> ne sont dus aux accords d'une adroite musique
> et ces paysages divers sont les jeux
> d'un pinceau que dirigea l'optique.
> Mais de ces arts ingénieux
> comment s'operent des merveilles?
> Servandoni ment a nos yeux
> et Rameau ment a nos oreilles.[17]

Meanwhile, Geminiani's work had taken him to Ireland from London and his first trip to Paris took place in 1732, while Servandoni was at a high point in his early career there as a result of the stage design successes. In March of that year a *Lettre Patente* from the Pope had granted him the Order of St John Lateran, after winning the competition for the design of a new facade for the fashionable large church on the Left Bank, S. Sulpice. The design and execution of that facade was the most important commission of his whole career, and gained him further patronage and increase in artistic status, as he could then pride himself on being not only a painter and set designer but also a practising architect. The design was Italianate in manner, though heavily influenced by Wren's St Paul's Cathedral, which he knew from his time in London in the early 1720s.[18]

★★★

As an immediate prelude to the years in Paris during which Servandoni tried to revive his theatrical glories of the '30s with the spectacle-pantomimes of which *La Forêt Enchantée* was one, we need now to turn back to London where he was again employed as set designer and where the circle of patrons

---

[17] [ANON.] 'Eloge du Mensonge', in: *Mercure de France*, July 1755; and quoted at the end of the section on opera by the neo-classical theorist, LAUGIER, Marc-Antoine. *Sentiment d'un Harmoniphile, sur différens ouvrages de musique*, Amsterdam, 1756. The verse may well be by Laugier himself.

[18] See COLVIN, Howard. *Biographical Dictionary of British Architects, 1600-1840*, London, J. Murray, 1978; and MIDDLETON, Robin D. 'Abbé Cordemoy and the Graeco-Gothic ideal', in: *Journal of the Warburg and Courtauld Institutes*, XXV (1962), p. 278, and XXVI (1963), p. 90. Its current appearance is far more 'neo-classical' than Servandoni intended, having been partially completed after the Revolution by Chalgrin, architect of the Arc de Triomphe.

and collaborators included several familiar names. He arrived in 1747 and was paid by John Rich as set designer at the Covent Garden theatre. There are no details of his work over these years, but it is known that he collaborated with Handel on an aborted project for a production of Smollett's *Alcestis* in 1749.[19] Letters in the State Archive at Vienna chronicle the building of a sculpture gallery designed by Servandoni in Hammersmith for Whig grandee Bubb Dodington and the artist's entrepreneurial activities in finding sculpture and mirrors from French collections to furnish it[20] — like Geminiani, he turned his hand to dealing in art.

His presence in London at this time was also documented by Henry Angelo in his *Reminiscences* published in 1828. He writes of the painter Richard Wilson:[21] "I remember being taken to his painting room when a boy by Signor Servandoni, a friend of my father [...] First I recollect his conversing with the Signor, partly in English and partly in Italian". Wilson was in Venice in 1751 on his way to Rome (in the company of another Geminiani portraitist, the artist and later art dealer Thomas Jenkins),[22] so this meeting would have taken place after February 1747 when Servandoni arrived in London[23] and before 1750 when Wilson left. It is likely that these four men met sometime during this period.

The most notable event for Servandoni of this second London period was the hugely expensive and notorious Royal Fireworks display of 1749 for which he provided the design for the *Machine for the Fireworks* and supervised its construction.[24] The event celebrated the Peace of Aix la Chapelle which had

---

[19] See review of a recording of the music: DEAN, Winton. '[Untitled]', in: *Musical Times*, CXXII/1663 (September 1981), p. 607.

[20] Osterreichische Staatsarchiv, Abt. Haus-, Hof und Staatsarchiv, Gesandlschaftsarchiv Rom-Vatikan, Fasz 138, 141-150 (Letters Albani-Dodington). See HORNSBY, Clare. 'Antiquarian Extravagance in Hammersmith: The Sculpture Gallery of George 'Bubb' Dodington', in: *Apollo*, CXXXIII/358 (December 1991), pp. 410-414.

[21] ANGELO, Henry. *Reminiscences*, 2 vols, London, Henry Colburn, 1828, vol. I, p. 256. Geminiani was 64, Servandoni 54, Wilson 37 and Jenkins about 30 in 1751.

[22] YARKER, Jonathan. Personal communication. For Jenkins see BIGNAMINI, Ilaria - HORNSBY, Clare. *Digging and Dealing in Eighteenth-Century Rome*, New Haven-London, Yale University Press, 2010.

[23] VERTUE, George. *Op. cit.* (see note 11), vol. III, p. 134.

[24] Much has been published on the Handel 'Musick for the Royal Fireworks' composed for this event; see the contemporary BOARD OF ORDNANCE. *Description of the Machine for the Fireworks*, London, 1749. There are also many contemporary engravings in the Coke Collection at the Foundling Museum in London and in the British Museum, Prints and Drawings Dept. Crace collection nos. 104-116. Also see HANDEL, George Frideric. *The Musick for the Royal Fireworks*, edited by Christopher Hogwood, Kassel, Bärenreiter, 2004, 'Introduction'; and HOGWOOD, Christopher. *Handel: Water Music and Music for the Royal Fireworks*, Cambridge, Cambridge University Press, 2005.

been signed the previous October. All Europe was involved in this treaty, and festivities were being undertaken in all the major capital cities. Servandoni had made an extravagant proposition for the Paris festivities which was rejected.[25] His plans for London were no less grand and consisted of a massive Doric temple-like structure being erected in Green Park, made of wood, canvas and stucco and lit up from within at night by thousands of lamps. These are the same techniques, of course, that were used to build stage sets.

The *Gentleman's Magazine* of that year gives an account of the event, including the anecdote telling how Servandoni was arrested as a result of drawing his sword in anger at the (unscheduled) explosion of one of the pavilions. This was only one of several mishaps that prompted much complaint in contemporary journals. Anti-Italian sentiment, often expressed against the opera in London in earlier years, was given free rein by critics.[26] The government was accused of wasting money on the costly enterprise and Servandoni was charged with stylistic plagiarism of one of Palladio's designs: "[he] made a Fair Sketch and call'd it New".[27] There were many collaborators on this vast project but two are of particular interest in the context of Servandoni's network of connections; firstly the Florentine and near contemporary of Servandoni, Andrea Soldi. This artist painted the *trompe l'oeil* architectural decoration on the firework structure and during these years Geminiani may have sat to him for his portrait. Another Italian painter working on the Fireworks, Andrea Casali, painted an altarpiece for the chapel of the Foundling Hospital where an 'indoors' arrangement of the Firework Music was performed some weeks after the Green Park event. The painting was eventually rejected as being too Catholic in appearance.[28] Servandoni finally left London, according to his own letter, on the 15th May 1751.[29]

★★★

---

[25] This despite the fact he had produced many such festivities for public events such as Royal births and weddings during the previous ten years; see Dezallier d'Argenville, Antoine-Nicolas. *Vies des fameux architectes depuis la Renaissance des arts, avec la description de leurs ouvrages*, Paris, 1787, pp. 463-465.

[26] See for example, Rogers, Pat. 'The Critique of Opera in Pope's Dunciad', in: *The Musical Quarterly*, LIX/1 (January 1973), pp. 15-30.

[27] A satirical poem included with one of the prints of the event.

[28] Nicolson, Benedict. *The Treasures of the Foundling Hospital*, Oxford, Clarendon Press, 1972, pp. 42-43 comments on the substitution of a painting by Benjamin West for the original Casali, reporting that "to the Governors of 1801 the Casali must have come to seem too theatrical, and the West more appropriate both in subject and restraint for the Foundlings' altar".

[29] Letter dated from *Paris Cour des Princes au Palais de Thuillerie ce 13 juin 1755*, Institut Néerlandais Paris, Fondation Custodia, Frits Lugt collection.

To place his work with Geminiani in context, we should look at the first ventures at the Salle des Machines des Tuileries.[30] As already noted, his design successes at the Opéra had been considerable and much written about by 1738, the year that the *S. Pierre de Rome* decoration inaugurated the first run of *spectacles;* the second series began in 1754 with the collaboration of Geminiani. These events are difficult to categorize in modern terminology; they were 'performance' in the sense that people were on stage, but they were restricted to movement only (though this was not mime as we know it); they were also 'spectacle' because the visual aspect was the dominant factor. They were clearly begun as a speculative financial venture; Servandoni's initial aim was to create a *spectacle d'optique*, capitalising on the public's taste for awe-inspiring illusion which had created the popularity of his Opéra sets, and having once identified his market he created the demand by timing the show to coincide with the annual closing of the theatres over the latter part of Lent and Holy Week immediately preceding Easter, secular theatrical entertainments being forbidden by the Church during this period. Also, the restrictions imposed by the rules forbidding vocal performances outside of the context of the Académie Royale de Musique did not affect his project.[31]

During the years of the first *spectacles*, Servandoni was in fact still employed at the Opéra; he left his post there in 1744. For the opening event, *S. Pierre de Rome*, his choice of an elaborate architectural set depicting, with a great concern for accuracy and show of scholarship, the most important church in Christendom, excited considerable public and educated interest; related matters such as perspective, scale and measurements of the structure were widely discussed.[32] Servandoni reproduced, with an accuracy that greatly impressed commentators, a scaled-down model of the church based, according to the *livret*, on the measurements given by Bonnani and

---

[30] See, most recently, OLIVIER, Marc. 'Jean-Nicolas Servandoni's Spectacles of Nature and Technology', in: *French Forum*, XXX/2 (Spring 2005), pp. 31-47; and LA GORCE, Jérôme de. 'Une initiative originale d'un artiste italien au XVIIIe siècle. Les spectacles de Servandoni dans la salle des machines des Tuileries', in: *Les artistes étrangers à Paris: De la fin du Moyen Âge aux années 1920. Actes des journées d'études organisées par le Centre André Chastel les 15 et 16 décembre 2005*, edited by Marie-Claude Chaudonneret, Bern-New York, Peter Lang, 2007, pp. 121-135. Also, on the various structures and institutions for music in Paris, see HEARTZ, Daniel. *Music in European Capitals: The Galant Style, 1720-1780*, New York-London, Norton, 2003, pp. 595-620: 603.

[31] LA GORCE, Jérôme de. 'Une initiative originale d'un artiste italien au XVIIIe siècle. [...]', *op. cit.* (see note 30), p. 124.

[32] For example the open letter on 'S. Pierre' in Bibliothèque de l'Arsenal, collection Bachaumont, Ms. 3505, f. 191.

Fontana in their 1696 description of the church. The *livret* also mentions that Servandoni took measurements "sur place". Although there is no evidence of his ever having returned to Rome, as a young student of Gianpaolo Panini he would certainly have visited the basilica to study its architecture and perhaps assisted in the taking of measurements, a frequent practice of students and amateurs. Panini's canvas on which the design was based was part of the Cardinal de Polignac's collection in Paris at the time,[33] and Servandoni used it as a reference for the architectural details. From three drawings by Servandoni in the Nationalmuseum in Stockholm (two reproduced in Neal Zaslaw's essay, pp. 51-52) which represent the positioning of the backcloths and wings on the stage, we see he did not follow his master's oblique-angled view of the interior, but rather presented it symmetrically; this was probably due to the exceptional narrowness as compared to depth of the Tuileries stage, as it diverged from the style of his designs for the Opéra, where he was famous for having introduced the Italian *scena per angolo* manner of creating space and depth in a stage set.[34] The financing of the project was fraught with difficulty from the very beginning, as the duc de Luynes noted regarding *S. Pierre*: "Servandoni m'a dit que les frais journaliers allaient déjà à environ 10,000 francs et cela independamment de la construction, bois, peinture etc."[35]

Developing from his first effort with *S. Pierre de Rome*, we can see a change in direction; with each subsequent show Servandoni devised at least four or five different decorations corresponding to the acts in a conventional drama or operatic production. Bergman has analysed the fashion for pantomime at the period, particularly the influence of the London exponents whom Servandoni may have seen during his early period at the Theatre Royal and who came to Paris to exploit a theatre-going public thirsty for new ideas. The success

---

[33] *Cardinal Melchior de Polignac (1661-1742) visiting St. Peter's in Rome,* 1730, Musée du Louvre, Paris; and *Rome: The Interior of St. Peter's,* before 1742, National Gallery, London. La Gorce, Jérôme de. 'Une initiative originale d'un artiste italien au XVIIIe siècle. [...]', *op. cit.* (see note 30), p. 125.

[34] Oddly, considering his general tone of harsh criticism for the sets of *La Forêt Enchantée,* Grimm praises exactly this aspect of the work of "les décorateurs italiens" in his review. See Grimm, Friedrich Melchior, Baron von. Private manuscript newsletter of 15 April 1754, published in: *Correspondance littéraire, philosophique et critique par Grimm, Diderot, Raynal, Meister,* edited by Maurice Tourneaux, 16 vols, Paris, Garnier, 1877-1882, vol II, pp. 343-347 (transcribed in Careri, pp. 207-210).

[35] Luynes, Charles Philippe d'Albert, Duc de. *Mémoires du duc de Luynes sur la cour de Louis XV, 1735-58,* Paris, Fermin-Didot, 1860, p. 102 (April 1738).

achieved by the Englishman Mainbray,[36] with his "pantomimes d'Arlequin" at the Foire S. Germain theatre must have played a part in Servandoni's decision to animate his spectacles.[37] The change from pure visual spectacle to pantomime necessitated Servandoni collaborating more widely, including with literary professionals, not only the artist-craftsmen familiar to him from his work at the Opéra. Pierre-Charles Roy appears, listed as "poète" on the production of the *Descente d'Enée aux Enfers* of 1740.[38] He wrote the *livrets* for ballets and operas at the Académie Royale de Musique, and must have been associated with Servandoni there. His task would have been to adapt the story to pantomime production, the actors being directed in their parts by Mainbray. It is also possible that the latter wrote the *livrets* for these Tuileries shows which frequently, aside from the usual 'blurb' vaunting their merits and the talents of their creator, deal at some length with the theoretical and philosophical intentions behind them.

The overt pretensions of this series of spectacles were scholarly; Bergman suggests that this attitude stemmed from an interest in the production of pantomime in the antique period — the use of dress contemporary with that era observed the 'unity of costume' which did not come until the late 1750s at the Opéra.[39] Perhaps Servandoni was showing a concern for naturalism in the depiction of certain scenes (such as the use of real animals for *Héro et Léandre* of 1742) that were part of the plan to "renouveler […] dans la capitale d'une nation rivale à tant de titres, et de Rome et d'Athènes, le goût d'un spectacle si vanté dans l'antiquité, et qui avait été négligé depuis plusieurs siècles." The *livret* for *Les Avantures d'Ulysse* of 1741, is by far the most eruditely written of all the programme notes, and unlike the others, exists in manuscript form.[40] A long dissertation mentioning classical authors such as Pindar leads up to an explanation of why the Homeric subject was chosen and why it was adapted in certain ways: "[Servandoni] a choisi les événements les plus propre à rendre son spectacle plus agréable par le contraste des scènes differents". An examination

---

[36]   There are no records of any other biographical detail on this artist.

[37]   See [PARFAICT, Claude.] *Dictionnaire des théâtres de Paris*, 7 vols, Paris, Rozet, 1767, vol. III, pp. 293-294; and for a list of his productions, <http://www.cesar.org.uk/cesar2/people/people.php?fct=edit&person_UOID=100963>.

[38]   *Procès verbal*, 23 August 1740, cited in BERGMAN, G. M. 'La grande mode des Pantomimes à Paris vers 1740 et les spectacles d'optique de Servandoni', in: *Theatre Research/Recherches Théâtrales*, II/2 (1960), p. 71.

[39]   *Ibidem*, p. 73. See also STATES, Bert Olen. 'Servandoni et la Salle des Machines', in: *Revue d'histoire du théâtre*, I (1961), pp. 42-44.

[40]   *Lettre au sujet du spectacle des Avantures d'Ulysse*, Paris, Bibiothèque de l'Arsenal, Ms 2727, 2e section, pp. 26-50.

of the decorations of each scene shows the contrasts were designed to excite in the audience a whole range of emotional reactions from horror to wonder. The appeal to classical antiquity in the adoption of the pantomime genre — making a virtue out of the necessity of not having voices — can be compared with Grimm's dislike and distaste for the very same notion in his acerbic comments on the spectacles published in the *Correspondence Littéraire*.[41]

For the second series, beginning in 1754, Servandoni added music provided by noted composers, and commissioned Geminiani for the opening pantomime, *La Forêt Enchantée*. Throughout the early 1750s Geminiani's works had been occasionally performed at the *Concert spirituel* and he published a French version of his treatise on violin performance;[42] these Parisian connections probably indicate that he visited the city from his base in Dublin, but we have no specific evidence to put him in Paris, either with or without meeting Servandoni, before 1754.[43]

There seems little doubt that the ageing Geminiani was unwilling to abandon his familiar and heretofore successful genre of the *concerto grosso* in order to create a composition that might have more suited the theatrical context. This failing would certainly have been perceived by the critics and must have been part of the negative response given, for example by Grimm in his comment about the "mauvaise musique". Were it possible to compare it with the music written for the subsequent *spectacles*, we might be in a better position to judge; it has all disappeared, apart from the sketches for *La Constance Couronnée*, examined below.

The following year, 1755, Servandoni's production was *Le Triomphe de l'Amour Conjugal* for which the music was composed by Charles-Guillaume Alexandre, a violinist like Geminiani, who played in the orchestra of the Opéra Comique.[44] The *spectacle* was based on the story of Alceste, first presented by Quinault and Lully at the Opéra in 1674. In his review of this Tuileries show, Fréron, who had been positive in his review of *La Forêt Enchantée,* noted that because of the designer's absence at the Polish court at Dresden, the decorations were not a great success and he bewails the lack of "imagination sublime de

---

[41]   See GRIMM, Friedrich Melchior, Baron von. *Op. cit.* (see note 34), vol. II, pp. 343-347 (transcribed in CARERI, pp. 207-210), criticised the whole production very severely; see Neal Zaslaw (pp. 49-87 in the present volume) who comes to somewhat different conclusions about the position of this *spectacle* within the contemporary dialectic on art theory.

[42]   GEMINIANI, Francesco. *L'art du jouer le violon*, Paris, 1752; see *Francesco Geminiani Opera Omnia*, vol. 13.

[43]   CARERI, p. 41.

[44]   BROOK, Barry S. et al. 'Alexandre, Charles-Guillaume', in: *NG*; and *CESAR: Calendrier électronique des spectacles sous l'ancien régime*, <http://www.cesar.org.uk/cesar2/home.php>.

cet inimitable décorateur" in the execution of the sets.[45] Alexandre also provided the music for the 1756 show, *La Conquête du Mogol,* a story of war and love set in India, which was produced during the period of Servandoni's absence abroad.

★★★

Although there is no record of the music that he wrote for these *spectacles, La Constance Couronnée,* the show of the following year (1757), is recorded in some detail in the archives of the Bibliothèque Historique de la Ville de Paris.

The documents for *Constance* form a detailed account of the production, revealing the working methods that lay behind the creation of spectacles such as *La Forêt Enchantée,* indicating the music that was to accompany each scene and demonstrating how extensive Servandoni's web of expatriate Italian collaborators was. They consist of three double sheets of text and one of musical notation. These briefly summarise the action of each of the five acts and their various scenes, noting "la musique de chaque acte doit durer environ 12 à 13 minute." For each scene within the act, a short phrase describes the mood of the music. These comments read as instructions to a composer or arranger on the character, length and scoring required for each act. For example, the first scene, which is of "les mauvais génies et leur chat" making spells in the forest, has the note "la musique doit être enthousiaste", while the third scene of act III set in a prison requires "musique exprimant tour à tour la tendresse, le mépris et le désespoir". The final scene of the last act, when the two lovers (simply referred to as a prince and princess in this original libretto, not having any connection with specific literary characters) are reunited and happy, is annotated and this time indicates the instrumentation: "musique exprimant le bonheur et la joye avec flustes [*sic*] et alternativement trompettes et timbales". An indication is given of the role of the author of this text by the inscription

---

⁴⁵ FRÉRON, Élie Catherine. *L'Année Littéraire,* II (1755), pp. 159-160. [PARFAICT, Claude.] *Op. cit.* (see note 37), vol. VII, pp. 726-727, mentions that the *spectacle* was a benefit for the "Sieurs Ruggieri" and that they executed some fireworks as part of the show which "y ajouterent beaucoup d'agrement dans la suite des representations". Charles Burney had visited the 'Waux-hall' set up at the Foire S. Germain (where the theatre of the *Comédie italienne* had been) in 1770. In BURNEY, Charles. *The Present State of Music in France and Italy,* London, T. Becket, 1771, p. 15, he describes the illuminations and decorations of the dance-hall and mentions that it was managed by the Ruggieri brothers, who had also created the Royal Fireworks in Green Park in 1749; so like Servandoni and Geminiani, many of the artists involved in opera and *fêtes* were also entrepreneurs.

on the verso "Monsieur Chevalier Servandoni fera copyer cecy promptement pour le musicien et me le renvoyera pour la composition de la pantomim." This writer is anonymous but might have been Mainbray, the librettist for the *Avantures d'Ulysse*[46] — if their collaboration had endured the twelve-year gap between the two series of *spectacles*. The handwriting is not that of Servandoni.[47] Fréron notes that the music in this case was by Carlo Sodi, born in Rome in 1715, who came to Paris in 1749 and worked as violinist in the orchestra of the *Comédie italienne*.[48] In this document, Servandoni — despite being again at the court of Dresden — appears as the producer and coördinator of the show, contrary to the impression given in the printed *livrets* that he created the whole production.

The first of the sheets consists of notes about which decorations were to be used and a rough sketch of the storyline that developed from them. It is headed "Projet de pantomime ajusté et relatif aux six décorations projettées" with the suggested title "Les enchantements ou le combat entre le génie bienfaisant et le chat des génies malfaisant". This rather unwieldy title is finally changed to "La constance couronnée" (with "la triomphe de la constance" crossed out below) on the next sheet. The decorations are described though no details of how they looked are given: "Une forest, le temple de la génie bienfaisant, une prison, une vaste mer, palais infernal ou image de l'enfer, vaste palais et gloire du génie bienfaisant" etc. The second sheet links these decorations together under the heading "spectacle proposée par le chev. Servandoni pour l'année 1757". An air of erudition is present in the way the subject is described, familiar from the *livret* to the *Fôret*, particularly as the writer explains why "un sujet de pure imagination" has been chosen.[49] The published *livret* ends with an apologia: "Ainsi, quoique ce spectacle ne paraîsse être fait que pour le plaisir des yeux, il n'en présente moins à l'esprit un Apologue dont on peut tirer ce sens moral: Que le Ciel protège la Vertu", thereby anticipating the challenge of frivolity that surely would be made by certain critics. This production of *La Constance Couronée* was a financial disaster and the result of the next and last

---

46   *Lettre au sujet du spectacle* […], *op. cit.* (see note 40), *2ᵉ section*, p. 46.

47   As seen on legal documents, reproduced in HORNSBY, Clare. *The Life and Work of Giovanni Niccolò Servandoni* […], *op. cit.* (see note 1).

48   FRÉRON, Élie Catherine. *Op. cit.* (see note 45), vol. II, p. 137 and COOK, Elisabeth. 'Sodi, Charles', in: *NG*.

49   However, one critic hinted at plagiarism, pointing out a close resemblance to a poem by Cahusac for Rameau's *Zoroastre*, successfully revived at the Opéra the previous year. From *Lettre sur le spectacle du chevalier Servandoni a Madame D.L.M. sur la Constance Couronnée, quo'on réprésente actuellement au Louvre*, 1757, p. 22, cited in LA GORCE, Jérôme de. 'Une initiative originale d'un artiste italien au XVIIIᵉ siècle. […]', *op. cit.* (see note 30), p. 134, n. 29.

spectacle in the series was the same. *La Chûte des Anges Rebelles* was based on Milton's *Paradise Lost*, featuring music for three hundred performers divided into several orchestras and written by the famed Italian composer of *opéras comiques* Egidio Duni.[50] This extravagance forced the final abandonment of the project.

The reasons for this can be adduced from an archival source that explains the debts that resulted from the failure of the first series in 1742. The total sum at that point amounted to 35,065 *livres* and the major creditors were de la Boullaye and Berthelin de Meuville, associates of the Académie Royale de Musique who had taken a gamble on the success of the shows.[51] As for the second and final failure, there exists a pleading letter written by Servandoni[52] to an unknown associate in February 1758, the year of the collaboration with Duni, in which he complains about the unreliability of his workmen, the little time left to him to complete his preparations before Easter and asks his correspondent to intervene on his [Servandoni's] behalf with his associates "comme vous avez deja [*sic*] fait une fois pour le spectacle des Travaux [crossed through] Avantures d'Ulysse". There is also mention of "votre diogramme", referring to a drawing or plan for the forthcoming performances. This correspondent was obviously someone of influence who was either an artistic collaborator in the production or who had been associated with Servandoni in some other capacity since 1741. Grimm noted gloatingly: "Il a été si mauvais qu'il est tombé sans ressources dès la première représentation".[53]

Luckily for Servandoni, there were still parts of Europe where his credit was good and reputation high and so the disastrous end of his shows at the Tuileries did not mark the end of his set-designing career. He had been recommended to Frederick the Great in 1748 as, "Peintre à talens [...] pour les tableaux d'architecture et les décorations des théâtres",[54] and his work in Paris

---

[50]   SMITH, Kent M. - COOK, Elisabeth. 'Duni, Egidio', in: *NG*: "Jean Monnet, director of the Paris Opéra-Comique, reported in his memoirs that in autumn 1756 he received a request from Parma for a French libretto for Duni, who wished to write an opera for Paris. The result, after hesitation on Monnet's part, was Louis Anseaume's *Le peintre amoureux de son modèle*, for the first performance of which on 26 July 1757 Duni went to Paris. This was a brilliant success and refuted Rousseau's claim that the French language was unsuitable for music: with its blend of vaudeville tunes and natural French expressive declamation within an Italian musical idiom, *Le peintre* served for several years as a model opéra comique".

[51]   See below for details of costs.

[52]   SMITH, Kent M. - COOK, Elisabeth. *Op. cit.* (see note 50).

[53]   See GRIMM, Friedrich Melchior, Baron von. *Op. cit.* (see note 34), vol. IV, p. 11 (15 June 1758).

[54]   F-Pa/ Ms. 3505, *op. cit.* (see note 32), f. 191.

had attracted attention all over Europe. For a ruler desirous of emulating the taste and fashion of the French capital there was no better way to achieve this than to employ one of France's most successful artists, as Augustus III, King of Poland, did in the mid-1750s. The yearly fee of 20,000 marks reflects the value he placed on Servandoni's talent[55] and these visits to the Dresden court helped ease Servandoni's fortunes considerably.[56] The productions were of *Aesio* or *Ezio* (*Aetius*) in the carnival season, January 1755, and of *Olympiade* the following year. Both were written by Metastasio and Hasse, and Servandoni collaborated with the decorator Adam Friedrich Oser on the second. There is archival evidence (reproduced below) that he employed another collaborator to write the text for *Aetius* who can probably be identified with his *livret*-writing associate on the *spectacle* series.[57] This document is the beginning of a programme note in the manner of the *livrets*.

The descriptions of this staging of *Aetius*, contemporary with the Tuileries *spectacles*, indicate that Servandoni used the same design vocabulary for the representation of well-established theatrical pieces as he did for the altered and adapted shows he produced himself.[58] The libretto suited Servandoni's predilections admirably and gave him the opportunity to show off his skills to the best advantage; the accounts mention the lavishness of the sets.[59]

A final example of Servandoni extending the shelf-life of the baroque manner of stage set-design by working outside France, away from the growing currents of *Encyclopédie*-driven neo-classical critique was his work in Stuttgart in 1763-1764 which is fully documented, thanks to an account by Joseph Uriot, the court librarian, of the birthday celebrations of the Herzog Karl Eugen.[60] The richness of the Duke's court, subsidised by France, was famous throughout Europe, and his wealth is reflected in the lavishness of his entertainments. The opera house was one of Europe's largest with an enormous budget — 200,000 *gulden* in 1763 — and 300 artists in its employ. Servandoni's collaborators in this

---

[55]   EDWARDS, Henry Sutherland. *History of the Opera*, London, W. H. Allen & Co., 1862, p. 178; THIEME, Ulrich - BECKER, Felix. *Allgemeines Lexicon der Bildenden Künstler*, 37 vols, Leipzig, Wilhelm Engelmann, 1907-1950, vol. XXX, p. 527 has *livres* not marks.

[56]   GREGOR, Joseph. *Wiener szenische kunst*, Vienna, Wiener Drucke, 1924-1925, p. 103; and ZUCKER, Paul. *Die Theaterdekoration des Klassizismus. Eine Kunstgeschichte des Bühnenbildes*, Berlin, R. Kaemmerer, 1925, p. 8.

[57]   See APPENDIX C for transcription of document.

[58]   This Dresden production was a new setting by Hasse, differing from the first at Naples in 1731.

[59]   NICHOLS, David J. - HANSELL, Sven. 'Hasse', in: *NG*.

[60]   Fully analysed in STATES, Bert Olen. 'Servandoni at Württemberg', in: *Theatre Survey*, v/2 (November 1964), p. 87.

production of Jomelli's version of Metastasio's *Il Demofoönte* were the designer Columba who contributed six of the twenty decorations, Louis Boquet the Paris-based costume designer, Noverre the choreographer and dancer whose four ballets came between each act of the opera, and Jomelli's son Jean Raphael as curtain painter. In such illustrious company Servandoni's art was completely at home, and for once the constraints of a limited budget were not a problem; he himself received 15,000 marks, expenses and a carriage in return for his services. The celebrations took place in February 1764 and lasted sixteen days, with several performances of the opera, fireworks, gala dinners and a Grand Ball. Servandoni's designs included both interior and exterior scenes, the two for the opera itself and others for the first of the *entr'acte* ballets — *La mort de Lycomède* — based on the story of Alceste which Servandoni had produced in his *Triomphe de l'Amour Conjugal* at the Tuileries in 1755. For this ballet Servandoni designed several sets: a rocky enclosure, a Doric colonnade leading to the sea, a marble palace chamber and the exterior of a walled town. The pair of drawings in Vienna attributed to Servandoni (see ILL. 1 and 2)[61] which show the siege engines and the fighting soldiers in the breach, are 'before and after' scenes, close to those clearly indicated in Uriot's description of the story as it was enacted at Stuttgart, thus giving us a glimpse of how things might have looked for the Salle des Machines set of 1755.[62]

There can be little doubt that the mood of the criticism in mid-century Paris was moving against Servandoni, *le merveilleux* and what came to be seen as the baroque excesses of the style in which he worked as a designer. His career was long and he travelled much; he seems to have outlived the taste for his work and on his death in Paris in 1766 he was massively in debt and was unlamented (except perhaps by his wife and children). As an artist, his greatest monument is the imposing façade of S. Sulpice,[63] which, ironically, given the way his decorative work was held in disfavour by the neo-classical polemicists such as Laugier and Grimm, has often been considered as a portent of that same movement in the field of architecture. If this is the case, it is not likely that the designer saw himself as a trail-blazer for the 'new' style; his career was spent in courts and on the stage. He was an archetypal eighteenth-century

---

[61] GREGOR, Joseph - HADAMOWSKY, Franz. *Katalog des Handzeichnungnen des Theatersammlung der Nationalbibliothek, Vienna*, Vienna, Höfels, 1930, catalogue nos. III/41 = A 1296 and III/42 = A 1297.

[62] STATES, Bert Olen. 'Servandoni at Württemberg', *op. cit.* (see note 60), p. 98, proposes these drawings as having been made for the Stuttgart performance.

[63] See the engraving by Pierre Patte, as reproduced in ERIKSEN, Svend. *Early Neoclassicism in France*, London, Faber, 1974, plate 16 and pp. 291-292.

ILL. 1: "Beseiged city", attributed to Giovanni Niccolò Servandoni, used at Stuttgart, perhaps also at Dresden. Vienna, Österreichischen Nationalbibliothek: Alb. Inv. 1296.

ILL. 2: "Duel", attributed to Giovanni Niccolò Servandoni, used at Stuttgart, perhaps also at Dresden. Vienna, Österreichischen Nationalbibliothek: Alb. Inv. 1297.

designer, a jack-of-all-trades who, for a number of years when Parisian public and critical taste coincided, was master of at least one, that of stage set-design. The project on which he employed Geminiani was only one of many such collaborative ventures undertaken throughout his working life; the fact that it was a financial failure should not be held against it — almost everything that Servandoni was involved with ended in financial disaster. The composer of *La Forêt Enchantée* has been luckier in his critical fortune than the designer; thanks to the contemporary publication of his works and recent recordings, we are able to hear the music for the show. The design, by contrast, disappeared, as did the sets themselves, which is the common fate of such artistic productions, whose ephemeral nature has to a large extent consigned Servandoni and other artists who worked in the same field, rather unjustifiably to the margins of any account of eighteenth-century art.

Appendix A

Servandoni's Work as Set Designer in Paris

[Production / volume reference in the *Mercure de France*]

Opera

Pyrame et Thisbe / 1726 oct. p. 2329
Proserpine / 1727 fév. p. 345
Orion / 1728 mars p. 561
Pénélope / 1728 sept. p. 2093
Tancrède / 1728 avr. p. 757, 770
Thésée / 1729 déc. II p. 3099
Thésée / 1730 jan. p. 146
Alcione / 1730 juin I p. 1188
Alcione / 1730 juill. p. 1621
Pyrrhus / 1730 nov. p. 2469
Phaëton / 1730 déc. I p. 2689
Phaëton / 1730 déc. II p. 2935
L'empire de l'amour / 1733 avr. p. 793
L'empire de l'amour / 1733 mai p. 998
(Pirithous) Jephté / 1734 avr. p. 756
Les Elémens / 1734 juill. p. 1601
Philomèle / 1734 déc. p. 2691
Les Indes Galantes / 1735 sep. p. 2035
Les Indes Galantes / 1735 oct. p. 2287
Scanderberg / 1735 nov. p. 2372
Scanderberg / 1735 déc. I p. 2704
Scanderberg / 1735 déc. II p. 2918
Scanderberg / 1736 jan. p. 30
Issé / 1741 déc, p. 2705

Spectacles

S. Pierre / 1737 déc. I p. 2653
S. Pierre / 1737 déc. II p. 2877
S. Pierre / 1738 fév. p. 319
Pandore / 1739 fév. p. 340
Pandore / 1739 mars p. 590
Descente d'Enée / 1740 mars p. 573
Descente d'Enée / 1740 mai p. 1016
Descente d'Enée / 1740 juin I p. 1210
Travaux d'Ulysse / 1741 fév. p. 393
Travaux d'Ulysse / 1741 juin I p. 1239
Héro et Léandre / (1742)
La Forêt Enchantée / 1754 mai p. 187

Le triomphe de l'amour / 1755 avr. p. 193
La conquête du Mogol / 1756 mai p. 244
La conquête du Mogol / 1756 juin p. 244
La Constance Couronné / 1757 avr. II p. 177
La Chûte des Anges Rebelles / (1758)

APPENDIX B

DEBTS ASSOCIATED WITH THE FIRST SERIES OF SPECTACLES

Paris, Centre d'accueil et de recherche des Archives nationals (CARAN)
Minutier Central XLII 397 16 août 1742

Convention et délégation entre les S. et D. Servandoni et leurs créanciers.

Jean Servandoni peintre et architecte du Roy et de l'Académie Royale de Musique et De. Anne Roots son épouse qu'il autorise à […] demeurant à Paris rue S.Thomas du Louvre, paroisse S.Germain l'Auxerrois d'une part […] long list of individual creditors follows] d'autre part. Le dit S. Servandoni represent à ses créanciers que le Roy lui ayant accordé il y a quelques anné le privilege de donner au public pendant le quinzaine de paques des représentations de décorations dans la salle des machines au chateau des tuileries, il a été obligé de faire de grands avances en dépendre à crédit de différent fournisseurs qui forment le plus grand nombre des dits créanciers nécessaires pour l'établissment de la spectacle.

(This document is signed by all creditors, by Servandoni and his wife, and all the sums owed are listed. Two of the major creditors are Mm. de la Boullaye – 7500 *livres* – and Berthelin de Meuville – 3673 *livres*. Total debts amounted to 35065 *livres*.)

APPENDIX C

SETS FOR *AETIUS* IN DRESDEN

Paris, Bibliothèque Historique de la Ville de Paris
Fonds Charles Read, N.A. 138, fol. 693. Spectacles divers G.N. Servandoni 1751–1756

Description du spectacle projettée par le Chev. Servandoni pour l'année 1756

Si il a été de tout temps non seulement permis mais mesme utile [...] dans l'empire des sciences et des arts d'emprunter des. [...] pais etrangers des lumieres et des modeles dans tous les genres on ne doit point avoir. [...] justifier aux yeus du public [...] en revendiquant sur eux les richesses que nous leurs avons nous mesmes communiqués, c'est ce que le chevalier Servandoni se propose de faire sous la protection de sa majesté en presentant à la capitale du royaume le plus puissant et le plus éclairée de [...] un spectacle qui lui a attirée les eloges d'un roy et d'une cour si etroitement unis avec la nostre qu'il semble que les mesmes arts et leurs ouvrages doivent leur estre commun, c'est donc du poeme 'Aetius' ecrite par le fameux Metastasio que le chev. Servandoni propose de tirer de sujet du spectacle qu'il prepare pour l'année 1756. Le sujet est susceptible de six décorations qui toutes peuvent offrir de grands objets aux spectateurs et fournir à l'artiste le moyen d'employer tout ce que l'architecture la perspective les ornemens et le mechanisme des théatres ont de plus magnifique et de plus recherché.

Premiere décoration. Le théâtre representera une place publique de Rome. [...] le throne imperial y sera placée sur un des cotés toute la place sera decorée pour le [...] des festes de annales (?) et ornée de tout ce qui peut la rendre plus magnifique et plus galante le prospectus de la ville de Rom [...] belles antiquitiés formera le fonds du théâtre cette grande ville paraitra illuminée de nuit et des arcs triomphant y seront disposés pour le retour d'Aetius vainqueur d'Attila. Le triomphe de ce guerrier illustre ajoutera par sa magnificence à la p[...] de ce spectacle.

Deuxième décoration. Le théâtre representera l'intérieur du palais impérial la perspective y fera appercevoir des suittes d'appartements différement ornés de statues, de colonnes, de vases precieux de peinture et tout ce qui marquera la magnificence et la richesse de l'empéreur Valentinien.

Troisième décoration. Le théâtre representera les jardins de l'empéreur digne de la magnificence de son palais ces jardins seront parées de plusieurs avenues, ornés de palissades de fleurs, d'octveillages (?) dorés d'arbustes, de differentes cascades, de vases et de statues le fonds representera de riches grottes avec une chutte d'eau qui formera un canal revestu de marbre et entouré de differents groupes de bronzes dorés.

Quatrième décoration. Le théatre representera une gallerie ornée de statues et de vases antiques avec tous les ornements dont on peut la rendre susceptible elle sera meublée de riches sièges dont un plus riches que les autres sera destiner pour l'empéreur et pour sa soeur.

Cinquième décoration. Le théâtre representera l'entrée d'une prison on y apercevra dans la perspective plusieurs voûtes souterrains garnies de grillages et de portes de fer avec des gardes placés aux avenues de ces differents cachots et l'art n'épagnera rien de ce qui peut augmenter l'horreur de ce spectacle.

Sixième décoration. Le théâtre representera le capitale le peuple y entrera en foule maxime les conjurés exciteront le peuple d'[…] la mort d'Aetius sur l'empéreur lui même ils entreprendront de meutes en capitole en combattant les gardes de Valentinien qui parait enfin lui même, l'épée à la main pour reduire les rebelles mais pret de succomber sur le nombre. Aetius qu'on croit mort arrive avec Varius (?) sauve l'empéreur defait les conjurés et merite que l'empéreur luy accorde enfin […] pour prix de sa fidelité reconnue.

APPENDIX D

SERVANDONI'S TROUBLES WITH THE *SPECTACLES*

Paris, Bibliothèque Jacques Doucet,
Autographes, carton 32 (architectes)

27 fevrier 1758.

Monsieur, Oserais je me flatter que vous me pardonnez si je ne vais pas moymeme vous faire ma cour? ouïy sans doute, puisque je scai que c'est vous la faire que de travailler beaucoup, en effet les travaux de mon spectacle sans si considerables et le tems qui me reste est si cours que la crainte de n'avoir pas fini pour le jour fais que je ne puis quitter mes ouvriers de vue. J'auray l'honneur de vous dire Monsieur que associes se sont ingérés [?] comptant me soulager, de faire a mon j […] [?] un diogramme de la piece de mon sujet, disan qu'ils ont cru bien faire, et que je ne pouvais vacquer [?] tout. Cela me met dans le cas Monsieur, de vous supplier d'avoir égard al Embaras ou cela me jette vis à vis d'eux, et de vouloir bien faire imprimer le votre en forme de lettre comme vous avez desja [sic] fait une fois pour le spectacle des Avantures d'Ulysse et de la quelle je joigns ici un imprimé. Je vous revoye paraillemen, Monsieur, l'original de votre diogramme, avec une copie au […] que j'en ay fait tirer, pour que vous puissiez y faire les corrections necessaires pour l'impression de cette lettre et auray attention de vous envoyer incessamens les […] notre imprimeur ord. pour qu'il le conforme aveque vous lui ordonnerez. Recevez en attendance s'il vous plaise les assurances du profond respect et del entier devouemen avec lequel j'ay l'honneur d'être Monsieur vostre tres humble tres obeissans serviteur Servandoni

The Dutch Publications of Francesco Geminiani

Rudolf Rasch
(Utrecht)

Introduction

WITHOUT SECURE PATRONAGE AND WELL–PAID positions for most of his life, earning income from his compositions must have been an important issue for Geminiani. And indeed, we see him constantly supervising the production, publication and sale of his musical works, primarily to ensure that they would contribute to his income rather than that of a publisher. Many works were first published in private editions and only later given to a commercial distributor. Several works published in England were engraved abroad, notably in France or Holland, certainly also to prevent unauthorized circulation and thereby unauthorized publication in England before his own publication. Some of these works were also published in those countries as separate issues, before or after the British issues. Geminiani obtained privileges to protect his works not only in England, but also in France and Holland.

Nearly every work of Geminiani therefore has a complicated publication history — where was it engraved, printed, and offered for sale, when, and by whom, if not by the composer himself? Old plates could be used to produce new copies immediately or any number of years later, with a different title-page, corrections in the music, or both, all factors further complicating the histories of the works involved. Simple lists of editions — as found, for example, in the RISM *Einzeldrucke* catalogues and in Careri's 1993 monograph — although fundamental to the study of the dissemination of the composer's work through the music trade, do not suffice to portray the stories behind them.[1]

This essay primarily discusses the publication histories of those works that were prepared — that is, engraved and often also printed — in Holland, before

---

[1] RISM G 1445-1569; *CARERI*, pp. 221-293. Abbreviations such as '*CARERI* 3a' refer to the editions as listed in Careri's thematic catalogue.

plates or printed copies were transferred to England. We will see that these procedures were used for the *Seconda parte* of the concerto grosso arrangements of the Sonatas Op. 5 by Corelli (published in 1729), for the Cello Sonatas Op. 5, the Violin Sonatas Op. 5 and the Concerti Grossi Op. 7 (all published in 1747-1748) and for the *Dictionaire harmonique* (published in 1756).[2]

Engraving was the sole printing method used by Geminiani for his musical works. In what follows, a clear distinction will be drawn between the terms 'edition' and 'issue'. An edition of a work comprises all the copies produced from the same plates; if certain sets of extant copies show similar characteristics (title-page, corrections, and so on) that differ from other sets of copies, such sets form 'issues' of that edition. An edition may therefore consist of several issues, sometimes created almost simultaneously, in which case one can speak of 'parallel issues' (since copies are printed one by one, perfect parallelism is impossible). In other cases when the changes were implemented after a longer interval, from a few years to more than a century, these will be described as 'serial issues'.[3] When plates were partially replaced, or editions were made up from plates of various sources, the result is somewhere between 'issue' and 'edition'. With the possibility of correction and replacement of single plates one should, ideally, study all extant copies of a certain edition, but this is rarely practicable.

Our concept of 'edition' is wider than that of the eighteenth century, when publishers did not have a specific word for 'issue', describing every new printing run as 'a new edition', even if identical to the previous one. An edition is then little more than a pile of newly produced copies.

Prices play an important role in this discussion; English prices are given in the form £0:10:6 (no pounds, 10 shillings, and six pence). Dutch prices will have the form *f* 10:5 (ten guilders and five stivers — *stuivers* in Dutch, *sols* or *sous* in French). Throughout the seventeenth and eighteenth centuries the exchange rate between British pounds and Dutch guilders was very simple, with one British pound equalling ten Dutch guilders, or one Dutch guilder = two British shillings.

The sources used for the present study should be mentioned; inspection of the extant copies was, of course, the first research step. Many editions are

---

[2]   To a certain extent also the Concerti Grossi Op. 3 is a 'Dutch publication': after John Walsh had published, apparently with the consent of the composer, their first edition in 1732 (RISM G 1466-1467; CARERI 3a), the Dutch music publisher Michel-Charles Le Cène published an edition that was "Nuovamente stampata e coretta per l'autore stesso" in 1733 (RISM G 1469; CARERI 3b). In this chapter, however, we will not discuss the publication history of Op. 3, especially as the Dutch edition is only an episode within a largely English story.

[3]   See the discussion in RASCH, Rudolf. 'Basic Notions', in: *Music Publishing in Europe: Concepts and Issues, Bibliography*, edited by Rudolf Rasch, Berlin, Berliner Wissenschafts-Verlag, 2005, pp. 21-30.

available in facsimile editions (often several alternatives for a single work) — a considerable help — while other works were studied from photocopies or from other reproductions. Publisher's catalogues, archival documents (relating, for example, to privileges and other legal procedures) and, in some cases extant, letters all revealed welcome information.

This study could certainly not have been written without the availability of the numerous advertisements in contemporary English, Dutch and French newspapers that announce the publication of works by Geminiani. For the Dutch newspapers I used my own collection of seventeenth- and eighteenth-century 'musical advertisements'. Announcements of musical publications in the French eighteenth-century periodical press are published in Anik Devriès' *L'édition musicale dans la presse parisienne du xviie siècle*, published in 2005.[4] No similar collection exists for Britain, but many advertisements related to Geminiani have been reproduced in works such as Careri's monograph and the bibliographies of the Walsh firm by William Smith and Charles Humphries.[5] The recently established database of Francesco Geminiani Newspaper References on the website of the *Opera Omnia* contains all these advertisements. The challenge of this study was to match the information derived from the various categories of sources — extant copies, catalogues, documents, announcements — and from it construct a coherent picture of the publication history of those works of Geminiani engraved and first printed in Holland.

THE CORELLI CONCERTOS

The first such works to be discussed here are Geminiani's concerto grosso arrangements after Corelli's Sonatas Op. 5, hereafter the 'Corelli Concertos'. These appeared in two volumes, a *Prima parte* (arrangements of the Sonatas Op. 5, Nos 1-6), and a *Seconda parte* (Nos 7-12). The *Prima parte* was first published in London by William Smith and John Barrett in 1726.[6] The edition was closely connected with the recently established musical-Masonic *Philo-Musicae et Architecturae Societas*, which was founded on 18 February 1725.[7] In fact, the publication of Geminiani's Corelli Concertos

---

[4]   DEVRIÈS, Anik. *L'édition musicale dans la presse parisienne au xviiie siècle: Catalogue des annonces*, Paris, CNRS, 2005.

[5]   *CARERI*; *SMITH1*; *SMITH2*.

[6]   Corelli Concertos, *Prima parte*, Smith-Barrett: RISM C 3866, G 1520; *Careri* 15a.

[7]   *CARERI*, p. 15. See PINK, Andrew. 'A Music Club for Freemasons: *Philo-musicae et -architecturae societas Apollini*, London, 1725-1727', in: *Early Music*, XXXVII/4 (2005), pp. 523-535,

and finding subscribers for it may have been one of the main purposes, if not the sole purpose of the *Societas*. With the *Prima parte*, the *Societas* certainly succeeded: an impressive list of 215 subscribers is recorded in the edition, including members of the nobility and royalty. Within six weeks of publication two unauthorized reprints had appeared in London, the first published by John Walsh, announced on 16 September 1726[8] and the second by Benjamin Cooke and Daniel Wright, announced on 19 September 1726.[9] Smith published a counter-announcement in the *Daily Courant* of 28 September, denouncing the inauthenticity and incorrectness of the two reprints. But since these reprints were selling for half a guinea, Smith reduced his price — originally probably a full guinea — to the same amount.[10]

Knowing the history of the *Prima parte* of the Corelli Concertos is necessary to understanding that of the *Seconda parte*, which is quite different. In March 1727 the *Societas* suspended its activities. On 17 August 1727 William Smith (probably on behalf of Geminiani) announced in the *Daily Journal* a subscription for the *Seconda parte*.[11] We assume that insufficient subscribers committed for this, since it was never published by Smith. Instead, the first edition was published in Amsterdam by Michel-Charles Le Cène, two years later, in 1729.[12] Le Cène also published a reprint of the *Prima parte*, but there are good reasons to believe that the *Prima parte* came *after* his edition of the *Seconda parte*, although planned with it to make up a set: advertisements which announce its publication do not mention the *Prima parte*, which would have been very unusual had it already been published. However, the first part has the publisher's number 549 and the second part 550, which clearly shows that it was Le Cène's intention to publish both parts.

In the literature, the Walsh edition of the *Seconda parte* is frequently but inaccurately listed as the first edition.[13] However, newspaper announcements

---

and the same author's essay in the present volume, pp. 369-398.

[8]   Corelli Concertos, *Prima parte*, Walsh: RISM C 3867, 3870, G 1522, 1524; *SMITH2* nos 433-436; *CARERI* 15e, 15g. Advertised *Daily Courant*, 16 and 21 September 1726.

[9]   Although the advertisement in the *Daily Courant* of 19 September 1726 mentions both Cooke and Wright as publishers, extant copies have either Cooke or Wright. Corelli Concertos, *Prima parte*, Cooke: RISM C 3872; not in *CARERI*. Corelli Concertos, *Prima parte*, Wright: RISM C 3871; *CARERI* 15d.

[10]   *Daily Courant*, 28 September 1724: see *CARERI*, p. 17.

[11]   *Daily Journal*, 17 August 1727: see *CARERI*, p. 17.

[12]   About le Cène see LESURE, François. *Bibliographie des éditions musicales publiées par Estienne Roger et Michel-Charles le Cène (Amsterdam, 1696-1743)*, Paris, Société française de musicologie, 1969.

[13]   *CARERI*, p. 269; and ID. 'Geminiani, Francesco', in: *NG*.

of the Amsterdam editions predate those of the Walsh edition by more than half a year. The *Flying Post, or the Weekly Medley* of 1 March 1729 contains the following interesting note:

> Amsterdam. We hear by our Correspondents from this Place, that the famous Mr. Geminiani has just publish'd here Concerti Grossi, con due Violini, viola e violoncello di concertini obligati, e due altri Violini e Basso di Concerto Grosso, quali contengono Preludii, Allemande, Correnti, Gigue, Sarabande, Gavotte e Follia composti della Seconda Parte del Opera quinta d'Arcangelo Corelli per Francesco Geminiani.

This can only refer to Le Cène's edition. In London this edition was sold by Nicolas Prevost, who advertised it in the same newspaper on 17 and 24 May 1729.[14] In Holland, Le Cène's edition was announced in the *Gazette d'Amsterdam* of 2 September 1729 and in the *Leidsche Courant* of 24 October and 11 November of the same year.[15] Walsh's edition was announced for the first time in the *Country Journal* of 1 November 1729,[16] eight months later than the first announcement of the works, six months later than Prevost's advertisements and two months later than Le Cène's announcements: Walsh's edition clearly came after the Amsterdam edition. It is interesting to note that Walsh's title-page is an imitation of Le Cène's, in a style that differs much from Walsh's own (see ILL. 1a and 1b).

The precedence of the Amsterdam editions strongly suggests that this edition was not only the first edition but also that it was an edition authorized

---

[14]   *Flying Post, or the Weekly Medley*, 17 May 1729: "Just Publish'd [...] At Nicolas Prevost's and Comp [...] Where may be had [...] Concerti Grossi, con due Violini, Viola e Violoncello di Concertini obligati, e due altri Violini e Basso di Concerto grosso, quali Contengono preludii, Allemande, Correnti, Gigue, Sarabande, Gavotte e Follia composti della Seconda Parte del Opera Quinta d'Arcangelo Corelli per Francesco Geminiani, Fol. Price One Guinée. N.B. The King's Patent is in Signor Geminiani's Hands". *Flying Post, or The Weekly Medley*, 24 May 1729: "Catalogue De Livres Nouveaux, que Nicholas Prevost & Comp^e [...] ont reçû des Pays Etrangers, pendant le Cours du Mois de April, 1729 [...] Concerti Grossi, con due Violini, Viola e Violoncello di Concertini obligati, e due altri Violini e Basso di Concerto grosso, quali Contengono preludii, Allemande, Correnti, Gigue, Sarabande, Gavotte e Follia composti della Seconda Parte del Opera Quinta d'Arcangelo Corelli per Francesco Geminiani, Fol.".

[15]   *Gazette d'Amsterdam*, 2 September 1729: see LESURE, François. *Op. cit.* (see note 12), p. 53; *Leidsche Courant*, 24 October, 11 November 1729: "Te Amsterdam by Michel Charles le Cene op de Boommarkt, zyn gedrukt en te bekomen [...] Corelli opera Quinta, parte Seconda Concerti grossi, con due Violini, Viola, e Violoncello di concertini obligati e due altri Violini e Basso di concerto grosso per Francesco Geminiani".

[16]   See CARERI, p. 23, n. 43.

Concerti Grossi

*Con due Violini, Viola e Violoncello
di Concertini Obligati, e due altri Violini
e Basso di Concerto Grosso*

Quali Contengono

Preludii Allemande Correnti
Gigue Sarabande Gavotte e Follia

Composti della Seconda Parte del

Opera Quinta

D'. Arcangelo Corelli

Per Francesco Geminiani

To be Sold

IN LONDON

att Nicolas Prevost Bookseller

*in ye Strand
Price one Guinée*

Ill. 1a: Geminiani, Concertos after Corelli Op. 5, *Seconda parte*, published by Le Cène and issued by Prevost, title-page.

by the composer, so that Walsh's edition cannot be anything other than an unauthorized reprint of either the Amsterdam edition or Prevost's London issue. These assessments are confirmed by further evidence.

Apparently, Geminiani visited Holland some time in 1728, although we know very little about this trip. Our sole source of information is the poem addressed "To Mr. Geminiani At The Hague" written by his pupil

CONCERTI GROSSI

Con due Violini, Viola e Violoncello
di Concertini Obligati, e due altri Violini
e Basso di Concerto Grosso

Quali Contengono

PRELUDII ALLEMANDE CORRENTI

GIGUE, SARABANDE GAVOTTE E FOLLIA

Composti della Seconda Parte del

Opera Quinta

D'ARCANGELO CORELLI

PER

FRANCESCO GEMINIANI

N.B. Where these are sold may be had the first Six Solos of Corelli
made into Concertos by Geminiani. and Twelve celebrated Solos
by the same Author for a Violin and a Bass.

London. Printed for and sold by I: Walsh servant to his Majesty at
the Harp and Hoboy in Catherine street in the Strand. and Ios: Hare
at the Viol and Hoboy in Cornhill near the Royal Exchange.

ILL. 1b: Geminiani, Concertos after Corelli Op. 5, *Seconda parte*, published by Walsh, title-page in imitation of Le Cène.

Henry Carey, and published in the latter's *Poems on Several Occasions* (London 3/1729).[17] Unfortunately, the poem only sings Geminiani's praises without providing any details or information about his journey to Holland. Of course, it is attractive to hypothesize that his motive was the printing of the *Seconda*

---

[17] CAREY, Henry. *Poems on Several Occasions*, London, E. Say, 1729, p. 111, reproduced in *CARERI*, p. 22.

parte of the Corelli Concertos, and most commentators so far have done so.[18] Fortunately, this proposition seems confirmed by the wording of the advertisement of 1 March quoted above: "Mr. Geminiani has just published here [= Amsterdam]" and in the absence of contrary evidence, we may assume that Geminiani was in Holland in 1728-1729 for the publication of the *Seconda parte* of his Corelli Concertos.

Le Cène produced the *Seconda parte* in two parallel issues, one mentioning Nicolas Prevost in London as its seller: "*To be Sold* | IN LONDON | att Nicolas Prevost Bookseller | *in ye Strand* | *Price one Guinée*". There are at least seven extant copies.[19] The other has the normal Le Cène imprint, with the publisher's number 550 in the lower right corner of the title-page.[20] Only one copy of this issue is extant today.[21] The imprint is the only difference between the two issues. The engraving of the London imprint is of similar style as the rest of the title-page so that the London title-pages must have been produced in Amsterdam. The Prevost title-page must have preceded Le Cène's 'own', otherwise he would have had to change the title-page twice. In addition, this order is confirmed by the chronology and by other evidence discussed below.

Who was the seller of the London issue, Nicolas Prevost? Born in 1697, his mother was Suzanne Vaillant, a daughter of François, later Francis Vaillant (1643-1721), a Huguenot émigré who had been, from about 1700 to 1711, the London agent of Estienne Roger (whose business Le Cène was continuing).[22] Prevost had collaborated as a publisher and bookseller in The Hague in the early 1720s with his uncles Paul Vaillant II (1671-1739) and Isaac Vaillant (1679-1753). In 1726 he returned to England and took over

---

[18]   *CARERI*, p. 22; RASCH, Rudolf. 'Il cielo batavo. I compositori italiani e le edizioni olandesi delle loro opere strumentali nel primo Settecento', in: *Italienische Instrumentalmusik des 18. Jahrhunderts: Alte und neue Protagonisten*, edited by Enrico Careri and Markus Engelhardt, Laaber, Laaber Verlag, 2002, pp. 237-266: 256.

[19]   Corelli Concertos, *Seconda parte*, Prevost: RISM C 3875, G 1526; not in *CARERI*. Copies in D-Bds (2x), GB-Ge, NL-Uim, S-LB, S-Uu, US-R.

[20]   Corelli Concertos, *Seconda parte*, Le Cène: RISM C 3877, G 1528; not in *CARERI*.

[21]   In The Hague, Nederlands Muziek Instituut (formerly Gemeentemuseum, Muziekbibliotheek).

[22]   On Prevost see PLOMER, Henry Robert - BUSHNELL, George Herbert - DIX, Ernest Reginald MacClintock. *A Dictionary of the Printers and Booksellers Who Were at Work in England, Scotland and Ireland from 1726 to 1775*, London, Bibliographical Society, 1932, p. 203; KOSSMANN, Ernst Ferdinand. *De boekhandel te 's-Gravenhage tot het eind van de 18de eeuw*, The Hague, Martinus Nijhoff, 1937, p. 90; SWIFT, Katherine. 'Dutch Penetration of the London Market for Books, *c*1690-1730', in: *Le magasin de l'univers: The Dutch Republic as the Centre of the European Book Trade*, edited by Christiane Berkvens-Stevelinck *et al.*, Leiden, Brill, 1992, pp. 265-279.

Paul Vaillant's bookshop in London. He was almost exclusively a bookseller, not a publisher, active especially in the Anglo-Dutch book trade. In 1733 he went bankrupt under suspicious circumstances and disappeared; the date of his death is unknown.

Prevost must have had some kind of business relationship with Le Cène by 1730. In the *Catalogo de' libri Italiani e Spagnuoli che si vendono da N. Prevost, & Comp. nel Strand* (London, 1730) there is, on the last page, a list of twenty-one musical titles, nearly all of them recent Le Cène publications. Among them, predictably, is the *Seconda parte* of the Corelli Concertos, while the *Prima parte* is not listed.

The imprint of the Prevost issue of the *Seconda parte* confirms the price of one guinea (£1:1:0) mentioned in the advertisement of 17 May 1729. This is a remarkable price: first, it is the same price as William Smith advertised for his failed subscription in 1727; second, it is much higher than Le Cène's price in Holland. Le Cène offered the two volumes of the Corelli Concertos in his catalogue for ƒ12 together — we assume ƒ6 for the *Prima parte* and ƒ6 for the *Seconda parte* as the *Prima parte* is only slightly larger than the *Seconda parte*, with 76 against 71 engraved pages of music. The guinea that Prevost asked for the *Seconda parte* alone corresponds to no less than ƒ10:10, almost twice the Dutch price. This suggests a direct involvement of Geminiani in the sale, since we frequently see that when Geminiani's music was sold by himself or on his behalf, the prices were approximately twice the norm for the size of the publication.

In Le Cène's catalogue, the two parts are listed and priced as a set and must have been sold thus, although only one set of both parts with a Le Cène imprint is known today. Five sets are known with a Le Cène *Prima parte* and a Prevost *Seconda parte*. One wonders if these 'mixed sets' were sold by Prevost or by Le Cène, assuming they were together from the beginning. That Prevost offered only the *Seconda parte* in his announcements of 17 and 24 May 1729 is inevitable, since Le Cène's *Prima parte* had not yet been published. But even in the 1730 catalogue still only the *Seconda parte* is mentioned. After all, the Smith and Barret edition of the *Prima parte* may still have been available in London in 1730. There is no evidence that Prevost ever sold the *Prima parte*. All the mixed sets may well have come from Le Cène's shop, as their present locations seem to confirm: three are in Continental libraries, two of which in Sweden, a typical outlet area of Le Cène. The two extant single copies of the Prevost *Seconda parte* are in Glasgow (Euing Library), a candidate to be a copy from Prevost's shop, and in Utrecht (University Library, from the former Collegium Musicum Trajectinum), certainly bought directly from Le Cène.

There is another puzzling aspect to the publication of the *Seconda parte* by Le Cène: when the latter's estate was inventoried after his death in 1743, there were found on his shelves no fewer than 218 printed copies of the *Seconda parte*[23] — an abnormally high, if not abnormal number for an engraved edition; normal stock numbers in the inventory would be below fifty, sometimes increasing to between fifty and one hundred. Since only six copies remained in 1743 of Le Cène's *Prima parte*, there is something suspicious about the publication of the *Seconda parte*. The only apparent explanation for such a large number of left-over copies is that Le Cène expected to sell *immediately* upon publication many more copies than normal. Perhaps Geminiani went to him with the list of the 215 subscribers of the *Prima parte*, or gave him a copy of the London *Prima parte* with the list in it and persuaded him to print a considerable surplus on top of the normal printing run. For the moment there is no precise answer. But the large left-over stock at least explains why Le Cène also sold copies with a Prevost imprint.

As mentioned above, Le Cène reprinted the *Prima parte* of the arrangements, so that he could offer the whole collection in his shop. His *Prima parte* must have appeared about a year after the *Seconda parte*, probably in late 1729 or early 1730; whether with or without Geminiani's consent is unclear. Whatever the case, it must be considered a standard reprint of an edition already published, presumably the Smith and Barrett edition. A copy of this edition is listed in the inventory of 1743.[24] It was offered for sale by the buyer of the estate, Emanuel-Jean de La Coste, as is apparent from its listing in the catalogue La Coste published in 1744.[25]

The fact that Geminiani selected William Smith as publisher for the *Prima parte* of his Corelli Op. 5 arrangements and Le Cène for the *Seconda parte* clearly shows that he was strenuously trying to avoid having John Wash as the publisher of his works. The journey to Holland in 1728 to have the *Seconda parte* of his Corelli Concertos published there would be the first in a series of foreign journeys with the same aim: to produce his music outside the reach of John Walsh and without the risk of reprinting even before the first edition had appeared.

---

[23] On the Le Cène estate see RASCH, Rudolf. 'I manoscritti musicali nel lascito di Michel-Charles le Cène (1743)', in: *Intorno a Locatelli. Studi in occasione del tricentenario della nascita di Pietro Antonio Locatelli (1695-1764)*, edited by Albert Dunning, 2 vols, Lucca, Libreria Musicale Italiana, 1995, vol. II, pp. 1039-1070. The inventory is to be found in Amsterdam, Amsterdam Archives, Notarial Archives, No. 10226 (Notary public Benjamin Phaff, May-August 1747), Item 536.

[24] Unless this is a copy of the Walsh edition, which seems unlikely.

[25] *Catalogue des livres de musique, imprimés à Amsterdam, chez Estienne Roger et Michel-Charles le Cène*, Amsterdam, Emmanuel-Jean de la Coste, [1745], p. 59: "[Geminiani] di Corelli parte prima Concerti London — *f* 6.0".

By the time of the publication of the *Seconda parte* of the Corelli Concertos Geminiani had in fact obtained a British privilege to protect his publications there. It is dated 26 March 1728 and should apply to "several Works consisting of Vocal and Instrumental Musick" for a period of fourteen years.[26] Its existence was mentioned by Prevost in his announcement of the *Seconda parte* in the *Flying Post* of 17 May 1729. However, it did not prevent a reprint by Walsh just a few months after the Le Cène/Prevost edition.[27] The reason may be that Walsh could maintain he was not reprinting a British but a foreign edition.[28] If this is the case, Geminiani's decision to publish the *Seconda parte* in Holland had the opposite effect to what he wished.

THE CELLO SONATAS OP. 5, THE VIOLIN SONATAS OP. 5 AND THE CONCERTOS OP. 7

At some point of time during the 1730s a form of agreement, understanding or even coöperation seems to have been established between Geminiani and the Walsh firm, judging from the Walsh publication of three original concertos by Geminiani (H. 121-123) in the third *Select Harmony* (concertos separately 1734, together 1735) and the concerto arrangements by the composer after Corelli's Sonatas Op. 1 and 3 (1736). These publications were followed by subscription announcements for Geminiani's Sonatas Op. 4,[29] and the republication of his Concertos Op. 2 "by John Walsh for the author" in 1737.[30] As later works by Geminiani are repeatedly mentioned in advertisements by Walsh and occasionally

---

[26]   See the reproduction in the facsimile edition of the Violin Sonatas Op. 4 by Fuzeau.

[27]   Corelli Concertos, *Seconda parte*, Walsh: RISM C 3876, G 1527; SMITH2, nos 436-440; CARERI 15f. Advertised in the *Country Journal* of 1 November 1729 (see CARERI, p. 23, n. 43).

[28]   As far as I know no extant copy of the Prevost issue of the *Seconda parte* contains the British privilege of 1728.

[29]   *London Evening Post*, 15-17 February 1737; *Dublin Newsletter*, 5 March 1737; *Faulkners Dublin Journal*, April 1738; see SMITH2, p. 159; CARERI, p. 31, n. 12.

[30]   *Country Journal*, 22 October 1737; see SMITH2, no. 691, p. 155; CARERI, p. 30, n. 11. The first issue of the Walsh edition of the Concerti Grossi Op. 2 is usually dated 1732 and then connected with the announcement in the *Daily Post* of 8 June 1732 (see SMITH2, p. 155, under no. 690; CARERI, p. 23), but this is incorrect. The latter announcement refers to Geminiani's private edition published in 1732 (RISM G 1455, not in CARERI), an edition not studied or noted at all, perhaps because RISM lists no extant copies in Great Britain (there is a copy in King's College, Cambridge). This edition has Geminiani's British privilege of 1728 and a short letter of dedication. (Exceptionally, the title-page is typeset, as are the privilege and the letter of dedication; only the Violino Primo has a title-page.) Walsh's edition of the works was first issued in 1737, in coöperation with Geminiani.

in catalogues, but no copies of them printed by Walsh are known to exist,[31] the existence of a agreement between the two cannot be denied.

Despite his growing coöperation with Walsh, Geminiani continued to issue his music in private editions first, and to have them engraved abroad. The Violin Sonatas Op. 4 and the revised Op. 1 Sonatas (both published in 1739) were engraved in Paris by Louis-Hector Hue,[32] the *Pièces de clavecin* in the same city by Mlle Vendôme. The works were issued both in London and Paris.[33]

For unknown reasons Geminiani went to Holland for the publication of a next group of works, a group that includes the Cello Sonatas Op. 5, the Violin Sonatas Op. 5 (a reworking of the Cello Sonatas) and the Concerti grossi Op. 7. They were engraved in The Hague in 1746 and issued there and in London. The two sonata volumes were subsequently re-engraved in Paris and published there. We will see that Geminiani was in The Hague in 1746-1747 to oversee the production of these Dutch publications; he used the occasion to apply for a Dutch privilege to protect his works, as a supplement to his British and French privileges. Let us first discuss the Dutch privilege before considering the engraving, printing and publication of this group of Dutch publications.

Typically, the first step towards obtaining a privilege in Holland was to have an employee of the States of Holland and West-Friesland write a request for consideration to the respective Lords of the States; for this Geminiani had the help of Reinier van Ouwenaller Junior (1722-1790).[34] The request is undated but since a handwritten note indicates that it was accepted for further

---

[31] Among these are the *Pièces de clavecin*, the Concertos Op. 4, the Cello and Violin Sonatas Op. 5 and the Concertos Op. 7. It is assumed that the unidentified listings in advertisements or catalogues of Walsh refer to lost editions. See, for example, SMITH2, no. 709, p. 158 (Cello Sonatas Op. 5) and no. 714, p. 159 (Sonatas Op. 4). But it seems improbable that no extant copy would exist of five separate editions of works by Geminiani published by Walsh.

[32] The engravings are not signed, but that they were made by Hue is clear from comparison with other, signed works engraved by him.

[33] The close coöperation with John Johnson only started in 1751; the Johnson issue of the Sonatas Opus 4 has the year "1739" on the title-page, simply because Johnson did not remove it when he added his own name to the imprint. Johnson's lengthy advertisement in the *General Advertiser* of 26 December 1751 marks the beginning of his systematic sale and re-issuing of Geminiani's work, especially those works that had been published privately by Geminiani from 1739 (Sonatas Opus 4) to 1751 (*The Art of Playing on the Violin*).

[34] The request is found in The Hague, National Archives, Archives of the States of Holland and West-Friesland, no. 1700 (Minutes-Patents for 1746). See *Geminiani Opera Omnia*, vol. 5, pp. 105-106. In The Hague there are two archives, the Nationaal Archief (the State Archives, hereinafter The Hague, National Archives) and the Haags Archief (the archives of the city of The Hague, hereinafter The Hague, City Archives).

processing on 30 July 1746 we assume it dates from that month. The privilege was requested for "several new works of music, consisting of concertos and solos, as well as a treatise, or dictionary on musical composition". It was granted almost half a year later, on 6 December 1746. The text was given to Geminiani, to be printed in full in every publication that he wished to protect. He was obliged to deposit one copy of each publication in the library of the University of Leiden. That library indeed still holds copies of the four editions that can be connected to the Dutch privilege: the Cello Sonatas Op. 5, the Violin Sonatas Op. 5, the Concertos Op. 7 and the *Dictionaire harmonique*.[35] The *Dictionaire* appeared only in 1756 — by which time more than half the span of the privilege had elapsed — and will be discussed below. We will now concentrate on the two Op. 5 sonata volumes and on the Concerti Op. 7.

The Cello Sonatas Op. 5 and the Violin Sonatas Op. 5 appeared in two editions, one Anglo-Dutch and one French. Both Anglo-Dutch editions can be split into Dutch and English issues: the musical parts are identical, that is, printed from the same plates, but the issues have different title-pages (and different privileges). The Dutch issues have title-pages in French, mentioning The Hague as the place of publication, 1746 as the year of publication and "the author" [Geminiani] as publisher (see ILL. 2a).[36] The Cello Sonatas mention on the title-page a dedication to the Prince D'Ardor[e,37] while the Violin Sonatas have no dedication. The Cello Sonatas are called Op. 5, the Violin Sonatas are without opus number. On the title-pages of both we read "Avec Privilege & & &" and the printed text of the Dutch privilege is included in all known extant copies of both publications.

The English issues of the Op. 5 Sonatas have title-pages in Italian giving London as the place of publication; the Violin Sonatas are now dated 1747, whereas the English issue of the Cello Sonatas is undated.[38] The English issues give no mention of a publisher, carry no dedication and include Geminiani's

---

[35] Shelfmarks: Cello Sonatas 545 B 29, Violin Sonatas 545 B 28, Concertos 680 A 44, the *Dictionaire* 680 A 45.

[36] Cello Sonatas Op. 5, The Hague, Geminiani, "1746" = 1747: RISM G 1508; not in *CARERI*. Facsimile editions: Florence, Spes, 1988 (Monumenta Musicae Revocatae), and New York, Performer's Facsimiles, no. 74, [1989]. Violin Sonatas Op. 5, The Hague, Geminiani, "1746" = 1747: RISM G 511; *CARERI* 5c.

[37] The Prince D'Ardore is the Calabrese nobleman Giacomo Francesco Milano (born Polistena, Calabria, 1699, died Naples 1780), Neapolitan ambassador in Paris from 1741 to 1753.

[38] Cello Sonatas Op. 5, London, Geminiani, n.d. = 1747: RISM G 1509; *CARERI* 5b. Violin Sonatas Op. 5, London, Geminiani, 1747: RISM G 1513; *CARERI* 5d. Facsimile edition: Huntingdon, King's Music, n.d.

SONATES
Pour le Violoncelle et Basse Continue
Par Monsieur
GEMINIANI
dans lesquelles il a fait une étude particuliere
Pour l'utilité de Ceux qui accompagnent.
Ouvrage Cinquieme
Dedié
à Son Excellence Monseigneur le
Prince d'Ardore
Chevalier des Ordres du St Esprit et de St Janvier,
Ambassadeur Extraordinaire de Sa Majesté Napolitaine
et Sicilienne à la Cour de France & & &

Gravees à la Haye
au depend de l'autheur
avec Privilege & & &
l'an MDCCXLVI

ILL. 2a: Geminiani, Cello Sonatas Op. 5, Dutch issue, title-page.

name on the title-page only as composer. Both the Cello Sonatas and the Violin Sonatas are called Op. 5, and no privilege is mentioned on either title-page. Nevertheless, several extant copies contain the British privilege of 1739.

The French editions of the Cello and the Violin Sonatas have title-pages in French,[39] that of the Cello Sonatas being a complete copy of the Dutch title,

---

[39]   Cello Sonatas Op. 5, Paris, Boivin-Leclerc, "1746" = 1747: RISM G 1510; *CARERI* 5a. Facsimile edition: Courlay, Fuzeau, 2007 (Collection FacsiMusic). Violin Sonatas Op. "6", Paris, Boivin-Leclerc-Castagnery, "1746" = 1748: RISM G 1512; not in *CARERI*.

VI SONATE

A

VIOLONCELLO SOLO e BASSO CONTINUO

COMPOSTE DA

GIACOMO HERMAN KLEYN

Amatore della Musica.

E DEDICATE

All Molto Illustre SIGNORE il SIGNOR

GIOUACHINO RENDORP

OPERA QUARTA

*Stampate a Spese
Di GERHARDO FEDERICO WITVOGEL
Organista della Chiesa nuova Luterana.*

A AMSTERDAM.

N.º 82.

ILL. 2b: Jacob Herman Klein, Cello Sonatas Op. 4, published by Witvogel in Amsterdam, 1745, title-page.

except for the imprint, while the French edition of the Violin Sonatas has a shortened version of the Dutch issue. The Cello Sonatas mention Madame Boivin and Monsieur Leclerc l'Aîné as publishers, or at least as sellers;[40] the

---

[40]   Madame Boivin is Elisabeth-Catherine Ballard (died 1776), daughter of Jean-Christoph Ballard, from the famous Ballard dynasty of printers. She married François Boivin in 1724. Boivin died in 1734, after which Elisabeth-Catherine continued the music business styling herself Madame Boivin or Veuve Boivin. Her shop "À la règle d'or" was on the rue Saint-

Violin Sonatas repeat these names but add that of Mlle Castagnerie. Geminiani is mentioned only as the composer of the sonatas, and both editions give a year of publication ("MDCCXLVI") at the bottom of the title-page. The Cello Sonatas mention the dedication to the Prince D'Ardore on the title-page, in the same words as the Dutch issue; the Violin Sonatas do not. The Cello Sonatas are called Op. 5, the Violin Sonatas Op. 6, a unique designation, and both volumes name Mlle Vendôme as the engraver.[41]

The various Op. 5 volumes raise several questions; first, whether both the Anglo-Dutch and the French editions were based on a manuscript by Geminiani or whether one is a copy of the other. In relation to the Anglo-Dutch edition we have to decide whether the music was engraved and printed in London or in The Hague, or perhaps even partially in both. In addition, we need a good chronology of these editions and issues.

A comparison of the engraving of the Anglo-Dutch and French editions, suggests strongly that one was made from the other, since it is implausible that two engraved editions made independently from one another from a manuscript would be so similar in result, especially in the division of the music between systems and pages. We must give priority to the Anglo-Dutch edition[42] since not only does it contain 'tr' for a trill, rather than the '+' sign as in the French issues, but it also mentions Geminiani as publisher (the Dutch issue) or has no publisher, which implies Geminiani as publisher (the English issue). Further evidence is provided by the tempo indications in roman type in the French editions, which

---

Honoré. See DEVRIÈS, Anik. *Édition et commerce de la musique gravée à Paris dans la première moitié du XVIIIe siècle: Les Boivin, les Leclerc*, Geneva, Minkoff, 1976, pp. 17-21; DEVRIÈS, Anik - LESURE, François. *Dictionnaire des éditeurs de musique français, Tome 1: Des origines à environ 1820*, Geneva, Minkoff, 1979, pp. 36-37. 'Leclerc L'aîné' is Jean-Panthaléon Leclerc (born before 1697, died after 1763), who had his shop "À la croix d'or" in the rue de Roule. He coöperated with Mme Boivin so closely that in practice everything available at one of the shops was available at the other. See DEVRIÈS, Anik. *Op. cit.* (see earlier in this note), pp. 25-34 and 87-93, and DEVRIÈS, Anik - LESURE, François. *Op. cit.* (see earlier in this note), pp. 95-97. Mme Boivin and Leclerc L'aîné were music dealers in the first place.

[41] This is Marie-Charlotte Vendôme, later Mme Moria, one of the most famous French eighteenth-century engravers.

[42] *CARERI*, pp. 248-249, lists the French edition of the Cello Sonatas as first edition, followed by the London issue of the Anglo-Dutch edition, without mentioning the Dutch issue. For the Cello Sonatas the Dutch issue is mentioned first, followed by the English. Here the French edition is not mentioned. Careri's article in *NG* repeats these views, by having the Cello Sonatas first appear in Paris and the Violin Sonatas first in The Hague. The presentation of the sources in the new edition of both the Cello and the Violin Sonatas by Christopher Hogwood (*Geminiani Opera Omnia*, vol. 5) extends Careri's views. For the Cello Sonatas the order is Paris (A), The Hague (B) and London (C), for the Violin Sonatas the order is The Hague (A), Paris (B) and London (C). RISM lists the Dutch issues before the English.

ILL. 3: Geminiani, Cello Sonatas Op. 5, Dutch issue, last engraved page of music with the signature "R. Denson".

is very unusual for a French engraved edition but easily explained if the Anglo–Dutch edition was Mlle Vendôme's example. The chronology presented below further corroborates the precedence of the Anglo–Dutch editions.

The Anglo–Dutch editions were therefore produced before the French editions, the latter being copied from them. At first the date 1746 on the French title-pages seems to contradict this, as the Anglo–Dutch editions were published only in 1747 (despite the dates 1746 on the title-pages of the Dutch issues; see below). But in fact the French editions did not appear before late 1747 or even early 1748, despite the dates 1746 on the title-pages (see below). These dates may simply be the result of copying the Dutch title-pages.

But were the Anglo-Dutch editions produced in The Hague or in London? The engraving of the two Anglo-Dutch editions is completely identical in style and form of symbols etc. and the style is clearly English, very similar to Walsh's editions, for example,[43] and certainly not Dutch[44] — a conclusion confirmed by the engraver's name added at the end of the Violin Sonatas: "R. Denson", apparently English (see ILL. 3). Although the first assumption would suggest that this engraving and printing was done in England, in fact, as will soon be clear, Denson did his work in The Hague; he may even have travelled to The Hague with Geminiani at some point in the spring of 1746.

A few words about Denson's work before he went to The Hague: he is known as the engraver of Charles Avison's *Two Concertos: The First for a Harpsichord, &c. in Eight Parts, the Second for Violins &c. in Seven Parts*, published in Newcastle in 1743, and the *Twelve Concerto's in Seven Parts* [...] *done from two Books of Lessons for the Harpsicord composed by Sig. Domenico Scarlatti* published in London in 1744.[45] Around 1745 he engraved and published in London two songs (perhaps his own compositions), *Advice to Brittish Sailors* and *The Maid is Blest*.[46] No British work by him is known after 1745.

Although Denson engraved all of the two sonata volumes Op. 5 and nearly all of the Concertos Op. 6, the coöperation between him and Geminiani

---

[43]   Walsh's engraving is characterized by verbal elements (titles, tempo indications, etc.) in roman lettering. Figuring is relatively small and very slightly italic; another characteristic is the H-shape of the C clef.

[44]   Dutch music engraving of the time has all words in italics, except titles at the beginning of works (Sonata, Concerto); C clefs consist of a vertical line with two hooks on the right side, one pointing upward, the other downward. These characteristics also hold for French engraving style of the first half of the eighteenth century. Dutch music engraving can be particularly recognized by the relatively large and clearly italic figuring. In addition there is the typical spiral bass clef, an imitation of the bass clef in Arcangelo Corelli's edition of his famous *Sonate a violino e violone o cembalo* [...] *opera quinta*, published privately in Rome in 1700. Estienne Roger initiated the 'Dutch style' with his reprint of this work in Amsterdam in 1702 and it was subsequently adopted by later eighteenth-century Amsterdam publishers of engraved music, among them Michel-Charles Le Cène, Gerhard Fredrik Witvogel, Arnoldus Olofsen and Siegfried Markordt. Elements of the Dutch style, such as the spiral bass clef, were also applied by some engravers in England, notably Benjamin Fortier and John Philips.

[45]   HUMPHRIES, Charles - SMITH, William C. *Music Publishing in the British Isles from the Earliest Times to the Middle of the Nineteenth Century*, London, Cassell, 1954, p. 131.

[46]   *Advice to British Sailors*: GB-Lbl G.316.a.(20.); *The Maid is Blest*: GB-Lbl G.312.(127.) and H.1994.c.(25.).

ended unpleasantly. On 18 October 1746 Richard Denson — we learn his first name for the first time here — engaged the lawyer Peter van Bekesteyn as his *procureur* (solicitor), to represent him in a lawsuit against Geminiani before the Court of Justice of The Hague.[47] Obviously Geminiani had broken up the relationship and Denson was now trying to get further payment. Unfortunately, the documents that supported Denson's case have not been preserved so we do not know the exact nature of the complaint. Denson's step was a so-called *rau-actie* (or *rauw-actie*, literally 'raw action'), a case without a specified amount claimed but designed to pave the way for a later case with a specified claim. Denson certainly chose this form to prevent Geminiani from leaving The Hague before being obliged by the Court to satisfy him.[48]

The protocols of the Court of Justice of The Hague make it possible to follow the trial week by week. The Court held sessions on Wednesday and apparently, only the solicitors of the two parties appeared in the court room. Geminiani was represented by the *procureur* Abraham Mens. On the following days the case *Denson* v. *Geminiani* was slated for hearing:

• 2 November 1746: Bekesteyn presented his procuration. He remarked that the opposite party was not present (which denied them certain means of defence) and asked for a second summons.

• 9 November: Mens asked for the case to be dismissed, and wanted to hear the claim. Bekesteyn consented, announced the claim, and asked for provision, as in the written documents. Mens asked for an adjournment, for copies of everything, and to inspect the original documents, if required. He wanted a guarantee for the costs and selection of *domicilium citandi et executandi* of the opposing party. Bekesteyn presented the guarantee and chose *domicilium* at the house of John Frost in the Korte Houtstraat in The Hague, being the house in which Denson lived.

• 16 November: Mens was present and requested an adjournment until the following week.

• 7 December: Mens asked for an adjournment to the next session.

Now a sworn statement was drafted at the request of Geminiani by Josua Bruyninx and Alida van Dalen, Geminiani's landlord and landlady in The Hague (see below).[49] The statement describes Denson's behaviour of the preceding

---

[47] The Hague, City Archives, Notarial Archives, No. 3299 (notary Anthony Deel), no. 12.

[48] The documents concerning *Denson* v. *Geminiani* are transcribed in the APPENDIX to this chapter.

[49] The Hague, City Archives, Notarial Archives, No. 3158, pp. 321-322, notary public Beukel Henricus den Dansser.

months and presents a very negative image of Denson's character: Bruyninx declared that some months previously, Richard Denson was so drunk that he lay down on the street, incapable of standing up, just outside the house of Charles-Bernard Lachy, a stucco-worker living in the Sint Jacobsstraat, in whose house Denson then lived. After this event, Lachy did not want Denson in his house any more and suggested that Bruyninx would take him, because Geminiani, Denson's employer, also lived there. Bruyninx at first refused, but later, on the repeated insistence of Geminiani, consented to take Denson in his house; but Denson continued to misbehave. Things got worse: first Denson sold some engraving plates as old tin; then he pawned two already engraved plates in an inn for two guilders, which he needed to pay the innkeeper for drinks consumed. Geminiani discovered this and asked Bruyninx to go to the inn to retrieve the plates and to stand security for the repayment of the two guilders. The passage about standing security was deleted and replaced by a statement that Bruyninx even paid the two guilders to rescue the plates.

 • 14 December: Mens read the sworn statement described above and lodged a copy with the Court.

 • 21 December: no progress.

 • 11 January 1747: no progress.

 • 18 January: Bekesteyn responded in defence of his client. Unfortunately, we do not know what arguments or facts he put forward.

 • 25 January: it was Mens' turn, but he declined it.

 • 1 February: Mens responded in defence of his client.

Now it was the turn of the Court, after having heard the solicitors and received and read the various documents, which took some time. On 19 July 1747 the case was slated again, now with a more explicit complaint, namely that "no goods of Geminiani, to be found at the premises of Gautier, would be moved until Geminiani had, under the pressure of the Court, given full satisfaction to Denson". Bekesteyn asked for sentence to be pronounced and asked for a provision. The sentence had already been established a few days earlier, on 13 July, to the effect that Denson would not get the requested provision. And that was the end of the case.

In the listings of the case on the role of the Court from 2 November 1746 to 1 February 1747 Denson is described as "music engraver, having lived in London, but now present here [The Hague]", Geminiani as "Italian musician, living here [The Hague]", descriptions actually copied from Bekesteyn's procuration, which was dated 18 October 1746. The descriptions were repeated to introduce the sentence of 13 July 1747, but they are missing in the listing of the case slated for the session of the Court on 19 July 1747: here the claim is to seize the possessions of Geminiani that could be found at Gautier's premises. This suggests that Geminiani had moved from The Hague, but had left certain possessions there, in the house of one Pierre Gautier, a French musician who ran a concert hall on the Buitenhof in The Hague.[50] In the declaration of 9 December 1746 Bruyninx stated that Denson had lived in his house for five or six months. If we assume that the coöperation between Geminiani and Denson ended in October 1746, Denson must have lived in Bruyninx's house from June or July until October. Before then he lived somewhere else and before that in the house of Charles-Bernard Lachy. All this seems to point to Geminiani and Denson arriving in The Hague in the first months of 1746.

The declaration of 10 December 1746 against Denson also informs us that Geminiani lived in the house of Josua Bruyninx and Alida van Dalen. Bruyninx was a Master Carpenter, who lived, at least in the period from 1742 to 1747, in the Wagenstraat, East-side.[51] The exact location of Bruyninx's premises can no longer be established, but the registration number suggests that it was between the Sint-Jacobsstraat and the Veerkade, near the present no. 100.[52]

Geminiani wrote a letter to Joseph Kelway dated "The Hague, 10 January 1747" which gives us further details about the various publications

---

[50] For more information on Pierre Gautier see the introduction to GAUTIER, Louis. *Six sonates pour le clavecin, Œuvre second*, edited by Rudolf Rasch, Utrecht, Koninklijke Vereniging voor Nederlandse Muziekgeschedenies, 2002.

[51] The Hague, City Archives, *Kohier van de Personele Quotisatie 1742*, nos. 4762-4763. The name of Bruyninx is written in many variant ways, Bruinis, Bruynincx, etc. He himself signed 'Bruynicx'.

[52] Although not of interest for the history of music, the following may have some human interest. Josua (or Joost) Bruyninx and Alida van Dalen were not youngsters anymore, when they decided to marry in 1731: Josua was born in The Hague in 1690 (baptized 28 June), Alida in 1686 (baptized 6 October). After registration of the marriage in The Hague on 11 March 1731, they married in the nearby village of Scheveningen on 26 March 1731. Not surprisingly, no children were born in the marriage. In 1742, Jan de Lanoy lived with them. When they got old, two nephews, Christiaan Remer (a son of Alida's sister Geertruida, employee of the Council of State of the Dutch Republic) and Daniel Bruyninx (1724-1787, a son of Josua's brother Laurens and a well-known miniature painter, both at the time and today) decided they should give up their household and enter into the Proveniershuis (Old People's Home) of Rijnsburg, a village a little west of Leiden. This happened in 1759, when Josua was 68 and Alida 72 years old. They bought themselves in with a sum of *f* 1150, an average amount. The Reformed Church in The Hague registered their departure on 18/19 June 1759. Josua died first (date not known), Alida on 28 May 1768; see The Hague, National Archives, Archive 3.01.06 (Archives of the Nobility of Holland), no. 1242. Their nephew Christiaan Remer refused the estate, saying it was just enough to pay the expenses of the burial; see The Hague, City Archives, Notarial Archives, no. 4218, no. 44, pp. 837-842, 5 July 1768.

produced in The Hague.[53] We learn that the Cello Sonatas were already printed and ready to be sent to London, but that Geminiani did not know to whom to send them to have them sold. He had already asked "Mr. Lawrence" some time earlier to announce them in the newspapers for September (presumably September 1746), but had not heard from him since. He now asked if he could send the books to Kelway or if he could recommend someone else, since it was too late to talk about September (probably meaning that he no longer had obligations to Mr Lawrence). He added that the Violin Sonatas had also been engraved and printed, but that the Concertos [Op. 7] although engraved, were not yet printed. This strongly suggests that both the Cello and the Violin Sonatas Op. 5 had not only been engraved in The Hague, but printed there too together with the copies that had to be sent for sale in London; additionally we can deduce that Geminiani had no imminent plans to go to London himself.[54]

The coöperation between Geminiani and Denson must have broken down in October 1746. What had happened between this month and January 1747 apart from waiting for the Dutch privilege, which was granted in December? It seems logical to assume that engraving and printing was done in the sequence Cello Sonatas — Violin Sonatas — Concertos. The two sonata volumes are clearly the work of the same engraver and the Violin Sonatas are signed "R. Denson" at the end, so there is no doubting Denson's hand here. The same engraving style is found in the Concertos, with the exception of the last one, Concerto VI. In all part-books the engraving is suddenly a little different, which is particularly clear in the clefs and the accidentals (see ILL. 4b). Since the engraving of the title "CONCERTO" before Concerto VI differs from Concertos I-V, Denson and Geminiani must have broken up just between work on Concerto V and Concerto VI.

---

[53] The letter is in GB-Lbl, Add. Ms. 21520; facsimile in CARERI, Plate 5, between pp. 114-115; Italian text and English translation in CARERI, pp. 36-37, and Geminiani Opera Omnia, vol. 5, pp. xiv-xv.

[54] At least some copies of the English issues of the Sonatas Opus 5 (Violin Sonatas in Cambridge, Cello Sonatas in London) were printed on the same paper as was used for the Dutch privilege included in the Dutch issues: bifolia with horizontal chain lines 28 mm apart and a clearly visible watermark consisting of a fleur-de-lys on a shield with a crown on top but no letters below (as is more usual). This differs considerably from the way Geminiani produced his English editions in London: they are always printed on single sheets. The London copy of the English issue of the Violin Sonatas is on different paper than the copies mentioned above and may have been printed later, in England. I wish to thank Ryan Mark (Cambridge) and Rupert Ridgewell (London) for providing information about the paper of copies of the English issues of the Opus 5 Sonatas in the Cambridge University Library and the British Library respectively.

ILL. 4a: Geminiani, Concertos Op. 7, published in London, 1746, Basso part-book, page 13. The three upper staves were engraved by Denson, the others by Philips; note the accidentals, the rests and the bass clefs.

Who completed the engraving of the Concertos Op. 7? A comparison of Concerto VI with the engraving of Geminiani's next works, *A Treatise of Good Taste in the Art of Musick* (1748) and *The Art of Playing on the Violin* (1751), both engraved by John Philips, strongly suggests that it was Philips who finished Op. 7, from the point where Denson had stopped.[55] Several part-books of Concerto VI have the 'upright sharp', typical for Philips, an emulator of Fortier, instead of the normal X-shaped sharp used by Denson.

---

[55] It is generally assumed that John Philips' wife Sarah worked with her husband in the engraving business.

CONCERTI GROSSI

Composti a 3, 4, 5, 6, 7, 8. Parti Reali, per
essere eseguiti da due VIOLINI, VIOLA, e
VIOLONCELLO, di CONCERTINO, e due
altri VIOLINI, VIOLA, e BASSO, di
RIPIENO, à quali vi sono annessi
due FLAUTI TRAVERSIERI
e BASSONE.

D A

F. GEMINIANI,

D E D I C A T I

*Alla Celebre Accademia della buona ed
Antica Musica*

Op.ᵃ VII.

*Stampate a spese dell' Autore con
Privilegio.*

M D C C X L V I I I.

ILL. 4b: Geminiani, Concertos Op. 7, Dutch deposit copy, title-page. Leiden, University Library: 680 A 4.

Philips worked on more than just Concerto VI; a comparison of the title-pages of the treatises and the title-pages of the English issues of the Cello and Violin Sonatas and the Concertos Op. 7 shows that he engraved these title-pages as well, confirmed by his signature "Philips sculp." around the word "*LONDRA*" on the title-page of the Cello Sonatas.[56]

---

[56] The title-pages of the English issues of the Opus 5 Sonatas seem to have been printed in London: they are on watermarked paper identical to that found in Geminiani's 1732 edition of his Concertos Opus 2. The watermark, a Strasburg lily with the letters LVG, is no. 1808

The title-pages of the Dutch issues of the Cello and the Violin Sonatas are quite different in layout from the English title-pages, yet the form of the letters and the engraving style of the various lines is similar to English title-pages. For these reasons we assume that these title-pages are also the work of Philips. Their layout differs considerably from the English title-pages because the Dutch title-pages try to imitate the layout of title-pages of musical works published in the Netherlands. This is particularly clear if one compares them with the title-page of music editions published some time previously in Amsterdam by Witvogel, such as that of the Cello Sonatas Op. 4 by Jacob Klein le Jeune, published in 1745, where the similarity is unmistakable (see ILL. 2b).

The title-page of the Dutch issues of the Cello and Violin Sonatas bear the date 1746, as does the title-page of the Concertos Op. 7. None of these publications was actually issued in that year, which means that 1746 rather is the year of engraving. Therefore Philips did his work in 1746 and in The Hague. In some part-books the end of Concerto v and the beginning of Concerto vi are on the same page, that is, on the same plate, so Philips must have come to The Hague to continue Denson's work.[57]

Geminiani's postscript to the letter to Kelway of 10 January 1747 provides a further delicate detail. Geminiani wrote that he just had discovered that his engraver had robbed him of four copies and had sold one of them to an Englishman. Geminiani feared that the buyer would in turn sell that copy to John Walsh who could then produce a reprint before his own edition had appeared in England. It is not clear which of the two engravers — Denson or Philips — is implicated. The date of the letter would point to Philips, but the continued coöperation with Philips speaks against it. The behaviour is rather Denson's, but then the theft must have taken place some months previously, before the two men ended their coöperation, but was only later discovered by Geminiani.

Since the Dutch issues of the two sets of sonatas were engraved and printed in Holland, it is to be expected that they would be available in The Hague earlier than in London; this is indeed the case. Daniel Joannes Langeweg, bookseller in the Vlamingstraat in The Hague, offered for sale

---

in HEAWOOD, Edward. *Watermarks mainly of the 17th and 18th Centuries*, Hilversum, Paper Publications Society, 1950. The plates have the same dimensions as those of the music pages of the publications, which suggests that they were engraved in The Hague (and then transferred to London before the printing). The British privileges found in the copies of the English issues will also have been printed in London, presumably together with the title-pages.

[57]   Unfortunately, I could not find an independent confirmation of John (and Sarah?) Philips' presence in The Hague.

both the Cello Sonatas and the Violin Sonatas in an announcement published in the *'s-Gravenhaagsche Courant* of 17 March 1747,[58] which fits perfectly into the chronology presented so far. Each volume cost *f* 6. In using Langeweg, Geminiani avoided the major music seller in The Hague at that time, Nicolas Selhof. Langeweg is not known for selling — let alone publishing — any musical publication except Geminiani's Sonatas. We assume that Geminiani left a small stock of the Dutch issues at Langeweg's, and also that he sent a deposit copy of both volumes to the University of Leiden before leaving the country.

The Dutch issues of the Cello and Violin Sonatas must have been distributed poorly, to put it mildly — apart from the two deposit copies, only one further copy of the Violin Sonatas is extant, and none of the Cello Sonatas. It is almost as if Geminiani wished to prevent reasonable distribution, by selecting someone outside the music trade and by asking a prohibitively high price.

The English issues of the Cello and Violin Sonatas became available only weeks after the Dutch ones: the Cello Sonatas were announced in the *Daily Advertiser* of 5 May 1747[59] and the Violin Sonatas in the *General Advertiser* of 11 May, both available at Kelway's house in King's Row, Upper Grosvenor Street.[60] The price of both Cello Sonatas and the Violin Sonatas was 12s 6d, which is slightly above the Dutch price (merely 12s in British currency). They were expensive in any case, and this may have contributed to their limited dissemination, although this was not as poor as the Dutch issues.

Geminiani's letter of 10 January 1747 appears — as we have seen — to suggest (correctly) that he had no immediate plans to go to England. By the end of 1747 the authorized French edition of the Cello Sonatas appeared and we may assume that from The Hague, Geminiani went to Paris to oversee the engraving and printing of both the Cello and the Violin versions of the Op. 5 Sonatas. The handwritten note "Vandome pour Mr. Giminiany" on the first

---

[58]   *'s-Gravenhaagse Courant*, 17 March 1747: "De SONATES pour Le Violon & pour le Violoncello, Nouveau Ouvrage de MONSR. GIMINIANI, zyn op heeden te bekomen by D. LANGEWEG, Boek- en Kaertverkoper in de Vlamingstraet in 's Hage. De prys van ieder Werk is 6 Guldens". For Daniel Joannes Langeweg (1710-1782) see Kossmann, Ernst Ferdinand. *Op. cit.* (see note 22), pp. 229-230. Langeweg did his business with varying degrees of success, to put it kindly.

[59]   *Daily Advertiser*, 5 May 1747: see *Geminiani Opera Omnia*, vol. 5, p. xv.

[60]   *General Advertiser*, 11 and 23 May 1747: "New Musick. This Day are published, Price 12s. 6d. Six Solos for a Violoncello, with a Thorough Bass for the Harpsichord. By Signor Francesco Geminiani. Opera V. The same Six Solos transpos'd and adapted with proper Alterations for the Violin, by the Author. To be had of Mr. Kebra [*sic* = Kelway], at his House in King's Row, Upper Grosvenor-Street".

music page of the only extant copy of the French edition of the Cello Sonatas suggests Geminiani's presence in Paris,[61] after which he must have gone back to The Hague, to collect the goods he had left there, and thence to England.

John Johnson produced, in 1751 or shortly after, a new issue of the Violin Sonatas Opus 5, based on the music plates of Denson and the title plate of Philips. He removed the date ("MDCCXLVI") and added the phrase "*Printed for* John Johnson *at the Harp and Crown in Cheapside*".[62] No Johnson issue of the Violoncello Sonatas is known, but it must be remarked that the Stockholm copy of the Johnson Violin Sonatas has after its title-page the music of the Cello Sonatas.[63]

The Violin Sonatas and the Cello Sonatas are both advertised at £0:13:6 in Johnson's catalogue of 1754, then at £0:10:6 in his catalogue of 1770. Later, Robert Bremner sold both volumes for the latter price.[64]

The French editions of both the Cello and the Violin Sonatas appeared some time after the Dutch and the English issues, despite — as previously mentioned — the date of 1746 printed on the title-pages. They were newly engraved, by Mlle Vendôme, and published by Mme Boivin and Leclerc L'aîné. The Cello Sonatas were advertised by Mme Boivin on 6 November 1747 in the *Affiches de Paris*.[65] No press announcement of the French edition of the Violin Sonatas is known, but we may assume from the presence of the name of Mlle Castagnery on the title-page that it appeared after the Cello Sonatas, probably not before 1748: her name occurs in conjunction with that of Mme Boivin primarily in the years 1748-1753.[66] Indirectly the opus number 6 indicates an appearance after the Cello Sonatas and one might imagine that they were issued before May 1748, when the Concertos Opus 7 were published. In the catalogue that Leclerc l'Aîné published in 1751,[67] both the Cello and the Violin Sonatas appear, and for £t 9 — prices mentioned on the

---

[61] Especially the spelling 'Giminiany', which may be unusual but may (not counting the final 'y', which is simply French) reflect the pronunciation of his name in Lucchese dialect. Langeweg's advertisement of 1747 also has Giminiani, as have several other sources.

[62] RISM G 1514.

[63] I did not check the two other copies, in Dresden and New York, in this respect.

[64] *A Catalogue of Vocal and Instrumental Music*, London, John Johnson, 1754; *A Catalogue of Vocal and Instrumental Music*, London, John Johnson, 1770; *A Catalogue of Vocal and Instrumental Music*, London, Robert Bremner, March 1782. The Violin Sonatas are also in John Welcker's catalogue of c1777.

[65] See DEVRIÈS, Anik. *Op. cit.* (see note 4), p. 211.

[66] On Marie-Anne Castagnerie (1722-1782) see DEVRIÈS, ANIK - LESURE, François. *Op. cit.* (see note 40), p. 47.

[67] See DEVRIÈS, Anik. *Op. cit.* (see note 40), p. 190.

title-pages as well —, which is certainly cheaper than f 6 for the Dutch issue of the Anglo-Dutch edition, or 10s 6d, the English price.[68]

What happened to Denson in The Hague after his unhappy ending first year there? Already in 1746 he had done other work than Geminiani's, notably Santo Lapis' *Sonnates pour le clavessin*,[69] and he continued working in The Hague, engraving there the *Chansons originaires des Francs Maçons* (The Hague, 1747, "Denson sculpt."),[70] *A Collection of New and Favourite English and French Songs, Adapted to the Voice, Violin, German-Flute and Harpsichord, engrav'd by R. Denson at the Hague. 1749. Recueil des chansons nouvelles, etc.*,[71] and perhaps other works as well. He would not live very long: on 5 March 1751 he signed his will before notary public Arent Lybreghts in The Hague, surely because he felt his end approaching.[72] His death was reported to the authorities in The Hague shortly afterwards, on 28 May of the same year, which means that he died some days earlier, only 30 years old, as the registration tells us.[73] The will mentions that he was born in the parish of St Paul, Covent Garden, in the Liberty of Westminster in London; the English-born shopkeeper and innkeeper John Frost and his wife Maria Clear were named sole heirs, with a legacy of f 150 for their son Peter, born in 1745.[74]

---

[68]   The French Livre Tournois is represented here by the symbol $£$t. The value of the Livre Tournois was not as strictly linked to the British and Dutch currencies as those two currencies were to each other, because the Livre Tournois was subject to a constant process of devaluation. For the second quarter of the eighteenth century, however, $£$t 1 for $£$0:1 or f 0:10 is a good approximation.

[69]   LAPIS, Santo. *XII Sonnates pour le clavessin*, The Hague, Lapis, [1746], "Denson sculp.", RISM L 662. Announced in the *'s-Gravenhaagsche Courant* of 15 and 17 October 1746 and 3 and 5 February 1747, with several sales addresses, of which Eustachius de Haen in The Hague is the most important. See the modern edition by Rudolf Rasch, Utrecht, Koninklijke Vereniging voor Nederlandse Muziekgeschiedenies, 2001 (Muziek uit de Republiek, 4).

[70]   A copy is in GB-Lbl, C.424.i. About this masonic songbook see DAVIS, Malcolm. *The Masonic Muse: Song, Music and Musicians Associated with Dutch Freemasonry: 1730-1806*, Utrecht, Koninklijke Vereniging voor Nederlandse Muziekgeschiedenis, 2005, pp. 72-77.

[71]   A copy is in GB-Lbl, C.756.gg.

[72]   The Hague, City Archives, Notarial Archives, No. 2138, pp. 1178-1180. An English translation was made in The Hague on 28 May 1751, of which a copy is in the Public Record Office, Prerogative Court of Canterbury Wills, no. 11/788. These documents are reproduced in full in the APPENDIX to this chapter.

[73]   The Hague, City Archives, Indexes of Burials.

[74]   John Frost had become a citizen of The Hague in 1738. That year he married Maria Clear (from Leeuwarden, her name also written Cler, Clair or even Le Clair). Several children were born and baptized in the German Reformed Church or in the Walloon Church of The Hague. "Pierre-Jean" was baptized 14 October 1745 in the Walloon Church. The taxing of 1742 calls Frost a tobacco shopkeeper and innkeeper in the Houtstraat. Maria Clear died June

The nomination was "for and in consideration of the many services done and assistance given unto him [...] when he was under difficulties and which he doubts not they will still continue doing" — certainly a reference to the conflict with Geminiani. In 1747, during the trial against Geminiani, he was living in their house, at the Korte Houtstraat, and we assume he lived there until his death in 1751.

Finally, some words must be said on the Concertos Op. 7, which were, as we have seen, engraved in The Hague by Denson and Philips. Neither a Dutch nor a French issue of the Concertos Op. 7 was produced, as far as we know. This suggests that Geminiani had sent the plates to England, or took them with him when returning from Paris to London via The Hague, and had the concertos printed in London. They are known in a single edition, which occurs with three different title-pages, so that we can speak of three issues. All title-pages are in Italian and all give title, composer's name and the dedication to the Academy of Ancient Music in exactly the same wording. One issue, presumably the first, mentions the protection by an English privilege ("con Privilegio di S.M.B.") and gives London 1746 as place and year of publication.[75] This title-page is clearly the work of John Philips. I presume that this is the issue prepared by Geminiani for the British market. Having not yet been printed in January 1747,[76] it cannot have been published in 1746. Geminiani advertised the edition at various times in England in 1747 — for example on 3 September in the *General Advertiser*, where publication in January 1748 is promised[77] — but in the end it was available to the subscribers only on 4 February 1748, as announced in the *General Advertiser* of 1 February of that year.[78] It was certainly printed in England. On a number of title-pages the date of 1746 has been changed into 1748 by adding 'II' in ink to the engraved "MDCCXLVI".[79] Copies of this issue normally include Geminiani's British privilege of 29 July 1739.

1751. Nothing could be found about any member of the family in The Hague after 1752, so I assume that Frost eventually left The Hague. (Information obtained from the standard indexes of the City Archives in The Hague.)

[75] RISM G 1481-1482; *CARERI* 7a. Facsimile edition: Huntingdon, King's Music, n.d.

[76] See Geminiani's letter to Kelway of 10 January 1747, discussed above.

[77] *General Advertiser*, 3 September 1747: "In January next will absolutely be published; SIX Grand CONCERTOS, Compos'd By Mr. GEMINIANI". I am indebted to Richard Maunder, editor of Op. 7 in: *Geminiani Opera Omnia*, for information on this and the following advertisement.

[78] *General Advertiser*, 1 February 1748: "On Thursday next Feb. 4, will be publish'd, (And delivered to the SUBSCRIBERS) the New Concerto's of Mr. GEMINIANI, at the Cabinet-Makers near New Slaughter's Coffee-House, St. Martin's Lane".

[79] I owe this observation to Richard Maunder.

In addition there are copies, with a newly engraved title-page with the same text, but without a date on the title-page and with the name of John Johnson in the imprint, though still "for the author".[80] These are copies to be sold in Johnson's shop, presumably from 1751. Johnson's catalogue of 1754 lists the Concertos Op. 7 at a price of £1:5:0, which may well have been the publication price in 1748.[81] Johnson's catalogue of 1770 offer the concertos at the reduced price of £1:1:0, for which price they are also found in Robert Bremner's catalogue of 1782.[82]

Finally, there is one copy of the Concertos Op. 7 with again a different title-page, type-set. Its text is the same as the first engraved one but the privilege is unspecified (only "con Privilegio"), and there is no place of publication, only the year, 1748 (see ILL. 4a). It is the deposit copy of the University Library of Leiden, where it was sent, we believe, to activate the Dutch privilege, and to prevent a Dutch reprint.[83] The copy itself does not include the text of the privilege, a requirement for the protection; the privilege may, however, have been sent on a separate sheet. We do not know of the existence of any other copy with this title-page, so we believe that this type-set title-page was prepared specifically for the deposit copy and that only one copy of it was ever printed.[84] The sending of this deposit copy to Leiden ends the 'second Dutch episode' of Geminiani's biblio-biography.

THE *DICTIONAIRE HARMONIQUE*

Geminiani published not only his instrumental works in parallel issues that became available more or less simultaneously in various countries, but also several of his treatises in this way. The *Art of Playing on the Violin*, for example, was produced in London first, in 1751, engraved by John Philips and published privately first and then by John Johnson "for the Author", then reissued in Paris, without publisher,

---

[80] Concertos Op. 7, Johnson: RISM G 1483; *CARERI* 7b.

[81] *A Catalogue of Vocal and Instrumental Music*, London, John Johnson, 1754.

[82] *A Catalogue of Vocal and Instrumental Music*, London, John Johnson, 1770; *A Catalogue of Vocal and Instrumental Music*, London, Robert Bremner, March 1782.

[83] Concertos Op. 7, Dutch deposit copy, 1748, Leiden, University Library, shelf mark 680 A 4; included in RISM G 1482; not in *CARERI*.

[84] The title-page was printed on paper that differs from everything else in the deposit copy: thinner, with vertical chain lines, and a beautiful watermark showing a Strasburg lily without any added letters or name, a mark not found in any of the major reference works. The same paper was used for the flyleaves, which is unusual and which means that it was bound immediately after the printing.

in 1752.[85] The word-text of the French edition (in French) was printed in France, while the musical examples were identical to those of the English issue, and must have been printed in England. Geminiani probably went to Paris to supervise the French publication at some point in the second half of 1751, since he applied for a new French privilege on 7 October 1751, which was granted on 25 January 1752.[86] He probably stayed there for several years, since no evidence connects him with London or elsewhere in Britain during this time, and in any case he was in Paris in March-April 1754, for the staging of *La Forêt Enchantée* and the publication of his *Art de bien accompagner du clavecin* in the same year.

The dating of Geminiani's next treatise, the *Dictionaire harmonique*, also known as *Guide harmonique* or *Guida armonica*, is a story in itself. Both Hawkins and Burney gave 1742 as the date of the London edition,[87] but Careri disagreed, arguing that Op. 10, the *Guida armonica*, must follow the *Art of Playing on the Violin* (Op. 9) of 1751[88] and at the same time citing a reference to the contents of the *Dictionaire* contained in William Hayes' *Remarks on Mr. Avison's Essay on Musical Expression*, published in 1753.[89] Since then, it has been assumed that the work was issued between 1751 and 1753. Nevertheless, the *Dictionaire harmonique* must have been written considerably earlier. It is not only mentioned in the Dutch privilege of 1745, where it is described as "een tractaat en woordenboek over de musicale Compositie", but, even earlier, subscriptions to the 'Harmonical Guide', had been invited in Dublin in April 1740, according to an announcement of 26 April in the *Dublin Newsletter*[90] — when, according to William Hayes, the high price discouraged all subscribers.

In Paris, subscription for the *Guide harmonique* opened with an announcement in the *Mercure de France* of April 1741.[91] Subscriptions were accepted at the shop of Prault, fils, bookseller at the Quay de Conti. Laurent-François Prault (1712-1780) was a bookseller and publisher occasionally connected with musical publications, among them Rameau's *Castor et Pollux* (1737).[92] A lengthy description of the

---

[85] Announced in the *Avis, Annonces et Affiches Divers* of 16 March 1752. See DEVRIÈS, Anik. *Op. cit.* (see note 4), p. 211.

[86] CARERI, p. 41.

[87] HAWKINS, V, p. 390; BURNEY, IV, p. 642.

[88] See CARERI, 1993, pp. 179-180.

[89] HAYES, William. *Remarks on Mr. Avison's Essay on Musical Expression*, London, J. Robinson, 1753, pp. 121-122; see CARERI, p. 180.

[90] See CARERI, p. 31.

[91] *Mercure de France*, April 1741, pp. 774-775; see DEVRIÈS, Anik. *Op. cit.* (see note 4), p. 211.

[92] With Mme Boivin, Leclerc l'Aîné, Duval and the composer. About Prault see DEVRIÈS, Anik - LESURE, François. *Op. cit.* (see note 40), p. 136.

Guide harmonique, of more than thirty duodecimo pages, appeared in the *Mémoires pour l'Histoire des Sciences et des Beaux Arts* or *Journal de Trévoux*, of August 1741, obviously with the intention to raise the number of subscribers.[93] This 'preview' mentioned that subscription was possible until 1 November 1741, and publication was promised in 1742. This must be the "dissertation" by the Jesuit Père Louis-Bertrand Castel mentioned by John Hawkins in his description of the work.[94] The *Mercure de France* of October 1741 repeated that the work would be available in April 1742 for those who subscribed before 1 November 1742, although without mentioning an address where one could subscribe.[95] Presumably, it was this notice that led Burney and Hawkins to declare that the work was published in 1742. Both notices in the *Mercure de France* seem to have been submitted by Geminiani himself, and Castel's article may have been written at his instigation. All this took place during Geminiani's stay in Paris from some point in 1740 to 1742, and the work was therefore probably written and complete by 1741.

Although the *Guide harmonique* was not published in 1742, a frontispiece was designed by Edmé Bouchardon and engraved by Simon François Ravenet. It shows a book with the title "GUIDA ARMONICA", lying on a sea-shore, and a flying herald with a banner displaying "ICH DIEN", the motto of the Prince of Wales, together with a coronet with three feathers, the Prince's crest. This suggests that it had been Geminiani's intention to dedicate the work to Frederick Prince of Wales (1707-1751), the eldest son of King George II. The plate would later be used in 1748 as frontispiece of *A Treatise of Good Taste in the Art of Music*, which was indeed dedicated to the Prince of Wales (as were the concerto versions of Op. 4 in 1743).

However, not only can Burney's and Hawkins' dating of 1742 be disregarded, but so can a publication date for the *Guide harmonique* of 1752. It was not until 1756 that subscribers in Amsterdam and London could collect their copies.

Subscription in Amsterdam was possible from November 1755, in the shop of Jean-François Joly (also written Jolly), a French bookseller at the Rokin, as indicated in an advertisement placed on behalf of Geminiani himself in the *Gazette d'Amsterdam* of 28 October 1755.[96] The wording suggests that

---

[93]   *Memoires pour l'Histoire des Sciences et des Beaux Arts*, August 1741, Article LXXI, pp. 1475-1509.

[94]   See *HAWKINS*, V, p. 391. Hawkins erroneously claimed that it was published in the *Journal des Savans*, a mistake repeated by many commentators after him.

[95]   *Mercure de France*, October 1741, pp. 2235-2236; see DEVRIÈS, Anik. *Op. cit.* (see note 4), p. 211.

[96]   *Gazette d'Amsterdam*, 28 October 1755: "Le Sr. Geminiani fait graver son œuvre un Dictiornaire harmonique ou guide à la vraye Modulation; avec le secours de ce Dictionnaire on pourra sans aucune connoissance de la musique, composer, la Basse Fondamentale pour

Geminiani was in Holland by that time. Joly is not known as a music publisher or music dealer, but was in the 1750s a publisher and seller of libretti of the French opéras-comiques and the Italian *opere buffe* that were performed in or near Amsterdam. At the same time, his was an address for the sale of tickets for concerts and opera performances, including subscriptions. Subscription to Geminiani's *Dictionaire* was open until 1 January 1756, for the price of *f* 10:10, the Dutch equivalent of a British guinea, half of it to be paid upon subscription, the other half upon publication.

Another advertisement was published by Geminiani in the *Amsterdamsche Courant* of 25 November 1755 without mention of any other names, but which simply referred back to the announcements published in the *'s-Gravenhaagsche Courant*.[97] This advertisement in particular seems to indicate a personal presence in Amsterdam. The next relevant advertisement appeared some days later, in the *Amsterdamsche Courant* of 29 November, again under the name of Geminiani.[98]

---

tous les Instrumens susceptibles d'Accoords. On y trouvera tous les Sons, les Consonances, les Dissonances, leur véritables rapports, et généralement tout ce qui est nécessaire pour la vraye Modulation ou bonne Composition. Cet ouvrage doit être imprimé sur du papier super royal-super fin d'Hollande. Le Sr. Geminiani offre ce Dictionnaire aux Amateurs de Musique et d'autres par voy de souscription à raison de 10 florins 10 sols d'Hollande l'Exemplaire. La moitié payable en souscrivant et le reste recevant les exemplaires pour lequel on aura souscrit. La souscription sera ouverte jusqu'au 1er du mois de Janvier prochain. Après l'expiration de ce terme le Dictionnaire coûtera 14 florins de Hollande. Ceux qui désirent souscrite peuvent s'adresser chez F. Jolly Libraire à Amsterdam sur le Rokin, lequel leur donnera une reconnaissance de l'argent qu'il recevra, ainsi que son Billet d'engagement pour leur délivrer en terme surdit les Exemplaires en question. On les devra à tous prendre chez ledit Jolly". The *'s-Gravenhaagsche Courant* of 3 (and 10) November 1755 repeats this advertisement in Dutch.

[97]   *'s-Gravenhaagsche Courant*, 25 November 1755: "Sr. F. Geminiani, adverteerd dat hy by inteekening op Koper laet graveeren en de Explicatie op best Royael Papier in de Hollandse en Franse tael drukken, Dictionarium Harmonicum, of zeker Wegwyzer tot de ware Modulatie, en wat tot een goede en fraeye compositie behoord; breeder in de Haegse Courant van den 3, en 10 November, gespecificeerd".

[98]   *Amsterdamsche Courant*, 29 November 1755: "Sig. F. Geminiani adverteerd dat by inteekening op Koper laet graveeren een Dictionarium Harmonicum, 't geen op best Royael Papier zal gedrukt werden breeder in de Haegse Courant vermeld, de Explicatie daer van is Hollands en Frans, de inteekening *f* 10-10 't Exemplaer, de eene helft te betaelen by de Soubscriptie, de andere by 't leveren des Exemplaers. de tyd van inschryving is tot ultimo December en zullen na verloop dier tyd *f* 14 kosten. NB. 't Zal maer een klyn getal in 't Duits en Frans gedrukt werden. Men zal kunnen inteekenen t'Amsterdam by J.Z. Triemer op de Blomgragt, en verder by de Boekverkoopers J. Cóvens Junior op de Vygendam, by H. Boussiere op den Dam, en by J.F. Joly op 't Rokkin, welke aennemen Quitantie van 't ontvangen geld te geven, en zig verbinden aen de Respectieve Inteekenaers, 't Exemplaer in de maend January 1756 te Leveren. NB. De Brieven buitens Lands moeten franco toegezonden worden".

The conditions of subscription are those described in the *Gazette d'Amsterdam* of some weeks earlier, but the number of addresses receiving subscriptions has increased to four. The musician and composer Johann Seewald Triemer, on the Bloemgracht, has now become the main address, while Henri Boussière (Dam), Jan Covens Jr. (Vijgendam) and Jean-Francois Joly (Rokin as before) are additional addresses; publication is promised for January 1756.

Johann Seewald Triemer was a musician — probably a violoncello player — and a composer of German descent, born in Weimar around 1705.[99] He settled in Amsterdam in the 1730s and published an Op. 1 with cello sonatas (Witvogel, c1735),[100] an Op. 2 with violin sonatas (probably as a private edition, 1748)[101] and an Op. 3 again of cello sonatas (offered for sale in manuscript, 1752).[102] He wrote melodies for the English Psalms of Tate and Brady, which were published in Amsterdam in 1753.[103] It is not clear how Geminiani and Triemer had met or how much contact they had, but in late 1755 and early 1756 Triemer was Geminiani's representative in Amsterdam. We assume that Triemer dealt in music in addition to being a practicing musician; he died soon after his dealings with Geminiani.[104] Johannes Covens Junior (1722-1794) was a music dealer and publisher who continued the business of Gerhard Fredrik Witvogel (see above). Henri Boussière was, like Joly, a French bookseller, not known as a music dealer or publisher, but a regular address for theatre and opera tickets.

It was Triemer who published an advertisement in the *Amsterdamsche Courant* of 12 February 1756 that Geminiani's *Dictionaire harmonique* had appeared and would be delivered to the subscribers.[105] Thereafter it would be for sale in the shops of Johannes Covens Junior (Vijgendam) and Arnoldus

---

[99]   Biographical data about Triemer were derived from the standard indexes of the Amsterdam Archives.

[100]   Witvogel's edition of Triemer's Op. 1, c1735, is lost; the French reprint is by Leclerc le Cadet, 1738: RISM T 1218.

[101]   Triemer's Op. 2 was advertised in the *Amsterdamsche Courant* of 11 November 1748. The Amsterdam edition is lost, but the work was reprinted in Paris by Maupetit, Mme Boivin, Leclerc and Mlle Castagnery: RISM T 1219. Note that except for Maupetit the Paris publishers are also those of the French edition of Geminiani's Violin Sonatas "Op. 6". The work was also published by John Johnson in London: RISM T 1220.

[102]   Lost. See the advertisement in the *Amsterdamsche Courant* of 17 October 1752.

[103]   TRIEMER, Johann Seewald. *A New Version of the Psalms of David by N. Tate & N. Brady, and set to musick by J. Z. Triemer*, Amsterdam, Antony Bruyn, 1753: RISM T 1215.

[104]   Triemer was buried in Amsterdam on 10 March 1756.

[105]   *Amsterdamsche Courant*, 12 February 1756: "Men adverteerd dat op heden door J.Z. TRIEMER, voor de respective inteekenaers het Dictionarium Harmonicum, van Sr. F. Geminiani, zal afgeleverd werden, en zyn vervolgens te bekomen by de Boekverkopers J. Covens Junior op den Vygendam en A. Olofsen in de Gravestraet, a f 14 't Exemplaer".

Olofsen (Gravestraat), for ƒ 14 per copy. Covens indeed included the *Dictionaire* in his advertisement in the *Amsterdamsche Courant* of 12 May 1756.[106] Arnoldus Olofsen (*c*1695-1768), the fifth Amsterdam dealer connected to the *Dictionaire*, had been a publisher and seller of books since the mid 1730s and had become a music dealer and publisher around 1750. The music of Antoine Mahaut and the books about music by Jacob Wilhelm Lustig were certainly his most important publications in this field.

The publication date of the Dutch version of the *Dictionaire* can thus safely be established as February 1756. The title-page is bilingual, French (*Dictionaire harmonique, ou Guide sur pour la vraie modulaison*) and Dutch, albeit that the latter begins with the main title in Latin: *Dictionarium harmonicum, of Zekere wegwyzer tot de waare modulatie* (see ILL. 5). On the title-page Geminiani is given as publisher of the work, with Amsterdam 1756 as place and year of publication. Triemer's advertisement suggests that by the time of the publication Geminiani had already left. After the title-page is the text of the Dutch privilege of 6 December 1746, followed by prefaces in French and Dutch, printed in parallel columns. We may assume that the French is Geminiani's or at least written under his personal supervision; the Dutch text is an accurate translation, presumably made in Holland during his stay there in November-December 1755. Following the preface is a brief introduction to the music examples that constitute the main part of the work, again with French in the left-hand column and Dutch in the right, and the three brief music examples centred, serving both languages.

The main part of the *Dictionaire harmonique* consists of thirty-four engraved pages of music examples. Where were these pages engraved? From the style of engraving, the spiral bass clef, the large italic figuring and especially the use of double-size plates, it is immediately clear it was according to Dutch principles. Since the double-size plate system assumes units of four pages on one bifolium, pages 33 and 34 were engraved as single plates. During the 1750s this style is found especially in the publications of Arnoldus Olofsen. Triemer, whose work was also sold by Olofsen after his death in 1756, may have been an intermediary between Geminiani and the engraver.

We can thus safely assume that the musical part of the *Dictionaire* was produced in Amsterdam. This leads us to expect that the English version was published later than the Dutch version — and indeed, the *Guida armonica* was advertised by Geminiani as a new publication some months after the availability

---

[106]   *'s-Gravenhaagsche Courant*, 12 May 1756: "Te Amsterdam bij Joh. Covens Junior op den Vygendam, zijn te bekomen de volgende Musicq Werken […] Geminiani Dictionarium Harmonicum, ƒ 14-0-0.".

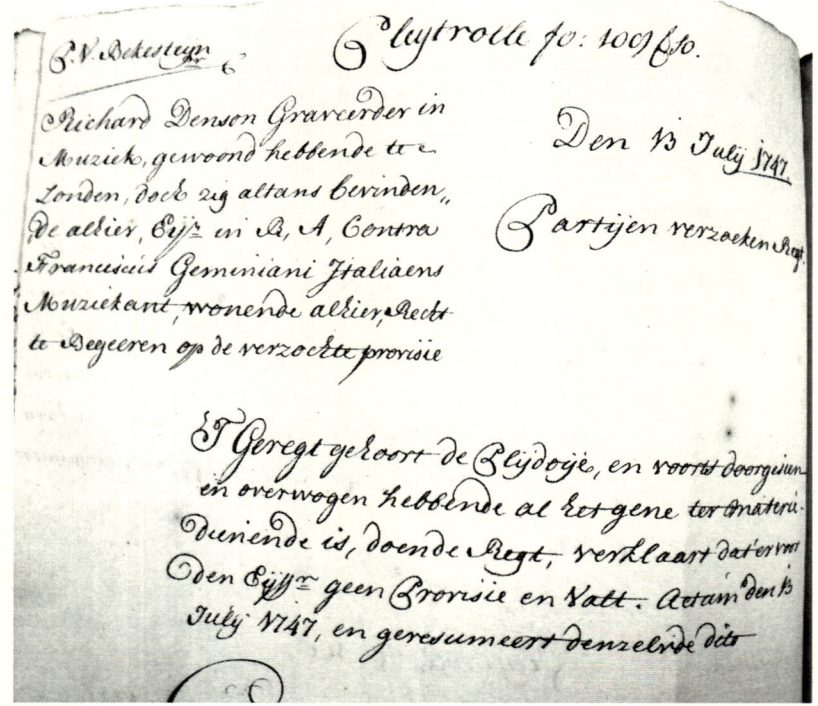

ILL. 5: Sentence in the case of Denson *v.* Geminiani, The Hague, 13 July 1747. The Hague, Archives, Archives of the Court of Justice: No. 244 (Sentences 1743-1750), fol. 18v.

of the Dutch version, in the *Whitehall Evening Post, or London Intelligencer* of 17 April 1756, in the *London Evening Post* of 20 April and in the *Gazetteer, and London Daily Advertiser* of 20 May of that year.[107] The London issue has a new, engraved title-page, in Italian (*Guida armonica, o Dizionario armonico*) and

---

[107] *Whitehall Evening Post, or London Intelligencer*, 17 April 1756; *London Evening Post*, 20 April 1756: "This Day was publish'd, Guida Armonica o Dizionario Armonico: Being a Sure Guide to Harmony and Modulation; in which are exhibited, the various Combinations of Sounds consonant and dissonant, Progressions of Harmony, Ligatures and Cadences, real and deceptive. By F. Geminiani. To be sold at the Author's Lodgings at Grange-Inn, in Carey-street, near Lincoln's-Inn Fields; and at all the Musick Shops in London and Westminster". *Gazetteer, and London Daily Advertiser*, 20 May 1756: "New Musick, This Day is published, Price Fifteen-Shillings. The Art of Accompaniament; or, A new and well digested Method to learn to perform thorough Bass on the Harpsichord, with Property [*sic*] and Elegance; composed by F. Geminiani, Opera 11th. Sold by the Author, at the Grange Inn, in Carey-street, near Lincoln's-Inn Fields; and by John Johnson, opposite Bow Church in Cheapside. Where may be had, just publish'd, Guida Armonica: Or, a Sure Guide to Harmony and Modulation: In which are exhibited, the various Combinations of Sounds Consonant and Dissonant, Progressions of Harmony, Ligatures and Cadences, real and deceptive, very necessary to all who study the Art of Composition, and desire to play the Organ and Harpsichord extempore. Opera 10th".

English (being *A Sure Guide to Harmony and Modulation*), describing the work as "Opera x" and that it was printed for the author by John Johnson. The preface and introduction are in English only, but these are not simple translations of the French texts of the Amsterdam edition, but new texts partially based on the earlier version. While this is not the place to present a detailed comparison of the two versions of the text, we cannot refrain from pointing to an interesting difference: in both it is stated that the guide is not complete, since it does not cover the major keys nor ascending or descending scales or imitation. Geminiani promises to publish a supplement, in the French text "si le tems me le permet", in the English text "if my Health permit". Had he fallen ill in the meantime? He was, after all, 75 years old in 1755. The supplement would indeed be written and published, but only in English, published by John Johnson in London.

Although the English *Guida armonica* was printed on the same paper as the Dutch *Dictionaire harmonique*, one must assume that it was produced in London on matching paper requested by Geminiani: the added engraved title-page certainly is British work (probably by Thomas Bennett — *cf.* VI *Sonatas* [...] *from the* VI *last Solos of his Op.ª 1.ª*) and the English introductory text would not have been prepared in Holland.

The high price will not have encouraged quick sales of the *Dictionaire*, neither in Holland nor in England. We do not know how long the stocks of Olofsen and Covens lasted, but in 1781 some copies of the *Dictionaire* must have come into the hands of the Amsterdam music dealer and publisher Johann Julius Hummel, who included the title in his 1781 catalogue, without a price.[108] Strangely enough, it is not found in later catalogues until those of 1802 and c1814. The 1802 catalogue was issued in Berlin and lists the *Dictionaire* for 2 Reichsthaler, 8 Groschen;[109] the c1814 catalogue was issued in Amsterdam and offers the *Dictionaire*, now more than half a century old, for *f* 5.[110] This is the last trace of its availability on the Dutch market.

The British issue, the *Guida armonica*, had a shorter life: it can still be found in Johnson's catalogue of 1770 and later, and at a reduced price, £0:10:6, half the original price given in Bremner's catalogue of 1782.[111]

---

[108] JOHANSSON, Cari. *J. J. & B. Hummel: Music-Publishing and Thematic Catalogues*, Stockholm, Almqvist & Wiksell, 1972 (Publications of the Library of the Royal Swedish Academy of Music, 3), vol. I, p. 36, n. 10a.

[109] *Ibidem*, vol. II, facsimile 40.

[110] *Ibidem*, vol. II, facsimile 41.

[111] *A Catalogue of Vocal and Instrumental Music* (London, John Johnson, 1770), *A Catalogue of Vocal and Instrumental Music* (London, Robert Bremner, March 1782).

Conclusions

The first conclusion to be drawn from this overview of Geminiani's Dutch publications is that he was intensely and personally — almost obsessively — occupied with the publication of his works. Most of his travels away from England were motivated by the wish to organize and oversee the production of his publications, and also control when they should appear in England. During these travels he never performed publically on the violin and kept a low profile, *quasi incognito*. For these reasons most of his foreign journeys are poorly documented.

Secondly, Geminiani tried to avoid being merely incorporated in some publisher's catalogue, beginning with John Walsh. Instead, he tried to publish his works in private editions, as *Selbstverlag* or *Eigenverlag*, before they were given to a commercial distributor. In the early years we see a number of these distributors. The Sonatas Op. 1 of 1716 were given, in 1718, to Richard Meares; the *Prima parte* of the Corelli Concertos were not privately issued but given to two novice publishers, William Smith and John Barrett; the *Seconda parte* was printed in Holland but distributed in London by Nicolas Prevost, a bookseller of no great importance and of no importance as music seller. Op. 3 was published by Walsh, and Op. 2 was privately issued before being transferred some years later to Walsh.

From about 1735 Geminiani organized the publication of his works with greater personal control. From that time, to 1757, nearly all his works (with the exception of some treatises) were engraved abroad, most often in Paris, and sometimes in Holland. The plates engraved in Holland were used first for producing Dutch issues, and thereafter for the British issues. At this time his relations with established publishers — notably John Walsh Junior and John Johnson — had been improved if not regularized. Most of his publications from before 1750 were sold by the Walsh firm, while Johnson's shop in London became, in 1751, the address for all of his works, from the very first (as reprints) to the last. The engraved plates of his works ended up in Johnson's shop, where further copies could be printed as necessary, a procedure which effectively restricted the amount of unauthorized reprinting. But it is also possible that Geminiani's style had become somewhat out of date in these years and publishers were less keen than before to reprint his works; no works that first appeared after 1740 were ever reprinted by other publishers.

APPENDIX

THE CASE *DENSON VERSUS GEMINIANI*

1. Procuration of Peter van Bekesteyn as solicitor for Richard Denson. The Hague, City Archives, Notarial Archives, No. 3299 (notary public Anthony Deel), No. 12.

Speciale procuratie *ad lites* door eene comparant betrekkelijk tot eene saeck.

Op huijden den 18 Octobter 1746 compareerde voor my, Anthony Deel, Openbaar Notaris by den Hove van Hollandt geadmitteert, in 's-Gravenhage resideerende, ter praesentie van de nagenoemde getuijgen, Richard Denson, Graveerder in musick, gewoont hebbende te Londen, dogh althans alhier, den twee ondergenoemde getuijgen bekent,
Dewelcke verklaarde te constitueeren ende magtig te maken D'Heer Pieter van Bekestijn Procureur voor den Ed. Agtb. Geregte van 's-Gravenhage, specialijck omme uijt sijn comparants naem en van sijnent wegen waer te neemen ende te defendeeren zoodanige zake ende instantie, als den Comparant genootsaakt is voor welgenoemt Geregt te moeten enthameeren als Eijsscher in R.A. [rau actie] ten eenre, op ende jegens Franciscus Geminiani, Italiaans Musikant, woonende alhier, Gedaegde int voorsz. cas, ter andere zijde; daar inne alle dagen ende termeijnen van Regten waer te neemen en te observeeren, vonnisse te versoeken ende hooren pronuncieeren, de voordelige te acquiesceren en ter executie te leggen, ende van de nadeelige te apelleeren of reformeeren, zoo als den geconstitueerde oordeelen zal te behooren, ende voorts generalijck daar inne verder te doen ende te verrigten 't geene vereijst zal worden, alles onder belofte van approbatie en ratificatie als naar Regte,
Aldus gepasseert in 's Hage voornoemt ter praesentie van Lodewijk Heijkoop en Johan Frost als getuijgen.

Richard Denson
L. Heijkoop
Frost A. Deel
Not. Publ. 1746

2. The Role of the Court of Justice of The Hague, 1746-1747. The Hague, City Archives, Archives of the Court of Justice, No. 200.[112]

The left-hand column is the official description of the case and was written before the session. The right-hand column is a summary of what happened during the session and is written in another hand. Pieter van Bekesteyn is Denson's solicitor, Abraham Mens is Geminiani's solicitor.

Fol. 107v: 2 November 1746	
P. V. Bekesteyn Richard Denson, Graveerder in Muziek, gewoont hebbende te Londen, doch zich althans bevindende alhier in Den Hage, Eiser in R.A. [rau actie], *contra* Franciscus Geminiani, Italiaens Muzikant woonende alhier, Gedaegde, Eisch doen en Provisie te begeeren.	Bekesteyn exhibeert procuratie, verzoekt voorts default, en tweede citatie. Schepenen *fiat*.
Fol. 111r: 9 November 1746	
P. V. Bekesteyn Richard Denson, Graveerder in Muziek, gewoont hebbende te Londen, doch zich althans bevindende alhier in Den Hage, Eiser in R.A., *contra* Franciscus Geminiani, Italiaens Muzikant woonende alhier, Gedaegde, het tweede default te begeeren.	Mens verzoekt purge, en Eysch te horen. Bekesteyn consenteert, mits etc., doet voorts Eysch, verzoekt provisie, en concludeert, alles *prout in scriptis*, en levert over. Mens dag en copie van alles, mitsgaders visie des noods, cautie van de kosten en electie van *domicilium citandi et executandi*. Bekesteyn presenteert cautie juratoire, en kiest *domicilium citandi et executandi* ten hyze van Johan Frost in de Houtstraat alhier, alwaer den Eyser is logerende.
Fol. 116v: 16 November 1746	
P. V. Bekesteyn Richard Denson, Graveerder in Muziek, gewoont hebbende te Londen, doch zich thans bevindende alhier in Den Hage, Eiser in R.A., *contra* Franciscus Geminiani, Italiaens Muzikant woonende alhier, Gedaegde, te antwoorden.	Mens *ad primam*, onvermindert zijne gedane verzoeken.

---

[112] KOSSMANN, Ernst Ferdinand. *Op. cit.* (see note 22), p. 90, quotes this archival document by mistake as no. 202.

Fol. 121v: 7 December 1746	
P. V. Bekesteyn Richard Denson, Graveerder in Muziek, gewoont hebbende te Londen, doch zich thans bevindende alhier in Den Hage, Eiser in R.A., *contra* Franciscus Geminiani, Italiaens Muzikant woonende alhier, Gedaegde, als noch te antoorden.	Mens ten naaste.
Fol. 126v: 14 December 1746	
P. V. Bekesteyn Richard Denson, Graveerder in Muziek, gewoont hebbende te Londen, doch zich thans bevindende alhier in Den Hage, Eiser in R.A., *contra* Franciscus Geminiani, Italiaens Muzikant woonende alhier, Gedaegde, ten derde mael te antwoorden.	Mens zegt, en antwoort, alles *prout in scriptis*, en levert over.
Fol. 130v: 21 December 1746	
P. V. Bekesteyn Richard Denson, Graveerder in Muziek, gewoont hebbende te Londen, doch zich althans bevindende alhier in Den Hage, Eiser in R.A. contra Franciscus Geminiani, Italiaens Muzikant woonende alhier, Gedaegde, te repliceeren.	In state.
Fol. 133v: 11 January 1747	
P. V. Bekesteyn Richard Denson, Graveerder in Muziek, gewoont hebbende te Londen, doch zich althans bevindende alhier in Den Hage, Eiser in R.A. *contra* Franciscus Geminiani, Italiaens Muzikant woonende alhier, Gedaegde, te repliceeren.	In state.
Fol. 136v: 18 January 1747	
P. V. Bekesteyn Richard Denson, Graveerder in Muziek, gewoont hebbende te Londen, doch zich althans bevindende alhier in Den Hage, Eiser in R.A., contra Franciscus Geminiani, Italiaens Muzikant woonende alhier, Gedaagde, te repliceeren.	Bekesteyn zegt, en repliceert, *prout in scriptis*, en levert over.
Fol. 139v: 25 January 1747	
P. V. Bekesteyn Richard Denson, Graveerder in Muziek, gewoont hebbende te Londen, doch zich althans bevindende alhier in Den Hage, Eiser in R.A., *contra* Franciscus Geminiani, Italiaens Muzikant woonende alhier, Gedaagde, te dupliceeren.	Mens ten naeste.

Fol. 143r: 1 February 1747	
P. V. Bekesteyn Richard Denson, Graveerder in Muziek, gewoont hebbende te Londen, doch zich althans bevindende alhier in Den Hage, Eiser in R.A., *contra* Franciscus Geminiani, Italiaens Muzikant woonende alhier, Gedaagde, te dupliceeren.	Mens dupliceert, *prout in scriptis*, en levert over.
Fol. 203v: 19 July 1747	
P. V. Bekesteyn Richard Denson, Graveerder in Muziek, Eiser Arrestant, op alle zodanige goederen en effecten, niets ter wereld uitgezondert, hoe genaemt of van wat Natuur dezelve ook zoude mogen wezen, als berustende zijn ten huize van Gotthier, wonende alhier, toekomende arngaende of eenigzins concerneerende Franciscus Geminiani, ten einde dezelve niet zullen werden getransporteert of elders vervoert voor en aleer de voornoemde Geminiani behoorlijke en suffisante Cautie subject de Judicature van deze Ed. Agtb. Geregte voor het uijtterlijke gewijsde in de procedure tusschen den Arrestant en Eiser ten eenre en den Gedaegde en gearresteerde *in bonis* ter andere zijde voor dezen Ed. Agtb. Geregte *lites pendent* te vallen zal hebben gestelt, Contra de voornoemde Geminiani, Gotthier, en alle anderen die hun op het arrest parthijen zoude willen stellen, gearresteerden en gedaegdens, Eisch doen, en dat enz.	Bekesteyn concludeert tot decretatie van het gedane arrest na etc.doende voorts Eysch en concludeert prout *in scriptis* en

3. Statement of Josua Bruyninx and Alida van Dalen, at the request of Geminiani and against Denson, 9 December 1746. The Hague, City Archives, Notarial Archives, No. 3158 (Notary public Beukel Henricus van den Dansser), No. 321.

Attestatie
No. 321
Den 9 December 1746 compareerde voor mij Beukel Henricus Den Dansser Notaris by den Hove van Holland geadmitteerd, in 's-Gravenhage residerende, present de getuijgen ondergenoemt, Monsr. Josua Bruninx, Mr. timmerman en juffw. Alida van Dale, egteliede, wonende alhier, my notaris bekent.
Dewelke verklaarde ter requisitie en de versoecke van D'Heer Franciscus Geminiani wonende alhier, waar en waarachtig te zijn, en wel hij eerste deposant, dat hij eenige tijd geleden heeft gesien, dat Richart Denson (als toen in dienst zijnde van den requestrant tot het gravere van

plate tot de muziek, en logerende by eene Monsr. Lachie in de St. Jacobstraat alhier) des avonts was legge, op de Straat regte by het gen. huys alwaer hy logierde, zodanig beschonken dat hy buyte staat was opstaan, dat daar op de Voorn. Mons. Lachie, daarmede by gekomen zynde en den eersten deposant ende tegens hem deposant zyde: "Neemt gy hem (denoterende daermede gem. Denson) in huys, want zyn heer woont bij u, en ik wil het beest niet meer in huys hebbe", dat de deposant zulx om het slegte leve van den zelven Denson, heeft gewijgert. Dog dat eenige tijd daarna, den requirant aan haar deposanten heeft versogt om den zelven Denson (also hij hem bij niemant in huys konde krijgen) in haar huys te neme, zeggende alsdan nog meer reguard op hem te konnen slaan en zulken levensmanier belette, dat zij deposanten op het aanhoudend versoek van de requirant, den gem. Denson hebben genome in haar huijs, om daar benevens den requirant te logiere, twelk ontrent 5 of 6 maanden heeft geduert, in welke tijt zy deposanten tezamen verklaren, den zelven Denson zig zodanig heeft gedrage en verschijde male zodanig beschonken is thuijs gekome, dat dezelve in het geheel ombequaam was om iets te konne doen, en zy deposante genoodsaak ware om deure en vensters te sluyten van wegen het brutaligere van gem. Denson, en hem te bedde te doen besorge, dat hij Denson, nadat hij alsdan nog wel een dag off ander moeste wagte eer hy wederom in staat was te konne werken;

dat gemelde Denson enige plate van den requestrant buyten desselfs kennis voor oud tin heeft verkogt, en ook eenige die alrede gegraveert waren in een kroegje alhier heeft verpant voor twee gulden die hij aldaar voor geconsumeerde drank schuldig was, en dus wederom andere moeste make, waardoor dubbelde tyd werd verspilt, welke gegraveerde plate eenige tyd daarna en nadat zulx aen den requestrant was bekent geworde door de eerste deposant syn wederom gehaalt ende voor de gen. twee gulden borge gebleve en op versoek van gem. Denson en ook aen die luyden betaelt.

~~Dat zy deposante de platen voor de requestrant zelf hebben gehaalt, uyt een kroegje alwaer gem. Denson dezelve had verpant voor twee gulden die hy zelve daer voor geconsumeerde drank schuldig was, en omme welke plate den requestrant ten uyterste verslagen was geweest, also hy dezelve hadde moeten gebruyken, zy deposanten voor de genoemde twee gulden voor denselve Denson hebbe borg gebleven, opdat hy dezelve plate den requestrant weder moge besorgen.~~ [crossed out and the following lines added after the cancellation]
Endigende zij deposanten deze hare gegeve verklaring gevende voor reden en wetenschap als in den staat van het zelve gesien, bijgewoont en gedaan te hebbe, presenterende het gedeposeerde desnoods en daertoe versogt zijnde met solemne ede te bevestigen.
Dit passeerde dus in presentie van Hendrik de Bruyn en Gerrit van Sull als getuygen

Josua Bruynicx
A V Dalen
H D Bruijn
gerrit van sull
B. H. Den Dansser, notarius Publicus

4. Sentence in the Case *Denson* v. *Geminiani*, 13 July 1747. The Hague, City Archives, Archives of the Court of Justice, No. 244 (Sentences 1743-1750).[113]

Pleytrolle fol: 108v	
P. V. Bekesteyn Richard Denson, Graveerder in Muziek, gewoond hebbende te Londen, doch zich altans bevindende alhier, Eiser in R.A., *contra* Franciscus Geminiani, Italiaens Muzikant woonende alhier, Recht te begeeren op de verzochte provisie.	Den 13 Julij 1747 Partijen verzoeken Regt.
't Geregt gehoort de Pleijdoije, en voorts doorgesien en overwogen hebben al het gene ter materie dienende is, doende Regt, verklaart dat er voor den Eijsser geen Provisie en valt. Actum den 13 Julij 1747, en geresumeert denzelvde dito.	

5. Testament of Richard Denson. The Hague, City Archives, Notarial Archives, No. 2138 (Notary public Arent Lybreghts), pp. 1178-1780.

Testament.
De Comparant verklaard beneden de vierduizend gulden gegoed te zijn, in 't amptgeld niet bekend te staan en werd in deze geen fideicommis gevonden.
Op huiden de vijfden Maart 1851, compareert voor my Arent Lybreghts, Openbaar Notaris, by den Edele Hove van Holland geadmiteert, in 's Hage resideerende, ter presentie van de nagenoemde getuigen, de Heer Richard Denson, Engelsman, musicq-graveerder, geboren in de Parochie van de St. Paulus Covent Garden, in de vryheid van Westminster te Londen, de nagenoemde getuigen bekend en wonende alhier.
Te kennen gevende genegen te zyn, om te disponeren van zyne natelatene goederen, mitsdien revocerende alle zyne voorgaande Testamenten en Codicillen, niettegenstaende in dezelve mochte gevonden werden eenige Clausule Derogatoir, als verklarende daarvan gene kennisse nochte geheugen te hebben.
Alvorens komende ter formele dispositie, zo legateert hy Comparant aan Peter Frost, zoon van zyne nagenoemde Erfgenamen, de somme van een-honderd-ende-vyftig guldens, welke allereerst zullen moeten werden uitgekeerd als den gelegateerden zal hebben bereykt d'ouderdom van vyf-en-twintig jaren ofte eerder huwelijken staat, zonder nochtans in deswegens eenige interesten te betalen.
Komende ter finale dispositie, zo verklaard hy Comparant tot zyne eenige en universele Erfgenamen *conjunctim*, wegens en uit hoofde van vele gedane diensten en assistentie in zyne ongelegenheden aan hem Comparant gedaan, en vertrouwt noch gedaan werden zal, te nomineren en t'instituëren Sr. John Frost, winkelier, en Juffrouw Maria Clear, echtelieden en wonende alhier in Den Hage, ende dat in alle zyne natelatene goederen, ende by vooroverlyden van de langstlevende hunne natelatene kind of kinderen by representatie.

---

[113]   *Ibidem*, p. 90, quotes this archival document by mistake as no. 242.

Verklarende hy Testateur tot voogden voor de gemelde kinderen te verkiezen zodanige personen als by de langstlevende van zyne respective Erfgenamen by Testament als anders zullen bevonden werden aangestelt te zyn.

Mitsdien uit zyne nalatenschap secluderende de Ed. Heren Weesmeesteren, waar zyn sterfhuis zoude mogen vallen en specialyk te dezer stede.

Al 't gunt voorsz. staat, den Comparant duidelyk voorgeleezen zynde, ende, zo hy zeide, 't zelve wel verstaan te hebben, begeert dat dit instrument zyn volkomen effect zal genieten, 't zy als Testament of Codicil, zo ende indervoegen 't zelve zal bestaan.

Aldus gedaan ende gepasseert, ter presentie van den Heer en Mr. David van Eversdyck, Advocaat voor den respective Hove van Justitie, en Monsr. Thomas Kerck, schoenmakersbaas, Lieden van eer en gelove, die my geassisteert hebben den Comparant dezelve te zyn, die hy zich in 't hoofd dezes heeft genoemd, als getuigen ten deze gerequireert.

Richd. Denson
D.v. Eversdyck
Thomas Kerck
A.Lybreghts Not. 1751.

6. The testament of Richard Denson, English Translation. Public Record Office, Probate 11/788.

Copy of Will. Translated out of Low Dutch. Richard Denson.

On this day the Fifth of Marche one-thousand-seven-hundred-and-fifty-one before me Arent Lybreghts Notary Publick admitted by the Court of Holland, residing in The Hague and in the presence of the witnesses hereinafter named, appeared Mr. Richard Denson, Englishman and Engraver of Musick, born in the Parish of St. Paul Covent Garden in the Liberty of Westminster at London, unto the undernamed witnesses known and dwelling here.

Who declared that he intends to dispose of his wordly estate, hereby revolting all his former Wills and Testaments notwithstanding any derogatory clauses might be found therin, whereof he declares not to have any knowledge or remembrance.

And before coming to a final disposition he the Appearer doth bequeath unto Peter Frost, son of his hereinafter named heirs the sum of one-hundred-and-fifty gilders, which shall not be paid until the said legatee shall have attained the age of twenty-five years or enter sooner into the Marriage State, nevertheless without paying any interest on that amount.

And coming to a final disposition he the Appearer declared to nominate and institute for his only and universal heirs jointly Mr. John Frost Shopkeeper and Mrs. Maria Clear Husband and Wife, dwelling here in The Hague and that in and to all the estate which shall leave behind him, and in case of the predecease of the survivor of them, the child or children which they shall leave behind them by representation and that for and in consideration of the many services done and assistance given unto him the Appearer when he was under difficulties and which he doubts not they will still continue doing.

He the Testator declaring to choose for Guardians to the said children such persons as shall be found to be appointed by the survivor of his respective heirs either by will or otherwise, hereby secluding from his estate all Gentlemen Orphan Masters wheresoever his mortuary house shall happen to be and specially those of this city.

All which as above written having been distinctly read over to the Appearer and he having as he sayd well understood the same he desired that this instrument may have and take full effect either as a Will or Codicil or in such manner as it can best subsist.

Thus done and passed in the presence of Mr. David van Eversdijck, Advocate in the respective Courts of Justice, and Mr. Thomas Kerck, Master Shoemaker, Persons of Honour and Credit, who affirmed unto me the Appearer to be the same person as he has called himself in the introduction hereof, as witnesses herunto required was signed Richd Denson, D.V. Eversdyck and Thomas Kerck. Lower: A. Lybreghts Not. 1751. After examination this was found to agree with the original remaining in the custody of Notary. Hague the 28th May 1751. A Lybreghts No. 1751.

We the underwritten Notarys residing in the City of The Hague in Holland do rectify that Arent Lybreghts before whom the aforegoing will is passed as a Notary in this city is a faithfull and lawfull Notary and that to all acts by him passed full faith is given both in Judgment Court and thereout. Done in The Hague the twenty-eighth of May one-thousand-seven-hundred-and-fifty-one. P. Coster Not. 1751. P.V.Bekesteyn 1751. Not.

GEMINIANI IN IRELAND

Barra Boydell
(MAYNOOTH)

IN THEIR RESPECTIVE ISSUES OF 4–8 DECEMBER 1733 *Faulkner's Dublin Journal*
and the *Dublin Evening Post* both reported: "Last Thursday the Rt Hon.
Lord Tullamore arrived here from his Travels. […] Signor Geminiani, a
Native of Italy, and a most famous Musician, arrived here with his Lordship".[1]
Geminiani was one of the most prominent Italian musicians and composers
to visit Ireland in the eighteenth century, living in Dublin between 1733 and
1740, returning to the country in 1759 and dying in Dublin in 1762. The
evidence for his activities during these two periods is limited, but it is clear
that he was held in high regard as a violinist and composer. Of particular
interest is Geminiani's posthumous reputation in the later eighteenth and
early nineteenth centuries within the context of the developing discourse
concerning the relative merits of Irish music (notably that of the harp tradition
epitomised by Turlough Carolan) and of Italian and European styles at a time
when antiquarian interest in the country's cultural heritage was laying the
foundations for the emergence of cultural nationalism.

In his detailed documentation of Geminiani's activities in Ireland,
Careri[2] cited W. H. Grattan Flood, whose article 'Geminiani in England and
Ireland' (1910) drew upon a number of original documentary sources which
were subsequently lost when the Irish Public Record Office was burnt down
in 1922.[3] Flood's writings need to be approached with considerable caution in
the light of his frequent inaccuracies both in the transcription of information
from primary sources and in the conclusions he drew on the basis of sometimes
flimsy evidence or flawed assumptions. Furthermore, he rarely cites sources

---

[1] Cited here after *Faulkner's Dublin Journal*. The *Dublin Evening Post* text varies only in minor details and differing abbreviations (e.g. 'Ld Tullamore' rather than 'the Lord Tullamore').

[2] CARERI, pp. 29-32 and 42-45.

[3] FLOOD, William Henry Grattan. 'Geminiani in England and Ireland', in: *Sammelbände der Internationalen Musikgesellschaft*, XII/1 (1910), pp. 108-112.

for his information. It is therefore important independently to validate any information given by Flood, in as much as this can be done given the subsequent loss of so many primary sources. Of particular significance in this respect is a set of notebooks containing information recorded by a Dr W. M. Graham in the Public Record Office shortly before it was destroyed.[4] While relating principally to Dublin violin makers, these notebooks also include information on Geminiani. Brian Boydell independently noted most of what survives in contemporary newspapers and related sources referring to Geminiani.[5] This chapter draws on the above sources in re-examining Geminiani's activities in Ireland, before considering his posthumous reception in the form of anecdotes related — and in some cases subsequently elaborated — by later authors in which he was cited in support of the technical artistry and musical achievements of Irish harpers and fiddle players.

Geminiani's arrival in Dublin in 1733 was not his first association with the country: according to Sir John Hawkins, Geminiani had been recommended by his then patron and former pupil Lord Essex (William Capel) for the post of Master and Composer of the State Music in Ireland following the death of John Sigismund Cousser in 1727. Geminiani however declined the position on the grounds that it was not tenable by a Catholic and, as Hawkins relates, it was given to Geminiani's pupil Matthew Dubourg:

> [...] upon enquiry into the conditions of the office, Geminiani found that it was not tenable by one of the Romish communion, he therefore declined accepting of it, assigning as a reason that he was a member of the catholic church; and that though he had never made great pretensions to religion, the thought of renouncing that faith in which he had been baptized, for the sake of worldly advantage, was what he could in no way answer to his conscience. Upon this refusal on the part of Geminiani, the place was bestowed on Mr. Matthew Dubourg, a young man who had been one of his pupils, and was a celebrated performer on the violin.[6]

---

4   Dublin, National Archives [IRL-Dna], M 3075-89.

5   BOYDELL, Brian. *Dublin: A Musical Calendar, 1700-1760*, Dublin, Irish Academic Press, 1988, *passim*.

6   *HAWKINS*, v, p. 241. Matthew Dubourg (1703-1767) held the post of 'Chief Composer and Master of the Music attending his Majesty's State in Ireland' until his death. He remained in Ireland until 1752 playing an active part as a violinist in Dublin's musical life. He was leader of the orchestra during Handel's visit, which included the first performance of *Messiah* (13 April 1742). Although he returned to London in 1752 to direct the Prince of Wales' Chamber Musick, and he became Master of Her Majesty's Band of Musick in 1761, he continued to visit Dublin, generally for performances of his royal birthday odes performed at Dublin Castle.

The Penal Laws then in force excluded Catholics from official office, but Careri suggests that Geminiani's refusal of the post in 1728 may have had as much to do with his desire to avoid the limitations that a regular commitment might entail and the requirement to write music "according to schedules and conditions imposed from without", as it had to do with his faith: his religion could have provided Geminiani with an honourable excuse, as it were.[7] It is of interest to note that Joseph C. Walker (identified as the later eighteenth-century author of an anonymous notebook now in the Royal Irish Academy) remarked of Matthew Dubourg that "Of his religion I cannot speak with certainty", suggesting that, in practice, the Penal Laws may not always have been strictly enforced.[8]

Although Geminiani had had no direct association with Ireland before 1728, his music was not unknown in Dublin. His pupil Dubourg is documented as having visited the city late in 1724,[9] but in December of the previous year the Dublin music publishers John and William Neale had announced the publication of "A Choice Collection of the Newest Airs, Minuets, and Play House Tunes",[10] an undated copy of which survives as "A Choice Collection of the Newest Airs and Minuets proper for the Violin German Flute or Hautboy". This, the Neales' earliest recorded music publication, includes "Geminiani's minuet with the adish[ional] graces by Mr. Duburg",[11] suggesting that Dubourg was already familiar to the Dublin musical public in 1723. By the mid-1720s Geminiani was at the height of his fame as a violinist and composer in London,

---

On 29 November 1759 (at the time of Geminiani's return to Ireland) he conducted the *Te Deum* and *Jubilate* performed at Christ Church cathedral to celebrate the British defeat of the French at Quebec.

[7]   *CARERI*, p. 21.

[8]   Dublin, Royal Irish Academy [IRL-Da], MS 12.B2.20, p. 18. The identification of Walker as the author of the anonymous notebook is based on its including corrected drafts of text that appear in his *Historical Memoirs of the Irish Bards* published in 1786 (Dublin, for the author). Non-conformist Protestants were excluded from official office by the Penal Laws, as were Catholics; thus, Walker could equally have been implying that Dubourg was a member of a non-conformist protestant sect as a Catholic.

[9]   BOYDELL, Brian. *Dublin* [...], *op. cit.* (see note 5), p. 41.

[10]   *Harding's Weekly Impartial News-Letter*, 28 December 1724. See NEALE, John - NEALE, William. *A Collection of the Most Celebrated Irish Tunes Proper for the Violin, German Flute or Hautboy*, Dublin, Neale, 1724; facs. ed. edited by Nicholas Carolan, Dublin, Irish Traditional Music Archive, ²2010, p. 25; BOYDELL, Brian. *Dublin* [...], *op. cit.* (see note 5), p. 41.

[11]   Dublin, National Library of Ireland [IRL-Dn], JM 5467[i], 10. This source is not cited amongst Careri's incipits of Geminiani's works, although the minuet itself circulated widely, both in instrumental forms (H. 177) and as the popular song "Gently touch the warbling Lyre" (H. 320) (*CARERI*, pp. 287 and 292).

so his music is likely already to have been known in Dublin (where musical tastes closely followed those of London), even if Dubourg had not played an active part in promoting it via the arrangement of his minuet. A tangential connection between Geminiani and Dublin in the mid-1720s is also present through Thomas Roseingrave. The latter's father, Daniel, had been organist at both Christ Church and St Patrick's cathedrals in Dublin. Thomas, who had left Dublin and settled in London by 1717 having previously visited Italy, applied (successfully) for the post of organist at St George's church, Hanover Square in 1725, on which occasion Geminiani was one of the examiners.[12]

The impetus for Geminiani's trip to Dublin in November 1733 was undoubtedly an invitation from the Irish aristocrat Baron Charles Moore of Tullamore (1712-64), who had been his patron in Paris and with whom he left for England in September 1733 en route to Ireland.[13] Geminiani remained in Dublin off and on until 1740, apparently living in Spring Gardens off Dame Street.[14] Here he established a concert venue referred to as "Geminiani's Great Room", which features as the venue for a number of musical and other events advertised in the Dublin newspapers both during the period he was in Dublin and for a number of years subsequently. Geminiani also dealt in paintings, his "Great Room" likewise serving as a venue for this activity.

Geminiani's first public performance in Dublin was announced in the *Dublin Evening Post* for 17 December 1733:

> By their graces the Duke and Dutchess of Dorset's Special Command. By Subscription. For the Benefit of Signior Geminiani. At the Great Room in Crow-Street.[15] On Monday the 17th of this Instant December, will be perform'd, A Consort of Vocal and Instrumental Musick, In which Signior Geminiani will perform several Solo's and Concerto's of His own Composition. The Vocal Part by Mrs. Davis. Subscriptions are taken in at Lucas's, the Globe, and the House of Commons Coffee-Houses,

---

[12] On the Roseingraves, see HOUSTON, Kerry. 'Roseingrave, Daniel', in: *Dictionary of Irish Biography*, 9 vols, Cambridge, Cambridge University Press-Royal Irish Academy, 2009, vol. VIII, pp. 610-612; on Geminiani's involvement in Thomas Roseingrave's appointment as organist, see CARERI, pp. 18-19.

[13] Letter from Thomas Pelham to William Capel, Paris, 1 October 1733, cited in CARERI, pp. 27-28.

[14] No longer in existence, Spring Gardens was situated off the south side of College Green, more or less opposite where the Central Bank building now stands.

[15] Built in 1731 at the request of the Musical Academy for the Practice of Italian Musick, Crow Street Music Hall was one of the first venues outside London specifically built for public concerts. It was to become one of the principal Dublin venues for oratorio and concert performances in the mid-eighteenth century, and was later converted into a theatre.

A Prospect of the Parliament House, in College Green DUBLIN. | Le Point de Vue de l'hotelle de Parlement dans le College vers de DUBLIN.

ILL. 1: View of College Green, Dublin, with Dame Street beyond, 1753; engraving by Joseph Tudor (author's collection). Geminiani lived in Spring Gardens, behind the third block of houses on the left, between 1733 and 1740. He died "at his lodgings in Dame Street" in September 1762.

> at one Guinea for Three Tickets, Single Tickets, half a Guinea each. To begin at the usual Hour.[16]

Thereafter Geminiani's activities in Dublin are difficult to trace. It is likely that, in addition to his primary duties (at least initially) as a musician under the patronage of Lord Tullamore, he may have performed principally at private concerts for the aristocracy — there is scant mention of him in contemporary Dublin newspapers — and he can be assumed also to have taught violin. Charles Burney wrote of Geminiani that he "was seldom heard in public during his long residence in England. His compositions, scholars, and the presents he received from the great, whenever he could be prevailed upon to play at their houses, were his chief support":[17] it would appear that he supported himself in like manner while in Ireland. Flood states without source that he "gave two concerts in the Spring of the following year [1734] and then returned to London, where he occasionally performed, in 1735, at Hickford's Room, but he devoted most of his time to composition".[18] Although there is no reason not to suppose that these concerts may have taken place, no documentation has come to light to substantiate this claim. Careri cites an undated letter from between 1728 and 1740 referring to Geminiani in London in support of the view that he was indeed there around 1735, but

---

[16] *Dublin Evening-Post*, 11-15 December 1733. See also CARERI, p. 29; BOYDELL, Brian. *Dublin* […], *op. cit.* (see note 5), p. 55.

[17] BURNEY, IV, p. 643.

[18] FLOOD, William Henry Grattan. 'Geminiani in England […]', *op. cit.* (see note 3), p. 109.

this clearly provides imprecise evidence at best.[19] Flood goes on to state, again without source, that Geminiani returned to Dublin in 1737 "at the urgent request of his pupil Dubourg", remaining there until 1740 and re-opening "his Academy in Spring Gardens, off Dame St., again known as 'Geminiani's Great Room', where he gave concerts as well as lessons".[20] Flood seems to have based his assertion on advertisements inviting subscriptions for "Twelve Sonatas, compos'd by Mr. Francis Geminiani, for the Violin and Bass" which appeared first of all in London in February 1737, then in the *Dublin Newsletter* on 5-8 March 1737, and subsequently in *Faulkner's Dublin Journal* on 18-22 April 1738. While the London advertisement mentioned the publisher John Walsh of the Strand, the Dublin advertisements invited subscriptions to be taken "by Mrs. Hyde, bookseller in Dame St. and by the printer hereof", the printer not being identified by name.[21] The issuing of these advertisements first in London in February 1737 and the following month and thereafter in Dublin does indeed suggest that Geminiani moved back to Dublin at this time, but this cannot be confirmed. In the event, this set of violin sonatas (Op. 4) was not published until April 1739.[22]

In April 1740 Geminiani advertised a proposal to publish by subscription his Harmonical Guide, subscriptions to be taken "at Bacon's Coffee-house in Essex-street, [and] by William Manwaring at Corelli's Head on College Green".[23] Manwaring was a prominent Dublin music publisher and seller. While this indicates that Geminiani was still in Dublin at this period, Careri incorrectly quotes this advertisement as stating that subscriptions were to be taken "*by* Mr. Francis Geminiani" [my italics], concluding that "it was therefore Geminiani himself who had the task of collecting in the subscriptions". Like his proposed set of twelve violin sonatas advertised in 1737 and 1738, this treatise was apparently advertised without success and was not published until twelve years later.[24]

---

[19] CARERI, p. 30, n. 11.

[20] FLOOD, William Henry Grattan. 'Geminiani in England [...]', *op. cit.* (see note 3), p. 109. Dr W. M. Graham's notes repeat this assertion, but he is clearly quoting Flood (Dublin, National Archives of Ireland [IRL-Dna], Graham, M3077, 'Notebook 3', [n.p.]).

[21] Mrs Hyde is identified as a bookseller in the advertisement in the *Dublin Newsletter*, 5-8 March 1736-1737, but not in the later *Faulkner's Dublin Journal* advertisement.

[22] CARERI, p. 31.

[23] *Dublin Newsletter*, 22-26 April 1740. See also CARERI, p. 31; BOYDELL, Brian. *Dublin* [...], *op. cit.* (see note 5), pp. 67-68.

[24] CARERI, p. 31. "By Mr. Francis Geminiani" appears in the advertisement at the end of the description of the *Harmonical Guide*, to identify the author. The information relating to the taking of subscriptions initiates the following (and final) paragraph: while Geminiani may indeed have taken the subscriptions himself at Bacon's Coffee House, this is not specified.

Despite the scant primary evidence for Geminiani's activities in Ireland during the 1730s, a number of undated reports and other sources reflect his presence there. James Latham (1696-1747), considered the leading portrait painter in Ireland at the time,[25] executed a portrait of "Geminiani, the composer" which, along with one of the actress Peg Woffington, was described by Anthony Pasquin in 1796 as being "painted in so pure a stile, as to procure him the title of the *Irish Vandyke*".[26] Since Latham was based in Dublin from 1725 until his death (apart from possible short visits to London and Paris),[27] it is likely that this portrait was painted in Dublin during the 1730s. Geminiani included an extended set of variations on "An Irish Tune" in his *Rules for Playing in a True Taste*, Op. 8, published in London *c*1748, as one of his "variety of compositions on the subjects of English, Scotch and Irish tunes".[28] The presence here of what Geminiani identifies as an Irish tune does not of itself constitute evidence for his having heard this melody in Dublin himself, since both Scottish and Irish tunes circulated widely in printed form throughout Great Britain and Ireland at this time. The tune itself is not in a style that can confidently be identified as traditional Irish of the period, although it could possibly be a harp tune (with the accidentals omitted it is compatible with the Irish harp).[29] Donal O'Sullivan (author of *Carolan: The Life, Times and Music of an Irish Harper* (1958) and *Songs of the Irish* (1960)) had earlier suggested that it might be a hybrid court dance which Geminiani could have heard in Dublin Castle and thus identified as Irish.[30]

An anonymous collection of pieces, now in the National Library of Ireland and apparently compiled in Dublin, includes Geminiani's popular Minuet (H. 177), entitled "Minuet by Geminiani". The collection contains (unaccompanied) popular song tunes, minuets (in most cases unattributed)

---

[25] CULLEN, Fintan. 'Latham, James', in: *The Dictionary of Art*, edited by Jane Turner, 34 vols, London, Grove-Macmillan, 1996, vol. XVIII, p. 829.

[26] PASQUIN, Anthony. *An Authentic History of the Professors of Painting, Sculpture, & Architecture, who have Practised in Ireland*, London, H. D. Symonds, 1796, p. 29. See also STRICKLAND, Walter. *A Dictionary of Irish Artists*, 2 vols, Dublin-London, Maunsel & Co., 1913, vol. II, pp. 2-3; also referred to by Flood who, with characteristic inaccuracy, gives Latham's date of death as 1756 (see FLOOD, William Henry Grattan. 'Geminiani in England […]', *op. cit.* [see note 3], p. 109). The present location of this portrait is unknown.

[27] MINCH, Rebecca. 'Latham, James', in: *Dictionary of Irish Biography*, *op. cit.* (see note 12).

[28] Incipit quoted in *CARERI*, p. 275.

[29] Private communication, Nicholas Carolan, director of the Irish Traditional Music Archive and reporting the opinions of Lisa Shields and Aibhlín McCrann of Cairde na Cruite ('Friends of the Harp'), an association for the revival and development of interest in the Irish harp, October 2010.

[30] Private communication, Brian Boydell, *c*1967.

and tunes from operas,[31] and appears to have been copied over several decades: Geminiani's minuet is on page [4], preceded and immediately followed by anonymous minuets, popular songs and dance tunes that are difficult to date. The earliest items to which a date *post quem* can be provided are a 'Minuet in Tamerlane' on page [11] (Handel's *Tamerlano* was premiered in London in 1724) and [Vivaldi's] 'Concerto Call'd the Cuckoo', which had been published in London in 1717. A tune on page [30] from Handel's *Arianna in Creta* ['in Ariadne'] (premiered in London in 1734), 'The Symphony of the Early Horn' on page [31] (the popular song 'The Early Horn' comes from John Galliard's pantomime *The Royal Chace* premiered at Covent Garden in 1736), and 'A Favourite Aire by Mr. Hendel in Atalanta' (premiered in London in 1736) on pages [35-37] indicate that the central part of the collection appears to have been copied during the mid- to later-1730s. A number of items towards the end of the volume can be dated to the 1740s,[32] and the date 1755 appears on one of the final pages. Since Geminiani's minuet occurs near the beginning of the collection it probably dates from the early 1730s, possibly after he arrived in Dublin, but it could be earlier, even from the late 1720s.

Geminiani's departure from Dublin in 1740 may have been related to the fact that Lord Tullamore had left Dublin, apparently following his marriage in October 1737 to Hester Coghill:[33] in September 1739 the house "in Abbey-street [...] where Lord Tullamore lately liv'd", described as a "large commodious House, exceedingly well finish'd, with large Stableing for Horses and Coach Houses, and all other convenient Offices [...]" was advertised "To be let for a Term of Years".[34] Whatever the reasons for his departure, by November 1740 Geminiani was in Paris, but he may not yet have considered permanently leaving Dublin, for it was not until March 1742 that his house "in Dame Street" (presumably referring to Spring Gardens, just off Dame St) was advertised "To be lett for any term of years, the house in Dames-Street,

---

[31] Dublin, National Library of Ireland [IRL-Dn], JM 5467[ii], [p. 4].

[32] For example, 'A Song made for ye Gentlemen Volunteers of the City of London, 1746' on page [57], the then-popular Irish tune 'Elin A Roon' on page [56] in a version apparently copied from Mathew Dubourg's setting published in Dublin in 1746 (see *Select Minuets. Collected from the Castle Balls, and the Publick Assemblies in Dublin [...] To which is added Eleen a Roon by M^r. Dubourgh, set to the harpsichord with his variations*, Dublin, W. Manwaring, 1746), or 'Minuet in the Oratoria of Saul: By Mr. Handel' on page [53] (*Saul* was first performed in London in January 1739 and in Dublin in 1749).

[33] DEBRETT, John. *The Peerage of the United Kingdom of Great Britain and Ireland*, 2 vols, London, J. Moyes, [13]1820, vol. II, p. 1064.

[34] *Faulkner's Dublin Journal*, 25-29 September 1739.

wherein Signor Geminiani lately dwelt. The whole house wainscoted, except the garrets; with Grates and Tiles ready set. Vaults proper for a Gentleman or Wine-Merchant [...]".[35]

The high regard in which Geminiani had been held in Dublin is reflected in the fact that his name continued to be attached to his former "great room" for many years after he had left the city. In July 1742 a furniture sale ("the Goods made up by a Person who is quitting the Paragon Kideminster Trade") was advertised "at Geminiani's Great Room",[36] and in November of the same year the premises again became the venue for musical activities when the Hungarian horn player Mr Charles took a lease on Geminiani's room which he used for instrumental lessons until he left Dublin after March 1743.[37] "Geminiani's Great Room" was still cited as the venue for an auction of paintings in December 1752, twelve years after Geminiani was last known to have been in Dublin.[38]

Geminiani returned to Ireland in 1759, reputedly as music master to the family of Charles Coote, whose house at Cootehill, Co. Cavan (built c1725-30 and renamed Bellamont Forest in 1767 following Coote's elevation to the title of Earl of Bellamont) is one of Ireland's finest Palladian villas.

Cootehill was the family's residence during the summer months, the winter season being spent in Dublin.[39] Although Burney gave the date of Geminiani's return to Ireland as 1761 (see below), Flood referred to an anecdote recorded by "Lee Lewis" which identified 1759 as the year of Geminiani's association with the Cootes, but without providing further details of this source.[40] Flood's source can be identified as the *Memoirs* of the actor Charles Lee Lewes published in 1805, over four decades after the events they record.[41] Independent evidence for Geminiani's position with the Cootes has not come

---

[35]   *Dublin Mercury*, 2-6 March 1742.

[36]   *Dublin Newsletter*, 13-17 July 1742. See also BOYDELL, Brian. *Dublin* [...], *op. cit.* (see note 5), p. 85.

[37]   *Dublin Newsletter*, 23-27 November 1742. See also BOYDELL, Brian. *Dublin* [...], *op. cit.* (see note 5), p. 87.

[38]   *Faulkner's Dublin Journal*, 5-9 December 1752.

[39]   On Bellamont Forest, see BENCE-JONES, Mark. *A Guide to Irish Country Houses*, London, Constable, rev. ed. 1988, p. 37.

[40]   FLOOD, William Henry Grattan. 'Geminiani in England [...]', *op. cit.* (see note 3), p. 111.

[41]   LEWES, Charles Lee. *Memoirs of Charles Lee Lewes* [...], 4 vols, London, Richard Philips, 1805, vol. I, pp. 213-223. I am grateful to Michael Talbot for identifying and bringing this reference to my attention.

ILL. 2: Bellamont Forest, Cootehill, co. Cavan (photograph by the author). Geminiani returned to Ireland in the summer of 1759 to work here as music teacher to Charles Coote, later Earl of Bellamont.

to light.[42] Lee Lewis' anecdote in relation to Geminiani at Cootehill deserves to be quoted at length:

> The late Mr. Joseph Younger, of truly respectable memory, related to me the following humorous circumstances, which happened to him at a place called Coot-hill, in the north of Ireland.
>
> The winter season being finished at Crow-street, Dublin, in the year 1759, he engaged himself and his wife to go with a company of itinerants on a summer excursion, until Barry and Woodward should open again the theatre in Dublin.
>
> Business proving very bad [...] The sensible and humane Younger, being unhappy at his own situation, and equally so for the distresses to which he saw the company constantly exposed, communicated their distressed condition to Mr. Coote, the late Lord Bellamont. The young gentleman was no sooner made

---

[42]   The family and estate papers for this period are not known to have survived (private communication from John Coote, October 2010).

acquainted with the circumstance, than he humanely ordered a play to be performed the next evening. He also, with some difficulty, prevailed upon the celebrated Geminiani, who then resided with him as teacher of the violin, to accompany him to the rural theatre.

Preparations being made to receive with due respect the worthy squire and his company, the house [footnote: This house was no other than a back stable, with a new laid malt-house floor: there was no raised stage, in consequence of the place not affording room for such a convenience.] was opened, and very speedily filled. But oh! grief of griefs! the company had no musicians with them, and some harmony was indispensably necessary to prevent the impending wrath of the offended gods. After a long search in vain for any kind of scraper or bagpiper, their fears rather subsided on seeing a girl leading in a poor old blind man, with signs of a *crowdy* [fiddle] beneath his coat. He was immediately engaged, and placed on a stool behind the scenes.

After thrumming his instrument to put it in tune, he drew from the strings such a series of discordant notes, as surely never before or since tormented the ears of mortals. All eyes were fixed on Geminiani, whose writhings of body and distortions of countenance were better to be imagined than described.

The poor fidler being informed by some wags behind the scenes, that the greatest violin player in the world was in the pit with Squire Coote, and that he was in raptures with the excellence of his playing, so exerted his skill and powers, as to cause the famed musician to start from his seat with the most rueful countenance, and with feelings almost bordering on convulsive agony. The harsh grating sounds, torn and rasped from the vilest of instruments, he at first avoided by stopping his ears; but the encreased exertions of the crowder broke every barrier, and assailed his hearing with all the combination of irritating discord. His torment was so great that it became intolerable, which caused him, with a pitiful aspect, to request that Mr. Coote would order the carriage to convey him from this cave of Cyclops. But the young squire was too much diverted with the enraged condition of his poor old tortured master, to comply with his request. The banquet was too mirthful to suffer him to end it by any retreat of Geminiani.

Crowdero,[43] considering the continual clapping of hands, the roars and shouts from every part of the house, as plaudits paid

---

[43]   The term 'crowdero' recurs elsewhere in late eighteenth- and early nineteenth-century Irish writings to refer to fiddle players. See for example a story recorded by Joseph C. Walker concerning Matthew Dubourg disguising himself as a "country fidler" at a fair in Ireland, where he "sallied forth among the Tents, another Crowdero". See Walker, Joseph Cooper.

to his merit, imagined his fortune was made, especially as he was informed that Mr. Coote was highly pleased with his playing: this was true information; for he was in a constant succession of fits of laughter to see the distressed son of scientific melody in an agony so unbecoming his age and gravity, while he accused his remorseless pupil of the greatest cruelty. Geminiani was however at last relieved, by an accident which threatened fatal consequences. Mr. Coote's violent fits of laughter were so great, and so continual, that he fell into a paroxysm of convulsion, which so alarmed his mother, who sat near him, that she immediately commanded the son of Carolan[44] to desist, on pain of her weighty displeasure.

The bell rang, the curtain drew up, and my friend Younger was seen seated at a table in the character of Lord Townley, in the Journey to London.[45] — His soliloquy being finished, Lady Townley entered, when he should have said —

"Going out so soon this morning, madam?"

But an unforeseen impediment suppressed his utterance, and withheld his approach towards his lady; the high heels of his stage shoes had made such an impression in the new made floor, and so tenacious was the clay of intruders, that although he extricated himself, he was obliged to leave his shoes fixed in the mire, until with might and main he compelled the earth to yield him up his property.

In this state of confusion, he ran off the stage, muttering curses and invectives against all the sluts and slovens in the kingdom. The tranquillity of the audience being thus broken again by this ridiculous accident, all attention to the

---

Historical Memoirs of the Irish Bards, op. cit. (see note 8), pp. 159-160, n. (k); see also BUNTING, Edward. *A General Collection of the Ancient Music of Ireland*, London, for the editor, 1809, p. 23, n. 'II', where he suggests the derivation from the Welsh 'crwth', corrupted to 'crowd'. Bunting also refers to *Hudibras*, a late seventeenth-century mock-heroic poem by Samuel Butler, a reprint of which had appeared in London in 1805; see Part 1, Canto 2, lines 106-122: 'I' the head of all this warlike rabble, | CROWDERO march'd, expert and able. | Instead of trumpet and of drum, | That makes the warrior's stomach come, | [...] | A squeaking engine he apply'd | Unto his neck, on north-east side, | [...] | His warped ear hung o'er the strings, | Which was but souse to chitterlings: | For guts, some write, e'er they are sodden, | Are fit for music, or for pudden'. 'Crwth/crowd/crowdero' is also cognate with 'cruit', an Irish word for the harp. In the absence of his subsequent identification as a "poor fidler", the earlier reference in this quotation to the itinerant musician having a "*crowdy* beneath his coat" could equally have been interpreted as referring to a small harp.

44   On the harper Turlough Carolan, see below. "Son of Carolan" is used here to designate an Irish itinerant musician rather than specifically a harper.

45   VANBRUGH, Sir John - CIBBER, Colley. *The Provok'd Husband; or, A Journey to London*, London, John Watts, 1728.

performance was entirely suspended, for the enjoyment of this more whimsical scene of humour. Even Geminiani forgot his own late ludicrous situation, and participated in the general mirth and jocund laugh [...].[46]

Charles Coote, aged twenty-one in 1759, had recently returned from the Grand Tour, subsequently affecting a foreign accent when speaking English and giving his maiden speech in the House of Lords in French.[47] His portrait by Joshua Reynolds (1773) reflects this self-important peacock of a grandee.[48] The background to Coote's engagement of Geminiani — then aged seventy-one — is not known, but it may reflect Coote's desire to enhance his self-image by attaching to his household an Italian musician who — if now elderly and no longer as famous as he once was — was still remembered as a celebrated violinist and musician. Coote was however an active musician: he played cello in the Musical Academy founded by Lord Mornington in 1758, an association exclusively comprised of "ladies and gentlemen" (and specifying in its statutes that "No public mercenary performer, professor, or teacher of music, shall ever be admitted into any rank of the Academy on any account whatsoever"), and which met in Dublin every week between November and May, giving public performances once a month.[49] Perhaps significantly in the context of Geminiani's employment by Coote, the Musical Academy clearly embraced Italian music, Mrs Mary Delany commenting of a performance she attended in December 1758 that "The Italian taste prevails too much, and takes off the pleasure I should otherwise have in their performance, which is better than I could have imagined".[50] The Coote family's musical interests are also reflected at Cootehill in the classical portico, which is thought to post-date the original construction of the house but nevertheless be of mid-eighteenth-

[46] LEWES, Charles Lee. *Op. cit.* (see note 41), pp. 213-222.

[47] LUNNEY, Linde. 'Coote, Charles', in: *Dictionary of Irish Biography, op. cit.* (see note 12), vol. II, pp. 831-832.

[48] <http://commons.wikimedia.org/wiki/File:Charles_Coote,_1st_Earl_of_Bellamont.jpg>: consulted 5 July 2010.

[49] WARBUTON, John - WHITELAW, James - WALSH, Robert. *The History of the City of Dublin*, 2 vols, London, Cadell and Davies, 1818, vol. II, pp. 906-908 (Charles Coote is anachronistically listed here as the Earl of Bellamont); see also GILBERT, John Thomas. *A History of the City of Dublin*, 3 vols, Dublin, James Duffy, 1861 (facs. repr., Shannon, Irish University Press, 1972), vol. I, pp. 77-79.

[50] *Letters from Georgian Ireland. The Correspondence of Mary Delany, 1731-68*, edited by Angélique Day, Belfast, The Friar's Bush Press, 1991, p. 267.

century date: its frieze features musical instruments, supposedly put there in reference to the noted musical interests of Charles Coote's sisters.[51]

Flood states that Geminiani settled in Dublin in the autumn of 1759 "at the invitation of Dubourg".[52] A move to Dublin from Cootehill would correspond with the Coote's return to the city from their country residence, and his presence in Dublin before the end of 1759 is confirmed by an advertisement which appeared first in *Faulkner's Dublin Journal* of 18-22 December for a benefit concert to be given by command of the lord lieutenant the Duke of Bedford and his wife on 4 February in Fishamble Street:

> On Monday the 4th of February, at the Great MUSICK-HALL in Fishamble-Street, will be a Grand CONCERTO SPIRITUALE, Tickets at Half a Guinea each. Mr. Geminiani will perform a Solo and Concerto on the Violin. After the Concert will be a Ball, with Tea, Coffee, Lemonade, Cards, &c. and the whole Performance will be conducted in the genteelest Manner. The Room will be illuminated with Wax. Tickets to be had of Mr. Geminiani, at Mr. Dobson's, Frame maker, in Abby-Street.

In the event, the concert was postponed until 3 March 1760, the relevant notice commenting that:

> Mr. Geminiani hopes to be excused for deferring his Concert, as he was under an absolute Necessity of doing so. By particular Desire he will perform a Concerto and Solo on the Violin, as he would endeavour by every Method in his Power to express the Sensibility he has of the Favour and generous Regards he met with in this Kingdom. — The Tickets printed for Monday the 4th of February will be taken the above Night.[53]

Mrs Delany's account of the concert in a letter written the following day is of particular interest:

> [...] there is a spirit of harmony and prettiness of fancy [in Geminiani's music] which no other music (besides our dear Handel's) has. He played one of his own solos most wonderfully for a man of eighty-six years of age,[54] and one of his fingers hurt; but the sweetness and melody of the tone of his fiddle, his fine

---

[51] Private communication from Sean Moran, estate manager at Bellamont Forest, July 2010.
[52] FLOOD, William Henry Grattan. 'Geminiani in England [...]', *op. cit.* (see note 3), p. 111.
[53] *Faulkner's Dublin Journal*, 26-29 January 1760; repeated *ibidem*, 26 February-1 March 1760.
[54] He was in fact 72.

and elegant taste, and the perfection of time and tune make full amends for some failures in his play [*sic*] occasioned by the weakness of his hand; and his clever management of passages too difficult for him to execute with the spirit he used to do was very surprizing. On the whole I was greatly entertained, though it is the fashion to shrug up the shoulders and say: "Poor old man! Did you ever hear such a close? No shake at all!" with impertinent etceteras. I felt quite peevish at their remarks. The great ladies and their attendant peers were so impatient to get to their cards and to their dancing, that a message was sent to Geminiani to "shorten the musical entertainment". I was quite provoked the concert was not above one hour; I could have sat three hours more with pleasure to have heard it. I have invited Geminiani to come and see me, and hope to hear this music again some way or other.[55]

Auctions of paintings were held at Geminiani's Great Room at this time, the first on 28 January 1760 of "a curious Collection of Flemish and other Pictures, consigned to a Merchant in this City by a Virtuoso in Holland",[56] the second on 11 February of "a large and curious Collection of most capital Paintings, lately imported into this Kingdom and bought in several Parts of Europe by one of the best Connoisseurs in England; there are many of them very large, fit for the most elegant Rooms, and are undoubted Originals [...]".[57] Given his well-documented interests in art dealing, it is tempting to read Geminiani's direct involvement into these art auctions, but this is nowhere mentioned nor implied in the advertisements. However, his continuing contacts within the art world are illustrated by tickets for his benefit concert being available "at Mr. Dobson's Frame Maker in Abbey St.".[58] In 1762, the year of Geminaini's death, his rooms were specifically described as "Geminiani's picture room" in a notice of an executor's auction on 19 April for one Capt. Bonfoy which included "a fine Chamber Organ, a Cremona Fiddle, marked Stainer [*sic*], 1699, and three large Fishing-Nets".[59]

In 1760 Geminiani travelled to Edinburgh, where he is first documented on 5 August. Michael Talbot suggests that the reason for this journey, and thence via Newcastle to London where he arrived around March 1761, was the publication of his *Art of Playing the Guitar or Cittra* in

---

[55]   *Letters from Georgian Ireland* [...], *op. cit.* (see note 50), p. 269.

[56]   *Faulkner's Dublin Journal*, 22-26 January 1760. The newspaper states "Monday 22nd Inst [January]", but this is clearly a misprint for Monday 28 January.

[57]   *Ibidem*, 5-9 February 1760.

[58]   *Ibidem*, 18-22 December 1759. See note 53.

[59]   *Ibidem*, 17-20 April 1762.

Edinburgh[60] and of a number of works including the *Two Unison Concertos*, the *Second Collection of Pieces for the Harpsichord* in London, and possibly *The Enchanted Forest*, the autograph manuscript of which he gave to the London merchant, amateur musician and collector of music James Matthias, to whom it is inscribed and dated 7 December 1761. Hawkins' statement that "In the year 1761 he [Geminiani] went over to Ireland, and was kindly entertained there by Mr. Matthew Dubourg, who had been his pupil, and was then master of the king's band in Ireland. This person through the course of his life had ever been disposed to render him friendly offices"[61] makes sense if it is understood to refer to his return to Ireland, presumably in December 1761, following this prolonged trip to Scotland and England, rather than providing an erroneous date for his coming to Ireland in 1759 in the service of Charles Coote. Burney clearly drew upon Hawkins when he stated that "In 1761, he went to Ireland, to visit his scholar Dubourg, master of the King's band in that kingdom, who always treated him with great respect and affection".[62] Hawkins is likewise the source for the story also related by Burney concerning the circumstances leading up to Geminiani's death:

> [...] it was but a short time after the arrival of Geminiani at Dublin that [Matthew Dubourg's] humanity was called upon to perform for him the last. It seems that Geminiani had spent many years in compiling an elaborate treatise on music, which he intended for publication; but, soon after his arrival at Dublin, by the treachery of a female servant, who it is said was recommended to him for no other purpose than that she might steal it, it was conveyed out of his chamber, and could never after be recovered: The greatness of this loss, and his inability to repair it, made a deep impression on his mind, and, as it is conjectured, precipitated his end; at least he survived it but a short time, the seventeenth of September, 1762, being the last day of his life.[63]

As Careri notes, this is just an anecdote, neither more nor less plausible than others such as that related by Burney about Corelli's death.[64] Geminiani died "at his lodgings in College Green" as reported in the Dublin newspapers

---

[60] TALBOT, Michael. 'Geminiani's Canon: A Souvenir of a Visit to Scotland?' in the present volume, pp. 215-232. I am grateful to Michael Talbot for communicating this information to me prior to publication.

[61] *HAWKINS*, V, pp. 424-425.

[62] *BURNEY*, IV, p. 644.

[63] *HAWKINS*, V, p. 425; *cf. BURNEY*, IV, p. 644.

[64] *CARERI*, p. 44.

(where his age is repeatedly given as 96 — he was in fact 74).[65] Flood's comments that he "was attended in his last moments by Rev. Dr. Reynolds, Catholic Pastor of St. Andrew's" and that "he was accorded a fine funeral, and his remains were interred in the churchyard of St. Andrew's, near College Green" are given without source, and it is very possible that whatever source he used may have been lost in the Public Record Office fire in 1922. Certainly, the parish records of St Andrew's church are known to have been lost on that occasion. It is however fortunate that Dr W. M. Graham's notes, taken in the Public Record Office shortly before its destruction,[66] include the extract from St Andrew's parish records: "Gemeniani Francis [buried] 19 Sept 1762", this providing independent confirmation of Flood's otherwise unsubstantiated claim.[67]

***

Despite the meagre information available to us today on Geminiani's activities in Ireland in the 1730s and following his return to the country in 1759, his importance at the time was great enough for his reputation to be invoked posthumously as the Irish sought to establish the prowess of their native musicians by depicting them as victors in combats of mythic proportions with Italian masters. The prime examples are the later eighteenth-century anecdotes associating the Irish harper Turlough Carolan, who died in 1738, with a violinist or musician, initially unnamed but later to be identified as Geminiani.[68]

---

[65] "Death — Yesterday in College Green aged 96 [*sic*], Mr. Francis Geminiani", *Faulkner's Dublin Journal*, 14-18 September 1762; "[Deaths:] last week at his lodgings in College Green aged 96 Signior Francisco Geminiani well known by the Lovers of Harmony for his Capital Performances on the Violin", *Pue's Occurrences*, 18-21 September 1762.

[66] As stated in a letter dated 17 May 1941 from Dr Graham's widow when presenting his notebooks to the National Archives of Ireland (Dublin, National Archives of Ireland [IRL-Dna], included with M3086, 'Notebook 12', [n.p.]).

[67] National Archives of Ireland, M3077, 'Notebook 3'; also a single sheet note included in *ibidem*, M3088. St Andrew's church, the eighteenth-century 'Round Church' of St Andrew's, was itself an important music venue in the eighteenth century, in particular for charity concerts. See BOYDELL, Brian. *Dublin [...]*, *op. cit.* (see note 5), *passim*. It was destroyed by fire in the nineteenth century and replaced by the current building. Deconsecrated in 1994, it is now the main Tourist Information Office for Dublin.

[68] On the identification of Carolan in the eighteenth century as the embodiment of Irish music, see in particular WHITE, Harry. *The Keeper's Recital: Music and Cultural History in Ireland, 1770-1970*, Cork, Cork University Press, 1998, pp. 15ff. On Carolan see also O'SULLIVAN, Donal. *Carolan: The Life, Times and Music of an Irish Harper*, 2 vols, London, Routledge-Kegan Paul, 1958; rev. ed., Cork, Ossian Publishing, 2001; O'Sullivan devotes a chapter to 'Carolan and the Italian Masters' (vol. 1, pp. 144-148).

The earliest anecdote to link Carolan with an "eminent musician" — at this stage without reference to Geminiani — appeared in an essay published in July 1760 by Oliver Goldsmith (who may have been born in Co. Roscommon, as was Carolan, but had settled in London in 1756). Goldsmith discusses Carolan ("Of all the bards this country ever produced, the last and the greatest") against the premise that "There can be perhaps no greater entertainment than to compare the rude Celtic simplicity with modern refinement". He recounts the following anecdote:

> Being once at the house of an Irish nobleman, where there was a musician present, who was eminent in the profession, Carolan immediately challenged him to a trial of skill. To carry the jest forward, his lordship persuaded the musician to accept the challenge, and he accordingly played over on his fiddle the fifth concerto of Vivaldi.[69] Carolan, immediately taking his harp, played over the whole piece after him, without missing a note, though he had never heard it before: which produced some surprize; but their astonishment increased, when he assured them he could make a concerto in the same taste himself, which he instantly composed, and that with such spirit and elegance, that it may compare (for we have it still) with the finest compositions of Italy.[70]

The piece by Carolan referred to here is presumably "Carolan's Concerto", otherwise known as "Mrs. Power" (or "Mrs. Poer"), one of Carolan's best-known pieces which clearly demonstrates the influence on Carolan of the Italian baroque style.[71] This anecdote uses the performance of a concerto by Vivaldi played by an anonymous violinist — who implicitly represents Italian music, whether or not he is understood to be an Italian himself — to confirm Carolan's musical reputation as measured by the accepted parameters of the time, namely of Italian music.

Geminiani's name was first linked to that of Carolan in 1777 when Thomas Campbell commented of the latter in his *Philosophical Survey of the*

---

[69] Presumably from *L'Estro Armonico*, Op. 3.

[70] GOLDSMITH, Oliver. 'The History of Carolan, the last Irish harper', in: *The British Magazine. Or Monthly Repository for Gentlemen and Ladies*, 1[/7] (July 1760), pp. 418-419. Reprinted in *The Field Day Anthology of Irish Writing*, edited by Seamus Deane, 3 vols, Derry, Field Day, 1991, vol. 1, pp. 667-668.

[71] O'SULLIVAN, Donal. *Op. cit.* (see note 68), vol. I, p. 245; vol. II, p. 97. Edward Bunting commented that "in Carolan's Concerto [...] the practitioner will perceive evident imitations of Corelli, in which the exuberant fancy of that admired composer is happily copied". See BUNTING, Edward. *A General Collection* [...], *op. cit.* (see note 43), p. [iii].

South of Ireland that "His ear was so exquisite, and his memory so tenacious, that he has been known to play off, at first hearing, some of the most difficult pieces of Italian music, to the astonishment of Geminiani".[72] Here, Goldsmith's "eminent musician" has become identified with Geminiani, fifteen years after the latter's death. This association of Geminiani with Carolan was developed by Joseph C. Walker, whose *Historical Memoirs of the Irish Bards* (1786) was the first book devoted exclusively to Irish music and which is recognised as a defining text in the development of Irish cultural identity in the late eighteenth and early nineteenth centuries.[73] Walker records two relevant anecdotes, the first being a variation of that given by Goldsmith. Citing "a letter which I lately received from a learned friend, containing many curious notices concerning Carolan",[74] Walker initially establishes Carolan's supposed international credentials by stating that "It was from a full conviction of his great powers, that the Italians have dignified him with the name of CAROLONIUS".[75] Who these "Italians" might have been remains unanswered, but Walker immediately goes on to relate an incident involving "an eminent Italian music-master in Dublin":

> [...] it is a fact well ascertained, that the fame of Carolan having reached the ears of an eminent Italian music-master in Dublin, he put his abilities to a severe test, and the issue of the trial convinced him, how well founded every thing had been which was advanced in favour of the Irish Bard. The method he made use of was as follows: He singled out an excellent piece of music, and highly in the style of the country which gave him birth; here and there he either altered or mutilated the piece, but in such a manner, as that no one but a real judge could make a discovery. Carolan bestowed the deepest attention upon the performer while he played it, not knowing however that it was intended as a trial of his skill; and that the critical moment was at hand, which was to determine his reputation for ever. He declared it was an admirable piece of music; but, to the astonishment of all present, said, very humorously, in his own language, ta se air chois air bacaighe; that is, here and there it limps and stumbles. He was prayed to rectify the errors, which he accordingly did. In this state the piece was sent from Connaught to Dublin; and

---

[72]   [CAMPBELL, Thomas.] *A Philosophical Survey of the South of Ireland, in a Series of Letters to John Watkinson, M.D.*, London, W. Strahan-T. Cadwell, 1777, p. 452.

[73]   WALKER, Joseph Cooper. *Op. cit.* (see note 43). On Walker see especially WHITE, Harry. *Op. cit.* (see note 68), pp. 20-24; and DAVIS, Leith. *Music, Postcolonialism, and Gender: The Construction of Irish National Identity, 1724-1874*, Notre Dame, University of Notre Dame Press, 2006, ch. 2.

[74]   WALKER, Joseph Cooper. *Op. cit.* (see note 43), Appendix [VI], p. 82.

[75]   *Ibidem*, Appendix [VI], p. 89.

the Italian no sooner saw the amendments, than he pronounced
Carolan to be a true musical genius.[76]

The second anecdote describes Carolan and "a celebrated Italian
performer" enjoying the patronage of Lord Mayo:

> Carolan, who was at that time on a visit at his lordship's,
> found himself greatly neglected; and complained of it one day
> in the presence of the foreigner. "When you play in as masterly
> a manner as he does, (replied his lordship) you shall not be
> overlooked." Carolan wagered with the musician, that though he
> was almost a total stranger to Italian music, yet he would follow
> him in any piece he played; and that he himself would afterwards
> play a voluntary, in which the Italian should not follow him. The
> proposal was acceded to; and Carolan was victorious.

Walker then comments, "The Italian alluded to in the first of these
relations, was the celebrated Geminiani".[77] However, some pages later he
cites Charles O'Conor, son of one of Carolan's principal patrons, as stating
that Carolan "excited the wonder, and obtained the approbation, of a
great Master, who never saw him; I mean Geminiani".[78] Notwithstanding
O'Conor's disclaimer, the legend of Carolan having met with Geminiani
became firmly established in the mythology of Carolan as the last and
most famous of the Irish harper-composers. In the extensive introductory
chapters to his third and final collection of Irish music, *The Ancient Music of
Ireland* (1840), Edward Bunting would repeat the anecdote first recounted
by Goldsmith in 1760 but specifically identifying "the eminent composer"
present who "played over on his violin the fifth concerto of Vivaldi" as
Geminiani, giving rise to Carolan's immediately improvising "that admirable
piece known ever since as Carolan's Concerto".[79]

Walker was writing half a century after the events he describes and with a
clear agenda to promote the musical reputation of Irish harpers and their music
through the example of their best-known exponent, Turlough Carolan. This
he does by direct comparison with and invoking the approval of Geminiani as a
renowned exponent of Italian music — the touchstone for eighteenth-century
musical taste. While little weight can be given to the historical accuracy of

---

[76] *Ibidem*, Appendix [VI], cited in Careri, pp. 31-32.

[77] Walker, Joseph Cooper. *Op. cit.* (see note 43), Appendix [VI], pp. 89-90.

[78] *Ibidem*, p. 97.

[79] Bunting, Edward. *The Ancient Music of Ireland*, Dublin, Hodges and Smith, 1840; facs.
repr., Dublin, Walton, 1969, p. 71.

these accounts (although this cannot be ruled out), the question as to whether Geminiani actually met Carolan or not is essentially irrelevant: what they do tell us is that during his stay in Ireland Geminiani established for himself a name as the foremost Italian musician in the country, a reputation that would continue to gather weight decades after his death in 1762.[80]

The story told by Charles Lee Lewes in 1805 concerning Geminiani's uncomfortable encounter in 1759 with a particularly second-rate Irish country musician at Cootehill was cited above. By 1832 an anonymous article (signed 'F.') in *The Irish Monthly Magazine of Politics and Literature* had expanded the theme of Geminiani's approval of Carolan to encompass the playing of an Irish traditional fiddle player Bob Meekins who, we are told, "was the best fiddler in Ireland during his time, and that his talents as a violin player were really of the first order, the following attestation, by the celebrated musical composer, Geminiani, will sufficiently prove".[81] The article relates a story "communicated to the writer, when a boy, by an old gentleman who had belonged to a convivial society, which held its sitting at Bath's in Pill-lane" in Dublin and set in "about the year 1760", in which Geminiani is called upon to adjudicate on the relative performances of Bob Meekins and an unnamed Italian violinist. Meekins played each evening at Mr Bath's tavern, where one evening a group of gentlemen who had come from a concert at the "music hall"[82] were discussing the relative merits of Meekins and "the Italian who led the band this night at the concert".[83] A "stranger" who was present and had also attended the concert agreed through a mutual acquaintance to invite Geminiani (described here as "the celebrated musical composer [...] [who] had sojourned for some time in Dublin, where he presided at several concerts") and "his countryman, the violin-player" to dine at a tavern outside Dublin, where Meekins would be secretly stationed in an adjoining room and "on a given signal he was to play an Irish air". Geminiani and the unidentified Italian violinist, who "seemed to think he had no rival in Ireland, and his

---

[80] O'Sullivan addresses the question of whether or not Geminiani and Carolan ever met. O'SULLIVAN, Donal. *Op. cit.* (see note 68), p. 147.

[81] 'F.'. 'Ireland and Italy: Bob Meekins and Geminiani', in: *The Irish Monthly Magazine of Politics and Literature*, 1/5 (September 1832), pp. 330-332.

[82] "Mr. Neal's Great Room", or the "Musick Hall" in Fishamble Street, Dublin's principal concert venue in the mid-eighteenth century.

[83] Possibly Signor Arrigoni, violinist and composer resident in Dublin, conductor of the band at the Great Britain St (later Rotunda Hospital) concerts between 1758 and 1762, and for whom benefit concerts were held in Fishamble St on a number of occasions around this period. See BOYDELL, Brian. *Dublin* [...], *op. cit.* (see note 5), p. 271, and ID. *Rotunda Music in Eighteenth-Century Dublin*, Dublin, Irish Academic Press, 1992, *passim.*

demeanour was commensurately arrogant with the consciousness of his own superiority", duly overheard Meekins playing, as was intended, and asked that he be brought into the room they were in. The two Italians "were equally astonished and mortified at the unrivalled powers of the country fiddler". Seeing the Italian violinist's instrument case on a table, Meekins asked if he would "just give them an ould Irish tune, or any other bit of a variation most agreeable to his honour?" The Italian declined, but "Geminiani here asked the stranger 'vat was de reason dat dis countra fidlere didn't play in de concerts, for he vas a great deal mush bettere player dan any Irish fidlere he ever saw?'" Meekins subsequently "played that night until the company separated at a late hour, delighted, by his extraordinary and original touches, which the Italians seemed to enjoy in a superior degree to the rest". The following day "when the stranger and the Pill-lane gentlemen waited on Geminiani, to hear his candid opinion whether the Irish fiddler or his own countryman were the better performer, the honest Italian declared, that 'the contra fidlere was a better violin player than his own friend'".

While again casting little light on Geminiani's activities in Dublin and doubtless elaborated over the intervening seventy years — not to mention the patronizing accents in which Geminiani's and the Irish fiddle player's speech is reported — this anecdote further attests to the lasting reputation Geminiani had established for himself in Ireland, even well into the nineteenth century, as the most highly-regarded Italian violinist-composer to have lived in the country. Lee Lewes' anecdote had contrasted what Goldsmith characterized as the "rude simplicity" of a (second-rate) local musician with Geminiani's "modern refinement" and musical sensibilities; the later eighteenth-century antiquarian retrieval of the 'ancient' traditions of the Irish harpers championed in particular by the example of Carolan had invoked Geminiani's approval in the service of establishing the credentials within the wider context of European music of this lauded exemplar of Irish musical culture;[84] by the 1830s the work of folklore and folk music collectors was beginning to widen the appreciation of Irish native musical traditions to embrace not only the early harp (which had by then all but died out), but also fiddle players, pipers and the song tradition.

The significance within the Irish context of Geminiani's having been offered the position of Master of the State Music in Ireland, his prolonged stay in the 1730s and his final years and death in Dublin go beyond the fact

---

[84]   This theme would continue to colour Irish musical historiography up to and including the writings of William Henry Grattan Flood in the early 20th century. See in particular FLOOD, William Henry Grattan. *A History of Irish Music*, Dublin, Browne & Nolan, 1905, [2]1906, [3]1913, [4]1927.

that, after Handel, he is certainly the most famous European baroque musician to have lived and worked in Ireland. Of particular interest is the extent to which he came to be regarded later in the eighteenth century as the paragon of Italian music, the "celebrated Italian musician" who would be invoked as a benchmark against whom to measure and validate Irish music and musicians as emerging cultural nationalism sought to claim, initially for Carolan and the Irish harpers and subsequently for other Irish traditional musicians, a place in the musical pantheon. Geminiani established a lasting reputation primarily through his largely undocumented contacts with, private performances for, and teaching of families of the gentry and aristocracy. This reputation is in marked contrast to the paucity of evidence for his activities in the newspapers and in other contemporary records. The fact that he appears to have given so few public performances is a reminder of the inadequacy of the public record for evaluating a musician's activities in the eighteenth century.

GEMINIANI, DAVID RIZZIO
AND THE ITALIAN CULT OF SCOTTISH MUSIC

Peter Holman
(LEEDS)

I N THE EIGHTEENTH CENTURY, WHEN MUSICAL history was in its infancy, all
sorts of unlikely stories circulated about composers and their lives. Thus
Charles Dibdin asserted that "CORELLI is said to have visited England
on purpose to see PURCELL, but hearing, at ROCHESTER, of his death,
he did not even visit the CAPITAL, but returned, saying — 'There can
be nothing worthy my curiosity since PURCELL is dead'".[1] According to
Richard Clark, Handel wrote his "Harmonious Blacksmith" variations after
hearing a blacksmith near the Cannons estate whistling the tune.[2] No-one
takes this seriously today, despite the presence of the mid-Victorian grave of
the blacksmith, William Powell, in the nearby churchyard of St Lawrence
Whitchurch, though other equally implausible stories have had much longer
lives, such as the idea that Charles Frederick Abel's viola da gamba was buried
with him after his death on 20 June 1787.[3] This only seems to go back as far as
a short story first published in 1866.[4] Three viols, including "A capital viol de
gamba, in a mahogany case, his best instrument", appear in the sale catalogue
of Abel's effects, sold on 12 December 1787.[5]

---

[1] DIBDIN, Charles. *The Musical Tour*, Sheffield, printed for the author by J. Gales, 1788, p. 190.

[2] CLARK, Richard. *Reminiscences of Handel*, London, s.n., 1836, especially pp. 6-11.

[3] For instance, OTTERSTEDT, Annette. *Die Gambe: Kulturgeschichte und praktischer Ratgeber*, Kassel, Bärenreiter, 1994; English translation by Hans Reiners, *The Viol: History of an Instrument*, Kassel, Bärenreiter, 2002, p. 94.

[4] HOLMAN, Peter. *Life after Death: the Viola da Gamba in Britain from Purcell to Dolmetsch*, Woodbridge, The Boydell Press, 2010, pp. 281-282.

[5] *A Catalogue of the Capital Collection of Manuscript and other Music [...] of Charles Frederick Abel, Esq. Deceased*, London, s.n., 1787, p. 4; see ROE, Stephen. 'The Sale Catalogue of Carl Friedrich Abel (1787)', in: *Music and the Book Trade from the Sixteenth to the Twentieth Century*, edited by Robin Myers, Michael Harris and Giles Mandelbrote, London-New Castle (DE), The British Library-Oak Knoll Press, 2008, pp. 105-143: 132.

PETER HOLMAN

THE RIZZIO MYTH

Another implausible eighteenth-century story was alluded to in Francesco Geminiani's *Treatise of Good Taste in the Art of Musick*, Op. 9 (London, 1749), p. 1:

> TWO Composers of Musick have appear'd in the World, who in their different Kinds of Melody, have rais'd my Admiration; namely *David Rizzio* and *Gio. Baptista Lulli*; of these which stands highest in Reputation, or deserves to stand highest, is none of my Business to pronounce: But when I consider, that *Rizzio* was foremost in point of Time, that till then Melody was intirely rude and barbarous, and that he found Means at once to civilize and inspire it with all the native Gallantry of the SCOTISH Nation, I am inclinable to give him the Preference.[6]

David Rizzio or Riccio is a familiar and tragic figure in the history of Scotland.[7] He was born near Turin in about 1533, the son of a musician, and arrived in Scotland in 1561 by way of the Savoy court at Nice. He became a court singer and *valet de chambre* to Mary, Queen of Scots, and then the queen's private secretary, arousing the jealousy of her husband, Lord Darnley; a conspiracy developed by Protestant nobles led by Lord Ruthven ended with his murder on 9 March 1566. The main contemporary source for Rizzio's musical activities is a passage in the memoirs of the diplomat Sir James Melville of Halhill (1535-1617), taken here from the first edition of 1683:

> Now there came here [to Scotland] in Company with the Ambassadour of *Savoy*, one *David Rixio* of the County of *Piedmont*, who was a merry fellow, and a good Musician. Her Majesty had three Valets of her Chamber who sung three parts, and wanted a Bass to sing the fourth part. Therefore they told her Majesty of this Man, as one fit to make the fourth in Concert.
>
> Thus he was drawn in to sing sometimes with the rest; and afterward when her *French* Secretary retired himself to *France*, this *David* obtained the said office.[8]

---

[6] An edition of *A Treatise of Good Taste*, edited by Peter Walls, can be found in: *Geminiani Opera Omnia*, vol. 12; I am grateful to Peter Walls for letting me read his introduction to the volume before publication. There is also a facsimile edition, with an introduction by Robert Donington, New York, Da Capo Press, 1969.

[7] See MARSHALL, Rosalind K. 'David Riccio', in: *Oxford Dictionary of National Biography* <http://www.oxforddnb.com>.

[8] *The Memoires of Sir James Melvil of Hal-hill*, edited by George Scott, London, Robert Boulter, 1683, p. 54. A rather different version, retaining the original Scots forms, is edited in *Memoirs of His Own Life by Sir James Melville of Halhill*, M.D.XLIX.–M.D.XCIII., *from the*

A painting supposedly representing Rizzio holding a violin is in the Royal Collection ILL. 1).[9] At the left-hand top corner is the inscription "DAVD RIZZO / MDLXIV.", though the costume suggests that it was painted around 1620, and Rizzio was a singer rather than a violinist. In an unfinished miniature said to be of him, but with rather different facial features and clothing, the instrument is a lute — more likely for a singer (ILL. 2).[10] It is likely that the inscription on the painting was added much later, perhaps to foster the Rizzio myth in the eighteenth century. Similarly, an elaborately decorated guitar, traditionally said to have been given to Rizzio by Mary Queen of Scots, is now dated *c*1650 and is attributed to René Voboam.[11] These artefacts, whether or not they were actually connected with David Rizzio, would have helped to foster the myth of him as a musician, though there seems to be no evidence that they were generally known in the eighteenth century.

It is not clear how the idea developed that Rizzio had a role in the creation of the Scots song repertory, though it was in existence several decades before 1749. Geminiani set "Ann thou were my ain thing" as a set of five variations for violin and continuo in his *Rules for Playing in a True Taste*, Op. 8 (London, *c*1746), ascribing it to "Davia Rizzi". Twelve more Scots tunes are in his *Treatise in the Art of Good Taste*, four set as songs with two flutes, four-part strings and continuo, four used as the basis of movements in three trio sonatas for two violins and continuo, and four set as "Airs for a Violin or German Flute Violoncello & Harpsichord". His source for them seems to have been William Thomson's *Orpheus Caledonius*, the most influential early eighteenth-century collection of Scots songs. It was first published as a single folio volume

---

Original Manuscript, Edinburgh, Bannatyne Club, 1827, pp. 131-132. There is a similar account in BUCHANAN, George. *Rerum Scoticarum historia*, Edinburgh, Alexander Arbuthnet, 1582; English translation, *Buchanan's History of Scotland [...] Revised and Corrected from the Latin Original by Mr. Bond*, 2 vols, London, J. Bettenham et al., ²1722, vol. II, p. 300. See also *HAWKINS*, IV, p. 2.

[9]   RCIN 401172 <http://www.royalcollection.org.uk/eGallery>. I am grateful to Karen Hearn, Tate Collections curator of Sixteenth- and Seventeenth-Century British Art, for helping me to assess the picture.

[10]   The miniature is reproduced at <http://tudorhistory.org/people/rizzio>. Three copies of a stipple engraving by Charles Wilkin, published in 1814, are in the National Portrait Gallery, D21382, D25583 and D25584 <http://www.npg.org.uk/collections>.

[11]   *Royal College of Music, Museum of Instruments, Catalogue Part III: European Stringed Instruments*, compiled by Elizabeth Wells and Christopher Nobbs, London, Royal College of Music, 2007, pp. 112-114, no. 32.

ILL. 1: *Portrait of a man known as David Rizzio* (British School, *c*1620), oil on canvas, 91.3 x 77.8 cm, The Royal Collection RCIN 401172 © 2012, Her Majesty Queen Elizabeth II.

containing 50 songs in 1726,[12] and was reissued as a two-volume octavo in 1733, its second volume containing a further instalment of 50 songs.[13] TABLE 1 sets out the concordances between the four publications.

[12]   It was entered in the Stationers' Register on 5 January 1725/1726; see *Music Entries at Stationers' Hall 1710-1818*, compiled by Michael Kassler, Aldershot, Ashgate, 2004, p. 9. There is a facsimile of the National Library of Scotland copy <http://digital.nls.uk/>.
[13]   There is a facsimile edition with an introduction by Henry George Farmer (see note 15). For Thomson and *Orpheus Caledonius* see especially JOHNSON, David. *Music and Society in Lowland Scotland in the Eighteenth Century*, London, Oxford University Press, 1972, pp. 140-

ILL. 2: Charles Wilkin, stipple engraving (1814), after an unfinished portrait said to be of David Rizzio (1564), National Portrait Gallery D25584 © National Portrait Gallery, London.

141, 155-157; FISKE, Roger. *Scotland in Music: a European Enthusiasm*, Cambridge, Cambridge University Press, 1983, pp. 15-17.

TABLE 1: THE SOURCES OF THE SCOTS TUNES USED BY GEMINIANI

OC1 = *Orpheus Caledonius* (London, 1726)
OC2 = *Orpheus Caledonius* [...] *the Second Edition*, 2 vols (London, 1733)

Rules for Playing in a True Taste

pp. 2-5	Ann thou were my ain thing	OC1, p. 23; OC2, i, no. 23

A Treatise of Good Taste

pp. 2-5	The lass of Peaty's Mill	OC1, p. 1; OC2, i, no. 1
pp. 6-8	The night her silent sable wore	OC2, ii, no. 14
pp. 9-11	When Phoebus bright	OC2, ii, no. 11
pp. 12-13	O Besse Bell	OC1, p. 2; OC2, i, no. 2
p. 14	The broom of Cowdenknows	OC1, p. 10; OC2, i, no. 10
pp. 14-17	Bonny Christy	OC1, p. 12; OC2, i, no. 12
pp. 18-21	[The] Bush aboon Traquair	OC1, p. 3; OC2, i, no. 3
pp. 22-5	The last time I came o'er the moor	OC1, p. 6; OC2, i, no. 6
p. 26	Auld Bob Morrice	OC1, p. 30; OC2, i, no. 30
pp. 26-7	The country lass	OC2, ii, no. 38
pp. 28-9	Lady Ann Bothwell's lament	OC2, ii, no. 17
pp. 29-30	Sleepy body	OC2, ii, no. 50

"Ann thou wert my ain thing", "The lass of Peaty's Mill", "Besse Bell", "The bush aboon Traquair", and "Auld Bob Morrice" are among seven tunes marked with an asterisk in the index of the 1726 volume, the asterisk signifying that "The Songs mark'd thus (★) were Composed by *David Rizzio*". The contents of the first volume of the 1733 *Orpheus Caledonius* are the same as the 1726 edition, though with the ascriptions to Rizzio omitted and with revised musical settings: by and large the tunes in the 1733 edition are less ornamented than in 1726 and the bass parts are simpler and more accomplished. Geminiani apparently accepted the Rizzio ascriptions from the 1726 edition, though where the versions of the tunes differed he tended to follow the 1733 edition, as can been seen by comparing the 1726 and 1733 versions of "The broom of Cowdenknows" with the opening of Geminiani's trio sonata setting (Ex. 1).

Ex. 1: The opening of "The broom of Cowdenknows": (a) *Orpheus Caledonius* (London, 1726), p. 10; (b) *Orpheus Caledonius… the Second Edition* (London, 1733), vol. 1, no. 10; (c) Francesco Geminiani, *A Treatise in the Art of Good Taste*, p. 14, Sonata 1 in F major.

Geminiani was not the only person to accept and promote the Rizzio myth. The developing interest in English and Scottish history meant that the story of his activities and murder would have been familiar from such publications as Daniel Defoe's *Memoirs of the Church of Scotland* (London, 1717), pp. 58-60; David Jones' *Secret History of White-Hall, from the Restoration of Charles II down to the Abdication of the late K. James* (London, ²1717), especially pp. 166-178; and Thomas Salmon's *Review of the History of England*, 2 vols (London, 1724), vol. 1, p. 291; Melville's *Memoirs* were republished in Edinburgh in 1735, in Glasgow in 1751, and in London in 1752.[14] Given the prestige of Italian music and the prominent position of *Orpheus Caledonius* in the developing Scots song repertory, it is not surprising that Rizzio was named as the author of particular tunes in printed collections over the next few decades, including John Watts'

---

[14] See the entries in *The British Library Integrated Catalogue* <http://catalogue.bl.uk>.

Musical Miscellany, 6 vols (London, 1729-1731), vols V and VI; John Walsh's *The Merry Musician, or A Cure for the Spleen*, 4 vols (London, 1716-1733), vol. IV; James Oswald's *Second Collection of Curious Scots Tunes* (London, 1743); *Apollo's Cabinet, or The Muses Delight*, 2 vols (Liverpool, 1756-1757), vol. I; and Francis Peacock's *Fifty Favourite Scotch Airs* (London, ?1762).[15] The setting of "Pinkie House" in Charles Burney's music for Mallet's play *Alfred* (1751) has a note in the score: "the above Melody is Old, & suppos'd to be David Rizzio's".[16]

The tide began to turn even before Geminiani published his endorsement of Rizzio in 1749.[17] It initially took the form of a suspicion that Oswald used Rizzio's name as an alias, much as he apparently attributed pieces to the French-Neapolitan composer Nicolas Dôthel and the Portuguese composer Antonio Pereya da Costa,[18] as well as using the name of the Society of the Temple of Apollo.[19] An allusion in a verse letter to Oswald, published in October 1741, shows that he was under suspicion even before he attributed six pieces to Rizzio in *A Second Collection of Curious Scots Tunes*:

> When wilt thou teach our soft *Aeidian* fair,
> To languish at a false Sicilian air;
> Or when some tender tune compose again,
> And cheat the town wi' *David Rizo*'s name?[20]

---

[15] See especially GLEN, John. *Early Scottish Melodies*, Edinburgh, Glen, 1900, p. 248; FARMER, Henry George. 'Foreword', in: THOMSON, William. *Orpheus Caledonius*, facsimile edition by Henry George Farmer, Hatboro (PA), Folklore Associates, 1962, pp. I-II; GELBART, Matthew. *The Invention of "Folk Music" and "Art Music": Emerging Categories from Ossian to Wagner*, Cambridge, Cambridge University Press, 2007, p. 34.

[16] FISKE, Roger. *English Theatre Music in the Eighteenth Century*, Oxford, Oxford University Press, ²1986, p. 227.

[17] GELBART, Matthew. *Op. cit.* (see note 15), pp. 34-35.

[18] DELIUS, Nikolaus. 'Nicolas Dôthel - oder ein janusköpfiger Oswald?', in: *Festschrift Hans-Peter Schmitz zum 75, Geburstag*, edited by Andreas Eichhorn, Kassel, Bärenreiter, 1992, pp. 53-61. That Oswald used da Costa's name was argued by Manuel Morais at the International Symposium on the Portuguese Guitar, Èvora, 7-9 September 2001; see MACKILLOP, Rob. 'The Guitar, Cittern and Guittar in Scotland, an Historical Introduction up to 1800', in: *Guitarre und Zister: Bauweise, Spieltechnik und Geschichte bis 1800. 22. Musikinstrumentenbau-Symposium (Michaelstein, 16. bis 18. November 2001)*, edited by Monika Lustig, Blankenburg, Michaelstein, 2004, pp. 121-148: 134.

[19] See especially KIDSON, Frank. 'James Oswald, Dr. Burney and "The Temple of Apollo"', in: *The Musical Antiquary*, II (1910-1911), pp. 34-41; PINK, Andrew. *The Musical Culture of Freemasonry in early Eighteenth-Century London*, Ph.D. Diss., Goldsmiths College, University of London, 2007, pp. 143-150.

[20] *Scots Magazine*, 3 (October 1741), p. 455. It has been attributed to Allan Ramsay senior; see MARTIN, Burns. *Bibliography of the Writings of Allan Ramsay*, Glasgow, Jackson, Wylie and Co. 1931, p. 52.

By the 1770s and '80s scepticism about the Rizzio myth had acquired heavyweight literary support, from the philosopher Lord Kames, the poet James Beattie, the music historian Sir John Hawkins, and the lawyer and antiquarian William Tytler, among others.[21] However, this was achieved only by advancing an equally unlikely theory: that the origin of the Scots song repertory lay with the Scottish King James I (1394-1437). Kames picked up on a passage in Alessandro Tassoni's *Dieci libri di pensieri diversi* (Carpi, 1620), p. 572 which claimed that James had "invented a new, melancholy, and plaintive kind of music, different from all other" that had been "imitated by Carlo Gesualdo, prince of Venosa".[22] This appealed to the developing nationalism of eighteenth-century Scotland, reversing the flow of influence from Italy, and had the advantage of putting back the origin of a clearly ancient type of music by more than a century. However both theories suffered from the same flaw: the desire, strong at the time and not unknown today, to pin an innovation onto a particular individual (christened "symbolic originator" or "symbolic creator" by Gelbart) even when evidence was lacking and could never be forthcoming.[23] Rizzio and then James I were recruits to a traditional pantheon of inventors featuring in musical 'creation myths', including Tubal-Cain, Jubal, Mercury and Hero of Alexandria (instruments), Pythagoras (the scale and the modes), Guido d'Arezzo (staff notation and the hexachords), St Ambrose and Pope Gregory the Great (chant), and Franco of Cologne (the notation of rhythm).[24]

Italian Musicians and Scottish Music

The Rizzio myth would be little more than a footnote in musical history were it not for the influence it seems to have had on Italian musicians. As we shall see, a remarkable number of them took an interest in Scots songs,

---

[21] Home, Henry, Lord Kames. *Sketches of the History of Man*, 2 vols, Edinburgh, Creech, 1774, vol. I, pp. 166-167; Beattie, James. *Essays on Poetry and Music, as they affect the Mind*, Edinburgh, Creech, 1776, pp. 187-189; *Hawkins*, IV, pp. 1-7; Tytler, William. 'Dissertation on the Scottish Music', in: *Transactions of the Antiquaries of Scotland*, I (1792), pp. 469-498, at pp. 474-475, 481-483. For the publishing history of Tytler's paper, see Nelson, Claire. 'Tea-Table Miscellanies: the Development of Scotland's Song Culture, 1720-1800', in: *Early Music*, XXVIII/4 (2000), pp. 596-618: n. 39.

[22] Translation from *Hawkins*, IV, p. 5.

[23] Gelbart, Matthew. *Op. cit.* (see note 15), pp. 38-39.

[24] *Hawkins*, I, *passim*, includes a convenient contemporary compilation of these 'creation myths'.

arranging, publishing or performing them.[25] The first seems to have been the cellist and composer Lorenzo Bocchi, who worked in Scotland on and off between 1720 and 1729.[26] I have argued that he collaborated with the Edinburgh poet Allan Ramsay senior in several works, including the masque *The Nuptials*, written for the marriage of James, Duke of Hamilton and Lady Ann Cochran on 14 February 1723.[27] If, as is likely, he composed or arranged all of its music, then it follows that he was already involved with Scottish music, for towards the end Bacchus introduces the customary dancing with the words: "Play up there Lassie, some blyth *Scottish* Tune, / Syne a' be blyth, when Wine and Wit gae round", and there is the rubric: "The Health about, Musick and Dancing begin".

Later in 1723 or in the spring of 1724 Bocchi moved to Dublin, where he became involved in the activities of John and William Neal or Neale, the first important music publishers in Ireland.[28] Among their early publications are *A Colection of the most Celebrated Irish Tunes proper for the Violin, German Flute or Hautboy* (Dublin, 1724), *A Colection of the most Celebrated Scotch Tunes for the Violin* (Dublin, 1724), and a collection of music by Bocchi himself, *A Musicall Entertainment for a Chamber* (Dublin, 1725; Edinburgh, ²1725-1726).[29] The first of these includes (pp. 6-9) a piece headed "Plea Rarkeh na Rourkough or yᵉ Irish weding improved with diferent divitions after yᵉ Italian maner with A bass and Chorus by Sigʳ: LORENZO BOCCHI", advertised on the title-page "*As performed at the* Subscription Consort by /

---

[25] The best survey is TINAGLI BAXTER, Sonia. *Italian Music and Musicians in Edinburgh c1720-1800: a Historical and Critical Study*, 2 vols, Ph.D. Diss., University of Glasgow, 1999, though it is limited to those who worked in Edinburgh.

[26] For Bocchi, see HOLMAN, Peter. 'A Little Light on Lorenzo Bocchi: an Italian in Edinburgh and Dublin', in: *Music in the British Provinces, 1690-1914*, edited by Rachel Cowgill and Peter Holman, Aldershot, Ashgate, 2007, pp. 61-86.

[27] Edited in *The Works of Allan Ramsay*, edited by Burns Martin, John W. Oliver, Alexander M. Kinghorn and Alexander Law, 6 vols, Edinburgh, Scottish Text Society, 1953-1974, vol. II (1953), pp. 85-87, 94-103. See also *ibidem*, vol. VI (1974), pp. 7, 72-73; BURDEN, Michael. 'The Independent Masque 1700-1800: a Catalogue', in: *Royal Music Association Research Chronicle*, XXVIII (1995), pp. 59-159: 88-89; HOLMAN, Peter. 'A Little Light on Lorenzo Bocchi [...]', *op. cit.* (see note 26), p. 66.

[28] For the Neals, see CAROLAN, Nicholas. 'Introduction', in: NEAL, John - NEAL, William. *A Collection of the Most Celebrated Irish Tunes Proper for the Violin, German Flute or Hautboy*, Dublin, Neal, 1724, facsimile edition by Nicholas Carolan, Dublin, Irish Traditional Music Archive, ²2010, pp. 15-28.

[29] For the complex bibliographic history of these publications, see especially HOLMAN, Peter. 'A Little Light on Lorenzo Bocchi [...]', *op. cit.* (see note 26), pp. 67-74; CAROLAN, Nicholas. *Op. cit.* (see note 28), pp. 25-28.

Senior Loranzo [*sic*] *Bocchi*"; subscription concerts were advertised by the Neals several times in the autumn of 1723.[30]

A Musicall Entertainment contains several other examples of Bocchi's engagement with popular culture: the last of twelve solo sonatas, in F major for viola da gamba and continuo, includes an "English Aire Improv'd after an Italian Manner", a setting of the tune "The parson among the peas".[31] At the end of the collection is an Italianate setting for soprano, unison violins and continuo of Allan Ramsay's Scots cantata "Blate Jonny faintly teld fair Jean his mind", the text of which was published in Ramsay's *Tea-Table Miscellany*, vol. 1 (Edinburgh, 1723), his influential collection of the words of Scots songs.[32] It is likely that Bocchi suggested the rather unlikely genre of the Scots cantata to Ramsay ("Blate Jonny" is the first-known example), and that he provided the Neals with their collection of Scots tunes. They were advertised on the title-page as "Being all Diferent from any yet Printed in Londo[n]", and many of them are in the musical supplement to *The Tea-Table Miscellany, Musick for Allan Ramsay's Collection of Scots Songs* (Edinburgh, 1725-1726).[33] Bocchi presumably became interested in Scottish music through his work with Ramsay, and may have been the person who provided the necessary musical expertise to turn Ramsay's pastoral play *The Gentle Shepherd* into a ballad opera in the winter of 1728-1729.[34]

Most Italian musicians who engaged with Scottish music encountered it while working in Scotland, though that is not true in every case. Geminiani is not known to have visited Edinburgh until 1760,[35] and therefore presumably developed his interest in Scottish music in London, perhaps through his contacts with Robert Bremner (*c*1713-1789). Bremner twice stated in print that he had been Geminiani's pupil. In his "Plan for instructing a Croud" in *The Rudiments of Music* (Edinburgh, ²1762), p. 61 he wrote: "I have often heard the celebrated *Geminiani* (whose Pupil I had the Honour to be) maintain, that the whole Art of Composition could be communicated in this manner; and from the Instructions I had from him, I discovered no Reasons to the Contrary".[36] He mentioned "The once eminent *Geminiani*, whose pupil I had the honour

[30]   HOLMAN, Peter. 'A Little Light on Lorenzo Bocchi [...]', *op. cit.* (see note 26), pp. 72-73.

[31]   Discussed in *ibidem*, pp. 81-83.

[32]   Edited in *The Works of Allan Ramsay*, *op. cit.* (see note 27), vol. III (1961), pp. 36-37.

[33]   For the collection, see JOHNSON, David. *Music and Society* [...], *op. cit.* (see note 13), pp. 140-141.

[34]   HOLMAN, Peter. 'A Little Light on Lorenzo Bocchi [...]', *op. cit.* (see note 26), pp. 76-77.

[35]   For a full account, see my introduction to *The Art of Playing the Guitar or Cittra* in: *Geminiani Opera Omnia*, vol. 16.

[36]   I am grateful to Michael Talbot for drawing this source to my attention.

to be" in the essay "Some Thoughts on the Performance of Concert Music", added to J. C. G. Schetky's *Six Quartettos for Two Violins, a Tenor, & Violoncello*, Op. 6 (London, 1777).[37] It is possible that these lessons took place in Edinburgh in 1760 (as Michael Talbot suggests in the present volume), though in my opinion it is more likely that Bremner studied composition with Geminiani as a young man, in London in the late 1720s or early 1730s.

The violinist and composer Francesco Veracini is a similar case: he is not known to have visited Scotland, though he worked in London several times between 1733 and 1745. He used "The lass of Peaty's mill" as the theme of an aria, "Oh inaspettata sorte", in his opera *Rosalinda*, produced at the King's Theatre in London on 31 January 1744.[38] Charles Burney thought that Veracini did so in order "to flatter the English" but that the ploy failed: "as few of the North Britons, or admirers of this national and natural Music, frequent the opera, or mean to give half a guinea to hear a Scots tune, which perhaps their cook-maid Peggy can sing better than any foreigner".[39] The aria was described as "a Favourite Italian Parody of the lass of Patie's Mill" when it was performed in a benefit concert for Nicolò Pasquali in Edinburgh on 15 January 1754.[40] In addition, a passage marked "Scozzeze" in No. 9 of Veracini's *Sonate accademiche*, Op. 2 for violin and continuo (London and Florence, 1744) turns out to be a setting with two variations of the tune "Tweedside"; it returns, more freely treated, as the final movement of the sonata.[41] It was evidently a party piece: Horace Mann, the British diplomatic representative in Florence, wrote to Horace Walpole on 8 May 1750 about "an elegant concert at which Veracini shone much, and particularly in a sonata in which he brings in Tweed's side, which he always plays when I am present".[42]

The oboist, flautist and composer Francesco Barsanti encountered Scottish music at first hand. He came to London from Lucca in 1714 with Geminiani and is first recorded in Edinburgh in June 1735 as an employee

---

[37] ZASLAW, Neal. 'The Compleat Orchestral Musician', in: *Early Music*, VII/1 (1979), pp. 46-57: 48.

[38] *Le delizie dell'opere*, 4 vols, London, John Walsh, 1746, vol. IV, pp. 95-98.

[39] BURNEY, IV, p. 451.

[40] TINAGLI BAXTER, Sonia. *Op. cit.* (see note 25), vol. I, pp. 65-66.

[41] There are two facsimiles of the collection, published by SPES (Florence, 1990) and King's Music (Wyton, n.d.). For "Tweedside" see GLEN, John. *Op. cit.* (see note 15), p. 69.

[42] *Horace Walpole's Correspondence*, edited by W.[ilmarth] S.[heldon] Lewis and Warren Hunting Smith, 48 vols, New Haven (CT)-London, Yale University Press, 1937-1983, vol. XX, 1960, p. 148.

of the Edinburgh Musical Society, returning to London in 1743.[43] While he was in Edinburgh he married a Scots girl and became attracted to Scottish music: his *Collection of Old Scots Tunes, with the Bass for the Violoncello or Harpsichord* was published in Edinburgh in 1742 and in London the following year.[44] It consists of 28 tunes arranged for an unnamed melody instrument (there are no words) and figured bass. Most of them do not go below *d'*, so Barsanti could have played them in concerts on the oboe or the flute or used them for teaching his Scottish flute pupils. Nearly all them were readily available in published collections, though his setting of "Johnnie Faa" (p. 6) seems to have been the first in print; John Glen suggested that he "had taken down a traditional set which he had heard sung or played".[45] In addition, Barsanti included the dance tune "Country bumpkin" (known in Scotland as "Babbity Bowster") as a subject in the fugue of the Overture in G major, No. 9 of his *Nove overture a quattro*, Op. 4 (Edinburgh, 1742); several of the other overtures in the collection use English popular tunes in a similar manner.[46] Barsanti did not mention the Rizzio myth in the preface to *A Collection of Old Scots Tunes*, though he wrote that he had discovered in "several ancient SCOTS TUNES, an Elegance and Variety of Harmony equal to the Compositions of the most celebrated Masters of those Times". He is another person who could have introduced Geminiani to Scottish tunes, on his return to London.

---

[43]   For Barsanti in Edinburgh, see especially TINAGLI BAXTER, Sonia. *Op. cit.* (see note 25), vol. 1, pp. 38-55; MACLEOD, Jennifer. *The Edinburgh Musical Society: Its Membership and Repertory 1728-1797*, Ph.D. Diss., University of Edinburgh, 2001, pp. 141-142. For the Edinburgh Musical Society, see especially HARRIS, David Fraser. *Saint Cecilia's Hall in the Niddry Wynd*, Edinburgh, Oliphant, Anderson, and Ferrier, 1911; repr. New York, Da Capo Press, 1984; BURCHELL, Jenny. *Polite or Commercial Concerts: Concert Management and Orchestral Repertoire in Edinburgh, Bath, Oxford, Manchester, and Newcastle, 1730-1799*, New York, Garland Publishing, Inc., 1996, pp. 31-100; MACLEOD, Jennifer. *Op. cit.* (see earlier in this note), *passim*.

[44]   See SMITH2, p. 34.

[45]   GLEN, John. *Op. cit.* (see note 15), p. 120. There is a modern edition in: JOHNSON, David. *Scottish Fiddle Music in the 18th Century: A Musical Collection and Historical Study*, Edinburgh, John Donald, 1984, p. 41.

[46]   Modern edition in: *The Symphony and Overture in Great Britain: Twenty Works*, edited by Richard Platt, Susan Kirakowska, David Johnson and Thomas McIntosh, New York, Garland, 1984, pp. 57-68. For the tune, see CHAPPELL, William. *The Ballad Literature and Popular Music of the Olden Time*, 2 vols, London, Chappell and Co., 1859; repr. New York, Dover, 1965, vol. II, p. 659.

The violinist and composer Nicolò Pasquali (1718-1757) also worked in Edinburgh, arriving in 1752 and remaining there until his death.[47] He did not publish a collection of Scottish tunes, though he wrote a cantata (now lost) based on "Tweedside",[48] and used the tune to demonstrate ornamentation in his *Art of Fingering the Harpsichord*, published posthumously in 1758 (ILL. 3).[49] In addition, he performed Scottish tunes in Edinburgh concerts, including variations on "Tweedside" (December 1753); "The Lass of Peaty's Mill" (the Veracini aria already mentioned) and "Concerto, Violin solo, in which is introduced a new Set of the Birks of Endermay" (15 January 1754); and "Concerto for Violins, Bassoon, &c. Tweed side, newly set in the Italian manner, (for the sake of Variety) by Signor Pasquali" (17 January 1755).[50] None have survived, despite Robert Bremner's statements in his preface to *The Art of Fingering the Harpsichord* that he had "purchased the whole Musical Effects of the Author, after his decease" and that many of them would "be printed from time to time".

ILL. 3: Nicolò Pasquali, *The Art of Fingering the Harpsichord*, plate 12, "Tweedside".

---

[47] For Pasquali in Edinburgh, see especially HARRIS, David Fraser. *Op. cit.* (see note 43), pp. 268, 271-272; TINAGLI BAXTER, Sonia. *Op. cit.* (see note 25), vol. 1, pp. 56-76; MACLEOD, Jennifer. *Op. cit.* (see note 43), pp. 142-143.

[48] JOHNSON, David. *Music and Society* [...], *op. cit.* (see note 13), p. 55.

[49] TINAGLI BAXTER, Sonia. *Op. cit.* (see note 25), vol. 1, p. 74.

[50] *Ibidem*, vol. 1, pp. 65-67.

The last two eighteenth-century Italians to publish settings of Scots songs were the violinist, keyboard player, singer and composer Domenico Corri (1746-1825) and the singer and composer Pietro Urbani (1749-1816). Corri and his wife, the singer known as "La Miniatrice", worked for the Edinburgh Musical Society between 1771 and 1788; in addition, he managed Comely Gardens, worked for the Theatre Royal, and in 1780 set up a music publishing business with James Sutherland.[51] He published his first Scots songs in *A Select Collection of the most Admired Songs, Duetts, &c.*, 3 vols (Edinburgh, c1779); there are more in vol. IV (Edinburgh, c1795).[52] Corri also published *A New and Complete Collection of the most Favourite Scots Songs*, 2 vols (Edinburgh, 1788), and some keyboard arrangements of Scots tunes, such as *Thou art gone awa, a Favourite Scots Song with Variations (One of which in Imitation of the Bag Pipes) and a Violin Accompaniment* (Edinburgh, 1785) and *My ain kind dearie with Variations* (Edinburgh, c1790).

The three Scots songs in *A Select Collection*, vol. II were taken from Ramsay's *The Gentle Shepherd* (pp. 72-73),[53] while those in vol. III are mostly the familiar ones, such as "The Lass of Peaty's Mill" (p. 69), "Lochaber" (p. 76), "The broom of Cowdenknows" (p. 83), and "Tweedside" (p. 92). However, among them are contemporary composed songs such as "The maid of Selma" (p. 100), a "Scotch Air" attributed to Oswald, and Tommaso Giordani's "Queen Mary's Lamentation", a setting popularised by Giusto Ferdinando Tenducci of words put into the mouth of the imprisoned Mary, Queen of Scots (p. 71).[54] Remarkably, there are also three songs marked "Galic Air", settings of fragments of Scots Gaelic (p. 45). There is a similar mixture in vol. IV, with genuine Scots songs such as "Here awa' there awa' Willie", labelled "Old Scotch Song" (p. 119), and "Duncan Gray" (p. 120) alongside Corri's own "Ballad in a Scotch Stile", "I come, O night" (p. 121). Corri made several innovations in *A Select Collection* to the way vocal music was published: in

---

[51] For the Corris in Scotland, see especially 'Life of Domenico Corri' in: *The Singer's Preceptor, or Corri's Treatise on Vocal Music*, London, Chappell & Co., 1810; Harris, David Fraser. *Op. cit.* (see note 43), pp. 131-148; Tinagli Baxter, Sonia. *Op. cit.* (see note 25), vol. I, pp. 140-178; Macleod, Jennifer. *Op. cit.* (see note 43), pp. 172-174.

[52] For the publishing history of *A Select Collection*, see Tinagli Baxter, Sonia. *Op. cit.* (see note 25), vol. I, pp. 164-165, 170.

[53] For the music of *The Gentle Shepherd*, see especially Fiske, Roger. *English Theatre Music* […], *op. cit.* (see note 16), pp. 111-112, 406-407; Holman, Peter. 'A Little Light on Lorenzo Bocchi […]', *op. cit.* (see note 26), pp. 76-77.

[54] *The British Library Integrated Catalogue* lists a number of copies of a score published by Preston in 1782 in which the work is said to have been "Sung by Sig. Tenducci at the Pantheon & Mr. Abel's Concert &c".

addition to figures under the bass line he provided a written-out right-hand realization in small notes to enable "every harpsichord-player […] at sight, and without a single lesson on the subject, to accompany any piece of music with taste and elegance".[55] He also provided the singer with unusually precise performance instructions, including dynamics, written-out ornamentation and breath marks (ILL. 4).

ILL. 4: Domenico Corri, *A Select Collection of the most Admired Songs, Duetts, &c.*, vol. III, p. 83, "The broom of Cowdenknows".

---

55 CORRI, Domenico. *A Select Collection of the most Admired Songs, Duetts, &c.*, 3 vols, Edinburgh, John Corri, *c*1779, vol. I, p. 6.

Urbani probably came to London in 1771, worked in Dublin and Glasgow between 1781 and 1784, and was hired by the Edinburgh Musical Society as a singer between 1785 and its dissolution in 1799; he subsequently became involved in promoting public concerts, though with diminishing success, and he returned to Dublin in 1806.[56] He was well known for his performances of Scots songs. Michael Kelly remembered that he was "a good professor, and, like his countryman, David Rizzio, very partial to Scotch melodies, some of which he sang very pleasingly, though in a falsetto voice".[57] Urbani also devoted much time and energy to publishing arrangements of them. He began with *A Selection of Scots Songs, Harmonized, Improved with Simple and Adapted Graces*, 4 vols (Edinburgh, *c*1792-1794) in which the tunes are set for voice with four-part strings and continuo or two voices, two violins and continuo; the written-out keyboard part serves as an alternative to the string parts (ILL. 5). It was reissued in 1804 with the addition of two more volumes entitled *A Select Collection of Original Scotish Airs with Select and Characteristic Scotch & English Verses, the Most Part Written by the Celebrated R. Burns*. In these the accompaniments are for the more modern combination of pianoforte, violin and violoncello, with the keyboard part printed in the score and separate violin and violoncello parts. Urbani also published *A Collection of New Reels* (Edinburgh, ?1790), *A Selection of Minuets, High Dances, Cottilions, Scots Airs &c.* [...] *Adapted for the Piano Forte or Harpsichord* (Edinburgh, 1796)*, A Favorite Selection of Scots Tunes* [...] *Properly Arranged as Duettos for Two German Flutes or Violins* (Edinburgh, 1797), and many individual publications of Scots songs and dances.[58]

The list of Italians attracted to Scots tunes can be lengthened by surveying those who performed them without acting as publishers or arrangers. Burney wrote that Filippo Palma's "manner of singing and varying 'The Lass of Paties Mill,' had more effect, even upon the most enthusiastic admirers of grand airs, than the performance of the greatest singers".[59] Palma, a tenor and harpsichordist, was employed by the Edinburgh Musical Society in 1741. The

---

[56]   For Urbani in Scotland, see especially HARRIS, David Fraser. *Op. cit.* (see note 43), pp. 123-131; TINAGLI BAXTER, Sonia. *Op. cit.* (see note 25), vol. I, pp. 245-268; MACLEOD, Jennifer. *Op. cit.* (see note 43), pp. 174-175.

[57]   KELLY, Michael. *Reminiscences of Michael Kelly*, 2 vols, London, Henry Colburn, 1826, vol. II, p. 67.

[58]   Many of them are listed in *The British Library Integrated Catalogue*.

[59]   'Filippo Palma', in: *The Cyclopedia*, edited by Abraham Rees, 39 vols, London, Longman, Hurst, Rees, Orme & Brown, 1802-1819; see also BURNEY, IV, p. 451. For Palma in Edinburgh, see TINAGLI BAXTER, Sonia. *Op. cit.* (see note 25), vol. I, pp. 92-95; MACLEOD, Jennifer. *Op. cit.* (see note 43), p. 156.

ILL. 5: Pietro Urbani, *A Selection of Scots Songs*, vol. 1, p. 44, the opening of "The broom of Cowdenknows".

tenor Gaetano Filippo Rochetti, employed by the Society between 1744 and 1753, sang Scots songs in Edinburgh public concerts, including "The bush aboon Traquair" (6 February, 14 June 1753).[60] The soprano Cristina Passerini was employed by the Society between 1751 and 1753 with her violinist husband Giuseppe,[61] and regularly sang Scots songs in Edinburgh public concerts,

---

[60] TINAGLI BAXTER, Sonia. *Op. cit.* (see note 25), vol. 1, pp. 100-101. See also MACLEOD, Jennifer. *Op. cit.* (see note 43), pp. 157-158.

[61] For the Passerinis in Scotland, see especially HARRIS, David Fraser. *Op. cit.* (see note 43), pp. 272-274; TINAGLI BAXTER, Sonia. *Op. cit.* (see note 25), vol. 1, pp. 103-114; MACLEOD,

including "Tweedside" (18 August and November 1752); "The bush aboon Traquair" and "The lass of Peaty's Mill" (9 January 1753).[62] The advertisement for the last concert stated that they were "set in Parts by Signor Geminiani" (presumably the published settings), while in November 1752 it was said that "Signor Passerini has dispersed some Scots Songs, and other Music, with fine words, in such manner as to afford Diversion to everybody". The harpsichordist Felice Doria and his wife, a singer, worked for the Society between 1763 and 1769.[63] She also sang Scots songs in Edinburgh concerts: on 18 December 1764 "Italian and Scotch songs by Signora Doria" were advertised.[64] The violinist Giuseppe Puppo was employed by the Society between 1774 and 1784, and his wife occasionally sang Scots songs in its concerts,[65] including "For the lack of gold she's left me".[66] "La Miniatrice" (Mrs Corri) sang "Will ye go to the ewe-bughts?" (9 February 1781; 8 August 1783; 28 May 1784) and "The broom of Cowdenknows" (4 June 1784) in the Society's concerts.[67]

Last but not least, the castrato Giusto Ferdinando Tenducci (c1735-1790) was particularly renowned for singing Scots songs. He worked for the Edinburgh Musical Society in 1768-1769, returning to the city in the summers of 1780, 1781 and 1785.[68] In addition to singing "The braes of Ballenden" and "Lochaber" to words by Robert Fergusson as Arbaces in a production of Arne's *Artaxerxes* at the Theatre Royal in July 1769,[69] he performed at least twelve Scots songs in concerts.[70] Having stated that "A Scots song can only be sung in taste by a Scottish voice", William Tytler observed:

Jennifer. *Op. cit.* (see note 43), pp. 158-162.

[62]   TINAGLI BAXTER, Sonia. *Op. cit.* (see note 25), vol. 1, pp. 110-113.

[63]   For the Dorias in Edinburgh, see *ibidem*, vol. 1, pp. 199-203; MACLEOD, Jennifer. *Op. cit.* (see note 43), p. 165.

[64]   TINAGLI BAXTER, Sonia. *Op. cit.* (see note 25), vol. 1, p. 201.

[65]   For the Puppos in Edinburgh, see especially HARRIS, David Fraser. *Op. cit* (see note 43), pp. 57-61; TINAGLI BAXTER, Sonia. *Op. cit.* (see note 25), vol. 1, pp. 209-216; MACLEOD, Jennifer. *Op. cit.* (see note 43), p. 148.

[66]   TINAGLI BAXTER, Sonia. *Op. cit.* (see note 25), vol. 1, p. 214. For the tune, see GLEN, John. *Op. cit.* (see note 15), p. 114.

[67]   MACLEOD, Jennifer. *Op. cit.* (see note 43), p. 135.

[68]   For Tenducci in Edinburgh, see especially HARRIS, David Fraser. *Op. cit* (see note 43), pp. 108-122; TINAGLI BAXTER, Sonia. *Op. cit.* (see note 25), vol. 1, pp. 120-139; MACLEOD, Jennifer. *Op. cit.* (see note 43), pp. 168-171. See also BALDWIN, Olive - WILSON, Thelma. 'Giusto Ferdinando Tenducci', in: *Oxford Dictionary of National Biography*, *op. cit.* (see note 7).

[69]   HARRIS, David Fraser. *Op. cit.* (see note 43), pp. 112-113; TINAGLI BAXTER, Sonia. *Op. cit.* (see note 25), vol. 1, pp. 129-130. See also *Artaxerxes, an English Opera, as it is Performed at the Theatre-Royal, Edinburgh*, Edinburgh, Martin & Wotherspoon, 1769.

[70]   NELSON, Claire. *Op. cit.* (see note 21), pp. 607-608.

We sometimes, however, find a foreign master, who, with a genius for the pathetic, and a knowledge of the subject and words, has afforded very high pleasure in a Scottish song. Who could hear with insensibility, or without being moved in the greatest degree, *Tenducci* sing *I'll never leave thee*, or *The Braes of Ballendine!* — or *Will ye go to the ewe bughts, Marion*, sung by Signora *Corri*?[71]

George Thomson (1757-1851) even wrote that performances by Tenducci and La Miniatrice inspired him to begin publishing his *Select Collection of Original Scotish Airs* (London, 1793-1841), best known today for their accompaniments by Haydn, Beethoven, Koželuch and others:

At the St. Cecilia Concerts I heard Scottish songs sung in a style of excellence far surpassing any idea which I had previously had of their beauty, and that, too, from Italians, Signor Tenducci the one, and Signora Domenica Corri the other. Tenducci's "I'll never leave thee" and "Braes of Ballenden," and the Signora's "Ewe-Bughts, Marion," and "Waly, Waly," so delighted every hearer that in the most crowded room not a whisper was to be heard, so entirely did they rivet the attention and admiration of the audience. Tenducci's singing was full of passion, feeling, and taste, and, what we hear very rarely from singers, his articulation of the words was no less perfect than his expression of the music. It was in consequence of my hearing him and Signora Corri sing a number of our songs so charmingly that I conceived the idea of collecting all our best melodies and songs, and of obtaining accompaniments to them worthy of their merit.[72]

Tenducci continued to sing Scots songs after his return to London, and John Christian Bach made a spectacular arrangement for him of "The braes of Ballenden" with oboe, violin, viola, violoncello and pianoforte obbligato, played respectively by J. C. Fischer, Wilhelm Cramer, Felice Giardini, John Crosdill and Bach himself.[73] Tenducci included it in his benefit at the Hanover Square Rooms on 10 May 1779.[74] In addition, Bach made simpler

---

[71]   TYTLER, William. *Op. cit.* (see note 21), pp. 495-496.

[72]   HADDEN, James Cuthbert. *George Thomson, the Friend of Burns: His Life and Correspondence*, London, John C. Nimmo, 1898, p. 20.

[73]   BACH, John Christian. *Braes of Ballanden as Sung by Mr. Tenducci at the Festino Rooms in Hanover Square in the Year 1779*, London, Cahusac, *c*1785; modern edition in: *Four Scotch Songs*, edited by Roger Fiske, 4 vols, London, Schott, 1969, vol. 1. See also FISKE, Roger. *Scotland in Music* [...], *op. cit.* (see note 13), pp. 28-29.

[74]   *The Public Advertiser*, 27 April 1779.

arrangements of "The broom of Cowdenknows", "I'll never leave thee" and "Lochaber" with two flutes, two violins and bass, each published as "Sung by Mr. Tenducci, at the Pantheon & Mr. Abel's Concert".[75] One of them was presumably the "favorite Scotch Air" Tenducci sang at a Pantheon concert on 18 February 1782.[76]

The engagement of eighteenth-century Italians with Scottish music is a remarkable phenomenon, though I do not wish to overstate the case that has been built up so far. Scottish musicians were always at the forefront of arranging and publishing their own music, and their dominance increased towards the end of the eighteenth century as the fashion for Italian performers lessened and more local musicians acquired the necessary skills to arrange the repertory.[77] The era of Corri and Urbani gave way to that of George Thomson, Stephen Clarke, the musical arranger for James Johnson's *Scots Musical Museum*, 6 vols (Edinburgh, 1787-1803), or Niel and Nathaniel Gow, authors of many publications of Scottish dance music. Also, musicians in England often arranged Scots tunes; examples not already mentioned include "The yellow hair'd laddie" in J. C. Bach's keyboard concerto Op. 13, no. 4 and Stephen Storace's *Gli equivoci* (1786); the "The Birks of Endermay" in John Mahon's F major clarinet concerto, and (arranged by Thomas Linley junior) in *The Duenna* (1775); and "Auld lang syne" in the overture of William Shield's *Rosina* (1782).[78]

IMPROVING THE MELODY OF RIZZIO

We have seen that Geminiani wrote in *A Treatise of Good Taste* that melody was "intirely rude and barbarous" until Rizzio had "found Means at once to civilize and inspire it with all the native Gallantry of the SCOTISH Nation". He went on to explain what this involved:

> But Melody, tho' pleasing to All, seldom communicates
> the highest Degree of Pleasure; and it was owing to this

---

[75]   BACH, John Christian. *A Favourite Scotch Song, Sung by Mr. Tenducci, at the Pantheon & Mr. Abel's Concert*, London, Cahusac, *c*1785; modern editions in: *Four Scotch Songs* (see note 73), vols II-IV.

[76]   *The Morning Chronicle and London Advertiser*, 18 February 1782.

[77]   This point is made in CRANMER, John Leonard. *Concert Life and the Music Trade in Edinburgh, c1780-c1830*, Ph.D. Diss., University of Edinburgh, 1991, pp. 345-346.

[78]   Listed in FISKE, Roger. *Scotland in Music* [...], *op. cit.* (see note 13), pp. 189-190, 198. Fiske suggested that "Auld lang syne" was a Northumbrian pipe tune that was popularised by Shield; see FISKE, Roger. *English Theatre Music* [...], *op. cit.* (see note 16), pp. 457-459.

Reflection, that I have lately undertaken to improve the Melody
of *Rizzio* into Harmony, by converting some of his Airs into
two, three, and four Parts; and by making such Additions and
Accompanyments to others as should give them all the Variety
and Fullness required in a Concert.

He was aware that Scots tunes frequently did not conform to the patterns
of Baroque harmony:

But how difficult it was to succeed in it, No-body can
judge better than myself (not to destroy the Simplicity and
Beauty, I found required some Discretion) But to add new
Parts on the same Principles, and to create Harmony without
violating the Intention of the Melody, required an equal Mixture
of Imagination and Judgment.

Of course, Scots tunes had long been harmonized, as can be seen in
seventeenth-century keyboard, lute and lyra viol manuscripts,[79] and the
"Additions and Accompanyments" needed to give them "all the Variety and
Fullness required in a Concert" were also developed before Geminiani. Sets
of written-down variations exist from about 1700 (David Johnson singled out
John McLachlan or McLauchland as an early exponent),[80] doubtless using
native traditions of improvised embellishment, English divisions and Italian
variations as models. Geminiani mentioned Corelli's *La folia* variations, Op. 5,
no. XII as a famous example, adding that he had "the Pleasure of discoursing
with him myself upon this Subject, and heard him acknowledge the Satisfaction
he took in composing it, and the value he set upon it"; William McGibbon's
variations on *La folia* is a direct imitation.[81] Sonatas for violin or flute and
continuo based on Scots tunes were developed in the 1730s, first in Alexander
Munro's *Collection of the Best Scots Tunes* (Paris, 1732), and then by Charles
McLean, James Oswald and William McGibbon.[82] The genre applied the

---

[79] The best study is STELL, Evelyn Florence. *Sources of Scottish Music 1603-1707*, Ph.D.
Diss., 2 vols, University of Glasgow, 1999. It is updated in EDWARDS, Warwick. 'The Musical
Sources', in: *Defining Strains: the Musical Life of Scots in the Seventeenth Century*, edited by James
Porter, Berne, Peter Lang, 2007, pp. 47-71; HOLMAN, Peter. *Life after Death* […], *op. cit.* (see
note 4), pp. 85-91.

[80] JOHNSON, David. *Scottish Fiddle Music* […], *op. cit.* (see note 45), pp. 15-16, 65-105. Many
of MacLachlan's settings, arranged for lute, are in the Balcarres manuscript; see *The Balcarres Lute
Book*, edited by Matthew Spring, 2 vols, Glasgow, Universities of Glasgow and Aberdeen, 2010.

[81] Edited in *Chamber Music of Eighteenth-Century Scotland*, edited by David Johnson,
Glasgow, Glasgow University Music Department Publications, 2000, pp. 33-39, no. 4.

[82] See JOHNSON, David. *Scottish Fiddle Music* […], *op. cit.* (see note 45), pp. 161-191;
Chamber Music of Eighteenth-Century Scotland, *op. cit.* (see note 81), pp. 55-63, no. 8.

formal patterns of the Italian sonata *da camera* as represented by Corelli's Op. 5, nos VII-XI to Scots tunes, transforming them into the rhythmic patterns of various dances — a technique used in courtly dance music since the early sixteenth century. The first trio sonata based on Scots tunes — the immediate starting point for Geminiani's sonatas — was the one in D major by Oswald, published in score in his *Curious Collection of Scots Tunes* (Edinburgh, c1739), pp. 28-31.[83]

Geminiani was rather unadventurous on the formal level in his sonatas on Scots tunes.[84] The second, based on "The bush aboon Traquair", consists simply of two statements of the tune, the second using more florid ornamentation. The third, based on the "The last time I came o'er the moor" also has two statements of the tune, the second marked Allegro, but a little variety is introduced by inserting a declamatory Grave between them, unrelated to the tune, in triple time rather than duple time, and in the relative minor. His first sonata is a little more sophisticated, consisting of a Grave based on "The broom of Cowdenknows", an Andante based on "Bonny Christy", a short unrelated Grave (again in triple time and in the relative minor), and a second, more florid version of "Bonny Christy" marked Presto. He never tried to intersperse statements of his tunes with concerto-like episodes of passage-work, as Bocchi did (in the "English Aire Improv'd" already mentioned),[85] nor to recast the tunes in the rhythms of different dances, like Munro, nor to use a Scots tune as the material for the outer section of a *da capo* aria, as Veracini did in "Oh inaspettata sorte". Nor did he follow Oswald in achieving sonata-like harmonic contrasts by juxtaposing two tunes in the minor, "Ettrick banks" and "She rose and let in me", with three in the major, "O mother what shall I do", "Cromlit's lilt" and "Polwart on the green".

Geminiani preferred to "improve" his Scots tunes by the addition of ornamentation, using florid variations as well as graces or "Ornaments of Expression" applying to a single note.[86] The florid ornamentation, mostly in the second statements of the tunes, would doubtless have struck his contemporaries as Italianate, but more surprising for an Italian composer

[83] Modern edition: Geminiani, Francesco - Oswald, James. *Trio Sonatas on Scots Tunes*, edited by Peter Holman, Edinburgh, Hardie Press, 1994, pp. 10-17, no. 1.

[84] Modern edition: *ibidem*, pp. 18-34, nos 2-4.

[85] See the analysis in Holman, Peter. 'A Little Light on Lorenzo Bocchi [...]', *op. cit.* (see note 26), pp. 81-83.

[86] Geminiani, Francesco. *A Treatise of Good Taste in the Art of Musick*, London, s.n., 1749, pp. 2-4 (for modern and facsimile editions see note 6).

is the care with which he indicated the graces, describing fourteen types, providing a table of "Examples of the Element of playing and singing in a good Taste", and sprinkling the signs liberally around the statements of the tunes (ILL. 6, 7). This may have been partly a legacy of repeated visits to Paris (French composers tended to specify ornaments more frequently and with more care than those in other countries, often providing tables of ornaments), though he also tapped into an established Scottish performing tradition: printed collections from the 1726 *Orpheus Caledonius* to Corri and Urbani often specify quite elaborate ornamentation, including trills, appoggiaturas, turns, and slides from the third below.

ILL. 6: Francesco Geminiani, *A Treatise in the Art of Good Taste*, p. [6], "Examples of the Element of playing and singing in a good Taste".

ILL. 7: Francesco Geminiani, *A Treatise in the Art of Good Taste*, p. 10, beginning of vocal section of "When Phoebus bright".

However, Geminiani broke new ground in *A Treatise of Good Taste* in the range of ornament signs used and in trying to classify the emotional effects of particular ornaments, characterizing the "TURNED SHAKE" as "fit to express Gaiety" and the "Superior APOGIATURA" as conveying "Love, Affection, Pleasure, &c."; the "BEAT" and the "close SHAKE" (vibrato) could "express several Passions" according to the way they were performed. It is not clear whether Geminiani was just using Scots tunes as a peg on which hang his ideas about ornamentation, or whether he was influenced by hearing Scottish singers and instrumentalists perform. He did not visit Scotland until after he had published his arrangements of Scots tunes, though he could have heard them played in London by Robert Bremner and Francesco Barsanti. Also, James Oswald moved from Edinburgh to London in 1741, and was noted for playing Scots tunes on the violoncello. Benjamin Franklin wrote, in a letter to Lord Kames dated 2 June 1765:

> Whoever has heard James Oswald play them on his Violoncello, will be less inclin'd to dispute this with me. I have more than once seen Tears of Pleasure in the Eyes of his Auditors; and yet I think even his Playing those Tunes would please more, if he gave them less modern Ornament.[87]

---

[87] *The Papers of Benjamin Franklin* <http://franklinpapers.org/franklin/>.

By "modern Ornament" Franklin was presumably thinking of the sort of ornamentation specified by Geminiani.

There is a tension here between simplicity (the tune) and complexity (the additions of the arranger or performer) that also applies to the textures of Scots song settings. Geminiani seems to have been the first composer to set them with "all the Variety and Fullness required in a Concert"; the four in *A Treatise of Good Taste* are scored for two flutes, two violins, viola and bass (ILL. 8). At first sight the solo and tutti marks in the first song, a setting of "The lass of Peaty's Mill", appear just to show how the violins and flutes should alternate and combine, but they are also applied to the viola and bass parts so it is likely that Geminiani envisaged more than one string player to a part. The scoring of two flutes, strings and continuo was commonly used in mid eighteenth-century English vocal music intended for the stage and public concerts, a notable early example being the trio "Hither turn thee, gentle swain" in Thomas Arne's *Judgement of Paris* (1740; published c1745).[88] Geminiani seems also to have been the first composer to offer flutes as an alternative to solo violins in seven-part concertos, in his *Concerti Grossi*, Op. 2 (London, 1732), and combined them with the solo violins in his *Concerti Grossi*, Op. 7 (London, 1748),[89] a texture also used in three of John Alcock's *Six Concerto's in Seven Parts* (London, 1750).

Geminiani's settings of Scots songs conform in outline to the pattern used by Arne and other English composer for two-section songs: the vocal sections are introduced and succeeded by instrumental passages or 'symphonies', though the repeat at the end of the first vocal section normally goes back to the entry of the voice rather than to the beginning, so the introductory symphony is heard only once. Scots songs were frequently published without the symphonies, though William Tytler stated that it was the normal practice to provide them *ad libitum* (as doubtless it was for other types of strophic song):

> Where, with a fine voice, is joined some skill and execution on either of those instruments [the harpsichord or guitar], the air, by way of symphony, or introduction to the song, should always be first played over; and, at the close of every stanza, the last part of the air should be repeated, as a relief for the voice, which it gracefully sets off. In this *symphonic part*, the performer may shew his taste and fancy on the instrument, by varying it *ad libitum*.[90]

---

[88]   Modern edition: ARNE, Thomas Augustine. *The Judgement of Paris*, edited by Ian Spink, London, Stainer and Bell, 1978 (Musica Britannica, 42), pp. 33-43, no. 5.

[89]   See *Geminiani Opera Omnia*, vol. 2, edited by Christopher Hogwood; vol. 6, edited by Richard Maunder.

[90]   TYTLER, William. *Op. cit.* (see note 21), pp. 496-497.

ILL. 8: Francesco Geminiani, *A Treatise in the Art of Good Taste*, p. 3, end of instrumental introduction to "The Lass of Peaty's Mill".

The more elaborate settings, such as those published by Corri and Urbani or those supplied by Thomas Linley junior for *The Duenna*,[91] put Tytler's prescriptions into practice, usually taking the first and last phrases of the tune as material for the symphonies. However, Geminiani goes further: his introductory symphonies are much longer and more complex, often departing from the tune, and in "The lass of Peaty's mill" and "O Bessy Bell" presenting it in the dominant near the end so that there can be a transition from dominant to tonic as the voice enters (ILL. 9). At the beginning of "When Phoebus bright" Geminiani shows a subtlety lacking in his trio sonatas on Scots tunes in the way he alludes to the first phrase of the song (ILL. 10). Geminiani's opening symphonies are only matched in sophistication by the one in J. C. Bach's setting of "The Braes of Ballenden", with its contrasted second subject in the dominant and its *galant* phraseology.

As the eighteenth century progressed, the feeling increased — influenced by Rousseau's ideas of simplicity in music[92] — that Scots songs were best performed in a style that matched the character of the tunes. In 1742 Barsanti

---

[91]   For the musical sources of *The Duenna*, see FISKE, Roger. *English Theatre Music* […], *op. cit.* (see note 16), pp. 416–418, 601–602.

[92]   See the discussion in NELSON, Claire. *Op. cit.* (see note 21), pp. 604, 607.

ILL. 9: Francesco Geminiani, *A Treatise in the Art of Good Taste*, p. 12, opening of "O Bessy Bell".

wrote: "I applied myself to do Justice to those ancient Compositions, by a proper and natural *Bass* to each Tune, with the strictest regard to the Tune itself, and without any Alteration of the *Tune* to accommodate it to the *Bass*", and put his ideas into practice by providing simple but effective bass lines, starting or finishing settings on the 'wrong' chord where necessary, as in his G major setting of "The broom of Cowdenknows" which begins and ends on D major chords.[93] Geminiani did the same thing with the tune in his first trio sonata, though his harmonization is much more complex, and the

---

[93]   Discussed and illustrated in FISKE, Roger. *Scotland in Music* [...], *op. cit.* (see note 13), pp. 18-19.

ILL. 10: Francesco Geminiani, *A Treatise in the Art of Good Taste*, p. 9, introduction to "When Phoebus bright".

ending sounds more conventional since it leads to the tonic chord of the next movement, the first setting of "Bonny Christy".

William Tytler thought that the "proper accompaniment of a Scottish song is a plain, thin, dropping bass, on the harpsichord or guittar",[94] while Benjamin Franklin, in the letter to Lord Kames already mentioned, asserted that "the Reason why the Scotch Tunes have liv'd so long, and will probably live forever (if they escape being stifled in modern affected Ornament) is merely this, that they are really Compositions of Melody and Harmony united, or rather that their Melody is Harmony. I mean the simple Tunes

---

[94]   TYTLER, William. *Op. cit.* (see note 21), p. 496.

sung by a single Voice". He explained: "the ancient Tunes" were "compos'd by the Minstrels of those days" to be sung to an undamped wire-strung harp "of the most simple kind [...] without any Half Notes but those in the natural Scale", which is why "almost every succeeding *emphatical* [i.e. stressed] Note, is a Third, a Fifth, an Octave, or in short some Note that is in Concord with the preceding Note". This, of course, is not literally true, though Franklin was right in thinking that many of the tunes are best served by an extremely simple harmonization that respects their modal characteristics.

Pietro Urbani seems to have been thinking along the same lines when he wrote (in the third person):

> He had often heard Scotch Songs performed at Theatres and in Concerts with false and unconnected Harmony, which entirely spoiled the beautiful simplicity of the original Air: to the following Songs, he has published the true harmony, which performers of every degree of proficiency may make use of.[95]

By "the true harmony" Urbani seems to have meant the *galant* idiom, with its elegant but simple progressions often using pedal-points, rather than the Baroque style, with its active bass lines and fast-moving harmony. The difference between the two can be seen by comparing extracts of the settings of "The last time I came o'er the moor" by Geminiani and Urbani (Ex. 2). Nevertheless, Geminiani was sometimes alert to the possibilities offered by *galant* harmony, as in the second strain of "When Phoebus bright", where a pedal-point passage sounds simultaneously modern and antique in its evocation of drones (ILL. 7). The possibilities of this new approach to Scots tunes, exploited to the full by J. C. Bach, Thomas Linley junior, Urbani and others, gave them a new lease of life in the 1770s.[96]

CONCLUSION

The engagement of Geminiani and other Italians with Scottish music may have begun with the Rizzio myth, and for those working in Scotland it was doubtless necessary to appeal to the concert-going and music-buying public. However, his settings show that there were deeper forces at work.

---

95 URBANI, Pietro. *A Selection of Scots Songs, Harmonized, Improved with Simple and Adapted Graces*, 6 vols, Edinburgh, Urbani & Liston, [1792-1804], vol. I, *c*1792, 'ADVERTISEMENT'.

96 A point made in FISKE, Roger. *English Theatre Music* [...], *op. cit.* (see note 16), pp. 416-417.

Ex. 2: The opening of "The last time I came o'er the moor": (a) Francesco Geminiani, *A Treatise in the Art of Good Taste*, p. 22, Sonata No. 3 in F major; (b) Pietro Urbani, *A Selection of Scots Songs*, vol. 1, p. 8.

He seems to have been attracted to the repertory partly because of its "Simplicity and Beauty", but also because of the opportunities it afforded for displaying good taste in ornamentation. In addition, the need to give Scots songs "all the Variety and Fullness required in a Concert" provided the opportunity for combining them with elements of the dominant Italian idiom, including variation techniques, sonata patterns and the *galant* style — which had originated in Italy in the early eighteenth century.[97] More generally, it can be seen as part of a developing interest in popular and exotic music across Europe in the middle of the eighteenth century, exemplified by such things as Telemann's sonatas and concertos in the Polish style, the Spanish elements in Domenico Scarlatti's harpsichord sonatas, Rameau's *Les Indes galantes*, the Turkish style in Viennese music, or (closer to home) Thomas Arne's vocal music, characterized by Burney as

---

[97]   See HEARTZ, Daniel. *Music in European Capitals: the Galant Style, 1720-1780*, New York, Norton, 2003.

"an agreeable mixture of Italian, English, and Scots".[98] This was, of course, merely the first wave of the great tide of exoticism and musical tourism that engulfed European music in the nineteenth century, inspiring such things as Schubert's settings of Ossian, Mendelssohn's *Hebrides* Overture and *Scottish Symphony*, and Bruch's *Scottish Fantasia*.[99]

---

[98]   *BURNEY*, IV, p. 673
[99]   For a survey, see FISKE, Roger. *Scotland in Music* [...], *op. cit.* (see note 13).

Geminiani's Canon:
A Souvenir of a Visit to Scotland?

Michael Talbot
(Liverpool)

O NE PECULIARITY OF MUSIC in eighteenth-century Britain is the dominance of the short piece, whether originally conceived as such or extracted from a longer composition. This phenomenon correlates closely with several others: the relative prominence of amateurs within the market for music and the performing domain; the importance of recreational as distinct from functional music; the absence of any hard-and-fast boundary between music for instruction and music for private or public performance (symbolized by the wide use of the term 'lesson' for instrumental pieces); the formation of a common musical repertory centred not so much on canonized composers or perceived masterworks (which was to become increasingly the case in the next century) as on 'favourite' pieces of surprisingly diverse nature and provenance.[1] In this kind of musical culture the anthology or miscellany forming a mosaic of several dozen short pieces became a major source of musical transmission within both manuscript and published traditions. Such collections were an inexpensive means of assembling popular pieces of the moment in a form convenient for amateurs.

For a modern student of Italian music, it can be a frustrating experience to investigate pieces attributed to the composer of particular interest contained in such collections. The movements are usually well known, adapted in ways that do not enhance their musical effectiveness (for example, they may be shorn of ornaments or lose inner parts in order to be accommodated within the number of staves available) and removed from their original context within

---

[1] This generalization needs qualification, since a few composers, among them Purcell, Corelli, Handel and even (briefly) Geminiani himself, attained the status of 'classics' in Britain during the eighteenth century. See WEBER, William. *The Rise of Musical Classics in Eighteenth-Century England*, Oxford, Clarendon Press, 1992, especially pp. 75-102.

a multi-movement framework. The examination and identification of these isolated movements is, for the scholar, more frequently a tedious duty than a cause for excited anticipation. Every so often, however, one receives a pleasant surprise: what was predicted to be merely an arrangement of movement X from the work numbered Y within the opus numbered Z turns out to be a previously unknown piece.

Such discoveries are commonly accidental by-products of investigation into other pieces. So it was in the present case. In July 2010 I decided to fill in time at the British Library by ordering an anthology containing a gavotta by Vivaldi taken from the first sonata (RV 73) of his Op. 1 trio sonatas. The presence of this movement was already known, and my inspection yielded no surprises — except that there was a further Vivaldi gavotta taken from the same opus that scholars had overlooked, perhaps because it was accidentally omitted from the collection's index. The anthology also contained, on pages 38-39, an unfamiliar three-part canon by Geminiani. Since I did not recall seeing any such composition in either the most recent *NG* (2001) work list or the published thematic catalogue by Enrico Careri,[2] I decided to transcribe it and seek further enlightenment. Learning from Careri and others that this was indeed a 'new' piece, I explored its context further and soon found that it could be related with some confidence to a visit paid by the elderly Geminiani to Edinburgh in 1760 — a visit frequently described in passing by previous scholars but hardly at all examined as a biographical episode in its own right.

A suitable starting point for the present account is 26 April 1755, when Robert Bremner, newly established as a music publisher in Edinburgh, advertised an anthology of 72 pieces entitled *A Collection of Airs and Marches for Two Violins, or German Flutes, Some of which have Basses*.[3] This was a periodical publication issued in twelve instalments (each comprising a gathering of eight pages), which was probably concluded in 1756. Bremner's formula was to mix pieces by local and other British composers with ones by Italians resident in Britain or particularly in fashion there. The "Airs" of the title refer to dance-movements as employed in chamber sonatas. Significant is the presence of two Edinburgh-based composers. The first, Hugh Clerk (a brother of the musically more famous Sir John Clerk of Penicuik), was a merchant active in the Edinburgh Musical Society, a thriving amateur association, from 1731

---

[2]   See *CARERI*; the 'Thematic Catalogue' comprising the second part of this study occupies pp. 221-293.

[3]   The collection was reissued in London from the same plates by Bremner, and by Preston and Son after Bremner's death.

to 1750, while the second, William McGibbon (1696-1756), was Scotland's premier violinist-composer, employed by the same society as one of its resident professionals since its inception in 1727-1728. As one would have expected, Bremner forged close and mutually advantageous links with the Musical Society right from the start. Between 1756 and 1762 either he or one of his sons of the same name was actually employed by it as a professional violinist and guitarist, while another son, James, also served it as a violinist.[4] Even after he moved to London in 1762 Robert Sr continued to supply it on a regular and official basis with music and musicians.

One of the five Italian composers represented in the collection was Geminiani, whose well-liked *Minuet* in C minor (H. 212; identified by Careri as "M/1") appears on page 80 as "Minuet by Mr. Geminiani", numbered 62.[5]

Geminiani, so far as is known, had not yet exhibited his talents as a violinist in Edinburgh, but the Musical Society had already taken him to its heart. As early as its first season, the society paid McGibbon for supplying one of his concertos.[6] Sonatas and concertos (as well as the expected *Scots Tunes*) by Geminiani were acquired intermittently in the succeeding decades, although it appears that the complete published Opp. 2, 3 and 7 concertos, ordered in duplicate or triplicate, were not in the Society's possession until shortly after Bremner's removal to London, doubtless stimulated by the erection of St Cecilia's Hall in 1762, which facilitated the rehearsal and performance of orchestral music.[7] We have, however, certain proof that Geminiani enjoyed special favour with the society already in the 1750s, since in a letter sent to Handel in December 1753 the directors averred: "The Performances of our Society have hitherto been confined to the compositions of Corelli, Geminiani and Mr. Handel".[8] In the second, augmented Edinburgh edition (1762) of his

---

[4]   McLEOD, Jennifer. *The Edinburgh Musical Society: Its Membership and Repertoire 1727-1797*, Ph.D. Diss., University of Edinburgh, 2001, p. 41n. This dissertation can be downloaded from the EThOS website of the British Library. McLeod identifies the Robert Bremner who served the society as the father, and this is indeed more likely if Robert Jr resided continuously in London around 1758-1759, as is implied by a minute of the society dated 11 July 1759 containing the information that he had been busy teaching guitar in London over the previous eleven months. On this, see COGGIN, Philip. '"This Easy and Agreable Instrument": A History of the English Guittar', in: *Early Music*, XV/2 (1987), pp. 204-218: 209.

[5]   This source is not listed in Careri's catalogue (*op. cit.* [see note 2]). I am grateful to Andrew Woolley for inspecting this collection on my behalf in the Scottish Studies Library at the University of Edinburgh.

[6]   McLEOD, Jennifer. *Op. cit.* (see note 4), p. 98.

[7]   On the acquisition from Bremner of the concerto sets, see *ibidem*, pp. 274-275; on St Cecilia's Hall, see *ibidem*, *passim*.

[8]   *Ibidem*, p. 122.

highly successful primer *The Rudiments of Music* Bremner identifies himself as a former pupil of Geminiani, whose positive opinion on the 'group' teaching of composition he quotes in connection with his advocacy of the same method of instruction for hymn singing.[9] In the past, it has been generally supposed, at least at a tacit level, that Bremner's period of study with Geminiani dated back several years from 1762, but, as we shall see, it may well have been much more recent and rather brief.

In 1759 Bremner's cosy monopoly over music publishing and resale in Edinburgh was broken by an interloper: Neil Stewart. An advertisement placed by Stewart in the *Edinburgh Evening Courant* of 20 October announced that, newly arrived from London, he was setting up in business in the city as a dealer in music and musical instruments.[10] As a publisher, Stewart right from the start challenged Bremner head-on: he produced rival editions of the same music (for instance, of McGibbon's *Scots Tunes*) or unauthorized sequels to Bremner publications that cheekily mimicked their title, format and content.[11] Such was the anthology entitled *A Collection of Marches & Airs for Violins, German Flutes, and Hautboys, the most of which has Basses for the Violoncello or Harpsichord* first advertised in the *Edinburgh Evening Courant* of 27 July 1761.[12] Like its model, this was a publication in twelve instalments running to 96 pages of music.

The title page of the volume reads: A | COLLECTION | of | MARCHES & AIRS. | For | VIOLINS, GERMAN FLUTES, AND HAUTBOYS. | the most of which has BASSES for the | VIOLONCELLO OR HARPSICHORD. | Published in Twelve Numbers | by NEIL STEWART. | At his Music Shop opposite the head of Black-fryers Wynd Edinburgh. Where may be had [there follows a list of publications "at the London prices", including notably McGibbon's *Scots Tunes* in three volumes, Pepusch's *Airs for two Violins*, *A Collection of Scots, English and Irish tunes for the guitar*, and various *Scots Reels and Minuets*] James Read Sculp.

A tabulation of the volume's content follows:

---

[9] BREMNER, Robert. *The Rudiments of Music* [...] *The Second Edition*, Edinburgh, Bremner, 1762, p. 61. The reference occurs during a section ('A Plan for Teaching a Croud') not included in the original edition of 1756.

[10] KIDSON, Frank. *British Music Publishers, Printers and Engravers: London, Provincial, Scottish and Irish. From Queen Elizabeth's Reign to George the Fourth's, with Select Bibliographical Lists of Musical Works Printed and Published within that Period*, London, Hill, [1900], p. 194.

[11] For other instances of this mimicry on Stewart's part, see *ibidem*, p. 195.

[12] Examples in the British Library (b.42.), the Central Library, Dundee, and the Library of Congress.

PAGE[a]	NO.	STAVES[b]	TITLE IN INDEX[c]	TITLE BEFORE PIECE	KEY[d]
1	1	2	Gavot by Mr MacLean[e]	Gavot by M.ʳ M.ᶜLean	G
2–3	2	3	March by Seg. Martini[f]	March by Sig.ʳ Martini	D
4a	3	3	March by Mr Collet	March by M.ʳ Collett	D
4b	[3 bis][g]	3	Minuet by Correlli	Minuet by Correlli	D
5	4	3	A Hessian March	A Hessian March	G
6–7a	5	2	Minuet by Mr Stanley	Minuet by M.ʳ Stanley	A
7b	6	3	Canon for 3 Violins or three Flutes	Canon for 3 Violins or 3 Flutes	D
8	7	3	Air in Alexander Severus[h]	Air in Alex.ʳ Severus	g
9a	8	2	Duet[i]	Duet	D
9b	9	2	Duet	Duet	D
10–11	10	2	March by Martini	March by Martini	D
12	11	2[j]	Gavot by Mr MacGibbon	Gavot by M.ʳ M.ᶜGibbon	A
13	12	2	Air by Mr Stanley	Air by M.ʳ Stanley	B♭
14–15a	13	3	Minuet by Mr Nardini	Minuet by M.ʳ Nardini	A
15b	14	2	Gavot by Humphries	Gavot by Humphries	D
16	15	3	The Old Buffs March	The Old Buffs March	G
17	16	3	Minuet by Jemelli	Minuet by Jomelli	D
18–19a	17	3	March and Gavot by Mr Handel	March and Gavot by M.ʳ Handel	D
19b	18	3	Gavot by Mr Vivaldi	Gavott by Vivaldi	g
20	19	3	Gavot in Amadis by Mr Handel	Gavotta in Amadis by M.ʳ Handel	c
21	20	3	March by Mr Smith[k]	March by M.ʳ Smith	D
22–23	21	2[l]	Minuet by Lockatelli	Minuet by Lockatelli	G
24a	22	2	Hessian March	Hessian Duett	D
24b	23	2	Duet	Duet	D
25	24	2	Minuet by Mr Stanley	Minuet by M.ʳ Stanley	A
26–27a	25	3	March by Mr Burney[m]	March by M.ʳ Burney	E♭
27b	26	2	Gavot by Mr MacLean[n]	Gavot by M.ʳ M.ᶜLean	B♭
28–29	27	3	Air by Mr Handel	Air by M.ʳ Handel	G
30–31	28	3	Minuet by Dominco Galo[o]	Minuet by Dominco Galo	G
32	29	3	Air by Bononcini	Air by Bononcini	G
33	30	3	General Handyside's March	Generall Handysides March	G
34–35	31	2	Duet by Mr Weideman[p]	Duet by M.ʳ Weideman	D
36–37a	32	2	Air by Mr Festing	Air by M.ʳ Festing	E♭
37b	33	2	Air in imitation of Val and Ceko	Air in Imitation of a Quail and Cokow	D
38–39	34	3	Canon by Mr Geminiani	Canone by M.ʳ Geminiani	D
40	35	3	March by Seg. Horner[q]	March by Sig.ʳ Horner	G
41	36	2	Gavot by Corelli	Gavot by Correlli	F

42–43a	37	4	March by Mr Abel	March by M.ʳ Abel	D
43b	38	2	Air by Mr Arne	Air by M.ʳ Arne	D
44–45	39	3	March by Dr Boyceʳ	March by D.ʳ Boyce	E♭
46–47	40ˢ	3	Air in Ariodante by Mr Handel	Air in Ariodante by M.ʳ Handel	g
48	41	3	Minuet in Julius Cæsar by Mr Handel	Minuet in Julius Cæsar by M.ʳ Handel	A
49	42	2	Air by Mr Handel	Air by M.ʳ Handel	G
50–51	43	3	March by Mr Avison	March by M.ʳ Avison	D
52	44	2	Gavot by Mr MacGibbon	Gavot by M.ʳ M.ᶜGibbon	D
53a	45	2	Duet by Mr Festing	Duet by M.ʳ Festing	D
53b	[45 bis]	2	[not indexed]	Duett	D
54–55	46	3ᵗ	Minuet by Seg. Lampugnani	Minuet by Sig.ʳ Lampugnani	A
56	47	2	Gavot by Mr Humphriesᵘ	Gavot by M.ʳ Humphries	D
57	48	3	Hornpipe by Mr Handel	Hornpipe by M.ʳ Handel	F
58–59	49	3	Air in Sosarmes by Mr Handel	Air in Sosarmes by M.ʳ Handel	A
60–61a	50	2	Minuet by Mr Smith	Minuet by M.ʳ Smith	D
61b	51	3	March by Mr Handel	March by M.ʳ Handel	D
62–63	52	2	Air by Mr Arne	Air by M.ʳ Arne	E
64	53	3	March	March	D
65	54	2	Minuet by Mr Hasse	Minuet by M.ʳ Hasse	D
66–67a	55	3	Air by Mr Handel	Air by M.ʳ Handel	D
67b	56	2	Air by Mr MacLean	Air by M.ʳ M.ᶜLean	F
68	57	3	Minuet by Mr Abel	Minuet by M.ʳ Abel	D
69	58	2	Air by Mr Handel	Air by M.ʳ Handel	F
70–71a	59	3	Gavot by Correlli	Gavot by Correlli	G
71b	60	3	Air in Pyrrhusᵛ	Air in Pyrrhus	D
72	61	2	Air by Dr Green	Air by D.ʳ Green	C
73	62	2	Minuet by Dr F.ʷ	Minuet by D.ʳ F.	D
74–75a	63	3	General Lampton's March	General Lampton's March	D
75b	64	3	The Duke of Rutland's March	The Duke of Rutland's March	D
76–77	65	2ˣ	Minuet by Mr MacGibbon	Minuet by M.ʳ M.ᶜGibbon	G
78–79a	66	3	Minuet by Jemelli	Minuet by Jomelli	G
79b	67ʸ	2	Duet	Duett	D
80	68	2	March by Dr F.	March by D.ʳ F.	D
81	69	2ᶻ	Minuet by Mr MacGibbon	Minuet by M.ʳ M.ᶜGibbon	A
82a	70	2	Air by Major Reidᵃᵃ	Air by Major Reid	d
82b–83a	[70 bis]	2	[not indexed]	Minuet	F
83b	71	3	[not indexed]	Gavot by Vivaldi	G
84–85	72	3	Saraband and Gavot by Correlli	Saraband and Gavot by Correlli	B♭
86–87a	73	2	Gavota del Seg. Castrucci	Gavota del Sig.ʳ Castrucci	A

87b	74	3	Bourre by Mr Handel	Bourre by M.ʳ Handel	g
88	75	2	Duet	Duet	D
89	76	2	Minuet by Mr Abel	Minuet by M,ʳ Abel	D
90-91	77	2ᵇᵇ	Air by Mr Cocklinᵃ	Air by M.ʳ Cocklin	E♭
92	78		Air by Mr Festing	Air by M.ʳ Festing	B♭
93	[78 bis]	2	[not indexed]	Minuet	B♭
94-95	79	3	Minuet by Martini	Minuet by Martini	G
96	80	3	Air by Mr Festing	Air by M.ʳ Festing	E♭

a. The letter 'a' following a page number denotes the upper part of the page, 'b' the lower part.

b. This column gives the number of staves per system, which remains constant for each piece unless otherwise noted.

c. Titles are given in diplomatic transcription. The order of the items as they appear in the index is generally alphabetical by title.

d. Upper case is used for major keys, lower case for minor keys.

e. Charles MacLean (*c*1712-*c*1772), a Scottish violinist employed by the Edinburgh Musical Society in 1737-1738.

f. Almost certainly the London-based Giuseppe Sammartini (1695-1750).

g. Numbered "3" only in the index.

h. Handel's pasticcio *Alessandro Severo* (1738).

i. All the pieces identified as duets are for two treble instruments without bass.

j. The variation to the gavotte is notated on a single staff (since the bass is simply repeated).

k. Identity uncertain: perhaps Handel's assistant John Christopher Smith (1712-1795).

l. A single staff is used for the variations.

m. Charles Burney (1726-1814), who in 1761 was still only 'Mr' Burney (his doctorate was awarded in 1769).

n. Charles MacLean (see above, note *e*).

o. The Italian composer Domenico Gallo.

p. The German-born flautist Carl Friedrich Weidemann (d. 1782).

q. Unidentified: the title 'Seg.' (for 'Sig.') implies continental origin.

r. 'Boyce' is corrected in ink from a misprinted original name in the British Library example.

s. Numbered "4" in error in the index.

t. A single staff is used for the variations.

u. The English violinist John Humphries (*fl*. 1726-1741), many of whose works were acquired by the Edinburgh Musical Society.

v. Perhaps the opera *Pyrrhus and Demetrius* based on an original by Alessandro Scarlatti given in London in 1708.

w. David Foulis (1710-1773), a physician and amateur composer who was a member of the Edinburgh Musical Society from 1737-1753.

x. A single staff is used for the variations.

y. Miswritten as "76" before the piece, but corrected in ink.

z. A single staff is used for the variations.

aa. John Reid (1721-1807), an army officer, flautist and composer who reached the rank of major in August 1759 and subsequently became a general. It was he who left the bequest establishing the chair of music at the University of Edinburgh that bears his name. He was a member of the Edinburgh Musical Society during 1742-1744.

bb. A single staff is used for the variations.

cc. Identity unknown — perhaps a local amateur composer. The piece is obviously composed for violin.

The fact that no fewer than 36 items in the collection out of a total of 84 (including four unnumbered items) are in D major is the first indication — there are many others — that the transverse flute was the instrument of choice for most of the pieces, although in a few instances the compass is extended at the lower end, or multiple stopping is employed, so as to demand the violin.[13] Each instalment of eight pages contains an assortment of ultra-simple, moderately simple and technically advanced pieces. Continental, British-born and local composers are fairly evenly distributed, as are novelties, 'favourite' pieces and established classics. The number of staves making up a system ranges from two to four (with eight or nine staves to the page), and the space occupied by a single item varies from a single system to two pages. Care has been taken to avoid inconvenient page turns. Quite often, unrelated pieces in the same key (though not always with the same scoring) are juxtaposed, almost as if the compiler wished to invent synthetic suites. The general tone is light, conforming to the recreational spirit of the age and place.

Even though this is a very diverse collection, Geminiani's *Canone* stands apart from its companions in two important respects: it is almost the only piece for three trebles, and one of only very few not classifiable even loosely as an 'air' or a march.[14] This suggests immediately that its inclusion was a matter of topical significance, and even that it was regarded as a specially valued ornament of the collection. It was certainly not a 'favourite' piece of the ordinary kind after the manner of his C minor *Minuet,* for otherwise we would know of it, as we do most of the other movements, from one or more earlier sources. Certainly, one should not take its authenticity absolutely for granted, but the presence of two similarly structured perpetual canons in Geminiani's *Art of Playing the Guitar or Cittra* (shortly to be discussed) is a very strong argument in favour. Was it perhaps a piece acquired not long before from the composer in Edinburgh and presented as a souvenir of the occasion, as if to 'cap' Bremner's publication of the ubiquitous C minor *Minuet?*

To answer this question, we need first to track Geminiani's movements and activities between 1759, when he moved back to Ireland from London, and the very end of 1761 (or perhaps the beginning of 1762) when, if my arguments hold, he returned to Dublin for the last time.

---

[13] The preference for D major is also related to the 'military' character that partly informs the collection.

[14] Its sole counterpart is a short, anonymous perpetual canon in D major for three violins or three flutes on p. 7. This utterly jejune piece, which may have been created especially for the purpose of making Geminiani's canon appear less isolated, does not escape even once from the chord of D major.

There seems no reason to doubt W. H. Grattan Flood's statement that it was in the late spring of 1759 that Geminiani returned to Ireland to take up the post of music master to Sir Charles Coote (1738-1800), the future Earl of Bellamont, whose elegantly Palladian country mansion stood (and still stands) at Cootehill, Co. Cavan.[15] That Geminiani was indeed in the service of Sir Charles by at least the summer of 1759 is proved by an amusing anecdote (to which Flood refers). The witness to the event was the actor Joseph Younger (1734-1784), who, between seasons at Dublin's Crow Theatre, was performing with a group of strolling players in the countryside.[16] Younger persuaded Coote to sponsor a performance in a barn by his troupe of Vanbrugh's comedy *The Provok'd Husband, or A Journey to London*, to which the young nobleman brought a reluctant Geminiani. The performance was rendered ludicrous by the energetic but execrable performance on the 'crowd' (or *cruit*, the Irish name for a fiddle) of an old and blind musician behind the stage. Coote was heartily amused, while Geminiani was mortified, cheering up only when Younger's shoes farcically became stuck in the mud.[17]

According to Flood, Geminiani moved to Dublin in November 1759, this coinciding with a tour by his former pupil and protégé Matthew Dubourg, who resided there.[18] Doubtless, Coote likewise occupied a town residence during the winter. He was a cellist in the Musical Academy founded in Dublin by Garrett Wesley, Lord Mornington, in 1757, and it is likely that through him Geminiani made contact with this body, although its exclusively amateur and well-heeled membership precluded any deep involvement on his part.[19]

On 22 December 1759 *Faulkner's Dublin Journal* announced a forthcoming benefit concert for Geminiani at Neale's Great Musick Room in Fishamble Street,

---

[15] FLOOD, William Henry Grattan. 'Geminiani in England and Ireland', in: *Sammelbände der Internationalen Musikgesellschaft*, XII (1910-1911), pp. 108-112: 111. It is generally recognized that some claims by Flood that today lack documentary confirmation are based on sources no longer extant, but equally that as a historian he was more than usually liable to simple error (for instance, on the previous page he makes Burney, not Hawkins, the author of the statement that Geminiani returned to Ireland in 1761).

[16] The episode is related, doubtless with embroidery, in *Memoirs of Charles Lee Lewes, Containing Anecdotes, Historical and Biographical, of the English and Scottish Stages*, edited by John Lee Lewes, 4 vols, London, Phillips, 1805, vol. I, pp. 213-223. Lewes (1740-1803) — Flood gives his surname incorrectly as 'Lewis' — was an actor, but achieved greater success as an author of books on the acting profession.

[17] See Barra Boydell's essay in the present volume, pp. 159-181.

[18] FLOOD, William Henry Grattan. *Op. cit.* (see note 15), p. 111.

[19] On this music society, see GILBERT, John. *A History of the City of Dublin*, 3 vols, Dublin, McGlashan, 1854-1859, vol. I, pp. 77-81.

where he was to play a 'solo' and a concerto.[20] In the event, the concert, originally planned for 4 February 1760, went ahead only on 3 March, Mary Delany giving on the next day a vivid account of the proceedings, in which she commented on the composer's frail physical state and paid tribute to his "clever management of passages too difficult for him to execute with the spirit he used to do".[21]

Until August 1760, when he turns up in Edinburgh, no further information on Geminiani's whereabouts has surfaced. For all we know, he may have spent time at Cootehill again in the spring and summer. At this point, we need to consider why Geminiani, for whom, as a septuagenarian, travel must have become an arduous business, conceived the plan of visiting Edinburgh and later London. In view of what we know about his activities in those two cities, it is a reasonable hypothesis that the twin 'pegs' on which he hung those visits, and the whole circular tour Dublin - Edinburgh - Newcastle - London - Dublin, were the publication of his *Art of Playing the Guitar or Cittra* in Edinburgh and of as many as three items (the *Two Concertos*, *The Enchanted Forest* and the second collection of *Pièces de clavecin*) in London. A study of the chronology of known events occurring during this tour suggests that Geminiani had time to deliver the manuscripts to the publisher and stay around long enough (except in the case of the last publication) to read proofs and take delivery of the result. Around this essential business various other professional and social activities took their place.

Bremner, who must have been keen to augment his list of works published for this newly fashionable instrument played not only by himself but also by his two sons, invited subscriptions to *The Art of Playing the Guitar or Cittra* on 12 July 1760, completing publication just before his advertisement of 26 November 1760.[22] Geminiani may not yet have reached Edinburgh at the time of the opening of subscriptions, but he was certainly there before 5 August, when the Edinburgh Musical Society recorded in its minutes the payment to him of £1-2-6 "By Expences with Mr. Geminiani & the Masters in the tavern Trying over his music".[23] The "Masters" were the professional

---

[20]   See *CARERI*, p. 43.

[21]   *The Autobiography and Correspondence of Mary Granville, Mrs. Delany*, edited by Lady Llanover (Augusta Hall), 6 vols, London, Bentley, 1861-1862, vol. III, pp. 586-587, quoted in *CARERI*, p. 43.

[22]   These dates were ascertained by Andrew Woolley for Peter Holman, editor of the forthcoming critical edition of *Art of Playing the Guitar or Cittra* (*Geminiani Opera Omnia*, vol. 16). I should like to thank the first scholar for permission to use the data, and the second scholar for letting me have sight of his draft introduction.

[23]   See TINAGLI BAXTER, Sonia. *Italian Music and Musicians in Edinburgh c. 1720-1800. A Historical and Critical Study*, Ph.D. Diss., 2 vols, University of Glasgow, 1999, vol. I, p. 48. This dissertation can be downloaded from the EThOS website of the British Library.

musicians retained by the society; the "tavern", *faute de mieux*, was the most suitable rehearsal space prior to the building of St Cecilia's Hall; the particular music rehearsed is not identified, but could well have been the *Two Concertos* (H. 124-125) written austerely in only two real parts (violins in unison and violas doubling the bass instruments) or even the suites formed from the music for *The Enchanted Forest*, neither of which Edinburgh had yet heard. On 11 August the society paid Geminiani £10-10-0 for unspecified "concertos".[24] This seems a surprisingly large sum, but if works from a number of different collections or multiple sets of parts were involved, it is not disproportionate. The *Two Concertos*, so unusual — indeed, probably unique — in their scoring, would certainly have conformed excellently to the needs of an amateur body possessing a large membership of mixed ability. Did Geminiani, one wonders, put his predilection for group teaching to the test with them in Edinburgh? Were these strange but musically very attractive concertos actually custom-written for the Edinburgh Musical Society?[25]

Geminani evidently lingered on in Edinburgh until late December — perhaps he was kept busy teaching (remembering that Bremner was a possible pupil) — but an anonymous letter published in *The Newcastle Journal* for 20-27 December 1760 confirms that he broke the journey to London in Newcastle, staying with his friend and former pupil Charles Avison and listening with admiration to the harpsichord playing of Avison's son Edward (1747-1776).[26]

How soon afterwards Geminiani reached London is uncertain. The first hint of his presence there is an advertisement placed in the *Public Advertiser* for 3, 10 and 11 April 1761 giving notice of a benefit concert at the concert room in Dean Street for "Signora Gambarini" — this was the admired singer and composer Elisabetta de Gambarini (1731-1765), a native of London — featuring as principal work *The Enchanted Forest*.[27] Presumably, Geminiani

---

[24]   *Ibidem.*

[25]   One must concede, however, that they would have been equally well suited to the Musical Academy in Dublin. But their connection with amateur music-making can hardly be questioned.

[26]   See SOUTHEY, Roz. *Commercial Music-Making in Eighteenth-Century North-East England: A Pale Reflection of London?*, Ph.D. Diss., 2 vols, University of Newcastle, 2001, vol. I, pp. 112-113. This thesis is not currently available on the EThOS website, but is published by the University of Newcastle at <https://theses.ncl.ac.uk/dspace/bitstream/10443/202/1/southey01v1.pdf> and <https://theses.ncl.ac.uk/dspace/bitstream/10443/202/1/southey01v2.pdf>.

[27]   To my knowledge, this performance has not been mentioned before in modern literature. No other performance of *The Enchanted Forest* is known to have taken place in Britain during the eighteenth century.

directed at least his own composition. The announcement describes him as "lately returned to England". If by "England" London is really meant (and it is hard to imagine special note being taken of the date of Geminiani's crossing into England from Scotland!), we have a hint that he arrived in London around March 1761, having wintered in Newcastle.

John Johnson, the publisher for whom the three remaining works after the guitar collection were destined, had been Geminiani's London publisher of choice since 1739, when he produced a second edition of the Op. 4 sonatas. His activity came to an end before 29 May 1761, when his widow announced in the *Public Advertiser* that, contrary to rumour, she was continuing her late husband's business. So the publication of the undated *Two Concertos* has to be fitted into a time-frame between summer 1760 and spring 1761. *The Enchanted Forest*, similarly undated, probably followed closely on its heels. As Careri notes, an autograph manuscript of this work (Royal College of Music, MS 822) was donated by Geminiani to James Mathias on 7 December 1761.[28] Mathias (1709/10-1782) was a merchant, amateur singer and keen collector of music who resided in London, and Geminiani's present makes sense only as a parting gift, the prime purposes of the manuscript (as printer's copy and, before that, as an *originale* from which to prepare manuscript orchestral parts) having been accomplished.[29] Both Burney ("about 1756")[30] and Hawkins ("around the same time [1755]"),[31] followed by more recent writers, place the date of publication much earlier — close, in fact, to the Parisian premiere of the pantomime. But these look like tentative guesses. The arguments in favour of publication in 1761 are much stronger. Geminiani would hardly have travelled to London with an autograph manuscript of *The Enchanted Forest* in his luggage unless this was for some special reason, and it was absolutely normal, in London musical life, for concert or staged performance of a longer work to be complemented soon afterwards by the engraving of

---

[28] *CARERI*, p. 113. Geminiani and Mathias may have become acquainted at the Academy of Ancient Music, of which both were members. See WEBER, William. *Op. cit.* (see note 1), pp. 72-73. On Mathias, see the obituary published in *The Gentleman's Magazine*, LII (1782), p. 311. Unlike the major part of Mathias' collection, which passed after his death to the British Museum, the autograph manuscript of *The Enchanted Forest* came into the possession of Benjamin Cooke Jr (1734-1793), at that time conductor of the Academy of Ancient Music. The Sacred Harmonic Society bought Cooke's collection from his heirs in 1845, and the Royal College of Music acquired it in 1883 following that society's dissolution.

[29] It is possible that the performance in Dean Street was able to employ the engraved parts, but this presupposes that Geminiani arrived in London closer to the start of the year.

[30] *BURNEY*, IV, p. 643.

[31] *HAWKINS*, V, p. 423.

the music.[32] To have published this 'concert' version of *The Enchanted Forest* in London in advance of April 1761 would have been contrary to custom and commercially risky.

Time was too short, alas, for Johnson to bring out the harpsichord pieces; this task was left to his widow, who issued them under her own name in 1762.

It was probably soon after 7 December 1761 that Geminiani undertook his homeward journey to Dublin. Hawkins' statement that he "went over" to Ireland in 1761, which has in the past seemed aberrant since it ignored his employment with Coote in 1759, may in fact be perfectly correct, referring to this second homecoming.[33] A letter to *The Newcastle Courant* for 17 September 1768 states that Geminiani's "last Excursion was from Edinburgh, by Newcastle and London, to the City of Dublin", so it does not appear that he tarried on the way back from London.[34]

The canon in the Stewart anthology fits into this eventful period as an occasional piece: a kind of musical visiting card. It is not out of the question that Geminiani had composed it already in Dublin for the Musical Academy (on whose programmes catches formed a staple ingredient) before his sojourn in Edinburgh, but given that such spontaneous, ephemeral pieces are by their nature unsuitable candidates for travel, it is far more probable that it came into being in the same city where it was shortly afterwards published. It could even have been solicited especially by Stewart, but its atypical nature within the collection argues against this. My surmise is that Geminiani wrote it for some amateur player or players, most likely members of the Musical Society, who later passed it on to Stewart for publication and preservation. Typically for the amateur repertory, Stewart's collection allows the treble instruments to be violins, flutes or oboes without distinction. Looking at the canon, the timbre and aesthetic of the flute seem far better suited to its *galant* and lilting manner than those of either the violin or the oboe. This was, after all, the heyday of the flute — a time when it almost seemed that this compact, highly portable instrument would supplant the violin as the 'gentleman's' instrument *par excellence*.

---

[32] This point is developed in TALBOT, Michael. '*The Golden Pippin* and the Extraordinary Adventures in Britain and Ireland of Vivaldi's Concerto RV 519', in: *Studi vivaldiani*, X (2010), pp. 87-124: p. 90n. It is conceivable that the musicians played from previously published parts, while Geminiani used his score simply for the purposes of rehearsal and direction, but this possibility seems to me more remote.

[33] *HAWKINS*, V, pp. 424-425.

[34] For the quotation, I am indebted to Peter Holman, who first made me aware of it, and to Roz Southey, who had earlier communicated it privately to him.

What is most interesting about Geminiani's unison canon is its hybrid nature. It is neither a repetitive circular canon (a wordless catch suitable for notation either as a single, continuous line or in the equally compact form of a score showing the disposition of the voices immediately after the final entry) nor a through-composed, finite canon (perhaps with a *da capo* repeat and a central modulation or two) in the manner of Telemann's *Canons mélodieux* (written for two similar instruments without bass) or the fast movements in the sonatas of Albinoni's Op. 8 (for two violins and 'free' bass part).[35] It derives the property of circularity from the first tradition, but the short time-interval between entries, the continuous thematic evolution and the idea of a central modulation from the second.

Ex. 1: *A Canon at the Unison for 3 Voices*, published in BREMNER, Robert. *The Rudiments of Music*, Edinburgh, Bremner, 1762.

Ex. 1, taken from Bremner's *Rudiments of Music*, illustrates the characteristic catch structure, even though in deference to its context and sacred words it is given the more decorous denomination of canon.[36] The three voices enter successively at the interval of ten bars, and the conclusion, after the desired

---

[35]   The high point of this tradition is the third movement of J. S. Bach's sonata for violin and obbligato harpsichord BWV 1015, which even manages to reintroduce the opening theme in a different key.

[36]   BREMNER, Robert. *Op. cit.* (see note 9), p. 64 of the music supplement.

number of repetitions,[37] may be either in all voices at once or 'tapered', according to the wish of the performers. Ironically, the object of the use of canon in such a piece is the very reverse of contrapuntal sophistication: rather, it is musical compactness, simplicity of utterance and kindness towards performers (since whoever has mastered the first voice has already learnt all the others as well). Bremner himself introduces his readers to the style in the following words,[38] which prefigure very closely the description given in Rousseau's *Dictionary*.[39]

Of CANON *or* CATCH.

A *Canon* or *Catch* in the Unison is performed by three or more *Voices*, each following one another at certain Distances: For *Example*, the first *Voice* begins the Piece alone; and by the Time that he has sung to the first *double Bar*, or *Repeat*, then the *second Voice* takes up the Piece also from the Beginning, the first still going on; and after the second voice has sung to the first *double Bar* or *Repeat*, the *third Voice* begins; and at this Distance they follow one another throughout the Piece, which they may sing over without stopping, as often as they please.

Ex. 2: Opening of Geminiani's *Canone*.

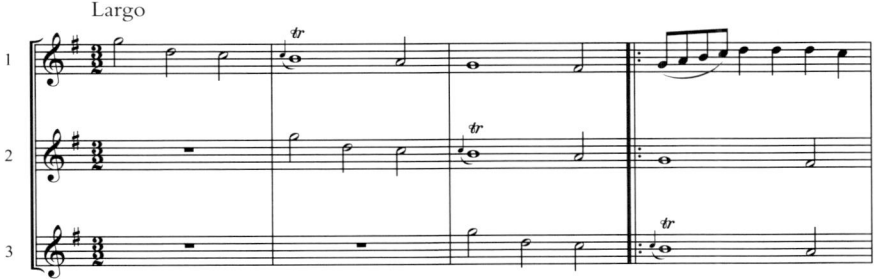

The second kind of unison canon can be illustrated directly from Geminiani's composition, which, apart from being circular and employing three rather than the two canonic voices more usual in instrumental music, is fairly conventionally structured. The complete canon is transcribed in single-line form as an appendix to this essay. Its opening, shown in score as Ex. 2, establishes its *galant* credentials immediately in the second bar. The short time-interval (one

---

[37]   Bremner notates the canon in single-line fashion, ending each ten-bar strain with a double barline.

[38]   BREMNER, Robert. *Op. cit.* (see note 9), p. 42.

[39]   ROUSSEAU, Jean-Jacques. *The Complete Dictionary of Music*, second edition translated by William Waring, London, French and others, [1779], p. 51.

bar) between entries is compositionally restrictive and inevitably makes for a bell-like oscillation between a few (in this instance, only two) harmonies. This potential weakness is commented on by Rousseau, who aptly observes:[40]

> To compose a canon where harmony may be a little varied, the parts must not follow each other too suddenly, and one must not enter till sometime after the other. When they follow one another with such velocity, as, at a pause, or demi-pause, there is no time for making several concords pass, and the canon cannot fail of being monotonous.

In fact, imitation at a bar's distance, and the resulting harmonic repetitiveness, can, through the composer's skill, be made musically quite appealing, as examples by Telemann and Albinoni (the opening movement in his Op. 8) show. However, the effect is improved if, in the middle of the piece, the tonality momentarily switches to one or more foreign keys, in particular the dominant (for a major-key movement). The technique for achieving this is very simple. The composition naturally moves forward in units equal in length to the time-interval between entries. That is, the first unit is written in Voice 1; it is immediately transferred to Voice 2, and a continuation-cum-counterpoint is written in Voice 1 as the second unit; this second unit is then transferred to Voice 2, and the first unit to Voice 3; and so on. To modulate, therefore, all one needs to do is to create a new unit or pair of units compatible harmonically with both the key of departure and the key of arrival. In Ex. 3, which shows bars 12-16 of Geminiani's *Canone*, the note A in bar 12 of voice 1 can function either in the dominant chord of G major or the tonic chord of D major; similarly, the note D in bar 13 (followed by rests that, as the cynic says, always make good harmony) exists within both the dominant chord of G and the tonic chord of D. The result is that the new unit arriving in bar 14 is able to sharpen the note C and effect the modulation. The return to G major in bars 21-24 is achieved by similar means.

Ex. 3: Bars 12-16 of Geminiani's *Canone*.

---

[40]   *Ibidem*, p. 53.

The other conventional task for the writer of extended unison canons is to introduce a reprise of the opening, which serves to counteract the natural tendency of canons towards thematic diffuseness. In Geminiani's case, unusually, this becomes a device for achieving circularity, whereas for most other composers (Telemann, Albinoni and J. S. Bach are cases in point) the *da capo* repeat is allowed to progress only up to a certain point before the piece concludes. Ex. 4 gives the last six bars of the canon. In preparation for the return of his opening theme, Geminiani has reduced the harmony to elaborations of a G major chord, and this, together with a generous dose of rests, allows the opening material to make a splendid return, revitalizing the by now slightly flagging musical discourse.

Ex. 4: Bars 41-46 of Geminiani's *Canone*.

Even if it does not turn out to be the last composition Geminiani ever completed, this rather undistinguished, if pleasant, canon is a welcome addition to the composer's 'canon' (in the other sense of the word) because it shows a different facet of the way in which he became acclimatized to the British environment. Like his Scottish songs, it represents a type of composition that could only have been written in these islands. But — looking at the question from another direction — it could only have been written by an Italian immigrant, or at least by a native composer well versed in Italian ways. So it is hybrid in national character as well as in musical structure.

There obviously remain many uncertainties about the exact way in which this little piece fits into the biography of Geminiani's last few years. But its connection with Edinburgh and the composer's visit there in 1760 seems more than probable. In its turn, this visit needs to be viewed in the wider context of Geminiani's surprisingly ambitious British tour of 1760-1761. The canon is a small detail in the fascinating picture of the composer as he neared the end of his life — still active, despite the physical difficulties observed by Mary Delany; still desirous of recognition; and, above all, still 'sociable'.

APPENDIX

GEMINIANI'S *CANONE* TRANSCRIBED IN SINGLE-LINE FORM

"The Road to Emulation": Geminiani's Elliptical Instructions

Peter Walls
(Wellington, NZ)

THE PREFACE TO GEMINIANI'S 1752 *L'Art de Jouer le Violon* provides early feedback on the reception given to *The Art of Playing on the Violin* (henceforth *APV*), published the preceding year:

> Allow me, before concluding, to respond to a reasonably widespread and somewhat plausible objection that is inherently quite misguided: it is said that I have given precepts for those who already play the instrument rather than for beginners; I submit, on the contrary, that the latter are precisely at the point where nature has need of art; they are much more ready to derive profit from this than the others, not having any bad habits to overcome, free, open-minded, and without fear and in an open field able to take the right path; they wouldn't know how to place obstacles in the way of progress that good rules inspire.[1]

From a modern standpoint, Geminiani's claims might seem disingenuous: how, really, could a beginner use *APV* to learn how to play the violin? The dizzying acceleration from basics to advanced techniques, with so much left out along the way, renders the treatise impractical for the novice. Hence, the judgement of history has tended to side with the unnamed critics whose views

---

[1] "Qu'il me soit permis, avant de finir, de répondre à une Objection assez générale, & quoique plausible, très-fausse en elle-même: on prétend que j'ai donné plutôt des préceptes pour ceux qui possedent déja l'instrument que pour les commençans; & je soutiens au contraire, que ceux-ci étant précisément au point où la Nature a besoin de l'Art, ils sont beaucoup plus à portée d'en profiter que les autres, n'ayant aucune mauvaise habitude à vaincre, libres, francs, & sans timidité, & en plein champ d'entrer dans la vraie route, ils ne sçauroient manquer d'y faire les progrès que les bonnes Regles inspirent". (All translations in this essay unless otherwise specified are by the author.)

are captured in Geminiani's French preface.[2] But posterity has not regarded Geminiani's failure to cater for novices as a negative. *APV* has been acclaimed as having broken new ground in addressing advanced violinists. David Boyden summed up the achievement of *APV* as "one of the first mature expositions of violin playing. Within the scope of its relatively few pages is covered quite completely the technical groundwork necessary to cope with almost any violinistic problem of its time".[3]

Something of Geminiani's genuine originality can be seen by looking at *APV* in the context of its antecedents. While these are mostly crudely amateur, mention needs to be made of the very sophisticated sections on the violin in those two great 17th-century musical encyclopaedias, Michael Praetorius's *Syntagma Musicum* (1617) and Marin Mersenne's *Harmonie Universelle* (1636). But, I use the term 'encyclopaedia' advisedly: neither Praetorius nor Mersenne have as their primary aim the instruction of practical musicians. Instead, they use their knowledge of acoustics, organology, composition and performance to document in great detail what could be established about contemporary and historical performance. Seen in this light, it seems safe to say that there are no genuine antecedents for *APV* as a volume addressed to performers wanting assistance with questions of technique and style relevant to idiomatic and even virtuoso repertoire for the violin.

Given the dual publication of *APV* in London and Paris, it seems appropriate to focus primarily on English and French pedagogical traditions. The earliest English-language manual was John Playford *An Introduction to the Skill of Musick*, which, from its second edition of 1658 onwards included "Instructions for the Treble Violin". In 1694, Thomas Cross published *Nolens Volens, or You shall learn to play the Violin whether you will or no*. This formed the basis, first, of another similar volume entitled *The Self-Instructor on the Violin or the Art of Playing on that Instrument* (1695) and then, 36 years later, was appropriated virtually word-for-word as "The Art of Playing on the Violin" in Peter Prelleur's *Modern Musick Master*. John Lenton's *Gentleman's Diversion, or the Violin Explained* appeared in 1694, the same year as *Nolens Volens*, and was then liberally quarried by "T. B." for the section on "Directions for Playing on the Violin" in *The Compleat Musick Master* (1722).[4] Given the degree of often

---

[2] This criticism that *APV* was unsuitable for beginners continued, most interestingly in JOUSSE, Jean. *The Theory and Practice of the Violin*, London, Birchall, 1811; see STOWELL, Robin. 'The Contribution of Geminiani's *The Art of Playing on the Violin* to "The Improved State of the Violin in England"', in this volume, pp. 257-300.

[3] BOYDEN, David. 'Preface', in: GEMINIANI, Francesco. *The Art of Playing on the Violin*, London, s.n., 1751, facsimile edition, London, Oxford University Press, [1952], p. v.

[4] In ID. 'Geminiani and the First Violin Tutor', in: *Acta Musicologica*, XXXI/3-4 (July-December 1959), pp. 168-170, Boyden provides a "Bibliography of treatises devoted in whole

overt plagiarism in this group of instruction manuals, we can cover the ground by focusing on three: (i) Playford, (ii) *Nolens Volens*/Prelleur, and (iii) Lenton.

The restricted ambitions of Playford's Instructions are clear from its opening sentence: "The *Treble-Violin* is a cheerful and spritely Instrument, and much practised of late, some by *Book*, and some *without* [...]". It then proceeds to a discussion of the advantages of being able to read music rather than simply playing by ear. As a reward for the reader's endeavours, the volume ends with a set of simple, popular "Tunes for the Treble Violin, by Letters and Note". Besides offering a rudimentary tablature (playing "by Letters") as an alternative to stave notation, Playford recommends that the violin be fitted with six frets like a viol, which, "though it be not usual, yet it is the best and easiest way for a Beginner who has a bad ear". The tunes — "Glory of the North", "Maiden Fair", "Step Stately", "Parthenia" and "The King's Delight" — never leave first position and, in fact, never once utilise the G string. They are followed by a set of four, similarly basic, Sarabands and then one slightly more ambitious piece, a set of divisions on "John Come Kiss Me Now", after which a note advises, "For Books of more Lessons for the Violin see in the Catalogue at the end of the Book".[5]

The title page of *Nolens Volens* likewise makes it clear that this little book is directed at beginners with limited musical horizons:

> *Nolens Volens*, or You shall learn to play the Violin whether you will or no. Being an new Introduction for the instruction of young Practitioners on that Delightful Instrument. Digested in a more plain and easy method than any yet extant [...].

The musical appendix to *Nolens Volens* is rather more advanced than that in Playford's "Instructions". There are slightly longer, more elaborate tunes, though none are technically difficult and, again, the G string is not utilised. For the most part, these popular tunes are drawn from similar stock to those chosen by Playford. Given Geminiani's use of Scottish melodies as the basis for so many of the compositions in the *Rules* and *Treatise*, it is interesting to see four "Scotch" tunes included in *Nolens Volens*. Only one of these (Ex. 1) has any of the melodic characteristics thought (in the eighteenth century anyway) to characterize such repertory: a mode that lacks a leading note in its nearest

---

or in part to violin instruction published in England 1658-1731".

[5]   Davis Mell and Thomas Baltzar both also wrote sets of divisions on this popular tune. Both (particularly those by Baltzar) are more challenging technically than the set in Playford's *Introduction*. See HOLMAN, Peter. 'Thomas Baltzar (?1631-1663), the "Incomperable *Luciber* on the Violin"', in: *Chelys*, XIII (1984), pp. 3-38.

diatonic scale equivalent and reverse dotted groups of the kind that came to be known as Scotch snaps. The "Suite of Ayres Made by Mr Courtville" with which the volume concludes, like Playford's divisions on "John Come Kiss Me Now", seems to be a point of entry into a more advanced musical environment. The Suite begins with a fully-fledged French Overture.

Ex. 1: *Nolens Volens*, p. [23], No. 26, "Scotch Tune".

TABLE 1

OPERA ARIAS FEATURED IN PRELLEUR'S "ART OF PLAYING ON THE VIOLIN", 1731

Minuet in Rodelinda	Handel, *Rodelinda*, 1725; revived 1731
A Favourite Air in the Opera of Siroe	Handel, *Siroe*, 1728
Air by Mr Handel in Julius Caesar	Handel, *Giulio Cesare*,1724; revived 1730 (and 1732)
Un lampo e la speranza	Handel, *Admeto*, 1727
In the Opera of Admetus | Si caro si in Admetus	Handel, *Admeto*, 1727
A Favourite Air in the Opera of Rodelinda	Handel, *Rodelinda*, 1725; revived 1731
Aure portate by Mr Handel in Ptolomy	Handel, *Tolomeo*, 1728
Air by Mr Bononcini in Astyanax	Bononcini, *Astianatte,* 1727
Air in Astyanax	Bononcini, *Astianatte,* 1727
A Favourite Air in Rhadamistus	Handel, *Radamisto*, 1720-1; revived 1728
A Favourite Air in the Opera of Rodelinda	Handel, *Rodelinda*, 1725; revived 1731

A Favourite Song in the Opera of Admetus	Handel, *Rodelinda*, 1725; revived 1731
A Favourite Air in Admetus	Handel, *Rodelinda*, 1725; revived 1731
A Favourite Air in the Opera of Tamerlano	Handel, *Tamerlano*, 1724; revived 1731
A Favourite Air in Siroe by Mr Handel	Handel, *Siroe*, 1728
A Favourite Air in the Opera of Siroe	Handel, *Siroe*, 1728
Furibondo in ye Opera of Parthenope	Handel, *Partenope*, 1730

Although the text is virtually identical to *Nolens Volens*, Prelleur's *Modern Musick-Master* provides its readers with much more challenging practice material. It shifts its focus, too, away from tunes that might loosely be regarded as folk tunes to — doubtless equally popular — hits from the Italian operas that had been staged in London in the years immediately leading up to publication (see TABLE 1). These compositions require a more advanced technique than those in Playford or *Nolens Volens*. In fact, they need a far more advanced technique than is envisaged in the written section of Prelleur's volume. One third of the pieces move beyond first position and they exploit the full range of the instrument (with seven including notes on the G string). Many demand considerable dexterity, with continuous semiquaver passages involving string crossing (see Ex. 2).

Ex. 2: Prelleur, *Modern Musick Master*, p. 47, "Furibondo in yᵉ Opera of Parthenope", bb. 51-63.

In each case, the musical content of these treatises cater to the tastes of the imagined user. The pieces are, presumably, intended as examples for practice, but there is an element of reward here, too ('observe my method, and look at what you will be able to play'). It is interesting to follow what these instruction manuals have to say on just two very basic but related issues: how to hold the violin and the function of the left-hand thumb, since this gives us two noteworthy points of comparison with Geminiani.

Playford begins in a way that (as with his openness to the use of frets) gives us a glimpse of the violin being taken up by amateur players with no idea even that it should be treated differently from a treble viol:

> First, The *Violin* is usually plaid above-hand, the Neck thereof being held by the left hand; the lower part thereof is rested on the left breast, a little below the shoulder [...].

What he has to say about the left-hand thumb is brief, unhelpful in its lack of specificity, and puzzling, given that none of the tunes in the volume ever require shifting away from first position:

> [...] place your Thumb on the back of the Neck, opposite to your forefinger, so will your fingers have the more liberty to move up and down in the several Stops.

Nolens Volens/Prelleur say nothing about how the violin should be held (though the latter has a frontispiece showing a player holding the instrument under his chin). But the role of the left hand in supporting the instrument is described in a way that suggests very little mobility (with the neck of the violin resting in the join between index finger and thumb). Indeed, nothing is said about shifting in *Nolens Volens*, though a fourth-finger extension to C on the E string (needed just once in the musical examples contained in the volume)[6] is countenanced:

> Hold the *Violin* with your left Hand, about half an inch from the bottom of its Head, which is usually termed the Nut, and let it lie between the root of your Thumb and that of your fore-finger [...].
>
> The 1ˢᵗ treble, or least string hath six Notes usually appropriated thereto [...] and lastly to stop *C sol fa ut* you must

---

6   In the Overture by Courtville.

stretch your little finger about a quarter of an inch farther than
you did for *B-fa-be-mi*.

(The title page of Prelleur's republication of this text makes false claims
in promising to show "how to stop every Note, Flat or Sharp, exactly in
Tune, and where the Shifts of the Hand should be made".)

John Lenton's *Gentleman's Diversion* is by far the most interesting of the
early English treatises.[7] Lenton was, in fact, a professional violinist — a member
(from 1681) of Charles II's Twenty-Four Violins.[8] In outline and much of its
content his treatise is not radically different from the other manuals. In fact,
it participates in the kind of intertextuality that might now result in lawsuits.
Where that is not the case, it is more colourfully written and reflects a level of
observation of what advanced violinists were doing that suggests a seriousness
of purpose. There is, in fact, a slightly contemptuous-sounding marginal gloss
at the end of the section "Of Bowing in Tripla Movements" that reads, "What
I have said in relation to Bowing, is in Relation to a Gentile manner of Musical
performance, those who perform to the Foot I leave to their own discretion".
The section that most distinguishes Lenton's treatise from rival
publications is "Of ordering the Bow and Instrument". Here we encounter
a practising violinist who combines a sense of personal modesty — "What I
have else to say, will be (by way of advice) my own opinion" — with strong
views about the methods adopted by other players:

> [...] as I would have none get a habit of holding an Instrument
> under the Chin, so I would have them avoid placing it as low
> as the Girdle, which is a mongrel sort of way us'd by some in
> imitation of the *Italians*, never considering the Nature of the
> Musick they are to perform.

Given that there is no evidence that Italians in general held the violin as
low as their girdles, Lenton must surely be complaining about the corrupting
influence of Nicola Matteis, whom Roger North described as holding his
violin down by his "short ribs".[9] Lenton continues

---

[7]   Regrettably, the only known extant copy lacks the title page and the first two pages of
text. See Boyd, Malcolm - Rayson, John. 'The Gentleman's Diversion: John Lenton and the
First Violin Tutor', in: *Early Music*, x/3 (1982), pp. 329-332.

[8]   Holman, Peter. *Four and Twenty Fiddlers: The Violin at the English Court 1540-1690*,
Oxford, Clarendon Press, 1993, p. 355.

[9]   See Wilson, John. *Roger North on Music*, London, Novello, 1959, p. 309 and n.

[…] but certainly for *English* Compositions, which generally carry a gay lively Air with them, the best way of commanding the Instrument will be to place it something higher than your Breast, your Fingers found and firm in stopping, not bending your joynts inward, and when you make a Shake let it be from the motion of the Finger alone, and not from any Squeeze of the Body or Wrist (except) it be a close Shake which is done by the consent and operation of all the Fingers.

While we might lament the lack of precision in a phrase like "something higher than your Breast", there is a stronger sense here than we ever find in Playford or Prelleur of the importance of a well-formed, relaxed left hand — one, moreover, that will need to be able to produce a relaxed vibrato (the close shake) from time to time.

What he has to say about management of the bow is similarly concerned with the development of fine motor skills:

[…] let your Bow be as long as your Instrument, well mounted and stiff Hair'd, it will otherwise totter upon the String in drawing a long stroke; hold it with your Thumb half under the Nutt, half under the Hair from the Nutt, and let it rest upon the middle of the first joynt, place all your fingers upon the Bow, pretty close, (or for the better guiding of it) you may place the out-side of the first joynt of the little Finger against the Wood, let the Bow move always within an inch of the Bridge directly forward and backward, let your Bow-wrist move loosly, (but nor much bent), and hold not up your Elbow, more than necessity requires.

This is the voice of a player/teacher who evinces a physical sense of how the bow must feel, and it captures two interesting historical details: first, the thumb is situated beneath the frog, not on the stick, and second, the elbow is to be kept low (a position that prevailed right through the nineteenth century).

For whom was Lenton writing? For all that there is considerable overlap in his treatise with the contents (and even the wording) of the other beginners' manuals, Lenton communicates a seriousness of purpose, a desire to help violinists develop a technique that will be genuinely serviceable. The Italians' approach to violin playing, he writes, "(in it self,) is the best manner in the World", but his explicit interest is in encouraging violinists to perform the music of his English confreres well and in an appropriate style. Interestingly, he makes oblique and passing reference to the rich ensemble repertoire available in late seventeenth-century England: "Stand or Sit upright, beware of unseemly actions, &c. The Time you beat let it be to your self, unless in Consort you are desired by the rest of the company".

Instead of the selection of popular tunes that normally conclude tutors of this kind, Lenton has provided a set of original compositions that he introduces by writing, "in hopes of rendring this undertaking the more acceptable to you, I have prevailed with several of the most Eminent Masters to adorn my Book with some Easie Lessons in Two Parts, made purposely upon this occasion, not wholly depending upon my own sufficiency". There are 28 pieces in total, nine by Lenton himself and the rest by colleagues.[10] The collection ends with a Prelude by "Mr Nicola"; this, too, seems to have been composed at Lenton's request, since it is not one of those included in Matteis' four volumes of *Ayrs*.

Taking text and practice pieces together, one could summarize the position of these various treatises as follows:
• Playford: a user-guide for absolute beginners with no aspirations to play more than very simple tunes.
• *Nolens Volens*: a rudimentary manual, perhaps not even written by a competent violinist, for those who may wish to work at slightly more difficult material in order to progress beyond a very elementary technique.
• Lenton: a thoughtful volume written by a violinist with a specific desire to equip learners to play the music of Purcell and his contemporaries.
• Prelleur's *Modern Musick Master*: a manual that promises far more in the music it provides than the text could possibly deliver.

The character and scope of the music included in each treatise give a fair indication of the target audience for each (see TABLE 2).

All, however, are clearly addressed to beginners and all adhere to a standard template. Although the order varies, all cover the following topics:

1. Topography of the fingerboard
2. Rudiments of music theory
3. Instructions on tuning the violin
4. Holding the violin and bow
5. Bowing rules
6. Ornamentation

Nolens Volens/Prelleur include a full-size (fold out) drawing of the violin fingerboard with notes and fingering indicated. The reader is encouraged to transfer markings from this to the fingerboard itself, if necessary moving the

---

[10]　See BOYD, Malcolm - RAYSON, John. *Op. cit.* (see note 7), p. 331.

TABLE 2

MUSICAL CONTENT OF EARLY ENGLISH VIOLIN TREATISES

PLAYFORD, *A Brief Introduction to the Skill of Musick* (1658)	*Nolens Volens* (1694)	LENTON, *The Gentleman's Diversion, or the Violin Explained* (1694)		PRELLEUR, *The Art of Playing on the Violin* (1731)
Tunes for the Treble Violin, by Letters and Notes	[...] *Together with a choice Collection of Ayrs compos'd by ye most Ingenious Masters of the Age.*	[...] *I have prevailed with several of the most Eminent Masters to adorn my Book with some Easie Lessons in Two Parts, made purposely upon this occasion, not wholly depending upon my own sufficiency.*		[TP] "[...] *To which is added A Collection of the finest Rigadoons, Almands, Sarabands, Courants, & Opera Airs extant*"
Glory of the North★	A Soldier and a Sailor	1	Mr P	Minuet
Maiden Fair★	Minuet	2	Mr P	Rigadoon
Step Stately★	The Duke of Gloucester's March	3		Minuet
Parthenia★	Minuet	4	Mr Forcer	Rigadoon
Freeman's Dance★	Borée	5	Mr Keller	Minuet
The Kings Delight★	Prince Lewis's March	6	Mr Williams	Minuet in Rodelinda
Sarabands (4)	Minuet	7		*The following Minuets by the most Eminent Masters* (9)
John Come Kiss with Division to each Strain	Minuet	8	Mr Banister	Rigadoon
	Jigg	9		Saraband by Sr Albinoni
	Oh! Fye what mean I foolish Maid	10	Mr King	Gavot by Sr Albinoni
	Ye Nymphs and Sylvan Gods	11	Mr S Eccles	Air by Sigr Masciti
	Young I am and yet unskill'd	12	Mr S Eccles	Air by Mr St Helene
★*tunes in tablature and staff notation*	A play house tune	13	Mr Crouch	Minuet
	Minuet	14	Mr H Eccles	Rigadoon
	Hornpipe	15	Mr J Eccles	Rigadoon
	Ayre	16	Mr Purcell	A Favourite Air in the Opera of Siroe
	A Scotch Tune	17	Mr Akeroyd	Air by Mr Handel in Julius Caesar
	Ayre	18	"on a Ground" J. L. [John Lenton]	Un lampo e la speranza
	Damon let a friend advise ye	19	J. L. [John Lenton]	In the Opera of Admetus	Si caro si in Admetus

	No.		
A Scotch Tune	20		A Favourite Air in the Opera of Rodelinda
Round O	21	J. L.	Minuet
Ayre	22	Duo treb & Base	Rigadoon
Horn Pipe	23	Duo 2 viol. J. L. [John Lenton]	Aure portate by Mr Handel in Ptolomy
Air	24	Duo 2 Viol	Air by Mr Bononcini in Astyanax
Horn Pipe	25	Duo 2 Viol J. L.	Air in Astyanax
Twas early one morning	26	2 in one Mr Collett	A Favourite Air in Rhadamistus
Minuet	27	Duo 2 viol J. L.	A Favourite Air in the Opera of Rodelinda
Borée	28	Prelude Mr Nicola	A Favourite Song in the Opera of Admetus
A Scotch Tune			A Favourite Air in Admetus
Scotch Tune			A Favourite Air in the Opera of Tamerlano
Horn Pipe			A Favourite Air in Siroe by Mr Handel
New Spanish Jigg			A Favourite Air in the Opera of Siroe
Jigg			Minuet
A Suite of Ayres Made by Mr Courtville			Rigadoon
Overture			Minuet
March			Minuet
Minuet			Furibondo in ye Opera of Parthenope
A Grave Ayre			
Jigg			

bridge to ensure that the vibrating string length exactly matches the diagram. Lenton originally included a similar diagram (and includes the same advice on moving the bridge.

The sections on rudiments merge with those on topography to the extent that explanations of diatonic or chromatic scales are always accompanied by basic first-position fingering for the notes.

The bowing rules all adhere strictly to the rule of the down-bow (though that expression is not used). *Nolens Volens*/Prelleur and Lenton both have separate sections on the method of bowing in (i) common time and (ii) triple time. The sections on ornamentation all describe what Playford (borrowing from Christopher Simpson) and *Nolens Volens*/Prelleur call "the usual graces".

One other aspect of these beginner manuals deserves comment: they often declare their own limits through disclaimers. This is most obvious in the treatment of bowing rules. *Nolens Volens*/Prelleur preface their discussion of this issue in the following way:

> It is difficult to lay down any certain Rules for yᵉ Use of
> yᵉ Bow by reason the direction of divers Masters and yᵉ Methods
> of Practioners are very different: nevertheless it may not be
> improper for yᵉ satisfaction of ingenious Learners to exhibit some
> few remarkable Observations on this subject [...].

Likewise, Lenton muses on the difficulty of dealing with this topic:

> It would be a difficult undertaking to prescribe a
> general rule for Bowing, the humours of Masters being very
> Various, and what is approved by one would be condemned
> by another, neither do I know any other way of bringing it
> into a method, but by Collecting all manner of Movements
> and setting marks over or under them, to direct the motion
> of the Bow; But this would be of tedious consequence, I shall
> therefore Hint at some things most material, and leave the rest
> to the Masters [...].[11]

Given that "setting marks over or under" notes has since become absolutely standard practice, this passage provides an interesting marker in the evolution of bowing conventions.

---

[11]   P. 7. The disclaimer makes a further appearance in T. B.'s 'Directions for Playing on the Violin', in: *The Compleat Musick Master*, London, William Pearson, 1722, p. 41: "The different Opinions of Masters concerning this point, renders it extreamly difficult to lay down any certain Rules for this purpose [...]".

An extreme statement made from the inside about the limitations of beginner manuals comes in Daniel Speer's *Gründrichtiger [...]* *Unterricht der musicalischen Kunst* (Ulm, 1697):

> [...] a true teacher will be sure to show his student what remains: how to hold the violin properly, how to place it on the breast, how to manage the bow, and how to play trills, mordents, slides and tremolos combined with other instruments.[12]

French violin methods tell much the same story. The most basic is Pierre Dupont's *Principes de Violon* (Paris, 1718). Its full title proclaims it as a "self instructor": *Principles of the Violin through Questions and Answers from which Anyone will be able to learn to play the said Instrument for themselves*.[13] The questions and answers mostly deal with bowing rules (and, as usual, these are all elaborations of the rule of the down-bow).

Michel Pignolet de Monteclair's *Méthode facile pour apprendre à joüer du violon* (Paris, 1711) also focuses, as its name implies, on basics. It fits the template for elementary tutors but it is not quite as crude as, say, *Nolens Volens*. Monteclair was a string player, though on *basse de violon* rather than violin.[14] The description of how to hold the violin would go some way towards encouraging a student to achieve a serviceable posture:

> The violin is held in the left hand, the neck placed between the thumb and the adjacent finger; it must not be held too tightly because that would make the fingers and the wrist too rigid. To hold it firm without moving, the button that holds the strings should be pressed against the neck under the left cheek. The elbow should be directly under the violin, the wrist well curved and the fingers nicely rounded so that their tips are placed on the strings while ensuring nevertheless that the fingernails do not touch them.[15]

---

[12]   Translation in HOWIE, Henry Eugene. *A Comprehensive Performance Project in Trombone Literature*, D.M.A. Diss., University of Iowa, 1971.

[13]   DUPONT, Pierre. *Principes de Violon par Demandes et Reponce par le quel Toutes Personne, pouront apprendre d'eux mêmes a jouer du dit Instrument*, Paris, Author, 1718.

[14]   See 'Monteclair, Michel Pignolet de', in: *NG*.

[15]   "Le Violon se tient de la main gauche, le manche posé entre le pouce et le doit suivant; il ne faut pas le trop serrer parce que cela roidiroit les doits et le poignet: Pour le tenir ferme et qu'il ne vacile point, il faut bien apuier le bouton qui tient les cordes contre le Col sous la joüe guache. Il faut que le Coude soit directement sous le Violon, que le poignet soit bien courbé et les doits bien ployez en arondissant, afin qu'ils posent sur les cordes par leur extremité, en evitant neanmoins de les toucher avec les ongles". MONTECLAIR, Michel Pignolet de. *Méthode*

Like his English equivalents, Monteclair avoids more complex questions by including a disclaimer at the end of the volume, this time indicating that he expected his volume to be used in conjunction with a teacher:

> The teacher, the application of the student, experience and taste will give a more thorough understanding of the different bow strokes and several other matters; that is why I move on here to Airs for Two Violins so that the student playing them with his teacher will be able to imitate the latter's approach and check the rhythm.[16]

The last French violin treatise before Geminiani's that deserves comment is Michel Corrette's *L'École d'Orphée* (Paris, 1738). This is one of the many treatises that Corrette produced for a variety of instruments, including a much later, more advanced violin manual, *L'art de se perfectionner dans le violon* (Paris, 1782). For all that his title pages are peppered with phrases promising simplicity ("apprendre en peu de tems", "…aisément", "…facilement", "méthode courte et facile"), Corrette is, from a violinist's perspective anyway, not just another Peter Prelleur.[17]

The complete title page of *L'École d'Orphée* indicates that this volume should be "useful to beginners and to those who wish to be able to perform

---

facile pour apprendre à joüer du violon avec un Abregé des Principes de Musique necessaire pour cet Instrument, Paris, Author, 1711, p. 2.

[16] "Le Maitre, l'aplication de l'Ecolier, l'experience et le gout doneront une conoissance plus etendüe des diferents coups d'archet et de plusieurs autres choses; c'est pourquoi je passe aux Airs à deux Violons afin que l'Ecolier joüant en partie avec son Maitre, puisse l'imiter dans le toucher et s'assurer de la mesure". *Ibidem*, p. 18.

[17] Corrette's other treatises comprise *Méthode théorique et pratique pour apprendre en peu de tems le violoncelle dans sa perfection*, Paris, Auteur-Me. Boivin-Le Clerc, 1741, expanded second edition, 1779; *Méthode pour apprendre aisément à jouer de la flûte traversière avec des principes de musique et les brunettes*, Paris, Boivin-Le Clerc, [c1742], expanded second edition with sections on oboe and clarinet, 1773; *Méthode pour apprendre facilement à jouer du par-dessus de viole à 5 et à 6 cordes*, Paris, Auteur-Boivin-Le Clerc, 1748; *Les dons d'Apollon, Méthode pour apprendre facilement à jouer de la guitarre par musique et par tablature*, Paris, Bayard-La Chevardiere-Castagnery, [1762]; *La belle Vielleuse, Méthode pour apprendre facilement à jouer de la vielle*, Paris, Castagnery, [c1782]; *Les amusemens du Parnasse, méthode courte et facile pour apprendre à toucher le clavecin avec les plus jolis airs à la mode où les doigts sont chiffrés pour les commençans ensemble des principes de musique*, Paris, Auteur, 1749, expanded second edition, 1779; *Le parfait maître à chanter, méthode pour apprendre facilement la musique vocale et instrumentale*, Paris, Auteur 1758, expanded second edition, 1782; *Méthode pour apprendre à jouer de la contre-basse […] de la quinte ou alto et de la viole d'Orphée*, Paris, Castagnery, [1773]; *L'Art de se perfectionner dans le violon où l'on donne à etudier des leçons sur toutes les positions*, Paris, Castagnery, [1782].

Sonatas, Concerto[s] pieces with double stops, and scordatura compositions".[18] In fact, the treatise effectively divides into two parts. The first part fits the template for beginner-manuals perfectly (rudiments, how to hold the violin and bow, topography of the fingerboard, etc.). The text is perhaps less sophisticated than Monteclair's (and may even borrow from it). Here, for example, is what he says about holding the instrument: "The violin must be taken in the left hand. Hold it with the thumb and the first finger without gripping it too tightly; curve the first, second and third fingers and extend the little finger slightly".[19] This passage, however, continues with the first mention in a French source (one of the earliest anywhere) of using the chin to stabilise the instrument when changing positions: "It is necessary to put the chin on the violin when changing positions; that frees the left hand completely especially when returning to the ordinary [first] position".[20]

The practice pieces following this section of the text create a transition into something more challenging. They are divided into "Lessons for learning to play the violin in the French manner" and "Violin lessons for learning to play in the Italian manner", the first section ending with a five-movement Suite for Two Violins (beginning with a French Overture) while the second culminates in a four-movement (Adagio, Allegro, Adagio, Presto) Sonata.

After these pieces there are further chapters dealing tersely with more complex bowings, shifting (up to seventh position), the performance of double stops and chords, and scordatura. A well-developed technique is needed for the later exercises in *L'École d'Orphée* (though Corrette's text will provide little help to any player wanting to acquire these skills). In this respect, it reflects the same disconnection between instruction and example (practice pieces) that we have already noted in Prelleur.

In the light of these other tutors, how does *APV* compare as a manual for beginners? It is Geminiani's preface to the 1752 French edition that provides the clearest statement of his aims:

> The principal aim of this work, is by reducing the art [of playing on the violin] to principles drawn from the nature of the

---

[18] "Ouvrage utile aux commencants et a ceux qui veule parvenir à l'execution des Sonates, Concerto, Pieces par accords et Pieces a cordes ravellées".

[19] "Il faut prendre le Manche du Violon de la main gauche, le tenir avec le pouce et le premier doigt sans trop serrer la main, arrondir le premier, deuxieme, troisieme doigt et tenir le petit plus allongé".

[20] "Il faut necessairement poser le menton sur le Violon quand on peut démancher, cela donne toutte liberté à la main gauche principalement quand il faut revenir à la position ordinaire".

instrument, and by expressing those principles in clear, concise, simple rules that are straightforward in their ramifications, and by overcoming difficulties, to get rid of the faults that have, up until now, essentially blocked progress in performance.

With this objective, I have tried to fill the common gaps in instruction by examples that are carefully selected and researched, and that get away from the usual routine [...].[21]

First, *APV* adheres quite closely to the template described above to which manuals that are unequivocally directed at beginners all seem to conform. It begins with the topography of the keyboard. Example A is Geminiani's own version of the fingerboard diagrams provided by *Nolens Volens*, etc. Like the authors of these handbooks, he also recommends that "the Learner [...] have the Finger-board of his Violin marked in the same Manner, which will greatly facilitate his learning to stop in Tune". So far, this is as basic as it gets.

Next, however, we encounter (as Example B) what has become known as the "Geminiani grip", the element of *APV* that has endured above all else. No earlier instruction book for violinists contains anything that could assist so directly in setting a left-hand position that would serve so well for virtuoso repertoire. Nevertheless, Geminiani's advice here is something that beginners would do well to note also. As he implies in his French preface, it is much better to begin correctly rather than acquire bad habits.

Next, still in conformity with the template, Geminiani moves on to rules for holding the violin and bow — all material that seems directed at beginners (though we will return to consider the implications of precisely what he is recommending here). We should acknowledge, too, that his instructions on holding the violin itself come closest to that most amateur of treatises, Playford's "Instructions".[22]

Example C takes us to Geminiani's equivalent of the sections in the earlier treatises setting out the scale (gamut) with violin fingerings. Here, however, he goes much further than any of his predecessors in describing seven "orders" or positions. (Only Corrette, in his one-page Chapter VI of *L'Ecole d'Orphée* even

---

[21] "Le but principal de cet Ouvrage, est d'en reduire l'Art à des Principes tirés de la nature de l'Instrument: d'en rendre les Regles sûres, courtes, simples & faciles dans toutes leurs étendues, & d'en supprimer les difficultés, en écartant les défauts qui jusqu'à présent ont arrêté essentiellement les progrès de l'exécution. | Pour cet effet, j'ai tâché de remplir les vuides communs de l'instruction, par des Exemples choisis, recherchés, & hors de la routine ordinaire [...]".

[22] For a fuller review of ways of holding the violin and their significance, see the introduction to *APV* in vol. 13 of *Geminiani Opera Omnia*.

attempts to illustrate the upper positions.) At this point, we part company with the "self instructors" of the previous century.

It should be noted that Geminiani does, nevertheless, systematically address the other topics listed in the template. He can be seen as responding to an agenda set by his predecessors, even though his views on "bowing rules" have a very different emphasis (in his vehement rejection of "that wretched Rule of drawing the Bow down at the first Note of every Bar"), and his section on Ornamentation represents a significant departure. It is here that *APV*'s real value lies, in the way it addresses questions of interest to advanced players. This is quite an original achievement, and in writing *APV* Geminiani was effectively inventing a new kind of discourse. It is extraordinary that, as his French preface illustrates, he was only half aware of the special character of his achievement.

The proposition that *APV* was the first advanced violin tutor needs contextualising. Not only did a volume like *L'Ecole d'Orphée* enter territory that is beyond the reach of real beginners, but *APV* itself was only just in front of an extraordinary wave of other manuals addressed to musicians who aspired to be able to perform sophisticated repertoire. Leopold Mozart's *Violinschule* followed hard on its heels in 1756 and incorporates material from a Tartini treatise that at this stage had been circulating in manuscripts that may well have pre-dated *APV*. (The Tartini was eventually published as *Traité des Agrémens* in Paris in 1771.) In the same year as the Mozart treatise, Joseph de Herrando's *Arte y puntual explicación del modo de tocar el violín* was published (thanks to the restrictions of the Spanish inquisition) in Paris. There, just six years later, the *Principes du violon* by the Abbé le Fils also appeared. At the same time as *APV*, the seminal treatises for flute by Johann Joachim Quantz (*Versuch einer Anweisung die Flöte Traversiere zu Spielen*, 1752) and for keyboard by Carl Phillipp Emanuel Bach (*Versuch über die wahre Art das Clavier zu spielen*, Part 1, 1753) were being published in Berlin.

The problem of writing for advanced players when the only models available were manuals for beginners is one that Geminiani shared with those other great pedagogues of the 1750s. Leopold Mozart, for instance, writes as if instructing initiates but progresses quickly to a discussion of matters that are relevant only to those who have already acquired considerable proficiency. Arguably, the transitions in Mozart's *Violinschule* are less abrupt than in *APV* and the management of various topics more systematic.

Geminiani's handling of complex topics is often so concentrated that it is easy to miss vital technical and musical advice. In fact, nothing could better reveal the radical achievement of *APV* than enquiring why Geminiani's instructions are so elliptical. In breaking new ground, Geminiani had to invent a new discourse. Perhaps the simplest way of illustrating this point is to jump forward 200 years to compare Geminiani's treatment of key topics with that of some of the great violin pedagogues of the second half of the twentieth century. The treatises that I have in mind are all, in some sense, descendants of the thoroughly systematic instruction manuals initiated by the Paris Conservatoire in the early years of the nineteenth century. The kind of discourse that I want to characterize here, one that sets out to convey a sense of complexity by breaking down each topic into micro-steps — was in the main established early in the nineteenth century. It is evident in Baillot's *L'Art du Violon* (1835), for example. But in choosing to focus on treatises written in the last 50 years or so, I hope to be able to compare Geminiani's instructions with those that at least some violinists reading this essay may well have encountered — relied on, even — in their formative years, such as Carl Flesch's 380-page *Violin Fingering* — a companion to his exhaustive (and exhausting) volume of violin scales.[23]

Some of these volumes pay homage to Geminiani. Joseph Szigeti, in *Szigeti on the Violin*, turns at one point in his 227 pages of personal commentary and advice to look at the Geminiani grip, noting its occurrence in a fingered passage of Bartók's Rhapsody No. 1.[24] I. M. Yampolsky in *The Principles of Violin Fingering* acknowledges the historical importance of *APV*.[25]

Ivan Galamian's *Principles of Violin Playing and Teaching* seems to have been held in particularly high regard by violinists seeking to perfect their technique.[26] Many of the students using Galamian's volume would simultaneously be attempting to master the concerto masterworks of the nineteenth century. Comparing what Geminiani and Galamian have to say on a single representative issue throws up some striking contrasts. Let us take the role of left-hand thumb in changing positions. Geminiani writes just two sentences. First, he describes its movement in upward shifts:

---

[23]   FLESCH, Carl. *Violin Fingering*, translated by Boris Schwarz with a foreword by Yehudi Menuhin, London, Barrie and Rockliff, 1960.

[24]   London, Cassell, 1969, p. 84.

[25]   YAMPOLSKY, Israel Markovich. *The Principles of Violin Fingering*, translated by Alan Lumsden with a preface by David Oistrach, London, Oxford University Press, 1967. The discussion of *APV* is on pp. 4-5 (where an erroneous publication date of 1739 is given).

[26]   GALAMIAN, Ivan. *Principles of Violin Playing and Teaching*, London, Faber, 1962. The text is "written by" Elizabeth H. Green. Galamian's credentials as a pedagogue rest partly on the fact that he taught both Pinchas Zukerman and Itzhak Perlman at the Juilliard School of Music in New York.

> After having been practised in the first Order, you must pass on to the second, and then to the third; in which Care is to be taken that the Thumb always remain farther back than the Fore-finger; and the more you advance in the other Orders the Thumb must be at a greater Distance till it remains almost hid under the Neck of the Violin.

In describing downward shifts he writes:

> It must here be observed, that in drawing back the Hand from the 5th, 4th and 3d Order to go to the first, the Thumb cannot, for Want of Time, be replaced in its natural Position; but it is necessary it should be replaced at the second Note.[27]

In contrast, Galamian goes into considerably greater detail:

> There are two main categories of shifts; they will be termed the *complete shift* and the *half shift*. In the complete shift, both the hand and the thumb move into the new position. In the half shift, the thumb does not change its place of contact with the neck of the violin. Instead it remains anchored, and by bending and stretching permits the hand and fingers to move up or down into other positions. This type of motion, the half shift, can be used in many instances where the fingers have to move into another position for a few notes only. Properly applied, it can greatly promote facility and security in passages that would otherwise be very cumbersome. Example 5 [Ex. 3 here] illustrates the point. At the asterisk, the third position is established, and the thumb then retains this point of contact, bending for the descent of the fingers into the first position, stretching for the return into the third position…

Ex. 3: Galamian, *Principles of Violin Playing and Teaching*, p. 24, Example 5: "Brahms: *Concerto in D major*, Op. 77 First movement (measures 338-39)".

Allegro non troppo

---

[27] Curiously, between these two statements Geminiani comments, "This is sufficient to shew what Transposition of the Hand is. I have only now to recommend a good Execution of the whole, both in rising and falling; and great Care in conducting the Hand, as also in the placing the Fingers exactly on the Marks. With all these the Practitioner must by Degrees acquire Quickness".

In performing the shift from the lower positions to the higher position, the thumb moves simultaneously with the hand and the fingers. As was pointed out before, the shape of the hand in moving up the fingerboard should remain basically the same, at least up to about the sixth or seventh position. The frame of the hand, however, will become gradually smaller as the string length shortens. The span of the frame of the eighth position will be half the size of that of the first position.

In making this shift from the lower to the higher positions, the thumb will gradually pass under the neck of the instrument as the hand glides through the third and fourth positions into the higher positions. This brings the elbow rather around the violin to the right. All of this should be done in one smooth movement. In the very high positions, above the seventh, the fingers can reach easily into several positions without actually shifting the hand. For the extremely high positions, if the player's thumb is short, he may have to let it come out from underneath the neck of the violin and find a comfortable place on the rib of the instrument. In this latter case, the head will have to hold the instrument very firmly.

In moving from third to first position, the thumb should slightly precede the hand. In a move from fifth position straight down to first, the same principle applies. But if the shift is from a higher position to the third, then it is often better to make use, at least partially, of the half-shift technique: keep the thumb in place while the finger and hand shift down, and then, after the shift of the hand is completed, let the thumb replace itself in the new position. The thumb thus acts as a pivot and bends during the shift but does not relinquish its contact until after the shift is completed. How soon after the shift the thumb readjusts itself will depend upon the character of the passage and especially upon the speed of the note sequence. In very fast shifts the move is almost simultaneous.

In a descending scale from the highest notes on the E string down to the first position, a player with a thumb of average length will have the ball of the thumb, at the outset, contacting the curve of the neck where it turns to join the body of the instrument. As the scale begins to descend, the thumb will exercise a slight pressure and, acting as a pivot, will pull the hand back until about the fifth position. In doing so, the thumb, which is stretched at first, gradually bends. For the further shift to about the third or fourth position the thumb still remains in place, bending a little farther and letting the hand precede, half-shift fashion. As soon as the hand completes the shift thus far, the thumb readjusts by stretching backward. It has to do so in order to be in time for the *leading* of the shift by slightly preceding the hand in the continued downward movement to the first position.

A hand with a short thumb will not be able to handle long shifts in this way. The short thumb will sooner reach its comfortable limit of bending and will therefore have to readjust more often [...].[28]

This is far from everything that Galamian has to say about shifting, but it does cover what he has to say about the thumb's role in this technique.

There is a crucial difference between the two writers' approach to this question. Geminiani's method of holding the violin precludes any assistance from the chin in shifting, while Galamian's advice is predicated on the violin being supported between collarbone and chin. Despite this there is, in fact, a strong element of agreement between Geminiani's two sentences and Galamian's much more expansive treatment of the subject. Geminiani's idea that in shifting into upper positions the thumb will gradually move under the neck of the violin (and thus be hidden from the player's view) is echoed by Galamian in saying that "the thumb will gradually pass under the neck of the instrument as the hand glides through the third and fourth positions into the higher positions". More significantly, Galamian recommends that in downward shifts from positions above third position the thumb should not be moved back immediately, but should instead act as a pivot during the shift and then move to its optimal position in the frame of the hand. This corresponds reasonably closely to the advice given by Geminiani in the second of the two sentences quoted above (though Galamian envisages more latitude in the timing of the thumb's readjustment to its normal position). There is another aspect of Galamian's advice that has parallels with *APV*, but these are not at all obvious from Geminiani's explicit commentary on the behaviour of the thumb in shifting. Galamian writes that in the "half shift" (i.e. a shift into second position), "the thumb does not change its place of contact with the neck of the violin. Instead it remains anchored, and by bending and stretching permits the hand and fingers to move up or down into other positions". The idea is that the fingers may extend forwards or backwards into neighbouring positions without involving any repositioning of the frame of the hand.

Geminiani's statement about not moving the thumb at the same time as the fingers in shifting down from high positions is made in relation to

---

[28] GALAMIAN, Ivan. *Op. cit.* (see note 26), pp. 23-25.

section E of *Essempio I* in *APV*. He introduces this section by saying that it "contains several different Scales, with the Transpositions of the Hand, which ought to be made both in rising and falling". It is not made absolutely clear whether these scales are meant to be regarded as a practical exercise or an illustration of the topography of the fingerboard (in the tradition of earlier violin treatises). But the fingerings themselves are far from straightforward and make no sense whatsoever simply as topographical illustrations. Practised as scales, however, they are very instructive. The first (using only first and second fingers) involves constant shifting between first and third positions. It would be possible for a player using chin and shoulder rest to make a series of orthodox shifts between these two positions but this is virtually impossible when the hand is simultaneously required to support the instrument. In such a situation, the thumb finds its way into an intermediate position where it can service both the third position notes and the first position notes — pretty much as Galamian prescribes for "half shifts". Any violinist sceptical about my interpretation of Geminiani's intention here might like to skip to the second to last scale in *Essempio I* section E (Ex. 4). Here the reliance on fingers I and 4 requires a process of alternating extensions and contractions of the hand with, once again, the thumb assuming a position that is pretty much where it would be for a prolonged second position passage.

Ex. 4: *APV*, p. I, "Essempio I°E", b. 22.

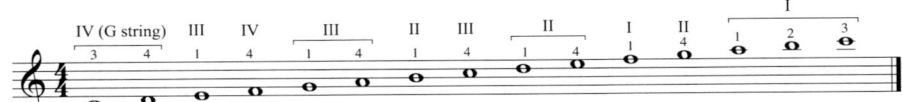

Besides the differences and similarities in shifting techniques as taught by Geminiani and Galamian, there is a huge difference in the level of detail in the information given with Geminiani appearing to fall short. My contention is that, taking the music examples together with the text, Geminiani shows a similar interest to Galamian in analysing the minute physical detail involved in shifting. Geminiani's music examples are an integral part of this process. It is worth noting just what a radical departure these are from the musical content of earlier treatises. Many of the examples in *APV* are concerned in various ways with the technique of shifting. *Essempio X* ("[...] calculated to render the Labour of Practice more pleasant") and *Essempio XI* (identical, but transposed up a tone to D major) are excellent for developing just the kind of independent relationship between thumb and fingers in shifting described above.

Comparing other issues would lead to similar conclusions. Galamian's extended discussion of vibrato begins with a four-page section on the various types. This is divided into sub-sections covering (i) The Hand Vibrato, (ii) The Arm Vibrato, (iii) The Finger Vibrato, (iv) The Finger Tip Vibrato and (v) Methods of loosening the Finger Joints.[29]

Geminiani's single paragraph on the Close Shake also deals with several varieties of vibrato:

> To perform it, you must press the Finger strongly upon the String of the Instrument, and move the Wrist in and out slowly and equally, when it is long continued swelling the Sound by Degrees, drawing the Bow nearer to the Bridge, and ending it very strong it may express Majesty, Dignity, &c. But making it shorter, lower and softer, it may denote Affliction, Fear, &c. and when it is made on short Notes, it only contributes to make their Sound more agreable and for this Reason it should be made use of as often as possible.

Apparently there is no distinction made here between the physical actions needed to produce a slow strong vibrato as against a faster, softer vibrato. Both require strong finger contact and movement from the wrist. Geminiani appears to be making a purely musical point in alluding to the expressive potential unlocked by varying the character of the close shake. Again however, I suspect that he is conflating two different kinds of advice. It is far easier to produce a slower and wider vibrato when bowing strongly and close to the bridge (particularly if the violin is being held without support from the chin). In other words, any violinist attempting to put Geminiani's expressive ideas into practice will discover that they have also been given a lesson in the mechanics of producing different kinds of vibrato. The paragraph in question has, almost since its first publication, caused a certain amount of controversy because of its concluding injunction to use the close shake "as often as possible".[30] Most of the problem lies in the advice being taken out of context. First, Geminiani's method of holding the violin means that his apparent enthusiasm for the close shake has a self-regulating aspect to it. It would be exceedingly difficult to produce a modern-sounding continuous vibrato without using chin and shoulder support to stabilize the instrument. More importantly, the paragraph on the close shake occurs as part of the discussion of the "ornaments of expression"

---

[29] *Ibidem*, pp. 38-41.

[30] See HICKMAN, Roger. 'The Censored Publications of the Art of Playing on the Violin, or Geminiani Unshaken', in: *Early Music*, XI/1 (January 1983), pp. 73-76.

in *APV* where we also read that the plain shake may also "be made upon any Note" and that the upper appoggiatura "will always have a pleasing Effect, and it may be added to any Note you will". In other words, the recommendation that vibrato be used as often as possible needs to be understood in exactly the same way as the similar advice about trills and upper appoggiature. Moreover, Geminiani says of "Holding a Note" that, "It is necessary to use this often; for were we to make Beats and Shakes continually without sometimes suffering the pure Note to be heard, the Melody would be too much diversified". One cannot imagine a modern pedagogue relying on the student to make these sorts of connections and thus remove any ambiguity that may be contained in the injunction to deploy vibrato as often as possible.

Galamian (Szigeti, Flesch, Dunis, *et al.*) have constructed a rhetoric of complication in which the level of detail given in the analysis of technique arguably goes beyond what could be helpfully verbalised for even the most advanced student. However, they vouchsafe it to their readers as their guarantee of authority. Geminiani's mode of discourse, by contrast, is one of extreme compression. He appears to omit vital pieces of information from his explanations of technical and musical points, and yet attentive practitioners can infer them from the musical exercises or by making connections that Geminiani himself neglects to make explicit. To what extent this is attributable to the lack of models — or the distraction of far less ambitious models — can only be a matter for speculation.

Towards the end of the preface to *A Treatise of Good Taste* Geminiani muses on his own ambition to do something to reverse what he saw as a worrying decline in musical values in London: "To say All in few Words, the Road to Emulation is both open and wide; the most effectual Method to triumph over an Author is to excel him; and he manifests his Affection to a Science most who contributes most to its Advancement". *APV* made an outstanding contribution to the advancement of violin pedagogy. The highest accolade one might bestow upon this volume is that it managed "to say all in a few words".

THE CONTRIBUTION OF GEMINIANI'S
THE ART OF PLAYING ON THE VIOLIN TO
"THE IMPROVED STATE OF THE VIOLIN IN ENGLAND"

Robin Stowell
(CARDIFF)

IN 1713 THE GERMAN COMPOSER AND CRITIC Johann Mattheson reported that "he who at the present time wants to profit from his music heads for England";[1] two years earlier, the respected English critic Joseph Addison had bemoaned the fact that the British were "transported by anything which is not English".[2] Unsurprisingly, therefore, foreign musicians dominated violin playing in eighteenth-century England, gaining considerable artistic and social prestige, and London boasted a cosmopolitan musical life unsurpassed in the rest of Europe. Italians in particular filled many of the leading musical posts in the capital, attracted principally by its flourishing concert life and the expanding music publishing industry. Their cultivation of the sonata and concerto and their styles of composition and performance, intended to "affect the mind and command the passions",[3] were enormously influential. English audiences treated Corelli "almost with the awed veneration of a religious cult",[4] Roger North remarking (*c*1710), "It [is] wonderfull to observe what a skratching of Corelli there is every where — nothing will relish but Corelli".[5]

---

[1]   MATTHESON, Johann. *Das neu-eröffnete Orchestre*, Hamburg, Benjamin Schillers Wittwe, 1713, p. 211.

[2]   *The Spectator*, 21 March 1711.

[3]   GEMINIANI, Francesco. *The Art of Playing on the Violin*, [hereafter *APV*], London, s.n., 1751, p. 1. For a facsimile edition with introduction by David Boyden, see note 7; for a modern edition with commentary by Peter Walls, see *Geminiani Opera Omnia*, vol. 13.

[4]   ALLSOP, Peter. *Arcangelo Corelli: 'New Orpheus of Our Times'*, Oxford, Oxford University Press, 1999, p. 188.

[5]   *Roger North on Music*, edited by John Wilson, London, Novello, 1959, p. xx. For more on Corelli's reception in England, see WALLS, Peter. 'Constructing the Archangel: Corelli in 18th-Century Editions of Opus V', in: *Arcangelo Corelli: fra mito e realtà storica*, edited by

Trained in Corelli's 'circle' in Rome, Francesco Geminiani came to London in 1714 and firmly grasped the opportunity to benefit from the popularity of Corelli's music in the capital.[6] He disseminated Corelli's technique and style through not only his own compositions but also his arrangements and re-workings of Corelli's music, his teaching, his performances, and his writings, particularly his *The Art of Playing on the Violin* (London, s.n., 1751),[7] hereafter abbreviated to *APV*.

DISSEMINATION

Geminiani's publications, social status and his position as one of the most respected violin teachers of his era in England and Ireland ensured the dissemination of his ideas throughout all levels of violin playing in those countries and elsewhere. His violin treatise appeared in several editions, as well as translations into French (first edition, *L'art de jouer le violon*, Paris, Aux adresses ordinaires, [1752]),[8] and German (first edition, *Gründliche Anleitung oder Violinschule*, Vienna, 1782). These translations were fairly faithful to the original text and such minor alterations as they contained largely reflected the instrument's developing technical and expressive vocabulary, influencing violin pedagogy in Europe until

---

Gregory Barnett, Antonella D'Ovidio and Stefano La Via, 2 vols, Florence, Olschki, 2007, vol. I, pp. 233-252; WALLS, Peter, 'Reconstructing the Archangel: Corelli "Ad Vivum Pinxit"', in: *Early Music*, XXXV/4 (2007), pp. 525-538; EDWARDS, Owain. 'The Response to Corelli's Music in Eighteenth-Century England', in: *Studia musicologica Norvegica*, II (1976), pp. 51-96; ALLSOP, Peter. *Op. cit.* (see note 4), esp. pp. 188-199.

[6] On Corelli and Geminiani's domination of the English musical scene *c*1730s onwards, see, for example, WEBER, William. *The Rise of Musical Classics in Eighteenth-Century England: A Study in Canon, Ritual, and Ideology*, Oxford, Oxford University Press, 1996, pp. 78-80, 96-97.

[7] David Boyden and Sonya Monosoff are among those who have speculated whether the examples, music, and perhaps even the text of Geminiani's treatise were prepared for publication in Italy prior to 1714, as the Italian captions, markings and abbreviations might suggest. However, Peter Walls convincingly scotches this possibility with his analysis of the text's development "through a series of (published) 'drafts'", confirming that Geminiani continued to use Italian as appropriate in his English publications and that the style of this treatise's plates (not least the inscription "Philips sculpt." on the last page of the examples) suggests their English mid-eighteenth-century origins. See BOYDEN, David. 'Introduction', in: GEMINIANI, Francesco. *APV, op. cit.* (see note 3); facsimile edition by David Boyden, London, Oxford University Press, 1952, p. xii; MONOSOFF, Sonya - WALLS, Peter. 'Violin fingering', in: *Early Music*, XIII/1 (1985), pp. 76-79.

[8] This date is not specified in the publication but has been suggested by both Robert Eitner (*Quellen-Lexikon*) and Lionel de La Laurencie (*L'École française de violon de Lully à Viotti*, 3 vols, Paris, Delagrave, 1922-1924, repr. Geneva, Minkoff, 1971, vol. III, p. 22).

well into the nineteenth century.[9] Various shortened, 'improved' and plagiarised versions were also issued; notable among these are an abridged version, *An Abstract of Geminiani's Art of Playing on the Violin* (Boston, New England, John Boyles, 1769) and an edited and improved version in French conforming to the demands of a more advanced technique.[10] The title-page of the latter states explicitly, "Composée primitivement par le Célèbre F. Geminiani" ("Originally composed by the celebrated F. Geminiani"), but its contents differ substantially from the original and are not a faithful representation of Geminiani's violin playing principles, raising doubts about some claims regarding the longevity of his treatise's significance.

RECEPTION

Clearly, though, Geminiani's *APV* occupies a pivotal position in violin history not only as "one of the first mature expositions of violin playing"[11] but also as the only violin method of an advanced technical standard to be compiled by a native of Italy and to be published in England in the eighteenth century. Charles Burney described it as "a very useful work in its day; the shifts and examples of different difficulties, and uses of the bow, being infinitely superior to those in any other book of the kind, or indeed oral instruction, which the nation could boast, till the arrival of Giardini".[12] Its impact and Geminiani's own presence to popularise and promote it in England ideally complemented the prevalence there of the 'Corelli style', otherwise known as the 'old' or 'ancient' style. Demonstrated in many works written for the instrument by English composers such as Joseph Gibbs, William Corbett, and Geminiani-pupils Michael Festing and Matthew Dubourg, this predominant Italian influence is endorsed in Thomas Gainsborough's famous portrait of Gibbs (*c*1755), which clearly shows two volumes of music, by Geminiani and Corelli respectively, behind the subject.[13] Some commentators considered works in the 'ancient' style to be dry and detached but most acknowledged

---

[9]   However, the French edition omits Geminiani's preface and substitutes for it an engraving of someone (unidentified) playing the violin. See below under 'Manner of holding the violin' and note 76.

[10]   GEMINIANI, Francesco. *L'Art du Violon ou Méthode raisonnée pour apprendre à bien jouer de cet instrument*, Paris, Sieber, ?1803.

[11]   BOYDEN, David. 'Introduction', *op. cit.* (see note 7), p. v.

[12]   *BURNEY*, IV, p. 643.

[13]   This portrait is housed in the National Portrait Gallery, London. It may be viewed at <www.npg.org.uk/collections/search/location.php?locid=232>. It is reproduced in:

that they had "a grand and intellectual air, that seems to ensure continual respect and admiration".[14] This style was preserved as a beacon of good taste in England throughout the eighteenth century and beyond and was only gradually eclipsed.

Echoing Burney's words that Geminiani's violin treatise was "a very useful work in its day", Jean Jousse acknowledged a considerable debt to the Italian "for the improved state of the Violin in England and for the advancement of Instrumental music during the first 50 years of the last century; he", Jousse continues, "with Veracini and Giardini, confirmed by their superior abilities the sovereignty of the Violin over all other instruments".[15] As will become evident, the influence of Geminiani's work on violin playing in England was actually to last considerably longer than even Jousse foresaw.

Geminiani's treatise was not without its critics, however. Some pointed out that it focuses on only a small number of precepts, placing taste before display and technique as the servant of expression. Its comparatively brief text is by far outweighed by musical content, in the form of exercises and "twelve Pieces in different Stiles for a Violin and Violoncello with a through Bass for the Harpsichord".[16] Although Geminiani claims to have prepared the violinist adequately for performing these pieces, considering his technical and expressive principles and musical examples "sufficient to qualify him to perform any Musick whatsoever",[17] numerous technical issues relevant to their performance remain unexplained, and doubtless would have required the guidance of a teacher.[18] Some perceived deficiencies of the treatise were outlined in the preface of the revised early nineteenth-century French edition mentioned earlier:

> The source of this method is by the celebrated Geminiani, but several well-informed artists and amateurs having rightly complained that: 1. the first edition was badly written, obscure, and beyond the range of understanding of young pupils; 2. the examples were for the most part too hard and there was a lack of clarity in what they were demonstrating; 3. several of these examples were lessons in composition and counterpoint rather

---

HOLMAN, Peter. 'The Colchester partbooks', in: *Early Music*, XXVIII/4 (2000), p. 581. See also p. 436 of the present volume.

[14]   *Quarterly Musical Magazine and Review*, II (1820), pp. 60-61.

[15]   JOUSSE, Jean. *The Theory and Practice of the Violin*, London, R. Birchall, [1811], p. xiv.

[16]   GEMINIANI, Francesco. *APV, op. cit.* (see note 3), p. 1.

[17]   *Ibidem*, p. 1.

[18]   See Peter Walls' essay, pp. 233-256, on the issue of self- versus tutor-instruction.

than genuine instructions in violin playing; 4. too little value was given to the kind of lessons which combine the useful and the pleasing in order to encourage pupils by making their study more enjoyable and less tedious.[19]

Elements of the first point (above) had already been aired by Stephen Philpot, a second-generation Geminiani pupil. While recognising the significance of the Italian's treatise, recommending it particularly in his discussion of "Characters of Musical Expression or Graces used in Playing", Philpot qualifies his enthusiasm by remarking that it "is too difficult for children or Young Beginners to attempt till they have made a good Progress in playing"; otherwise, he continues, "there has not appeared any rational Treatise upon this Subject, that has been of any other Use, than as a Gamut to shew the Notes, and something of the different sorts of time".[20]

The significance of Geminiani's treatise is magnified by some appreciation of the context in which it was conceived and published; for it appeared as a giant amongst a myriad of pedagogical methods, most of which were sparked by the demise of the viol in favour of the violin and were intended for use by amateur musicians.[21] Most of these methods were brief and designed for self-instruction;[22] few had much value or significance as a means of achieving proficiency on an instrument. They largely combined elementary instruction on musical rudiments, tuning, basic technique and ornamentation with a collection of popular melodies and/or dances for the student to play. Plagiarism was rife and what little textual instruction was included tended to be replicated with little, if any, modification from method to method.[23]

---

[19]   GEMINIANI, Francesco. *L'Art du Violon* […], *op. cit.* (see note 10), p. [1]. "Le fond de cette méthode est du Célèbre Geminiani, mais plusieurs artistes et amateurs éclairés s'étant plaints avec justice que la première Edition étoit 1. mal rédigée, obscure, et nullement à portée de l'intelligence des jeunes Elèves; 2. les exemples pour la plus-part trop sévères et manquant de Clarté dans leur démonstrations; 3. que plusieurs de ces exemples étoient plutôt des Leçons de composition et de contrepoint que de véritables instructions pour le Violon; 4. trop peu riche dans la partie de Leçons qui doivent réunir l'Utile à l'Agréable, pour encourager les Elèves en leur rendant l'Etude plus aimable et moins rebutante".

[20]   PHILPOT, Stephen. *An Introduction to the Art of Playing on the Violin*, London, Randall and Abell, ?1767, p. 6.

[21]   See LEPPERT, Richard. *Music and Image: Domesticity, Ideology and Social-Cultural Formation in Eighteenth-Century England*, Cambridge, Cambridge University Press, 1988, pp. 67-70.

[22]   See BOYDEN, David. *The History of Violin Playing from its Origins to 1761*, London, Oxford University Press, 1965, pp. 244-247.

[23]   For more on the content of treatises that preceded Geminiani's *APV* see Peter Walls' essay, pp. 233-256.

ROBIN STOWELL

SUPPOSITITIOUS WORKS

In that kind of publishing climate, it is hardly surprising that several other violin treatises were ascribed to Geminiani, particularly the various versions and editions of Part v of Peter Prelleur's *The Modern Musick-Master* (London, 1731), the anonymous author of which discussed technical and other issues relating to the violin and used the same title as Geminiani's treatise. It is also unsurprising that the positive reception and impact of Geminiani's treatise influenced the content of several subsequent English treatises for the 'amateur violinist', as well as prompting the publication of various supposititious works in Geminiani's name. Most of the latter still derived from Prelleur and comprised little more than finger-board charts, basic musical rudiments, definitions of musical terminology, and the table of ornaments from Geminiani's violin treatise,[24] as well as several short pieces (airs, dances) of elementary demand. Boyden notes that they differ externally from Prelleur et al. "in typography, in the frontispieces which (according to Heron-Allen) exhibit costumes of a later period, in the format which is lengthwise, in the inaccurate reproduction of the fingering chart, in differences in the concluding pieces of music, and in the fact that the title-page claims Geminiani as author".[25]

Various supposititious works continued to be published after Geminiani's death and well into the nineteenth century,[26] the use of his name justified only by the fact that his table of embellishments (see Ill. 1) and/ or some fingering exercises and bowing instructions from *APV* commonly appear therein. Boyden provides a list of such works with approximate dates, suggesting that these methods represent "probably a mere sampling of the posthumous Geminiani that may be still extant".[27] The differences between these works are of minor detail and significance but generally include "the frontispiece, a small deletion or addition here and there, and a different set of complete pieces at the end".[28] Nevertheless, such an implied association with the much respected Italian maestro attracted the interest of amateurs and proved an effective sales ploy during a period of striking

[24] The original source of this table is: GEMINIANI, Francesco. *A Treatise of Good Taste in the Art of Musick*, London, s.n., 1749, p. [6]; see *Geminiani Opera Omnia*, vol. 13.
[25] BOYDEN, David. 'Introduction', *op. cit.* (see note 7), pp. x-xi.
[26] For an assessment of these by Boyden, see *ibidem*, pp. ix-xi.
[27] *Ibidem*, pp. x-xi.
[28] *Ibidem*, p. xi.

ILL. I: *APV*, p. 26, "Essemp. xviii".

development both in the construction of the violin and bow and in violin playing styles. Whether or not publishers felt justified in pursuing such a marketing policy because of the inclusion of an extract from Geminiani's work (e.g. his table of ornaments), or because they believed Geminiani to be the author of Part v of Prelleur's *magnum opus*, is unclear.

These supposititious publications reflect Geminiani's teaching with little, if any, fidelity; and, despite claims of completeness, they fail to describe the fundamental aspects of technique in sufficient detail, if they describe them at all. They also emphasize not only the immense difference in technical standards between amateur and professional violinists in eighteenth-century England, giving added credence not only to the comments of Jousse, Philpot, and others, but also to the general standards of available treatises in England at that time as compared with, for example, the very thorough and comprehensive volumes by Leopold Mozart and Quantz. One-to-one instruction was undoubtedly a necessary supplement to using such methods if any worthwhile progress on the instrument was to be made.

General Influence on Selected British Treatises

Despite the negativity surrounding these supposititious works, Geminiani's treatise seems gradually to have prompted in England a more serious and systematic approach to the compilation of violin methods and to violin instruction in general. Its move away from the prevalent format of including basic musical rudiments and popular melodies and its cultivation of a more theoretical and practical approach directly influenced many of the more progressive instruction manuals for amateurs written by some of his pupils and disciples, as well as by others who came under his influence. Philpot's violin treatise,[29] for example, is essentially a simplified version of Geminiani's, the Italian's principles having been transmitted to the Englishman through his teacher, Michael Festing. Like many of its successors,[30] it explicitly states its aim of "laying a Regular Foundation for Young Beginners,[31] facilitating their Early Progress [...] more especially in the Art of Bowing",[32] and "the improvement of amateurs",[33] as opposed to catering for the gentleman. Philpot intends his method merely as an introduction to violin playing and not "as a regular System of finished Rules", which, he presumes, "whoever attempts after that celebrated Master Geminiani must expect to draw upon himself the Censure of the Musical World".[34]

Significantly, too, Philpot's treatise reflects his own experiences as a violin teacher; not only does it advocate using the "Assistance of a Master"[35] but its content also seems to signal a move away from self-instruction, giving more attention to the teacher's contribution to the cause and incorporating some duos for master and pupil to perform. Its influence, together with that of Geminiani's treatise, extends well into the nineteenth century, as attested by the publication of a new edition as late as *c*1820 by Goulding, D'Almaine, Potter & Co. and an anonymous treatise, *The Violin Preceptor, or Compleat Tutor [...] / Judiciously selected from the treatises of Geminiani and Philpot, / to which is added a select collection of songs, airs, marches &c.* (London, *c*1835), issued by Z. T. Purday.

Two relevant theoretical works by the Scottish music publisher Robert Bremner — *The Compleat Tutor for the Violin* (London, *c*1770) and *Some Thoughts*

---

29   PHILPOT, Stephen. *Op. cit.* (see note 20).

30   For example: KEITH, Robert W. *A Violin Preceptor on an Entirely New Principle*, London, Jauncey, 1813; SANDERSON, James. *A Celebrated Study for the Bow and Fingerboard of the Violin*, London, Keith, 1825.

31   PHILPOT, Stephen. *Op. cit.* (see note 20), title-page.

32   KEITH, Robert W. *Op. cit.* (see note 30), title-page.

33   SANDERSON, James. *Op. cit.* (see note 30), title-page.

34   PHILPOT, Stephen. *Op. cit.* (see note 20), p. 13.

35   *Ibidem*, pp. 13-14.

on the Performance of Concert Music, which forms a preface to his edition of Johann Georg Christoph Schetky's *Six Quartettos* Op. 6 (London, 1777) — were also based firmly on the principles of his teacher Geminiani and those of Tartini. However, they occasionally express some contrary views; and in his reissue of Geminiani's violin treatise (after 1777)[36] Bremner seems to have exercised 'publisher's licence' to omit three significant passages from the original — concerning the placement of the thumb in third position, the execution of the superior appoggiatura, and the use of vibrato or the 'close shake' — to align his mentor's text with his own opinions. The third deletion complements Bremner's views regarding vibrato, expressed in *Some Thoughts*.[37]

Although the text of John Tashanberg's *The Compleat School or Art of Playing the Violin* (London, [1796]) is far from 'compleat' as an instructional method and shows rather less of Geminiani's influence, its musical content is more in the mould of the Italian's treatise. Selected from different genres and styles, it includes some passages of considerable technical demand.

Towards the end of the eighteenth century the predominance of Geminiani's treatise was challenged by a clutch of methods issued by foreign musicians who were resident in England. Some of their works sparked further improvement in the general level of teaching materials. The Belgian Joseph Gehot, for example, published many treatises, including his *The Art of Bowing* (c1790), which consists of progressively more challenging variations on a theme;[38] and the French violinist François-Hippolyte Barthélemon, renowned for his interpretations of Corelli's sonatas, published his *A New Tutor for the Violin* (c1798) not only "for the improvement of the Lovers of that Instrument" but also, significantly, to satisfy his perceived need for a tutor "to introduce the Performer to the Ancient as well as Modern Authors".[39] Again, the textual content is sparse, particularly in respect of technical issues, but the musical material is suitably challenging, culminating in six 'capricios', which Barthélemon hopes may "be instrumental to lead the student to an exact and powerful Performance of both Ancient and Modern compositions".[40]

---

[36]   The treatise was later reissued by Preston and Son after this publisher had bought the plates from Bremner in 1789. On the background, see HICKMAN, Roger. 'The Censored Publications of *The Art of Playing on the Violin*, or Geminiani Unshaken', in: *Early Music*, XI/1 (1983), p. 73.

[37]   On these points, see discussion below and *ibidem*, pp. 73-76.

[38]   For example, GEHOT, Joseph. *Complete Instructions for Every Musical Instrument*, London, Dalmaine, c1780; ID. *A Complete Instructor for Every Instrument*, London, Dalmaine, 1790.

[39]   BARTHÉLEMON, François-Hippolyte. *A New Tutor for the Violin*, London, the Author, c1798, Preface.

[40]   *Ibidem*.

The music of Tartini was also influential in London, demonstrating, in Hogarth's view, "a knowledge of the violin, both in regard to the bow and the finger-board, which Corelli had not been able to attain".[41] Nevertheless, Tartini's letter to Maddalena Lombardini-Sirmen (1770), translated by Burney and published on his return from his Italian sojourn, served to sustain the pedagogical role of Corelli's violin works for practice and study.[42] Felice Giardini, a disciple of G. B. Somis, also perpetuated the Corelli/Geminiani tradition in England from 1751 but laced it with more progressive elements of Tartini's style, particularly with regard to bowing and expression. One nineteenth-century commentator claimed that Giardini "reformed, or rather founded, a school for the violin in England", introducing into the orchestra of the Italian Opera at the King's Theatre "a new discipline, and a new style of playing more congenial with the poetry and music of Italy than the languid manner of his predecessors".[43] The influence of Viotti in England advanced technical and expressive performance still further, perpetuating the Corellian tradition (through Pugnani) but with some additional French seasoning.

A Teutonic style also infiltrated British violin playing in the 1770s, not least on account of a royal preference for German musicians. Simon McVeigh discusses the rivalries that ensued, the resultant dichotomy between "German intensity and Italian lyricism" and how these developments marked a turning point in the London career of Giardini and his "Roman legion".[44] Particularly influential were the Mannheim violinist Wilhelm Cramer, who resided in London from 1772 until the early 1790s, and the German violinist, impresario and composer Johann Peter Salomon, who settled in London early in 1781, secured Haydn's visits to the capital in 1790-1791 and 1794-1795, and played such a leading role in English musical life that Friedrich Rochlitz opined that

---

[41] HOGARTH, George. *Musical History, Biography and Criticism*, 2 vols, London, Parker, 1835, vol. I, p. 166.

[42] *Lettera del defonto Signor Giuseppe Tartini alla Signora Maddalena Lombardini inserviente ad una importante lezione per i suonatori di violino*; English translation by Charles Burney, *A Letter From the Late Signor Tartini to Signora Maddalena Lombardini (now Signora Sirmen) Published as an Important Lesson to Performers on the Violin*, London, R. Bremner, 1771. See TARTINI, Giuseppe. *Traité des agrémens de la musique*, Paris, l'Auteur, 1771; edition by Erwin R. Jacobi and English translation by Cuthbert Girdlestone, *Treatise on the Ornaments of Music*, Celle-New York, Hermann Moeck Verlag, 1961, pp. 132-138.

[43] [ANON.] 'Memoir', in: *The Harmonicon*, V (1827), p. 215. JOUSSE, Jean. *The Theory and Practice* […], *op. cit.* (see note 15), p. xiv.

[44] 'Giardini', in: *The Cyclopaedia*, edited by Abraham Rees, 39 vols, London, Longman-Hurst-Rees-Orme & Brown, 1802-1819; quoted in McVEIGH, Simon. 'Felice Giardini: A Violinist in Late Eighteenth-Century London', in: *Music and Letters*, LXIV/3-4 (1983), p. 167.

"among all purely executant musicians of this age none has had so wide, so decisive and so beneficent an influence as he".[45]

This diversity of foreign influences had considerable impact on the English concert stage and prompted a greater interest in and demand for instrumental instruction in general and instrumental treatises in particular. However, it affected relatively little the content and standards of violin treatises published in Britain in the first quarter of the nineteenth century, even if progressive influences from France and elsewhere occasionally filtered through into some publications.[46] Frenchman Jean Jousse compiled several instrumental instruction manuals for the English market, some of which were extremely popular and appeared in several editions;[47] but much of his *The Modern Violin Preceptor* (1805?) is underpinned by eighteenth-century concepts, especially those of Geminiani, Philpot and their followers. Jousse's focus is on "the art of bowing with propriety elucidated by examples and exercises", for which he retains the customary "selection of favourite Songs, Marches, Rondos and Duetts" in various major keys up to three sharps and three flats.[48]

Jousse's later *The Theory and Practice of the Violin* (1811), dedicated to Salomon "as a Mark of Real Esteem", expands substantially upon his previous work but retains the focus on the "progress of Learners in the Art of Bowing with propriety and elegance".[49] He bemoans the neglect of the violin by English gentlemen, attributing it partly to "the want of a proper book of Precepts for the Violin; for, except Geminiani's *Art of Playing on the Violin*, in which the Instructions are very incomplete, and the Exercises above the capacity of learners, there is no compleat Tutor for the Violin published in this country".[50] Integrating some of the precepts of, amongst others, Leopold Mozart, Geminiani, l'Abbé le Fils and Rode, Baillot and Kreutzer with his own ideas, his second violin treatise comprises a considerably more thorough exploration of the art of violin playing, its first part theoretical and its second

---

[45]   ROCHLITZ, Friedrich. 'Johann Peter Salomon', in: *Allgemeine musikalische Zeitung*, XVIII (1816), pp. 132-137. On Cramer, Salomon *et al.* and London life as a professional musician, see MCVEIGH, Simon. *Concert Life in London from Mozart to Haydn*, Cambridge, Cambridge University Press, 1993, pp. 182-205.

[46]   See, for example, JOUSSE, Jean. *The Theory and Practice* […], *op. cit.* (see note 15).

[47]   See POOLE, Edmund – HALTON, David. 'A catalogue of musical instruments offered for sale in 1839 by D'Almaine & Co., 20 Soho Square', in: *The Galpin Society Journal*, XXXV (March 1982), pp. 2-36.

[48]   JOUSSE, Jean. *The Modern Violin Preceptor*, London, Goulding, Phipps, D'Almaine & Co., ?1805, title-page.

[49]   ID. *The Theory and Practice* […], *op. cit.* (see note 15), title-page.

[50]   *Ibidem*, p. v.

practical. Its advice is also rather more teacher-orientated, requiring the guidance of an "intelligent" and "judicious Master" and including sections such as "Recommended Music for the Student's Practice".[51] Interestingly, this time Jousse has purposely not "swelled the work with Airs, or Elementary Pieces, which every Master may easily get for his pupils";[52] rather, the second part of his method comprises exercises with a second violin accompaniment for the teacher. Like Philpot, Jousse refers to the "Requisites in an Artist" as "Genius Taste and Application".[53] Typically, he advocates Corelli's works for "forming the hand of a young practitioner", and he borrows Geminiani's vocal analogy and expressive intentions verbatim in his overview of the art of violin playing.[54]

Most native contributions to the British pedagogical literature for the violin in the first third of the nineteenth century reveal the influence of Geminiani in their nurturing of elements of the "ancient style". Many encouraged the involvement of a teacher, not least by including pieces in duet form for master and pupil to play; and some attended also to more current trends in violin playing, a few demonstrating a more systematic approach to instruction. Thomas Goodban's *A New and Complete Guide to the Art of Playing on the Violin* (1810) incorporates a mixture of precepts culled largely from Geminiani and Leopold Mozart, focusing in particular on bowing, fingering and shifting and concluding with four challenging variation sets, arranged as duets or solos. *A Violin Preceptor on an Entire New Principle* (1813) by Robert William Keith, a pupil of Barthélemon, is also largely 'old school' in its pedagogical principles, incorporating various elements derived from Geminiani. "Calculated to lay a regular and stable foundation for Young Practitioners and to Facilitate their Early Progress on that Instrument more especially in the Art of Bowing",[55] it also replicates some of Jousse's precepts and includes some duets and other progressive features such as a brief discussion of natural and artificial harmonics.

John Paine's *A Treatise on the Violin* (c1815) adopts a dialogue format as if to replicate a violin lesson.[56] Although he acknowledges that his method

---

[51]   *Ibidem*, pp. v and xx.

[52]   *Ibidem*, p. v.

[53]   *Ibidem*, pp. xix-xx; Philpot, Stephen. *Op. cit.* (see note 20), pp. 3–6.

[54]   Jousse, Jean. *The Modern Violin* [...], *op. cit.* (see note 48), p. v. Geminiani, Francesco. *APV, op. cit.* (see note 3), p. 1.

[55]   Keith, Robert. *Op. cit.* (see note 30), title-page.

[56]   Pierre Dupont (*Principes de violon par demandes et par reponce*, Paris, L'Auteur, 1718) had adopted a similar dialogue approach, which was to be emulated also in Hamilton, J.[ames] A.[lexander] *Catechism for the Violin*, London, Cocks, c1835; and Thomson, Andrew. *New and Improved Violin Instructor with a Catechism for the Violin*, London, Wood & Ivy, c1840.

is no self–instructor, he aims to provide "a fundamental system" to which the "gentleman" may refer in any part of the world he may be.[57] As the "Inventor and Manufacturer of the Gamut Fingerboard and Bow Guide", Paine incorporates discussion of the merits of these inventions as part of a beginner's practice regime.[58]

In the preface to his *General and Comprehensive Instruction Book for the Violin* (1824), dedicated to Paolo Spagnoletti,[59] John David Loder bemoans both the paucity of pedagogical material for the violin and the manner in which treatise writers have traded on Geminiani's name:

> The acquirement of skill upon an Instrument, confessed by the most difficult of attainment, having never been facilitated by any introductory system beyond a collection of common place tunes subjoin'd to a Gamut and dignified by the Title of 'Geminiani's art of playing the Violin' and the time lost in writing, together with the difficulty of procuring good progressive lessons having long been pressing considerations with the Author of the present collection has induced him to present it not as any addition to the information of his Brethren in the profession, but as a means of smoothing their path in a career, in which pecuniary remuneration however ample, can scarcely be call'd an adequate recompense.[60]

Loder's treatise marks a step forward with regard to the logical progression of its content and was evidently in considerable demand, appearing in numerous editions into the early twentieth century.

Later English violin methods suggest a gradual weakening of Geminiani's predominance. Neville Butler Challoner's *Instructions for the Violin* (1825), compiled with the intention "of facilitating the progress of the Pupil and preventing unnecessary trouble to the Master",[61] focuses on the importance of the duet for study purposes, integrating more closely the role of the teacher with the pedagogical material and musical requirements such as accuracy of intonation and strict time-keeping. The Bristol luthier Thomas Howell

---

[57] PAINE, John. *A Treatise on the Violin*, London, the Author, c1815, Preface, p. v.

[58] *Ibidem*, title-page, pp. 13, 47.

[59] Paolo Spagnoletti (1773-1834) came to London c1802 and soon became renowned as an orchestral leader (he was Paganini's choice for his London concerts in 1831) and chamber musician.

[60] LODER, John. *General and Comprehensive Instruction Book for the Violin*, London, D'Almaine & Co., 1824, Preface.

[61] CHALLONER, Neville B. *Instructions for the Violin*, London, Mayhew & Co, 1825, title-page.

also emphasises the important role of the teacher in his *Original Instructions for the Violin* (1825), notably in demonstrating and guiding the assimilation of its precepts. He bemoans the facts that "there is scarcely an intelligible definition to be met with on the Rudiments of the Science" in violin instruction books in the English language and that "there is a general want of progressive arrangement".[62] He despises "the confused manner" in which instructive matter "is strewed through their pages, and of the almost immediate introduction of popular airs" and opts instead for a more systematic approach with "original progressive examples calculated to lead the pupil by gentle steps through his difficulties".[63] Accordingly, his *Practical Elementary Examples for the Violin* ([1828]), "Designed as an Auxiliary Work" to his *Original Instructions*, comprises a "Systematic Progression of Original Lessons with copious Rules for obtaining an effective and elegant Method of Bowing".[64]

Although the content of three "new", "improved", or "original" treatises by native British writers Henry Blagrove, Robert Hack and Andrew Thomson is substantially elementary and retrospective,[65] these writers all emphasise the importance of the teacher in the pedagogical equation, as "proficiency [...] cannot be gained from books alone, without personal examples and illustrations".[66] Hack reinforces his point by including some duets for master and pupil to play.

As seems clearly evident from the above brief overview of selected British treatises, Geminiani's violin treatise remained, in general terms, a significant influence on violinists and violin playing in the British Isles well into the nineteenth century. The core of this essay will evaluate the extent of Geminiani's influence on each of the principal technical and expressive issues discussed in the text of his treatise and implied by its musical examples.

POSTURE

The main principles of Geminiani's prescription "that the Head of the Violin must be nearly Horizontal with that Part which rests against the

---

[62] HOWELL, Thomas. *Original Instructions for the Violin*, Bristol, s.n., 1825, Introduction.

[63] *Ibidem*, p. 1.

[64] ID. *Practical Elementary Examples for the Violin*, Bristol, Mori & Lavenu, 1828, title-page.

[65] BLAGROVE, Henry. *A New and Improved System of the Art of Violin Playing*, London, s.n., 1828; HACK, Robert. *New and Original Instructions for the Violin*, London, s.n., c1835; THOMSON, Andrew. *Op. cit.* (see note 56).

[66] HACK, Robert. *Op. cit.* (see note 65), p. 52.

Breast, that the Hand may be shifted with Facility and without any Danger of dropping the Instrument"[67] seem to have been absorbed and developed by most of his immediate successors, even though eighteenth-century English treatises are generally vague regarding postural issues. Howell, for example, later recommends "a graceful position" which "gives freedom" to the action of the bow arm; Paine opts for "an easy and graceful attitude, similar to a soldier standing at ease"; and Keith simply urges students to "avoid all motions with the Head, or any other part of the Body".[68] However, nineteenth-century sources generally reveal an increasing trend towards moving the elbow away from the trunk and holding the instrument straight out in front; Jousse, for example, warns against moving the head and body, and his advice that "the head of the Violin should face the middle of the left shoulder" suggests the influence of one of his principal sources of inspiration, the method of Baillot, Rode and Kreutzer.[69] Thomson later provides a considerably more detailed description, recommending the cultivation of

> a noble and easy attitude of the body and head, such as to permit grace to accompany the motions of the fingers, and of the bow. The head and body should be held in an upright position fronting the music, the left shoulder advanced as little as possible and the right side quite disengaged so that the arm may act without causing the least motion of the body. Avoid an affected manner or ungraceful negligence.[70]

MANNER OF HOLDING THE VIOLIN

The eighteenth century witnessed a wide variety of ways of holding the violin, ranging from the surprisingly progressive chin-braced hold originally suggested by Johann Jacob Prinner in 1670 to various methods, some with occasional and most without any stabilising support from the chin.[71] Once

---

[67] GEMINIANI, Francesco. *APV*, *op. cit.* (see note 3), p. 2.

[68] HOWELL, Thomas. *Original Instructions* [...], *op. cit.* (see note 62), p. 22; PAINE, John. *Op. cit.* (see note 57), p. 9; KEITH, Robert. *Op. cit.* (see note 30), p. 13.

[69] JOUSSE, Jean. *The Theory and Practice* [...], *op. cit.* (see note 15), p. 3; BAILLOT, Pierre – RODE, Pierre – KREUTZER, Rodolphe. *Méthode de violon*, Paris, Au Magasin de Musique, 1803, art. 1, p. 5.

[70] THOMSON, Andrew. *Op. cit.* (see note 56), p. 13.

[71] On Johann Jacob Prinner's instructions, see MEDLAM, Charles – ALMOND, Clare. 'On Holding the Violin', in: *Early Music*, VII/4 (1979), pp. 561-563. On the progressive instruction of another source before Geminiani, see BRENDSTRUP, Mogens. 'Danish Violin Testimony', in: *Early Music*, VIII/3 (1980), pp. 429-430. See also Peter Walls in the present volume.

again, Geminiani's instructions are brief and not very informative; but they do offer some foundations for future development, recommending a relatively old-fashioned violin hold with the instrument "rested just below the collarbone" without chin support, but with the instrument tilted slightly for convenient bowing on the G string.[72] Five years after the appearance of Geminiani's treatise, Leopold Mozart considered such a method of holding the violin at the collar-bone "natural and pleasant to the eyes of the onlookers but somewhat difficult and inconvenient for the player as, during quick movements of the hand in the high position, the violin has no support and must therefore necessarily fall unless by long practice the advantage of being able to hold it between the thumb and index-finger has been acquired".[73]

Geminiani's old-fashioned manner of holding the instrument was an additional factor in David Boyden's speculation that this particular section of the treatise may have been written some years before 1751. His suspicions were reinforced by the fact that the frontispiece engraving to what he believed to be the first French edition (1752) of the treatise failed to support Geminiani's text.[74] However, Peter Walls has confirmed that this engraving, which is actually a copy of the frontispiece of José Herrando's *Arte, y puntual explicación del modo de tocar el violin* (Paris, 1756), did not appear until the third French edition of Geminiani's work, published by La Chevardière et les Frères le Goux probably well after Geminiani's death.[75] Interestingly, the first version of Geminiani's violin treatise in German recommends that "the violin must be held between the collar-bone and the jaw-bone" and "with the chin at the right and not at the left side of the tailpiece".[76]

Methods of holding the violin clearly remained variable until well into the nineteenth century. In 1761, l'Abbé le Fils proposed that the chin should be positioned on the G string side of the instrument,[77] but this practice was apparently still not completely accepted by the end of the eighteenth century. Treatises based on Part v of Prelleur's text provide the model for most, if

---

[72]   BOYDEN, David. 'Introduction', *op. cit.* (see note 7), p. vi; GEMINIANI, Francesco. *APV*, *op. cit.* (see note 3), p. 1.

[73]   MOZART, Leopold. *Versuch einer gründlichen Violinschule*, Augsburg, Johann Jacob Lotter, 1756; English translation by Editha Knocker, *A Treatise on the Fundamental Principles of Violin Playing*, London, Oxford University Press, 1951, p. 54.

[74]   BOYDEN, David. 'Introduction', *op. cit.* (see note 7), p. xii.

[75]   On Boyden's unfounded speculation, see WALLS, Peter. 'Violin Fingering in the Eighteenth Century', in: *Early Music*, XII/3, (1984), pp. 303-304.

[76]   GEMINIANI, Francesco. *Gründliche Anleitung oder Violinschule*, Vienna, Christoph Torricella, 1782, Ex. 1 (B), p. 1.

[77]   L'ABBÉ LE FILS. *Principes du violon*, Paris, chez l'Auteur, 1761, p. 1.

not all, of the sources attributed to Geminiani, and they omit mention of the chin or collar-bone positions. The instruction given in other English publications varied considerably, Philpot confirming that "different Masters give different Directions" and recommending the method he learnt (from Festing/Geminiani?) of resting the instrument "upon the Collar-bone, the Tail-piece rather of the Left-side of the Chin".[78] No mention is made, however, of the chin securing the violin in any way, although Robert Crome subscribed to the concept of a chin-braced grip, developing observations in Prelleur's Part v through various editions of his *The Fiddle, New Modell'd* from the 1740s onwards.[79]

Of early nineteenth-century writers, the prescriptions of Paine and Hack are largely retrospective, Paine for example advising the pupil, "keep your left elbow close to your side, and your arm elevated from the elbow to the wrist" and "throw the hand back from the wrist, so as to form a cradle for the neck of the violin".[80] Jousse combines the comments of Prelleur, Geminiani, and Philpot in his *The Modern Violin Preceptor* (1805?),[81] but in his later work opts for the "lean gently" route for the chin on the left side of the tailpiece, advocating a chin-braced grip only when shifting.[82] His descriptions are detailed for their time, amalgamate past practices (even allowing holding the violin at the chest, but pointing out the problems of shifting and keeping the instrument stable) with more contemporary trends, notably some inspired by Baillot, Rode and Kreutzer's *Méthode de violon*, and are supported by some informative illustrations.[83] Keith seems to have gained inspiration from Jousse's descriptions and illustrations, reproducing some of them in his own method. He particularly advises the student to place "your left elbow before your stomach under the Violin leaning your arm against the upper ribs", and recommends that the chin "should lean lightly on the left side of the tailpiece".[84] Howell's advice to lower the right side of the instrument a little to facilitate bowing on the lower

---

[78]   PHILPOT, Stephen. *Op. cit.* (see note 20), p. 6.

[79]   CROME, Robert. *The Fiddle, New Modell'd, or A Useful Introduction for the Violin*, London, J. Tyther, *c*1740, p. 34.

[80]   PAINE, John. *Op. cit.* (see note 57), p. 9. See also KEITH, Robert. *Op. cit.* (see note 30), p. 12; HACK, Robert. *Op. cit.* (see note 65), p. 11.

[81]   JOUSSE, Jean. *The Modern Violin* [...], *op. cit.* (see note 48), p. 8. See PRELLEUR, Peter. *The Modern Musick-Master*, London, for the Author, 1731, Part v, p. 2; GEMINIANI, Francesco. *APV*, *op. cit.* (see note 3), pp. 1-2; PHILPOT, Stephen. *Op. cit.* (see note 20), p. 6.

[82]   JOUSSE, Jean. *The Theory and Practice* [...], *op. cit.* (see note 15), p. 3.

[83]   *Ibidem*, pp. 2-3.

[84]   KEITH, Robert. *Op. cit.* (see note 30), p. 12.

strings doubtless has its roots in Geminiani's text,[85] but his recommendation of a central chin position, "with the tailpiece immediately under the chin", looks forward to advice given in Spohr's *Violinschule*.[86]

THE GEMINIANI GRIP

Geminiani's "Method of acquiring the true position of the Hand"[87] was emulated by several of his English successors as a guide to the optimum position of the fingers and thumb on the fingerboard in first position. Among them were Philpot, Jousse and Keith, Jousse providing detailed explanation of the violin hold with illustrations.[88] This 'Geminiani grip', as it was known, allowed some flexibility for different hand and finger sizes, ensured that the elbow was positioned well under the middle of violin, and permitted the fingers to fall naturally and perpendicularly onto the strings. Significantly, Leopold Mozart adopted it for the very first time in the 1769-1770 edition of his *Versuch*, incorporating it into an exercise for perfecting the playing position. He mirrored Geminiani in claiming that it offers "the shortest way to acquire the true position of the hand and that thereby one achieves an extraordinary facility in playing double-stopping in tune when the moment arrives".[89] Goodban offers a variation on the 'Geminiani grip' to establish the hand-position, with the fingers differently placed.[90]

The "Geminiani grip" was also perpetuated in the relatively advanced treatises of Campagnoli, Baillot, Rode and Kreutzer, Baillot, and David.[91]

---

[85] HOWELL, Thomas. *Original Instructions* [...], *op. cit.* (see note 62), p. 22. GEMINIANI, Francesco. *APV*, *op. cit.* (see note 3), pp. 1-2.

[86] Unlike Spohr, however, Howell makes no mention of a chin rest. On this and associated matters, see STOWELL, Robin. *Violin Technique and Performance Practice in the Late Eighteenth and Early Nineteenth Centuries*, Cambridge, Cambridge University Press, 1985, pp. 29-30.

[87] GEMINIANI, Francesco. *APV*, *op. cit.* (see note 3), p. 1. 1st finger on *f"* (*e"* string); 2nd on *c"* (*a'* string); 3rd on *g'* (*d'* string); 4th on *d'* (*g* string).

[88] PHILPOT, Stephen. *Op. cit.* (see note 20), p. 6; JOUSSE, Jean. *The Modern Violin* [...], *op. cit.* (see note 48), p. 8; ID. *The Theory and Practice* [...], *op. cit.* (see note 15), pp. 3 and 5; GOODBAN, Thomas. *A New and Complete Guide to the Art of Playing on the Violin*, London, Preston, 1810, p. 5; KEITH, Robert. *Op. cit.* (see note 30), p. 13. Jousse's Figures 5, 6, 8 and 9 are reproduced on the title-page of Keith's method, which also mirrors Jousse's instructions.

[89] MOZART, Leopold. *Op. cit.* (see note 73), p. 57, n. 2.

[90] GOODBAN, Thomas. *Op. cit.* (see note 88), p. 15. 1st finger on *b natural'*, 2nd on *c"* (both *a'* string); 3rd on *g'* and 4th on *a'* (both *d'* string).

[91] CAMPAGNOLI, Bartolomeo. *Nouvelle méthode de la mécanique du jeu de violon*, Leipzig, Breitkopf & Härtel, 1824, p. 2; BAILLOT, Pierre - RODE, Pierre - KREUTZER, Rodolphe. *Op.*

Interestingly, Spohr does not subscribe to it in his *Violinschule*, which eventually became the preferred text of the nineteenth-century English school of violin playing.

FINGERBOARD CHART AND INTONATION SYSTEM

Geminiani's inclusion of a fingerboard chart "for learners" seems at odds with his treatise's status as one for the advanced player, and the fact that it is so "perfunctory and carelessly drawn", when compared, for example, with that given in Part v of Prelleur's *The Modern Musick-Master*, points to his making "the traditional gesture to those who wished to adorn their fingerboards in order to play in tune"[92] (see ILL. 2). The custom in English sources of including charts or attaching intonation aids such as frets on fingerboards, lasted well into the nineteenth century.[93] Playford had earlier recommended that beginners should use instruments with frets to accustom fingers for intonation.[94] Paine perpetuated that suggestion with his fretted "Patent finger-board", and Challoner provided a chart for the pupil to use as a template for marking up his fingerboard with a penknife![95] Hack included a "paper fingerboard" with his treatise, an option recommended also by Jousse and others to assist the beginner in "finding the distances".[96]

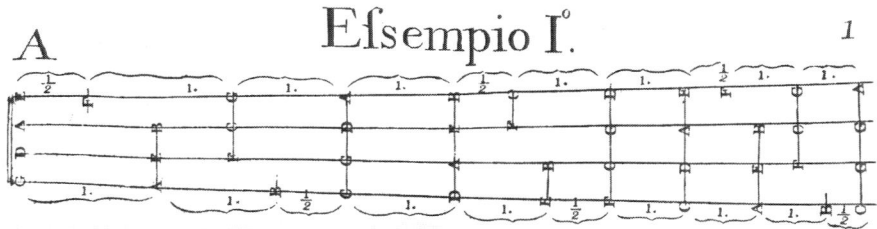

ILL. 2: *APV*, p. 1, "Essempio 1°A".

cit. (see note 69), p. 7; BAILLOT, Pierre. *L'art du Violon: nouvelle Méthode*, Paris, Au dépôt centrale de la musique, 1835, pp. 15 and 18; DAVID, Ferdinand. *Violinschule*, Leipzig, Breitkopf & Härtel, 1864, p. 5.

92   BOYDEN, David. 'Prelleur, Geminiani and Just Intonation', in: *Journal of the American Musicological Society*, IV/3 (1951), p. 211.

93   Among the many examples, see GOODBAN, Thomas. *Op. cit.* (see note 88), p. 17; KEITH, Robert. *Op. cit.* (see note 30), pp. 14 and 16.

94   PLAYFORD, John. *A Briefe Introduction to the Skill of Musick for Song and Viol*, London, Printed by W. Godbid for John Playford, 1658.

95   PAINE, John. *Op. cit.* (see note 57), pp. 13 and 47; CHALLONER, Neville B. *Op. cit.* (see note 61), p. 7.

96   HACK, Robert. *Op. cit.* (see note 65), p. 5; JOUSSE, Jean. *The Theory and Practice* [...], *op. cit.* (see note 15), p. 6.

Geminiani employed a flexible kind of just intonation system, used also in Part v of Prelleur's treatise (1731) and by Tartini in his *Trattato di musica* (1754). This system, in which the sharpened note of enharmonic pairs was considered slightly lower in pitch than its flattened equivalent and was generally not stopped by one and the same finger, can scarcely have been universally adopted. Philpot, for example, acknowledged that only advanced players could be expected to make such a distinction in their tuning.[97] In the nineteenth century a move took place towards the sharpened note of enharmonic pairs being considered higher than its flattened equivalent and, of course, towards equal temperament. Indeed, Howell suggests that harmonic equivalents should sound the same but be created with different fingering.[98] Vestiges of the older systems were retained in, for example, English translations of Spohr's treatise, John Bishop's edition mentioning major and minor semitones while acknowledging equal temperament as the norm.[99]

FINGERING

Geminiani's violin treatise was significant in disseminating information about issues of violin fingering in the eighteenth century, particularly in relation to scales and position-work generally. It demanded facility in seven hand positions (or "orders") on all four strings and various approaches to shifting according to musical context, mastery of double and multiple stopping as well as of scales in various forms, and familiarity with finger extensions and contractions.

Positions

Geminiani considers seven "orders" in his treatise. Jousse also writes about "orders" and, like Keith, extends his use of them to nine, including

---

[97]   PHILPOT, Stephen. *Op. cit.* (see note 20), p. 13. On intonation issues, see BOYDEN, David. 'Prelleur, [...]', *op. cit.* (see note 92), pp. 202-219; BARBOUR, James Murray. 'Violin Intonation in the 18th Century', in: *Journal of the American Musicological Society*, v/3 (1952), pp. 224-234; CHESTNUT, John H. 'Mozart's Teaching of Intonation', in: *Journal of the American Musicological Society*, xxx/2 (Summer, 1977), pp. 254-271.

[98]   HOWELL, Thomas. *Original Instructions* [...], *op. cit.* (see note 62), pp. 60-61.

[99]   SPOHR, Louis. *Violinschule*, Vienna, Tobias Haslinger, 1832; English translation and edition by John Bishop, *Louis Spohr's Celebrated Violin School*, London, R. Cocks & Co., 1843, pp. ii-iii, footnote.

the "natural position".[100] Most other English sources adopted the term "natural position" to denote modern first position, "half shift" for modern second position, and "whole" or "full shift" for modern third position, and Howell, among others, perpetuated the use of this terminology well into the nineteenth century.[101]

The Mechanics of Shifting

The mechanics of shifting were dependent upon such a variety of technical and musical considerations that Tartini famously sat on the fence over the issue, claiming, "it is impossible to give any hard and fast rules. The student should adopt whatever method he finds more comfortable in each case, and he should therefore practise the hand shifts in every possible way so that he is prepared for every situation that may arise".[102] Crucial in the equation, clearly, was whether or not the violin was held with a chin-braced grip. Geminiani's relaxed and natural posture and 'chin-off' technique led to his adoption of a shifting mechanism which stresses the importance of the independence of the thumb from the fingers:

> After having been practised in the first Order, you must pass on to the second, and then to the third; in which Care is to be taken that the Thumb always remain farther back than the Fore-finger;[103] and the more you advance in the other Orders the Thumb must be at a greater Distance till it remains almost hid under the Neck of the Violin.[104]

Downward shifts also called for a special technique requiring the left thumb to play an independent role in the "transposition of the Hand":

> It must here be observed, that in drawing back the Hand from the 5th, 4th and 3d Order to go to the first, the Thumb cannot, for Want of Time, be replaced in its natural Position; but it is necessary it should be replaced at the second Note.[105]

---

[100] JOUSSE, Jean. *The Theory and Practice* [...], *op. cit.* (see note 15), p. 25; KEITH, Robert. *Op. cit.* (see note 30), p. 33.

[101] HOWELL, Thomas. *Original Instructions* [...], *op. cit.* (see note 62), p. 41.

[102] TARTINI, Giuseppe. *Op. cit.* (see note 42), p. 56.

[103] Interestingly, this phrase was omitted in Robert Bremner's reissue of Geminiani's violin treatise in 1777.

[104] GEMINIANI, Francesco. *APV*, *op. cit.* (see note 3), p. 2, re: Example 1C.

[105] *Ibidem*, p. 3, re: Example 1E.

Geminiani's examples exploit every conceivable kind of shift and explore the fingerboard up to seventh position. He seems to favour bold leaps and large hand movements (such as 123, 123, or 1234, 1234) in his annotated fingerings for the scales and exercises in his treatise, running counter to the general eighteenth-century trend towards small upward shifts, often using adjacent fingers (23-23 or 12-12). The advent of using the chin as a stabilising agent for the instrument affected shifting practices only very gradually. As Peter Walls deduces, "The consistency of rules about shifting and of shift markings in studies and sonatas throughout the [eighteenth century] suggests that it was a long time before the chin came to be used as anything more than a supplementary aid".[106] As a consequence, large hand movements seem to be favoured by most writers for downward shifts in the eighteenth century.

Some nineteenth-century treatises in English offer more detail regarding shifting mechanisms by providing some text, fingerings, scales, exercises and/or fingering charts, but in most cases the instruction given was insufficient without the benefit of additional teaching. Jousse provides exercises for shifts of various kinds, explains the role of the thumb as a facilitator in shifting and recognises the stablising potential of "leaning gently the chin on the violin to prevent its falling".[107] As with several technical issues, Keith mirrors some of Jousse's instructions but, in contrast to Geminiani, comes out in favour of smaller shifts of the hand. Like Paine, he looks back to Leopold Mozart and exploits the use of open strings for ease of shifting, whereas Goodban particularly flags up the importance of maintaining the geography of the fingerboard for intonation purposes in shifting, keeping the first finger down on the string as much as possible as a guide.[108] He continues: "After Shifting, the Hand must be brought back into its natural position by means of the wrist; or by pressing the chin upon the instrument to contain it while the hand is moved — the latter is certainly the most easy to a Learner, but the former is the most graceful and proper". Following the likes of Leopold Mozart and Galeazzi, he also suggests that the open strings may be taken advantage of in shifting, "when they can be used with propriety".

---

[106] WALLS, Peter. 'Violin Fingering [...]', *op. cit.* (see note 75), p. 305.

[107] JOUSSE, Jean. *The Theory and Practice [...]*, *op. cit.* (see note 15), pp. 3 and 22.

[108] KEITH, Robert. *Op. cit.* (see note 30), pp. 34-35; PAINE, John. *Op. cit.* (see note 57), p. 43; MOZART, Leopold. *Op. cit.* (see note 73), p. 138; GOODBAN, Thomas. *Op. cit.* (see note 88), pp. 38-39.

Scales

It was not until the second half of the eighteenth century that writers really began to appreciate the importance of scales in the training and discipline of the left hand. Geminiani (Examples I-VIII) was one of the first to incorporate a detailed survey of scales in a violin treatise; his successors generally followed his lead, most including scales in some form in their methods in order to encourage the cultivation of accurate intonation, independence and agility of fingers, strong finger action for tonal clarity and many bowing disciplines, notably those of tone-quality, bow division, and dynamics.[109]

Unnecessary activity of the fingers was normally avoided, the general rule applying that the fingers should not be raised from the strings without good reason.[110] Thus, Geminiani's "constant Rule to keep the Fingers as firm as possible, and not to raise them, till there is a Necessity of doing it, to place them somewhere else"[111] was followed by the vast majority of English writers.[112] Howell, for example, writes that the four fingers "must form an arch, bringing their points in contact with the strings, and acting in a right line with them, so as not to pull them aside, but for the pressure of the fingers to be perpendicular".[113] His alignment of finger pressure with tonal quality represents a relatively rare occurrence in the pedagogical literature of the period, mentioned previously only by Philpot, who recommended "stopping the fingers firm upon each String" for optimum tonal clarity.[114]

Finger Elasticity: Extensions and Contractions

Geminiani's various exercises place particular importance on cultivating flexibility of the fingers in order to facilitate extensions and contractions smoothly and thereby to move the left hand freely around the fingerboard. His Example ID (see ILL. 3) illustrating "the different Ways of stopping the

---

[109] HOWELL, Thomas. *Original Instructions* [...], *op. cit.* (see note 62), pp. 12ff.

[110] GOODBAN, Thomas. *Op. cit.* (see note 88), p. 15; KEITH, Robert. *Op. cit.* (see note 30), p. 12.

[111] GEMINIANI, Francesco. *APV, op. cit.* (see note 3), p. 2.

[112] JOUSSE, Jean. *The Theory and Practice* [...], *op. cit.* (see note 15), p. 6; PAINE, John. *Op. cit.* (see note 57), pp. 21-22; HOWELL, Thomas. *Original Instructions* [...], *op. cit.* (see note 62), p. 25; HAMILTON, J.[ames] A.[lexander] *Op. cit.* (see note 56), p. 32; THOMSON, Andrew. *Op. cit.* (see note 56), p. 12; LODER, John. *Op. cit.* (see note 60), p. 46.

[113] HOWELL, Thomas. *Original Instructions* [...], *op. cit.* (see note 62), p. 22.

[114] PHILPOT, Stephen. *Op. cit.* (see note 20), p. 6.

same Note" is but one example, and his fingerings for the C major scales at the end of Example IE seem to ignore the whole concept of positions, requiring minimal hand movement and remarkable digital elasticity.

ILL. 3: *APV*, p. 1, "Essempio 1°D/E".

He also recommends various extensions and contractions of the hand as a means of enlarging its range in a given position, notably in his examples involving double stopping (see ILL. 4). Although unsupported by explanatory text, such fingerings often reduced the need for formal shifts and were particularly helpful to those violinists who did not use a chin-braced method of holding the violin.

Many writers after Geminiani emphasized the need for a strong, hammer-like finger-action with minimal uplift of the fingers in order to obtain clear articulation and tone production,[115] but none came close to reproducing his complex web of extensions and contractions or his innovative one-finger-per-

---

[115] See, for example, JOUSSE, Jean. *The Theory and Practice* [...], *op. cit.* (see note 15), p. 3.

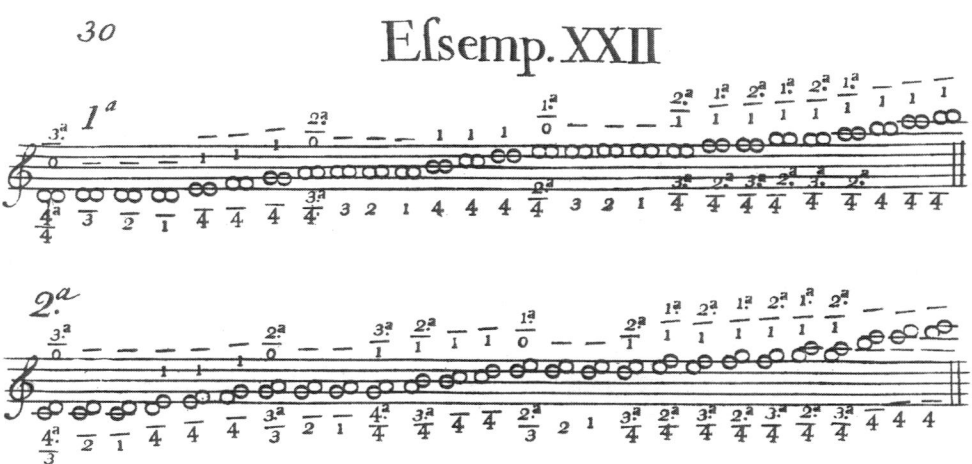

ILL. 4: *APV*, p. 30, "Essemp. XXII 1ª/2ª".

note policy for the execution of chromatic scale passages, even though this latter offered greater evenness, articulation and clarity than the traditional 'slide' fingering. As Boyden remarks, this chromatic fingering was so progressive that it "had to be rediscovered in the twentieth century by Joseph Achron and expounded by Carl Flesch".[116]

Although open strings were sometimes necessarily employed in the execution of shifts, double and multiple stopping and other such technical elements in the eighteenth century, they were not generally adopted in instances where stopped notes were technically viable. Peter Walls concluded from his study of early eighteenth-century fingering that "the indication of fourth fingers seems often to have been the only fingering choice that composers felt any need to make themselves".[117] One treatise attributed to Geminiani discusses using the fourth finger to attain good intonation rather than for sonority, referring to occasions when that finger is more "equal in tune" than the open string.[118] However, the principal reason for indicating the use of the fourth finger reflects an increasing interest in eliminating the tonal difference between open and stopped strings and thereby cultivating homogeneous tone quality and sonority; this interest was encouraged thereafter in England by the likes of, among others, Philpot, Goodban, Jousse, Challoner and Howell. Goodban claims that the fourth finger "ought always to be preferred in playing Piano or Soft — and as passing or crossing the Strings unnecessarily is to be avoided, it should also be

---

[116]   BOYDEN, David. 'Introduction', *op. cit.* (see note 7), p. vii.

[117]   WALLS, Peter. 'Violin Fingering […]', *op. cit.* (see note 75), p. 307.

[118]   GEMINIANI, Francesco, attrib. *Compleat Instructions for the Violin*, London, G. Goulding, *c*1800, p. 2.

used where ye preceeding and succeeding Notes are both below it", whereas Howell concedes that "the open string occasionally gives variety, strength and brilliancy to certain passages".[119]

Writers in England were not backward in emulating those in other countries who exploited the higher positions for increased sonority and expression. Goodban considers shifting "highly useful in the performance of such passages as require sweetness of Tone or Delicacy in Playing, for although the Notes of which such passages consist may all lie within the compass of the natural position of the hand, yet it often occurs that they cannot be Played with so much facility or with so good an effect as upon the Shift".[120] Jousse, meanwhile, maintains that "the Rules for shifting depend on the expression to be given to a passage and on the quantity of notes, which for the sake of smoothness ought to be played on the same string", and Hack recommends in slow movements playing as many notes on one string as the passage will permit in order to achieve "a firm and even quality of tone, which cannot be gained by playing across the strings".[121]

Portamento

Portamento can often be a natural outcome of the shifting process and practical experiments suggest that it was a likely outcome from Geminiani's various fingerboard manoeuvres. However, a comment from Charles Burney negates this suggestion and points to the fact that Geminiani may well have been hostile to an effect that was to play an increasingly significant artistic role in violin playing:

> Geminiani, however, was certainly mistaken in laying it down as a rule, that "no two notes on the same string, in shifting, should be played with the same finger"; as beautiful expressions and effects are produced by great players, in shifting, suddenly, from a low note to a high, with the same finger on the same string.[122]

Some annotated fingerings of the period certainly imply, like Burney's text, that the potential resultant slide was most probably intended to be

---

[119] Philpot, Stephen. *Op. cit.* (see note 20), p. 10; Goodban, Thomas. *Op. cit.* (see note 88), p. 27; Jousse, Jean. *The Theory and Practice* […], *op. cit.* (see note 15), p. 35; Howell, Thomas. *Original Instructions* […], *op. cit.* (see note 62), p. 26.

[120] Goodban, Thomas. *Op. cit.* (see note 88), p. 38.

[121] Jousse, Jean. *The Theory and Practice* […], *op. cit.* (see note 15), p. 70; Hack, Robert. *Op. cit.* (see note 65), p. 52.

[122] Burney, IV, p. 643n.

heard.[123] Indeed, Clive Brown claims that portamento was "very strongly associated with the Italian style of performance and in particular with Italian and Italian-influenced musicians",[124] so it is likely to have played a prominent part in performance practices in England from the latter half of the eighteenth century.[125] Indeed, by the beginning of the nineteenth century the use of portamento by string players was widespread throughout Europe and remained so until well into the twentieth century. Howell, for example, remarks that shifting "gives opportunities of gliding the fingers along the strings so as to produce a continuity of sound between distant degrees that constitutes one of its chief ornaments when introduced and executed with judgement, it being as successful an imitation of this beautiful effect in a fine Human Voice, as any instrument whatever is capable of producing".[126] Brown provides evidence that portamento even infiltrated into orchestral playing, despite condemnation by many prominent theorists and composers, including Spohr.[127]

BOW MANAGEMENT

The fundamental principle in Italian violin pedagogy appears to have been to establish and develop left-hand before right-hand technique. Consequently, Geminiani encourages practice of his initial exercises in the various positions without the bow, "which you should not meddle with till you come to the 7th Example, in which will be found the necessary and proper Method of using it. It cannot be supposed but that this Practice without the Bow is disagreeable, since it gives no Satisfaction to the Ear; but the Benefit which, in Time, will arise from it, will be a Recompence more than adequate to the Disgust it may give".[128] When Geminiani does bring the bow into play in the fourteen scales of Example VII, the player is

---

[123]   One of many examples appears in: MOZART, Leopold. *Op. cit.* (see note 73), Ch. XI, Sec. 7, p. 206.

[124]   BROWN, Clive. *Classical and Romantic Performance Practice 1750-1900*, Oxford, Oxford University Press, 1999, p. 561.

[125]   For more on Italian/European exploitation of portamento in the late eighteenth century and thereafter see also WALLS, Peter. *History, Imagination and the Performance of Music*, Woodbridge, Boydell Press, 2003, pp. 90ff.; STOWELL, Robin. *Op. cit.* (see note 86), pp. 98-103.

[126]   HOWELL, Thomas. *Original Instructions* [...], *op. cit.* (see note 62), p. 41.

[127]   BROWN, Clive. *Classical and Romantic Performance Practice* [...], *op. cit.* (see note 124), pp. 561-562. SPOHR, Louis. *Op. cit.* (see note 99), Vienna, 1832, p. 248.

[128]   GEMINIANI, Francesco. *APV*, *op. cit.* (see note 3), pp. 2-3.

immediately substantially challenged with string crossings, in addition to the demands of the various "Transpositions of the Hand".[129]

The Manner of Holding the Bow

Geminiani describes the typical early eighteenth-century Italian manner of holding the bow "at a small Distance from the Nut, between the Thumb and Fingers, the Hair being turned inward against the Back or Outside of the Thumb, in which Position it is to be held free and easy, and not stiff".[130] As with the manner of holding the violin, there are inconsistencies between the text and the frontispiece from the third French edition of his method, with the original description of a bow hold "a small distance from the nut" illustrated as a rather large distance. Although Geminiani's bow hold has been criticised as being retrospective for its time, especially when compared with Leopold Mozart's somewhat firmer grip, in which the bowstick was held "at its lowest extremity, between the thumb and the middle joint of the index-finger, or even a little behind it",[131] the treatises of, amongst others, Philpot, Jousse, Goodban, Keith, Challoner and Hack were clearly indebted to his instruction.[132] Philpot's recommendations, for example, closely resemble Geminiani's, suggesting that the bow should be "held between the Thumb and the fingers of the right hand, the hair being turned inwardly against the outside of the Thumb which is to support the whole weight of the bow, and must be placed on the stick about an inch from the Nut, facing the 2nd finger".[133] Similarly, Keith recommends:

> The bow is to be held at a small distance from the Nut,
> between the thumb and fingers of the right Hand, the hair being
> turned inward against the back or outside of the thumb which

---

[129]   *Ibidem*, p. 4.

[130]   *Ibidem*, p. 2.

[131]   MOZART, Leopold. *Op. cit.* (see note 73), pp. 58-59. Note that this description was slightly modified in the 1787 edition. This lower position on the stick was combined with pressure from the second joint of the index-finger (instead of Geminiani's first joint — see frontispiece illustration). And Leopold Mozart's bow-hair was "more straight than sideways on the violin" (*ibidem*, p. 60) in his quest for a powerful "honest and virile tone" (*ibidem*, p. 58).

[132]   JOUSSE, Jean. *The Modern Violin* [...], *op. cit.* (see note 48), p. 8; GEMINIANI, Francesco. *APV, op. cit.* (see note 3), p. 2; PHILPOT, Stephen. *Op. cit.* (see note 20), p. 6; GOODBAN, Thomas. *Op. cit.* (see note 88), p. 15; KEITH, Robert. *Op. cit.* (see note 30), p. 12; CHALLONER, Neville B. *Op. cit.* (see note 61), p. 6; HACK, Robert. *Op. cit.* (see note 65), p. 11.

[133]   PHILPOT, Stephen. *Op. cit.* (see note 20), p. 4.

is to support the whole weight of the bow, and must be placed
pressing on the Stick facing the 2nd finger.[134]

Geminiani's text about "the right Management of the Bow" is
reproduced in the various sources attributed to him and underpins many
of the pedagogical materials published in England well into the nineteenth
century. Philpot, for example, embraces the main principles of Geminiani's
basic bowing philosophy in his instruction that "the thumb should be
placed just above the Nut, the Hair resting on the Back of the Thumb,
and the Fingers on the Outside of the Bow, some little distance from each
other, that thereby the whole Length of the Bow may be Commanded
at Pleasure".[135] Others, such as Jousse, Goodban, and Keith repeat much
of Geminiani's advice, particularly emphasising the role of the wrist in
cultivating a straight bow-stroke.[136] They use some of Geminiani's
phraseology practically verbatim,[137] whilst occasionally introducing some
small modifications. In order to develop flexibility in the wrist and avoid
bowing "from the shoulder" Jousse, for example, points out, "In drawing
the bow [i.e. in a down-bow] the hand must recede from the body, the
Wrist raising upwards with ease; but when the bow is pushed [i.e. in an
up-bow], the Hand is brought closer to the body, the Wrist inclining
downward".[138] However, Keith all but replicates Geminiani by specifying
that "the motion of the bow is to proceed from the joints of the wrist and
elbow in playing quick notes, and very little or not at all from the joints of
the Shoulder; but in playing long Notes, where the Bow is drawn from one
end of it to the other the joint of the Shoulder is also a little employed".[139]

Some of the 'modifications' mentioned above concern the position of
the thumb, which Jousse, Goodban, Keith and Howell place opposite the
second finger;[140] and some concern the placement of the elbow in relation to
the body, Jousse, for example, prescribing an elbow position "always at a little

---

[134]   Keith, Robert. *Op. cit.* (see note 30), p. 12.

[135]   Philpot, Stephen. *Op. cit.* (see note 20), p. 6.

[136]   For example, Jousse, Jean. *The Theory and Practice* [...], *op. cit.* (see note 15), p. 14;
Howell, Thomas. *Original Instructions* [...], *op. cit.* (see note 62), p. 22.

[137]   For example, the first three lines of Robert W. Keith's instructions (p. 12) are very
similar to those of Geminiani (p. 2).

[138]   Jousse, Jean. *The Theory and Practice* [...], *op. cit.* (see note 15), p. 14.

[139]   Keith, Robert. *Op. cit.* (see note 30), p. 12.

[140]   Jousse, Jean. *The Theory and Practice* [...], *op. cit.* (see note 15), p. 4; Goodban,
Thomas. *Op. cit.* (see note 88), p. 15; Keith, Robert. *Op. cit.* (see note 30), p. 12; Howell,
Thomas. *Original Instructions* [...], *op. cit.* (see note 62), p. 22.

distance from the body".[141] Most other writers are consistent with Geminiani regarding the largely non-participatory role of the upper arm and shoulder and the need for flexibility of the wrist in order to cultivate a straight bow-stroke.[142] Paine, who invented his 'bow guide' as an aid to ensure that the bow was drawn parallel to, and at a suitable distance from the bridge, illustrates a high hand position with the hand turned "a little outwards",[143] and Jousse similarly expresses the concern that the knuckles should be kept "rather high above the Stick". Perhaps unsurprisingly, given his French background, Jousse is one of the first of the 'English' writers to replicate l'Abbé le Fils' prescription that the joints of the fingers should be kept free "to obey all those necessary, though imperceptible motions, which serve to draw a fine tone from the violin".[144] He also gives a special mention to the role of the little finger, which "must be placed on the Stick over the Nut [...] but so lightly as to be able to leave or retake its position at the performer's will, without hindering the action of the other fingers, or altering their position".

Writers continually stress Geminiani's instruction that the control of bow pressure, and hence tonal quality and volume, should come from the index finger (or forefinger) and not from the weight of the hand.[145] Geminiani makes no mention of bow speed in, for example, swelling the sound, but Howell's treatises are especially significant in highlighting the need "to proportion the pressure to the Velocity".[146] Many of Geminiani's successors add to his basic instructions that the index finger should be separated slightly from the other fingers on the bow stick in order for it to control the tonal volume by applying or releasing pressure as required.[147] Interestingly, though, Spohr later warned

---

[141]   JOUSSE, Jean. *The Theory and Practice* [...], *op. cit.* (see note 15), p. 4.

[142]   GOODBAN, Thomas. *Op. cit.* (see note 88), p. 15; KEITH, Robert. *Op. cit.* (see note 30), p. 12; HOWELL, Thomas. *Original Instructions* [...], *op. cit.* (see note 62), p. 22; CHALLONER, Neville B. *Op. cit.* (see note 61), p. 6.

[143]   PAINE, John. *Op. cit.* (see note 57), title-page and p. 9. On the 'bow guide' see pp. 13 and 47. Paine may have been inspired by Georg Simon Löhlein's recommendation in LÖHLEIN, Georg Simon. *Anweisung zum Violinspielen*, Leipzig-Züllichau, Auf Kosten der Waysenhaus- und Frommanischen Buchhandlung, 1774, Ch. 5, sec. 34, p. 21.

[144]   JOUSSE, Jean. *The Theory and Practice* [...], *op. cit.* (see note 15), p. 4. L'ABBÉ LE FILS. *Op. cit.* (see note 77), p. 1.

[145]   GEMINIANI, Francesco. *APV, op. cit.* (see note 3), p. 2; JOUSSE, Jean. *The Modern Violin* [...], *op. cit.* (see note 48), p. 8; HACK, Robert. *Op. cit.* (see note 65), p. 21; GOODBAN, Thomas. *Op. cit.* (see note 88), p. 15.

[146]   HOWELL, Thomas. *Original Instructions* [...], *op. cit.* (see note 62), p. 22. ID. *Practical Elementary Examples* [...], *op. cit.* (see note 64), p. 1.

[147]   However, the stretching out of the index finger was universally recognised as a technical fault, causing constrictions in the free movement of the wrist and fingers and

specifically against separating the index finger from the others on the bow stick, recommending that "the tips of all four fingers should be so brought together that there is no space between them".[148] With the advent of the Tourte bow and its powers of even pressure-distribution throughout its length, it was no longer necessary to separate the index finger from the others in order to realise adequate pressure at the point.

Other General Bowing Issues

Geminiani illustrates a wide range of bow strokes, most notably in Examples IX, XVI and XVII, but the true meanings of his classifications "good" [buono], "bad" [cattivo] and "middling" [mediocre] for his various strokes in Example XX are confusing and unclear. Boyden also questions Geminiani's views on staccato, detached strokes played on the string, and "plain" legato.[149] Most other English writers refrain from providing detailed descriptions of individual bow strokes, hoping doubtless that the music included in their treatises would make the stroke required, and its execution, self-explanatory. Jousse, for example, claims that "the puntato (pointed notes), the staccato (notes detached in the same bow) and the legato (slurred notes)" comprise the principal bowing styles and he gives some basic observations about each, strangely claiming that the thumb alone should press against the stick in staccato bowing.[150] Some, and most notably Hamilton, build on Leopold Mozart's so-called divisions of the bow, four types of nuanced bowings (Division 1 = <>; Division 2 = >; Division 3 = <; and Division 4 = <><>), using them as a basis for exercises to help the player "to apply strength and weakness in all parts of the bow" and to cultivate tonal purity and variety of nuance and expression.[151]

Few writers go quite as far as to emulate Geminiani's encouragement to players to "make Use of the whole of it [the bow], from the Point to that Part of it under, and even beyond their Fingers".[152] However, Jousse encourages his readers "to draw the bow smooth and even, from end to end", and Howell similarly urges use of "the whole extent of the Bow"

---

impeding the player's bow control.

[148]   SPOHR, Louis. *Op. cit.* (see note 99), p. 25.

[149]   BOYDEN, David. 'Introduction', *op. cit.* (see note 7), p. viii.

[150]   JOUSSE, Jean. *The Theory and Practice* […], *op. cit.* (see note 15), p. 20.

[151]   MOZART, Leopold. *Op. cit.* (see note 73), Ch. 5, secs 4-8, pp. 102–104. HAMILTON, J.[ames] A.[lexander] *Op. cit.* (see note 56), pp. 43-44.

[152]   GEMINIANI, Francesco. *APV, op. cit.* (see note 3), p. 2.

whenever possible, because of the impression of grandeur that such liberal usage imparts to a performance.[153]

Rule of Down-Bow

Geminiani rejected the restrictive, yet long-standing, rule of down-bow,[154] formulated by the Italians early in the seventeenth century or even before but very much a hallmark of French playing of the period, in favour of a more flexible bowing regime. He warns "the Learner against marking the Time with his Bow", on account of the "most disagreeable Effect" that can result, whether through stressing the first note of every bar or through destroying a composer's intended syncopations;[155] elsewhere he urges avoidance of "that wretched Rule of drawing the Bow down at the first Note of every Bar"[156] and provides exercises designed to encourage greater equality of accentuation between up and down strokes. Quantz and Reichardt were among those who likewise encouraged such equality.[157] One of Geminiani's exercises involves a repeated section which requires the player to adopt bowing completely contrary to that used in his first playing.[158] Jousse also later rejects the "wretched method of taking the first note of every bar in a down-bow", not only because it is "liable to many exceptions" but also because it can "give to the performance a monotonous regularity, and cramp the powers of the performer".[159] He provides sets of rules for governing up- and down-bow usage.[160]

Another Italian with influence in England, Tartini, adopts a more flexible compromise, claiming that "there are no definite rules for determining whether one should begin with a down bow or up bow", and he urges that "all passages should be practised in both ways, in order to gain complete mastery of the bow

---

[153] JOUSSE, Jean. *The Modern Violin* [...], *op. cit.* (see note 48), p. 8. HOWELL, Thomas. *Original Instructions* [...], *op. cit.* (see note 62), p. 23.

[154] This rule requires the first note of each bar, or effectively every accented beat or part thereof, with a down bow, so far as tempo considerations allow.

[155] GEMINIANI, Francesco. *APV*, *op. cit.* (see note 3), p. 9.

[156] *Ibidem*, p. 4.

[157] QUANTZ, Johann Joachim. *Versuch einer Anweisung die Flöte traversiere zu spielen*, Berlin, Johann Friedrich Voß, 1752, 1789; facsimile edition by Hans-Peter Schmitz, Kassel, Bärenreiter, 1953; English translation by Edward R. Reilly, *On Playing the Flute*, London-New York, Faber & Faber, 1966, pp. 222-223. REICHARDT, Johann Friedrich. *Ueber die Pflichten des Ripien-Violinisten*, Berlin-Leipzig, Decker, 1776, p. 28.

[158] KEITH, Robert. *Op. cit.* (see note 30), pp. 39ff. reproduces some of Geminiani's exercises, along with others by the likes of Corelli and Tessarini.

[159] JOUSSE, Jean. *The Theory and Practice* [...], *op. cit.* (see note 15), pp. 17 and 15.

[160] *Ibidem*, pp. 15-17.

in both up and down strokes".[161] However, successors such as Goodban, Keith, Challoner, Paine, Hack and West do not subscribe to such flexibility, even if some of them acknowledge, in Challoner's words, that the rule "cannot always be attended to".[162] Hack, for example, claims that "The first note of every measure [...] must be played with a down bow, unless marked to the contrary", later emphasising that "accents are indispensably essential to all music, and are most forcibly and accurately produced in drawing the bow downwards".[163] Certainly, the rule of down-bow remained a guiding principle in bowing throughout the nineteenth and twentieth centuries, even if Geminiani's loosening of its imperatives generally allowed some degree of flexibility in its application.

Expression, Ornamentation (Including Vibrato) & Taste

Hawkins reported that Geminiani "had none of the fire and spirit of the modern violinists, but that all the graces and elegancies of the melody, all the powers that can engage attention, or that render the passions of the hearer subservient to the will of the artist, were united in his performance".[164] Thus, Geminiani maintained and furthered the Corelli tradition of violin playing as much from an expressive and tasteful standpoint as from a technical one. Despising virtuosity for its own sake, as well as technical trickery, including the French tendency towards the imitation of extra-musical ideas, Geminiani emphasised the performer's responsibility to convey the composer's intentions with accuracy, expression and good taste.[165] His ideal model for violin playing was the human voice, in both a singing and a spoken role, and he sought to encourage a highly expressive, emotional style of performance through the imaginative, yet controlled employment of specific and extempore ornamentation, dynamic markings, varied and nuanced bowings, vibrato and other expressive means. Acknowledging Geminiani's survey of his own expressive practice, Charles Avison remarked that in his "useful" treatise Geminiani "has communicated to the musical World, as much of his superior

---

[161]   Tartini, Giuseppe. *Op. cit.* (see note 42), p. 56.

[162]   Goodban, Thomas. *Op. cit.* (see note 88), pp. 18 and 21; Keith, Robert. *Op. cit.* (see note 30), p. 16; Challoner, Neville B. *Op. cit.* (see note 61), p. 10; Paine, John. *Op. cit.* (see note 57), p. 24; Hack, Robert. *Op. cit.* (see note 65), p. 22; West, William Henry *The Art of Playing the Violin, on a new principle by which the progress of the learner is greatly facilitated*, London, s.n., 1840, p. 8.

[163]   Hack, Robert. *Op. cit.* (see note 65), pp. 22 and 50.

[164]   *Hawkins*, V, p. 393.

[165]   Geminiani, Francesco. *APV, op. cit.* (see note 3), pp. 1 and 6.

Taste and Method of Execution, as could possibly be expected from such an Undertaking".[166]

Geminiani's *APV* also incorporates essentially the first reasonably detailed survey of ornamentation in a violin treatise and particularly emphasises the role of ornaments (including vibrato and dynamic indications) in expressing affective sentiments in performance. Believing that a violinist should strive to develop a tone which rivals "the most perfect human voice", he describes how music should imitate "a Discourse"; and he considers that *piano* and *forte* "are designed to produce the same Effects that an Orator does by raising and falling his voice".[167] Along with these close parallels between violin and vocal performance, Music's power to "strike the Imagination, affect the Mind, and command the Passions" is especially highlighted. Nowhere is this more evident than in Geminiani's brief description of each of the fourteen ornaments, in which he relates how some change their character or affect according to their manner of execution. His description of the 'beat' (or mordent) is a case in point:

> If it be perform'd with Strength, and continued long, it expresses Fury, Anger, Resolution, &c. If it be play'd less strong and shorter, it expresses Mirth, Satisfaction, &c. But if you play it quite soft, and swell the Note, it may then denote Horror, Fear, Grief, Lamentation, &c. By making it short and swelling the Note gently, it may express Affection and Pleasure.[168]

Such variation in the expressive realisation of individual specific ornaments (other than vibrato) means that their discussion in more than general terms is essentially beyond the scope of this survey. Suffice it to say, though, that Geminiani's table of ornaments and supporting text in Example XVIII, reproduced from his earlier *Treatise of Good Taste in the Art of Musick* (1749), were disseminated widely (see ILL. 1). The table featured in most of the later treatises attributed to him[169] — indeed, it was one of the

---

166   AVISON, Charles. *An Essay on Musical Expression*, London, C. Davis, 1753; facsimile edition, New York, Broude Brothers, 1967, p. 127.

167   GEMINIANI, Francesco. *APV*, *op. cit.* (see note 3), p. 7 and music p. 26.

168   *Ibidem*, pp. 7-8.

169   For example, several late eighteenth- and early nineteenth-century publications which appeared as *The Compleat Tutor for the Violin: containing the easiest and best methods for learners to obtain a proficiency, with some useful directions, lessons, graces &c. by Geminiani* […], or with a similar title, issued at various times by publishers such as S. A. and P. Thompson, C. and S. Thompson, Thompson and Son, and John Preston.

principal attributable aspects of those publications — and was also imitated with varying degrees of fidelity by many of his 'English' successors.

As styles and tastes changed, so did the expressive role of each ornament and their various individual descriptions. Philpot, for example, makes reference to Geminiani's treatment of ornaments but briefly describes only about five ornament types, and in very different, and rather more simple, terms; Jousse, meanwhile, includes "the proper use of Graces" as one of the six principal means of expression,[170] discussing various types of trill (shake) and, like Leopold Mozart, incorporating an extract from Tartini's 'Devil's Trill' sonata to illustrate double trills.[171] He recommends Geminiani's embellishments of Corelli's sonatas as models for extempore ornamentation, and his treatise is also significant, along with Tashanberg's, for its inclusion of some suggestions for cadential and other embellishments.[172]

Many writers were at pains to warn against overusing ornaments, lest the melody become "too much diversified" or the performer be "guilty of a breach of harmony".[173] As Goodban confirms, "it requires Caution not to use too many as well as Judgement and Taste to perform those introduced with elegance and correctness".[174]

Geminiani's pupil, Robert Bremner, contrasts the respective approaches of the soloist and the orchestral musician towards ornamentation in general, as well as to individual specific ornaments. Whereas the soloist may apply "all the different graces of the bow and finger [...] when and where he pleases", the orchestral player should consider the fingers "as meer [*sic*] stops to put the notes in tune" so that "every tone should be as void of ornament as if produced by an open string". Bremner's distinction between these two different approaches goes some way towards explaining his apparent disagreement with his mentor over vibrato and its usage (see below).

---

[170] The other means concern the proper modification of sounds, the strict observance of accentuation, a knowledge of the principal movements, matters of style, and variety of bowing.

[171] PHILPOT, Stephen. *Op. cit.* (see note 20), pp. 9-10; JOUSSE, Jean. *The Theory and Practice* [...], *op. cit.* (see note 15), pp. 41, 46-52.

[172] JOUSSE, Jean. *The Theory and Practice* [...], *op. cit.* (see note 15), pp. 51-52; TASHANBERG, John. *The Compleat School or Art of Playing the Violin*, London, R. Wornum, 1796, pp. 5ff.

[173] GEMINIANI, Francesco. *APV*, *op. cit.* (see note 3), p. 7.

[174] GOODBAN, Thomas. *Op. cit.* (see note 88), p. 11. JOUSSE, Jean. *The Theory and Practice* [...], *op. cit.* (see note 15), p. 52.

Geminiani considered vibrato (or the "close shake", as he termed it)[175] as an ornament and also associated it with affective performance: "When it is long continued swelling the Sound by Degrees, drawing the Bow nearer to the Bridge, and ending it very strong", he writes, "it may express Majesty, Dignity, *&c*. But making it shorter, lower and softer, it may denote Affliction, Fear, *&c*.". Such an association was not unusual in the first half of the eighteenth century but had little influence on later writers, most of whom recommended employing vibrato sparingly for its expressive qualities.[176] More controversial has been Geminiani's proposed use of vibrato "as often as possible", not least because it can make the sounds of short notes "more agreeable".[177]

This advice has been interpreted by many as *carte blanche* for the adoption of a continuous vibrato.[178] Such an interpretation is highly debatable; no contemporary evidence has come to light that Geminiani's tone was in any way unusual or unique — in fact, Hawkins actually praises Geminiani's tone production[179] — and, as Neal Zaslaw comments, Geminiani could equally well have written "all the time", "continuously", or any similar expression had he wished to convey such an interpretation.[180] Interestingly, too, Geminiani specifically cites one occasion when shakes would be inappropriate in the section headed "Of Holding a Note", where he states, "were we to make Beats and Shakes [i.e. vibrato] continually without sometimes suffering the pure Note to be heard, the Melody would be too much diversified".[181] Further, he indicates in his treatise's Compos.^{ne} I^{a} and Essemp. XVIII "all the Ornaments of Expression, necessary to the playing in a good Taste",[182] but indicates vibrato usage only once — on a long, tied *g''* in bar 9 of a 13-bar

---

[175]   His use of the term tremolo in GEMINIANI, Francesco. *APV*, *op. cit.* (see note 3), music p. 26, Essemp. XVIII, is an exception.

[176]   HOWELL, Thomas. *Original Instructions* [...], *op. cit.* (see note 62), p. 48. Here, Howell retains the term close shake for vibrato and claims that it "is expressive of dignity, and also has a pathetic effect when judiciously introduced and dexterously managed".

[177]   GEMINIANI, Francesco. *APV*, *op. cit.* (see note 3), p. 8. This passage on vibrato is identical to one in Geminiani's earlier *A Treatise of Good Taste* [...], *op. cit.* (see note 24), p. 3. See *Geminiani Opera Omnia*, vol. 12.

[178]   For example, Robert Donington ('Vibrato', in: *NG*) misleadingly claims that Geminiani's recommendation "corresponds to modern usage".

[179]   *HAWKINS*, V, p. 393.

[180]   ZASLAW, Neal. 'Some Thoughts on the Performance of Concert Music', in: *Early Music*, VII/1 (1979), p. 48.

[181]   GEMINIANI, Francesco. *APV*, *op. cit.* (see note 3), p. 7.

[182]   *Ibidem*, music pp. 33 and 26.

ILL. 5: *APV*, p. 33, "Compos.^ne 1^a".

Adagio. Earlier, too, he had differentiated between vibrato on the German flute, which "must only be made on long Notes", and violin vibrato, "which may be made on any Note whatsoever",[183] the latter phrase having very different implications from "as often as possible".

Geminiani certainly seems to have ploughed a lone furrow by recommending the introduction of vibrato "as often as possible"; all other writers either criticise such use, recommending only sparing use of vibrato as if an ornament, or omit discussion of the device entirely.[184] As mentioned earlier, Geminiani's pupil Robert Bremner even appears to have used his influential position as a publisher to modify his master's instruction, republishing Geminiani's violin treatise in 1777 with three significant passages omitted. One of these omitted passages, the last two lines of the first paragraph of Geminiani's consideration of the 'close shake', removes his reference to the introduction

---

[183] GEMINIANI, Francesco. *Rules for Playing in a True Taste*, London, s.n., c1746, Preface. See *Geminiani Opera Omnia*, vol. 12.

[184] For example, Thomas Howell (HOWELL, Thomas. *Op. cit.* [see note 62], p. 48) discusses vibrato only as an ornament, and John Loder (LODER, John. *Op. cit.* [see note 60]) makes no mention of vibrato whatsoever.

of vibrato on short notes and the "more agreeable" sound thereby produced, his recommendation to use it "as often as possible"[185] and his qualification "when it is long continued" regarding the use of the swell.[186] By contrast, Bremner himself seems to have allowed the soloist the freedom to apply "all the different graces of the bow and finger [...] when and where he pleases".[187]

The later sources attributed to Geminiani generally describe the close shake but do not recommend its application beyond that of any other ornament.[188] Although some of his text describing vibrato serves as the basis for Jousse's brief 1805 mention of the "close shake" under the heading "of Graces",[189] Geminiani's recommendation to use vibrato "as often as possible" [in solo playing] failed to find favour with his successors, either in England or abroad. Philpot, for example, limits the "close Shake or Swell" to "long Notes in an Adagio";[190] and in his later 1811 treatise Jousse pronounces the "tremolo (improperly called by Geminiani and others the Close Shake)" as "an obsolete grace"[191] that may be introduced "for the sake of variety [...] on a long note in a simple melody"; like Leopold Mozart, he equates its overuse with a singer with the "Palsy", and takes Bremner's stance (see below) regarding its introduction "in a piece of harmony", where "it becomes hurtful and disgustful".[192] Keith chastises Geminiani, Philpot and others for calling vibrato "the close shake", preferring the descriptor "tremolo shake", but he nevertheless maintains that it "should only be introduced on long notes".[193] Such prescribed limitations on the use of vibrato support the implication of a wide variety of critical sources and reviews that vibrato was employed rather more in practice than was approved by the most authoritative writers of the period.[194]

---

[185] Compare GEMINIANI, Francesco. *APV*, op. cit. (see note 3), p. 8, with BREMNER, Robert. 'Some Thoughts on the Performance of Concert Music', in: SCHETKY, Johann Georg Christoph. *6 Quartettos*, Op. 6, London, Robert Bremner, 1777, pp. i–ii.

[186] Remarkably, T. C. Bates' treatise (*Bates' Complete Preceptor for the Violin*, London, s.n., *c*1845, p. 14) reproduces this section, and other parts of the hybrid model, almost verbatim.

[187] BREMNER, Robert. *Op. cit.* (see note 185), p. ii.

[188] For example, *The Compleat Tutor for the Violin* [...], London, C. & S. Thompson, *c*1770, p. 13 (see note 169).

[189] JOUSSE, Jean. *The Modern Violin* [...], *op. cit.* (see note 48), p. 15.

[190] PHILPOT, Stephen. *Op. cit.* (see note 20), p. 9.

[191] Jousse's reference to obsolete may be to the close-shake, as distinct from the tremolo (vibrato).

[192] Compare JOUSSE, Jean. *The Theory and Practice* [...], *op. cit.* (see note 15), p. 48 and BREMNER, Robert. *Op. cit.* (see note 185), p. 1.

[193] KEITH, Robert. *Op. cit.* (see note 30), p. 10.

[194] For example, LÖHLEIN, Georg Simon. *Op. cit.* (see note 143), p. 51; REICHARDT, Johann Friedrich. *Op. cit.* (see note 157), p. 35.

Vibrato was still viewed principally as an expressive tool by Spohr in 1832 when he advocates it for giving "more force and expression to long sustained notes", for characterising "passages of a tender or impassioned character", or "for giving intensity to the powerful accentuation of notes marked *sforzando*". He aligns vibrato with singing and distinguishes four different varieties — rapid, "for intensifying passionate expression and adding vehemence to accentuated notes"; slow, "for imparting tenderness to sustained and pathetic melody"; accelerating, for use with the crescendo; and decelerating, for use with the diminuendo. His instructions, and not least his warning against using vibrato "too often, or in unsuitable places" proved to be the strongest influence on British use of vibrato and taste throughout the second half of the nineteenth century.[195] Spohr even differentiates between the responsibilities of soloists and orchestral players in cultivating vibrato, stating categorically that "those means of expression so effective in solo and concerted playing are out of place in the orchestra", and including in his exclusion list tempo rubato, portamento (except in certain places), vibrato (called "tremolo") and any unprescribed timbres, bowings, or accentuations that may "destroy the unity of performance".[196]

Whereas Geminiani's treatise includes no separate instruction for orchestral players, his pupil, Robert Bremner, bemoaned the fact that "many gentlemen players on bow instruments are so exceeding fond of the tremolo, that they apply it wherever they possibly can". Bremner rejected his mentor's pervasive "close shake" in an ensemble situation out of concern that vibrato (which he calls "tremolo") destroyed the purity of harmony and affected adversely considerations of tuning. While allowing its use from time to time as an ornament in solo playing ("on a long note in simple melody"), he advised that it be used with discretion in the interests of harmonic clarity and gave it no place whatsoever in orchestral playing, because if "introduced into harmony, where the beauty and energy of the performance depend upon the united effect of all parts being exactly in tune with each other, it becomes hurtful".[197] The German translator of Bremner's prefatory essay, Carl Friedrich Cramer, felt the need to make some qualifying remarks about it, basing his judgement on vocal models:

> The author of these remarks seems to me to be entirely
> too much prejudiced against vibrato [...]. The application of

---

[195] SPOHR, Louis. *Op. cit.* (see note 99), pp. 175-176.
[196] *Ibidem*, p. 248.
[197] BREMNER, Robert. *Op. cit.* (see note 185), p. 1.

this [vocal technique] to instrumental execution is easy to make. Because however much *vocal* performance (also the model and ideal for the instrumental) and passionate expression allow of it, so much more does the indefiniteness of the naked, wordless tone [of instrumental music]. Thus it follows irrefutably that, in such passages where the singer would apply vibrato, the instrumentalist not only *may* make use of it, but *must*. That this, however, like all niceties and ornaments, must occur not too frequently but with discretion and upon reflection, I have no desire to argue about with our author.[198]

LONGEVITY OF INFLUENCE

Although Geminiani's *APV* is retrospective in many of its precepts and is far from being a comprehensive or systematic survey of violin technique in the first half of the eighteenth century as compared with, for example, Leopold Mozart's well-organised, roughly contemporary *Versuch einer gründlichen Violinschule*, the strength and longevity of its influence were ensured by its pedigree and its 'fit' with the predominant musical taste of English society. Its relatively sparse textual content "conceals the true technical magnitude of the work as a whole";[199] for its various, substantially advanced technical and expressive foci consolidated and furthered the 'ancient' Corellian style in England and laid firm foundations for the developing English violin 'school' of the nineteenth century. As Boyden points out, "Geminiani must have realised that the very lack of concrete and mechanistic detail would force students to a healthy exercise of imagination and self-reliance in performing the examples and the music".[200] His inclusion of "twelve Pieces in different Stiles" confirmed the higher artistic aims of his treatise, as compared with those which presented only short airs as musical practice materials. Dances and pieces in contrapuntal and/or concertante style intermix with slow pieces of a highly expressive character, scrupulously annotated with dynamic indications, echo and other special effects.

Although challenged by a few of the multitude of pedagogical works issued by the booming publishing industry of its time, Geminiani's treatise was the predominant influence in England for over three-quarters of a century. Many of its principles maintained their currency in England even if they had

---

[198] *Cramers Magazin der Musik* (1 December, 1783), quoted in ZASLAW, Neal. *Mozart's Symphonies: Context, Performance Practice, Reception*, Oxford, Clarendon Press, 1989, p. 479.

[199] BOYDEN, David. 'Introduction', *op. cit.* (see note 7), p. viii.

[200] *Ibidem*, p. viii.

long been superseded elsewhere. Its predominance during that period was assisted by the continued reverence for the 'ancient style' of Corelli's Sonatas Op. 5, which served as ideal models and teaching materials for composers and performers of conservative taste. As mentioned earlier, Jousse considered them invaluable material for the training of the left hand;[201] and Hogarth commented (1838) that if Corelli's music were ever "thrown aside or forgotten, it will be the most unequivocal sign of the corruption of taste and the decay of music in England".[202] Later still, George Dubourg recommended Corelli's sonatas "for the acquisition of *tone* and *steadiness*", but considered them "not a sufficient authority as to the varieties and subtleties of *bowing*; for [...] much that relates to these has been added *since* his time to the province of the violin".[203] Even towards the close of the nineteenth century Paul David was still referring to Corelli as the "norm and model of violin-playing" and the source of all of value that succeeded him. Further, he still considered Geminiani's *APV* as a work "of the greatest interest" as "the only direct evidence of Corelli's method and principles".[204]

DEMISE

Geminiani's method was eventually superseded in England by the availability from 1833 of an English translation of most of Louis Spohr's *Violinschule* (Vienna, 1832). Spohr had come to England in 1820 at the behest of the London Philharmonic Society, at whose concerts several of his works were performed and warmly received; but he gained even more acclaim for his performances as a violinist and director.[205] His violin playing amalgamated the expressive performance of the Mannheim School (through his teacher Franz Eck) with the lyrical and brilliant style of Viotti (himself a descendant of the Corellian tradition) and Pierre Rode. Hogarth endorsed Spohr's reputation as "the first violinist of the age", and he recorded that Spohr "was particularly distinguished for his pure and delicate tone, the smoothness and facility of his execution, his expression, and the vocal

---

[201]   JOUSSE, Jean. *The Theory and Practice* [...], *op. cit.* (see note 15), p. xx.

[202]   HOGARTH, George. *Op. cit.* (see note 41), vol. I, p. 154.

[203]   DUBOURG, George. *The Violin*, London, Robert Cocks and Co., 1852, p. 330.

[204]   DAVID, Paul. 'Geminiani, Francesco', in: *A Dictionary of Music and Musicians*, edited by George Grove, 4 vols, London, Macmillan, 1879-1889, vol. I, pp. 291-292.

[205]   See BROWN, Clive. *The popularity and influence of Spohr in England*, Ph.D. Diss., Oxford, University of Oxford, 1980; ID. *Louis Spohr: a Critical Biography*, Cambridge, Cambridge University Press, 1984.

character of his style".[206] Others singled out for comment his refinement of style and "classical taste" and described him as "the rock against which the so-called *virtuosity* of his time could make no head".[207] The practical, theoretical and pedagogical precepts discussed in his *Violinschule* were eagerly absorbed by English violinists, courtesy of the first of the English translations by C. Rudolphus ([1833])[208] and later those of John Bishop ([1843]) and Florence A. Marshall (1878, edited by Henry Holmes).[209] Various condensed versions of Spohr's treatise were also published in England to ensure that the influence of its technical and interpretative instruction endured;[210] inevitably, too, some publishers could not resist making easy money by using Spohr's name to market material that was passé.[211]

Spohr's return visits to England in 1830, 1837 and 1839 were as a conductor/director, but his violin performances in 1843 maintained his overall reputation amongst English musicians. Although virtuosi such as Paganini enjoyed many successes in England in the early 1830s, most writers of the time tended to spurn their bravura approach in favour of Spohr's noble playing style, not least because he preserved "the great qualities of the Classical Italian and the Paris Schools",[212] using technique as the servant of taste and expression rather than as a virtuoso tool. He was considered "second to none as a profound teacher"[213] and exerted a powerful influence on English pedagogy. In addition to his English pupils Henry Blagrove,

---

[206]   HOGARTH, George. *Op. cit.* (see note 41), vol. II, p. 187.

[207]   *The Harmonicon*, II (1824), p. 215.

[208]   Rudolphus' translation is virtually complete, but a small amount of Spohr's original text has been omitted and there is some additional instruction and an illustrated example concerning bow division.

[209]   SPOHR, Louis. *Op. cit.* (see note 99); English translation by C. Rudolphus, *Louis Spohr's Grand Violin School*, London, Wessel & Co., 1833; English translation by John Bishop, *Louis Spohr's Celebrated Violin School*, London, R. Cocks & Co., 1843; English translation by Florence A. Marshall, revised and edited by Henry Holmes, *Spohr's Violin School*, London, Boosey, 1878.

[210]   For example, *Spohr's Hand-book for the Violin, with numerous Studies and Exercises, and a Selection of 40 Melodies*, London, s.n., c1860.

[211]   For example, the supposititious *Spohr's Celebrated Instructions for the Violin, containing a variety of progressive examples, on the various styles of bowing and fingering, for the use of amateurs & professors, to which is added thirty six favorite [sic] melodies*, London, s.n., [1854]. This presents material from Spohr's *Violinschule* in an antiquated arrangement which also incorporates instructions from the treatises of Geminiani, Philpot and Jousse (?1805).

[212]   On Spohr's visits to England, see BROWN, Clive. *The Popularity and Influence of Spohr* [...], *op. cit.* (see note 205); DAVID, Paul. *Op. cit.* (see note 204), pp. 294-295.

[213]   *Musical World*, XXXIV (1859), p. 712.

Henry and Alfred Holmes *et al.*, and the teaching material published by those influenced by him, several foreign disciples held prominent positions and perpetuated Spohr's methods in various institutions. Notable amongst these were Bernhard Molique (Royal Academy of Music)[214] and eventually August Wilhelmj (Guildhall School of Music and Drama), along with the English violinist Henry Holmes (Royal College of Music).[215] Joseph Joachim, too, disseminated Spohr's principles to a considerable degree, citing (with Andreas Moser) some of Spohr's precepts verbatim in their collaborative *Violinschule*.[216]

RENAISSANCE

Spohr's treatise was itself superseded in Britain in the early years of the twentieth century by, among other pedagogical methods, the *Violinschule* of Joseph Joachim and Andreas Moser, Carl Flesch's *Die Kunst des Violin-Spiels*,[217] works by Leopold Auer,[218] and various treatises slanted more towards scientific and physiological rather than musical and technical principles.[219] Dormant for about a century, Geminiani's *APV* was to re-emerge into the spotlight in the early 1950s through the research of David Boyden, who attributed its neglect at that time largely to the fact that "it describes a technique quite different from that of the present".[220] Having suggested that Geminiani's treatise is merely of archaeological use and that its contents are often meaningless or misleading if considered apart from the original instrument,[221] Boyden published his research on its background and content

---

[214]   The management committee of the Royal Academy of Music, under the presidency of Lord Burghersh, became patrons of John Bishop's translation of Spohr's treatise when it was published in 1843. See DUBOURG, George. *Op. cit.* (see note 203), appendix, p. 3.

[215]   Holmes was appointed violin professor at the newly founded Royal College of Music in 1883.

[216]   JOACHIM, Joseph – MOSER, Andreas. *Violinschule*, 3 vols, Berlin, N. Simrock, 1905.

[217]   FLESCH, Carl. *Die Kunst des Violinspiels*, 2 vols, Berlin, 1923, 1928; English translation by Frederick Martens, *The Art of Violin Playing*, 2 vols, New York, Carl Fischer, 1924, 1930.

[218]   AUER, Leopold. *Violin Playing as I Teach it*, New York, Frederick A. Stokes, 1921; ID. *Violin Masterworks and their Interpretation*, New York, C. Fischer Inc., 1925; ID. *Graded Course of Violin Playing*, New York, C. Fischer Inc., 1926.

[219]   The various publications of Demetrios Dounis come into this category, especially DOUNIS, Demetrios. *The Artist's Technique of Violin Playing*, Op. 12, New York, C. Fischer, 1921; ID. *The Absolute Independence of the Fingers* Op. 15, London, Strad Edition, 1924; and ID. *The Staccato*, London, Strad Edition, 1925, based entirely on études by Kreutzer.

[220]   BOYDEN, David. 'Introduction', *op. cit.* (see note 7), p. v.

[221]   *Ibidem*, p. v.

and made it available in a facsimile reproduction, complete with scholarly trappings, just at the time when the burgeoning early music movement was beginning to gather steam in professional musical life. Along with Editha Knocker's English translation of Leopold Mozart's *Versuch einer gründlichen Violinschule* (1756), Edward R. Reilly's of Johann Joachim Quantz's *Versuch einer Anweisung die Flöte traversiere zu spielen* (1752), and William J. Mitchell's of Carl Philipp Emanuel Bach's *Versuch über die wahre Art das Clavier zu spielen* (1753), eager exponents of historical performance adopted it as one of their principal seminal eighteenth-century texts.

Boyden's facsimile edition of Geminiani's *APV* initially proved enormously influential in awakening interest in historically informed performance on period instruments and has grown in stature with the seemingly ever-increasing thirst for knowledge about Baroque performing methods. It has acted as a vital catalyst in uncovering the riches of the early music repertory, providing strong roots for the development of early music performance from a cult phenomenon into a major sector of the music industry,[222] and once again contributing to "the improved state of the [baroque] Violin in England".[223]

---

[222] On this re-awakening of interest in early music, see HASKELL, Harry. *The Early Music Revival: A History*, London, Thames and Hudson, 1988.

[223] JOUSSE, Jean. *The Theory and Practice* [...], *op. cit.* (see note 15), p. xiv.

"You are my Heir": Geminiani's Influence on the Life and Music of Charles Avison

Mark Kroll
(Boston, MA)

I N December of 1760, a glowing report appeared in the *Newcastle Journal* of an encounter with Francesco Geminiani at the home of Newcastle's most famous musician, Charles Avison.[1] The writer began by explaining that Geminiani was in Newcastle "on his Road from Edinburg", and also took the opportunity to remind readers that Avison was "a favourite Disciple, whom he had not seen for many Years". We learn that at some point during this apparently warm and enjoyable gathering, Geminiani became

> so much delighted with the Performance of Mr. Avison's eldest Son upon the Harpsicord, (a boy 13 Years old) that he took him to his Arms with an Earnestness which affected them both. Then turning to his Father, he said, 'My Friend, I love all your Productions. You are my Heir. This boy will be yours. Take Care of him. To raise up Geniuses like him, is the only way to perpetuate Music'.[2]

---

[1] Information about Avison's life and works, and his relationship with Geminiani, can be found in a number of sources, including: Burchell, Jenny. *Polite or Commercial Concerts?*, New York, Garland, 1996; *Music in the British Provinces, 1690-1914*, edited by Rachel Cowgill and Peter Holman, Aldershot, Ashgate, 2007; *Charles Avison's Essay on Musical Expression*, edited by Pierre Dubois, Aldershot, Ashgate, 2004; Horsley, P. M. 'Charles Avison: The Man and His Milieu', in: *Music and Letters*, LV/1 (1974), pp. 5-23; Avison, Charles. *Concerto-Grosso Arrangements of Francesco Geminiani's Sonatas for Violin and Basso Continuo, Op. 1, Nos. 1-10 and 12*, edited by Mark Kroll, Middleton (WI), A-R Editions, 2010; Southey, Roz. *Music-Making in North-East England During the Eighteenth Century*, Aldershot, Ashgate, 2006; Southey, Roz - Maddison, Margaret - Hughes, David. *The Ingenious Mr Avison*, Newcastle, Tyne Bridge Publishing, 2009; and Stephens, Norris Lynn. *Charles Avison: An Eighteenth-Century English Composer, Musician and Writer*, Ph.D. Diss., University of Pittsburgh (PA), 1968.

[2] The son described in this report was Edward Avison (1747-1776), an accomplished musician who succeeded his father as organist at St Nicholas and director of the Newcastle

Among the colourful descriptions found in this report, the most striking are the claims that Avison was Geminiani's "favourite Disciple" and that Geminiani considered him to be his "heir". Are they justified, or was the writer merely engaging in embellishment and hyperbole to further raise the stature of Newcastle's favourite son? This essay will attempt to determine if Charles Avison was indeed Geminiani's most prominent student and the heir to his musical legacy.

If we search through all of Avison's voluminous written output for the answer, we will be disappointed. Not once does Avison specifically refer to Geminiani as his 'teacher', nor for that matter does Geminiani ever call Avison his 'pupil'. Nevertheless, an examination of contemporary accounts and historical evidence, and a comparative analysis of the music of the two composers allows us to arrive at the conclusion that the description in the *Newcastle Journal* of 1760 is accurate: Geminiani *was* Avison's mentor and model throughout his life, and Avison in turn enthusiastically assumed the role of Geminiani's staunchest defender and advocate. Moreover, the two men enjoyed a close personal and professional relationship, one that is all the more remarkable when we consider that their backgrounds, personalities and lifestyles could not have been more different: Geminiani, the temperamental, somewhat disorganized Italian–Catholic émigré soloist who travelled widely in the British Isles and the Continent; and Avison, the sober, responsible Anglican church musician, a faithful family man who rarely strayed far from his native city of Newcastle, and who was a capable manger of several long-running concert series.[3]

Musical Society that Avison père had founded in 1735. Avison's younger son Charles (1751-1795) was also a musician, but less successful than his older brother. The full text that appeared in the *Newcastle Journal*, 20-27 December 1760 reads: "To the PUBLISHERS of the NEWCASTLE JOURNAL. | GENTLEMEN. | I HAD the Pleasure a few Days ago to pay my Devoirs to the celebrated Geminiani, who was on his Road from Edinburgh, and lodged with Mr. Avison of this Town, (a favourite Disciple, whom he had not seen for many Years). I cannot describe the Satisfaction I felt in observing this illustrious Artist, at the Age of 88 [*sic*], possessed of all his Faculties, and of so lively an Imagination, as to keep up an entertaining Conversation for several Hours together. His Spirits seemed greatly elevated, in the Company of all his Friends, and Family, and so much delighted with the Performance of Mr. Avison's eldest Son upon the Harpsicord, (a boy 13 Years old) that he took him to his Arms with an Earnestness which affected them both. Then turning to his Father, he said, 'My Friend, I love all your Productions. You are my Heir. This boy will be yours. Take Care of him. To raise up Geniuses like him, is the only way to perpetuate Music'. I send you this little Anecdote, as it may entertain some of your Readers, and as it also does Honour to our Organist, and is a recent Proof of the Fame of his Music, I hope you will favour it with a Place in your Paper. I am, &c.". The letter is unsigned.

³ Several commentators assert that Avison travelled to Italy, or perhaps to some other city on the Continent, at some point during his early years. Burney, for example, writes that Avison "visited Italy early in his youth". See BURNEY, IV, p. 670. However, no records exist

The Conventional Wisdom

Although we have observed that Avison does not actually write that Geminiani was his teacher, his status as Geminiani's pupil seems to have been a fact generally accepted by the rest of Great Britain. For example, in 1759, one year before Geminiani's visit to Avison, a letter sent to *The Newcastle Journal* also used the term "disciple" to describe Avison's relationship to the illustrious Italian composer, and pointed out that Geminiani had recommended Avison for two vacant organist positions in Dublin.[4] Even stronger confirmation comes from the Oxford professor and notorious Avison critic William Hayes, who wrote in his *Remarks on Mr. Avison's Essay on Musical Expression* of 1753 that Avison had received "the principal Part of his Education from Geminiani".[5] The perception that Avison was Geminiani's student persisted long after

---

to confirm this. See also Southey, Roz - Maddison, Margaret - Hughes, David. *Op. cit.* (see note 1), p. 30 and Stephens, Norris Lynn. *Op. cit.* (see note 1), pp. 4-5. Geminiani could be mercurial indeed and, in contrast to Avison, had few skills when it came to managing money or organizing concerts. An indication of Geminiani's haphazard approach to concert management comes to us from Hawkins' description of Geminiani's ill-fated attempt to raise money by producing a benefit at the Drury Lane Theatre on 11 April 1750. See *Hawkins*, v, p. 421. In a footnote, Hawkins also gives an example of Geminiani's inability to remain in a single place for any length of time, which is again in stark contrast to Avison, who was born, worked and died in Newcastle: "The late prince of Wales greatly admired the compositions of Geminiani, and at the same time that he retained Martini [Sammartini] in his service, would have bestowed on him [Geminiani] a pension of a hundred pounds a year, but the latter affecting an aversion to a life of dependence, declined the offer".

4   This letter, signed 'Marcellinus' and dated 17 March 1759, appeared in *The Newcastle Journal* on 20 March. The writer also tells us that Avison had been offered many other distinguished positions during his career, but chose to remain in his native Newcastle. The most notable sections are provided below. The full text can be found in Stephens, Norris Lynn. *Op. cit.* (see note 1), pp. 39-40. "I have been told, when one organist was elected to serve at St. Nicholas', that he has a favourable prospect of establishing himself in London. But it seems his inclination to fix in New castle prevailed above all other considerations. I could never otherwise account for his refusing the offers that have since been made him. First, he had the offer to be organist of the Cathedral of York when it was given to Dr. Nares [...] soon after, Mr. Avison was applied to by Sigr. Geminiani, whose disciple he had been, to accompany him to Dublin, having a promise to succeed as organist to two churches vacant in that city. Afterwards he had a proposal from Edinburgh to perform in the concerts there, and to teach upon the harpsichord, the proposers engaging to procure him two hundred pounds sterling per annum. Lastly, on the death of Dr. Pepusch he was desired by several gentlemen in London to offer himself a candidate for the place of organist in the Charter House [...] but all of these opportunities of advancement himself he declined, though he had friends and character to support him".

5   Hayes, William. *Remarks on Mr. Avison's Essay on Musical Expression*, London, J. Robinson, 1753, p. 111.

Avison's death in 1770. Burney, whose comments would continue to carry a great deal of authority, wrote in 1789 that Avison "received instructions from Geminiani", and his statement found its way into the 1808 obituary for Anne Ord, one of Avison's patrons in Newcastle and the dedicatee of his 6 Concertos in 7 Parts, Op. 3.[6] Clearly, for many if not all of Avison's contemporaries the Italian violinist was the dominant influence on the organist from Newcastle.

AVISON IN PRINT

Avison certainly made no effort to hide the fact that he considered Geminiani to be his mentor. In fact he took every possible opportunity to tell his colleagues that he was his model in all things musical, often scolding them that Geminiani should be theirs as well. Avison put it bluntly in the preface to the Opus 3 concertos: Geminiani was "the greatest Master of Instrumental Musick (whose inimitable Works ought to have been much more our Pattern) [...] the Publick are indebted for several excellent Rules for playing that kind of Composition in Taste".[7] Avison's adulation of Geminiani is expressed with even greater force in his *Essay on Musical Expression*: Geminiani's

> [...] Elegance and Spirit of Composition ought to have been much more our Pattern; and from whom the public Taste might have received the highest Improvement, had we thought proper to lay hold of the Opportunities which his long Residence in the Kingdom has given us. The Public is greatly indebted to this Gentleman, not only for his many excellent Compositions, but for having as yet parted with none that are not extremely correct and fine. There is such a Genteelness and Delicacy in the Turn of his musical Phrase, (if I may so call it), and such a natural Connection in his expressive and sweet Modulation throughout all his Works, which are every where supported with so perfect a Harmony, that we can never too often hear, or too much admire them.[8]

---

6 See BURNEY, IV, p. 670. Ord was apparently a fine musician in her own right and Avison described her playing as "elegant". See STEPHENS, Norris Lynn. *Op. cit.* (see note 1), p. 5, and SOUTHEY, Roz - MADDISON, Margaret - HUGHES, David. *Op. cit.* (see note 1), p. 60.

7 Reprints of Avison's prefaces can be found in STEPHENS, Norris Lynn. *Op. cit.* (see note 1), pp. 309-334, and selections in *Charles Avison's Essay* [...], *op. cit.* (see note 1), pp. 159-185.

8 AVISON, Charles. *An Essay on Musical Expression*, London, C. Davis, 1753; facsimile edition, New York, Broude Brothers, 1967, p. 103. The second edition is quoted here since it also contains Avison's reply to William Hayes. The full title is *An Essay on Musical Expression* [...] *The Second Edition, with Alterations and Large Additions. To which is added, A Letter to the*

Avison continued to heap praise on Geminiani throughout his life, as we can read in the preface to his 6 Sonatas for the Harpsichord, Op. 8, published in 1764. This begins with an appraisal of the music of Domenico Scarlatti, Rameau and C. P. E. Bach, thus revealing Avison's considerable musical sophistication, despite the fact that he lived in a provincial English city far from the major musical centres of London, Paris and Berlin: "Among the various Productions of foreign Composers for the Harpsichord, the Sonatas of SCARLATTI, RAMEAU AND CARLO-BACH have their *peculiar* Beauties. The *fine Fancy* of the Italian — the *spirited Science* of the Frenchman — and the German's *diffusive Expression* are the distinguishing Signatures of their Music". True to form, however, Avison saves the best for last: "But if we examine the Lessons of GEMINIANI we shall find them fraught with *every* Beauty, and therefore, worthy of the Attention of Those who would improve a true taste, and acquire a graceful and fluent Execution".

Editing Geminiani:
Avison's Workbooks and the Gentlemen Amateurs of Newcastle

Some of the most convincing musical evidence for the influence of Geminiani's "lessons" on Avison can be found in the recently discovered Avison workbooks. These seem to have been begun at some point in the 1730s, and additional entries were made by Avison (and his son Edward) for the next forty years. Taken together, the two books provide eloquent testimony to the importance of Geminiani and the Italian style to Charles Avison.[9]

What one first notices in the workbooks is that they are dominated by copies or arrangements of music by Italian composers, including no fewer than three members of the Scarlatti family — Francesco (1666-1741); Stephani (n.d.) and Domenico (1685-1757).[10] Not surprisingly, however, the name

---

Author, concerning the Music of the Ancients [...]. Likewise, Mr. Avison's Reply to the Author of Remarks on the Essay on Musical Expression. In a Letter from Mr. Avison, to his Friend in London.

[9] For further information on the workbooks, including the dramatic events leading to their discovery, see KROLL, Mark. 'Two Important New Sources for the Music of Charles Avison', in: *Music and Letters*, LXXXVI/3 (2005), pp. 414-431. The two workbooks are currently owned by the Charles Avison Society of Newcastle, England and housed in the Charles Avison Archives of the Newcastle Public Library.

[10] Very little is known about Francesco Scarlatti, the uncle of Domenico. He was born in Palermo on 5 December 1666, lived in London after 1719, and died in poverty in Dublin at some point in 1741. For further information, see DENT, Edward Joseph. *Alessandro Scarlatti: His Life and Works*, London, Edward Arnold, 1905, rev. Frank Walker, 1960; PROTA-GIURLEO,

that appears more frequently than any other composer is Geminiani, who is represented by six large-scale works. Workbook I contains copies in score of Geminiani's Concerti Grossi Opp. 2 and 3, and score versions of his concerto arrangements of Arcangelo Corelli's Sonatas for Violin and Basso Continuo, Op. 5. Workbook II includes copies in full score of Geminiani's Concerti Grossi, Op. 7, and Avison's concerto arrangements of Geminiani's Sonatas for Violin and Basso Continuo, Op. 1 (nos. I-X, XII) and Sonatas for Violin and Basso Continuo, Op. 4.

Avison's orchestral arrangements of Geminiani's Opus 1 sonatas provide particularly important insights about Avison's approach to and understanding of Geminiani's music, and into his own compositional process.[11] Compare, for example, the following excerpts from Geminiani's Sonata in C minor, Op. 1, no. 7 in sonata and concerto versions with Avison's arrangement of the work:

Ex. 1a: Geminiani, Sonata in C minor, Op. 1/VII/i/1-12 in the original 1716 version (H. 7).

Ulisse. *Alessandro Scarlatti, "il Palermitano" (la patria & la famiglia)*, Naples, Lubrano, 1926; SCARLATTI, Francesco. *Six Concerti Grossi*, edited by Mark Kroll, Middleton (WI), A-R Editions, 2010; and PAGANO, Roberto. *Alessandro e Domenico Scarlatti: due vite in una*, Milan, Arnoldo Mondadori, 1985; English translation by Frederick Hammond, *Alessandro and Domenico Scarlatti: Two Lives in One*, New York, Pendragon, 2006. The name of Stephani Scarlatti was completely unknown until the discovery of the Avison workbooks. I have been unable to find any further information on the man or his music.

[11]   For further information on the complicated history of these sonatas see *Geminiani Opera Omnia*, vol. 1, edited by Rudolf Rasch.

Ex. 1b: Geminiani, Sonata in C minor, Op. 1/vii/i/1-12 in the 1739 revision (H. 19).

Ex. 1c: Geminiani, Sonata in C minor, Op. 1/vii/i/1-12 in the Barsanti arrangement [1736].

Ex. 1d: Geminiani, Sonata in C minor, Op. 1/vii/i/1-12 in the Geminiani 1757 arrangement for trio (H. 31) with a ripieno bass (H. 43) (as bb. 1-11).

Ex. 1e: Geminiani, Sonata in C minor, Op. 1/vii/i/1-12 in the Avison arrangement.

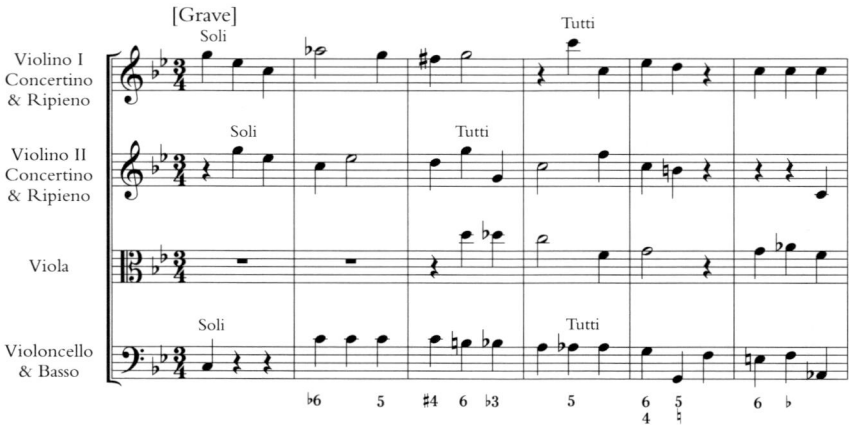

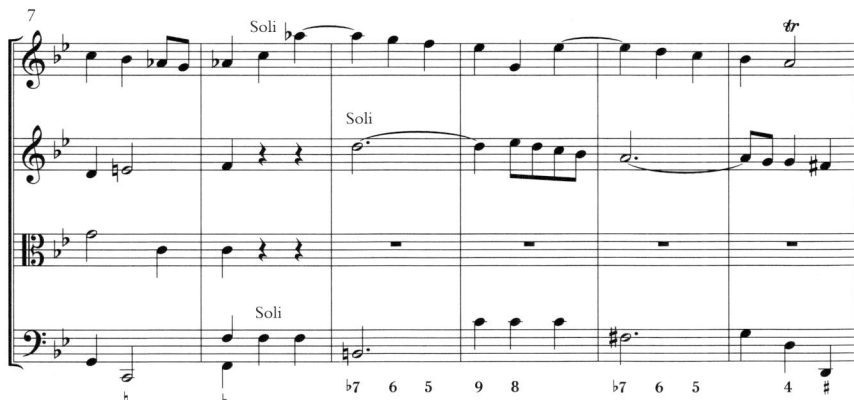

Ex. 2a: Geminiani, Sonata in C minor, Op. 1/VII/iv/51-58 in the original 1716 version (H. 7).

Ex. 2b: Geminiani, Sonata in C minor, Op. 1/VII/iv/51-58 in the 1739 revision (H. 19).

Ex. 2c: Geminiani, Sonata in C minor, Op. 1/VII/iv/51-58 in the Barsanti arrangement [1736].

Ex. 2d: Geminiani, Sonata in C minor, Op. 1/VII/iv/51-58 in the Geminiani 1757 arrangement for trio (H. 31) with a ripieno bass (H. 43) (as bb. 49-56).

Ex. 2e: Geminiani, Sonata in C minor, Op. 1/vii/iv/51-58 in the Avison arrangement.

It will be noted that Avison's arrangements remain relatively faithful to the Geminiani originals, using little embellishment and usually avoiding the complex and technically demanding style of writing found in Geminiani's later revised versions of this work. The same observation can be made when comparing the various versions of the sonata in B minor, Op. 1, no. viii and the Sonata in E major, Op. 1, no. x, including its keyboard transcription (for some reason Avison has transposed his arrangement of the E-major sonata to D major).

Ex. 3a: Geminiani, Sonata in B minor, Op. 1/viii/iii/0-4 in the original 1716 version (H. 8).

Ex. 3b: Geminiani, Sonata in B minor, Op. 1/VIII/iii/0-4 in the 1739 revision (H. 20).

★ '3' added editorially

Ex. 3c: Geminiani, Sonata in B minor, Op. 1/VIII/iii/0-4 in the Barsanti arrangement [1736].

Ex. 3d: Geminiani, Sonata in B minor, Op. 1/VIII/iii/0-4 in the Geminiani 1757 arrangement for trio (H. 32) with a ripieno bass (H. 44) (as bb. 0-3).

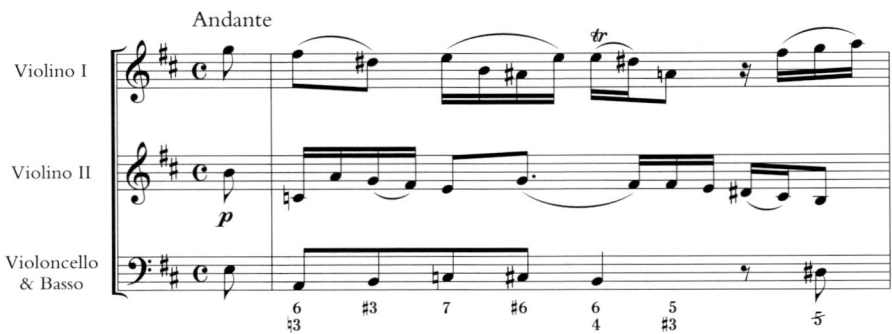

Ex. 3e: Geminiani, Sonata in B minor, Op. 1/VIII/iii/0–4 in the Avison arrangement.

Ex. 4a: Geminiani, Sonata in E major, Op. 1/x/i/10-12 and ii/1-11 in the original 1716 version (H. 10).

Ex. 4b: Geminiani, Sonata in E major, Op. 1/x/i/10-12 and ii/1-11 in the 1739 revision (H. 22).

Ex. 4c: Geminiani, Sonata in E major, Op. 1/x/i/10-12 and ii/1-11 in the Barsanti arrangement [1736].

Ex. 4d: Geminiani, Sonata in E major, Op. 1/x/i/10-12 and ii/1-11 in the Geminiani 1757 version for trio (H. 34) with a ripieno bass (H. 46) (as i/7-9 and ii/1-11).

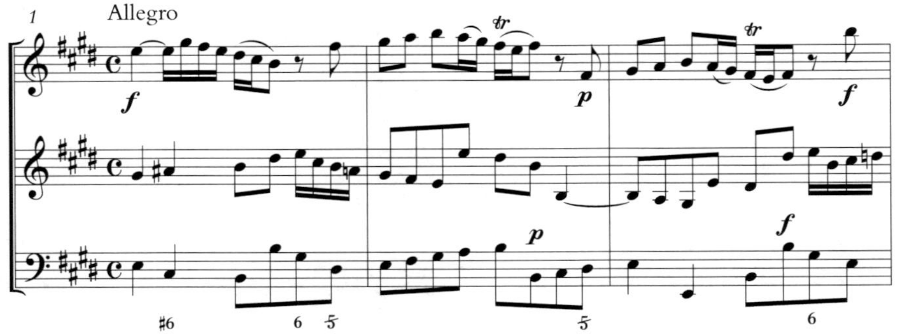

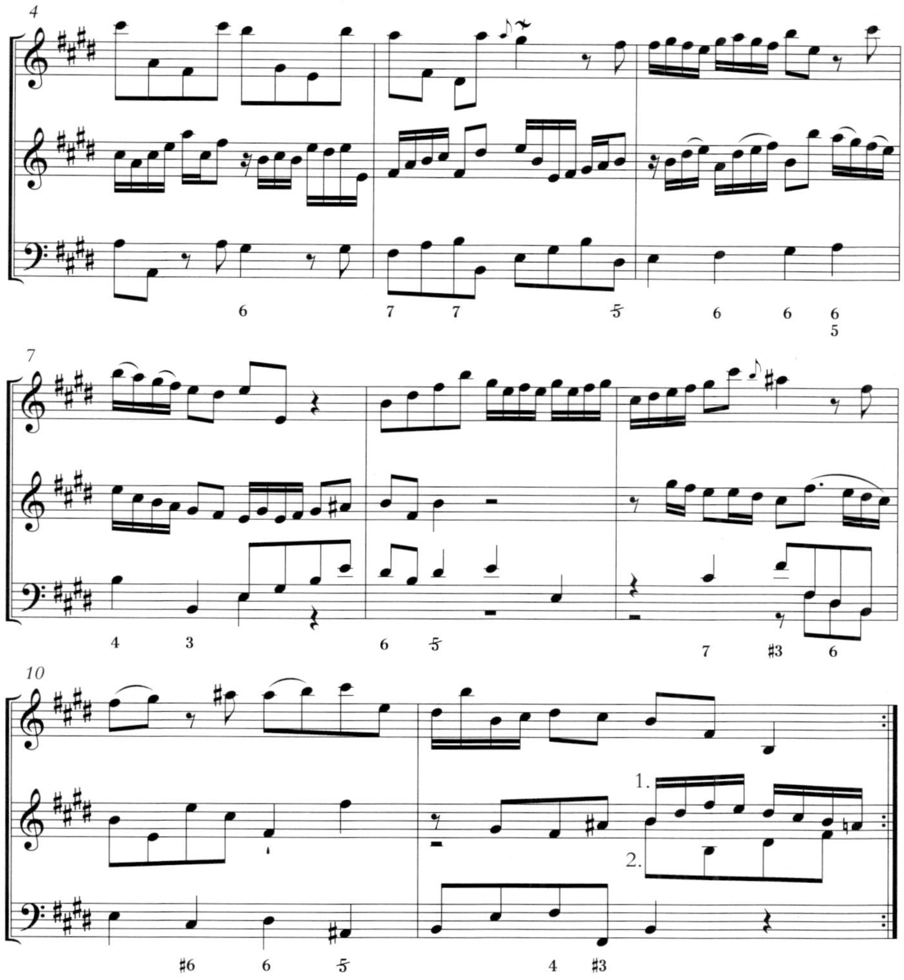

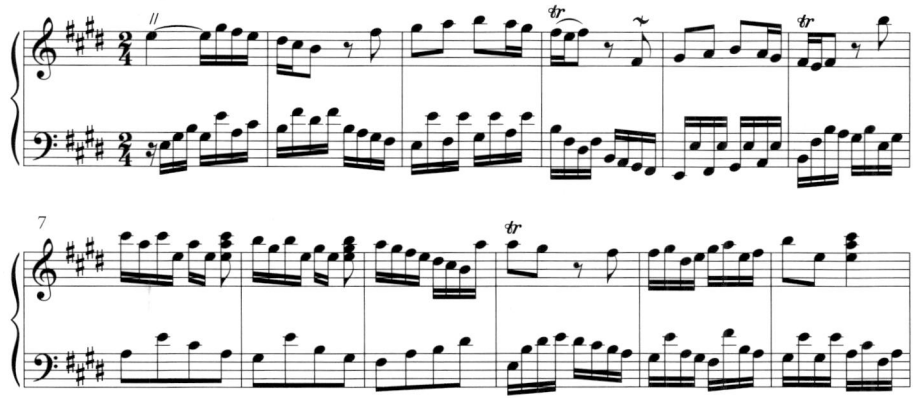

Ex. 4e: Geminiani, Sonata in E major, Op. 1/x/i/10-12 and ii/1-11 in the Geminiani 1762 keyboard transcription (H. 251) (as bb. 1-24).

Allegro moderato

Ex. 4f: Geminiani, Sonata in E major, Op. 1/x/i/10-12 and ii/1-11 in the Avison arrangement (in D major).

★ nn. 3-4 F, B in original

Several general conclusions can be drawn from these examples. One is that Avison based his arrangements of Opus 1 on the original 1716 edition of Geminiani's sonatas, since his workbook versions feature none of the exuberant ornamentation that Geminiani added to the subsequent edition of these compositions. Another is that Avison tended to favour simpler textures, and limits virtuosic display to the first *concertino* violin. A possible reason for these stylistic choices might be traced to the nature of Avison's audiences in Newcastle. Avison was a good businessman, and the Newcastle music society was a risky entrepreneurial venture, so he may well have tailored his arrangements to satisfy the tastes of his ticket-buying public. Another explanation is more likely, however: the musicians he had at his disposal in Newcastle were few in number and of poor quality. Most were "gentlemen amateurs", people of wealth or social status who might also be patrons of Avison, but who had little musical training, and he knew from experience that he could give them only the simplest parts to play.

However, these simple parts apparently could still present challenges for Avison's "unexperienced performers", as he diplomatically calls his gentlemen. Avison describes many of the problems in the prefaces to his works, and one can glean from his comments the sense the frustration he must have felt, particularly since he could hardly dismiss people from his orchestra who were either his social superiors or provided financial support for his concerts. Avison's private reaction can therefore only be imagined when the gentlemen who appointed him as director of the Newcastle Music Society publicly announced that they would continue to "assist him with their performance".[12]

The mistakes Avison mentions in his prefaces are those typical of amateurs. One was the habit of slowing down during decrescendos and speeding up while playing a crescendo, as he describes in the preface to his *Eight Concertos in Seven Parts*, Op. 4 (1760): "[…] it is almost a general Practice to *abate* the *Time* where the Sounds are *diminished*; as also where the Sounds are *encreased* to *quicken* the *Time* […] we should neither *retard* the *Piano*, nor *precipitate* the *Forte*". Another complaint concerned rhythm, or the lack of it; his players could not play in time. This seems to have been true not only of the *ripieno*, but of the *concertino* as well, even though this group presumably consisted of professionals or trained musicians, as he describes in the preface to Opus 3: "In the four principal Parts, there ought to be four Performers of almost equal Mastery; as well in regard to *Time*, as Execution; for however easy it may seem to acquire the former, yet nothing more shews a Master than a steady Performance throughout the whole Movement".

It is also in this preface that we discover Avison's low opinion of viola players, whom he considered the most unreliable musicians of the ensemble

---

[12]   Avison was appointed director in 1738; see *Newcastle Courant*, 29 July 1738, cited in SOUTHEY, ROZ - MADDISON, Margaret - HUGHES, David. *Op. cit.* (see note 1), p. 33.

because they had "[…] one of the worst Hands". In fact, Avison's violists were so weak that he was forced to shift all challenging passages to the cello: "[…] it is from a Difficulty of finding a Performer, equal to what is required on this Instrument, that I have been induced to throw the principal Points, and Fugues of this Part into the Violoncello". Avison's viola complaint is somewhat ironic, since it was Geminiani who expanded the role of the viola in the concerto grosso ensemble. Here is one instance where Avison did not follow in the footsteps of his mentor; his viola parts remained simple throughout all of his compositions.

It should not be implied here, however, that Avison was solely concerned with the needs and abilities of his Newcastle audiences and musicians when writing or conducting music. He was, after all, an accomplished composer in his own right, and many of Avison's decisions reflect his own artistic preferences. For example, in his arrangements he will often re-distribute the double stops of the solo violin part between *concertino* violins I and II differently, but no less creatively, than do Geminiani or Barsanti. He was also not hesitant to make substantial changes in the structure and form of the Geminiani originals when he felt them to be necessary or appropriate. A prime example can be found in the final movement of his concerto arrangement of Geminiani's Sonata in G minor, Op.1, no. VI, an orchestral andante followed by a set of two-part variations based on its harmonic progression, and to which Avison adds the inscription "Da Capo il Minuet" at the end. The music for these variations is not found in any version of Geminiani's G-minor violin sonata, which always concludes with a third movement Allegro in triple time. However, we do find the Avison minuet and variations in three printed sources of Geminiani's keyboard music.[13] Thus Avison has created his own final movement for his concerto arrangement of this sonata by orchestrating one of Geminiani's keyboard minuets and variations (H. 213). Moreover, it is safe to assume that the variations are intended for keyboard performance in Avison's concerto, since they are in two parts and there is no indication of instrumentation. This leads us to a further observation: since the keyboard player in every other Avison orchestral work, either original or arrangement, was always assigned the task of realizing the basso continuo and had no solo duties, the inclusion of a two-part solo harpsichord section in Avison's G-minor concerto is unique in all of the composer's orchestral output.

---

[13]   *Menuetti con variazioni composti per il cembalo da F. Geminiani* […] [c1740]; *Pièces de Clavecin Tirées des differens Ouvrages de M.r F. Geminiani* […] MDCCXLIII; and *HANDEL's Celebrated WATER MUSICK Compleat. Set for the Harpsicord. To which is added, Two favourite MINUETS, with Variations for the Harpsicord, By GEMINIANI* […] [1743].

Ex. 5: Geminiani, Minuet (H. 213) for keyboard, as arranged by Avison, bb. 201-208.

Avison's novel approach to Geminiani is also apparent in his decision to place Geminiani's concerti grossi Opp. 2, 3 and 7, and the concerto arrangements of Corelli's Sonatas for Violin, Op. 5, into score in the workbooks rather than in parts as they were originally published.[14] In fact, it is probable that Avison was the first person to do this, since he was such a strong advocate for publishing orchestral works in this format, as he explains in the *Essay*:

> I know not a more effectual Test than a good Harpsichord and Performance from the *Score*, where the Eye will assist the Ear through all the Defects of this Instrument, and give a better Idea of the Composer's Design than any unsuccessful Attempt in Concert. For this Reason, were the Printers of Music to publish the best *Concertos* and *Sonatas* in *Score*, as are those of CORELLI, perhaps this very Expedient, though it may seem hazardous at first, would contribute more to a general good Taste and Knowledge of Music, than any yet thought of […] I have heard the first Publisher of CORELLI'S Works in Score, very frankly acknowledge, that the Profits received from the Sale of these

---

[14]   For further information on these works, see *Geminiani Opera Ominia*, vols 2, 3, 6 and 7.

> Books, were greater than could have been expected: And, as the
> Public has had almost twenty Years Trial of the Advantages that
> have accrued from an intimate Acquaintance with this classical
> Composer; it cannot, I think, be doubted but a like good Effect
> might also attend a Publication in Score of GEMINIANI'S
> Concertos; and of other Compositions in Parts.[15]

It is also safe to say that Avison based his scored workbook versions of Opp. 2 and 3 on the first edition of 1732, rather than Geminiani's 1755 revision, since he did not incorporate the substantial revisions Geminiani made to his work in the later publication, as we observe in examples 6a and 6b.[16]

Ex. 6a: Geminiani, Concerto in D major, Op. 3/1/i/1-3 in the original 1732 version (H. 73) as copied by Avison.

AVISON'S COMPOSITIONAL STYLE AND ITS CONSEQUENCES

Geminiani's influence can also be felt in Avison's original orchestral compositions, especially because the vast majority are in the Italian concerto grosso style. Avison composed more than fifty works in the genre, writing concertos long after they had gone out of fashion as the new classical symphony began to supplant older orchestral forms. Avison's fidelity to the Italian concerto-grosso style, even as the English public was listening to symphonies by Haydn, can be traced to a number of factors. One was the

---

[15]   AVISON, Charles. *An Essay on Musical Expression*, *op. cit.* (see note 8), pp. 149-150.

[16]   Burney also put Geminiani's Op. 2 concerti grossi into score, but long after Avison, as he describes in his *General History*: "This edition was prepared from a score which I had made for my own improvement, and of which, upon Geminiani's complaining, in 1750, that he had lost his *original*, I was much flattered by his acceptance". The date also leads us to assume that Burney, like Avison, based his score version on the 1732 edition. See BURNEY, IV, p. 644n.

Ex. 6b: Geminiani, Concerto in D major, Op. 3/1/i/1-3 in the Geminiani 1757 revision (H. 79).

nature of Newcastle audiences as described above. Another can certainly be ascribed to the aforementioned musical abilities of his "Gentlemen Amateurs"; since they were so limited, the *ripieno* section of the concerto grosso, with its relatively simple parts, was the perfect place to put them. It is also possible that Avison was influenced by a tendency in Britain during this period to look backwards in all of the arts, as manifested by the popularity of the Academy of Antient Music, the rise of romanticism and the gothic novel in England, and the burgeoning interest in antiquarian scholarship.[17]

Avison's fidelity to Geminiani and his style was on the whole a very good thing, but it did have the unintended consequence of leaving Avison open to considerable criticism, some of it quite vicious. John Hawkins, for example, felt that all of what he considered to be Avison's flaws as a composer could be traced to an excessive devotion to Geminiani: "The music of Avison is light and elegant, but it wants originality, a necessary consequence of his too close attachment to the style of Geminiani, which in a few particulars only he was able to imitate".[18] Burney was equally critical, writing that Avison was simply so close to Geminiani, that his "[…] judgement was warped by many prejudices. He exalted Rameau and Geminiani at the expence of Handel".[19] Burney also extended the criticism to Avison's own musical style, and traced these faults to an overdependence on Geminiani: "[…] a bias in

---

[17] For a full discussion of this issue, see *Music in Eighteenth-Century Britain*, edited by David Wyn Jones, Aldershot, Ashgate, 2000, p. 10 and *passim*.

[18] *HAWKINS*, IV, p. 419.

[19] *BURNEY*, III, p. VI.

[Avison's] compositions for violins, and in his *Essay on Musical Expression*, towards that master is manifest".[20]

The most incendiary criticism comes from William Hayes, who attacks Avison at every level, both personal and professional. He is particularly critical of Avison's insufficiently high regard for Handel, which Hayes ascribes to Geminiani's bad influence, writing that whenever Geminiani "has affected to hold Mr. Handel's Compositions cheap [...] *Charles* (or the more familiar Name *Charley*) Avison" takes the same position. Hayes goes even further and accuses Geminiani or a "*Junto*" of being the true author of Avison's *Essay*, noting that in Geminiani's "Treatise on *good Taste in Music*, and the Dedication of his last Concertos [...] the same Pen hath been employed that writ the Essay; the Style very exactly corresponding, the same haughty and contemptuous Expressions abound in each, and they alike seem calculated more to depreciate the Performances of other Men, and to magnify those of the supposed Author, than any thing beside".[21]

Avison might have been the sober, responsible Anglican church musician as described earlier, but he was no less of an artist than Geminiani when it came to assaults on his musical judgement and character. He was also a better writer. There were, in fact, few people at the time, either English or foreign-born, who could match his verbal skills in this arena. Avison was therefore able to publish a "Reply" to Hayes in 1753, the same year in which Hayes' "Remarks" appeared, where he refutes almost all of Hayes' accusations, including those mentioned above, with passion and eloquence. It is beyond the scope of this article to provide a detailed discussion of Avison's response. Suffice it to say that he used his sharpest tongue to defend himself against Hayes, whom he describes as a "vain, disappointed, snarling Doctor of the Science", and a "pur-blind Critic".[22]

Geminiani in Newcastle

In light of Avison's vigorous and uncompromising advocacy of Geminiani, one would assume that Avison frequently programmed his music during the thirty-two years he served as director of the Newcastle Musical Society, but there is little documentation to support this. Information about

---

[20] *Ibidem*, IV, p. 670.
[21] HAYES, William. *Op. cit.* (see note 5), pp. 111-113.
[22] AVISON, Charles. *An Essay on Musical Expression, op. cit.* (see note 8). The two quotations cited come from pages 2 and 21 respectively of the *Reply*.

Avison's programs and repertoire is fragmentary, and the overwhelming majority of his concert advertisements merely provide the "when" and "where" of the event, and how much the tickets cost. If there is any mention of the repertoire at all, it was quite general, usually being described as "a concert of vocal and instrumental music".[23]

One would have also presumed that Avison's mentor and friend played frequently in his student's series, but the name of Geminiani as a performer does not turn up in any Newcastle records. Perhaps Geminiani's absence from the Newcastle stage as a violinist can be explained by his well-known reluctance to appear in public, especially during his later years, or possibly because his abilities as a virtuoso performer had diminished with age. Avison seems to imply the latter when he diplomatically describes Geminiani's waning powers in his *Essay*: "And notwithstanding the uncertain Duration of this Talent, a Circumstance common to every Performer, he will ever live in those Rules above referred to, and in his *Art of playing on the Violin*".[24]

This, however, still does not explain the apparent absence of Geminiani's music in Newcastle. There is however some evidence, although admittedly circumstantial, to suggest that Geminiani's works were indeed performed there. For this we need to turn to the neighbouring city of Durham and the diaries of George Harris. In an entry on 21 October 1748, Harris tells us that he heard the music of Geminiani in Durham at "A private concert at the Deanery in the evening. — Lord Cowper & a Paxton, fiddles — another Paxton, violoncello. Hasleden, harpsichord. — Corelli, Boyce, Geminiani".[25] Since Durham often shared orchestral personnel, singers and soloists with Newcastle, and programmes and repertoire were frequently repeated in both cities as well,

---

[23]   We do know that Avison programmed works by Rameau and Handel, as well as his own compositions. One listing that appeared in the *Newcastle Journal* of 24 November - 1 December 1759 gives an indication of the repertoire typically performed there: "The same Evening at Mr. Avison's Concert, which was honoured by a very numerous and splendid Company, were perform'd several excellent Pieces of Music suitable to the Occasion; and each Act was closed [with] Songs, such as *Britons strike Home*, *Rule Britannia*, *God save the King*, &c. The Songs were several Times encored; and the Company, at the Close of the Concert, expressed their high Approbation of the Whole by three Huzzas". The patriotic air of this concert reflected the difficult political situation in England at the time and the war in Europe. I am grateful to Roz Southey for this information.

[24]   AVISON, Charles. *An Essay on Musical Expression, op. cit.* (see note 8), p. 127.

[25]   *Music and Theatre in Handel's World: The Family Papers of James Harris, 1732-1780*, edited by Donald Burrows and Rosemary Dunhill, New York, Oxford University Press, 2002, p. 251. "Hasleden" is James Hesletine, the organist of Durham Cathedral from 1711-1763 and incidentally, one of Avison's antagonists. Spencer Cowper was Dean of Durham Cathedral at this time.

it is not unreasonable to hypothesize that the music by Geminiani that George Harris heard in Durham would have also been performed in Newcastle, perhaps played by the Geminiani himself.[26] A more definitive answer to this question will have to await the discovery of new information or documents.

Lessons with Geminiani

We return to the question of whether Avison actually studied with Geminiani. Although this is another aspect of their relationship that is difficult to prove with absolute certainty, it is highly probable that Avison *did* take lessons with Geminiani, and these probably occurred at some point between 1730 and 1735, during Avison's first trip to London.[27] Avison may well have made the trip to London specifically to study with Geminiani, who was at the height of his fame as a violinist and composer at this time, but their collaborations could not have been regular or frequent, considering Geminiani's mercurial personality and penchant for travel. The most extended period for their meetings would have been possible between 1730 and April

---

[26] In a letter of 10 December 1752, Cowper describes a concert in the Durham subscription series of John Garth, a close friend and colleague of Avison; it tells us much about Avison's programming in Newcastle as well: "The Musick was chiefly Instrumental performers at least equal to our own; but the choice of it wretched. It open'd with the Overture of Clothilde, an Opera many ages older than Camilla, and consisted of Concertos and solos, from Rameau, Giardini and Avison". From *Letters of Spencer Cowper, Dean of Durham 1746-1774*, edited by Edward Hughes, Durham – London, Andrew & Co. – Bernard Quaritch, 1950 (Surtees Society, 165), p. 161. I am grateful to Roz Southey for information about this letter.

[27] Little is know about Avison's early life and training. He certainly received musical instruction from his father, who was a Newcastle town wait, and perhaps also benefited from his association with Ralph Jenison (1696-1758), Member of Parliament for Northumberland from 1724 to 1741 and the dedicatee of Avison's first published work, the *Sonatas for Two Violins and a Bass*, Op. 1 (c1737). Although a career politician, evidence of Jenison's patronage of the arts is confirmed by the number of works dedicated to him, such as CORELLI, Arcangelo. *The Score of the Twelve Concertos* [...] *revised by D' Pepusch*, London, c1732. See STEPHENS, Norris Lynn. *Op. cit.* (see note 1), pp. 2-3. Avison also may have received training from a Colonel John Blathwayt (or Blaithwaite), who served for a time as director of the Royal Academy of Music. Hawkins tells us that he "had when a child been a pupil of Alessandro Scarlatti. His proficiency on the harpsichord at twelve years of age astonished every one." (HAWKINS, v, p. 273). Avison, in the preface to his *Six Concertos, Op. 2*, refers to the "valuable opportunities of improving" that he had received through Blathwayt's "generous assistance". See SOUTHEY, Roz - MADDISON, Margaret - HUGHES, David. *Op. cit.* (see note 1), p. 30.

1732, the conclusion of Geminiani's successful series of concerts in Hickford's Room.[28] By the end of that year, Geminiani was in Paris and any chance for further contact would have been delayed until October 1733, when Geminiani returned to London.[29] But even then he and Avison would have had only two more months to work together, since Geminiani was in Dublin by 6 December of that year.[30]

Regardless of the exact time of study and its duration, Avison would have clearly profited from contact with Geminiani in London, and perhaps from his teacher's connections there as well. The twenty-five year old Avison presented his own London benefit concert at Hickford's Room in 1734, performing on no fewer than three instruments — transverse flute, violin and harpsichord — in a program that featured concertos by Corelli and Geminiani, songs by Handel and various instrumental solos.[31] It is also possible that Avison continued his studies when Geminiani once more returned to London, in 1735, but again this would probably have not been for an extended time. Avison had to be back in Newcastle by October 1735, if not earlier, to assume his first position there as organist of St John the Baptist.[32]

AVISON, GEMINIANI AND THE ITALIAN CONNECTION

Charles Avison also played an important role in the lives of other Italian musicians who made England their home in the eighteenth century, chief among them Felice Giardini, who served as leader of Avison's orchestra in Newcastle on several occasions. Avison probably had some connections with Francesco Scarlatti as well, and it might very well have

---

[28] See CARERI, pp. 22-25.

[29] We learn this from a letter of Charles Stanhope to William Capel on 3 November 1732, who wrote to contradict erroneous reports that Geminiani had died: "I left him in Paris alive, and well, and I believe he will be here in a day or two". According to Capel, Geminiani remained in Paris until 20 September 1733, and on 1 October he reported that he "went from hence ten days ago […] for England". See CARERI, p. 27.

[30] See CARERI, p. 29.

[31] Cited in SOUTHEY, Roz - MADDISON, Margaret - HUGHES, David. Op. cit. (see note 1), p. 31, and Charles Avison's Essay […], op. cit. (see note 1), p. x.

[32] Although Avison was in Newcastle by October of 1735, he could not begin his duties at St John's until nearly nine months later, on 24 June 1736, when the newly acquired organ had become playable. Information from the Newcastle Common Council Book for 13 October 1735, f. 296 and 12 July 1736, f. 316, cited in STEPHENS, Norris Lynn. Op. cit. (see note 1), p. 7.

been Geminiani who had given Avison the Scarlatti concertos that appeared in the workbooks. Avison was also a source of employment to the many less illustrious Italians trying to earn a living in England. Like Geminiani in 1760, they too would find themselves stopping in Newcastle as they travelled on the main road north from London to Edinburgh, where they could pick up a few shillings playing for Avison's Newcastle Music Society. At least five touring Italians are documented during the 1739-1740 Newcastle season: the violinist Giovanni Piantanida and his wife the singer Costanza Posterla; and the violinists Alexander Bitti, Giovanni Cattanei, and Joseph-Marie-Clément Dall'Abaco (1710-1805).[33] When Giardini was unable to perform in Newcastle, Avison turned to yet another Italian, Giovanni Battista Noferi, to replace him.[34] Avison was also adept at engaging famous vocal soloists as they passed through the town, since he had so few singers to draw upon in Newcastle. One guest artist was the soprano Clementina Cremonini, an Italian of course, who performed in his series in 1762.[35]

No Italian musician, however, would have as profound an influence on Avison as Geminiani. We have observed this in Avison's writings, in his music, in their personal interactions, and in reports by their contemporaries. Geminiani and Avison also shared a favourite publisher: John Johnson. Of Avison's ten published works with opus numbers, eight (nos. 1, 3, 4, 5, 7, 8 and 9) received their first of second printing from "John Johnson [...] in Cheapside", or were sold or advertised by either John or Robert Johnson. The list also includes Avison's *Twenty Six Concertos* that he printed himself in 1758.[36]

Geminiani's death in 1762 did not diminish Avison's admiration for his mentor, and his gratitude for all that he had learned from him. Six years later, in 1768, and two years before his own death, Avison wrote

---

[33] SOUTHEY, Roz. 'The role of gentlemen amateurs in subscription concerts in north-east England during the eighteenth century', in: *Music in the British Provinces* [...], *op. cit.* (see note 1), p. 121. For a comprehensive discussion of the numerous Italian musicians wandering the British Isles during this period, see McVEIGH, Simon. 'Italian Violinists in Eighteenth-Century London', in: *The Eighteenth-Century Diaspora of Italian Music and Musicians*, edited by Reinhard Strohm, Turnhout, Brepols, 2001 (Speculum Musicae, 8), pp. 139-176.

[34] SOUTHEY, Roz. *Music-Making in North-East England* [...], *op. cit.* (see note 1), pp. 34-35.

[35] *Ibidem*, p. 36.

[36] The full title is *Twenty Six CONCERTOS Composed for Four Violins, One Alto-Viola, a Violoncello and Ripieno Bass. Divided into Four Books in Score for the use of PERFORMERS, On the Harpsichord.*

two separate articles to express his feelings in writing. One describes Geminiani's artistry and his generosity to other musicians, including Avison: "He loved the Arts, and assisted many artists. I speak for one, and revere his Memory".[37] The other is an eloquent and heartfelt eulogy to his departed friend and master:[38]

> *For the* LITERARY REGISTER.
>
> On viewing a portrait of the late celebrated GEMINIANI.
>
> WHILE contending nations alarm the world abroad, and interiour commotions at home, I peruse *thy* pacific page, and wonder where the powers of music are fled, not to harmonize the passions of men ; yet still the dulcet strains will live in congenial souls, to smooth the path of life which providence has given to lovers of harmony.
>
> *Newcastle.*   C. A.

---

[37] *Newcastle Courant*, 17 September 1768.
[38] The eulogy appeared in *The Literary Register, or Weekly Miscellany Literary Register*, vol. I, 1768, p. 278.

Geminiani the Arranger: A Re-Evaluation

Sandra Mangsen
(North Bennington, VT)

O VER THE COURSE OF A CAREER AS COMPOSER, teacher, performer and dealer in fine art, Geminiani must have expended at least as much effort on arranging his earlier compositions as he did on writing new ones. Such adaptations were hardly unusual at the time: Handel, Bach and Telemann all re-arranged and re-used their earlier compositions to suit new scorings and even radically different musical contexts. The title page of Telemann's *Six Concerts et Six Suites* (1734) specifies several performance possibilities: harpsichord and flute, with or without cello; violin, flute and cello or continuo; or harpsichord, violin, flute and cello. Rameau's *Pièces en concerts* (1741) allow for solo harpsichord or trio performance; the keyboard player simply plays the part used in the trio version, except in the five movements where the string parts are critical, for which Rameau provided a separate arrangement for solo performance.[1] Although Handel's borrowings, Bach's organ transcriptions and Telemann's or Rameau's multiple performance options seem to have attracted little contemporary comment, both Charles Burney and Sir John Hawkins criticized Geminiani for relying too frequently on arrangements of existing compositions, a habit they attributed to a deficiency in his imagination. As Burney saw it,

> Geminiani, for all his harmonical abilities, was so circumscribed in his invention, that he was obliged to have recourse to all the arts of musical cookery, not to call it quackery, for materials to publish. In his younger days, when imagination

I am grateful to my colleagues and graduate students at the University of Western Ontario for their helpful responses to an earlier version of this essay, to my colleague Edmund Goerhing for his written comments on that draft, and to Mary Cyr for her helpful critique of a more recent version.

[1] See MANGSEN, Sandra. 'Rameau's *Pièces en concerts*: Trios or Accompanied Keyboard Music?', in: *Early Keyboard Journal*, II (1983-1984), pp. 21-40.

is most fertile, sixteen years elapsed between the publication of his first book of solos and his first six concertos. Indeed, during that period, he achieved what a plodding contrapuntist of inferior abilities might have done as well: he transformed Corelli's solos and six of his sonatas into concertos, by multiplying notes, and loading, and deforming, I think, those melodies, that were more graceful and pleasing in their light original dress.[2]

Burney also devalued the keyboard arrangements, arguing that the original pieces had been "rendered impracticable by crouded harmony and multiplied notes".[3] Hawkins' view, while not quite as harsh as Burney's, is also negative:

> Notwithstanding the fine talents which as a musician Geminiani possessed, it must be remarked that the powers of his fancy seem to have been limited. His melodies were to the last degree elegant, his modulation original and multifarious, and in their general cast his compositions were tender and pathetic; and it is to the want of an active and teeming imagination that we are to attribute the publication of his works in various forms. Perhaps it was this that moved him to compose his first opera of solos into sonatas for two violins and a bass, notwithstanding that the latter six of them had been made into sonatas by Barsanti many years before; and also to make into concertos sundry of the solos in his opera quarta. In the same spirit of improvement he employed the latter years of his life in varying and new molding his former works, particularly he made two books of lessons for the harpsichord, consisting chiefly of airs from his solos; and it was not always that he altered them for the better.[4]

Such critiques of Geminiani as composer were hardly new; in fact, both Burney and Hawkins echoed similarly disparaging remarks made a generation earlier by one of the composer's chief rivals, the Italian violinist Francesco Veracini (1690-1768). Veracini spent much of 1714 in London, just as Geminiani was establishing himself there, and returned in 1733 for several more years. He was heard frequently as a solo performer and saw four of his operas produced in London between 1735 and 1744.[5] Although his later remarks do not mention Geminiani by name, Veracini seems to have had him in mind when he complained of composers who reheat their 'eternal stews' made up of bits and pieces of their own earlier works and borrowings from

---

[2]   *BURNEY*, IV, p. 644.
[3]   *Ibidem*, IV, p. 643.
[4]   *HAWKINS*, V, p. 424.
[5]   HILL, John Walter. 'Francesco Veracini', in: *NG*.

those of others. In Veracini's view, "The reheaters were so called because on every occasion when they had to produce new works they always 'reheated' the same works that they had heated up on other occasions".[6]

Criticism of Geminiani's over-reliance on arrangements continued far into the twentieth century. Editions of *Grove's Dictionary of Music and Musicians* from the first (1880) through the fifth (1954) echo Burney and Hawkins in calling him a composer "wanting in originality and individuality". William S. Newman's characterization of Geminiani's arrangements is quite dismissive; in the concertos, he claims, "the changes are minimal" and the harpsichord pieces typically involve "no other transcription than that of assigning the 'solo' to the right hand and the b.c. to the left".[7] By 1980, however, Geminiani's harpsichord collections had come to be called "fascinating essays in the possibilities of adapting one medium to another".[8] If his arrangements might justifiably be regarded either as evidence of a lack of imagination, or as fascinating transformations, perhaps it is time to look more carefully at them and at their critical role in his career.

As Enrico Careri noted in his 1993 study of the composer, "If we exclude all his numerous elaborations and transcriptions, the musical output of Geminiani seems rather exiguous: two sets of violin sonatas (Opp. 1 and 4), one of cello sonatas (Op. 5), three of concerti grossi (Opp. 2, 3 and 7), *The Inchanted Forrest*, and the compositions published in his treatises".[9] Especially significant here are the two volumes of violin sonatas and the single volume of cello sonatas, which together provided much of the raw material for the two collections of harpsichord arrangements, published as *Pièces de Clavecin* in 1743 and *The Second Collection of Pieces for the Harpsichord* in 1762. The violin sonatas were also transformed into trio sonatas and concertos, the cello sonatas into sonatas for violin. Indeed, in pre-1945 discussions of Geminiani's works the violin sonatas were taken to be the originals and those for cello

---

[6]   "I Rifriggiatori furono così chiamati perché, in ogni occasione di dover fare nuove Composizioni, rifriggevano sempre le medesime, altre volte rifritte". The remarks are drawn from a manuscript in I Fc, 'Il trionfo della pratica musicale', c1760, excerpts from which are quoted and translated in CARERI, pp. 52-55 and 136. See CARERI, Chapters 5 and 8, for a more extended discussion of Geminiani reception and of Veracini's criticism, and *Geminiani Opera Omnia*, vol. 6. See also FABBRI, Mario. 'Le acute censure di Francesco M. Veracini a *L'Arte della Fuga* di Francesco Geminani', in: *Accademia Musicale Chigiana*, XX (1963), pp. 186-187.

[7]   NEWMAN, William S. *The Sonata in the Baroque Era*, New York, Norton, ⁴1983, pp. 322 and 324.

[8]   BOYDEN, David D. 'Francesco Geminiani', in: *The New Grove Dictionary of Music and Musicians*, edited by Stanley Sadie, 20 vols, London, Macmillan, ⁶1980, vol. VII, p. 226.

[9]   *CARERI*, p. 59.

the arrangements.[10] Although as an arranger Geminiani focused mainly on his own music, he also transformed Corelli's solo violin sonatas and some of the trio sonatas into concertos, published in three sets between 1726 and 1735. Finally we might include among Geminiani's arrangements the sonatas from the *Treatise of Good Taste in the Art of Music* (1749). The three "Airs made into Sonatas for Two Violins and a Bass" may arguably be regarded as creative transformations of the songs, in which Geminiani the composer took precedence over Geminiani the arranger, for his raw material consisted simply of the borrowed melodies.

What should we make of this series of adaptations and re-workings of existing musical material? In arranging Corelli's sonatas and many of his own compositions, Geminiani was certainly responding to an already established market in which musical works were regularly transferred from one medium to another. By 1700, the practice of performing solo and trio sonatas as concertos, or vice versa, was already well established in adaptations made by performers taking a piece from one context to another. In the preface to his *Ausserlesene Instrumental-Music*, Georg Muffat explained how concertos could be reduced to chamber proportions simply by leaving out the ripieno instruments, or enhanced for larger venues by adding winds to double the strings.[11] Four decades later, Michel Corrette suggested that cellists could easily play the treble parts of violin sonatas (an octave lower than written) by utilizing thumb position.[12] Geminiani's keyboard adaptations of his own violin sonatas belong within a similar tradition, in which all kinds of vocal and instrumental music was made more accessible to solo keyboard players. Harpsichordists in eighteenth-century England could be counted upon to purchase such ready-made arrangements, which made it easier for them to enjoy arias or violin repertoire they would otherwise have had to adapt directly from the original songbooks or sonata prints and orchestral

---

[10] See, for example, the article on the composer in *Grove's Dictionary of Music and Musicians*, edited by John Alexander Fuller-Maitland, London, Macmillian, ²1904-1910; the error is repeated in *Grove's Dictionary of Music and Musicians*, edited by Henry Cope Colles, London, Macmillan, ³1927.

[11] Muffat transformed his own sonatas à 5 "for few or many instruments" from *Armonico Tributo* (1682) into concertos in *Ausserlesene Instrumental-Music* (1701) in a manner not so far from Geminiani's arrangements of Corelli's sonatas. See my article, 'Ad Libitum Procedures in Instrumental Duos and Trios', in: *Early Music*, XIX/1 (1991), pp. 28-40.

[12] By placing the thumb in such a way as to transform the 'open' strings into *e'-a-d-G*, the cellist could simply read violin parts (and the violin fingerings), transposing by an octave at sight: "ainsi en se servant du pouce on jouera aisément les dessus des sonates de violon". See CORRETTE, Michel. *Méthode théorique et pratique pour apprendre en peu de tems le violoncelle dans sa perfection*, Op. 24, Paris, chez l'Auteur *et al.*, 1741, p. 41. I am indebted to Mary Cyr for this reference.

repertoire for which they would have had to make their own transcriptions. Even late in the century Geminiani's own concertos, Opp. 2 and 3, were arranged for solo keyboard "as perform'd by Mr. Cramer" and presented at the Concerts of Ancient Music.[13] Such public performances of arranged works make it clear that the market for arrangements was not confined solely to domestic contexts. In fact, transforming sonatas into concertos provided a convenient vehicle for transporting private music into the public sphere.

An examination of the publications of John Walsh in the first decades of the eighteenth century readily demonstrates the critical importance of transcriptions to English music making in private and public contexts. Walsh published arrangement after arrangement of arias and instrumental music from the London stage, which both exploited and enhanced the popularity of Italianate opera in London. Among composers of instrumental music, Corelli was especially marketable. Between 1700 and 1706, Walsh advertised editions of Corelli's solo and trio sonatas, not only for violins, but also arranged for recorder and for harpsichord alone.[14] Beyond filling an empty niche in an established market, Geminiani's concerto arrangements of Corelli's sonatas certainly must have helped to keep his own name before the public during the period Burney called fallow. Given the success of his Corelli arrangements, it should not surprise us that Geminiani subsequently transformed so many of his own works from one medium to another. Finally, it may be useful to recall, as we think about his 'reheatings', that in an era before recordings, playing works in keyboard or chamber reduction was one of the few ways to experience them repeatedly and 'on demand'. In addition, turning sonatas into concertos not only gave them a public face, but also increased their stature, which in turn would likely have boosted sales of the original sonatas.

My aims in this essay are twofold: to examine Geminiani's arrangements and then to analyse our own attitudes and those of his contemporaries toward them. Why did he make them? How did he proceed? What effect did they have on the dissemination of his compositions and on his reputation? And, finally, how should we regard them today? I begin by examining in detail some of the solo violin and cello sonatas that were destined to appear as concertos or keyboard suites. The first set of violin sonatas, published in 1716, appeared in a revised edition in 1739, which clearly illustrates the "spirit of improvement" noted by Hawkins. (See TABLE 1 for a list of Geminiani's sonata volumes and their various transformations.) The sonatas had been "carefully corrected", and were provided

---

[13] *Geminiani's Celebrated Six Concertos as Perform'd by Mr. Cramer* [...] *Adapted for the Harpsichord, Organ, or Pianoforte, Op. 3*, London, G. Goulding, *c*1788. The practice of publishing arrangements for the domestic market remained strong until the advent of recordings, when multiple rehearings no longer depended on live performance.

[14] See SMITH1, nos 31, 85, 107, 135, 181 and 205.

with ornamentation as well as fingerings. Many short slurs, as well as a few dynamic markings were added, some tempo markings were changed, and a few passages were more thoroughly recomposed. This spirit of improvement may also be reflected in what Peter Walls has characterized as a French cast evident in Geminiani's revisions.[15] Ex. 1a shows the opening bars of Op. 1 No. 3 as they appeared in the 1716 and 1739 editions. Note that Geminiani has replaced the Italianate ornament in the first bar with ornament signs, which are provided in abundance in the slow movements of the revised sonatas.

TABLE 1

SELECTED PUBLISHED COLLECTIONS AND THEIR TRANSFORMATIONS

Op. 1

Sonate a violino, violone, e cembalo [...], London, 1716 (the date of dedication; another edition from the same plates was advertised in 1718).

Le prime sonate a violino, e basso, di F. Geminiani nuovamente ristampate, e con diligenza corette, aggiuntovi ancora per maggior facilità le grazie agli adagi, ed i numeri per la trasposizione della mano, London, 1739.

Six sonatas for two violins & a violoncello, or harpsichord with a ripieno bass, to be used when the violins are doubled [...] *from the* VI *first solos of his Op.ª 1ª*, London, Johnson, 1757.

The Ripieno parts belonging to the six sonatas composed by F. Geminiani from the VI *first solos of his opera prima*, London, Johnson, 1757.

VI *Sonatas for two violins & a violoncello, or harpsichord; with a ripieno bass, to be used when the violins are doubled* [...] *from the* VI *last solos of his Op.ª 1ª*, London, Johnson, 1757.

Op. 4

Sonate a violino e basso [...] Opera IV, London, 1739.

Concerti grossi a due violini, due viole e violoncello obligati con due altri violini, e basso di ripieno [...] *Questi concerti sono composti dalle Sonate a Violino e Basso dell'Opera* IV, London, 1743.

Op. 5

Sonate pour le violoncelle et basse continue [...] *dans les qu'elles il a fait une etude particuliere pour l'utilié de ceux qui accompagnent*, Paris, 1746 [*recte* 1747].

Sonates pour le violon avec un violoncelle ou clavecin lesquelles ne sont pas moins utiles a ceux qui jouent le violon, qu'à ceux qui accompagnent, The Hague, 1746 [*recte* 1747].

VI *Sonate di violoncello e basso continuo* [...] *Opera* V *Nelle quali egli a procurato di renderle non solo utile a quelli che bramano perfettionarsi sopra il detto stromento ma ancora per quelli che accompagnano di cembalo*, London, c1747.

Six sonates transposés pour le violon avec des agrement propres pour l'instrument [...] *Œuvre* VIͤ, Paris, 1746 [*recte* 1747].

---

[15]   Peter Walls attributes some of these changes to Geminiani's increasing fascination with French style, which makes good sense considering what we now know about his sojourns in Paris. See WALLS, Peter. '"Ill-Compliments and Arbitrary Taste?": Geminiani's Directions for Performers', in: *Early Music*, XIV/2 (1986), pp. 221-235.

Le VI Sonate di Violoncello e Basso Continuo Composte da F. Geminiani Opera V Sono dallo stesso trasposte per il Violino con cambiamenti proprij e necessarij allo stromento, London, 1747.

In 1757 Geminiani published trio arrangements of all twelve Op. 1 sonatas.[16] Here we encounter still further changes, including more altered tempo markings and a simpler approach to ornamentation. For instance, *moderato* is added to four of the original *allegro* markings, and *andante*, which appeared only once in the 1716 version of Op. 1, is used six times in the trios (twice for substitute movements). *Piano* and *forte* indications are fairly plentiful in some of the trio versions (although not in the passage shown here), but are almost completely absent in the solo sonatas. Ex. 1b shows the opening bars of Sonata No. 3 in the trio version; Exx. 1c–d illustrate some of the recomposition evident in the 1739 solos and 1757 trios. In the revised solos, some details of the violin writing in the *Presto* were reworked and the triple metre bars have additional ornaments. In the trio version of the same passage (Ex. 1d), marked *Allegro* in the violin parts and *Presto* in the basso continuo, the first violin inherits the somewhat abbreviated figuration, and the short triple metre section is rewritten in $\frac{3}{2}$. In addition, these three sections are elided in the trio, whereas there are strong cadences at equivalent points in the solo sonata. Striking evidence of recomposition is also found in the sixth sonata, when the third movement was expanded from thirty-eight to sixty-one bars in the 1739 revision. The trio also transmits the more extended version, but the intervening movement is entirely new. Geminiani replaced the $\frac{6}{8}$ *Adagio* (marked *Andante* in 1739) with a brief transitional movement marked *Adagio-Presto-Adagio-Presto-Adagio*.

Ex. 1a: Geminiani, Sonata in E minor, Op. 1/III: i/1-6 in 1716 (H. 3) and 1739 (H. 15) versions.

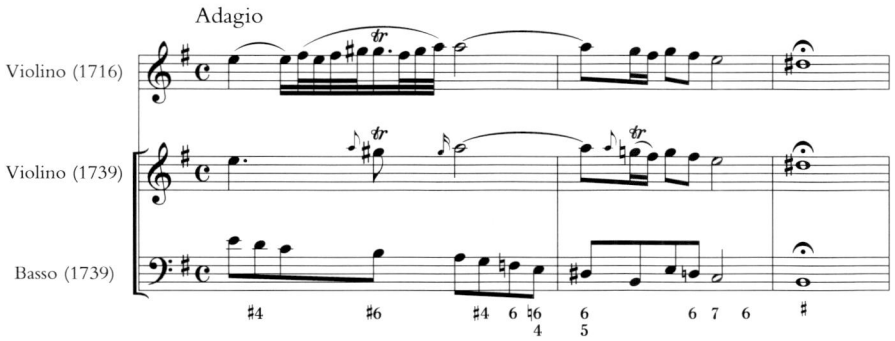

---

[16] Six of those sonatas (nos 7–12) had already been arranged as trios by Francesco Barsanti (*c*1728). See SMITH2, p. 159, nos 710 and 711. Walsh reprinted those arrangements *c*1742, without the attribution to Barsanti.

Ex. 1b: Geminiani, Sonata in E minor, Op. 1/III: i/1-6 in the 1757 arrangement for trio (H. 27).

Ex. 1c: Geminiani, Sonata in E minor, Op. 1/III: i/40-50, ii/0-2 in 1716 (H. 3) and 1739 (H. 15) versions.

Ex. 1d: Geminiani, Sonata in E minor, Op. 1/III: i/48-56, ii/1-2 in the 1757 arrangement for trio (H. 27).

Ex. 2a: Geminiani, Sonata in A minor, Op. 4/v: i./0–10 in the original 1739 version (H. 89).

Six of the twelve solo sonatas of Op. 4, which had been issued in the same year as the revised edition of Op. 1, were soon arranged as concerti grossi (see TABLE 1). They were published in eight part books, and advertised in the *London Daily Post and General Advertiser* on 20 May 1743. In contrast to the concertos playable from the trio parts for the Op. 1 sonatas, these concerti have two newly composed viola parts. Geminiani's experience in rewriting Corelli's solo and trio sonatas as concertos must have served as a useful training ground both for adapting his own sonatas and for composing the first two of his three concerto collections, published in 1732. According to Marion McArtor, "The arrangements [of six Op. 4 sonatas] are the most faithful and literal adaptations that Geminiani ever published. Beyond the addition of inner voices, modifications are limited to omissions of more difficult and florid ornamentations, simplification of phrasing, and reconstruction of melodic lines whenever the original was written above *d''''*".[17] Yet there was still a lot of recomposition involved. A brief example from Sonata 5/Concerto 4 will serve to illustrate how the ripieno violin parts are related to the original solo violin part.

Ex. 2 shows the opening bars of the *Adagio* from Sonata No. 5 in its original version for solo violin and the parallel passages from the concerto. In the sonata the repetition of these bars is not written out, but in the concerto, the solo first violin, liberated from the sonata's double and triple stops, plays a melodic elaboration of the opening passage (bars 9–16). Of course this may have been the approach for the sonata violinist as well, but we have no way of knowing how the first repeat was actually performed. In Ex. 2b the rich harmony originally provided by the multiple stops is distributed among all of the strings; bars 16–24 show that sometimes Geminiani simply divided double stops between the two concertino violins, and then provided more active counter melodies for the ripieno violinists and the violists. In the final movement of the concerto, the first violin and cello preserve most of the original sonata material, but here again Geminiani composed quite active inner parts (see Exx. 3a–b). The transformed tempo marks are a bit confusing: the *Allegro Affettuoso... Non Tanto* of the Sonata, are marked *Allegro* and *Affettuoso* in the Concerto. In the *Affettuoso* Geminiani has the ripieno strings simply doubling the concertino in some repeated passages (Ex. 3c). The two violas once again have independent parts. As in the Sonata, the movement ends with a restatement of the opening rondo theme, including the elaborate cello line shown in Ex. 3b.

In 1747 Geminiani published his only set of cello sonatas in The Hague, Paris and London (using the plates from the Dutch edition).[18] Geminiani must have been encouraged to produce sonatas for cello by the spate of such

---

[17] MCARTOR, Marion Emmett. *Francesco Geminiani: Composer and Theorist*, Ph.D. Diss., Ann Arbor (MI), UMI Research Press (51-107), 1951, p. 335.

[18] See Christopher Hogwood's Introduction to *Geminiani Opera Omnia*, vol. 5, pp. xiv-xv for a discussion of these publications and Geminiani's attempts to avoid pirated editions. For the re-dating of these publications, despite the evidence of the title-pages ("MDCCXLVI"), see the essay by Rudolf Rasch in the present volume, pp. 123-141.

Ex. 2b: Geminiani, Sonata in A minor, Op. 4/v: i/0-24 in the 1743 arrangement as Concerto IV (H. 100).

* Minor differences between concertino and ripieno parts are ignored in Exx. 2b and 3a–c.

publications that had appeared in London and on the Continent in the 1730s and early 1740s.[19] It is no surprise, however, that he adapted these sonatas for the violin at the very same time. The violin versions are, as one might expect, quite similar to those for cello, but four are transposed (two by a major third

---

19   See *Geminiani Opera Omnia*, vol. 5, pp. xi–xii for a capsule history.

and two by a perfect fourth) and, as promised, most movements are provided with "ornaments appropriate for the instrument". But there are many other changes, as shown in Ex. 4.

In the opening movement of Sonata No. 2, the cellist is immediately presented with four chords, for the execution of which Geminiani gives no particular advice; for the violinist, however, the composer writes out precisely how to negotiate the passage (Ex. 4a). In the third movement he again gives more detailed advice to the violinist than to the cellist with respect to melodic ornamentation, an arpeggiated outline of the harmony (bar 7), swells, and

Ex. 3a: Geminiani, Sonata in A minor, Op. 4/v arranged as Concerto IV (H. 100): iii/1-8.

a reduction in dynamic level at the end of the passage (Ex. 4b). In the final movement of the Sonata, mm. 55-60 are recomposed for the violin (three of the four cello chords are replaced by melodic figuration). Similar recomposition is found in several other sonatas in this collection; in Sonata No. 4 cellist and violinist approach the "Fantasia ad libitum" in the second movement quite differently, when the cellist's wide leaps are replaced by a stepwise descent through an interval of a twelfth in the violin (Ex. 5a). In the opening *Andante* and in the third movement *Grave*, Geminiani again provides a descending

Ex. 3b: Geminiani, Sonata in A minor, Op. 4/v arranged as Concerto IV (H. 100): iii/17-24.

scale for the violinist in place of the cellist's chords. The two versions of Op. 5 illustrate what Geminiani thought appropriate to each instrument, and indeed how the continuo line might also be altered when it is accompanying a violin rather than a solo cello, where elaboration in the bass register might simply be in the cellist's way (Ex. 5b). His characterization of the two instruments is hardly rigid, since in bar 3 of this example, it is the violinist who leaps and plays a chord while the cellist has a stepwise passage. And at the end of the final movement, Geminiani actually requires more athletic broken chords

Ex. 3c: Geminiani, Sonata in A minor, Op. 4/v arranged as Concerto IV (H. 100): iii/73-104.

from the violin than he does from the cello; but then, as if by way of apology, he extends the coda for another four bars in the violin version, employing only stepwise figuration. That extension turns up in the harpsichord arrangement in the 1762 collection, almost unaltered.

Having examined the various transformations of the string sonatas within the same family, so to speak, we turn now to the keyboard arrangements of some of these pieces. The *Pièces de Clavecin* (1743) and *The Second Collection of Pieces for the Harpsichord* (1762) show us yet another side of Geminiani as

Ex. 4a: Geminiani, Sonata Op. 5/II, in versions for cello (H. 104) and for violin (H. 110): i/1-2.

arranger of his own works. TABLE 2 takes us from the sonata collections to the keyboard volumes, showing which sonatas Geminiani chose to transcribe for keyboard, and the various changes of key and tempo marking he introduced.[20] The *Pièces* contain fourteen separate items, twelve of which are grouped by key into four suites; two minuets with variations close the volume. The Op. 4 violin sonatas provided material for the first three suites; Geminiani then turned to his first set of violin sonatas for Suite 4. The first minuet (H. 212)

---

[20] *CARERI*, Table 8.1 organizes this information in the opposite way, taking us from keyboard pieces and apparent suites back to their sources in the sonatas and other works.

Ex. 4b: Geminiani, Sonata Op. 5/ɪɪ, in versions for cello (H. 104) and for violin (H. 110): third movement.

Ex. 5a: Geminiani, Sonata Op. 5/IV, in versions for cello (H. 106) and for violin (H. 112): ii/33-36.

comes from his Concerto grosso, Op. 2 No. 1; the source of the second (H. 213), written *sopra un soggetto datogli* (on a subject given to him), is unknown. The minuets had already been printed and may have served simply to fill out this collection.[21] The second volume includes other movements from Opp. 1, 4 and 5, but also draws on the guitar and the violin treatises. As in the first collection, movements are often grouped by key, with the original sonatas transposed as necessary, but few suites include more than two movements

---

[21]   *Handel's Celebrated Water Musick Compleat. Set for the Harpsicord. To which is added Two favourite Minuets, with Variations for the Harpsicord, by Geminiani*, London, Walsh, 1740.

Ex. 5b: Geminiani, Sonata Op. 5/IV, in versions for cello (H. 106) and for violin (H. 112): first movement.

and only one sonata (Op. 4 No. 11) is transferred relatively intact. Occasional dance names (minuet, allemanda, giga) substitute for tempo markings in the 1762 volume, but in comparison with the *Pièces* this collection seems less a deliberate selection and careful regrouping into keyboard suites than a hodgepodge, perhaps quickly assembled.

TABLE 2
VIOLIN AND CELLO SONATAS ARRANGED FOR HARPSICHORD

Pièces de clavecin, tirées des differents ouvrages de M.ʳ F. Geminiani adaptées par luy meme a cet instrument, London, 1743, and Paris.

The Second Collection of Pieces for the harpsichord. Taken from different works of F. Geminiani and adapted by himself to that instrument, London, 1762.

Op. 1

			Pièces de clavecin			*Second Collection*		
Sonata 1/ii	A	----				xxxiii	A	Fuga per l'organo, Allegro
Sonata 1/iv	A	Allegro				xxxiv	A	Allegro
Sonata 4/iv	D	Allegro				xxxvii	D	Per l'organo, Allegro
Sonata 6/i	g	Affettuoso	xi	g	Tendrement			
Sonata 6/iii	g	Allegro	xii	g	Vivement			
Sonata 7/iv	c	Allegro				xxxvi	c	Allegro
Sonata 9/i	F	Allegro				xxii	F	Allemanda, Allegro moderato
Sonata 9/iii	F	Allegro				xxiv	F	Allegro assai
Sonata 10/ii	E	Allegro				xxxviii	E	Allegro moderato
Sonata 10/iv	E	Allegro				xxxix	E	Allegro

Op. 4

			Pièces de clavecin			*Second Collection*		
Sonata 1/i	D	Adagio	i	D	Prelude, Lentement			
Sonata 1/ii	D	Allegro	ii	D	Gayment			
Sonata 1/iv	D	Allegro assai	iii	D	Vivement			
Sonata 2/iv	e	Allegro				xiv	c	Allegro
Sonata 3/ii	C	Allegro				viii	Bᵇ	Allegro
Sonata 5/i	a	Andante	iv	a	Tendrement			
Sonata 5/ii	A	Presto	v	A	Vivement			
Sonata 5/iii	a	Allegro affettuoso [non tanto]	vi	a	Vivement			
			vii	A	Tendrement			
Sonata 6/ii	D	Allegro				ix	Bᵇ	Allegro
Sonata 6/iii	d	Andante	x	d	Moderement			
Sonata 6/iv	D	Allegro				xxi	Bᵇ	Giga Allegro
Sonata 8/ii	d	Allegro				xvi	d	Allegro
Sonata 8/iv	d	Allegro	viii	d	Amoureusement			
Sonata 9/iv	c	Allegro				xii	a	Allegro moderato
Sonata 10/iii	A	Allegro				xiii	A	Minuet Allegro
Sonata 11/i	b	Largo				xxvii	b	Adagio
Sonata 11/ii	D	Allegro				xxviii	D	Allegro assai
Sonata 11/iv	D	Allegro				xxix	D	Allegro
Sonata 12/iv	A	Presto				xxvi	G	Giga Allegro assai

Op. 5			*Pièces de clavecin*	Second Collection		
Sonata 5/iv	A	Allegro		xi	A	Allegro
Sonata 3/iii	c	Affettuoso		xvii	c	Affettuoso
Sonata 3/iv	C	Allegro		xviii	C	Allegro
Sonata 4/ii	B♭	Allegro moderato		iii	B♭	Allegro moderato
Sonata 4/iii	g	Grave		iii	g	Andante
Sonata 4/iv	B♭	Allegro		x	B♭	Minuet Allegro

Nonetheless, there is substantial evidence of Geminiani's efforts to ensure that the music suited the new instrument, even in the *Second Collection*. Violin and cello chords or large leaps tend to be compacted in deference to keyboard technique. Ex. 6 shows some typical passages, drawn from one of the cello sonatas we have already examined. The passage shown in Ex. 6a, from the Op. 5 No. 4, leads for the violin or cello to a fermata marked "Fantasia ad libitum". In the harpsichord version, not only is the material rewritten so that it lies more conveniently under the hand, but the improvised Fantasia is replaced by newly composed figuration. Moreover the entire da capo is also written out. At the end of the da capo, Geminiani elides this movement with the *Andante* (marked *Grave* in Op. 5) that follows, again rewriting some of the material to better suit the keyboard. (Ex. 6b shows harpsichord and cello versions of the *Grave*.) For some reason, he concludes this three-movement suite with a new *Allegro* in ⅜, reserving the original movement from the cello sonata for another point in the collection.

Ex. 6a: Geminiani, Sonata in B flat major, Op. 5/IV: second movement, in the arrangement for keyboard (H. 216a, bb. 66-76).

Ex. 6b: Geminiani, Sonata in B flat major, Op. 5/IV: third movement, in the original cello version (H. 106), and in the arrangement for keyboard (H. 216a, bb. 121-131).

While the second set can be put aside for the moment as part of Geminiani's efforts to exploit an established market late in his career, the first collection demands more attention. At first glance, what seems most striking about the *Pièces* is the use of French movement titles in place of the Italian tempo words in the violin sonatas, certainly a deliberate attempt to appeal to the market for French harpsichord music. Geminiani had established contacts in Paris during his initial stay there from November 1732 until September 1733, but he began to publish there only in the 1740s.[22] Careri reports that the composer twice received privileges for Parisian publication of his instrumental works, the first granted on 31 December 1740 and the second on 25 January 1752.[23] Opp. 1-4, which had appeared between 1716 and 1739, all enjoyed Parisian editions in the 1740s; Op. 5 and the *Pièces* probably appeared at about the same time in London and Paris. The Parisian editions carry dedications (Op. 5 to *Monseigneur Le Prince d'Ardore* [...] *Ambassadeur Extraordinaire de sa Majesté Napolitaine et Sicilienne a la Cour de France* and the *Pièces* to *Mademoiselle de Saint Sulpix*), while no dedicatees are named in the London prints, nor do they appear in the edition of Op. 5 printed in The Hague. The Paris edition of the *Pièces* has not been precisely dated, but the composer could have overseen the engraving by Mlle Vendôme before the autumn of 1741, when he returned to London.[24] The Op. 4 violin sonatas (1739), some of which appear transformed in the *Pièces*, were printed in Paris *Avec Privilege du Roy c*1742; it would have made sense to issue the harpsichord collection around the same time. Since the London edition used the same plates, they must have been transferred in time for the 1743 edition to be printed there, with the new title page.[25]

Geminiani must have enjoyed his sojourns in Paris. Titon du Tillet describes performances at the Duhallay home, where the most famous Italian and French musicians could be heard.[26] Although this passage from

---

[22] *Careri*, p. 27. Geminiani was in Paris for two subsequent periods, for at least a year beginning in November 1740 and again from October 1751 until the spring of 1754.

[23] *Careri*, pp. 32 and 41.

[24] *Careri*, p. 34.

[25] The Catalogue of the Bibliothèque nationale gives *c*1742 as the date of publication of Op. 4 (F-Pn Vm7 1092). Given that RISM lists only one copy of the Paris print of the *Pièces de Clavecin* (F-Pn D-4524), it seems likely that the press run there was quite limited. I am grateful to Edward Smith for confirming that the same plates were used for the Paris and London printings of the *Pièces* (personal communication, 21 November 2010). Of course, the plates could have travelled from Mlle Vendôme to London and then back again to Paris for the French edition, which would then have to be dated somewhat later; however, this seems the less likely alternative. See Rudolf Rasch in the present volume (p. 141) for evidence of such transfers. Ronald Broude drew my attention to the presence of more than one engraver's hand and clarified for me the practice of 'coöperative printing', in which separate issues were produced from a single set of plates, which in this case were likely owned by the composer (personal communication, 7 December 2011).

[26] See *Careri*, p. 33, where a passage from Titon du Tillet is translated and quoted, which describes the salons of the Duhallay family, where mother and daughter are deemed "*virtuose* on the harpsichord".

the *Parnasse françois* does not mention Jean Barrière (c1705-1747) among the individual French composers and performers who frequented salons where Italianate music was in favour, one has to wonder if Geminiani may have become acquainted with the cellist-composer in 1740-1741. Geminiani's own cello sonatas were published only in 1747; perhaps they were influenced by his exposure to Barrière's four sets. Both composers' harpsichord transcriptions were engraved in Paris, probably in the early 1740s; Barrière's collection draws primarily on five sonatas from his fifth book, for *pardessus de viole*. The two composers share some similarity of approach to arranging for the harpsichord, including a habit of writing out extravagant cadenzas and a peculiar manner of notating arpeggiated chords, encountered not only in the harpsichord volumes but also in Geminiani's accompaniment treatise.[27] If they were in close contact, it is not clear which one had the overriding influence, since in this particular *goût réuni* each would have had much to learn from the other.

Geminiani's Op. 4 collection begins with a four-movement sonata in D Major; the same sonata, minus its brief third movement (*Largo*), opens the *Pièces*.[28] The second suite begins with an equally lovely and very much re-composed *Tendrement* (*Andante* in the Sonata), in which all of the repetitions of the opening rondo are written out in full for the harpsichordist. Apparently the violinist would have been able to provide his own elaborations, whereas the harpsichordist needed help. The help Geminiani provided is not so much in terms of melodic elaboration, but more in terms of how chords and melody should be integrated by the keyboard player. In both the sonata and its keyboard transformation, sonority is more critical than melody in this movement, but violinist and harpsichordist must approach this problem in their individual ways. The violinist is left to his own devices, but Geminiani chose to help the harpsichordist by showing more clearly how certain chords should be arpeggiated. The rest of the sonata is arranged to complete this suite, the *Presto* of the second movement now marked *Vivement*, and the *Allegro affettuoso... non tanto* transformed into *Gracieusement* and *Tendrement*. ILL. 1 shows the first page of the opening *Tendrement*, while Ex. 7 shows excerpts from the *Gracieusement-Tendrement* parallel to those given in Ex. 3 from the concerto version. The *Gracieusement* transmits the violin sonata without significant

---

[27]   BARRIÈRE, Jean. *Sonates pour le pardessus de viole avec la basse continüe. Livre V^e*, Paris, after 1740. Geminiani's use of three staves for the two pieces drawn from Op. 1 is also unusual. His claim that the three staves would be easier to read is questionable and he did not repeat the experiment.

[28]   The violin sonata, harpsichord and concerto versions of this piece are compared in CARERI, p. 143 and several facsimile reproductions are found on the following pages.

ILL. 1: Geminiani, *Pièces de clavecin* (1743), p. 8, No. IV (H. 203), *Tendrement*, bb. 1-24.

alteration, save filling in some of the harmony that the continuo player would have supplied. However, in the concluding *Tendrement* (see ILL. 2 and EX. 3c), Geminiani writes out the repeated sections, replacing the solid chords with broken ones, and carefully notating the concluding arpeggio. In general, one might say that more of what the performer has to do is actually written

ILL. 2: Geminiani, *Pièces de clavecin* (1743), p. 13, No. VII (H. 206), *Tendrement.*

down in the harpsichord version in comparison with the string sonatas, where ornamentation and continuo realization are typically left to the performers' improvisatory fancy.

Two complete manuscript copies of the *Pièces* survive, both apparently made from the print or from a source close to the print. In addition the British Library holds an autograph manuscript containing the *Prelude* and *Vivement*

Ex. 7a: Geminiani, Sonata in A minor, Op. 4/v, arranged for harpsichord (H. 205), bb. 1-8.

Gracieusement

from the first suite, and a few bars of the A-minor *Tendrement* from the second (GB-Lbl Add. MS 32587). The complete copy (GB-Lbl Add MS 16155) made by John Burton (1730-1782) is very accurate, but curious in that it provides staves for the sonata version in the opening movements of each of the first two suites.[29] Only in the opening *Prelude* did Burton actually notate the violin and bass parts. Perhaps he intended them to serve as a convenient way of studying Geminiani's keyboard arrangement technique. The other complete manuscript copy (GB-DRc E25/xiv, lacking the minuets) was made by Richard Fawcett (1714-1782), probably while he was in Oxford (1730-1754);[30] it too transmits readings quite close to the printed version, although several small differences suggest that Fawcett may have been working from an earlier exemplar. Another copy in Fawcett's hand transmits two movements from the opening suite (*Prelude* and *Vivement*) in readings nearly identical to those in the autograph manuscript cited above, including a different version of the cadenza in the *Prelude*. Both this copy of the first suite and the autograph also lack many of the ornaments found in the 1743 print and the complete manuscript copies.[31] The notation of the arpeggiated chords also differs among these sources. The print and Burton's manuscript array the note heads along an oblique axis with a wavy line above them (as seen in ILL. 1), whereas the other manuscripts mentioned simply stack the note heads vertically or write out the

---

[29] I am grateful to Christopher Hogwood for confirming that Burton was the copyist of this manuscript (personal communication, 10 November 2010), which is wrongly identified as autograph in CARERI, p. 291. There is one interesting error in the 1743 London print, which is correct in this manuscript: in the penultimate bar of the fourth piece, the note *c'* is printed as a crotchet, whereas a quaver is required. In GB-DRc E25.xiv (discussed below) the passage was originally copied correctly (with a quaver), and then corrected at some later point to accord with the reading in the print.

[30] For a discussion of Richard Fawcett's activities as a Handel copyist in Oxford, see BURROWS, Donald. 'Sources for Oxford Handel Performances in the First Half of the Eighteenth Century', in: *Music and Letters*, LXI/2 (1980), pp. 177-185.

[31] WALLS, Peter. *Op. cit.* (see note 15), p. 226, compares the readings in GB-Lbl Add. MS 32587 and the 1743 print.

Ex. 7b: Geminiani, Sonata in A minor, Op. 4/v, arranged for harpsichord (H. 205), bb. 17–25.

arpeggiation in ordinary note values. In any case, however the manuscripts and prints may be related to one another, the existence of earlier versions suggests that Geminiani's arrangements evolved over some time rather than being created as quickly as possible for the printed collection.

Why Geminiani chose certain movements and ignored others for the harpsichord collections remains a mystery, but the care with which he transformed particularly the first collection into idiomatic harpsichord pieces is quite remarkable. And the French influence cannot be denied: the opening *Prelude* and the *Tendrement* in A minor (ILL. 1) succeed in exploiting the sonority of the harpsichord as well as any unmeasured prelude; the elegant ornamentation and rondo forms make some of the transformed sonatas seem nearly indistinguishable from the contemporary harpsichord arrangements of sonatas and suites by Barrière and Forqueray.[32] Moreover, were we unaware of the origins of most of Geminiani's pieces as string sonatas, we might be fooled into accepting several of them as compositions made expressly for the harpsichord. At the very least, they are definitely creative arrangements rather than simple transcriptions.

The two minuets with variations that conclude the *Pièces* had already appeared in print alongside a keyboard arrangement of excerpts from Handel's *Water Music*, and they were also copied in several manuscripts. The borrowed

---

[32]   BARRIÈRE, Jean. *Sonates et pieces pour le clavecin, Livre VI*, Paris, Auteur-Vve Boivin-Le Clerc, after 1740; FORQUERAY 'LE PÈRE', Antoine – FORQUERAY 'LE FILS', Jean-Baptiste-Antoine. *Pieces de viole composées par Mr. Forqueray le Pere, mises en pieces de clavecin*, Paris, Auteur-Veuve Boivin-Le Clerc, 1747.

concerto minuet (H. 212) is found not only in the one of the manuscript sources already mentioned (GB-Lbl Add. MS 16155), but also in radically simpler versions in many other manuscripts.[33] Shortly after the concerto volume was printed, this 'Favourite Minuet' was printed with a text by Mr. [Richard] Leveridge, 'Know, Madam, I never was born'.[34] Following the composer's death, it was employed in a 1763 pasticcio, *Love in a Village*, with the text 'If ever a fond inclination', and was also parodied in French printed and manuscript sources as 'Oui, vous en feriez la folie'.[35] We might note as well that the $\frac{3}{8}$ *Allegro affettuoso* and *Non tanto* from Sonata 5 discussed above also acquired a text, 'Welcome all who sigh with Truth', for use in *The Island of St. Marguerite*, by John St John (1746-1793), which premiered at Drury Lane on 13 November 1789. The song was printed separately by Preston & Son in the same year.[36] Although the composer himself did not arrange these minuets as vocal music, their existence does suggest at least some of Geminiani's tunes were regarded as eminently singable and thus suitable to use on the stage throughout the century, or, as Hawkins, characterized them "to the last degree elegant".

It remains to mention Geminiani's use of Scottish tunes in the three sonatas included in his *Treatise of Good Taste in the Art of Music* (1749). The four tunes used for these sonatas had all appeared in a collection published in London, but mere accessibility does not explain adoption.[37] Geminiani may have had more than one reason for basing all of his examples in the treatise on Scottish music. The vogue for Scottish tunes with Italianate accompaniment was well established in Edinburgh by the late 1720s. The frontispiece to Alexander Stuart's collection, *Musick for Allan Ramsay's* [...] *Scots Songs* (Edinburgh, c1728), depicts an "Edinburgh drawing room with gentleman fiddler, lady harpsichordist, and fawning spaniel, which at least makes clear the social image that the collection was trying to create".[38] In 1741, James

---

[33]   For example, GB-Lbl Add MS 47446, ff. 80-81r, and Add MS 31814, f. 96v.

[34]   *A Favourite Minuet by Geminiani The Words by M.r Leveridge. Set for y.e German Flute*, London, s.n., c1735. See CARERI, p. 287 for references to copies in England and France. Richard Leveridge was a singer and a composer of theatre songs who enjoyed a career on the English musical stage that encompassed Restoration drama and Purcell's 'semi-operas', Italian opera and pasticcio in the early eighteenth century, and the pantomimes mounted in competition with the Italian opera. See BALDWIN, Olive - WILSON, Thelma. 'Richard Leveridge, 1670-1758', in: *The Musical Times*, III (June, September and October 1970), pp. 592-594, 891-893 and 988-990.

[35]   See CARERI, pp. 289 and 292 for these manuscript references.

[36]   Copy at GB-Lbl g.809n.(20).

[37]   THOMSON, William. *Orpheus Caledonius*, London, Author, 1725, rev. 1733.

[38]   See JOHNSON, David. *Scottish Fiddle Music in the 18th Century*, Edinburgh, John Donald, 1984, p. 36.

Oswald, a Scottish violinist and composer, had moved from Edinburgh to London. He had published a 'Sonata of Scots Tunes' in 1739, which consists of a medley of four tunes, the last of which is followed by three variations; in 1747 he began to issue in London *The Caledonian Pocket Companion*, which would reach fifteen volumes by 1769.[39] Perhaps more importantly, Francesco Barsanti, who had probably known Geminiani in Lucca and had arranged some of his Op. 1 sonatas as trios, had returned to London in 1743 after several years in Edinburgh, where he too had published a collection of Scots tunes, ornamented and provided with figured bass accompaniment.[40] Finally, Geminiani's rival, Francesco Veracini, had included a set of variations on a Scottish tune in his *Sonate accademiche* (Florence and London, 1744).[41] Scottish tunes were apparently considered fashionably exotic in mid eighteenth-century London.

Geminiani included in his treatise not only the three sonatas based on Scottish tunes, but also arrangements of four more Scottish songs for voice, two flutes, strings and continuo, as well as variations on four others for violin or flute, cello and continuo. Indeed, all of the music in the Treatise is of Scottish origin. In the first sonata, 'The Broom of Cowdenknows' serves as the first movement, in which the first violin presents the tune simply, while the second violin is given an active contrapuntal line. Geminiani used 'Bonny Christy' for the next section, again presenting the tune simply and slowly at first and concluding with a fast movement in which the tune is varied by the first violin. A short *Grave* connects these two movements. The approach in the other two sonatas is similar, although they are based entirely on a single tune and Sonata 2 has no slow passage to connect the two movements. As one might expect, Geminiani was careful to include many slurs and ornament signs, as well as a few dynamic markings in the sonatas and in the four Airs that follow. Since the Airs for solo instrument and continuo adopt a formal strategy similar to that in the sonatas, presenting the tunes simply and then in *allegro* variations, it is not clear why the terminology is altered. Whatever they are called, these arrangements do illustrate the fascination Scottish music seems to have held for Geminiani and some other London violinists, and they may

---

[39] See the modern publication of Oswald's sonata, and those of Geminiani, in GEMINIANI, Francesco – OSWALD, James. *Trio Sonatas on Scots Tunes*, edited by Peter Holman, Edinburgh, Hardie Press, 1994 (Orpheus Caledonius, 3).

[40] BARSANTI, Francesco. *A Collection of Old Scots Tunes*, Edinburgh, Alexander Baillie, 1742.

[41] The final movement of Sonata 9, labeled *Scozzese*, is a set of variations on the ballad tune, 'Tweed's Side'. See HILL, John Walter. *Op. cit.* (see note 5).

have something to tell us about the typical approach Italian-trained violinists took to playing Scottish music; however, they add little to our picture of Geminiani as arranger. Nonetheless, that Scottish music provides all of the examples in this Treatise does seem somewhat peculiar; perhaps, Geminiani was attempting to show that even these simple Scottish tunes could be made tasteful by following his guidelines for ornamentation and expression.

The question of how his efforts have been received lingers. As suggested at the beginning of this essay, opinion has frequently been divided. With respect to the keyboard arrangements, Luigi Torchi asserted that he was careful to provide "qualche piccolo effetto" in order to sustain the harpsichord sound; however, Torchi also criticized his treatment of the keyboardist's left hand, calling it "absolutely inelegant", a criticism that cannot be entirely discounted.[42] On the other hand, Gabriela Sartini, in the preface to a facsimile edition of the two sets of harpsichord pieces, claimed that the pieces do not seem like "re-elaborations" but rather like pieces "composed and conceived for keyboard instruments".[43] I think the truth lies somewhere in between. Most keyboard players would not be fooled into thinking of these as originally composed for them; they do look and feel like transcriptions. But Geminiani certainly succeeded in making them work in a medium very different from that of the bowed strings.

We have noted criticism of his arrangements in his own day from Veracini and later from Burney and Hawkins. During his last stay in Paris, his works were performed at the *Concert spirituel*, where his concertos as well as his arrangements of Corelli's Op. 5 sonatas remained in the repertory until at least 1758. Among newly arrived foreign composers, he was heard more often than most.[44] Late eighteenth-century London concert programs seem to have favoured his arranged concertos over those newly composed. Thus the concertos based on his solo sonatas from Op. 4 appear on concert programs of the Academy of Ancient Music, along with his arrangements of Corelli's Op. 5 sonatas, and favourite concerti grossi by Corelli. For instance, the Concert

---

[42]   "[…] l'assoluta ineleganza e nullità della parte composta per la mano sinistra". TORCHI, Luigi. *La musica istrumentale in Italia nei secoli XVI, XVII e XVIII*, Turin, Bocca, 1901, repr. Bologna, Forni, 1969, p. 257. Quoted in SARTINI, Gabriella. 'Preface', in: GEMINIANI, Francesco. *Pièces de clavecin/Pieces for the Harpsichord*, facsimile edition by Gabriella Sartini, Bologna, Forni, c1975, p. 6.

[43]   SARTINI, Gabriella. *Op. cit.* (see note 42), p. 13. "Il compositore ha saputo cogliere così bene lo spirito e la tecnica del clavicembalo, che questi pezzi non danno assolutamente l'idea di rielaborazioni, ma sembrano direttamente composti e pensati per lo strumento a tastiera".

[44]   PIERRE, Constant. *Histoire du concert spirituel 1725-1790*, Paris, Société française de musicologie, 1975, p. 109.

of Ancient Music held on 30 April 1781, included vocal music by Purcell, Handel and Hasse, along with two instrumental works, both concertos based on sonatas. Geminiani's is listed as the "4th Concerto, from his own Solos". That work appeared on at least four other such concerts in the years to come, listed variously as "from his Solos, Op. 4" (9 March 1798), or simply "from his solos" (16 March 1796; 18 March 1795; 7 March 1792). This was not information to be hidden: the concert attendees had perhaps heard or played the sonata more than once at home; now it could be seen and heard on the big screen, so to speak. Presenting an arrangement in that context was not an embarrassment; rather, the virtuoso soloist has now simply acquired in the orchestral accompaniment a more impressive backdrop. Perhaps a desire for virtuosity ensured that these concertos were more often performed than the more old-fashioned concerti grossi of Opp. 2 and 3. In these solo sonatas transformed into concertos, the first violinist retains pride of place, able to play the diva as much as the singer who has just been heard in a Handel aria.

Despite the criticism of Burney and Hawkins, as well as early twentieth-century authors, it must be acknowledged that Geminiani was regarded by some of his contemporaries as the equal of Corelli and Handel. In his *Essay on Musical Expression* (1752), Charles Avison (1709-1770) offered up Benedetto Marcello and Francesco Geminiani as the pre-eminent composers of vocal and instrumental music, respectively. William Hayes (1708-1777) regarded that claim as a direct affront to Handel. In his hostile (but anonymous) response, Hayes went so far as to suggest that Geminiani himself might have authored at least part of Avison's *Essay*.[45] Avison had of course studied with Geminiani, whereas Hayes was a lifelong devotee and promoter of Handel's music.

If not quite as prominent as Avison suggested, Geminiani certainly boasted some success as a composer of instrumental music and especially as a teacher. Why was he not more successful? And why does he not hold a place in the canon parallel to those occupied today by Corelli and Handel, with whom he was so often compared? Hawkins had proposed that his lack of participation in the fashionable opera scene may have limited his reputation, but certainly the criticism of his 'reheatings' cannot be entirely ignored. We might recall here that Handel also re-used his own and other composers' works; however, he did not announce his borrowings from the rooftops. In fact, there was for

---

[45] Avison's *Essay* was initially published in London in 1752; the 1753 edition included William Hayes' *Remarks on Mr. Avison's Essay on Musical Expression* and Avison's *Reply to the Remarks on the Essay on Musical Expression*. See AVISON, Charles. *Essay on Musical Expression*, edited by Pierre Dubois, Aldershot, Ashgate, 2004; and also the discussion in CARERI, pp. 47-49.

a time a minor scholarly industry devoted to searching out and publishing Handel's sources in the works of others. In contrast, Geminiani proclaimed his transcriptions directly on his title pages, as in his own arrangement of the Op. 1 solo sonatas: *VI sonatas for two violins & a violoncello, or harpsichord with a ripieno bass, to be used when the violins are doubled* [...] *from the VI first solos of his Op.ª Iª*. Much like the early twentieth-century advocate of transcription, Ferruccio Busoni, he seems to have regarded arrangements and original versions of his musical works as equally valid.

Geminiani, Handel and in particular the music publisher John Walsh well understood the value of creating multiple versions of a work in order to sustain and even to enhance its cultural capital. Contemporary stage music, for instance, was widely marketable in formats designed to suit specialized environments. Thus, we find Walsh publishing collection after collection of 'Favourite songs from the Operas', appropriately arranged for performance at home, alongside versions without text for the amateur harpsichordist or recorder player. Instrumental music also found its niche, as overtures were made available in chamber and keyboard arrangements, violin sonatas transformed into concertos, and vice versa, concertos arranged for the chamber. Without recordings, these were vehicles for continued appreciation of works already heard in the theatre or in professional concerts; they permitted those geographically removed from the city to remain abreast of the latest musical styles in London.

But where do this shifting collections of original versions and multiple arrangements leave the concept of the musical work, a concept often associated with a definitive hierarchical arrangement of original and derivative sources, ultimately stemming from the composer's autograph? In fact, the notion of a well-defined musical work is distinctly problematic, so much so that Nicholas Cook asserted in a 2003 essay that we have no 'original' for Beethoven's Ninth Symphony. Instead we have "a variety of largely contradictory sources (the autograph, copyists' scores, early printed editions, and so on) [...] [and] that while these historically privileged texts have a particular significance and authority within the field encompassed by the 9th Symphony, they do not exhaust the work's identity [...]".[46] Cook proposes that there are only, in Wittgenstein's sense, sets of texts that bear a family resemblance to each other. We regard each different version as representative of a particular musical work, just as each of your siblings and cousins, who differ from you

---

[46] COOK, Nicholas. 'Music as performance', in: *The Cultural Study of Music: A Critical Introduction*, edited by Martin Clayton, Trevor Herbert and Richard Middleton, New York, Routledge, 2003, p. 207.

in many respects physically, may still be recognizable as family members. As Wittgenstein argued, there can be no complete and consistent set of essential characteristics common to the entire family — whether of your relatives or of musical works. The opening prelude in the *Pièces de Clavecin* belongs to the set of versions that collectively define Geminiani's Op. 4 no. 1; in this view the violin sonata is not to be privileged over the keyboard arrangement, since each represents the work equally. This may seem radical enough, but Ferruccio Busoni offered a much more outrageous suggestion early in the last century.[47] Busoni asserted, if we continue with the family metaphor, that there is only one such musical family, of which all particular works are members. Each composition is merely a specific instantiation of what he called the Ur-Musik from which composers draw their more specific musical ideas. The composer merely manipulates that which already exists, shaping it into particular forms, creating its particular boundaries. For Busoni, there is really only one Work. For Geminiani, it seems, each of his works might take a variety of forms without any damage to its value or identity.

Nonetheless, if we wish to retain our allegiance to the idea of musical works, we will no doubt feel compelled to place their instantiations — their arrangements — in a hierarchy according to whether they are 'better' and 'worse', faithful and not-so-faithful. Thus, Barsanti's arrangements of Op. 1 seem less successful than Geminiani's own, although not because Geminiani as the original author in some sense owns the ideas. The composer's versions are simply more interesting transformations of the solos. Both of these arrangements, Geminiani's and Barsanti's, preserve the essence of the solo sonatas (enough for us to recognize the piece), so must be admitted to the family that defines these works. We might also regard the composer's violin or keyboard arrangements of the cello sonatas as closer the centre of the work's family than would a radically simplified version that might be found in a domestic manuscript (or in a modern keyboard tutor).

Geminiani apparently saw no reason to restrict any of his compositions to a single version, and had good reasons for making several arrangements equally available. Thus, when we think about his Op. 4 solo sonatas, it seems critical to consider not only the solo version, but also the arranged ones, which reveal his musical ideas in a new light. If a version should be judged out of bounds, banished from the family, that decision will be made by the musical community to which it is presented. So Burney and Hawkins were entitled

---

[47]   BUSONI, Ferruccio. *Entwurf einer neuen Aesthetik der Tonkunst*, Trieste, Schmidt, 1907; English translation by Theodore Baker, *Sketch of a New Esthetic of Music*, New York, G. Schirmer, 1911.

to devalue Geminiani's 'reheatings' in comparison with his original versions, and to call him deficient for relying on them too frequently, but the public apparently had no problem accepting them, since they offered a convenient means of getting to know the pieces. Today we rely on recordings, a much more passive experience, and one perhaps offering less insight. Geminiani's motivation for reheating existing compositions likely went beyond mere profit seeking, although that can hardly be discounted. Careri suggested several, with which I find no reason to disagree: "a desire to improve a composition *tout court*; a desire to bring it up to date in matters of taste and style; a desire to exemplify the composer's theoretical tenet; a desire to bring a work before a wider audience, a desire to remain in the public eye; a desire to make money".[48] And of course, these are not mutually exclusive. In his day, they surely made him and his works much better known than either would have been had he confined himself to publishing just the 'original' versions. Even today they offer us a new window on those compositions and on contemporary performance practices as well.

For example, one might look closely at Geminiani's translation of the Italian tempo words in the string sonatas into French terms in the first keyboard collection. Since the Op. 4 and Op. 1 volumes precede the *Pièces* by only a few years, one can't assume these changes are aimed at updating the music. But are they translations to be taken at face value? Not quite, I think, since there is also the matter of adding a French veneer to the volume and of changing its performance medium. After all, Couperin tells us in *L'Art de toucher le clavecin* that we must play somewhat faster on the harpsichord than on instruments that can sustain the sound. Similarly, one might ask why he sometimes alters the metre in the harpsichord version of a piece. And these fully composed harpsichord parts surely have something to tell us about realization of continuo and possible elaboration of bass lines; indeed, the arrangements look very similar to some of the examples in the accompaniment treatise on both counts. On a more detailed level, one notices what seem to be alternate ways of notating apparently identical figures, which speak to questions about the meaning of ornament signs. It may also be worth recalling that many brief, transitional slow movements are eliminated in the harpsichord versions. Are they generally more ephemeral and inessential to the concept of the work? One is also struck by the detail provided for the harpsichordist, compared to the relatively bare sonatas. Surely violinists would have added rich ornamentation to the slow movements in the sonatas.

---

[48]   *CARERI*, p. 159.

Did Geminiani think it necessary to write out more for harpsichordists than for violinists? Or is it simply that he aimed the keyboard versions at the community of amateur players rather than the professionals he hoped would perform his violin sonatas. Finally, when we look at the adaptations in detail, do his transcriptions bespeak a profound interest in sonority and timbre or a cavalier attitude toward them? Given the trouble he took to create them, it would seem to be more the former than the latter.

I would assert that the idea of a transcription or arrangement, a re-casting of the 'original' version to make it suitable for some other medium or performance situation, or simply to update it so that its place in the repertoire can remain comfortably secure, is something to celebrate boldly rather than to bemoan as a departure from the composer's intentions. The latter is of course especially absurd when it is the composer himself who has made the departure. Whether created to make the music available at home, or in a chamber version more affordable to perform, or as a vehicle for the virtuosic public performer, such arrangements are today often ignored and even devalued, if not by their various amateur consumers, then by performers and scholars seeking to identify and reproduce the one definitive version. While we all appreciate having a trustworthy modern edition, regarding it as completely definitive (and so discounting alternates) seems to be stretching the point and unduly limiting our concept of the musical work. In his many arrangements, Geminiani has left us a large collection of his own musical ideas, and those of Corelli, viewed from different angles. We should put them to good use.

Francesco Geminiani and Freemasonry

Andrew Pink
(London)

FRANCESCO GEMINIANI BECAME A FREEMASON in London on 1 February 1725, in a lodge that met at the Queen's Head tavern, Holles Street,[1] an area of London's West End now occupied by Cavendish Square. We have no way of knowing why Geminiani made the decision to become a freemason, and — as far as we can tell — none of the members of that lodge had any professional association with music. However, almost immediately after joining the lodge, Geminiani and others from it set up a new lodge devoted entirely to music-making by its members, and located at another Queen's Head tavern, close by the Temple Bar, in an area now covered by the Royal Courts of Justice (see ILL. 5). The presence of Geminiani among these amateur musicians makes an interesting contrast to the more common image of him employed by the great and good, as London's foremost independent musician and the most respected violin teacher of his time.[2]

The *Philo-musicae* lodge, London

The new lodge established by Geminiani and his brethren was given the imposing name of *Philo-musicae et -architecturae societas Apollini* [The Apollo Society for Lovers of Music and Architecture]. According to the lodge's minute book, now in the British Library,[3] the Queen's Head tavern was soon

---

[1] RYLANDS, Harry. *The Book of the Fundamental Constitutions and Orders of the Philo Musicae et Architecturae Societas, London, 1725-27*, London, Quatuor Coronati Lodge, 1900 (Antigrapha Masonic Reprints, 9), p. 7.

[2] WEBER, William. *The Rise of Musical Classics in Eighteenth-Century England: A Study in Canon, Ritual, and Ideology*, Oxford, Clarendon Press, 1992, p. 80.

[3] GB-Lbl Add. 23202: The Fundamental Constitution and Orders of the Society Intitiled [*sic*] Philo-musicæ et Architecturae Societas Apollini.

renamed the Apollo tavern in honour of its masonic musical clientele, with a new sign painted by the French-born artist and lodge member James (Jacques) Parmentier (1658-1730).[4]

At this time in London there were around sixty masonic lodges, their number having grown rapidly from a handful in 1717,[5] and so it is not surprising to find that particular lodges developed particular interests, or attracted members from particular walks of life. For example, in the period 1733-1734 at the *Old King's Arms* lodge, at Seven Dials, scientific papers were regularly given on such themes as "The Structure and Force of Muscles", "The Water Clock", and "Optics".[6] (Newtonian science had a popular audience in several English masonic lodges at this time.)[7] In the same period, it seems that the lodge meeting at the *Bear and Harrow* tavern in the Butcher Row, Strand,[8] had an interest in theatre and the arts. It brought together influential courtiers such as Viscount Montagu (1690-1749) and Georg Ludwig von Kielmansegg (1705-1785), painters such as William Hogarth (1697-1764), and theatrical people such as the actor-manager Theophilus Cibber (1703-1758), the actor-singer-songwriter Richard Leveridge (1670-1758) and the dancer François Nivelon (active 1723-1739).[9] So, as a masonic lodge attracting men with shared interests, the *Philo-musicae* lodge was entirely in keeping with other lodges of the period.

However, in making music *Philo-musicae* was unique, "a hybrid";[10] part music club for freemasons, and part masonic lodge. For while singing was common to all masonic lodges — a common repertoire of simple unaccompanied songs formed part of the normal routine of a lodge meeting[11] — the *Philo-musicae* lodge was the only lodge to make performance of instrumental music a part of its work, and fashionably contemporary music too. The lodge minutes

---

[4]   Rylands, Harry. *Op. cit.* (see note 1), p. 79.

[5]   Clark, Peter. *British Clubs and Societies, 1580-1800: The Origins of an Associational World*, New York, Oxford University Press, 2000, p. 310.

[6]   Ashby, John. *Freemasonry and Entertainment. The Prestonian Lecture 1999*, London, s.n., 1999, p. 12.

[7]   Jacob, Margaret. *The Radical Enlightenment: Pantheists, Freemasons and Republicans*, Morristown (NJ), Temple Books, 2003, pp. 132-133.

[8]   Butcher Row, now built over, lay on the north side of the Strand, due east of St Clement Danes church.

[9]   Songhurst, William John. *The Minutes of the Grand Lodge of Freemasons of England, 1723-1739*, London, Quatuor Coronati Lodge, 1913, pp. 177-178.

[10]   Clark, Peter. *Op. cit.* (see note 5), p. 339.

[11]   For a discussion of lodge music in this period, see Pink, Andrew. 'When They Sing: The Performance of Songs in English Lodges of the 18th Century', in: *Freemasonry in Music and Literature*, edited by Trevor Stewart, London, Canonbury Masonic Research Centre, 2005, pp. 1-14. Available via UCL Discovery: <http://eprints.ucl.ac.uk/1756/>.

reveal a particular devotion to Italian repertoire comprising not only orchestral sonatas and concerti by composers such as Albinoni, Torelli and Geminiani, but also music from Italian operas performed in London, such as Bononcini's *Camilla* and *Pharnaces*, and Handel's *Radamisto*.[12]

Some basic biographical details about most of the *Philo-musicae* lodge's founders can readily be deduced since each man had his own coat of arms ('ensign') copied into the minute book (Ill. 1),[13] together with a drawing of the medal ('token of distinction') that was worn on a black ribbon by each Director when in the lodge. Each medal is personalised and in some cases gives additional clues about each individual's origins. (Ill. 2).[14] Thus, we have:[15]

1. WILLIAM GULSTON, a wine and timber merchant, the son, or possibly grandson, of the Rev. William Gulston of Wymondham, who was Bishop of Bristol from 1679 until his death in 1684.

2. COORT KNEVIT, was part of an ancient family of squires from Buckenham, Norfolk, and an antecedent of the better-known musical Knevitts: Charles, (1710-1782), Charles (1752-1822), and Charles (1773-1852). Coort was later a lieutenant and then a captain in the 3rd Regiment of the Scots Guards.

3. WILLIAM JONES, apothecary.

4. EDMUND SQUIRE, gentleman, later replaced by ISAAC THURET, gentleman.

5. CHARLES COTTON, Esquire, probably the fifth son of George Cotton and grandson of Sir George Cotton of Combermere.

6. E. PAPILLON BALL, West India merchant and later a director of the Royal Exchange Assurance Company.

7. THOMAS MARSHALL, gentleman, later replaced by JOSEPH MURDEN, Esquire.

8. FRANCESCO GEMINIANI.

9. THOMAS SHUTTLEWORTH JUNIOR, a government employee, later replaced by JOHN ELLAM.

10. THOMAS HARBIN, a stationer on the Strand.

11. JAMES MURRAY, gentleman, of Pulrose, Sutherland, later replaced by WILLIAM GRANT, attorney.

12. ANTHONY CORVILLE, gentleman.

13. JOSHUA DRAPER, gentleman, owning property in West Harling, Norfolk.

---

[12]   RYLANDS, Harry. *Op. cit.* (see note 1), pp. 89-90.

[13]   PLATES 1-4 are reproduced in colour in PINK, Andrew. 'A Music Club for Freemasons', in: *Early Music*, XXXVIII/4 (2010), pp. 523-536.

[14]   Such medals, to distinguish masonic rank and honours, are still in use by freemasons today, and termed 'jewels'.

[15]   More detailed biographical information can be found in the discussion of the *Philo-musicae* lodge in PINK, Andrew. *The Musical Culture of Freemasonry in early Eighteenth-century London*, Ph.D. Diss., University of London, 2007, and also in RYLANDS, Harry. *Op. cit.* (see note 1), pp. xlii-l.

In addition to these thirteen founders, the *Philo-musicae* lodge steadily acquired additional ordinary members (some of whom were made freemasons at the *Philo-musicae* lodge), and visitors from other lodges were welcomed, particularly during the first year of the lodge's existence. All appear to have been of similar rank and station to the founders, drawn mostly from among city lawyers and merchants, government officials, and the minor gentry,[16] creating a group of socially respectable musical amateurs, meeting together to foster a shared love of music under the mantle of freemasonry. The relationship between music and freemasonry as they saw it, was clearly stated in the *Philo-musicae* minute book:

> Musick and Architecture, the Happy produce of Geometry, have such Affinity, they Justly may be Stil'd Twin Sisters, and Inseparable; Constituting a perfect Harmony by Just Rules, Due proportion, & Exact Symmetry, without which neither can arrive to any Degree of perfection.
>
> A Structure form'd according to the Nice Rules of Architecture, having all its parts disposed in a perfect & pleasing Harmony, Surprizes the Eye at every different View, Elates our Fancy's to Sublime Thoughts, & imprints on our Imaginations Vast Ideas.
>
> So Musick in its effect divine charms every Sence, Transports our Thoughts, & Captivates the Soul, & Bury's all Misfortunes in its Harmony.
>
> If Harmony gain such an Ascendant over our passions to charm our Senses, let it preside over our Actions, and produce in us those Social Virtues, Friendship and Loyalty.[17]

It is no surprise, therefore, to find that having such a figure as Geminiani in their midst, the *Philo-musicae* lodge members gave him sole charge of the music-making in perpetuity, as we read in the Articles that preface the *Philo-musicae* minute book:

> Article VII: That our most Deserving and Justly Applauded Brother Seign.ʳ *Francesco Xavier Geminiani* be the Sole *Director* and perpetual *Dictator* of all our *Musical* Performances and in his absence the *President* for the time being; but in case of his Death or leaving the Society his Token of Distinction shall ever be worn by the *President* who shall by that Authority act or depute some other to perform that Office for the night.[18]

---

[16]   A full list of visitors can be found in RYLANDS, Harry. *Op. cit.* (see note 1), pp. l-lvi.
[17]   *Ibidem*, pp. 1-2.
[18]   *Ibidem*, p. 15.

As a member of the *Philo-musicae* lodge Geminiani received no money for attending meetings, but the minutes reveal that on the lodge's behalf he was able to exercise a certain degree of patronage. Thus, he provided custom for the music dealers and instrument sellers Richard Meares and John Barrett, and gave employment to five additional musicians variously employed to attend the lodge meetings as required, each a significant professional in his own right: Francesco Barsanti (1690-1777), David Boswillibald (d. 1729), John Eccles (*c*1668-1735), Charles Pardini (d. 1756), Gaetano Scarpettini (*fl.* 1730-1755), and John Smith — possibly John Christopher Smith (1683-1763). It seems that the lodge did not require these men to be freemasons, their connections being purely musical.

Francesco Barsanti was born in Lucca, and after studying science in Padua, he took up music, travelling to London in 1714 with Geminiani, a fellow Lucchese. Barsanti played the oboe in the orchestra of The Royal Academy of Music under Handel.[19] By 1735 Barsanti was settled in Edinburgh where he was the chorus master of the Edinburgh Music Society concerts and highly regarded as a composer of concerti grossi. By 1743 he had become a freemason since on 2 March that year he appeared as "Brother Francis Barsanti" in the minutes of the Edinburgh *Canongate Kilwinning* lodge.[20] On his return to London, later in 1743, he became an orchestral viola player,[21] although we have no further mention of him as a freemason. Given the string-based repertoire of the *Philo-musicae*, we assume Barsanti played the viola in the lodge.

David Boswillibald is principally known as a double-bass player, listed as such among the musicians in the Lord Mayor's Day concert, both in 1714 and 1727, in the orchestra of the Royal Academy in 1720, and in the Chapel Royal during Handel's time there in the 1720s. He is also identified as a viola da gamba player at a concert in Wells in 1718.[22] Boswillibald was probably part of the family of German musicians of the same name, and it

---

[19]   LASOCKI, David. 'The French Hautboy in England, 1673-1730', in: *Early Music*, XVI/3 (1988), pp. 339-358: 350.

[20]   MACLEOD, Jennifer. 'Freemasonry and Music in Eighteenth-Century Edinburgh', in: *Freemasonry on Both Sides of the Atlantic: Essays Concerning the Craft in the British Isles, Europe, the United States, and Mexico*, edited by R. William Weisberger, Wallace McLeod and S. Brent Morris, New York, Columbia University Press, 2002, pp. 123-152: 127.

[21]   JOHNSON, David. 'Barsanti, Francesco', in: *NG*.

[22]   HOLMAN, Peter. *Life after Death: the Viola da Gamba in Britain from Purcell to Dolmetsch*, Woodbridge, Boydell & Brewer, 2010, p. 110. Various sources give Bosswillibald, Boeswillibald, Beswillibald, Besswillibald, and Williwald. His will, however, clearly gives the family name as Boswillibald: see Public Record Office, London, PROB 11/630, f. 130.

is likely that he came to England as part of the Hanoverian entourage after the succession of George I.

John Eccles was a well-known theatre musician, both as composer and musical director. His father Simon and brother Henry were violinists, while another brother John was a tavern musician.[23] In 1700, he became Master of the King's Music for William III and following his royal appointment retired from the theatre to live near the Thames at Kingston, restricting himself to the composition of court odes.[24] He retained his royal appointment under Queen Anne, King George I and King George II. Without evidence to the contrary, it may well be reasonable to assume that Eccles' primary role at the *Philo-musicae* lodge was as a keyboard player.

Charles Pardini was a cellist who had been a musician at Canons — the country estate at Edgware of James Brydges (1673-1744), Earl of Carnarvon (and later Duke of Chandos) — during Handel's time there.[25] In 1736 he accompanied one of Handel's singers, Domenico Annibali (1705-1779), probably with Handel at the harpsichord, in a performance for the Queen and Princesses at Kensington Palace, even though at the time he appears to have been employed in the orchestra of the Opera of the Nobility, the rival opera company to Handel's Royal Academy.[26] He was later named in Court documents as "Musick Master" to Frederick, Prince of Wales (1707-1751),[27] and in 1739 was a signatory of the Declaration of Trust for the Society of Musicians, which later became The Royal Society of Musicians. Furthermore, he became one of the first Governors of that Society.[28]

Gaetano Scarpettini was, from 1717 until 1721, the first violinist of the orchestra based at Canons. He too was a signatory of the Society of Musicians' original Declaration of Trust,[29] and was active in the Society until his death.

It is entirely possible that the John Smith, whose name appears amongst the musicians employed by the *Philo-musicae* lodge, was John Christopher

---

[23] *HAWKINS*, V, p. 66.

[24] LAURIE, Margaret - LINCOLN, Stoddart. 'Eccles, John', in: *NG*.

[25] BEEKS, Graydon. 'Handel and Music for the Earl of Carnarvon', in: *Bach, Handel, Scarlatti: Tercentenary Essays*, edited by Peter Williams, Cambridge, Cambridge University Press, 1985, pp. 1-20: 8, 17.

[26] BURROWS, Donald - DUNHILL, Rosemary. *Music and Theatre in Handel's World: The Family Papers of James Harris 1732-1780*, Oxford, Clarendon Press, 2002, p. 19.

[27] DAUB, Peggy. 'Handel and Frederick', in: *The Musical Times*, CXXII/1665 (1981), p. 733.

[28] MATTHEWS, Betty. *The Royal Society of Musicians of Great Britain List of Members, 1738-1984*, London, The Royal Society of Musicians, 1985, pp. 183-184.

[29] *Ibidem*, p. 183.

Smith, Handel's copyist and amanuensis, and later a music publisher, who played the viola. He too was a founder of the Society of Musicians,[30] as well as a signatory of the Society's Declaration.[31]

Thus we have: Geminiani, violin; Scarpettini, violin; Barsanti, viola; John Smith, viola; Pardini, cello; Bosswillibald, double bass; and Eccles, keyboard; all eminently capable of taking the more difficult solo parts and bolstering the ripieno. We have no idea by what means Geminiani came to select these musicians, and the differing payments due to each performer, often paid on different dates, suggests that they did not always all attend the same lodge meetings. (See TABLE 1, p. 391).

One occasion when additional musicians were required was in the summer of 1725, when the lodge met outside the confines of its tavern home to enjoy a trip on the River Thames. In the minutes of 10 June 1725 we read: "that Four Persons be appointed by [...] Geminiani in order to Assist our Musical Performance, & to be paid for their Attendance out of the Publick Treasury of the Society" for an "Entertainment" for St John the Baptist's Day "and that the Society do go up the Water in Barges, if the Weather should be proper for that Purpose". This date, St John the Baptist's day (24 June), was the traditional mid-summer holiday and ordinarily was the occasion for all London freemasons to meet for their yearly Grand Feast, but in 1725 it did not take place.[32] This may explain why the *Philo-musicae* lodge organised its own 'Entertainment'. The boat trip itself was not unusual, since we find evidence of other groups, including masonic lodges, making such pleasure trips. For instance, in *Reads Weekly Journal*, 13 July 1734, we read that "the Honourable Society of Free and Accepted Masons, who hold their Lodge at the Prince of Orange's Head in Jermyn Street, went on board the Cloth Workers Barge at Whitehall, and from thence proceed [sic] up the River to Fulham, attended by an elegant Concert of Musick", and in the middle years of the century a masonic boat trip, with musicians, took place annually in Norwich, heading downstream for a venison feast.[33]

Another noteworthy occasion when additional musicians were employed in the *Philo-musicae* lodge occurred in 1726. On 17 February, the

---

[30] *Ibidem*, p. 171.

[31] *Ibidem*, p. 183.

[32] Dates and locations of the London freemasons' annual Grand Feast during the period concerned here can be found in ANDERSON, James. 'The History of Masonry: Part 3', in: *The New Book of Constitutions [...] of Free and Accepted Masons*, London, Brothers Cæsar Ward and Richard Chandler, 1738, pp. 97-139.

[33] FAWCETT, Trevor. *Music in Eighteenth-century Norwich and Norfolk*, Norwich, Centre of East Anglian Studies, University of East Anglia, 1979, p. 32.

lodge members decided to organise an entertainment to celebrate the lodge's first anniversary, and the lodge meeting instructed the lodge President,[34] William Gulston, to arrange the event, and to "take Particular Care to have Sufficient Performers to make a Concert both Vocal and instrumental". On this occasion, the minutes report that members' ladies (wives) were to be invited, probably the earliest known instance of what is nowadays termed by freemasons "a Ladies Night".

The *Philo-musicae* lodge minute book also shows payments made to a copyist, Thomas Shuttleworth who, according to the music historian John Hawkins, was known for his production of manuscript copies of Corelli.[35] Thomas was the father of the composer and violinist Obadiah Shuttleworth (d. 1734) who was a freemason in a lodge that met at the *Queen's Head* tavern, Hoxton.[36] Hawkins records that Thomas had two other sons who also played the violin, but does not name them. One of these two has to be the Thomas Shuttleworth junior, who was a member of the *Philo-musicae* lodge. (See ILL. 3.) The other son is probably the John Shuttleworth who, according to the Grand Lodge membership lists of 1723, belonged to lodges at the *Greyhound* in Fleet Street, and the *Blew Posts* tavern in Devereux Court,[37] and in 1730, along with Hawkins, belonged to a lodge that met at the *Three Tuns and Bulls Head*, Cheapside.[38] Unlike Obadiah, neither John nor Thomas junior were known as professional musicians. One, so Hawkins tells us, was "a Clerk in the South-sea-house, a very gay man", probably John who seems to have enjoyed the conviviality of masonic life. The other son is therefore likely to have been Thomas junior, and according to Hawkins, "had a place in some other of the public offices and was remarkably grave".[39] He only appears as a freemason at the *Philo-musicae* lodge.

The lodge maintained some instruments of its own, together with a collection of music, all stored at the tavern between meetings. We know this because at a meeting of the *Philo-musicae* on 4 March 1725, it was proposed and agreed to have a cupboard made, at the cost of 15 guineas, to store the furniture, candlesticks and general equipment of the lodge, together with books, music, and musical instruments. There are also several references to stringed

---

[34] 'President' is a very unusual term in this context; the senior officer in a lodge was usually referred to as Master.

[35] *Hawkins*, IV, p. 312n.

[36] Songhurst, William John. *Op. cit.* (see note 9), p. 175.

[37] *Ibidem*, pp. 8 and 42.

[38] *Ibidem*, p. 165.

[39] *Hawkins*, V, p. 181.

instruments in the *Philo-musicae* minute book. For example, on 16 December 1725 the minutes show that the lodge acquired a violin, the gift of William Gulston, which was described as:

> a Violin and Bow the makers Name Writ on the Back within Side Edward Pamphillon To the use of this Right Wor[shi]pfull and Highly Esteem'd Society for Ever [...].

A minute from 30 December 1725 shows that amongst several items the lodge agreed to buy was a "Tenor Violin Case and Bow" suggesting the need for a second viola in lodge performances. The following year, on 25 August 1726 "Barrat and Meers" were paid £3-13s-6d for cases and bows and for mending instruments. It appears that the lodge also stored members' instruments, for in September 1726 when Thomas Shuttleworth junior resigned from the lodge, he requested the return of the "Violin Case and Bow I left in the Society it belonging to my Father".[40] The minutes do not mention the presence of a keyboard, but we do know that some taverns in this period possessed an organ — a tradition dating back to the Commonwealth period at least, when some of the organs removed from churches were installed in taverns[41] — while others kept a harpsichord.[42]

An indication of the lodge's repertoire comes from a minute of 16 December 1725 that recorded William Gulston's presentation to the lodge of a collection of printed music as follows:

> 1.st   Seven Volumes Stich'd and Bound in Pasteboards Containing.
> The Second Opera of Tomazo Albinoni Consisting of Six Sinfonies and Six Concerto's.
> The fifth Opera of Said Author Consisting of Twelve Concerti Grossi

[40]   RYLANDS, Harry. *Op. cit.* (see note 1), p. 160.

[41]   See ELKIN, Robert. *The Old Concert Halls of London*, London, Edward Arnold Ltd, 1955, pp. 13-14, and also *HAWKINS*, IV, p. 379. FAWCETT, Trevor. *Op. cit.* (see note 33), p. 3, describes a tavern in Norwich setting up a music room with instruments and an organ in 1711 (*Norwich Gazette*, 25 August 1711) and in WROTH, William. *The London Pleasure Gardens of the Eighteenth Century*, London, Macmillan, 1896, we read several references to organs in the Long Rooms of the London pleasure gardens. See also KING, Alexander Hyatt. 'The London Tavern: A Forgotten Concert Room', in: *The Musical Times*, CXXVII/1720 (1986), pp. 382-385: 383, for a description of the organ in the concert room of The London Tavern.

[42]   The Queen's Head tavern in St Paul's churchyard, noted in THORNBURY, Walter – WALFORD, Edward. *Old and New London*, 6 vols, London-New York, Cassell-Peter & Galpin, [1872-1878], vol. I, <http://www.british-history.ac.uk/source.aspx?pubid=339>.

The Third Opera of Carlo Antonio Marini Consisting partly of Sonata's and partly of Concerto's.

The Sixth Opera of Said Author Consisting of Sonata's and Concerto's as before.

The Sixth Opera of Giuseppi Torelli Consisting of Twelve Concerto's

The Seventh Opera of Henrici Albicastro Consisting of Twelve Concerto's.

The Second Opera of Gio: Bianchi Consisting of Six Sonata's and Six Concerto's

2.ᵈ One Large Book bound in red Calves Leather and Gilt Containing the Opera's of Rinaldo Etearco Hydaspes et Almahide

Three books bound in Sky Marbled Paper Containing the Symphony's to Sᵈ Opera's

3.ᵈ The Opera's of Camilla Thomyris-Clotilda Astartus & Radamistus, Stitch'd

The Symphonys to Said Opera's also Stich'd

It seems fair to assume that Geminiani advised on this selection, and the operatic vocal music would have provided a stark contrast to the functional repertoire of simple, unaccompanied masonic songs commonly used in masonic lodge meetings at this time. On 23 December 1725, just seven days after the donation of this music, Thomas Harbin was paid £10-19s-3d for binding and embossing it with golden letters proclaiming the name of the lodge and of the benefactor. At the same time Thomas Shuttleworth senior was paid £14-5s-6d "for Writing Severall Select Pieces of Musick as by his Bill is Specified"; the bill does not survive, but we presume it refers to instrumental parts made from Gulston's music.

On 21 June 1726 the lodge agreed to buy the overture to Bononcini's *Pharnaces*,[43] and on 25 August 1726 it was agreed that Thomas Shuttleworth should receive £8-17s for writing "several pieces of Musick"; probably individual parts from the score of *Pharnaces*. This payment may also have included the cost of parts for Geminiani's recently published concerti grossi, arranged from the first six of Corelli's Opus 5 violin sonatas, and which had appeared in print in August 1726 published by Smith and Barrett.[44] The extensive subscription list attached to the concertino first violin part of this latter work included the names of the founder members of the *Philo-musicae* lodge and the

---

[43] Bononcini's opera *Farnace* (*Pharnaces*) was premiered in London in November 1723. Only ten arias were issued in print (London, Walsh and Hare, 1724), and so the overture referred to here was probably prepared for the lodge from manuscript copies.

[44] See *Geminiani Opera Omnia*, vol. 7.

name of the lodge itself. These concertos had been in the planning for some considerable time since they had been mentioned at the very first meeting of the lodge on 18 February 1725 — eighteen months before they made their appearance in print:

> Order'd.
> That the First Six Solo's of Corelli made into Concerti Grossi by our Dictator Sign^re Francesco Xaverio Geminiani be Subscrib'd for in the Name of the Society.
> To be paid for out of the Publick Treasury of this Society.

No other works by Corelli can be associated with the lodge, but it is probable that the lodge already had some of Corelli's own concerti grossi. These much-loved concertos, although few in number, formed the basic repertory for musical societies across the country,[45] not least because they permitted most amateurs to take the ripieno part, while the better players took the concertino parts.[46] Thus, Geminiani's Corelli arrangements of 1726 served to extend this relatively small repertoire. The fact that Geminiani was reputed to have been a pupil of Corelli added greatly to the musical value of his arrangements, not just to the members of the *Philo-musicae* lodge, but also to amateur musicians in general. The arrangements achieved considerable success (re-printed several times, including unauthorised editions),[47] and they became a staple of the repertory, not only in concerts but also as entr'acte music in the theatres.[48] In 1726 Obadiah Shuttleworth published two Corelli-style concertos arranged from two sonatas of the same Corelli Opus 5: numbers 1 and 11.[49] This can have been no mere coincidence, given Obadiah's family connections with the *Philo-musicae* lodge.

According to Peter Holman and Richard Maunder, before Corelli's concertos achieved widespread popularity in Britain, the prevailing concerto model seems to have been that of Albinoni, with scoring for a single concertino violin and two ripieno violins. Holman and Maunder have suggested that Geminiani's concerto arrangements of 1726 were the first Corelli-style concertos published in England, with scoring for two concertino and two

---

[45] WEBER, William. *Op. cit.* (see note 2), p. 82.

[46] PLATT, Richard. 'New Light on Richard Mudge, 1716-63: Some Aspects of Social Status and Amateur Music Making', in: *Early Music*, XXVII/4 (2000), pp. 531-545: 531.

[47] *CARERI*, p. 17.

[48] WEBER, William. *Op. cit.* (see note 2), p. 81.

[49] Published by Cross and Hare (London, 1726); see *Geminiani Opera Omnia*, vol. 7, 'Appendix' for a modern edition of these works edited by Andrew Pink.

ripieno violins;[50] Shuttleworth's of the same year are the first such published in England by a native to use this scoring.[51] In 1729, Geminiani arranged the remaining six of Corelli's Op. 5 sonatas (nos 7-12), but they do not seem to have achieved the same level of success as the earlier set. As John Hawkins put it: "he made the remaining six of Corelli's Solos also into Concertos, but these having no fugues and consisting altogether of airs, afforded him but little scope for the exercise of his skill, and met with but an indifferent reception".[52]

The subject of Geminiani's concerto arrangements raises the question of the number of performers at *Philo-musicae* lodge meetings. While the lodge was open to all music-loving freemasons, the eight founder members (who referred to themselves as Directors) immediately made the decision that there would eventually be thirteen such Directors:

> Resolved That This Society doe consist of Thirteen Directors (which shall be Compleated and filled up by Such persons as We the Eight Founders and Every New Director admitted shall approve of).[53]

This implies more than one player to a part, in what was largely a seven- or eight-part repertoire, based on the details we have of it. The two violas owned by the lodge further suggest the possibility of such doubling. Certainly, Geminiani himself had no problem with instrumental doubling, to judge from the evidence of the 1735 edition of his second set of concerto arrangements of Corelli Op. 5 where the title page clearly states that the parts "may be doubled at pleasure".

Despite its well-to-do connections, its coherent structure and its place in the rapidly growing masonic community of London, the *Philo-musicae* lodge survived barely two years, and its demise seems to have stemmed from the very source that might otherwise appear to be its strength: freemasonry itself. The foundation of the *Philo-musicae* lodge took place eight years after the formation of an English Grand Lodge, established to be a governing body for English freemasonry at a time when numbers of freemasons, and of lodges, were fast increasing. During the first six years of its existence (1717-1723) the Grand Lodge seems to have been relaxed about its own rules and regulations,

---

[50]   HOLMAN, Peter - MAUNDER, Richard. 'The Accompaniment of Concertos in Eighteenth-Century England', in: *Early Music*, XXVIII/4 (2000), pp. 636-652: 639.

[51]   The concerto in eighteenth-century England is discussed fully in MAUNDER, Richard. *The Scoring of Baroque Concertos*, Woodbridge, The Boydell Press, 2004.

[52]   *HAWKINS*, v, p. 242.

[53]   RYLANDS, Harry. *Op. cit.* (see note 1), p. 12.

to the extent that it kept no minutes or other records of its meetings. Perhaps this was because initially the activity of the Grand Lodge comprised only the election of officers and the organisation of an annual Grand Feast, in effect an umbrella organisation under which the members of the London lodges could meet socially.[54] The Grand Lodge showed no particular interest in the day-to-day work of local lodges, or their recruitment of freemasons; indeed, it had always been the custom for the proper number of masons in a lodge "to make Masons if they wished to [...] by a right which they considered they had always held".[55]

After 1723, when the number of London lodges was growing fast, the Grand Lodge became more business-like in its commitment to ensure conformity in matters of local lodges' day-to-day organisation and ritual. The Grand Lodge began to keep detailed minutes of its own meetings and, in June 1723, published the first edition of *The Constitutions of the Freemasons* to provide a single version of masonic tradition and practice. The Grand Lodge now began to make a clear distinction between Regular lodges that recognised its authority, and Irregular lodges that did not. The *Philo-musicae* lodge was formed just as a hitherto loose collection of self-governing lodges began to come under the scrutiny of the new Grand Lodge looking to control them.[56]

On 21 November 1724, the Grand Lodge declared:

> [...] if any Brethren shall meet Irregularly and Make masons at any place within ten miles of London, the persons present at the making (The New Brethren Excepted) shall not be admitted even as Visitors into any Regular Lodge whatsoever Unless they come and make Such Submissions to the Grand Ma[ste]r and Grand Lodge as they shall think fit to impose on them.[57]

It was because of this edict that in May 1725 the Grand Lodge summoned members of the *Philo-musicae* lodge, including Geminiani, to attend its next quarterly meeting, due in November of that year. The Grand Lodge was concerned not that the *Philo-musicae* lodge was running a music club for freemasons, but that masons were made there without it having formally associated with the Grand Lodge. During the autumn of 1725 the *Philo-musicae*

---

[54]   HAMILL, John. *The History of English Freemasonry*, Addlestone, Lewis Masonic Books, 1994, pp. 47-48.

[55]   RYLANDS, Harry. *Op. cit.* (see note 1), p. xxviii.

[56]   See HAMILL, John. *Op. cit.* (see note 54), pp. 47-50 for the detail of this paragraph.

[57]   SONGHURST, William John. *Op. cit.* (see note 9), p. 59.

minutes show that there were visits to the lodge by several Grand Officers, perhaps to prepare matters in advance of the November meeting of the Grand Lodge. These visits were to no avail because Geminiani and his fellows never attended the November meeting, and as a result a letter was sent to the *Philo-musicae* lodge from the Duke of Richmond (Grand Master) and George Payne (Grand Warden), which formally admonished the 'Directors' of the *Philo-musicae* for unlawfully making men freemasons. Even so, at the very same meeting at which the lodge minuted receipt of this letter (16 December 1725), more men became freemasons, and in the *Philo-musicae* record of that meeting the Duke of Richmond was referred to as "a Pretended Authority". The lodge appears to have been confident that Masonic tradition prior to the creation of the Grand Lodge justified its conduct.

Nevertheless, the conflict developing between *Philo-musicae* and the Grand Lodge clearly took a toll on the lodge's membership. During 1725, up to the time that the Grand Lodge sent its letter of reprimand, the *Philo-musicae* minutes recorded visits to the lodge by 41 freemasons from other London lodges, but in 1726 that number was just two, and in 1727 only three. Also, the lodge began to delete Directors and members for non–attendance, while others resigned; for example, Thomas Shuttleworth junior left at the end of July 1726, professing he had too much work to do. The sudden reduction in numbers suggests that such men did not wish to risk losing their masonic recognition by attending what the Grand Lodge considered to be an 'irregular' lodge. Certainly, *Philo-musicae* lodge never featured in any of the official printed lists of lodges that were circulated from time to time, although on a copy of one early list the lodge has been added by hand (ILL. 4).

The *Philo-musicae* lodge minutes end abruptly in March 1727 without any hint of the lodge's demise. Indeed, the last minute refers to the upcoming election of officers. We must assume that the conflict between the *Philo-musicae* lodge and the Grand Lodge depleted the membership to such an extent that it was no longer viable. However, several of the *Philo-musicae* lodge Directors and members did continue in freemasonry elsewhere, as members and officers of 'regular' London lodges.[58]

Geminiani remained a freemason, and although evidence of his subsequent membership is fragmentary and to an extent speculative, his masonic story does continue, as we shall see. However, we must be aware that such incomplete traces of a masonic career as Geminiani's are not unusual in this period. Until the third quarter of the eighteenth century, English freemasons'

---

[58]   RYLANDS, Harry. *Op. cit.* (see note 1), pp. xxxvii–xl.

records were not kept in any systematic, centralised fashion, and today very few lodge records survive from the first half of the eighteenth century. The handful that do survive in the archives of the United Grand Lodge of England are there more by chance than design, and precise information about how many yet remain in the custody of local lodges is unknown.[59]

The *Perfect Union* lodge, Naples

An intriguing aspect of Geminiani's later masonic life is his association with a new English lodge founded in Naples, *c*1728, the first such masonic lodge in Italy[60] (Naples was then a Viennese Hapsburg territory). It seems that in May 1728 Geminiani, together with a George Olivaros,[61] was warranted to establish a lodge in Naples by the then Grand Master, Henry Hare, Lord Coleraine (1693-1749), a three-times Grand Tourist and lover of Italian art and architecture.[62] Details of this warrant emerged in Italy in the 1880s,[63] when it was first published as follows:

> Coleraine G[rand] M[aster] (L.S.)
> Whereas, a petition has been presented to us, and signed by several Brethern residing in and about *the city of Naples in Italy*, humbly praying that they may be constituted into a regular lodge [...] These are therefore to Impower and Authorize our Rt.

---

[59]   Some early lodge records have been deposited in the archive of the United Grand Lodge of England (UGLE), but such action is entirely at the discretion of local lodges. In 2010 UGLE authorities approved a survey of local lodge records, but this is an entirely voluntary process on the part of the local lodges, reliant on local masonic volunteers. Even so, it will only give headline data and date ranges for records with no precise details of content.

[60]   Francovich, Carlo. *Storia della Massoneria in Italia. Dalle origini alla rivoluzione francese*, Florence, La Nuova Italia, 1974, p. 40.

[61]   Is Olivaros a mis-transcription of the surname Oliverson? A Thomas Oliverson is identified in the *Philo-musicae* lodge minutes as the landlord of the Queens Head/Apollo tavern. Is George thus a relative?

[62]   Boyd-Haycock, David. 'Hare, Henry, Third Baron Coleraine (1693-1749), Antiquary', in: *DNB*.

[63]   The warrant was later re-published in Maruzzi, Pericle. 'Sulla prima loggia massonica', in: *Rivista massonica*, XLVIII (1918), pp. 128-131: 129 (copy at GB-Ob, Per.24791.d.107). Here we learn that it was first published in the journal *Luce e concordia* (Naples), June 1886, p. 29 — of which no copies appear to be extant — where it is described as having been a copy of the original, made during some anti-masonic trials of 1776, and preserved in the Neapolitan State Archives; present whereabouts unknown. See recent discussion in Di Castiglione, Ruggiero. *Alle sorgenti della massoneria*, Rome, Editrice Atanòr, 1988, p. 85, fn. 86.

Worshipful and well beloved Brethern Mr. George Olivaros and Sig. Francesco Saverio Germiniani, or either of them to convene our Brethern at Naples, aforesaid who have signed the said Petition; and that the said Mr. George Olivaros or Sig. Francesco Saverio Germiniani do in our place and stead Constitute a regular Lodge in due form (they the said Mr. George Olivaros and Sig. Francesco Saverio Germiniani taking special care that they and every of them have been regulary made Masons); and that the[y] be required to conform themselves to all and every the Regulations contained in the printed *Book of Constitutions* of our most ancient and right Worshipful Fraternity and observe such other Rules and Regulations as shall from time to time to [*sic*] transmitted to them by us or Al[exander] Choke Esq., our Deputy Grand Master, or the Grand Master or his Deputy for the time being. And that they do send to us or our Deputy a List of the Members of their Lodge together with the Regulations agreed on to be by them observed, to the end, that they may be entered in the Grand Lodge Book. And upon the due Execution of this our Deputation, the said Mr. George Olivaros or Sig. Francesco Saverio Germiniani is hereby required to transmit to us or our said Deputy a Certificate under both or either of their hands, of the time and place of such Constitution. In order that it may be entered in the Book of Regular Lodges.

Given under our hand and seal of Office, this Eleventh day of May, 1728, and in the Year of Masonry 5728.

By the Grand Master's Command,
Will. Reid, Secretary
Al[exander] Choke, D[eputy]. G[rand]. M[aster].
Nathaniel Blackesby [Blackerby]
Jo[seph] Highmore   G[rand] Wardens.

Since the transcription was made, the original document has been lost, and no other records of the lodge have ever been found, either in Italian or English archives — despite the survival of other primary material from this time relating to the establishment of English lodges overseas: a lodge in Madrid, February 1728;[64] Gibraltar, November 1728;[65] and Fort William in Bengal, December 1728.[66]

Scholars of Italian masonic history suggest that the lodge in Naples was named *Perfetta Unione* (Perfect Union) and was already in existence by the early 1730s catering largely to the city's English residents.[67] If so, its absence

---

[64] SONGHURST, William John. *Op. cit.* (see note 9), p. xv.

[65] *Ibidem*, p. xv.

[66] *Ibidem*, p. 95.

[67] For further details of the *Perfect Union* lodge in Naples, see the description in FRANCOVICH, Carlo. *Op. cit.* (see note 60), with further details added in DI CASTIGLIONE,

from the records of the Grand Lodge of England may simply indicate that no formal notification of its activity was ever sent back to London as Coleraine's warrant required. This was a turbulent period in Neapolitan history, not least for the British there. Austrian rule ended suddenly in 1734 when a Spanish army appropriated the city to install Charles Bourbon, a younger son of King Philip V of Spain, as King of Naples and Sicily, and so complying with Grand Lodge bureaucracy may not have been easy.

While we have no way of knowing if Geminiani ever visited the lodge or merely lent his famous name to its establishment, there is no evidence precluding his presence in Naples between 1727 and 1731.[68] Of his foreign travel in this period we know for sure only that *c*1728-1729 he was in The Hague, on the basis of a poem by Henry Carey (1687-1743) called *To Mr. Geminiani at The Hague* (published in London in 1729).[69] Hawkins reports that it was also in 1728 that Geminiani was offered the position of Master and Composer of the State Music in Ireland, through the intervention of his pupil William Capel, Lord Essex. Hawkins goes on to record that Geminiani declined the post because of its requirement that all Crown appointees should be members of the Church of England, and so refusing to disavow his Catholic beliefs, Geminiani nominated his pupil Matthew Dubourg (1707-1767), who took up the post instead. Is this perhaps only part of the story? It is conceivable that Geminiani's decision was also influenced by plans to set off on an extended European trip, not only to The Hague but also (as seems likely) to Naples.

In this context it is intriguing to note that in January 1728 Count Broglio, the French Ambassador in London, wrote to a senior British Government civil servant, Charles Delafaye (1677-1762), also an active freemason,[70] to inform him that "Francois Xavier Geminiani de Lucca" had been taken into his service. Delafaye was First Secretary to Thomas Pelham-Holles (1693-1768), Lord Newcastle, the Secretary of State for the Southern Department. Pelham-Holles' ministerial responsibilities included not only management of Government interests in southern England, Wales and Ireland, but also British interests in Catholic Europe.

Ruggiero. *Op. cit.* (see note 63) and ID. *La massoneria nelle due Sicilie e i "Fratelli" meridionali del '700*, Rome, Gangemi, 2006. I am grateful to Dr. Bernardino Fioravanti, Librarian of the Biblioteca del Grande Oriente d'Italia, Rome, for directing my attention to these authors.

[68] See CARERI, Enrico. 'Francesco Geminiani, primo massone italiano', in: *Hiram*, II (2002), pp. 63-69: 68.

[69] *CARERI*, pp. 21-22. See pp. 118-120 of the present publication for more details of Geminiani's trip to Holland.

[70] SAINTY, John Christopher. 'Delafaye, Charles (1677-1762) Public Servant', in: *DNB*.

We have no record of Geminiani's duties for the French Ambassador, musical or otherwise, but for Geminiani the diplomatic status such a post entailed would have facilitated his European travels. It can be no coincidence that in March of that same year, while still in London, Geminiani met with Pelham-Holles, at Capel's instigation, on the premise of seeking a music-printing licence.

> Mr. Geminiary [*sic*] who has the honour to bring your grace this, is the gentleman you promised me the patent for the sole printing of his own music, which if your grace will be so good to order him, I shall take it as a particular favour, the sooner he has it the more service it will be to him.[71]

It seems odd that the British Secretary of State for the Southern Department would be concerned with obtaining a music printing licence for Geminiani — not least since Geminiani had no obvious difficulty in publishing his own music, and no particular connection with Pelham-Holles. It seems more likely that with Delafaye's (and Capel's) knowledge of Geminiani's new diplomatic status, this letter served as a subterfuge to bring Geminiani and the Minister together, not only to discuss his post with the French Ambassador but also — we can imagine — to discuss his willingness to work in the British interest.

Certainly, if Geminiani was to carry an English Grand Lodge warrant to Naples, probably not necessarily with the French Ambassador's knowledge, the Ambassador's protection would have been very useful. Masonic materials (not least from England) were not always viewed as benign in mainland Europe, and stringent penalties could be applied to those who carried them across politically sensitive European borders.[72]

Lord Capel was soon to be initiated into freemasonry (in November 1731) at the Norfolk home of Prime Minister Robert Walpole (1676-1745), along with Pelham-Holles and Francis, Duke of Lorraine (1708-1765), who was to become Hapsburg emperor and the Holy Roman Emperor.[73] For the next five years Capel was minister-plenipotentiary and then ambassador-extraordinary to the king of Sardinia at Turin.

---

[71]   Public Record Office, SP 36, Secretaries of State: State Papers Domestic, George II, Folio 220, 1728 March 20.

[72]   JACOB, Margaret. *Op. cit.* (see note 7), pp. 219-221.

[73]   *Freemasons and the Royal Society; Alphabetical List of Fellows of the Royal Society who were Freemasons*, MS typescript, 120 pp., compiled by Bruce Hogg, London, Library and Museum of Freemasonry, 2010. Online resource: <http://tinyurl.com/3rqmube>, accessed July 2011.

So, while the reality of the situation between Geminiani, Broglio, Capel, and Pelham-Holles remains obscure, it does seem clear that at this time Geminiani was known among the highest diplomatic and masonic circles.

The *Swan and Rummer* Lodge, London

Geminiani was again in London on 13 October 1731 when "Brother Geminiani" appeared as a visitor in the minute book of the *Swan and Rummer* lodge, Finch Lane, close to the Royal Exchange, in the City of London.[74] From this we learn not only that Geminaini was still a freemason but also that he was then living at the King's Head tavern, Tyburn Row. As we shall see, the *Swan and Rummer* was a rather well connected lodge, and many of the lodge members' interests related to Geminiani's own: Ireland, finance, publishing, and the London stage.

Among the members of the *Swan and Rummer* lodge there was a distinct Irish connection including the two Irish nobles James King (1693-1761), 4th Baronet Kingston, and Gerald de Courcy (1700-1759), 24th Baron Kingsale, as well as a number of eminent Iberian and German Jews, who included several of the Mendes da Costa family of financiers, and Dr Meyer Schomberg (1690-1761), an eminent surgeon.[75] A Joseph Hare — possibly Geminiani's publisher (d. 1735) whose business was nearby — regularly attended lodge meetings, as did a John Hawkins (was this the music historian?) and a Jonathan Tyers (was this the same Jonathan Tyers (1702-1767) who later became the proprietor of Vauxhall Gardens?). A number of masonic actors' names appear in the minutes as members: [James] Bencraft (d. 1765), [Dennis] Delane (d. 1750),[76] James Oates (d. 1751), Thomas Oddell (1691-1749) and William Pinkethman (d. 1740). Others appear only as occasional visitors: James Excell (*fl.* 1730-1741), Henry Giffard (1694-1772), and [Charles] Shephard (1675-1748).[77] Handel's

---

[74] [Anon.] *The Minute Book of the Swan and Rummer Lodge*, FMH SN66, Library and Museum of Freemasonry, London. I am grateful to Susan Snell, archivist at the Library and Museum of Freemasonry, London, for helping me to obtain permission to study these minutes from The Lodge of Philanthropy, Stockton-on-Tees, the current owner.

[75] Hughan, William James. 'The Three Degrees of Freemasonry', in: *Ars Quatuor Coronatorum*, x (1896), pp. 127-154: 142-143.

[76] I have assumed these to be James and Dennis from the context.

[77] The minutes identify his lodge as *The Sun*, Clare Market. *The Sun* lodge records (Songhurst, William John. *Op. cit.* [see note 9], p. 28) also show Charles Shephard as a member. This lodge was popular with theatre folk.

virtuoso recorder player from Canons, Lewis Mercy (*fl.* 1708-1751),[78] and the rather more hazy musical figure of Thomas Lansa (*fl.* 1720-1750) — both of whom we shall meet again — each visited the lodge on at least two occasions.

We can only guess at Geminiani's reason for attending this lodge in October 1731, since the names of those who were there on that occasion offer us no immediate clues.[79] Was it in the hope of meeting his publisher Joseph Hare, who did not attend that evening? Perhaps Geminiani and the other musicians and actors who attended this lodge were encouraged there by a good fee to provide support for singing and for entertainment, or simply because of their celebrity status.

FRANCE, HOLLAND AND IRELAND

Towards the end of 1732 Geminiani travelled to Paris, becoming a regular visitor there, and appearing no less than sixteen times as a performer at the *Concert spirituel*,[80] a fact that can be partly explained by Geminiani's masonic connections. Freemasons had not been slow to establish themselves in senior positions at the *Concert spirituel*, and effectively ran the organization;[81] they included musicians such as Michel Blavet (1700-1768), Michel Corrette (1707-1795), Louis-Nicolas Clérambault (1676-1749), Jean-Pierre Guignon (1702-1774), Pierre Jelyotte (1713-1797) and Jacques-Christophe Naudot (*c*1690-1762).[82]

A letter from Pelham-Holles to Capel tells us that Geminaini returned to London about 20 September 1733 in the company of the Irish aristocrat Charles Moore (1712-1764), second Baron Moore of Tullamore.[83] Although we have no information about whether Moore was a freemason at this time we assume he was since within a few years he was the Grand Master of Irish

---

[78] For his Cannons connections see BEEKS, Graydon. *Op. cit.* (see note 25), pp. 8 and 10.

[79] On the occasion of Geminiani's visit those present were recorded as follows: James Berrington, Master *Pro Tempore*; Doctor [*Meyer*] Shomberg - Warden; Bro. [*Noah*] Roul - Warden; Bro. [*James*] Stiles; Bro. [*David*] Atkinson; Bro. [*Thomas*] Beach; Bro. [*James*] Oates; Bro. [*Robert*] Littlebury; Bro. [*William*] Tomkinson; Bro. [*Malachi*] Postlethwaite; Bro. [*William*] Bell; Bro. [*Francis*] Baker; Bro. Phillip Mendez da Costa. Visiting brethren: Bro. West, Crown, Snow Hill; Bro. D'Almeide, Kings Head, Chancery Lane; Bro. Geminiani, Kings Head, Tyburn Row; Bro. [*Moses*] Adolphus, Bricklayers Arms, Barbican. Italicised first names given in square brackets are taken from other entries in the same minute book.

[80] GEFEN, Gérard. *Les musiciens et la franc-maçonnerie*, Paris, Fayard, 2003, p. 42.

[81] *Ibidem*, p. 42.

[82] *Ibidem*, pp. 36-51.

[83] *CARERI*, p. 27.

Freemasons, 1741-1743, and again in 1761-1764.[84] Geminiani then set out for Dublin, arriving on 6 December 1733.

In 1746 Geminiani was in Holland to supervise the engraving of the plates for his cello sonatas (Op. 5) and his concerti grossi (Op. 7). He planned to combine this trip to Holland with a twelve-concert tour with the London-based Italian musician and freemason Thomas Lansa, accompanied by Lansa's daughter, a harpsichord prodigy then performing in Paris, and the young François-André Danican Philidor (1726-95), a Parisian composer, chess prodigy[85] and later a freemason.[86] Lansa was a member of the French lodge of London, where the Master was Lewis Mercy.[87] It was probably as a result of this trip to Holland that Geminiani collaborated with Lansa on producing the masonic songbook *Chansons Originaires des Francs-Maçons* (London, 1749), dedicated to the Orange lodge in Rotterdam. This is effectively the third edition of a song book of the same name first published in The Hague in 1744 by Vincent La Chapelle (d. 1746) and then re-issued by Lansa in 1746 following Chapelle's death.[88] Comparison of the 1749 book with its predecessors shows it to be little changed despite Lansa's claim in the preface that this edition was revised and corrected "par le celébre Frére, dont le Nom commence par la Lettre G" [by the famous Brother, whose name begins with the letter G].[89] While any involvement by Geminiani amounted at most to adding slight melodic decorations here and there to the musical text, he thereby fraternally lent his reputation to support Lansa's project.

Here it is worth noting that, with the exception of John Walsh (1665/6-1736) and Benjamin Cooke senior (d. 1742/3),[90] all Geminiani's British publishers were known freemasons: Robert Bremner (1713-89), Joseph Hare (d.1733), John Johnson (d. 1762), James Oswald and William Smith (d. 1765?); none of the continental ones were.

---

[84] COKAYNE, George Edward, et al. *The Complete Peerage of England, Scotland, Ireland, Great Britain and the United Kingdom, Extant, Extinct or Dormant*, Gloucester, Alan Sutton Publishing, 2000, vol. III, p. 140.

[85] ALLEN, George. *The Life of Philidor*, New York, Da Capo Press, 1971, pp. 20-22.

[86] GEFEN, Gérard. *Op. cit.* (see note 80), p. 66.

[87] DAVIES, Malcolm. *The Masonic Muse: Songs, Music and Musicians Associated with Dutch Freemasonry, 1730-1806*, Utrecht, Koninklijke Vereniging voor Nederlandse Muziekgeschiedenis, 2005, p. 40.

[88] PINK, Andrew. 'Masonic Songs in Performance (2)', in: ID. *The Musical Culture of Freemasonry, op. cit.* (see note 15), pp. 70-97.

[89] DAVIES, Malcolm. *Op. cit.* (see note 87), pp. 79-80.

[90] Unless he is the 'Mr. Cook' mentioned in the Grand Lodge of England's minutes of 1723 as a member of the *Horn* Lodge Westminster, along with the bass-viol player Francisco Goodsens (d. 1741); SONGHURST, William John. *Op. cit.* (see note 9), p. 5.

Once more in Ireland in the Spring of 1759, Geminiani spent some time as music master to Charles Coote (1736-1800), later the first Earl of Bellamont, at his estate at Cootehill.[91] We cannot discount a masonic connection here too, since although we have no lodge records or other membership information to show that Coote was a freemason, the records of the Grand Lodge of Ireland show that there was a lodge at Cootehill from 1734-1801.[92] This lodge must have run with the tacit agreement of Coote, if not with his active participation, for which the lodge's closure the year after the Earl's death without a legitimate heir, is a strong indicator.

In November that year Geminiani moved to Dublin, where his last public appearance was on 3 March 1760. This was a benefit for Geminiani that took place at the Great Musick Hall in Fishamble Street, arranged by command of the Lord Lieutenant of Ireland, and freemason,[93] John Russell (1710-1771) Duke of Bedford.[94] Geminiani died unmarried at his home in Dublin on 17 September 1762, "attended in his last moments by Rev. Dr. Reynolds, Catholic Pastor of St. Andrew's, who had been Tutor for a time to Prince Charles Edward in Rome (1728-1730)".[95] Geminiani was buried two days later at St Andrew's church, with — as far as we know — no masonic ceremony.

Modern scholarship, particularly the work of Enrico Careri, has led to a new awareness of the significance of Geminiani to the development of eighteenth-century English music. We can now begin to see that freemasonry played a part in forming the international network of patronage and support that sustained Geminiani's career, even if — for now — the picture remains incomplete.

---

[91]   CARERI, p. 42.

[92]   *Lodges of County Cavan*, MS typed, 3 pp., Grand Lodge of Ireland, 2009. I am grateful to Rebecca Hayes, archivist of the Grand Lodge of Ireland, for supplying this information.

[93]   *Freemasons and the Royal Society* [...], *op. cit.* (see note 73).

[94]   BOYDELL, Brian. *A Dublin Musical Calendar 1700-1760*, Dublin, Irish Academic Press, 1988, p. 254.

[95]   FLOOD, William Henry Grattan. 'Geminiani in England and Ireland', in: *Sammelbände der Internationalen Musikgesellschaft*, XII/1 (1910), pp. 108-112: 111.

Table 1

Payments to Supernumerary Musicians of the *Philo-musicae* Lodge

	Reporting periods				
	10 June 1725 – 14 October 1725 [approx. 4 months]	15 October –23 December 1725 [approx. 3 months]	24 December 1725 – 31 March 1726] [approx. 3 months]	1 April 1726 – 22 December 1726 [approx. 9 months]	23 December 1726 – 23 March 1727 [approx. 3 months]
Pardini	£3–3s (paid Oct. 28)	£3–3s (paid Dec 27)	£3–3s*	£4–4s	£4
Scarpettini		£3–3s (Dec 27)	£3–3s*	£4–4s	£4
Boswillibald		£2–8s (paid Dec 30)	£3–3s*	£4–4s	£4
Barsanti	£2–2s (Nov 11)	£3–3s (paid Dec 30)			
Smith			£4–2s–6d**		£4
Eccles			£4–2s–6d**		
Total	£5–5s	£11–17s	£17–14s +	£12–12s +	£16+

★ based on previous, known quarterly payments
★★ the balance remaining, shared in two after the sum of the other three is removed
★★★ based on the given total
+ the sum alone is given in the minutes

ILL. I: Arms of the Directors of the *Philo-musicae* lodge, as shown in the lodge minutes. Geminiani's shield, second row, centre, is blank. (RYLANDS, Harry. *Op. cit.* [see note 1], frontispiece.) Image ©2009 The Library and Museum of Freemasonry, London. Reproduced with permission.

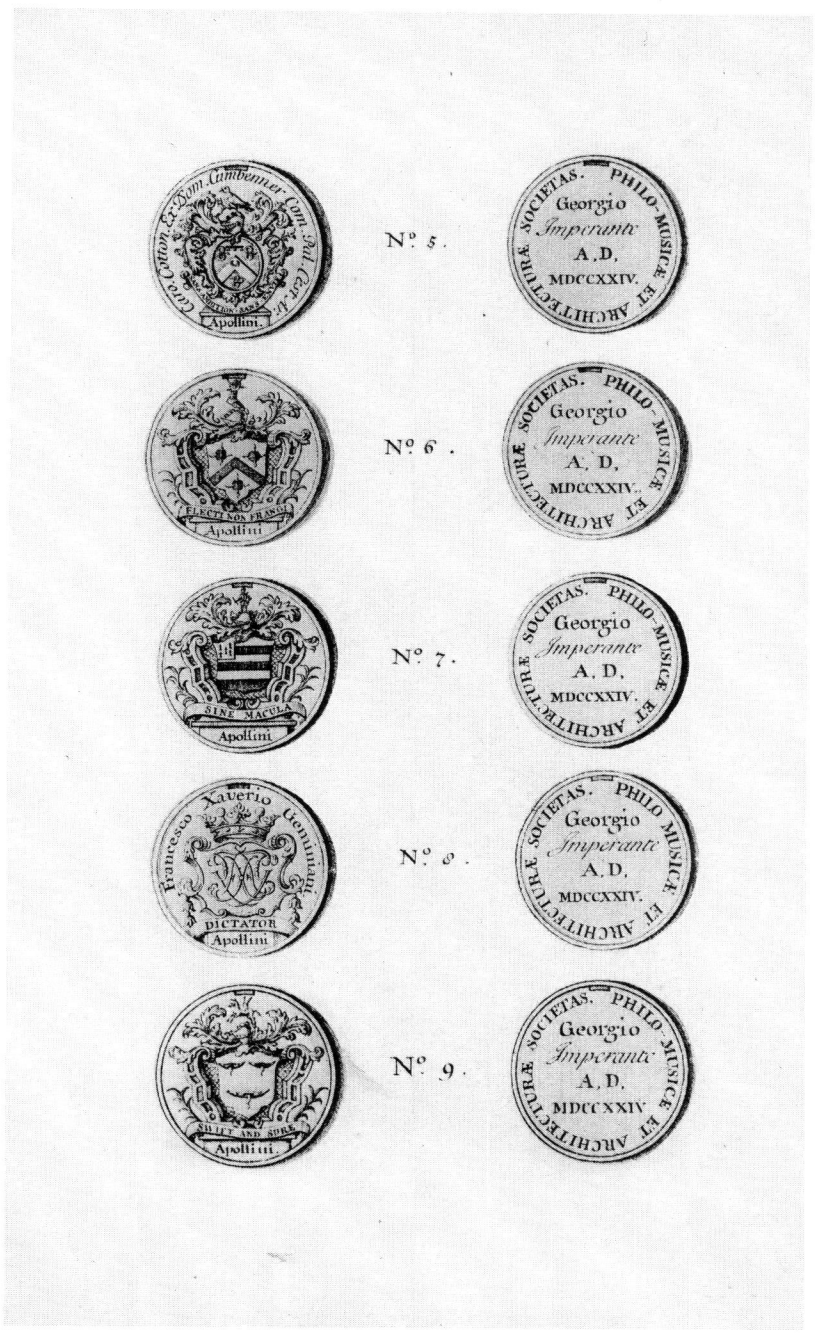

ILL. 2: Five of the thirteen 'tokens of distinction' worn by each of the Directors. Geminiani's is shown at no. 8. (RYLANDS, Harry. *Op. cit.* [see note 1], plate 2.) Image ©2009 The Library and Museum of Freemasonry, London. Reproduced with permission.

ILL. 3: Thomas Shuttleworth junior's request for admittance as the ninth Director of the Philo-musicae lodge, together with the signatures of the other eight Directors. (RYLANDS, Harry. *Op. cit.* (see note 1), plate 16.) Image ©2009 The Library and Museum of Freemasonry, London. Reproduced with permission.

	Dutchy-lane in the Strand	Second Fryd. & last Monday in every Month
24	Chancery lane	First Monday in every Month
	Clare Market	First Wednesday in every Month
	South-side of St. Pauls	First & Third Tuesday in every Month
	behind the Royal Exchange	Second Thursday in every Month
	Newgate street	First & Third Wednesday in every Month
P D	Cavendish street	every other Mond from ye 18th of Novr. inclusive
	Vere-street	last Wednesd. in every Month
	Bow Lane	First Tuesday in every Month
	St. Pauls Church-yard	First Fryday in every Month
	Great Queen street	First & Third Thursday in every Month
Ditto Temple Barr	Philo-musical & Architecture societs.	Every other thursday from St. John Bapts.

ILL. 4: extract from an official list of London lodges, engraved and published for the Grand Lodge by John Pine (London, 1725), with handwritten additions concerning the *Philomusicae* lodge. Image ©2009 The Library and Museum of Freemasonry, London. Reproduced with permission.

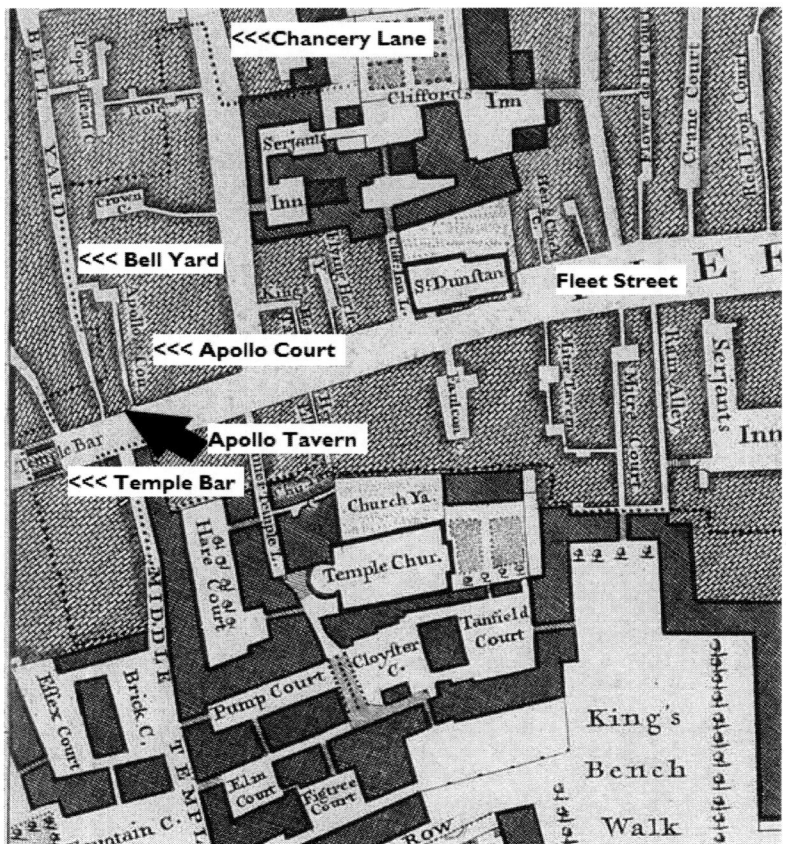

Ill. 5: the Temple Bar area from John Roque's *A Plan of the Cities of London and Westminster* [...] (1746). The Apollo tavern was located on Fleet Street between Bell Yard and Apollo Court, opposite the Middle Temple Gate.

Evidence for the Queen's Head/Apollo Tavern is patchy. The earliest known mention of it is in the diary of Narcissus Luttrell (1657-1732) for March 1682: "The 2nd, in the morning early, a fire broke out in the back part of the Queen's Head Tavern, by Temple Bar, but was mastered in a little time, so that it consumed only the back part".[96] The tavern is noted in 1709 as the location of demonstrations in experimental philosophy presented by James Hodgson (1672-1755).[97] It seems that already in May 1725 this tavern had seen better days, being subdivided for use by a tallow chandler.

---

[96] CHANCELLOR, Edwin Beresford. *The Annals of Fleet Street, Its Traditions and Associations*, London, Chapman & Hall Ltd., 1912, p. 308.

[97] STEWART, Larry. 'Other Centres of Calculation, or, Where the Royal Society Didn't Count: Commerce, Coffee-Houses and Natural Philosophy in Early Modern London', in:

Richard Lutwych hath open'd a new Warehouse, being a Part of the House, formerly the Queen's Head Tavern near Temple-bar, opposite to the Middle Temple-gate, where will be sold the very best sorts of tallow candles at the price of 5d per Dozen; where constant Attendance will be given.

Daily Post, Wednesday 5 May 1725

We learn from the *Philo-musicae* lodge minutes, that the tavern was run by a Thomas Oliverson (d. 1731),[98] during whose time it was named Apollo, after the lodge that met there. We assume that Apollo Yard was so named at this time. Apart from the lodge minutes we have no news of the tavern for another decade.

In 1736 a series of press advertisements indicate that the Apollo tavern had become the Apollo coffee house, and was known as a venue for auction sales, still occasionally identified as having been "formerly the Apollo tavern".

Around 1737 the Apollo seems to have briefly changed its name, when, according to a concert announcement of December 1737: "tickets are to be had at Will's Coffee House, formerly the Apollo in Bell Yard near Temple Bar". It seems that this Wills Coffee House contained an Apollo Room,[99] and from this we can confidently assume the concert announcement is describing the building associated with the *Philo-musicae* lodge. However, this is the only mention we have of the location being associated with Wills Coffee House, and as we shall see, it seems to have been a temporary change of name, the former soon being reinstated. There have been several other London coffee houses named Wills, e.g. at Scotland Yard Gate, Whitehall, in the 17th century (noted by the diarist Samuel Pepys) and, in the 18th century, at Russell Street, Covent Garden, the well-known haunt of Dryden and other literary figures.

During 1738, advertisements again refer to the Apollo as a coffee house, "formerly the Apollo tavern", and as the site of auction sales, which continued until 1749 when in the *London Evening Post*, Tuesday, 3 October 1749, we read of the death of Mr Kingsman, "Master of the Apollo Coffee House, in Apollo Court, near Temple Bar".

On 5 October 1745, a government spy called Haldanby Moore was staying at the Apollo Coffee House, Apollo Court near Temple Bar, when he wrote to the Prime Minister, Lord Newcastle, with details of disaffected persons residing in Stockport, Cheshire.[100]

The British Journal for the History of Science, XXXII/2 (June, 1999, special issue: *Did the Royal Society Matter in the Eighteenth Century?*), pp. 133–153: 144.

[98]   See his will at Public Record Office, London, PROB 3/30/41

[99]   CHANCELLOR, Edwin Beresford. *Op. cit.* (see note 96), pp. 251–252.

[100]   Public Record Office, London, SP 36/70, Secretaries of State, State Papers Domestic, George II, Letters and Papers; Folio 175.

From a press advertisement in 1752 we know the Apollo was again home to auction sales:

> To be sold by auction by B. Dickinson, tomorrow, the 21st instant, at five o'clock, at the Apollo Coffee-House, in Apollo-Court, Temple Bar, the copper-plate stock of Mess. Stewart and Woodgate, late of London Bridge, deceas'd [...]
>
> *Daily Advertiser*, 20 July 1752

On 27th February 1760 the proprietor of the Apollo Coffee house, a John Ambery, was found guilty of fraud at the Old Bailey.[101]

The next mention of the Apollo comes in 1765, when an advertisement appeared in the *Gazetteer and New Daily Advertiser* on Friday 19 April 1765:

> A Leasehold Estate in Apollo-Court, near Temple-Bar, consisting of a substantial Brick House, which was lately the Apollo coffee-House, lett to Mr. Lumley, Carpenter, on Lease at £26. a Year, Ground rent £10. 22 Years of the lease are unexpired.

The last information we have about the Apollo shows that it was still open for business as a coffee house in 1782, when *Parker's General Advertiser and Morning Intelligencer* announced on Friday 10 May that a reward for a lost dog could be claimed there.

---

[101] *Old Bailey Proceedings Online*, <http://www.oldbaileyonline.org/>, accessed 1 July 2011.

Geminiani v. Mrs Frederica: Legal Battles with an Opera Singer

Cheryll Duncan
(Manchester)

T HE TITLE OF THIS ESSAY SITS A LITTLE UNCOMFORTABLY with regard to a composer whose reputation today rests exclusively on his sonatas, concertos and treatises.[1] Geminiani's preference for instrumental over vocal genres did not escape the notice of later commentators such as Sir John Hawkins:

> [...] his compositions, elegant and ornate as they were, carried in them no evidences of that extensive genius which is required in dramatic music; nor did he make the least effort to show that he was possessed of the talent of associating music with poetry, or of adapting corresponding sounds to sentiments [...][2]

This single-mindedness had serious repercussions for Geminiani's public appeal, as Hawkins later points out:

> [...] it must be observed, that as he had never attempted dramatic composition of any kind, he drew to him but a small share of the public attention, that being in general awake only to such entertainments as the theatres afford. The consequence whereof was, that the sense of his merits existed only among those who had attained a competent skill in the practice of instrumental harmony [...][3]

---

[1] Only one original vocal work, an early cantata, *Nella stagione appunto*, for soprano and basso continuo (H. 300) is definitely attributed to Geminiani in CARERI, p. 292. However an aria *Primo Cesare, ottomano* (H. 310) is found as the last item in SMITH, John Stafford. *Musica Antiqua*, 2 vols, London, Preston, 1728, vol. II, p. 208. Other attributed vocal works, including one number, *If ever a fond inclination* (H. 321), in the ballad-opera *Love in a Village*, are adaptations of Geminiani's instrumental compositions.

[2] *HAWKINS*, v, pp. 239-240.

[3] *Ibidem*, pp. 420-421.

Geminiani may not have left us any operas, but he was not a total stranger to the theatre. A number of references in contemporary letters and newspapers bear witness to his association with various productions on the London stage, and his instrumental works were performed as entr'acte music on many occasions. However, his efforts to develop a career in the theatre were largely unsuccessful and short-lived. Documents recently discovered among the legal records held by The National Archives at Kew in London help us to understand why that was the case.

Hawkins' view that Geminiani enjoyed the patronage of a coterie of admirers rather than the acclaim of wider audiences is substantiated by Charles Burney, according to whom "Geminiani was seldom heard in public during his long residence in England".[4] The restriction that this must have placed on his earning power as a performer was doubtless the reason why he chose to forge a largely independent living through a portfolio of varied activities. He continued to give occasional concerts in London, and during the early 1740s played a number of times at the Little (or "New") Theatre in the Haymarket. However, for the 1744-1745 season there he was preoccupied with an altogether more ambitious project — the production of a new pasticcio opera in three acts entitled *L'Incostanza Delusa*. On 6 February 1745 *The General Advertiser* carried the following announcement:

> MR. GEMINIANI proposing to have a Pastoral Opera,
> call'd L'INCOSTANZA DELUSA, Perform'd at the *New Theatre*
> in the *Haymarket*, the 9th Instant, and Having neither spared Pains
> nor Expence to render it an agreeable Entertainment, he hopes
> his Endeavours will merit the Approbation and Encouragement
> of the Publick.

The libretto of this 'Pastoral Opera' was by Francesco Vanneschi (d. 1759), who had worked for Lord Middlesex's opera company as poet and impresario at the King's Theatre since 1741.[5] Geminiani's precise role in the production is unclear, but he probably put the music together and acted as director for the performances, all of which took place on Saturdays (February 9, 16 and 23, March 2, 9, 16, 23 and 30; April 6 and 20). Certainly he did not lead the orchestra on these occasions, that particular task being entrusted to the Italian violinist Nicolò Pasquali (*c*1718-1757), who came to England about 1743. Burney recounts how, at a rehearsal of the opera, "Geminiani [took] the violin

---

4   BURNEY, IV, p. 643.
5   WEAVER, Robert Lamar. 'Vanneschi, Francesco', in: *NG*.

out of [Pasquali's] hands, to give him the style and expression of the symphony to a song, which had been mistaken, when first led off".[6] According to the fourth Earl of Shaftesbury, the only music contributed by Geminiani himself was the overture and a concerto (possibly one of his new Concerti Grossi Op. 7 which were intended for publication the following year) performed between the acts.[7] The main musical content of the pasticcio consisted of new songs by the enigmatic Count of Saint Germain (d. 1784), together with two arias by Giuseppe Ferdinando Brivio (d. *c*1758) taken from his earlier opera *L'Incostanza Delusa* (Milan, 1739).[8] Six of these arias were published by John Walsh as *The Favourite Songs from the Opera Called "L'Incostanza Delusa"* (London, 1745); Walsh also names the singers who performed the arias, which is particularly useful as the wordbook, published by J. Hughs (London, 1745), contains no cast list: four of the arias were sung by Giulia Frasi (soprano), and two by Caterina Galli (mezzo-soprano).[9] By comparing Walsh's texts with the wordbook it is possible to ascertain that Galli sang the role of Filandro (first man) and Frasi that of Corina (first woman). One of the arias sung by Frasi, Saint Germain's 'Per pietà bell'Idol mio', was evidently encored every night.[10] Further testimony to the popularity of this aria is evident from a house in Richmond occupied by Handel's associate Johann Jacob Heidegger, where an extract from the music serves as the subject for a wall painting; this was probably the work of Antonio Joli (*c*1700-1777), who was employed as a scene-painter at the King's Theatre during the 1740s.[11] Overall, however, *L'Incostanza Delusa* was not well received; three days after the opening night, the fourth Earl of Shaftesbury reported that "Geminiani's opera [...] went off I hear most wretchedly last Saturday, and people don't seem inclined to favour it at all".[12] Thomas Harris further confirmed that "Geminiani's new opera had but bad success, there being a thin house on Saturday last".[13]

---

[6]   BURNEY, IV, p. 452.

[7]   Letter of 12 February 1745 from the fourth Earl of Shaftesbury to James Harris; see BURROWS, Donald - DUNHILL, Rosemary. *Music and Theatre in Handel's World: The Family Papers of James Harris 1732-1780*, Oxford, Oxford University Press, 2002, p. 214.

[8]   HANSELL, Sven. 'Brivio, Giuseppe Ferdinando', in: *NG*.

[9]   For more information on the latter singer, see DUNCAN, Cheryll - MATEER, David. 'An Innocent Abroad? Caterina Galli's Finances in New Handel Documents', in: *Journal of the American Musicological Society*, LXIV/3 (2011), pp. 495-526.

[10]   BURNEY, IV, p. 452.

[11]   CROFT-MURRAY, Edward. 'The Painted Hall in Heidegger's House at Richmond: II', in: *The Burlington Magazine for Connoisseurs*, LXXVIII (May 1941), p. 155.

[12]   Letter to James Harris, 12 February 1745; see BURROWS, Donald - DUNHILL, Rosemary. *Op. cit.* (see note 7), p. 214.

[13]   *Ibidem*; letter to James Harris, 14 February 1745.

Apart from Frasi and Galli, the only other singer who can be identified with any certainty is a "Mrs. Frederica", for whose benefit the performance of *L'Incostanza Delusa* was given on 6 April; from the wordbook it is possible to identify her role as that of Orsinda, the only other female part.[14] Very little is known about Mrs Frederica apart from her various London addresses; according to *The Daily Advertiser*, she was living "in Sherrard-Street, facing Queen-Street, near Golden-Square" at the time of her benefit. She is not heard of again until July 1750, when she gave two concerts in Amsterdam with her seven-year-old daughter Cassandra, who played the harpsichord.[15] Evidently something of a prodigy, Cassandra gave a number of concerts in London in which she used the Anglicized form of her surname, "Frederick". Tickets for these events were advertised as being available from "Mrs. Frederick's in Wardour-Street, Soho, near Meard's Court".[16] In the autumn of 1750 Mrs Frederica presented her daughter at the fashionable spa resort of Bath, and sang in Cassandra's benefit concert at Wiltshire's Room on 26 November alongside the up-and-coming alto castrato Gaetano Guadagni.[17] The Fredericas returned to Bath the following year when Cassandra's benefit on 11 November listed her mother and Francesca Cuzzoni as principal vocalists.[18] Two weeks later, "Seigniora Frederica" and her daughter were in Bristol for a benefit at the Assembly Room, St Augustine's Back, in which the young harpsichordist played "a Concerto of Mr. Rameau, the first Concerto of Mr. Handell, and several Lessons from the Great Masters".[19] On 15 October 1755 mother and daughter advertised themselves as music teachers in *The Public Advertiser*:

---

[14] A letter from the fourth Earl of Shaftesbury to James Harris on 17 January 1745 states that, alongside "chief singers" Galli and Frasi, "Bettina the dancing woman is also to sing". This presumably referred to the Neapolitan dancer Signora Bettina who first came to England in 1741 to perform at the King's Theatre. Burrows and Dunhill suggest that her involvement is unlikely because Bettina was advertised as dancing at Drury Lane on nights when *L'Incostanza Delusa* was playing (*ibidem*, p. 211).

[15] DEAN, Winton. 'Frederick, Cassandra', in: *NG*. Cassandra Frederick went on to enjoy a successful career as a mezzo-soprano, being engaged by Handel as an oratorio singer from 1758. Dean is unsure about the relationship between Mrs Frederica and Cassandra, but it can now be confirmed that they were mother and daughter.

[16] See, for example, *The General Advertiser*, 26 March 1750.

[17] JAMES, Kenneth Edward. *Concert Life in Eighteenth-Century Bath*, Ph.D. Diss., University of London, 1987, p. 617; and *The Bath Journal*, 19 November 1750.

[18] JAMES, Kenneth Edward. *Op. cit.* (see note 17), p. 571; and *The Bath Journal*, 4 November 1751.

[19] JENKINS, John S. 'Leopold Mozart's Madame Wynne: Look to the Lady', in: *The Musical Times*, no. 142 (Spring 2001), p. 29.

> MRS. FREDERICA, and her Daughter CASSANDRA,
> propose to instruct on reasonable Terms, all such Ladies, and
> young Persons (not under five Years of Age) as may be desirous
> of being taught the Harpsichord, or Singing, at her Lodgings at
> Mr. Paradie's, in Wardour-street, Soho.[20]

The final mention of "Signora Frederica" in the press is on 20 April 1762, when she sang in a benefit concert for the flautist Joseph Tacet at the Great Room in Dean Street, Soho, performing alongside the beneficiary and the violinist Felice de' Giardini.[21] Surviving evidence, therefore, suggests that *L'Incostanza Delusa* was the only operatic venture in which Mrs Frederica participated. Even so, her involvement in the season was cut short when she and Geminiani fell out over the agreement they had struck regarding the terms of her benefit, and he took her to court. In the theatre his retribution was swift; a newspaper advertisement for the next and (as it happened) final performance of *L'Incostanza* on 20 April announced that: "Signora Frederica's Part will be perform'd by Mrs. Arne".[22] In court, on the other hand, the legal proceedings were considerably more protracted and much less decisive.

Geminiani lost no time in bringing a bill of complaint against Frederica in the court of King's Bench. The singer was summarily arrested and would have been incarcerated had she been unable to find bail. Sureties were at first provided by "Christian Avolio Widow", though the court later ordered that her name be removed from the bail piece, that is, the document recording the nature of the bail granted to the defendant.[23] Geminiani had to wait until Michaelmas 1745 before presenting his case, and even then it was immediately adjourned to the following term.[24] The preamble to the litigation states that this is an action in trespass on the case, that is, an action to recover damages that are not the immediate result of a wrongful act but rather a later consequence. Geminiani states that on 6 February 1745 he obtained a licence from Charles

---

[20] Domenico Paradies (1707-1791) arrived in London in 1746 and, according to Leopold Mozart, took charge of Mrs Frederica and her children after the death of her husband; see *The Letters of Mozart and His Family*, edited by Emily Anderson, London, Macmillan, 1988, p. 92.

[21] *The Public Advertiser*, 3 April 1762.

[22] *The Daily Advertiser*, 20 April 1745. Mrs Arne was formerly Cecilia Young, one of Geminiani's pupils.

[23] The National Archives (hereafter TNA): KB125/129, King's Bench Rules and Orders. This volume is unpaginated, but the relevant heading is "Wednesday next after fifteen Days of the Holy Trinity in the 20th [*recte* 19th] year of King George the 2d", i.e. 26 June 1745. Christina Maria Avoglio is best remembered today for singing the principal soprano part at the first performance of *Messiah* in Dublin on 13 April 1742.

[24] TNA: KB122/213 (Hilary 1746), rot. 667.

Fitzroy, Duke of Grafton, the then Lord Chamberlain, to perform "a certain Italian Opera called in the Italian Tongue by the Name of La Inconstanza Delusa on Twelve different Times at a certain House or Theatre scituate in the Parish of St. James [...] Westminster [...] called the little Theatre in the Hay Markett". In fact, the opera received only ten performances, probably because of disappointing audience numbers. On the same day, Geminiani agreed that one of the performances should be a benefit for Mrs Elizabeth Frederica; it is only from these and other legal proceedings, to be discussed later, that we learn her given name.

The term 'benefit' is used here to describe a special theatrical performance intended to benefit financially a playwright, actor/singer, theatrical employee, or charitable cause. The benefit was of vital importance to performers in the eighteenth-century London theatre, since the income it produced was a crucial supplement to their ordinary salary. Originally such occasions arose in response to special needs; theatre managements allowed actors in their companies or their families who found themselves in straitened circumstances to canvass public support, but by the end of the eighteenth century the system of annual benefits for all members of the theatre, including its lesser personnel, had become part of the regular season. It was much vilified on the grounds that managers were able to depress performers' salaries by the promise of a benefit, and that it forced performers and others who hoped to augment their meagre incomes to become virtual beggars in soliciting audiences. Nevertheless, the system whereby performers and managers negotiated a share of the gross proceeds persisted throughout the nineteenth century. Basically there were five types of benefit. The most desirable, but also the rarest, was the 'clear' benefit by which the beneficiary received all the receipts, the management picking up the bill for the house charges, i.e. for printing, lighting and the use of the theatre, as well as the wages of stage staff, other performers, orchestra, front of house officials, and the like. In the 'half-clear' benefit the beneficiary made an equal division of the gross receipts of the night with the manager, the latter paying the charges. The most common form was the 'whole' benefit, which involved the deduction from the receipts of a sum sufficient to meet the house charges. A variant of this arrangement more favourable to the performer was the 'guaranteed' benefit, in which he/she received an agreed sum, with the management making up the difference even if the house takings did not cover the sum assured. In a fourth kind, the 'half' benefit, profits above the charges were shared equally between performer and management. Finally, there was the group benefit, in which several minor functionaries of the theatre were joined together as recipients of a 'whole' or 'half' benefit.[25] However, these categories were not rigidly set, and great variety was possible in the terms negotiated between management and performers.

For Mrs Frederica's benefit it was agreed that she should have the use of the performing materials — the so called 'Musick Books' — that Geminiani had put together. In recompense she was to pay him 12 guineas out of the profits on the night, but should those profits come to less than that sum, then he was to receive them all. (This is an interesting variation on the 'whole' benefit, with the performer having to bear additional costs to protect Geminiani's share.) A third party, one Samuel Righton, was appointed to receive and distribute the money under the terms of the agreement. Geminiani and Mrs Frederica then pledged to uphold their respective sides of the undertaking, and the said benefit took place as agreed on 6 April following. However, although the profits from this performance "then and there amounted to a large Sum of Money", they came to less than the specified 12 guineas, "to wit to the sum of twelve Pounds and Eleven Shillings"; the closeness of this sum to the required 12 guineas should alert one to the possibility that we are dealing here with a legal fiction. We then come to the essence of Geminiani's complaint, which is that "the said Elizabeth not regarding her said last mentioned Promise and Undertaking but contriving and fraudulently intending craftily and Subtilly to deceive and Defraud the said Francis in this respect[,] hath not yet paid the said last mentioned Sum of twelve Pounds and Eleven Shillings or any part thereof [...] nor permitted the said Samuel to pay him".

The litigation then does something characteristic of seventeenth- and eighteenth-century pleas of trespass on the case: it repeats the first count virtually word for word. We read for a second time how, on 6 February 1745, Geminiani obtained a licence to perform the said opera twelve times; how he agreed that Elizabeth Frederica should have one of the performances as her benefit; how she was to have use of the 'Musick Books' for which she was to pay him either 12 guineas out of the profits, or all the profits should they not come to so much; and how they had both agreed to keep their side of the bargain. The second count differs from the first only in one important respect: the profits from Mrs Frederica's benefit on 6 April amounted this time "to twelve Guineas and more". Geminiani complains once more that the singer has refused to pay what had been agreed should be paid in the circumstances.

These allegations are then reiterated almost *verbatim* in a third count. One might reasonably ask oneself at this stage: what is going on here? How can the

---

[25] This paragraph draws on TROUBRIDGE, St Vincent. *The Benefit System in the British Theatre*, London, Society for Theatre Research, 1967.

same performance on the same day in the same venue produce profits that are at once above and below the twelve guinea benchmark? What is the reason for such prolixity and redundancy? Contemporary handbooks of legal practice provide an explanation; they tell us that it is usual, particularly in cases of debt and simple contract, and in actions on the case, to set forth the plaintiff's cause of action in various shapes in different counts, so that if the plaintiff should fail in the proof of one count he/she may succeed on another. Thus in an action for a breach of promise of marriage, if the defendant promised to marry upon a particular day, the first count is framed accordingly, but for fear the plaintiff should not be able to prove such particular promise, it was usual, where the evidence may probably support the allegation, to add a count to marry on request, another to marry in a reasonable time, and another to marry generally. In other words, the pleader had to frame in alternative counts all the possible forms which an implication might take, in the hope that one of them would be upheld on the evidence.

This use of multiple counts can clearly be seen as Geminiani's case unfolds. He next claims that on 1 May 1745 Elizabeth owed him £20 which she promised to pay (count 4). He then states that, on the same day and year aforesaid, she owed him another £20 "for the Use of divers Theatrical Habits Dresses and Musick Books of the said Francis by the said Francis before that Time let to hire to the said Elizabeth" (count 5). And finally Geminiani claims that, on the day and year aforesaid, at Elizabeth's instance and request, he hired to her "certain other Theatrical Habits Dresses and certain other Musick Books of the said Francis to be used by the said Elizabeth in and about her Business" (count 6). He states that these items had been used "for a long Time then elapsed", and that Elizabeth had promised to pay him "so much money as he reasonably deserved to have", which Geminiani says was £20.[26] He claims that by 10 May she had "not yet paid the three last mentioned several Sums of Money or any part thereof"; in fact, there was only one sum of £20, not three — so he claims his loss amounts to £20.

The case reached court in the Hilary term of 1746, until which time Elizabeth had leave to imparl to Geminiani's bill, that is, she was granted time to consider what answer she should make to the plaintiff's action. Geminiani was represented in court by his attorney, but Elizabeth appeared in her proper person. She denied any wrongdoing and said "that she did not take upon herself and promise in manner and form as the said Francis hath above declared against her And of this she puts herself upon the Country", that is, she was

---

[26] This count is known in legal parlance as a *quantum meruit* ('as much as he has deserved'). It was used as a possible measure of restitution where a contract had not fixed a price.

prepared to submit her case to trial by jury. A date was then fixed for this, namely, the Monday after Ascension (i.e. 12 May 1746). However, proceedings never reached that stage, and the record of the case, so far as the plea roll is concerned, simply peters out. One can often assume, in instances where no judgment is entered, that an out-of-court settlement was brokered between the parties before the date of trial. However, that cannot have happened here, as the court's rules and orders demonstrate. Under the heading for Wednesday 16 April 1746, the following entry appears against a list of cases that includes Geminiani v. Frederica: "Monday next after three Weeks from Easter Day [21 April] is given to the P*laintiff* to reply and enter the Issue[;] otherwise Let a Non pross be Entered".[27] Geminiani failed to comply with this order and was consequently "nonprossed", i.e. the court ruled that proceedings should be halted because of the discovery of some error or defect in them, and the plaintiff was obliged to renounce his suit. The nature of the flaw that proved so fatal to his case would soon be revealed.

Nothing daunted, Geminiani presented another bill of complaint against Elizabeth at Easter 1747, this time in the Court of Exchequer, consisting essentially of the same set of grievances.[28] The Exchequer was primarily the place where the King's debtors were called to account; secondarily it was a court of law in which cases affecting the rights and revenues of the Crown were heard and determined. The Exchequer Court had two sides — a common law jurisdiction (the 'Exchequer of Pleas') and an equity side. In the latter anyone could file a bill against another claiming that he was the King's accountant; a person indebted to the Crown could sue in this Court upon a suggestion of *quominus*, that is, of his being 'the less' able to satisfy the Crown by reason of the cause of action he had against the defendant. Until the middle of the seventeenth century, litigants had to have some genuine connection with the royal revenue, but from 1649 this connection persisted only as a legal fiction for most plaintiffs, and the application of the writ of *quominus* was eventually so far extended that practically everyone might institute in the Exchequer proceedings in any personal action. This is why Geminiani's bill begins: "Francis Geminiani of the Parish of Saint Ann Soho in the Liberty of Westminster and county of Middlesex Gentleman Debtor and Accountant to his Majesty".

There are significant as well as minor differences between the King's Bench and Exchequer bills. In the latter, after claiming to have "composed or set

---

[27] TNA: KB125/129, *s.v.* "Wednesday next after fifteen Days from Easter in the 19th year of King George 2[d] 1746".

[28] TNA: E112/1211/2409

to Musick a certain Italian Opera called […] L'Incostanza Delusa", Geminiani provides a more detailed account of how he and Elizabeth negotiated the terms of the singer's benefit night. At first she wanted "one of the said twelve Nights for the mutual Benefit of her […] and your Orator" [i.e. Geminani]; she proposed "that all the clear gains and profits […] should be equally divided between the said Elizabeth Frederica and your Orator in equal Moieties"; and she offered to pay half of the house charges. This is a 'half-clear' benefit, but with the performer paying half the charges.

In order to persuade Geminiani to agree to this proposal, Elizabeth assured him that she "had great Interest with many persons of Quality and Fortune and by means thereof would procure a full Audience at the performance". This first attempt to reach an agreement fell through because she insisted on employing someone to receive the night's takings of whom Geminiani did not approve. Elizabeth then came back with the proposition we know about from the King's Bench bill, namely that the performance should be "for the Sole benefit and advantage of the said Elizabeth Frederica and that your Orator would let her […] have the use of the Orator's said Musick Books for the Several performers […] and the said Several Cloths Habits and Dresses to be worn by the several Singers in the said Opera". In return she was to give Geminiani 12 guineas from the takings after charges had been deducted. In addition, she was to pay out of her own pocket the wages of two of her fellow singers, Giulia Frasi and Caterina Galli — a clause omitted from the King's Bench bill. One can understand why Geminiani was so insistent that their salaries should not be reckoned as part of the house charges, but should be met by Frederica alone. The size of his cut depended on the size of the profits (the greater the profits, the greater his chances of receiving 12 guineas); but the size of the profits depended on the house charges (the fewer of those there were the greater his chances of getting his 12 guineas); so to minimize the assessed charges Geminiani made Frederica responsible for the fees of his two leading singers. However, if the profits did not amount to 12 guineas, then Geminiani was to receive whatever profits there were. He stipulated that his cut should be paid directly to him by the person appointed to receive the money, i.e. by Samuel Righton, who we learn was a jeweller of St Martin-in-the-fields. Frederica's benefit went ahead as planned and, although Geminiani claimed that the monies that remained after payment of house charges "amounted to a very large Sum", Frederica and Righton "hath absolutely refused either to pay your Orator the said Sum of Twelve Guineas or to come to a just and fair Account with your Orator". Geminiani states that the singer had tried to justify her actions by claiming, amongst other things, that he never obtained a licence from the Lord Chamberlain, that he did not "compose or Set to Musick the said Opera nor had any property therein", that she never had the use of his music books and costumes, and that the box–office receipts were insufficient to defray the cost of mounting the opera.

He then touches on what was undoubtedly the reason for the removal of his suit from King's Bench a year earlier, and why he is now resorting to equity:

> Elizabeth Frederica pretends that she is not accountable to your Orator for the said Sum of Twelve Guineas in Regard that she was a Feme Covert at the time of making the said Agreement[,] being then Married to one John Frederica who was then and is still living in Petersbourgh in the Kingdom of Russia and therefore that she the said Elizabeth Frederica was not bound by her said Agreement with your Orator.

In law French a *feme covert* was a married woman, as opposed to a *feme sole* (a spinster or widow); her husband was her *baron* (lord), and her 'coverture' was the state of being a married woman under the protection of her *baron*. Today a married woman has a separate legal identity with full power of acquiring, holding, and dealing with any kind of property; but this has not always been the case. Before the Married Women's Property Act (1882), husband and wife were one person in law, the legal personality of the woman being subsumed in that of the man. Accordingly, a married woman was in general incapable of acquiring, holding, or alienating any property. Money and personal chattels belonging to the wife at the time of her marriage, or acquired by her during it, were vested in the husband absolutely. During coverture she lost the capacity to own separate property or make contracts; and crucially she could not sue or be sued at common law without her husband.

Almost certainly Frederica invoked her coverture as a defence against Geminiani's bill in King's Bench, thus causing the case to be discontinued. Having initially failed to achieve justice at common law, Geminiani was driven to seek relief on the equity side of the Exchequer. The word 'equity' is synonymous with natural justice, and is often used in contrast with the strict rules of the common law. Equity is therefore recourse to principles of justice that seem naturally fair and right in order to correct or supplement the law as applied to particular circumstances.[29]

In his Exchequer bill Geminiani puts the case even more forcefully than he did in King's Bench, claiming that in the presence of witnesses

---

[29]   In England the major court of equity was Chancery, but the Exchequer also exercised an equitable jurisdiction until 1841.

[...] the said Elizabeth Frederica did declare [...] before the making of the said Agreement that her said Husband was Dead[,] and did Wear Mourning Cloths on Account of the Death of her said Husband [...] and did pass for a Widow[.] And your Orator Charges that in case [i.e. if] the said Elizabeth Frederica was ever married and her Husband is now living[,] that he never resided in his Majestie's Dominions but at some remote place beyond the Seas and not amenable by the process of this honourable Court.

Geminiani is making an important legal point here, which we find most clearly expressed in the first book of Sir William Blackstone's *Commentaries on the Laws of England*. After defining a married woman's position before the law and emphasizing that she cannot be sued without making her husband a defendant, Blackstone adds the following qualification:

> There is indeed one case where the wife shall sue and be sued as a feme sole, viz. where the husband has abjured the realm, or is banished: for then he is dead in law; and, the husband being thus disabled to sue for or defend the wife, it would be most unreasonable if she had no remedy, or could make no defence at all.[30]

Geminiani's legal team is arguing that, even if Elizabeth is married, she *is* still suable as a single woman because her husband is beyond the reach of British justice.

Finally, Geminiani insists that, since Frederica and Righton had collected the takings for her benefit night, she "ought to pay the Expences thereof or indemnify your Orator from the same". He repeats his demand for the 12 guineas (or the residue of the profits after charges had been deducted), and complains that, since Frederica had neglected to pay the other performers and the landlord or owner of the theatre, they were threatening to sue him for their money. He claims that should they try to sue her, she would plead her coverture in bar of such actions. He declares that "All of which Actings doings and pretences are contrary to Equity and good Conscience", and that he is "wholy remedyless in the premises by the Strict Rules of Law". He therefore petitions the court to issue writs of subpoena to secure the attendance of Frederica and Righton to answer his complaint. Most frustratingly, however, Geminiani's bill is all the documentation we have for the case in its Exchequer version. Indeed, one suspects that that is all there ever was, and that Mrs Frederica quickly settled out of court.

---

30 BLACKSTONE, William. *Commentaries on the Laws of England*, 4 vols, Oxford, Clarendon Press, 1765-1769; facsimile edition, Chicago, University of Chicago Press, 1979, vol. I, p. 431.

The litigation discussed above throws new light on the activities and character of one of the most versatile figures in the musical life of eighteenth-century Britain. Geminiani *v.* Frederica illuminates the circumstances surrounding the production of *L'Incostanza Delusa*, a hitherto obscure corner of the London operatic scene in the mid-1740s. As the person who negotiated the terms of Frederica's benefit, and the owner of the performing materials and costumes used for the run, it is possible to identify Geminiani as the managerial force behind the venture. Undaunted by the singer's legal ducking and weaving, he tenaciously pursued her through two courts, convinced by the rightness of his cause. The documents show how a woman prior to the 1882 Married Women's Property Act could manipulate the law on coverture in order to plead immunity from prosecution for breach of contract. Whereas hitherto Frederica was known only by the title of 'Mrs.', the documents specify her first name, Elizabeth, and suggest a reason why she was summarily dropped after her benefit performance and replaced by Mrs Arne for the final night. The case provides a valuable insight into the benefit system, about which far less is known for musicians than for actors, and demonstrates the shifting demands and compromises that management and performer were required to make in order to reach an agreement.[31]

---

[31]   Mrs Frederica was not the only singer with whom Geminiani engaged in litigation. For an account of his legal battle with the castrato Giuseppe Manfredini in 1751, see DUNCAN, Cheryll. 'Castrati and impresarios in London: two mid-eighteenth-century lawsuits', in: *Cambridge Opera Journal*, XXIV/1 (2012), pp. 43-65.

Geminiani and Fine Art

Christopher Hogwood
(Cambridge)

ONE DAY IN THE AUTUMN OF 1757 a visitor called unexpectedly on Geminiani in his lodgings at the Grange Inn in Carey Street, near Lincoln's-Inn Fields, wanting to buy the new editions of his Opp. 2 and 3 concertos which had just been published:

> I found him in a room at the top of the house half filled with pictures, and in his waistcoat. Upon my telling him that I wanted the score and parts of both operas of his concertos, he asked me if I loved pictures; and upon my answering in the affirmative, he said that he loved painting better than music, and with great labour drew from among the many that stood upon the floor round the room, two, the one the story of Tobit cured of his blindness, by Michael Angelo Caravaggio; the other a Venus, by Correggio. These pictures, said Geminiani, I bought at Paris, the latter was in the collection of the duke of Orleans; they are inestimable, and I mean to leave them to my relations: Many men are able to bequeath to their relations great sums of money, I shall leave to mine what is more valuable than money, two pictures that are scarcely to be matched in the world.[1]

This rare glimpse of the elderly Geminiani at home (he was nearly 70) is reported second-hand in a footnote by Sir John Hawkins, who added (without identifying the visitor):

> After some farther conversation, in which it was very difficult to get him to say any thing on the subject of music, the visitor withdrew, leaving Geminiani to enjoy that pleasure which seemed to be the result of frenzy.[2]

---

[1] The identity of these two paintings is uncertain; the provenance of the Duc d'Orléans may well have been used to add credence to the attribution.

[2] *HAWKINS*, V, p. 423.

Such a picture of enthusiasm and (judging from the two paintings he so valued) good taste contrasts with the much repeated but more malicious description of Geminiani by Burney which has generally been accepted as gospel:

> It is well known how much he preferred the character of a picture-dealer, without the necessary knowledge or taste in painting, as very good judges asserted, to that of a composer of Music, by which he had subsisted and acquired all his fame and importance. It is to be feared that a propensity towards chicane and cunning, which gratified some dispositions more by outwitting mankind, than excelling them in virtue and talents, operated a little upon Geminiani; whose musical decisions ceasing to be irrevocable in England, determined him to try his hand at buying cheap and selling dear; imposing upon grosser ignorance with false names, and passing off copies for originals.[3]

Burney had earlier tried out the paragraph privately in a letter to Thomas Twining, again suggesting (wrongly) that Geminiani began art dealing only when his compositions ceased to be popular, and describing him as variable and

> as a Critic, *jamais de bonne Foi*, changing his opinions according to his Interest, as often as Caprice. One Day he w^d set up French Music against all other — the next, English — Scots — Irish, anything but the best Compositions of Handel & Italy. You know, I dare say, how much he preferred the Character of a Picture-dealer, without the least knowledge or Taste in Painting, to that of a Musician, by which he had acquired his reputation & importance. I am afraid there is such a *penchant* in the generality of Italian artists towards Chicane, that they w^d rather trick a Man out of a Guinea than get it fairly, in a John-Trot way. & when Geminiani's Musical decisions ceased to be irrevocable, he tried his Hand at Painting.[4]

Burney's assessment, which was taken up and has been quoted ever since without question, is certainly the most derogatory of his contemporaries. Hawkins employed the more measured phraseology of a lawyer, but came to an equally pessimistic conclusion:

---

[3] *BURNEY*, IV, p. 645.

[4] Burney to Twining, 30 August 1773 in: *The Letters of Dr Charles Burney*, edited by Alvaro Ribeiro, SJ, 4 vols, Oxford, Oxford University Press, 1991, vol. I, p. 144.

The relation between the arts of music and painting is so near, that in numberless instances, those who have excelled in one have been admirers of the other. Geminiani was an enthusiast in painting, and the versatility of his temper was such, that, to gratify this passion, he not only suspended his studies, and neglected the exercise of his talents, but involved himself in straits and difficulties, which a small degree of prudence would have taught him to avoid. To gratify his taste, he bought pictures; and, to supply his wants, he sold them; the necessary consequence of this kind of traffic was loss, and its concomitant, necessity.[5]

Despite the obvious contradiction — Burney accuses him of "buying cheap and selling dear", while Hawkins describes the opposite process — both historians are unanimous in censuring Geminiani for spending his life "employed in pursuits that had no connections with his art"[6] and "neglecting the exercise of his talents" — a very eighteenth-century underlining of the assumed obligations of musical genius, and the low moral status of mercenary trade (cognate with "chicane and cunning").

A similarly high moral obligation for musical talent was posited by William Hayes in 1753 in his explanation of Geminiani's 'failure' — a refusal to accept the divine hand of Providence and relish his position as the leading violinist in Europe; but since Hayes was in open opposition to Geminiani's pupil Avison, an inclination to exaggerate must be expected:

> […] for many Years he was wavering between *Music* and a kind of *Merchandize*, by which he hoped to have made his Fortune, independent of it; namely, buying and selling Pictures. So long as this Frenzy continued (for such it may justly be called) he disdained the Thought of being regarded on the Footing of a Musician, and never condescended to embrace the Means which Providence had reached out so visibly for his Support; except when he was broken down, and incapacitated for pursuing his other Trade. It is true, he frequently employed himself in composing for his Amusement, and his Concertos got abroad, but rather by Stealth than his Permission: Which seems to evince an eager Disposition in the Public, to catch at any Productions of his, rather than to manifest the least Slight, Contempt, or Disregard. On the contrary, he has been courted and solicited to apply himself wholly to Music; to make it his Profession; in order that the Public might reap some Advantage from his Instruction and Example; but such was the

---

[5] *Hawkins*, v, p. 240.
[6] *Ibidem*, p. 421.

Capriciousness and Inconstancy of his Temper, that he was
seldom prevailed upon, unless to gratify some favourite Whim
or Conceit of his own, or perhaps to supply his unbounded
Extravagance; a very prevailing Argument.[7]

Prevailing, maybe — but not well-founded, given that Geminiani in
fact provided more "Instruction and Example" in his seven published treatises
than any of his contemporaries, and personally supervised the publication of
his compositions to ensure they "got abroad". Nor is Hayes convincing in
suggesting that Geminiani showed contempt for the musical public as such,
but rather a completely understandable distaste for grovelling to patrons, and
a preference for securing his independence via another art form he admired
("a kind of *Merchandize*" to Hayes). Hawkins himself documented this self-
sufficiency: "The late prince of Wales greatly admired the compositions of
Geminiani, and at the same time that he retained Martini [Sammartini] in his
service, would have bestowed on him [Geminiani] a pension of a hundred
pounds a year, but the latter affecting an aversion to a life of dependence,
declined the offer".[8]

Independent and self-sufficient would seem to be better descriptions for
Geminiani than the character of a 'reluctant prima donna', but the prosecution's
charge of irresponsibility was further compounded by frequent recourse to the
term 'frenzy', implying that to refuse the normal path must have been the
result of some mental instability — divine penalty for neglecting his appointed
metier. But Hawkins' nicely euphemistic comment on "the versatility of
his temper" was perhaps no more than a chauvinistic response to normal
Italian capriciousness or artistic expression. All musicians when inspired in
performance were thought to be 'possessed'; witness the vivid descriptions of
Corelli playing, when "his Countenance will be distorted, his *Eye*-Balls *roll* as
in an Agony".[9] Tartini is supposed to have devised the epithet "il furibundo
Geminiani",[10] but this again was for his playing manner, not his life-style.
Charles Jennens remarked similarly on Handel's "maggots", which turn out

---

[7] [HAYES, William.] *Remarks on Mr. Avison's Essay on Musical Expression. Wherein The
Characters of several great Masters, both Ancient and modern, are rescued from the Misrepresentations of
the above Author; and their real Merit asserted and vindicated. In a Letter from a Gentleman in London
to his Friend in the Country*, London, J. Robinson, 1753, pp. 119-120

[8] *HAWKINS*, v, p. 421n.

[9] [RAGUENET, François.] *A Comparison between the French and Italian Musick and Opera's*,
London, William Lewis, 1709, p. 21n.

[10] Mentioned in the first edition of *A Dictionary of Music and Musicians*, edited by George
Grove, London, Macmillan, 1878, p. 587; always quoted thus, although "furibondo" is better
Italian.

to be little more than passing enthusiasms for exotic musical instruments such as the carillon. Neither Geminiani nor Handel came close to the genuine instability of, for example, Louis-Gabriel Guillemain, the French violinist, whose uncontrolled extravagance and passion for buying rare carpets ended with his suicide in a coach travelling from Paris to Versailles.

It is sobering, however, to note that these dissections of Geminiani's failings were openly made while he was still alive — so far had he lapsed from his once prime position, that period in the 20s and 30s to which Burney looked back when he reminisced that "Handel, Geminiani & Corelli were the sole Divinities of my Youth".[11] But the aim of this essay is not to trace the decline in public enthusiasm for Geminiani's music but to examine the almost universally negative reaction to his sustained enthusiasm for fine art.

★★★

For a member of the upper classes (Hawkins) or a social snob (Burney), it was clearly difficult to accept, or perhaps even realize, that while most men of property flaunted fine art as a demonstration of their wealth, Geminiani's paintings *were* his wealth, to be redeemed when needed. His expenses for a trip to Paris in 1733, for example, were in part covered by art dealing, according to a letter to William Capel from Thomas Pelham:

> My Lord, Paris Oct.ʳ 1.ˢᵗ 1733
>
> Geminiani went from hence about ten days ago with L.ᵈ Tullamore for England. I believe he got just money enough here, with the help of some Pictures, to defray his Expences. After the P. of Orange's wedding is over, they are to go to pass the winter in Ireland.[12]

This is not, *pace* CARERI (p. 28), the first mention of Geminiani's art dealing — earlier documentation can be found in both a 1723 advert and a 1725 catalogue (see below) — but certainly the first description of his unusual financial strategy in practice.

---

[11]   Burney to Twining, 14 December 1781. See *The Letters of Dr Charles Burney, op. cit.* (see note 4), vol. 1, p. 328.

[12]   *A Collection of several private letters received by His Excellency the Earl of Essex during his Embassy at Turin, 1732-36*, GB-Lbm Add. MS 27732, f. 239. Capel, Earl of Essex, was Geminiani's pupil and patron; Pelham[-Holles], a leading Whig, was Duke of Newcastle and Secretary of State.

Geminiani's status with his patrons was, like Handel's, supported but unattached; Baron Kilmansegg (who also assisted Handel) offered help when he first arrived in England (Op. 1 is dedicated to him); the Earl of Essex, William Capel was both protector and violin pupil; and Lord Tullamore (Charles Moore) and later Charles Coote provided refuge in Ireland. But, rather like Handel at Canons or Burlington House, Geminiani accepted accommodation (on the footing of family rather than servant) and protection, but reserved the right to come and go as he pleased. From the letter quoted above it is clear that while he accompanied Lord Tullamore abroad, he was independent and responsible for his own expenses. Only once do we find a record of him invoking immunity as a member of the Earl of Essex's household, and then only as a last resort. Hawkins reports the incident:

> The late earl of Essex was a lover of music, and had been taught the violin by Geminiani, who at times had been resident in his lordship's family; upon this ground the earl was prevailed on to inroll the name of Geminiani in the list of those servants of his whom he meant to screen from the process of the law.
>
> The notification of the security which Geminiani had thus obtained was not so general as to answer the design of it. A creditor for a small sum of money arrested him, and threw him into the prison of the Marshalsea, from whence, upon an application to his protector, he was, however, in a very short time discharged.[13]

Despite later assumptions that this was the result of fraudulent dealing in pictures, this is nowhere documented (and the incident, being undated, may actually have taken place before he started art dealing); in fact a "small sum of money" is hardly commensurate with the price of any painting that would have been considered worth faking.

In his character assassination, Burney guardedly cites, without names, "very good judges" for ratification of his opinion that Geminiani lacked expertise in fine art, and concludes that it was by "chicane" he managed to profit. Hawkins merely mentions a lack of prudence (presumably financial rather than artistic) and Hayes ventures no opinion on his skills, merely deploring "the Capriciousness and Inconstancy of his Temper".[14] Obviously

---

[13] HAWKINS, v, pp. 240-241. A graphic account of a fellow-musician who was also imprisoned in the Marshalsea, in 1729, can be found in *Handel's Trumpeter: the Diary of John Grano*, edited by John Ginger, Stuyvesant (NY), Pendragon Press, 1998.

[14] And Hayes, to give him his due, while comparing Handel to Rubens did admit Geminiani to be "the *Titian* in music" ([HAYES, William.] *Op. cit.* [see note 7], p. 128) — a comparison which must have gratified both composers.

other documented facts are needed against which to test Burney's thesis and answer the obvious questions which arise: can we discover which paintings he owned and sold? If so, are these pictures examples of bad or uninformed taste? Were they willfully misdescribed? Most important, were the prices that Geminiani got notably lower than other dealers achieved or substantially different from earlier or later selling prices for the same work?

★★★

The most detailed documentary evidence of paintings that passed through Geminiani's hands can be found in auction catalogues, two printed (1725, 1742) and two others (1741, 1743) whose details are preserved in the Houlditch MS;[15] the 1742 sale ("Monsr de Piles's Sale of Pictures brought over and sold by Geminiani") is also found in the Houlditch MS, where not only the hammer prices but also the names of many of the purchasers are listed.[16] Supplemented by mentions in the popular press, we can create at least a partial chronology of the composer's commercial art activities.

Charles Avison claimed that Geminiani had arrived in England in 1714 already "in the Capacity of an Italian Merchant" and "without any Intention of professing the Art [of Music]",[17] so we may imagine his first ten years in London included some private trading in pictures. The earliest mention of a public sale comes from a London newspaper advertisement (as yet no catalogue has been located) for an auction in 1723 which seems to have been a combined household clearance and art sale:

Daily Post, Tuesday, 19 March 1723

> To be Sold by AUCTION, On Thursday the 21st Instant, a curious Collection of Paintings, by the most eminent Italian and other Masters, with some very good Household Furniture, as large Peer and Chimney Glasses, Walnut-Tree Chairs, cover'd with Silver Brocade, &c. being the entire Collection of Mr. Geminiani, will be sold on Thursday the 21st Instant, at his Lodgings, the Blue Ball in Duke-Street, York-Buildings. The Collection may be seen at the House aforesaid this Day, to Morrow, and Thursday till the Time of Sale, which will begin at

---

[15]   Victoria and Albert Museum, London, MSL/1938/868: *Sales Catalogues of the Principal Collections of Pictures Sold by Auction in England 1711-1759.*

[16]   See APPENDIX I (pp. 439-460) for full transcriptions of the catalogues and additional comments.

[17]   *Newcastle Courant*, 17 September 1768.

11 a-clock in the Forenoon. Catalogues may be had Gratis at the Place of Sale, and at Mr. Cock's the Upper End of Broad-street near Golden-Square.

The sale of his "*entire* collection" including furnishings rather than select art works suggests some pressure on Geminiani. Could this be related to the Marshalsea incident described above? May Geminiani have been planning to leave London? Or might there be a connection with plans for the formation of the Masonic Lodge called "Philo-Musicae et Architecturae Societas",[18] in preparation for which Geminiani was initiated early in 1725? One of the prime objectives of this Lodge seems to have been to encourage subscriptions to Geminiani's first set of arrangements of the Corelli Op. 5 sonatas as concertos, and it is possible that the 1723 sale was needed to finance the engraving of this collection.

On Wednesday, 21 April 1725, another auction is announced in the *Daily Courant* of

[...] The valuable and exceeding fine Collection of Mr. Geminiani's Choice Paintings, by the most Eminent Italian and other Masters; at the Green Door in the Little-Piazza, Covent-Garden [...].

This may have been Geminiani's modest official start at public dealing, since the auctioneer Christopher Cock felt the need to add an apology in a footnote:

N.B. This Collection consists but of 98 Pictures, which will be Sold in two Days, so that the Sale will end each Day before Three in the Afternoon; and on Saturday next will be sold likewise, a valuable Library of Books. Catalogues to be had at the Place aforesaid.[19]

Two copies of the printed catalogue for this picture sale have survived (in the Frick Collection and the J. Paul Getty Museum: see pp. 443-446, and a full transcription in APPENDIX I, pp. 439-442). Unlike his later sales recorded in the Houlditch MS, the 1725 auction consists primarily of Dutch and Flemish pictures with a few canvases attributed to fashionable Italian *Seicento* painters

---

[18]   See Andrew Pink's study of 'Francesco Geminiani and Freemasonry' in the present volume, pp. 369-398.

[19]   Geminiani's later sale in 1743 contained over 160 items; that of 1742 offered a mere 83 (but from the Piles collection). No copy of the catalogue for the sale of books mentioned by Cock has yet been located.

such as Carlo Dolci. The generic titles and presence of undoubted copies, such as the version of Van Dyck's portrait of the Earl of Strafford, suggest it was a collection of modest value assembled in Britain. In 1729 an incidental mention of Geminiani in an announcement for a sale (6 May) of the estate of the late Hewer Edgley Hewer mentions, amongst several hundred lots, "[…] The famous Picture of TINTORET, once belonging to Mr. Geminiani, several Sea Pieces of the best Vanderveld's, and many other Paintings by several Italian and other Masters", in addition to "two fine Organs, a Harpsichord, and a small Library".[20] Clearly the Tintoretto was sufficiently known in the art-world to need no identification other than the name of its previous owner. In the catalogue for the eleventh day of the sale it is similarly incognito — "Lot 57. A very large and celebrated Picture by Tintoret."[21] — but it can probably be equated with the single canvas attributed to Tintoretto listed in Geminiani's 1725 sale: "Lot 93. St. *Francis* and a Glory by *Tintoret*". From the number of musical instruments advertised in 1729 we might also hazard that Mr Hewer had been part of Geminiani's personal circle.

Geminiani was evidently active in the London art market; occasional mention of him making purchases from other vendors can also be found in the Houlditch MS, such as: from Samuel Paris' "Sale of Pictures 1738/9 […] Lot 10 C. Lorrain Architecture and Ships £6 10s" and from the sale of the enigmatic dealer "Major" in April 1751, "Lot 29 Hans Holbein A portrait £1 13s" and "Lot 36 Rembrandt Our Saviour £2 2s".[22]

If the ascriptions are correct this shows fine classical taste and an interest in the new French style, in addition to a very modest outlay. However, the three catalogues from the early 1740s copied into the Houlditch MS provide the richest evidence of Geminiani's dealings and give us invaluable information on prices and even purchasers for three consecutive years. All three sales present Geminiani selling in his own right; although the Houlditch MS describes that of 1742 as "Monsr de Piles's Sale of Pictures brought over and sold by Geminiani", the printed catalogue specifically states the more commercially astute: "Lately purchased and Brought from *Paris* by Mr. Geminiani".

There is some debate as to whether "de Piles" refers to the critic and amateur Roger de Piles (1635-1709) or Jacques André du Pille, Vicomte du Monteuil (1680-1740). The latter's collection, for which little documentation

---

[20]   *Daily Journal*, Tuesday, 22 April 1729.

[21]   From *A Catalogue of all the Houshold Furniture and other valuable effects of Hewer Edgeley Hewer* […] *Brought from his seat at Clapham, to his house in Buckingham street, York-Buildings, etc.* GB-Lbl: S.C.330.(5.); entries are unpriced.

[22]   For Samuel Paris and his dubious dealings, see below, p. 431.

has survived, was apparently dispersed on his death, possibly directly to Geminiani. Although neither Charles Blanc nor Lugt record a public auction of the de Piles' collection, the Courtauld catalogue clearly states "*Monsieur De Piles'* celebrated Gallery of Capital Pictures". The association has not previously been questioned by scholars, who have accepted that de Piles' collection was dispersed in London by Geminiani. Indeed, the internal evidence of the 1742 catalogue at first supports this claim, particularly two items: Lot 77, listed as "A Girl leaning att a Window" attributed to Rembrandt and apparently purchased by the Duke of Bedford for the substantial sum of £67 4s and Lot 65, a "Venus and Adonis" attributed to Paolo Veronese and sold to Frederick Prince of Wales for £68 5s.

The first is still in the collection of the Duke of Bedford at Woburn Abbey where a bill survives, dated 29-30 April 1742 for £67 4s, agreeing with the Houlditch figure.[23] This has in the past been identified as the painting mentioned by Roger de Piles in his *Cours de Peinture par Principes*, first published in 1708: "Rembrant, par exemple, se divertit un jour à faire le portrait de sa servante, pour l'exposer à une fenêtre & tromper les yeux des passans. Cela lui réüssit; car on ne s'apperçût que quelques jours après de la tromerie. Ce n'etoit comme on peut bien se l'imaginer de Rembrant, ni la beauté du dessein, ni la noblesse des expressions qui avoient produit cet effet", further adding: "je l'achetai, & il tient aujourd'hui une place considerable dans mon cabinet".[24]

The Veronese is also still identifiable in the Royal Collection and is now at Holyrood House.[25] First recorded in an inventory of paintings at Kew made in 1800-1805 for Frederick's son, George III,[26] Shearman (p. xxiv) describes it bleakly as "a hard, characterless and somewhat damaged version of a composition known from an etching by S. F. Ravenet after a canvas attributed to Veronese in the 'Cabinet M Dupille'".

Although both Rembrandt's "Cook at an open door" and Veronese's "Venus and Adonis" apparently point to Roger de Piles, closer investigation suggests that Jacques André du Pille is a more likely candidate. Firstly, whilst de Piles' description of Rembrandt's cook fits the painting now attributed to Rembrandt's pupil Samuel van Hoogstaten at Woburn, there are in fact

---

[23]   Reference: 4D-A1-2-40-44; box reference: NMR 2/38/6. The painting is documented in the catalogue: *Paintings and Silver From Woburn Abbey, lent by the Duke of Bedford*, London, The Arts Council, 1950, cat. no. 78, *A Girl at a House Door*.

[24]   DE PILES, Roger. *Cours de peinture par principes*, Paris, Jacques Estienne, 1708, pp. 10-11.

[25]   SHEARMAN, John. *The Early Italian Pictures in the Collection of Her Majesty the Queen*, Cambridge, Cambridge University Press, 1983, cat. no. 321.

[26]   Manuscript in The Surveyor's Office, entitled "A Catalogue of the Pictures at Kew House".

several more convincing candidates for the painting described by de Piles, the one accepted by most scholars being Rembrandt's *Girl at a Window* (now in the Dulwich Picture Gallery).[27] Recent provenance research has revealed that the Dulwich picture was probably sold by Gersaint on 17 December, 1747 as Lot 435; Gersaint quotes de Piles' words and adds:

> Ce Tableau, depuis la mort de M. de Piles, a passé successivement dans les Cabinets les plus fameux, où rien n'entroit qui ne fût décidé assez parfait, pour mériter d'y trouver place. Il y a tout lieu de penser qu'il aura encore aujourd'hui le même avantage. C'est M. Duvivier, Officier dans les Gardes Françoises, & Oncle de M. de Fonspertuis, qui l'a possedé après M. de Piles. Delà il passa a M. le Compte d'Hoym, après le décès duquel M. de Morvil en fit l'acquisition; & enfin M. de Fonspertuis s'en rendit l'Acquéreur à la vente que l'on fit après la mort de ce Ministre.[28]

The picture was apparently purchased by J.-B. P. LeBrun who in turn sold it to the founders of Dulwich, Noel Desenfans and Francis Bourgeois.[29] Secondly, the engraving of the Veronese from the *Recuil Crozat* is inscribed "Cabinet M Dupille", not de Piles, and was published in 1729, long after de Piles' death.

By the 1740s Roger de Pile's collection had evidently been dispersed, since works of this provenance can be identified in earlier sales catalogues.[30] Most of his collection of drawings seems to have passed to his friend and supporter Pierre Crozat, and several lots are listed as having a de Piles provenance in

---

[27] See ABBING, Michiel Roscam. 'De trompe-l'oeil-anekdote over Rembrandts dienstmeisje van Roger de Piles,' in: *Kroniek Van Het Rembrandthuis*, XLIV/2, 1992, vol. II, pp. 2-22; and CAVALLI-BJÖRKMAN, Görel. 'Rembrandt's *The Kitchen Maid*; Problems of Provenance and Iconography', in: *Rembrandt and His Pupils*, edited by Görel Cavalli-Björkman, Stockholm, Nationalmuseum, 1993, pp. 68-76.

[28] *Catalogue raisonné, des bijoux, porcelaines, bronzes [...] provenans de la Succession de M. Angran, Vicomte de Fonspertuis, [...] Par E. F. Gersaint*, Paris, Pierre Prault, 1747, pp. 201-202.

[29] Other candidates appeared during the nineteenth century, including Willem Drost's *Cook at a Window* now in Lille. For an excellent discussion of the provenance of the Drost picture see: BIKKER, Jonathan. *Willem Drost; A Rembrandt Pupil in Amsterdam and Venice*, New Haven (CT)-London, Yale University Press, 2005, cat. no. 11.

[30] For example, in the inventory of the collection of Charles d'Hoym (d. 1736), no. 580 is listed as "Une figure de bronze de 2 pieds de hauteur, representant l'Antinous, faisant pendant au petit Flûteur ci-devant, no 577, Venant de chez M. du Pile, Achetée du Sieur Hébert 350*l.*" (PICHON, Jérôme. *Vie de Charles-Henry Comte de Hoym, Ambassadeur de Saxe-Pologne en France, et célèbre amateur de livres*, Paris, Société des bibliophiles François, 1880, vol. II, p. 113).

Mariette's catalogue of the 1741 Crozat sale[31] (for example Lot 840, Rubens: "Ces quatre-vigne-quatorze Têtes formoient cidevant un volume que M. de Piles avoit apporte de Flandres").[32]

On the other hand the entry for Du Pille in the 1776 *Dictionnaire de la noblesse*[33] reads: "Jacques André du Pille, Ecuyer, Vicomte de Monteil dans la Marche, Seigneur de Saleuillete, Tresorier Général de l'Extraordinaire des Guerres, & des Troupes de la Maison du Roi, moert le 17 Mai 1740 [...]". The date of Geminiani's sale would therefore seem to support the case for Du Pille as the still uncertain origin of this collection.

Several of the paintings sold in 1742 can be identified and located today; the following selection offers specific evidence of Geminiani's taste, attributions and prices realised. Titian's *A Venetian Nobleman, half Length*, bought by the Duke of Bedford for £52 10s was possibly one of the pictures seen by Horace Walpole in the "common eating-parlour" at Woburn in October 1751: "Salon 'A man by Titian, very fine'". This portrait is still at Woburn, but now relegated to "Venetian School".[34] The Duke also purchased a pair of works by Poussin, *A Large Landschape and Figures* (£90 6s) and *It's Companion* (£105), which may be Scharf cat. nos 408, 409 or 410[35] and possibly the pictures seen by Horace Walpole in the 'salon' at Woburn in October 1751: "Two fine large Gaspar Poussin's". If so, they were sold from Woburn in 1951 (Christie's, 19 January 1951, Lots 47 and 95). Lot 47 was purchased by J. A. Tooth and eventually acquired by the Birmingham City Museum and Art Gallery (inv.104.51); it is a coastal scene with brigands, dated by Boisclair to 1657.[36] Lot 95 was with Richard L. Feigen & Co, New York in 1984, and is dated by Boisclair to c1670.[37] The pictures were probably called pendants only by Geminiani as they are clearly not related, although both are still considered autograph. Waagen on his visit to Woburn in 1854 observed:

---

[31] Drawn up by Pierre-Jean Mariette in 1741, this is the first example of the modern descriptive sale catalogue.

[32] See EIDELBERG, Martin. 'An Album of Drawings from Rubens' Studio', in: *Master Drawings*, XXXV/3 (Autumn 1997), pp. 234-266.

[33] CHESNAYE-DESBOIS, François-Alexandre Aubert de la. *Dictionnaire de la Noblesse*, Paris, Veuve Duchesne, 1776, vol. II.

[34] Information kindly provided by the archivist, Chris Gravett.

[35] SCHARF, Sir George. *A Descriptive and Historical Catalogue of the Collection of Pictures at Woburn Abbey*, London, Bradbury, Agnew & Co., 1877.

[36] BOISCLAIR, Marie-Nicole. *Gaspard Dughet 1615-1675, Sa vie et son œuvre*, Paris, Arthéna, 1986, cat. no. 148.

[37] *Ibidem*, cat. no. 329.

The saloon. 3. A sea view. On the left a chain of hills receding one behind the other. Pictures by this master in which the sea is the principal subject are seldom met with. This equally bears witness, however to the grandeur of his mode of conception. Unfortunately dark in some parts.[38]

The Duke of Devonshire bought *A Man's Head with a Turban* by Rembrandt (£78 15s), listed by Robert Dodesley in 1762 as hanging in the 'Withdrawing room' of Devonshire House, and known as "An old man in a Turkish dress, Rembrant".[39] It is now called *King Uzziah Stricken with Leprosy*, still accepted as an autograph Rembrandt and still in the Devonshire Collection, Chatsworth. In 1999 it was established that the painting came from the collection of the Saxon Count Charles Henry d'Hoym (1694-1736) in Paris. It had originated from the "palais Mazarin", indicating the painting had been owned by Cardinal Jules Mazarin.[40] When in Mazarin's collection it was called a portrait of a Pasha, and in a letter from Elpidio Benedetti to Mazarin, dated 8 February 1661, he refers to "col ritratto di quell Bassa che V[otre] Em[inence] Desidera". The presence of the painting in d'Hoym's collection also suggests that not all the pictures in Geminiani's sale came via the collection of Roger de Piles — an alternative explanation is that at least this picture passed directly from d'Hoym to du Pille.

The Prince of Wales made eleven purchases in all at the 1742 sale: *Diana and Acteon* by Bassano (£73 10s) is possibly the painting recorded as being cleaned in 1747 by John Anderson ("Nymphs Bathing Bassan").[41] George Vertue mentioned two paintings by Bassano in the Prince's closet at Leicester House in 1749 (Vertue, vol. I, p. 11), and in 1750 he noted a painting of "Diana Bathing" by Bassano in the Prince's collection (BL Add. MS 19027, f.20).

The *Diana and Acteon* by Titian, on the other hand, is a mystery; it was clearly highly regarded (£173 5s was a substantial price in the eighteenth century), yet there is no mention of it ever entering the Royal Collection. Wethey records

---

[38]   WAAGEN, Gustav Friedrich. *Galleries and Cabinets of Art in Great Britain: being an account of more than forty collections of paintings, drawings, sculptures, MSS., &c. &c.*, London, John Murray, 1857, p. 333.

[39]   *London and its Environs Described Containing an Account of Whatever is most Remarkable for Grandeur, Elegance, Curiosity or Use*, 6 vols, London, R. and J. Dodsley, 1761, vol. II, p. 226.

[40]   MICHEL, Patrick. *Mazarin, prince des collectionneurs*, Paris, Réunion des Musées Nationaux, 1999, p. 333, no. 179. There is a copy at Kingston Lacy, Dorset, which was made in Rome for Sir Ralph Bankes by N. Wray, before 1659 when it is recorded in his London house. See ABBING, Michiel Roscam. *Rembrandt 2006: New Rembrandt Documents*, 2 vols, Leiden, Foleor Publishers, 2006, vol. I, pp. 77-78.

[41]   Duchy of Cornwall Office, XVIII, p. 548. See RORSCHACH, Kimerly. 'Frederick, Prince of Wales (1707-51) as Collector and Patron', in: *Walpole Society*, LV (1989-1990), p. 58.

it under "literary reference" but provides no solution.[42] It might be that, like the Wouvermans below, Frederick sold it soon after the sale; if so, it could be any of the copies listed by Wethey with no provenance before 1742, or it could be that the compiler of the Houlditch MS was mistaken in the buyer's name.

The Holy Family by Cignani (£98 12s) is possibly the painting still in the Royal Collection and catalogued by Michael Levey (cat. no. 421) as Simone Cantarini, *The Virgin with Child Showing Her a Cross*, which was recorded at Buckingham House in the reign of George III, but later attributed to Carlo Cignani. Vertue also mentioned a painting by Cignani in Prince Frederick's collection in 1750 (BL Add. MS 19037, f. 20).

A Stag Hunting and *It's Companion*, both by Wouverman (£73 10s and £110 5s) were acquired by the Staatliche Kunstsammlungen, Gemäldegalerie Alte Meister, Dresden.[43] They were apparently purchased by the painter and dealer, Hyacinthe Rigaud and Louis Le Leu in 1743; the pictures are given a de Piles provenance in the engraving by Le Bas.[44]

★★★

Armed with such documentation it should now be possible to isolate and answer the questions of price, competence and honesty in Geminiani's art dealings with specific comparisons.

In the sales of 1741 and 1743 Geminiani offered three pairs of works by Chardin, including what must have been versions of either *Un jeune dessinateur* or *Un jeune dessinateur taillant son crayon*. On the first day of the 1741 sale, Lots 19 and 20 (*A boy at his Drawing* and *A Girl at Needle Work, its companion*) made £24 3s. On the first day of the 1743 sale two "sketches" of these same compositions (Lot 21, *A Girl at her Needle, a sketch* and Lot 22, *Its Companion*) made only £0 14s. However, on the second day Lot 104, *A Girl with Needlework* made £12 12s. and Lot 105, *Its companion* made £7 1s 6d, prices which suggest that they may be identical with Lots 19 and 20 in the 1741 sale. The progress of these pictures through later auctions and collections, traced by David Carritt in *The Burlington Magazine*,[45] shows that Lots 104 and 105 later formed part

---

[42]   WETHEY, Harold. *The Paintings of Titian: III; the Mythological and Historical Paintings*, London, Phaidon, 1975, cat. no. 9, literary reference no. 5.

[43]   WOERMANN, Karl. *Katalog der Königlichen Gemäldegalerie zu Dresden*, Dresden, Hoffmann, 1905, cat. nos 1414 (now lost) and 1443.

[44]   See *Dresde ou le rêve des Princes, La Galerie de peintures au XVIIIᵉ siècle*, exhibition catalogue (Musée des Beaux-Arts de Dijon), Paris, Réunion des musées nationaux, 2001, p. 254.

[45]   CARRITT, David. 'Mr. Fauquier's Chardins', in: *The Burlington Magazine*, CXVI/858 (September 1974), pp. 507-508.

of the collection of one Roger Harenc (a name found in the subscription lists of Geminiani's music publications) which was sold after his death in 1764 by Langford and Sons (1–3 March); there they made £4 14s 6d and £9 19s 6d respectively which, given the increased fame of Chardin in the intervening two decades, demonstrates Geminiani's ability to achieve an impressively high market price.

The 1742 sale, the best annotated of the Houlditch accounts, stands out as a social and political occasion; amongst the named purchasers were the leading Whig supporters of Robert Walpole, including George, Earl of Cholmondeley (son-in-law of Walpole), Francis Seymour-Conway, Marquess of Hertford (Walpole's nephew by marriage), Thomas Winnington (a profligate Whig supporter of Walpole), James Cavendish, Duke of Devonshire and John Russell, Duke of Bedford. Less aligned were John Boyle, 5th Earl of Cork and Orrery, a Tory biographer and writer, plus Frederick, Prince of Wales, who at this date was a focus for anti-Walpole Whig politics.

With the marked absence of dealers from this sale, and a concentration of not only fashionable aristocrats but politically active ones, it is interesting to speculate on the auction house as an arena to act out personal and political rivalries — to the advantage of the seller. George Vertue noted of this auction that "in the sale of Geminiani's pictures Peter Lance showd away. Bought many high priced pictures — for himself or by commission. After an extravagant manner".[46] The high prices of the 1742 sale are confirmed by subsequent appearances of the same pictures in almost contemporary sales: Sir John Rawdon, the Irish politician and connoisseur who is recorded as a purchaser in the Houlditch MS, sold part of his collection in an auction organized by Christopher Cock in 1744, including two pictures which had been purchased from Geminiani two years earlier: Lot 45, "A sacrifice" by Rembrandt, was sold for £21 to Bellis, having been purchased for £39 8s, and Lot 49, "St. Peter in prison", which can probably be identified as "Joseph and Pharaoh's cup bearer" from the 1742 sale, attributed to Ribera (called Spanioletto), Rawdon bought for £175 7s and sold for £89 5s, also to Bellis. Rawdon therefore made substantial losses of almost 50% on his purchases from Geminiani.

In most areas Geminiani's taste is fairly conventional although the presence of a number of contemporary French paintings (including the Chardins discussed above) in the 1741 sale is unusual and probably reflects his experience and connections in Paris — the Boucher (1743, Lot 59) appears to

---

[46] Mr Lance is probably the miniaturist Bernard Lens III, according to the annotation in VERTUE, George. *Notebooks*, 6 vols, London, The Walpole Society, 1929-1950, vol. III (The Walpole Society, 22), p. 109 (May 1742).

be the earliest example of the artist's work in an English sale. In the 1742 sale, Lot 7, the picture of *St. Jerome* attributed to J. Bellini and purchased by Lord Duncannon stands out since at this date Bellini was not a common name and the taste for *quattrocento* Italian painting had yet to develop. That said, Bellini, as Titian's master would have been of art historical interest.[47] Otherwise the high prices achieved by Geminiani for Dutch and Italian paintings of the 16th and 17th centuries are entirely consistent with other contemporary sales and the composition of contemporary collections.[48]

Although there is surely more documentation to be unearthed on Geminiani's auctions, the dated evidence we now have can help in suggesting a pattern to his dealing and some possible reasons for the timing of his sales. Several of the documented sales, for instance, seem to have preceded a period of lavish music publication; the 1725 sale took place just as subscriptions opened for the first instalment of his concerto arrangements of Corelli's Op. 5 which appeared the following year (his last publication had been Op. 1 in 1716, shortly after his arrival in England), the 1740s sales before an intensive period of publication over several years with the Opp. 4 and 7 concertos, the Op. 5 sonatas (both cello and violin versions), the *Pièces de Clavecin* and the beginning of his sequence of treatises. This suggests better financial discipline than many accounts impute, and a realistic attitude to maintaining his independence, comparable with Handel, who took his risks in the world of opera rather than becoming indentured, and as a result suffered accordingly. Geminiani prudently took care not to initiate the actual printing of a volume until sufficient subscribers had committed to the venture — hence the delayed appearance, for example, of the Op. 7 concertos which were offered for subscription in 1746 (and were in fact engraved with an over-optimistic 1746 title-page), but only issued in 1748. The *Guida Armonica* had an even more protracted genesis, with subscriptions first solicited in 1740 but publication delayed until 1756.

Contrary to the claims of Burney and Hawkins that he gave preference to his frenzy for art, it appears that Geminiani deliberately planned to sell his paintings in order to pay for the publication of his music, just as he had earlier used them to cover travelling expenses. It seems that he simply saw investing in paintings as a safer alternative to banking or the Stock Exchange — and he would not have been unaware of Handel's narrow

---

[47] Duncannon was William Ponsonby, later second Earl of Bessborough, but the Bellini does not appear in his posthumous sale (Christie's, 5 February 1801).

[48] PEARS, Iain. *The Discovery of Painting; The Growth of Interest in the Arts in England 1680-1768*, New Haven (CT)-London, Yale University Press, 1988, remains the most authoritative collation of prices from the period.

escape from financial calamity when the South Sea Bubble burst in 1720 and ruined many speculators.

Despite Burney's analysis of Geminiani's problems and mismanagement, and Hawkins' prediction of "loss… and necessity", it would seem that Geminiani had soon accumulated sufficient resources to set up his own Great Room in Dublin for the double purpose of art sales and concerts — exactly the recipe which, by Burney's reckoning, should have already bankrupted him. This venture was modelled on the London establishments which he knew well (such as Hickford's Great Room near the Haymarket in which he had begun a concert series in 1731) and was a rival to the nearby Great Room in Crow Street, Dublin, built in 1731 at the request of the Musical Academy for the Practice of Italian Musick. See p. 173 of the present volume for a summary by Barra Boydell of the art auctions held in "Geminiani's Great Room" up to the last years of the composer's life.

Geminiani was not alone in his twin enthusiasms — Handel,[49] Valentini, Locatelli, Nicola Haym[50] and Geminiani's violinist rival in Paris, Giovanni Battista Somis (another Corelli pupil) were also well-known musical art-collectors, as was Corelli himself (who was also notorious for defaulting on payment).[51] But while none of these was even a *marchand amateur*, Geminiani aspired to be — and was accepted as — a professional; the international aspect of such a career was much aided by his musical connections through which he had the advantage of being equally at home in the upper echelons of several countries. In short, the others *collected* for pleasure, whereas Geminiani *dealt* in order to survive.

A number of less well-connected French dealers tried to sell paintings directly in Britain; in 1749 Pierre Rémy and Jean-Baptiste Slodtz jointly purchased Veronese's *Venus and Adonis* (the original as opposed to the

---

[49]   Handel's private collection is reconstructed and illustrated in McGeary, Thomas. 'Handel as Art Collector: Art, Connoisseurship and Taste in Hanoverian Britain', in: *Early Music*, XXXVII/4 (2009), pp. 533-576.

[50]   *Hawkins*, V, p. 169, states that Haym "abandoning the profession of music, betook himself to another, viz., that of a collector of pictures". He was employed by distinguished patrons such as Robert Walpole and the Duke of Bedford, and his personal collection ultimately included "between ten and twenty thousand fine drawings, etchings, and engravings". See Lindgren, Lowell E. 'Introduction', in: *Nicola Francesco Haym: Complete Sonatas Part 1*, edited by Lowell E. Lindgren, Middleton (WI), A-R Editions, 2002, p. xii.

[51]   Wolfe, Karin. 'Il pittore e il musicista. Il sodalizio artistico tra Francesco Trevisani e Arcangelo Corelli', in: *Arcangelo Corelli: fra mito e realtà storica*, edited by Gregory Barnett, Antonella D'Ovidio and Stefano La Via, 2 vols, Florence, Olschki, 2007, vol. I, pp. 169-188. Corelli was a close friend of the painters Carlo Cignani and Carlo Maratta, both of whose works feature in Geminiani's lists.

copy included in Geminiani's sale) at the Malson d'Bercy sale for 3,000 livres; however, it was apparently unsuccessful in London, and remained in Rémy's collection after Slodtz's death. According to Wildenstein, the Veronese "devait être envoyé à Londres à leurs risques et périls pour y être vendu".[52] Precisely how it was offered for sale in London is unclear, or whether Rémy had an English business partner, but it is certain that the Veronese was not a lone venture. At the Crozat/Tugny sale in 1751 both Slodtz and Rémy are listed as major purchasers.[53] Titian's *Adoration of the Shepherds* bought by Rémy for 280 livres was successfully sold in London to a British collector,[54] General John Guise, passing from his collection to Christ Church, Oxford in 1765; the painting is recorded at Guise's George Street house, off Hanover Square, in 1761.[55]

In turn, it was already established that most major English dealers were buying pictures in France to sell in England. Andrew Hay is often seen as the first professional art dealer in Britain.[56] In 1719 he overreached himself on a buying trip to Paris and his brother, George, was forced to ask his patrons to advance Hay credit.[57] Hay made over fifteen buying trips to France, according to Vertue, but Pears points out that he avoided speculating too deeply, by dealing increasingly in low value paintings. In 1738 Hay wrote: "as to the virtu, the profitts are far short of what they used to be, and I am not yet determined whether to log another journey. I see several pictures sold here att sales cheaper than I would pay for them abroad".[58] Between 1738 and 1745 the average value of painting sold by Hay was between £7 15s and £11 5s and only on one occasion did a picture fetch more than £60 — very poor returns compared with Geminiani's sale prices.[59]

---

[52] WILDENSTEIN, Daniel. *Documents inédits sur les artistes français du XVIIIᵉ siècle*, Paris, Les Beaux Arts, 1966, p. 127.

[53] *Catalogue des Tableaux et sculptures, Tant en Bronze qu'en Marbre, du Cabinet de feu M. le President de Tugny, & de celui de M. Crozat*, Paris, Louis-François Delatour, 1750.

[54] Lot 45: Titian, 'Les Bergers adorant l'Enfant Jesus dans l'etable de Bethleem. Tableau qui a appartenu a Charles Ier, roi d'Angleterre. Il y en a une estampe gravee du temps meme du peintre. Trois pieds sur quarante et un pouces'. See YARKER, Jonathan. 'Copies after Titian and the Market in late 18th-century England', in: *The Reception of Titian in Britain, 1769-1877*, edited by Peter Humfrey, Turnhout, Brepols, 2011.

[55] *London and its Environs Described [...]*, *op. cit.* (see note 39), vol. VI, pp. 26-27. SHAW, J. Byam. *Paintings by Old Masters at Christ Church Oxford*, London, Phaidon, 1967, cat. no. 79.

[56] PEARS, Iain. *Op. cit.* (see note 48), p. 77.

[57] *Ibidem*, p. 79.

[58] Letter 10 June 1738, Scottish Record Office, *Clerk of Penicuick MSS*, GD/18/4665/2 quoted in PEARS, Iain. *Op. cit.* (see note 48), p. 89.

[59] *Ibidem*, pp. 84-85.

Some trade was certainly conducted with dishonest intent; Samuel Paris lived in France specifically buying paintings to be exported, but was reported in a letter from a French dealer to be making and selling copies as originals in England. Writing to Robert Walpole on 15 April 1733, the French dealer de Roussel reported that:

> il y a ici un appellé Paris peintre quy achète des tableaux pour les vendre il vint chez moy il vut mes tableaux admirables il me tendit un piège [...] il me dit que comme je ne recevois pas beaucoup de monde sais que le les envoyer mes tableauz chez lui qu'il avoit fait vendre je sais que l'etoit pour les faire copier et puis il avoit vendu les copies pour des originaux.[60]

We have noted above that Geminiani bought a "Lorrain" from one of Paris' English sales, but at a price which suggests it could not have been a genuine Claude. Later dealers like Richard Bragge also found it expedient to form a partnership with a local associate, importing pictures purchased on his behalf at the Potier sale in 1757 and Tallard sale in 1756 by the French dealer Rémy.[61]

Geminiani's activities differ from these examples in several respects: most tellingly, his level of financial commitment overall was considerably greater than Hay's — to finance expenditure in Paris on the level of the 1742 'de Piles' sale in particular, he would have needed considerable capital, or the backing of an influential patron. Nor is there any evidence (other than Burney's generic assumption that all Italians were crooks) that he emulated Samuel Paris in encouraging faking; nor are more works known to be misattributed in his lists than in other catalogues of the period (and in most cases it is only recent research which has been responsible for many reattributions). Geminiani's descriptions (it is assumed they were written by him) in fact contain a slightly *higher* proportion of "school of", "after", "disciple of", "stile of" or "in the manner of" disclaimers than others recorded in the Houlditch MS.

★★★

Geminiani was known to many professional painters, and sat for more of them than most of his contemporaries, Handel excepted. Surviving

---

[60] Letter de Roussel to Walpole, 15 April 1733, Cambridge University Library, Cholmondely (Houghton) Papers, C(H) Correspondence 1968, quoted in *Ibidem*, pp. 88-89.

[61] *Ibidem*, p. 247, n. 143. They are listed in the annotated catalogues as "pour l'Angleterre" or "pour Dr Bragge".

portraits, or mentions of portraits are listed in APPENDIX II (pp. 461-475), and while precise dates are in most cases difficult to establish, an approximate chronological order would place the Soldi as the earliest representation, followed by Latham, Jenkins, Anon (Royal College of Music, London), Bouchardon and Hoare.

Although Geminiani always had the accoutrements of a composer included in his portraits, he is noticeably never shown with a violin;[62] in the early Andrea Soldi portrait, however, it is not even his own music that he is holding, as would be normal for a composer, but that of his teacher Corelli. The choice of the individual work was evidently of great significance to Geminiani, since the sheet music portrayed does not represent any actual printed edition but is cleverly reformatted by Soldi to feature the opening of the famous (and most recognizable) *Christmas Concerto* on a right-hand page. In the printed sources, *Concerto VIII* begins less conveniently on a left-hand page, and there are ten staves to the page rather than the eleven of Soldi's very convincing imitation. In other respects, however, the music and the engraving style are imitated with exactitude and notational accuracy. Some problems surrounding this portrait remain as yet unexplained: Geminiani, for example, is clearly in his mid-thirties, but when Soldi first arrived in England in 1736, Geminiani was 49. On the other hand, Geminiani left Italy when he was 32 but Soldi was only about 11. So far no evidence has come to light for him revisiting Florence in the 1720s, and in 1738, the most productive year of Soldi's career in England, when, according to Vertue, he produced "above thirty portraits" from April to August alone, Geminiani was 51. However the favourite blue coat is an authentic touch and is found in most other portraits (except that by Hoare where he wears brown): according to John O'Keeffe, remembering Geminiani later in life in Dublin, he was "a little man, sallow complexion, black eye-brows, pleasing face; his dress blue velvet heavy with gold embroidery".[63] The only surviving documentation of the picture is the seller's printed label on the reverse — J. Leger & Son (est. 1892), 13 Old Bond Street — filled in with sitter and artist and dated March 1956.

---

[62] The later frontispiece added to the posthumous Paris issue of *The Art of Playing on the Violin* (c1770) is, contrary to popular impression, not a portrait of Geminiani, but a remake of an engraving from HERRANDO, José. *Arte y puntual explicacion del modo de tocar el violin*, Paris, Joannes a Cruce faciebat, 1756.

[63] O'KEEFFE, John. *Recollections* [...] *written by Himself*, 2 vols, London, Colburn, 1826, vol. I, p. 57.

The 'Soldi problem' is further complicated by the portrait of Geminiani now in the Royal College of Music, London (estimated c1735) which was donated by Walter Goldsmith in 1966. At that time it too was recorded as being by Soldi, confirmed by an extant typed note on the reverse, although it is now catalogued by the RCM as anonymous. The suspicion cannot be stifled that some form of confusion or substitution might have taken place, the more glamorous 'Corelli' acquiring the pedigree of the Goldsmith picture.

William Hoare's portrait features, in addition to a page of illegible manuscript music with quill and inkstand, a bound volume titled in gold. Hoare was the leading portrait-painter in Bath before the arrival of Gainsborough (and painted other musicians, including Handel); he was described blandly as "an ingenious and amiable English artist". His patron, the Duke of Newcastle, Thomas Pelham-Holles also administered the allocation of Royal Privileges, including that granted to Geminiani to protect him from copyright piracy, for which he first petitioned in 1728.[64]

The Jenkins picture (at Gosford House in the collection of the Earl of Wemyss, but more widely known from the 1777 engraving by James MacArdell) also shows Geminiani at about the same age (late 40s), with quill, paper and inkstand (executed somewhat in the manner of Richard Wilson),[65] and in the Latham portrait, much applauded in Irish circles along with the same artist's portrait of the notorious actress Peg Woffington, he is simply holding a rolled-up scroll of paper with music notation. Although described by "Anthony Pasquin" (a pseudonym for John Williams) in 1796 as being "painted in so pure a stile, as to procure him the title of the *Irish*

---

[64] Geminiani's pioneering use of Privileges to protect his music has yet to be fully investigated; for the texts issued between 1739 and 1746 and utilised for Op. 5, see the Appendix of *Geminiani Opera Omnia*, vol. 5. However, Geminiani made application for such protection as early as 1728; the State Papers for Secretaries of State hold an introductory note from the Earl of Essex to the Duke of Newcastle: "Mr. Geminiary [*sic*] who has the honour to bring your grace this, is the gentleman you promised me the patent for the sole printing of his own music, which if your grace will be so good to order him, I shall take it as a particular favour, the sooner he has it the more service it will be to him." (20 March 1728, SP 36/5/). I am grateful to Andrew Pink for drawing my attention to this document.

[65] Pointed out by Jonathan Yarker, who speculates that Jenkins may have worked with Richard Wilson before they are both recorded in Venice in 1751; "Comparing the highly polished table, quill and silver ink-well with similar props in Wilson's portrait of *George III and the Duke of York* dated to 1749 in the Tate, suggests they might well have trained together".

Vandyke",[66] Latham's Geminiani portrait was mistaken for some time as the work of Thomas Hudson.[67]

Additional references to portraitists of Geminiani include James Parmentier, who was commissioned to paint a group portrait of the Directors of the Masonic Lodge *Philo-musicae et -architecturae societas Apollini* which was established in 1725; according to the Minutes of 14 October 1725[68] it was ordered

> That a Picture of the President Censors & Directors be painted on one large Canvas The Expence not to Exceed Three Hundred Pounds to [be] paid for out of the Publick Treasury of this Society.
>
> ORDERED
> That Bro[r] Parmentier do perform the same

However, after several part-payments had been made, Parmentier apologised for the "multitude of difficulties in carrying on the Design of painting [...] the Pictures in one Canvas" and proposed to "paint them separately in three Quarters Cloth for five Guineas each" (Minutes for 27 October 1726). No more is heard of this assignment and no portraits have been identified. Equally tantalising is the report from 1782 that in his will Joseph Kelway (a pupil of Geminiani and a leading keyboard player in London) "had given his picture of Germiniani [*sic*] and his own portrait to his 'faithful servant, Ann Phillips'".[69]

The message conveyed by a portrait in the eighteenth century was much more than a simple representation of a face; if the subject were still alive, it could indicate aspiration, pedigree, achievements and hobbies, tastes and wealth, close connections and matrimonial availability; if it was *post mortem*, then status, position in history, summary of achievements and in many instances a bulwark against the barbarians and the degeneration of standards since the subject's lifetime.

Charles Avison, Geminiani's most enthusiastic English disciple, typified this last reaction in a short burst of purple prose in the *Newcastle Literary Register*

---

66   PASQUIN Anthony. *An Authentic History of the Professors of Painting, Sculpture, & Architecture, who have Practised in Ireland; Involving Original Letters from Sir Joshua Reynolds, Which Prove him to have been Illiterate*, London, H. D. Symonds, Paternoster-Row - P. M'queen - T. Bellamy, King-Street, Covent-Garden [1796], p. 29.

67   See, for example, CARERI, plate 1, and the catalogue of The Royal Society of Musicians, London.

68   GB-Lbl, Add. MS 23202: *The Fundamental Constitution and Orders of the Society intitled* [*sic*] *Philo-musicæ et Architecturæ Societas*. See Andrew Pink's essay in the present volume, pp. 369-398, for fuller details of these Masonic activities.

69   *DNB*, London, 1921-1922, pp. 1248-1249.

seven years after Geminiani's death — but sadly without identifying which portrait raised these thoughts:[70]

> For the LITERARY REGISTER.
> On viewing a portrait of the late celebrated
> GEMINIANI.
> WHILE contending nations alarm the world abroad, and interiour commotions at home, I peruse *thy* pacific page, and wonderwhere the powers of music are fled, not to harmonize the passions of men; yet still the dulcet strains will live in congenial souls, to smooth the path of life which providence has given to lovers of harmony.
> *Newcastle.*   C.A.

★★★

One feature that separated Geminiani from his colleagues in the art-world was not only his enthusiasm for, but also a personal acquaintance with some of the most important contemporary French artists. The results can be seen both in the portrait sketch made of him in 1737 by Edmé Bouchardon, the great sculptor, and also in the way Geminiani carried over this resource into his music publications. Not only did the Bouchardon sketch feature in a much larger frontispiece for the 1739 issue of Op. 1 — Geminiani's features, in a medallion, are supported by the Genius of Music and the Three Graces, with Apollo above — but two other elaborate (and doubtless expensive) full-page engravings were designed by the same artist, and engraved by Ravenet for *A Treatise of Good Taste* and by Jean Aubert for Op. 7. The original *sanguine* studies for these designs are now in the Musée du Louvre, Paris (Inv. 23855 and 23856). In their final engravings as frontispieces, both scenes were filled with symbols, many of them suggesting Masonic connections (the Zodiac, the "Royal Arch", the waterfall — a standard ingredient of the "Petit Elu" degree —, Apollo etc.) if one is inclined to hunt for them. Since these are not found in the original sketches, one must assume they were added by the engraver on Geminiani's instructions, along with the additional tributes to the Prince of Wales in *Good Taste* (although his motto, "Ich Dien" is included in Bouchardon's sketch).

---

[70] *The Literary Register*, Newcastle, 1769, p. 278. See p. 330 of the present volume for a facsimile reproduction of this source.

Geminiani clearly cared as much about the appearance of his publications as for his own features on canvas. Moving beyond the frontispieces, his careful choice of the best available music engravers (including Marie-Charlotte Vendôme — sometimes spelled Vandome — the doyenne of French engravers) and elaborately designed title-pages show a determination to present his works in the best possible dress. Even his Op. 1 sonatas he had engraved by Thomas Cross (junior), once the best of the English craftsmen, but by 1716 well past his prime; Hawkins says that "he stamped the plates of Geminiani's solos and a few other publications, but in a very homely and illegible character, of which he was so little conscious that he set his name to every thing he did, even to single songs". Thereafter Geminiani whenever possible sought out French engravers and brought the plates back to England for publication (see Rudolf Rasch's description of some of these transactions in the present volume, pp. 113-150).

Two incidental pictorial compliments to Geminiani should be noted by way of postscript: in a portrait by Gainsborough of his friend the Ipswich organist and composer Joseph Gibbs, two volumes of bound music are included in the background, one titled "Corelli" the other (only partly visible) "Gem [...]"[71] — twin indicators of his musical taste; and in "The Sense of Hearing" by Philip Mercier, four anonymous ladies are playing flute, violin, cello and harpsichord with scores on the music desk marked "Hendel Operas" and "Geminiani's Sonates".[72] As another foreign artist in England, Mercier may well have selected these names as evidence of the two most famous musical immigrants who prospered in a British setting.

***

In sum, Geminiani may have seemed volatile in character and feckless with money (he would certainly not be the first Italian with these flaws) but after one brief brush with the Marshalsea he remained solvent all his life; in his art dealings he was demonstrably far from the frenzied amateur that Hawkins and Burney would have us believe, nor did he in the process neglect his personal musical ambitions. Most importantly, he showed that an

---

[71] Purchased from Gibbs' descendants by the National Portrait Gallery in 1928 (NPG 2179) and now on display at Beningbrough Hall; see KERSLAKE, John. *Early Georgian Portraits*, London, HMSO, 1977, p. 98; and SAYWELL, David - SIMON, Jacob. *National Portrait Gallery: Complete Illustrated Catalogue*, London, Unicorn Press, 2004, p. 244. It may be viewed at <http://www.npg.org.uk/collections/search/location.php?locid=232>.

[72] Mellon Collection, Yale, painted *c*1744-1747.

artist could be financially independent of patronage at a time when almost all were either indentured or in debt. If anything, his financial fluctuations were less precipitous than Handel's since he chose to avoid the fashionable but treacherous world of opera. Contrary to the inherited and accepted verdict, it may be that — after the recent traumas of Ponzi schemes and hedge-fund collapses — Geminiani's strategy has something recommendable in it even to the present age.

Acknowledgements

I am especially grateful to Jonathan Yarker for guiding me through the minefields of modern fine art research; also to the Victoria and Albert Museum (London), The Frick Collection (New York), and Clare Hornsby, Anthony Mould, Colin Coleman, Hilary Wilkie (Gosford House), Chris Gravett (Woburn), Ryan Mark, Barra Boydell, Andrew Pink, Anthony Fabian, Paul Lindenauer, Roz Southey, Paul Spencer-Longhurst, Richard Stephens and Heather Jarman.

APPENDIX I

AUCTION CATALOGUES FOR 1725, 1741, 1742 AND 1743

1725 Geminiani Auction Catalogue

A / Catalogue / Of The / Valuable and Exceeding Fine / Collection / Of / Mr. Geminiani's, / Choice Pictures; / By the most Eminent Italian and other Masters. / Will be Sold by Auction on Wednesday the 21st of this Inst. / April, 1725, at the Green-door in the little Piazza Co- / vent- Garden. / The Collection may be view'd / on Monday the 19th, Tuesday / the 20th, and Wednesday the 21st till the Hour of Sale, / which will begin at Twelve a Clock in the Forenoon. / Catalogues to be had at / Mr. Cock's in Broad-street near Golden- / Square, and at the place of Sale. [rule] N.B. This Collection consists but of 98 Pictures, which will be / Sold in two Days, so / that the Sale will end each Day before three / in the afternoon; and in a few Days will be sold likewise, a / Valuable Library of Books.

comments

[p. 2]
		comments
1	A Sea piece, *Italian*.	
2	A Masquerade, *Flemish*.	
3	*Lott and his two Daughters*, *Italian*.	
4	A Battle by *Borgognone*.	Jacques Courtois (1621–1676?)
5	Ditto.	
6	A Landskip by *Griffier*.	Jan Griffier (1652–1718)
7	A Landskip by *Genoese*.	probably Bernardo Strozzi (Pietr Genoese, 1581–1644)
8	Ditto.	
9	An Inn &c. by *Borgognone*.	
10	*Bacchus* and *Ariadne* by *Nicolas Poussin*.	
11	A Venus with other Figures by *Bourdon*.	Sebastien Bourdon (1616–1671)
12	A Diana by *Guerchino*.	Giovanni Francesco Barbieri il Guercino (1591–1666)
13	A Fruit piece by *Michael Angelo*.	Michelangelo Pace ditto il Campidoglio (c1610–1670)
14	A Nymph with young Satyrs by *Pietro da Cortona*.	Pietro Berrettini da Cortona (1596–1669)
15	A picture by *Luca D'hollande*.	Lucas van Leyden (c1494–1533)
15★	Its Companion	
16	A Fruit piece by *Deheem*.	probably Cornelis de Heem (1631–1695)
17	A Landskip with Cattel by *Castiglione*.	Giovanni Benedetto Castiglione (1609–1664)
18	A Mans Head by *Michael Angelo de Carravaggio*.	Michelangelo Merisi da Caravaggio (1571–1610)

No.	Description	Attribution
19	A Landskip by Annibal Carrats.	Annibale Carracci (1560-1609)
20	St Jerome by old Palma.	Palma Vecchio (1480-1528)
21	Ditto by Carlo Lotti.	Johann Carl Loth (1632-1698)
22	Adam and Eve by Bloemart.	Abraham Bloemaert (1566-1651)
23	A Fortune by Vandyke.	Anthony Van Dyck (1599-1641)
24	Venus and Adonis by Felice Ciniani.	Felice Cignani (1660-1724)
25	Procris and Meleager, by Pelegrino Tibaldi.	Pellegrino Tibaldi (1527-1596)
26	The five Senses by Teniers.	David Teniers (1610-1690)
27	A little Landskip with Figures by Velvet Brughel.	Jan Bruegel the elder (1568-1625)
28	Ditto.	
29	A little picture by Vanderwerf.	Adrian Van der Werf (1659-1722)
30	The Holy Family by Titian.	Tiziano Veccelli (1488-1576)
31	A Landskip upon copper by Schoevaerdts.	Mathys Schoevaerdts (1665-1723)
32	A Head of Spagnoletto.	Jusepe de Ribera (1591-1652)
33	An Adoration of the Kings by Rubens.	Peter Paul Rubens (1577-1640)
34	Gamesters by Pasqualino.	possibly Pasqualino Ottino (1685-1734)
35	A Head by Rembrant.	

[p. 3]

No.	Description	Attribution
36	Europa by Giacomo Bassano.	Jacopo Bassano (1510-1592)
37	A Bacchanal manner of Philippo Lauro.	Filippo Lauri (1623-1694)
38	A Gardner with Fruit and Herbs by Mr. Angells.	[not identified]
39	A Conversation by Van Loe.	Carle Vanloo (1705-1765)
40	The Earl of Strafford by Van Dyck.	
41	A little Landskip with Figures by Vincabone.	
42	Ditto.	
43	St. Sebastian by Bassano.	
44	A Flower piece by Mario de Fiori.	Mario dei Fiori (1603-1673)
45	Ditto.	
46	The Adoration of Bacchus by Julio Romano after Raphael.	Giulio Romano (1499-1546)
47	A little Landskip with Figures by Velvet Brughell.	
48	A Landskip with Figures by Paul Brill.	Paul Brill (1554-1626)
49	The four Seasons by Rubens.	
50	A Battle in the manner of Borgognone.	
51	A Conversation by Teniers.	

52	St. *Agnes* by *Teniers* in the manner of *Corregio.*	Antonio da Correggio (1489–1534)
53	*David* with *Goliah's* Head by *Carlo Dulci.*	Carlo Dolci (1616–1686)
54	A Landskip by *Claude Lorrain.*	Claude Lorrain (1602–1682)
55	Christ and the Samaritan Woman by *Francisco Bolognese.*	Francesco Monti il Bolognese (1685–1768)
56	A picture by *Rubens.*	
57	An Ecce Homo by young *Palma.*	Palma Giovane (1548–1628)
58	*David and Abigal* by *Jordans D'Andversa.*	probably Jacob Jordaens (1593–1678)
59	The Shepherds offering, the School of *Raphael.*	
60	A piece of Cattle by *Rosa of Tivoli.*	
61	Christ and St. Magdalen, the School of *Barroccio.*	Federico Barocci (1526–1612)
62	A Bacchanal of *Nichola Rosso*	
63	*Apollo and Daphne*, by *Cavalier Liberi.*	Pietro Liberi (1605–1687)
64	St. *John* by *Leonardo da Vinci.*	
65	The last Supper, the *Florantin* School.	
66	A Magdalen by *Mola.*	Pier Francesco Mola (1612–1666)
67	A little Figure, by *Sebastian Richi.*	Sebastiano Ricci (1659–1734)
68	A Flower piece with Insects by *Alex. Adrian.*	
69	Two Sybils by *Guido Cagniacci.*	Guido Cagnacci (1601–1663)
70	A Man studying, neatly done.	
[p. 4]		
71	A picture by *Antonio More.*	Antonis Mor (1545–1576)
72	*David and Saul* by *Ciro Ferri.*	Ciro Ferri (1634–1689)
73	A Madona by *Carlo Morat.*	Carlo Maratta (1625–1713)
74	A Flower piece by old *Baptist.*	Jean-Baptiste Monnoyer (1636–1699)
75	*Herodias* the first manner of *Domen[s]chino.*	
76	A picture the School of *Rubens.*	
77	An old Man's head *Italian:*	
78	*Bachus and Ariadne* by *Scarcelino Du Ferrara.*	Ippolito Scarsella (1550–1620) called Scarsellino
79	An Assumption by *Domenichino.*	
80	A Landskip with Figures, by *Nicholas Poussin.*	
81	A Landskip Flemish, neatly done.	
82	A Battle by *Michael Angelo.*	
83	A Bachanal by a Disciple of *Rubens.*	
84	The Burial of Christ by *Valerio Castelli.*	Vallerio Castello (1624–1659)

85	*Solomons* Judgment by *Francisco Salviatti.*	Francesco Salviati (1510-1563)
86	A Charity by *Francesco Flora.*	
87	A Landskip by *Moïsa Vanderbrook.*	
88	The Angel appearing to the Shepherd by *Pietro Facini.*	Pietro Facini (1562-1614)
89	The holy Family by *Michael Angelo.*	possibly M. Buonarroti or Pace
90	An Adoration by *Bonane da Ferrara.*	Carlo Bonone (1569-1632)
91	The four Seasons by *Rubens.*	
92	The holy Family by *Titian.*	
93	St. *Francis* and a Glory by *Tintoret.*	Jacopo Robusti, Tintoretto (1518-1594)
94	A Picture by *Sebastian del Piombo.*	Sebastiano Luciani (1485-1547)
95	A Landskip by *Paul Brill.*	Paul Brill (1554-1626)
96	The flight into *Egypt* by *Mola.*	Pier Francesco Mola (1612-1666)
97	The four Seasons by *Velvet Brughel* and *Vanballen.*	Jan Bruegel (1568-1625)

FINIS.

442

A
CATALOGUE
OF THE
VALUABLE and Exceeding FINE
COLLECTION
OF
Mr. *GEMINIANI's,*
Choice *PICTURES;*
By the moſt Eminent *Italian* and other Maſters.

Will be Sold by Auction on *Wedneſday* the 21ſt of this Inſt. *April,* 1725. at the Green-door in the little *Piazza Co-vent-Garden.*

The Collection may be view'd on *Monday* the 19th, *Tueſday* the 20th and *Wedneſday* the 21ſt. till the Hour of Sale, which will begin at Twelve a Clock in the Forenoon.

Catalogues to be had at Mr. *Cock's* in *Broad-ſtreet* near *Golden-Square,* and at the Place of S A L E.

N. B. *This Collection conſiſts but of 98 Pictures, which will be Sold in two Days, ſo that the Sale will end each Day before three in the afternoon; and in a few Days will be ſold likewiſe, a Valuable Library of Books.*

PICTURES.

1 A Sea piece, *Italian.*
2 A Masquerade, *Flemish.*
3 *Lott* and his two Daughters, *Italian.*
4 A Battle by *Borgognone.*
5 Ditto.
6 A Landskip by *Griffier.*
7 A Landskip by *Genoese.*
8 Ditto.
9 An Inn &c. by *Borgognone.*
10 *Bacchus* and *Ariadne* by *Nicolas Poussin.*
11 A Venus with other Figures by *Bourdon.*
12 A Diana by *Guerchino.*
13 A Fruit piece by *Michael Angelo.*
14 A Nymph with young Satyrs by *Pietro da Cortona.*
15 A picture by *Luca D'hollande.*
15 * Its Companion
16 A Fruit piece by *Deheem.*
17 A Landskip with Cattel by *Castiglione.*
18 A Mans Head by *Michael Angelo de Carravagio.*
19 A Landskip by *Annibal Carrats.*
20 St *Jerome* by old *Palma.*
21 Ditto by *Carlo Lotti.*
22 *Adam* and *Eve* by *Bloemart.*
23 A Fortune by *Vandyke.*
24 *Venus* and *Adonis* by *Felice Ciniani.*
25 *Procris* and *Meleager,* by *Pelegrino Tibaldi.*
26 The five Senses by *Teniers*
27 A little Landskip with Figures by *Velvet Brughel.*
28 Ditto.
29 A little picture by *Vanderwerf.*
30 The Holy Family by *Titian.*
31 A Landskip upon copper by *Schoevaerats.*
32 A Head of *Spagnoletto.*
33 An Adoration of the Kings by *Rubens.*
34 Gamesters by *Pasqualino.*
35 A Head by *Rembrant.*

36 *Europa*

[3]

36 *Europa* by *Giacamo Baffano.*
37 A Bacchanal manner of *Philippo Lauro.*
38 A Gardner with Fruit and Herbs by Mr. *Angells.*
39 A Converfation by *Van Loo.*
40 The Earl of *Strafford* by *Van Dyck.*
41 A little Landskip with Figures by *Vincabone.*
42 Ditto.
43 St. *Sebaftian* by *Baffano.*
44 A Flower piece by *Mario de Fiori.*
45 Ditto.
46 The Adoration of *Bacchus* by *Julio Romano* after *Raphael.*
47 A little Landskip with Figures by Velvet *Brughell.*
48 A Landskip with Figures by *Paul Brill.*
49 The four Seafons by *Rubens.*

The Second Day's Sale.

50 A Battle the manner of *Borgognone.*
51 A Converfation by *Teniers.*
52 St. *Agnes* by *Teniers* in the manner of *Corregio.*
53 *David* with *Goliah's* Head by *Carlo Dulci.*
54 A Landskip by *Claude Lorrain.*
55 Chrift and the Samaritan Woman by *Francifco Bolognefe.*
56 A picture by *Rubens.*
57 An Ecce Homo by young *Palma.*
58 *David* and *Abigal* by *Jordans D'Andverfa*
59 The Shepherds offering, the School of *Raphael.*
60 A piece of Cattle by *Rofa* of *Tivoli.*
61 Chrift and St. Magdalen, the School of *Barroccio.*
62 A Bacchanal of *Nichola Roffo* Difciple of *Luca Jordano.*
63 *Apollo* and *Daphne*, by *Cavalier Liberi.*
64 St. *John* by *Leonardo da Vinci.*
65 The laft Supper, the *Florantin* School.
66 A Magdalen by *Mola.*
67 A little Figure, by *Sebaftian Richi.*
68 A Flower piece with Infects by *Alex. Adrian.*
69 Two Sybils by *Guido Cagniacci.*
70 A Man ftudying, neatly done.

71 A,

[4]

71 A picture by *Antonio More*.
72 *David* and *Saul* by *Ciro Ferri*.
73 A Madona by *Carlo Morat*.
74 A Flower piece by old *Baptiſt*.
75 *Herodias* the firſt manner of *Domenchino*.
76 A picture the School of *Rubens*.
77 An old Man's head *Italian*:
78 *Bacchus* and *Ariadne* by *Scarcelino Du Ferrara*.
79 An Aſſumption by *Domenichino*.
80 A Landskip with Figures, by *Nicholas Pouſſin*.
81 A Landskip Flemiſh, neatly done.
82 A Battle by *Michael Angelo*.
83 A Bachanal by a Diſciple of *Rubens*.
84 The Burial of Chriſt by *Valerio Caſtelli*.
85 *Solomons* Judgment by *Franciſco Salviatti*.
86 A Charity by *Franceſco Flora*.
87 A Landskip by *Moiſa Vanderbrook*.
88 The Angel appearing to the Shepherd by *Pietro Facini*.
89 The holy Family by *Michael Angelo*.
90 An Adoration by *Bonane da Ferrara*.
91 The four Seaſons by *Rubens*
92 The holy Family by *Titian*.
93 St. *Francis* and a Glory by *Tintoret*.
94 A Picture by *Sebaſtian del Piombo*.
95 A Landskip by *Paul Brill*.
96 The flight into *Egypt* by *Mola*.
97 The four Seaſons by *Velvet Brughel* and *Vanballen*.

F I N I S.

[Houlditch MS, p. 135]

Geminiani's Sale of / Pictures 1741.

Lott.			£	s	[d]	comments
1.	A Seaport with Figures	Vandercable	2	2		Adriaen van der Cabel (1631-1705)
2.	It's Companion	Ditto	2	2		
3.	A Landschape, with an Arch	Patell	3	11		Pierre Patel (1605-1676)
4.	A Landskip, a Sea view, and Fig:s	Swanevelt	4	11		Herman van Swanevelt (1603-1665)
5.	The Flight into Egypt	Young Palma	4	13		Jacopo Palma, Il Giovane (c1548-1628)
6.	A Woman att a well, and Still Life	Kalf	4	10		Willem Kalf (1619-1693) still-life painter.
7.	The Assumption of the Virgin	Procaccino	4	4		Giulio Cesare Procaccini (c1574-1625)
8.	Woman Bathing	Swanevelt	5	12		
9.	A Dead Hare and Birds	Bol	3	13	6	Ferdinand Bol (1616-1680)
10.	It's Companion	Ditto	4	1		
11.	A Landschape and Figures	G. Poussin	6	15		Gaspard Dughet (1615-1675)
12.	Mount Parnassus	L. Carracci	4	8		
13.	A Landskip with a woman on a mule, Stile of	G. Poussin	6	15		
14.	A Land Storm	Fran. Millè	8	2	6	Jean-Francois Millet the elder (1642-1679)
15.	Princess Mary, half Length	S.r P. Lely	7	0		Sir Peter Lely (1618-1680)
16.	A Holy Family	C. Maratti	24	13	6	Carlo Maratta (1625-1713)
17.	The Finding of Moses	Le Sueur	4	5		Eustache Le Sueur (1617-1655)
18.	School of Athens	a Disciple of Raphael	12	12		Copy of fresco in the Vatican
19.	{A Boy att his Drawing	Chardin }	24	3		Jean-Baptiste-Siméon Chardin (1699-1779)
20.	{A Girl att Needle Work, it's Companion	Ditto }				
21.	A Man, with a Vase, his best manner	Rubens	10	10		
22.	The Incendio di Borghi, after	Rafaelle	6	10		Copy of fresco in the Vatican
23.	{					
24.	{ Bronzes &c.					
25.	{					

447

[p. 136]

No.		Artist				
26.	A large Landschape, and Figures	Gas. Poussin	20	9		
27.	A Large Sea Storm	Sal. Rosa	5	18	6	Salvator Rosa (1615-1673)
28.	The Virgin, with Angels in the Clouds, Sch. of	Vandyck	2	0		Anthony Van Dyck (1599-1641)
29.	A Landskip and Fig.ˢ	An. Caracci	12	12		Annibale Carracci (1560-1609)
30.	Salmacis and Hermap[h]roditus	Albano	9	9		Francesco Albani (1578-1660)
31.	A Landskip with Men Fishing	G Poussin	10	10		
32.	A Seaport with Architecture and Fig.ˢ	Claude, Viviano, J. Miele	19	19		Viviano Codazzi (c1606-1670), Jan Miel (1599-1663)
33.	A Landschape and Figures	N. Poussin	17	17		Nicolas Poussin (1594-1665)
34.	The Massacre of the Innocents, after Guido	Albano	13	—		
35.	A Landschape with a Stag Hunting	P. Brill	12	15		
36.	A large Landschape	D. Teniers	26	5		David Teniers (1610-1690)
37.	A Landschape and Figures	C. Lorrain	37	16		Claude Lorrain (1602-1682)
38.	The Virgin, Christ, and S.ᵗ John, big as Life	Bronzino	12	12		Agnolo di Cosimo (1503-1572), usually known as Il Bronzino
39.	A Sea-port, and Figures	Claude & J. Mielle	33	—		
40.	{A Nobleman, half Length	Vandyke }	126	—		
41.	{His Lady ... ditto	Ditto }				
42.	Jacob's Journey into Egypt	Gia. Bassano	78	15		Jacopo Bassano (1510-1592)
43.	The Family of Jeronimo Grimani	Titian	120	15		

<u>Finis.</u>

[Houlditch MS, p.76]

Monsr de Piles's Sale / of Pictures brought / over and sold by / Geminiani 1742.

1st Day's Sale.

Lott.			£	s	[d]	comments
1.	The Transformation, on marble		1	10		
2.	A Garland of Flowers		1	0		
3.	The good Samaritan		0	11		
4.	A Boy playing with a Lamb, Style of	Correggio	2	10		Antonio da Correggio (1489–1534)
5.	An Old Woman's Head	Guido	5	5		Guido Reni (1575–1642)
	D. Bedford.					
6.	A Landschape	Fouquiere	4	5		Jacques Fouquier (c1591–1659)
7.	Saint Jerom	J Bellini	3	3		Giovanni Bellini (c1430–1516)
	Ld Duncannonn.					
8.	Two Small Landskips	Patel	14	14		Pierre Patel (1605–1676)
9.	The Adoration, Style of	P. Veronese	2	10		Paolo Veronese (1528–1588)
10.	A Man's head	Vandyck	4	14	6	Anthony Van Dyck (1599–1641)
11.	A Lady dressing	Raous	13	13		Palma Vecchio (1480–1528)
12.	Saint Apollonius	Old Palma	7	7		
	Jennings.					
13.	A Small Landschape	Bartolomeo	4	0		possibly Bartolomeo Pedon (1665–1733)
	D. Bedford.					
14.	Saint Peter denying Christ	G. Segre	20	10		
	Ld Duncannonn.					
15.	A Landskip and Fig^s	Mola	6	10		Pier Francesco Mola (1612–1666)
	Marshal.					

449

16.	A Landskip and Fig:s *Winnington.*	D. Teniers	17	17		David Teniers (1610-1690)
17.	The Virgin and Christ *D. Bedford.*	Guercino	28	6		Giovanni Francesco Barbieri (1591-1666)
18.	A Small Landschape and Figures *Winnington.*	Brouwre¹	8	8		Adriaen Brouwer (1605-1638)
19.	A Large Landskip	Wannde [?]	16	10		
20.	A Battle piece	Ustenbourg	7	15		
21.	It's Companion	Ditto	18	5		
22.	Christ and the Woman of Samaria, on copper	M. Angelo	2	15		possibly Michelangelo Buonarroti (1475-1564)
23.	Bacchus with Figures dancing	G. Baptista Viola	2	6		Giovanni Battista Viola (1576-1622)
24.	A Seapiece, on Copper *Burgess.*	C. Lorrain	19	8	6	Claude Lorrain (1602-1682)
25.	It's Companion *Ditto.*	Ditto	11	11		
26.	A Landskip and Figures *D. Bedford.*	The two Boths	25	4		Jan Both (1615-1652) and Adries Dirksz Both (1611-1641)
27.	A Landskip and Fig:s *Ditto*	Jac. Bassano	16	5	6	Jacopo Bassano (1510-1592)
[p.77]						
28.	{Jacob's Vision	J.Mielle }	22	11	6	Jan Miel (1599-1663)
29.	{Moses and the burning Bush, it's Companion *L.d Cholmondeley.*	Ditto }				
30.	A Sacrifice *S.r J. Rawdon.*	Rembrandt	39	8		Rembrandt van Rijn (1606-1669)
31.	Herodias with the head of Saint John	Scipio Gaetan	16	16		Scipione Pulzone il Gaetano (1550-1598)
32.	Abraham's Servant and Rebecca *D. Bedford.*	P. Veronese	42	0		Paolo Veronese (1528-1588)
33.	Susanna *Ditto.*	Le Moyne	61	19		François Lemoyne (1688-1737)

¹ "w" inserted

No.	Description	Attribution (sale)				Artist (scholarly)
34.	A Landscape and Figures	Swanevelt	29	8		Herman van Swanevelt (1603-1655)
35.	Christ bearing his Cross *S.r Jn.o Rawdon.*	Vandyck	58	16		
36.	A Man's Head with a Turban *D. Devonshire.*	Rembrandt	78	15		Tiziano Vecellio (c1488-1576)
37.	A Venetian Nobleman, half Length *D. Bedford.*	Titian	52	10		
38. {	The Flight into Egypt, an Oval	Gobbo Caracci }				Pietro Paolo Bonzi known as il Gobbo dei Carracci (1576-1636)
39. {	It's Companion *L.d Cholmondeley.*	Ditto }	22	1		
40.	Diana and Acteon *P. Wales*	Titian	173	5		
41.	A Boar Hunting	Teniers & Rubens	48	6		David Teniers (1610-1690) and Peter Paul Rubens (1577-1640)
	Cooke.					
42.	A Large Landschape and Figures *D. Bedford.*	Gas. Pousin	90	6		Gaspard Dughet (1615-1675)
43.	It's Companion *Ditto.*	Ditto	105	—		

2.d Day's Sale

Lott.	Description	Attribution (sale)				Artist (scholarly)
44.	The Virgin Mary	Italian	1	8		
45.	Two Small Landskips		1	10		
46.	A Small History piece	Van Houc	2	6		
47.	A Girl's Head		8	10		
48.	A Landschape and Figures	Fouquiere	2	12	6	Jacques Fouquier (c1591-1659)
49.	It's Companion	Ditto	3	8		
50.	A Landskip and Figures	Poelenburch	4	4		Cornelis van Poelenburgh (c1594-1667)
51.	Two Heads *Heidegger.*	Rubens	15	15		
52.	The Decollation of S.t John		2	2		

No.	Title	Attribution				Artist
53.	A Small Landskip and Figures	Flemish		18	4	
54.	Leda and the Swan			12	2	
55.	Atalanta and Hippomanes	Boulogne		10	8	Louis de Boulogne (1654–1733)
56.	Saint Catharine, on Copper / *P. Wales.*	Guido		8	29	Guido Reni (1575–1642)
57.	The Angel Appearing to the Shepherds / *Cooke.*	G. Bassano		18	39	Jacopo Bassano (1510–1592)
58.	A Landskip and Fig:ˢ / *S.ʳ J. Rawdon.*	C. Poelenburch		4	25	
59.	It's Companion / *Ditto.*	Ditto		9	24	
60.	Cleopatra	Le Moyne		2	23	François Lemoyne (1688–1737)
[p.78]						
61.	The Ark of the Covenant / *D. Bedford.*	Old Parrocel		18	18	Joseph Parrocel (1646–1704)
62.	A Small Landschape	Rembrandt		15	5	
63.	Children dancing / *P. Wales.*	Van Houc	6	18	18	
64.	The Holy Family / *Ditto.*	Car. Cignani		12	98	Carlo Cignani (1628–1719)
65.	Venus and Adonis / *Ditto.*	P. Veronese		5	68	Paolo Veronese (1528–1588)
66.	A Small Head / *S.ʳ Jn.ᵒ Rawdon.*	Vandyck	6	11	22	
67.	Artemisia / *L.ᵈ J. Cavendish:*	Rembrandt		5	26	
68.	Saint John in the Wilderness / *L.ᵈ Cholmondeley.*	Mola	6	0	11	Pier Francesco Mola (1612–1666)
69.	Men playing at Cards / *P. Wales.*	Ad. Brouwer		3	45	Adriaen Brouwer (1605–1638)
70.	Return from Hunting / *L.ᵈ Conway.*	D. Teniers		2	170	David Teniers (1610–1690)

No.	Title	Location	Artist				Attribution
71.	Cleopatra	*L.ᵈ Orrery.*	A. Veronese	18	0	6	
72.	Diana and Acteon	*P. Wales.*	Jac. Bassano	73	10		
73.	A Descent from the Cross	*L.ᵈ Cholmondeley.*	Rottenhamer	16	16		Hans Rottenhammer (1564–1625)
74.	Jacob and Rachael	*P. Wales.*	Seb. Bourdon	68	5		Sebastien Bourdon (1616–1671)
75.	Joseph and Pharoah's Cupbearer	*S.r Jn.° Rawdon.*	Spagniolet	175	5		Jusepe de Ribera (1591–1652)
76.	Venus and Adonis	*P. Wales.*	N. Poussin	47	5		Nicolas Poussin (1594–1665)
77.	A Girl leaning att a Window	*D. Bedford.*	Rembrandt	67	4		
78.	Venus, Cupid, and a Satyr	*L.ᵈ Duncannonn.*	Jul. Romano	26	15	6	Gulio Romano (1499–1546)
79.	A Nobleman, Half Length, with a Dog	*D. Bedford.*	Titian	33	12		
80.	The Prodigal Son	*Townsend.*	D. Teneirs	116	11		
81.	A Stag Hunting	*P. Wales.*	P. Wouverman	73	10		Philip Wouwerman (1619–1668)
82.	It's Companion	*Ditto.*	Ditto	110	5		
83.	Cain and Abel	*D. Bedford.*	Guido Reni	73	10		Guido Reni (1575–1642)

Finis.

[Houlditch MS, p. 187]

Geminiani's Sale of / Pictures 1743.

1st. Day's Sale.

Lott.			£	s	[d]	comments
1	Two Small Sea pieces	Italian	1	2		?Paolo Veronese (1528-1588)
2.	Two Heads	A. Veronese	2	0		Sébastian Bourdon (1616-1671)
3	Boys att Cards	Bourdon	2	0		Jacques Fouquier (c1591-1659)
4.	A Winter piece	Fourquiere	0	8		
5.	Venus and Adonis	Italian	1	1		
6.	A Woman's Head	Vandyck	1	11	6	Anthony Van Dyck (1599-1641)
7.	A Landschape and Figures	Italian	3	4		
8.	It's Companion	Ditto	3	7		
9.	A Woman's Head, in a Round	Holbein	3	11		Hans Holbein the younger (1498-1543)
10.	An old Man's Head, small oval	Carrache	1	17		Annibale Carracci (1560-1609)
11.	Two Parrots	Flemish	1	16		
12.	A Conversation	Boulogne	1	3		Louis de Boulogne (1654-1733)
13.	A Moon-light	Van der Meer	1	2		Jan Van der Meer (1632-1675)
14.	A Landschape and Fig.	F. Millé	3	15		Salvator Rosa (1615-1673)
15.	{A Landscape, with a Sea View, Stile of	Sal. Rosa	1	4		
16.	{It's Companion	Ditto	"	"		
17.	Saint Cecilia, on Copper	Stella	1	11	6	Jacques Stella (1596-1657)
18.	Bacchus, Venus, Cupid, and Ceres	Van Balen	1	7		Hendrick Van Balen (1575-1632)
19.	Two Oval Flower-pieces	Baptiste	2	2		Jean Baptiste Monnoyer (1636-1699)
20.	Saint Jerome	Carrache, & P. Brill	1	17		Annibale Carracci (1560-1609)
21.	{A Girl at her Needle, a Sketch	Chardin	0	14		Jean-Baptiste-Siméon Chardin (1699-1779)
22.	{It's Companion	Ditto	"	"		
23.	St. Francis in a Landskip	Mola	2	7		Pier Francesco Mola (1612-1666)
24.	{A Landskip, Cattle and Fig.5	Rosa of Tivoli	3	15		Philipp Peter Roos (1651-1706)
25.	{It's Companion	Ditto	"	"		

455

[p.188]

No.							Artist
26.	Fishermen	Agos. Caracci	4	6			Agostino Carracci (1557-1602)
27.	{A Landschape and Figures	Swanevelt	17	17			Herman van Swanevelt (1603-1655)
28.	{It's Companion	Ditto	17	17			
29.	Ruins and Figures	Patel	4	19			Pierre Patel (1605-1676)
30.	A Landschape and Figures, manner of	C. Lorrain	3	1			Claude Lorrain (1602-1682)
31.	Fruit, and Dead Game	Fyt	1	14			Jan Fyt (1611-1661)
32.	A Battle piece	Tempesta	5				Antonio Tempesta (1555-1630)
33.	A Head Sketch'd	Rembrandt	2	5			Rembrandt van Rijn (1606-1669)
34.	Fruit and Dead Birds	Snyders	2	11			Fran Snyders (1579-1657)
35.	Architecture	Vivians	2	2			Francois Vivares (1708-1780)
36.	A Large Landschape and Fig.s	Momper	2	3			Joos de Momper (1564-1635)
37.	It's Companion	Ditto	3	8			
38.	The Building the Ark	Cav.r Calabrese	1	15			Mattia Preti (1613-1699)
39.	Apollo &c.	Verdier	1	7			Francois Verdier (1651-1730)
40.	A Landschape and Cattle	Berghem	1	19			Nicolaes Berchem (1620-1683)
41.	A Landskip with ruins	Gobbo Carracci	3	6			Pietro Paolo Bonzi (1576-1636)
42.	A Conversation in a Landskip	Watteau	2	2			Antoine Watteau (1684-1721)
43.	The Virgin with angels, after Guido	Albano	5				Francesco Albani (1578-1660)
44.	Flowers, and Still Life	Maria de Fiori	6	15			Mario Nuzzi (1603-1673)
45.	A Landschape, and Figures dancing	Theodore	3	0			
46.	Flight into Egypt, First Manner	Poelenburch	6	0			Cornelis van Poelenburgh (1594-1667)
47.	Dead Game	Chardin	1	14			Jean-Baptiste-Siméon Chardin (1699-1779)
48.	A Landschape	Patel	2	18			
49.	Cosmo di Medici, D. of Tuscay, when Young	Vandyck	7	12	6		
50.	A Large Landskip, Architecture, & Fig.s	De la Hyre	14	0			Laurent de La Hyre (1606-1656)
51.	Time and Truth, Emblematical	Le Sueur	2	5			Eustache Le Sueur (1617-1655)
52.	A Landschape and Figures	S. Bourdon	2	10			Sebastien Bourdon (1616-1671)
53.	A Lobster, and Still Life	Deheem	2	2			Jan Davidsz de Heem (1606-1684)
54.	Hippomanes, and Atalanta	Le Mere & N. Poussin	12	5			
55.	Pan and Syrinx	Rubens	4	14	6		Peter Paul Rubens (1577-1640)

[p.189]

2ᵈ. Day's Sale.

			£	s.	d.	
56.	A Landscape and Figures	Fouquiere	0	11		Jacques Fouquier (c1591-1659)
57.	A Sketch, with Ornaments	Watteau	1	1		
58.	Flowers	Baptiste	0	14	6	
59.	A Woman's head, Crayons	Boucher	0	17		François Boucher (1703-1770)
60.	A Landskip and Figˢ, manner of.	Bartolomeo	1	12		possibly Bartolomeo Biscaino (1632-1657)
61.	It's Companion	F. Millè	2	11		
62.	Lot, and his two Daughters	Italian	1	11	6	
63.	A Winter Piece	Breughel	1	11	6	probably Pieter 'velvet' Bruegel (1568-1625)
64.	A Venetian Nobleman	Holbein	0	13		Hans Holbein (1498-1543)
65.	A Martyrdom	P. Bourdon	0	13		Paris Bordone (1500-1571)
66.	A Woman with a Frying pan, a Sketch	Chardin	0	12		Jean-Baptiste-Siméon Chardin
67.	A Landskip and Figˢ, in manner of	Berghem	1	7		
68.	A Small Fruit piece	M. Angelo	4	6		Michelangelo Pace da Campidoglio (c1610-1670)
69.	A History	A. Schiavoni	1	0		Andrea Schiavone (1510-1563)
70.	Apollo, and Daphne, in a Landskip	Vander Cable	1	6		Adriaen van der Cabel (1631-1705)
71.	It's Companion	Ditto	1	15		
72.	A Landskip, Cattle and Figˢ.	Van Blomen	3	3		Jan Frans van Bloemen (1662-1749)
73.	It's Companion	Ditto	3	8		
74.	The Crucifixion	A. Durer	2	19		Albrecht Durer (1471-1528)
75.	Two Flower pieces	M. di Fiori	1	11	6	Mario dei Fiori (1603-1673)
76.	Jupiter and Europa on Copper	Flemish	2	5		
77.	Cattle	Rosa di Tivoli	3	0		Philipp Peter Roos (1651-1706)
78.	It's Companion	Ditto	3	5		
79.	Flora	Guido Cagnacci	1	18		Guido Cagnacci (1601-1663)
80.	Saint Ursula	Vouet	1	6		Simon Vouet (1590-1649)
81.	A Man's Head	Holbein	1	13		
82.	An old Woman dressing	Boulogne	2	10		Louis de Boulogne (1654-1733)
83.	Flowers	Baptist	2	6		Jean-Baptiste Monnoyer (1636-1699)
84.	Dead Game	Chardin	[blank]			

457

[p.190]

No.	Title	Attribution				Artist
85.	A Landschape with Horsemen	Van der mulen		2	9	Steven Van der Meulen (fl.1543-1564)
86.	A Landschape, with the Repose	Stella		5	5	Jacques Stella (1596-1657)
87.	A Landskip and Figures	B. Castiglione		2	15	Giovanni-Benedetto Castiglione (1609-1664)
88.	Lot, and his Daughters	Guido Cagnacci		9	9	Guido Cagnacci (1601-1663)
89.	The Adoration of the Magi	Rottenhamer		4	11	Hans Rottenhammer (1564-1625)
90.	A large Landschape and Fig.ˢ	Otho Voenius		5		Otto van Veen (1556-1629)
91.	A View of the Campo Vaccino	C. Lorrain		22	11	
92.	A round Landschape	F Laura		2	2	Filippo Lauri (1623-1694)
93.	Sᵗ. Peter denying Christ	Le Valentine		8	8	
94.	A Landskip with a view of the Rhine	Momper		2	2	Joos de Momper (1564-1635)
95.	Sᵗ. John in a Landskip, on Copper	Gobbo Carrache & P. Brill				
96.	It's Companion	Ditto	6	4	6	
97.	A Landschape, and Figures	D. Teneirs	6	3	13	David Teniers (1610-1690)
98.	{A Conversation in a Landskip	J. Le Bel [?]		7	10	
99.	{It's Companion	Ditto		11	11	
				"	"	
100.	A Magdalen	Correggio	6	9	11	Antonio de Correggio (1489-1534)
101.	The Holy Family, on Copper	C. Maratti		4	15	Carlo Maratta (1625-1713)
102.	Cain and Abel	Domenichino		4	4	Domenico Zampieri (1581-1641)
103.	A Landschape and Figures	C. Poelenburgh		16	16	Cornelis van Poelenburgh (1594-1667)
104.	A Girl with Needlework	Chardin		12	12	
105.	It's Companion	Ditto	6	7	1	
106.	Venus dressing	Albano		6	10	Francesco Albani (1578-1660)
107.	Our Saviour in the Garden	J. Bassano		8	8	Jacopo Bassano (1510-1592)
108.	A Nympth [sic] with a Burning Glass	Le Moine		10	10	François Lemoyne (or Le Moine) (1688-1737)
109.	Saint John preaching in the Wilderness	L. Jordans	6	23	12	Jacob Jordaens (1593-1678)
110.	Saint Simeon	Rembrandt		4	5	
111.	Venus and Aeneas	N. Poussin		21	0	Nicolas Poussin (1594-1665)

[p.191]

3.ᵈ Day's Sale.

No.		Attribution	£	s	d	Artist
112.	Two Small Landskips and Fig.ˢ.	Van der Meer	4	4		
113.	Two Flower pieces	Old Baptiste	1	11	6	
114.	A Landscape with a Water-fall, manner of	Gobbo Carrache	1	1		
115.	A Landscape and Figures	Flemish	1	15		
116.	A Sea Calm	Zeeman	1	18		Reinier Nooms (1623-1667)
117.	Beggars	Bourdon	2	12	6	
118.	Two Small round pieces of Architecture	Clevenbroeke	1	15		
119.	Diana and Endymion	Le Sueur	2	0		
120.	A Landskip and Figures	F. Millè	1	10		
121.	{Architecture, and Fig.ˢ. manner of	Viviano	6	0		
122.	{It's Companion	Ditto	"	"		
123.	Bacchus, and Ceres	La Force	1	18		
124.	Flowers	M. di Fiori	1	17		
125.	It's Companion	Ditto	1	16		
126.	A Landskip, Stile of	G. Poussin	4	4		Gaspard Dughet (1615-1675)
127.	Ditto, the Figures Nicolo	Ditto	4	4		
128.	Women and Children	Boucher	2	2		François Boucher
129.	A Small Landschape and Fig.ˢ.	Poelenburch	2	5		Cornelis van Poelenburgh (1594-1667)
130.	It's Companion	Ditto	2	5		
131.	Flowers	Flemish	2	3		
132.	Fruit, and Still Life	Deheem	3	5		Cornelis de Heem (1631-1695)
133.	It's Companion	Ditto	2	15		
134.	Our Saviour in the Garden	C. Maratti	7	11	6	Carlo Maratta (1625-1713)
135.	Venus, and Cupid Sleeping	C. Poelenburch	3	16		
136.	Savoyards dancing	Chardin	2	15		
137.	A Landschape and Figures	N. Poussin	5	5		
138.	The Sketch for the Monument of Cav.ʳ Calabrese	Solimeni	[blank]	5		Francesco Solimena (1657-1747)
139.	S.ᵗ Francis dying	F. Mola	12	10		Pier Francesco Mola (1612-1666)
140.	The Holy Family	Proccacino	1	13		Andrea Procaccini (1671-1734)
141.	Jupiter and Europa	Flemish	3	5		
142.	It's Companion	Ditto	3	8		

[p.192]

No.	Title	Artist				Attribution
143.	A Landschape and Cattle, Style of	Berghem	4	11		
144.	A Sibyl's Head	M. Ang. Carravagio	1	11	6	Michelangelo Merisi da Caravaggio (1571–1610)
145.	Boors Smoaking	D. Teniers	3	13	6	David Teniers the Younger (1610–1690)
146.	A History	Solimeni	2	3		Francesco Solimena (1657–1747)
147.	Meleager and Atalanta, school of	Vandyck	5	18		
148.	A large Landskip, with Cattle	Rosa of Tivoli	4	19	6	
149.	A Landskip and Figures	Bott	2	10		Jan Both (1615–1652)
150.	Dutch Boors	D. Teniers	3	13		
151.	A Boy playing with a Totum	Chardin	6	6		
152.	Charity Emblematical	A. del Sarto	11	11		Andrea del Sarto (1486–1530)
153.	Death of Adonis	Tintoret	10	10		Jacopo Robusti, Tintoretto (1518–1594)
154.	The Virgin, Christ, St. John, Sch: of	Correggio	24	0		Antonio da Correggio (1489–1534)
155.	The Pope, and Cardinals	P. da Cortona	5	18		Pietro da Cortona (1596–1669)
156.	The Virgin and Others, in a Landskip	Poelenburgh	13	0		Cornelis van Poelenburgh (1594–1667)
157.	The Nativity	B. Murillo	18			Bartolome Esteban Murillo (1617–1682)
158.	Bacchus, with Satyrs and Nympths [sic]	Rubens	5	6		
159.	Our Saviour att Emaus	Titian	24	13	6	Tiziano Vecelli (1488–1576)
160.	{Bronzes					
161.	{					

Finis.

In the following listing of Geminiani portraits, engravings derived from paintings are grouped after the original portrait; all plates, which are for identification purposes only, are reproduced by kind permission of their current owner (where known).

EDMÉ BOUCHARDON (1737)
Red chalk, signed and dated 1737, 445 x 323 mm.
San Francisco University, California: de Bellis Collection.

Sold at Sotheby's, Thursday 28 March, 1968, Lot 143. The collector's mark demonstrates it was formerly owned by Pierre-Jean Mariette (L.1852).

Pierre Aveline, after Bouchardon

Medallion depicting Geminiani, supported by the Genius of Music and the Three Graces, with Apollo above. Engraving by Pierre-Alexandre Aveline (Paris, 1702 – Paris, 1760) after E. Bouchardon.

E. Bouchardon invenit *An.1751.* *P. Aveline Sculpsit.*

Debent Charites hæc pignora Vati.

Used by Geminiani as frontispiece for Op. 1, 1739 version.

J. B. Lucien, after Bouchardon

J. B. Lucien, sculpsit.

Plate caption: Francois Xavier Geminiani Célebre Musicien Italien, Dessiné par Edme Bouchardon… porte-feuille de Mr. De Villemorien. A Paris chez Chereau rue des Mathurins aux 2 Piliers d'Or.

ANDREA SOLDI

Oil on canvas, signed "Soldi. Pittore", 620 x 750 mm.
Foundling Museum, London: Gerald Coke Handel Collection, Art. No: DEC84534.

Andrea Soldi (c1703-1771) was born in Florence and came to Britain in 1736. Ingamells stresses the lightness of his art in contrast to the prevailing style of portraiture derived from Kneller.[73] By 1744 he had acquired, according to Vertue, "high mind and *conceptions grandisses* willing to be thought a Count or Marquis, rather than an excellent painter." After success in the 1740s, his art went into decline and by 1771 he was forced to apply for charity from the Royal Academy; according to Whitley, Soldi's funeral was paid for by Reynolds.

---

[73] See INGAMELLS, John. 'Andrea Soldi – A check-list of his works', in: *The Forty-Seventh Volume of the Walpole Society*, London, The Walpole Society, 1980, pp. 1-21.

WILLIAM HOARE OF BATH (*c1735*)
Oil on canvas, dimensions unknown.

Present location unknown; reproduced in BETTI, Adolfo. *La vita e l'arte di Francesco Geminiani*, Lucca, G. Giusti, 1933.

William Hoare (1707-1792) worked principally in Bath; originally from Suffolk, he studied in London and Italy with the portraitist Giuseppe Grisoni. The portrait of Geminiani, if dated 1735, was completed after his return to Britain and before he established a lucrative practice in Bath in 1738. In Bath he painted several visiting musical celebrities. There appears to be no trace of the portrait of Geminiani, although no authoritative list of his works survives.[74]

---

[74] See SLOMAN, Susan. *Pickpocketing the Rich: portrait painting in Bath 1720-1800*, exhibition catalogue, Bath, Holbourne Museum of Art, 2002, pp. 37-42.

THOMAS JENKINS (c1750)

Oil on canvas, 38½ by 28½ inches.

Gosford House (East Lothian) in the collection of the Earl of Wemyss.

Thomas Jenkins (1722–1798), a painter who became a wealthy art dealer and banker, lived in Rome and engaged in securing commissions for the British artists residing there and in buying works of art for noblemen on the Grand Tour. The portrait was probably painted in London c1750 before Jenkins embarked for Rome; it is demonstrably not the painting mentioned by Ingamells as being dispatched from Rome in 1751.

James MacArdell, after Jenkins (1777)
Mezzotint, 349 mm x 249 mm.

MacArdell (c1728-1765) was the major mezzotinter of the second half of the 18th century.

Charles Grignion, after Jenkins (*c*1776)

Engraving in circular frame, inscribed "T. Jenkins pinxit" and "C. Grignion sculp.", diameter 96 mm.

Reproduced in *HAWKINS*, v, p. 238.

FRANCESCO GEMINIANI.

Charles Grignion (*c*1721-1810) studied in Paris under J. P. Le Bas and then at Gravelot's drawing school in Covent Garden, alongside Thomas Gainsborough, after which he developed a career as a historical engraver and book illustrator. He produced a number of plates for *HAWKINS*.

JAMES LATHAM *c*1730-39 (misattrib. Hudson)
Oil on canvas, 76 x 62 cm.
Royal Society of Musicians, London.

James Latham (1696-1746) was a native of Tipperary. When young he studied art at Antwerp, and about 1725 began to practise portrait-painting in Dublin. Latham was the earliest native artist who gained any repute in Ireland, and from his skill in painting portraits he was called the "Irish Vandyck." It is stated that he also worked for a short time in London. Latham's works are seldom met with out of Ireland, but are to be found in many family mansions there. His portraits of Margaret Woffington and of Geminiani attracted much notice. Several of his portraits were engraved, including those of Bishop ditto Berkeley and Sir John

Ligonier by John Brooks, Sir Samuel Cooke by John Faber Jr., and Patrick Quin by Andrew Miller. Latham died in Trinity Street, Dublin, about 1750.

Provenance: bequeathed by Redmond Simpson (?1730-1787). Portraits of Handel, Corelli, Purcell and Geminiani were placed by Simpson in the Royal box at the Concerts of Antient Music sometime in 1785 or 1786, and upon the dissolution of the Concerts they were handed over to the Royal Academy of Music. However, Simpson had wished the portraits to the RSM and written documentation was provided by the Society in 1851 to prove their claim. The portraits were received in July 1851 and have been displayed in the Society's rooms (presently 10 Stratford Place, London) since that time.

The earlier provenance of the portrait(s) is speculative: a sale of paintings was held at Matthew Dubourg's house in Dublin in January 1748 and Simpson may have acquired one or all then although he would have been only about 18 years of age. Simpson was to marry Dubourg's daughter, Elizabeth, on 22 September 1753 which may have entitled Simpson in the future to Dubourg's retained paintings; Dubourg passed away in 1767 and had, early in life, been a pupil of Geminiani's.

ANONYMOUS (RCM) (*c*1735)

Oil on canvas, 602 mm x 488 mm.
Royal College of Music, London.

This painting appears to have been donated by Mr Goldsmith, the then owner of Salisbury Hall, London Colney, St Albans, Hertfordshire. Although the painting was at first to be purchased by the RCM from him for £100, this later changed due to a shortage of funds and it was agreed that the painting would be given out from a trust fund. By this time the person writing was Ian Morrison, living in Grosvenor Sq, London but assumed to be related [to] or working for Mr Goldsmith.

At the time of donating the painting, it was recorded as being by Andrea Soldi, an Italian painter, about 1703-1771, active in Great Britain. This attribution was never recorded by the RCM and at a later date the RCM noted that the painting was by an unknown artist. A typed label on the back records that the work is by Soldi and is of Geminiani. There is a Witt mount of a portrait by Soldi which is also thought to be of Geminiani. It was sold at Christie's, London, 27 May 1952, lot 28 but is signed 'Soldi Pittore'. [Note by Madeleine Korn].

UNKNOWN ENGRAVER [?ROBERT LAWRIE] (c1785)
Engraved double portrait within individual roundels, 155 x 95 mm.

Inscription: HENRY / PURCELL. / FRANCESCO / GEMINIANI.

Line engraving by an unidentified engraver (?Robert Lawrie, c1755-1836) after an unidentified artist (?Jenkins), possibly for inclusion in the *Universal Magazine*.

ANONYMOUS (*c*1756)
Engraved frontispiece to GEMINIANI, Francesco. *L'Art du Violon*, Paris, ?1763.

Based on an engraving that appears as the frontispiece to HERRANDO, José. *Arte Y Puntual Explicacion Del Modo de Tocar El Violin*, Paris, 1756, and inscribed "Mat. Salvador Carmona, Sculp. 1756". The Geminiani version does not appear until the de la Chevardière/Frères le Goux edition — well after Geminiani's own 1752 *L'Art de Jouer le Violon*.

THOMAS HUDSON [*recte* Latham, see above]

Portrait of Geminiani once attributed to Thomas Hudson (in the possession of the Royal Society of Musicians).

JAMES PARMENTIER

The Minutes of the Masonic Lodge *Philo-musicae et -architecturae societas Apollini* mention a group portrait including Geminiani who was the "perpetual Dictator" of their musical performances; later, because of difficulties, individual portraits were proposed, but there is no evidence that they were ever executed (see essay by Andrew Pink in the present volume).

On 14 October 1725 it was ordered "That a Picture of the President Censors & Directors be painted on one large Canvas The Expence not to Exceed Three Hundred Pounds to [be] paid for out of the Publick Treasury of this Society. | ORDERED | That Bro^r Parmentier do perform the same".

A first payment was made on 27 December; later it was resolved that the picture "should not be mov'd to any place to be finish'd Except to the house of Bro^r W^m. Gulston [...] and there to be kept by him till the Society think proper to remove it. Resolv'd that the Said Picture be mov'd as soon as Convenient to Mr. Reg^r. Gulstons new house in Ste Marie La Bonne fields in Ord^r to be there intirely Compleated and finished".

On 27 October 1726 a third payment was made, Parmentier having blamed the "multitude of difficulties in carrying on the Design of painting [...] the Pictures in one Canvas" and proposed to "paint them separately in three Quarters Cloth for five Guineas each".

UNIDENTIFIED

Portrait of Geminiani bequeathed by the composer Joseph Kelway in 1782.

He had given his picture of Geminiani and his own portrait to his "faithful servant, Ann Phillips", as evidenced by his will, signed 14 April 1779 and proved 5 June 1782 (quoted in *DNB*, under "Kelway, Joseph").

VALENTINE GREEN

Engraved portrait (?mezzotint) by Valentine Green (1739-1816) listed by William Richardson in a sale catalogue of 1800 which was later issued with interleaved pages giving the purchaser and price of each lot in manuscript. The comprehensive title reads: "British Portraits. A Catalogue of a Genuine and Extensive Collection of English Portraits Consisting of the Royal Families, Peers, Gentry, Clergy, Lawyers, Military, Literary, Artists, Actors, Writing-Masters, Musicians, Female Sex, Phenomena, Convicts, Monsters, &c. From Egbert the Great to the Present Time; Comprising the Choicest Works of Delaram, Elstrack, Faithorne, Hollar, Loggan, Lumley, the Pass's, Place, Smith, Rob. White, &c. And nearly the whole that have been engraved after Sir Joshua Reynolds, and other Modern Artists, most of them Proofs, many Private Plates, and Unique Prints, not to be found in any other Collection, with Biographical and Genealogical Remarks. By an Eminent Collector, During the last Forty Years…".

In the section devoted to "Artists, Actors, Musicians, Painters, Writing-Masters, Mechanicians, &c…" on the twenty-third day of sale we find Lot 110 (p. 234): "Three — Geminiani, by V. Green; Sir Balthasar Gerbier, Mistress, and Children, from Rubens, by McArdell; and Richard Gomeldon, mez. by W. Fairthorne".

On the interleaved page the purchaser is given as "Tyson", a frequent purchaser throughout the 31 days of the sale, at a price of 12s and 6d; since no artist is mentioned, the original painting from which the engraving was made cannot be identified.

Curiously, in the final day of sale, otherwise devoted to "Convicts, Phenomena, &c.", we find "Romain a violinist" and "Italian singers" included.

Are We Ready for Francesco Geminiani? Thoughts on Performing Geminiani Today

Wiebke Thormählen
(Southampton)

To say All in few Words, the Road to Emulation is both open and wide; the most effectual Method to triumph over an Author is to excel him; and he manifests his Affection to a Science most who contributes most to its Advancement.[1]

With these words Francesco Geminiani closed the preface to his *Treatise of Good Taste in the Art of Musick* (1749). Taste, in this context, was a measurement applied to the evaluation of performance rather than composition; today, in a culture of 'classical' music still used to evaluating works first, and then evaluating performances of a particular work against the work's inherent value, the idea that performances were seen as being the work still provides a seemingly insurmountable hurdle for performers. Whereas a tasteful performance today might be one that 'interprets' the composer's intentions to its best effects, in the eighteenth century the compositional process itself assumed a large amount of input from the performer. For the eighteenth-century musician the idea that the work as such might exist apart from the performance would have been puzzling. In late eighteenth-century descriptions by theorists such as Heinrich Christoph Koch and Johann Georg Sulzer, the compositional process entailed three stages: 'Anlage' (first conception of a piece of music), 'Ausführung' (elaboration) and 'Ausarbeitung' (surface detail) with the latter left largely to the performer.[2] The composer, then, saw himself as the supplier of ingenious ideas and melodies brought into particular forms and combinations, yet it was

---

[1] Geminiani, Francesco. *A Treatise of Good Taste in the Art of Musick*, London, s.n., 1749, p. 4.

[2] Koch, Heinrich Christoph. *Versuch einer Anleitung zur Composition*, 3 vols, Rudolfstadt, 1782; Leipzig, Adam Friedrich Böhme, 1787 and 1793, vol. II, pp. 51-69.

up to the performer to supply the necessary taste to furnish these shapes and forms with grace, elegance and, ultimately, with meaning.[3]

Today's performers largely still suffer from the 'interpretation' heritage of the nineteenth century, based on a self-image that places the performer lower than the composer within a strict hierarchy. As such, tasteful performances remain within boundaries that place the work higher than the particular spectacle of performance. Geminiani, on the other hand, was aiming for spectacle in his own playing, and his oeuvre — compositions, arrangements, treatises — suggests that he attempted to inspire similar freedom in others' performance. Geminiani's own words as quoted above highlight that his focus was on emulation, excelling and advancement rather than on re-creating someone else's balanced shapes, forms and melodies. Today, reviews of concerts and recordings alike betray that 'taste' is all too often equated with 'beauty', and 'beauty' with a classical balance of the shapes and melodies that make up the composition itself. Yet, Geminiani's 'excelling' and 'advancement' are a call to place the process of creating itself at the top of the hierarchy, not the compositional product. As such, today's renditions of Geminiani's music regularly feature beautiful playing in the shape of considered and certainly historically-informed performances. Yet, they raise the question whether Geminiani's ideal of beauty, particularly as it pertained to performance, is to be unquestioningly equated with today's common notions of beauty in music. What do the reports of his own performance — positive and negative — in combination with his compositions, arrangements and treatises tell us of his own objectives for the art of music? Assessing these questions through a critical historical assessment of what a tasteful performance meant for Geminiani ought to be the job of today's performers so as to reach above and beyond an understanding of 'historical performance' as a set of technical rules. Geminiani, perhaps more than any other eighteenth-century performer (and, perhaps, in anticipation of the Romantic virtuoso) raises the question of how excelling and advancement become part of a concept of beauty.

It may have been this very feature of Geminiani's ideal of beauty in performance which placed him at the centre of much controversy in the eighteenth century. Frequently cited and easily accessible to today's performers is Charles Burney's account of Geminiani's life in his *General History of Music*.[4] Burney's account of the musician, a fascinating diatribe against the Italian, in which he gradually writes himself into a Geminianian frenzy, reveals as much

---

3   BENT, Ian. 'The Compositional Process in Music Theory 1713-1850', in: *Music Analysis*, III/1 (March 1984), pp. 29-55.

4   *BURNEY*, IV, pp. 641-645.

about the author's values as it contributes to our knowledge of Geminiani. As such, it is unclear whether Burney's jaundiced observations on Geminiani's career were shared as generally across Europe as he would have us believe. To be sure, recounting the violinist Francesco Barbella's account of Geminiani's ineptitude when placed at the head of the orchestra in Naples would have provided a field-day for many writers, yet in part, surely, because it made for a good story about a famous musician. But behind the criticism of being "so wild and unsteady a timist, that instead of regulating and conducting the band, he threw it into confusion" linger the rather more suggestive descriptions of his *tempo rubato* and "other unexpected accelerations and relaxations of measure".[5] If Geminiani was henceforth to be relegated to the viola part by the disaffected orchestra this says as much about his approach to performance as it does about the orchestra's inability to adapt to a perhaps revolutionary manner of playing. If we are not to discredit Geminiani altogether, his erratic behaviour must have remained within the bounds of a wider arch of unity that comprised libertine excess, yet not total incompetence.

In fact, Burney himself gave much credit to Geminiani, describing his "powerful hand" and "bolder modulation" and granting indebtedness to him for "the improved state of the violin" in England and "for the advancement of instrumental Music in general".[6] As a player he rated him higher than Veracini, yet indicated that neither violinist's style was in line with "the taste of the English at this time".[7] These assessments of Geminiani as a performer appear in Burney's section on Veracini, whereas his (much longer) musing on Geminiani focuses almost exclusively on his compositions, a fact which bears witness to Burney's own manner of working when compiling this history: in assessing the music of the past he arduously collected and compiled written records of musicians' work. As such, his history presents one of the first modern music histories in that it has, fundamentally, a work-based approach to music history, with a narrative and evaluations founded on compositions rather than performances. Whereas this characterises him essentially as a modern writer in his times, his prejudices against instrumental music as he recounts them in his critique of *The Enchanted Forest* simultaneously show his conservatism.[8] Geminiani, however, was a performer and a composer of instrumental music, both classifications which made it difficult for Burney to rate him highly. But the Italian contravened Burney's (and possibly other English writers') sensitivities in other ways: his

---

[5] *Ibidem*, p. 641.
[6] *Ibidem*.
[7] *Ibidem*, p. 640.
[8] *Ibidem*, p. 643.

concertos were "laboured, difficult, and fantastical", his taste erratic and his sentiments frequently changing.[9] When Geminiani's productions are described as "the offspring of whim, caprice, expedients, and an unprincipled change of style and taste", Burney had intended a criticism where we — stepping back from the particular English sensitivities of the eighteenth century for which Burney wrote — can now detect Geminiani's true value. For Burney's critique of Geminiani's lack of consistency both within a piece of music and from one musical event or proclamation of his taste to the next, speaks on the one hand of Geminiani's refusal to be type-cast and on the other of his love of surprise and astonishment in performance.

Today's performers should seek to capture the same sense of "rhapsody or extemporaneous flight, rather than a polished and regular production" and convey the desire to "outwit".[10] Geminiani emerges from the descriptions of Burney and his contemporaries as a proto-romantic libertine, whereas extant compositions betray a multitude of musical influences mingled into a personal style that defied the constricts of national style, performance setting (such as the traditional church, chamber and theatre distinction) and of a particular compositional heritage (in his case Corelli's). The fact that many of his pieces were too difficult for others to perform goes hand in hand with Peter Walls' observation that Geminiani's treatises addressed not only the usual amateur audience but the advanced player (see p. 249 of the present volume): in his six treatises Geminiani gave plenty of instruction to those already accomplished in the ground rules of both composition and performance. The point of his didactic works, then, was a further education that would equip the performer with the necessary tools and inspire him intellectually into ever more daring freedom in performance.

Geminiani's arrangements and transcriptions of his own and others' music must be read in a similar vein. Sandra Mangsen, in her essay on Geminiani as arranger in the present volume, points out that Geminiani furnished the keyboard version of his Op. 4 collection with more detailed performance instructions than the violin version. This implies that he expected violinists who were sufficiently accomplished to play his pieces to be able to supply their own ornamentation and embellishment; simultaneously, it suggests an intended integration of his three types of output — his own playing as model or inspiration, his treatise as a further step towards learning his type of freedom, and his written records or 'pieces'. His "carefully corrected" first set of violin sonatas as it reappears in 1739 (see MANGSEN, pp. 335ff.) may equally have been

---

[9]   *Ibidem*, p. 642.

[10]   *Ibidem*, p. 645.

inspired by his didactic vision more than by the necessity to improve on his earlier compositions. Supplying an abundance of performance marks must therefore not be taken as an early example of a composer dictating a single vision of a finished work; rather, Geminiani intended to furnish the performer with ideas and models for performance. Mangsen argues convincingly that his arrangements can only be understood in this light: as a myriad of equally viable versions or, as I might like to extend it, as a myriad to which Geminiani would have wished to see many more added by each performer approaching his material. The sheer density of performance markings in some sources, even including the invention of new expression marks such as a sign for the swelling of sound (such invention in itself not having been an unusual practice within the French harpsichord context that influenced him), makes them difficult to read in performance. Therefore it seems unlikely that they were meant for direct and faithful reproduction; instead, they may show an intention to educate and instruct each player into his or her own flights of fancy by merely illustrating the level of intricacies possible.

Today we have whole-heartedly embraced the idea that the text of much eighteenth-century music provides a skeleton which needs fleshing out with our own improvisations and embellishments, and performers are versed in providing these ornamentations with recourse to eighteenth-century treatises, descriptions of performances and other sources of written-out ornamentation. Performers, then, adhere to rules of both taste and style which these eighteenth-century sources appear to dictate. Yet how do we approach Geminiani who himself defied the rules of his times and his contemporaries? And are his over-zealous ornamentation and expression marks merely an exemplar for the manner in which he transgressed these boundaries? And if we transgress with him how do we answer to the inevitable accusation of jaggedness, disjunction, asymmetry and confusion of the whole? Need we willingly become "bad mental arithmeticians, or calculators of time"?[11]

Burney, in line with many of his contemporaries, had begun to posit unity as the highest order of a composition. As such Corelli's sonatas, "models of simplicity, grace, and elegance in melody", were valued higher than Veracini's "wild and flighty" compositions.[12] In later treatises melody was openly posited as the most important element of invention which alone could display the genius of the composer. For Geminiani, however, unity lay in the act of performance, in the tempo fluctuations and the "whim, caprice,

---

[11] *Ibidem*, p. 644.
[12] *Ibidem*, p. 640.

expedients"[13] inspired by the moment of performance and by its narrative, not by the narrative of the melodic material *per se*. Geminiani's performance might have been more akin to the stand-up comedian's acting and reacting, directing his ensemble on impulse and in accordance with each current context. As such, his excessive *accelerandi* would have served to bring out particular passages in the music and to either emphasise or juxtapose the often irregular phrase lengths of his written melodies. The detailed performance directions in some sources, then, instruct performers first and foremost to steer the music through their own detailed strength of vision. Geminiani's idea of performance may not have been dissimilar to Carl Philipp Emanuel Bach's vision as the latter hoped to convey it in his *Versuch über die wahre Art das Clavier zu spielen*, not only in regard to the performance of the fantasia, but also with respect to performing in a larger group, as his frequent reference to accompanying illustrates. Ultimately, Bach's fantasias, which employ no bar lines and hence appear incoherent at first sight, gain unity through the performer's voice and physical motion. Performers today have embraced Bach's ideal of the free fantasia as a semblance of improvisation that is applicable to solo music; his treatise, however, is primarily concerned with the art of accompanying for which he demands similar freedom and strength of vision and seeks to provide all the tools to gain both. Both composer-performers, Bach and Geminiani, shared a vision of control through improvisatory freedom that could follow the performers' narrative rather than the measured narrative of the notated text, a 'work concept' based not on notation but on the performer's larger vision.

The recent Geminiani revival has yet to address this vision of performance. Part of the problem may lie in the nature of performance today which has to live up to the challenges of the recording industry. Deprived of the visual element of performance, recordings seem to fare better if they retreat behind today's standard notions of beauty, taste, balance and unity which have been established by later repertoire. Enrico Careri, in his review of Geminiani scholarship in the present volume, rightly applauds the high quality of many recent Geminiani recordings. Many are certainly excellent, but very few are daring. In live performance, many performers excel in the manner Geminiani hoped for, yet on their recordings deeply ingrained notions of beauty and unity frequently supersede an understanding of those elements of Geminiani's musical language and vision which demand a more thorough historical ideology critique. Andrew Manze's direction of the Academy of Ancient Music in the Concerti Grossi after Corelli Op. 5 (Harmonia Mundi,

---

[13]   *Ibidem*, p. 644.

HMX2907262, 2007) remains faithful to the Corellian mould of "simplicity, grace and elegance",[14] yet it shows little of Geminiani's surpassing of his former master. A Corellian account is often an understandable, if safe, choice; after all, Geminiani consciously cast Opp. 2 and 3 in the Corellian mould, while arranging Corelli's Opp. 1, 3 and 5 for other concerto collections. Yet, in some concerti, such as those of Op. 7, and in *The Enchanted Forest*, we may hope to hear Geminiani's voice but are invariably rewarded with bland beauty. The latter concerti, almost pantomimic in nature, bear Geminiani's voice clearly in the actual compositional framework, but Ryo Terakado's direction of the Orchestra Barocca Italiana (Stradivarius, STR 11014, 1994) sounds at times as though he feared being relegated to the viola if he dared too much: there is a palpable embarrassment at the oddities of Geminiani's music, and the music's descriptive, conjuring elements are left unexploited. Although the recording is highly skilled, professional and must be rated as a good performance of music, it is not necessarily a good performance of Geminiani. Michael Schneider with La Stagione Frankfurt (Capriccio, capriccio / 67 081, 2004) brings out the music's fantastical element in a detailed attention to its colours, yet many curious moments are lost to an overriding perception of the music's frequent dance characteristics. The group's recording of the Concerti Grossi Op. 7 nos. 4 and 6, from the same disc, is similarly colourful and enjoyably energetic, yet at the expense of the repertoire's concerto element: the soloists do not give us our money's worth in competitive fiddling. This recording, along with other excellent renditions of Op. 7, seems to rectify the potential for Geminiani's excessive accelerations and relaxations of tempi, instead of embracing them as an inherent feature of Geminiani's style. It makes one wonder whether Geminiani became so precise in his notation because his contemporaries, similarly, were too happy with being perfect arithmeticians to narrate in the manner he envisaged. Even in his solo repertoire performers frequently fail to break through the strictures of tactus and tempo — while some are so tame as to sound at best un-narrative and at worst careless despite the high quality of their technical playing, others, such as Alison McGillivray in her recording of the Op. 5 Cello Sonatas (Linn Records, CKD 251, 2004), and Lyriarte's recording of select Violin Sonatas from the Op. 4 set (Oehms Classics, OC 356, 2004), seem to fall short of translating the spontaneity of the live performance to the recording, while also drawing parallels to Corelli instead of illustrating where and how the music passes beyond his idiom. Moments of instability and disquietude frequently remain unexploited; Bruno Cocset's recording of

---

[14]   *Ibidem*, p. 640.

Op. 5 (Alpha, ALPHA 123, 2008) perhaps advances furthest into understanding the composer's demand for performative control.[15] Cocset crafts the album as an almost symphonically unified whole by giving much consideration to a variety of instruments used both by the soloist and the continuo group, and by clearly paying attention to the music's surface details. Op. 5 no. 4 is truly convincing in its Geminianian style, presenting an exceptional moment on all these recordings in which the notion of beauty is re-interpreted into an aesthetic experience that incorporates the grotesque. Similarly daring and vibrant is Anton Steck's account of the violin version of Op. 5 (CPO, DDD, 2004); it is a rare recording which manages to surmount the hurdle between live performance and recording and captures the tension and spontaneity of the former on disc. The violinist's vibrancy and his daring to imitate Geminiani in his more erratic performance manner enables the listener to imagine the spectacle of the visual performance, and Steck is not afraid to sacrifice beauty and evenness of sound to this overall effect.

The newly-launched critical edition of *Geminiani Opera Omnia* (published by Ut Orpheus Edizioni) for the first time makes the performer-composer's repertoire available to study as a whole, thereby offering up many of the conflicting elements of Geminiani's contrary style.[16] A serious engagement with these conflicts will have to comprise an ideology critique of our notions of beauty and taste. Translating these critiques into performance may in the past have been hampered by the petrification of performance on recordings, a much-debated issue ever since T. W. Adorno's critique of listening practices and the commodification of music.[17] Perhaps the latest revolutions in the new media, however, and with them audience's new listening habits might revolutionise performers' approaches to recording again. While YouTube clips

---

[15]   A more extensive review of Bruno Cocset's recording of Op. 5 appears in THORMÄHLEN, Wiebke. 'Francesco Geminiani (1687-1762): Sonates pour Violoncelle avec la Basse Continue Opus v', in: *Eighteenth-Century Music*, VI/2 (2009), pp. 287-289. The review touches on several issues discussed here.

[16]   *Francesco Geminiani Opera Omnia*, edited by Christopher Hogwood, 16 vols, Bologna, Ut Orpheus Edizioni, 2010—.

[17]   See for example, ADORNO, Theodor W. *Einleitung in die Musiksoziologie. Zwölf theoretische Vorlesungen*, Frankfurt am Main, Suhrkamp, 1962, English translation by E. B. Ashton, *Introduction to the Sociology of Music*, New York, Continuum, 1989; ID. 'On the Fetish-Character in Music and the Regression of Listening (1938)', in: *Essays on Music*, selected and edited by Richard Leppert, English translation by Susan H. Gillespie, Berkeley (CA), University of California Press, 2002, pp. 288-317; STOCKFELT, Ola. 'Adequate Modes of Listening', in: *Keeping Score: Music, Disciplinarity, Culture*, edited by David Schwarz, Anahid Kassabian and Lawrence Siegel, Charlottesville (VA)-London, University Press of Virginia, 1997, pp. 129-146.

offer the visual along with the aural, the iPod generation rarely ever listens to an entire CD in one sitting, opting instead for the random mix of favourites carried on their MP3 devices. Eighteenth-century listeners, likewise, would not have listened to six consecutive concerti grossi — a listening experience that might stretch one's ability to be excited by Geminiani's erratic manner and make one wish for a more balanced, unchallenging beauty; re-creating a broader mix not only in performances but also on recordings, a mix that escapes the symphonically-inspired ideals of unity within the variety of movements and replaces it with the unity provided by the performer's voice, might open up both performers and audiences to new visions of beauty in the more extreme performances.

In order to give Geminiani his true credit, we must perform not his pieces but his vision of musical performance which provided integration whether its material basis was a melody of his own invention, Corelli's famous Op. 5 sonatas, or a Scottish folk tune. To do so, however, performers as much as audiences have to break the restrictions imposed by a market of recording-led performance.

CONTRIBUTOR BIOGRAPHIES

GREGORY BARNETT is Associate Professor of Musicology at the Shepherd School of Music, Rice University. He is the author of *Bolognese Instrumental Music, 1660-1710* (Ashgate Press) and is a contributor to *The Cambridge History of Western Music Theory* and to *The Cambridge History of Seventeenth-Century Music*. He has also published articles in the *Journal of the American Musicological Society*, *Early Music*, and the *Journal of Musicology*. His interests include the history of modal theory, Baroque-era instrumental music and instruments, and the music of Handel. His research has been supported by grants from the American Council of Learned Societies, the National Endowment for the Humanities, the Fulbright Program, and the American Musicological Society.

BARRA BOYDELL retired in 2010 from a professorship in music at the National University of Ireland, Maynooth. His extensive publications include *The crumhorn and other renaissance windcap instruments* (1982), *Music and paintings at the National Gallery of Ireland* (1985), *Music at Christ Church before 1800: documents and selected anthems* (1998), *A history of music at Christ Church Cathedral* (2004) and *Music, Ireland and the Seventeenth Century* (2009, with Kerry Houston). He is co-general editor of the forthcoming *Encyclopaedia of Music in Ireland* (University College Dublin Press, 2013).

ENRICO CARERI is Professor of Musicology at the University of Naples "Federico II". He studied music and musicology in Rome and took his Ph.D. in Liverpool (1990) with a thesis on Geminiani which later became the standard book on this composer (OUP, 1993; LIM, 1999). He has published several articles on Italian Baroque music, critical editions of Vivaldi's *La verità in cimento*, Bonporti's trio sonatas and Geminiani's *The Inchanted Forrest*, two catalogues of Renaissance and Baroque music preserved in Rome (*Catalogo del fondo musicale Chiti-Corsini*, 1998; *Catalogo dei manoscritti musicali dell'Archivio Generale delle Scuole Pie*, 1987), essays on notated silences and their modern interpretation in Haydn, Mozart, Beethoven and Schubert, a book on musicology (*Beni musicali, musica, musicologia*, LIM, 2006) and a collection of essays on eighteenth-century music (*Dopo l'opera quinta*, LIM, 2008). He is director of *Centro Studi sulla Canzone Napoletana* and a member of the scientific committee of *Edizione Nazionale delle Opere di Giovanni Battista Pergolesi* and *Centro Studi Luigi Boccherini*. He is a member of the editorial board of *Geminiani Opera Omnia* and the critical edition of Vivaldi's operatic works.

CHERYLL DUNCAN has taught at a number of UK universities, including the Open University, and is currently a tutor in Academic Studies at the Royal Northern College of Music in Manchester. She is working on legal documents in relation to the operatic and concert life of London in the early eighteenth century, and has recently published in the *Journal of the American Musicological Society* a study of the financial affairs of Caterina Galli, one of Handel's oratorio singers.

Christopher Hogwood is General Editor of the *Francesco Geminiani Opera Omnia* project and divides his time between musicology and performance. With the Academy of Ancient Music (which he founded in 1973) he has made over 200 recordings, including the complete symphonies of Mozart and Beethoven. Recent editions include Mendelssohn Symphonies, the *Kenner und Liebhaber* sonatas of C.P.E. Bach, Brahms' String Sextets and Stravinsky's final composition, arrangements of four Preludes and Fugues by J. S. Bach. Latest writings include *Handel: Water Music and Music for the Royal Fireworks* (Cambridge Music Handbooks), *Haydn's Visits to England* (Thames & Hudson) and 'Musical Identity' in *Identity* (Darwin College Lectures Series, CUP). He is Honorary Emeritus Professor of Music at Cambridge University.

Peter Holman is Emeritus Professor of Historical Musicology at Leeds University. He has wide interests in English music from about 1550 to 1850, and the history of instruments and instrumental music. He is the author of the prize-winning *Four and Twenty Fiddlers: The Violin at the English Court 1540-1690* (1993), and studies of Henry Purcell (1994), and Dowland's *Lachrimae* (1999), as well as numerous scholarly articles. His most recent book, *Life after Death: the Viola da Gamba in Britain from Purcell to Dolmetsch*, was published by Boydell in November 2010. As a performer he is director of The Parley of Instruments, the Suffolk Villages Festival and Leeds Baroque.

Clare Hornsby is an art historian who has published widely on eighteenth-century art and on the Grand Tour. For many years she researched and worked for the British School at Rome and her recent book, "Digging and Dealing in Eighteenth-Century Rome" (Yale University Press, 2010; with the late Ilaria Bignamini) discusses the antiquities market and connoisseurship in Rome and London. Her doctoral thesis examined the life and career of the eighteenth-century Italo-French set designer and architect Giovanni Niccolò Servandoni. Her current academic focus is on the relationship between music and art in terms of patronage and aesthetics; she has been an Honorary Research Fellow at the Royal Academy of Music in London, teaching a postgraduate course on the cultural and artistic contexts for music, 1050-1800, and a member of the Foundation Committee of Benedictus Trust.

Mark Kroll, an award-winning harpsichordist, fortepianist, scholar and educator, performs worldwide, has made forty recordings, and is harpsichordist for the Boston Symphony Orchestra. His books include *Playing the Harpsichord Expressively*, *The Beethoven Violin Sonatas* and *Johann Nepomuk Hummel: A Musician's Life and World*, and he has published editions of the music of Hummel, Francesco Scarlatti and Charles Avison. Kroll is Professor Emeritus at Boston University, where he was founder and chair of the Department of Historical Performance, and has also served as Visiting Professor in the USA and Europe. He is currently writing a biography of Ignaz Moscheles and was recently appointed editor of the *Historical Harpsichord Series* for Pendragon Press.

Sandra Mangsen taught musicology and historical performance at the University of Western Ontario from 1989 until her retirement in 2011. Holding degrees in both harpsichord performance and musicology, she has recorded cantatas and trio sonatas of Buxtehude as well as *Entretiens*, a CD devoted to harpsichord music of seventeenth-century France. Her research focuses on issues in performance practice and the dissemination of music; her book in progress is tentatively entitled *Music, Meanings and Markets: Keyboard Arrangements of Vocal Music in England, 1560–1760*. Sandra Mangsen now lives in North Bennington, Vermont.

Andrew Pink, independent researcher, is an alumnus of the Royal Academy of Music and Goldsmiths, University of London (Ph.D. Diss., 2007: *The Musical Culture of Freemasonry in Early Eighteenth-Century London*). Publications include: 'Robin des Bois et ses joyeuses femmes : une société de francs-maçons dans un jardin d'agrément de Londres au dix-huitième siècle', in: *La Pensée et les Hommes*, LV/82-83 (2011); 'Order and Uniformity, Decorum and Taste: Sermons Preached at the Anniversary Meeting of the Three Choirs, 1720-1800', in: *The Oxford Handbook of the British Sermon, 1689-1901* (OUP, 2012); biographical entries for *Le Monde maçonnique des Lumières* (Champion, 2013); chapters on theatre and songs in *British Freemasonry 1717-1813* (Pickering and Chatto, 2014).

Rudolf Rasch studied musicology in Amsterdam with Profs Karel Philippus Bernet Kempers and Joseph Smits van Waesberghe. He wrote a dissertation on seventeenth-century polyphonic carols in the Spanish Netherlands (Utrecht, 1985) and from 1977 to 2010 was affiliated with the Institute of Musicology of Utrecht University. His main research interests are the musical history of the Netherlands, tuning and temperament, and the works of composers such as Corelli, Vivaldi, Geminiani and Boccherini. His publications in these fields include editing a collection of essays on *Music Publishing in Europe 1600-1900* (2005), *Driehonderd brieven over muziek* (letters about music to and from Constantijn Huygens (2007), *Beyond Notes: Improvisation in Western Music of the Eighteenth and Nineteenth Centuries* (2011), critical editions of *Duetti per 2 Violini Opus 3* and *Sonate per tastiera e violino Opus 5* by Luigi Boccherini (2007, 2009) and a facsimile edition with introduction of Johann Georg Neidhardt's *Beste und leichteste Temperatur 1706* (2010).

Robin Stowell is a Professor of Music at Cardiff University. Educated at the University of Cambridge and the Royal Academy of Music, he has performed, broadcast and recorded as a violinist/period violinist. Since his pioneering book on *Violin Technique and Performance Practice* (Cambridge University Press, 1985) he has published widely on issues of performance practice, organology, music of the 'long 18th century', violinists, chamber music, and string-playing in general. His more recent major publications include *The Cambridge Companion to the String Quartet* (CUP, 2003), *The Early Violin and Viola* (CUP, 2001), and, with Colin Lawson, *The Historical Performance of Music: an Introduction* (CUP, 1999). His second collaboration with Lawson, *The Cambridge History of Musical Performance* was published (CUP) in 2012.

Michael Talbot is Emeritus Professor of Music at the University of Liverpool and a Fellow of the British Academy. His research focuses on Italian music of the late seventeenth and eighteenth centuries, and he is most widely known for his writings and editions connected with Vivaldi. His recent projects include a reference work on Vivaldi (*The Vivaldi Compendium*) and a study of Giovanni Stefano Carbonelli, a violinist-composer contemporary with Geminiani in England.

Wiebke Thormählen received her doctorate in musicology from Cornell University in 2008. She is currently an AHRC Early Career Research Fellow in the School of Humanities at the University of Southampton. Her articles have appeared in the *Journal of Musicology*, *Early Music*, *Acta Mozartiana*, and *Neues Musikwissenschaftliches Jahrbuch*, and she has contributed numerous reviews to *Notes* and *Eighteenth-Century Music*. Her research focuses on the role that music as social practice played in educating individuals and social groups emotionally during the mid-eighteenth to mid-nineteenth centuries. Recent research on the social, sociological and psychological functions of various forms of performance, such as the playing of musical arrangements and the display of virtuosity, was funded by the Wellcome Trust.

PETER WALLS is Emeritus Professor of Music at Victoria University of Wellington and from 2002-2011 was Chief Executive of the New Zealand Symphony Orchestra. A baroque violinist and conductor, he is the author of *Music in the English Courtly Masque* (1996), *History, Imagination and the Performance of Music* (2003) and numerous articles on historical performance practice. He is the editor of *Baroque Music* (2011) in the Ashgate series "The Library of Essays on Music Performance Practice".

NEAL ZASLAW is the Herbert Gussman Professor of Music at Cornell University (Ithaca, NY). His *Köchelverzeichnis: Chronologisch-thematisches Verzeichnis sämtlicher Tonwerke Wolfgang Amadé Mozarts / Neuausgabe* will be published in 2013 as a German-language book (Breitkopf & Härtel) and an English-language web site <http://www.mozarteum.at>.

INDEX OF NAMES